DREAM-WEAVER

Jonathan Wylie

CORGI BOOKS

DREAM WEAVER
A CORGI BOOK 0 552 13757 X

First publication in Great Britain

PRINTING HISTORY
Corgi edition published 1991

This book is set in 9½/10½pt Mallard
by Busby The Printers Ltd, Exeter

Corgi Books are published by Transworld Publishers Ltd,
61–63 Uxbridge Road, Ealing, London W5 5SA, in Australia by
Transworld Publishers (Australia) Pty. Ltd, 15–23 Helles
Avenue, Moorebank, NSW 2170, and in New Zealand by
Transworld Publishers (N.Z.) Ltd, Cnr Moselle and
Waipareira Avenues, Henderson, Auckland.

Printed and bound in Great Britain by
Cox & Wyman Ltd, Reading, Berks.

PROLOGUE

At first they thought it was snow. But it was too warm, too dry, and the white crystals crunched underfoot. There was a tang in the air, sharp and familiar, yet it was some time before anyone realized what was falling on their city.

The sky was raining salt.

At first, the inhabitants treated the dry rain as a novel joke, just one more nuisance in an already tense and worried city. But the salt did not stop. The first light sprinklings were followed by increasingly heavy falls, which in their turn became an unstoppable downpour. The crystals got everywhere, fouling the water supplies and choking the gardens. It seeped into every house, clogging up the streets and alleys. No matter how hard the people of Derith tried to keep their homes clear, the salt always gained on them, filling the days with a deadly haze and the nights with a horrible rustling.

Discomfort and inconvenience turned to anger and bewilderment, and finally to terror as they realized the fate that awaited their city. Those who stayed died. Most of those who fled also died. They had left their escape too late, unable to believe the extent of the catastrophe which had overtaken them. They died of thirst in a white, sliding desert. Half-blind and half-mad, many turned on their fellow citizens, killing them for just a few drops of water, a mouthful of untainted food. Yet more simply gave up, their minds no longer able to cope with the unequal struggle. They lay down to die, and let the salt cover them slowly in a crystalline shroud.

A very few *did* escape. The lucky ones were the merchants and artists whose nomadic way of life meant that they were far from home. A royal envoy and his party also survived, having been dispatched on an unexplained mission to the far south. But they were the exceptions. To the rest, the salt showed no mercy.

The streets grew quiet – the same streets which, only a few days earlier, had echoed to the drums and wailing of the king's funeral cortège. Tyrrell had been interred in the heart of his city in a great pyramid, built of black torgrist hewn from the quarries at Blackator. He had designed his immense tomb himself, with great attention to detail, planning ahead as though he had known the very day on which he was to die.

Tyrrell had died without an heir, and there had been an ugly rumour circulating through the city about the way in which the young prince, the king's only child, had met his death. Other rumours spoke of sorcery and of a power struggle between warring factions in the court. The nobility and the wizards were believed to have been opposed to each other in matters of policy and over the uncertain succession even when Tyrrell was alive. After his death, the reality of civil war became inevitable, and the situation was made infinitely worse by the terrible disaster that was soon to fall upon the city. It was to be many years before the bloodshed in the country ended and a new capital chosen for the land of Ahrenia.

The streets grew quiet. Then ceased to be streets. The salt filled every crevice, erasing every detail of the landscape. Soon only the tallest buildings remained, jutting from the dead, pristine plain. But still the salt did not relent. It was determined to bury Derith completely. Eventually a vast white sea extended for scores of leagues to east and west, as still and as silent as death.

One tower remained visible longer than the rest. One tower, its solitary inhabitant working feverishly in the few hours left to him. His last act, after hurriedly completing his final carving, was to ring the great golden bell, tolling the doom of the city. Then he too fell victim to the shifting crystals, and no one was left alive in the whole city.

No one alive in any conventional sense, that is . . .

The numbness of defeat began to creep through Rebecca's limbs. She stared down at the ground, unable to face the world. Salt whispered beneath her feet.

The noise of the crowd faded, becoming a spectral echo of its former tumult; colour no longer existed in this world of despair – the very idea of it seemed absurd. The pearly whiteness of the rustling crystals dominated everything.

The salt began to shift. Then squirmed. It was a whirlpool now, and Rebecca fell into the realms of nightmare.

When she finally looked up, she saw two worlds, both frozen in time. One was the scene in Edgefield Square, the fateful game stilled, hundreds of pairs of eyes peering, mouths agape in mid-shout. The other was cold and constricting, superimposed on the real world of warmth and sunlight like a gossamer web of darkness. In that realm the black king was a glistening monster, the knight a blind painter; a castle juggled black letters, and the queen was a crystal demon of black flame. The monk wore his usual enigmatic smile.

I can't fight them all.

Also by Jonathan Wylie

SERVANTS OF ARK
Book One: THE FIRST NAMED
Book Two: THE CENTRE OF THE CIRCLE
Book Three: THE MAGE-BORN CHILD

THE UNBALANCED EARTH
Book One: DREAMS OF STONE
Book Two: THE LIGHTLESS KINGDOM
Book Three: THE AGE OF CHAOS

and published by Corgi Books

Part One
EDGE

CHAPTER ONE

The picture was dead. Rebecca had seen that at a glance, and closer inspection had only confirmed her initial impression. As she stared at it now, willing the colour and texture of the painting to come to life, she knew her task was hopeless. For a moment, she imagined that she could see a twinkle in the eyes of the old hunting dog, and could hear a faraway echo of his excited barking. But even that faded as Rebecca looked at him more closely. The only things visible were the painter's brush strokes and his artfully applied flecks of light.

The young artist had placed Old Growler in the lower right-hand corner of the portrait, without having been asked to do so, but this deviation from his original brief had met with Baldemar's instant approval. Rebecca's father had always considered hunting to be one of the most proper pursuits of a noble gentleman; though he rode little these days, he liked the implication provided by seeing his favourite hound at his feet.

However, Baron Baldemar would have liked the painting well enough even without that inclusion. The portrait was a good likeness, though flattering. It made him look strong and arrogant, his large hands resting on the pommel of his great sword. Rebecca knew that her father could hardly lift the heavy blade now; he had grown overweight in recent years, losing much of his physical power, and he had needed assistance to place the sword so that it seemed to rest nonchalantly in his hands, the tip on the floor between his feet. Yet the artist, Kedar, had succeeded in giving the impression of a mighty warrior, and even though Rebecca saw through the tricks he had used, she

8

admired his technical expertise.

Baldemar had always been a big man, tall and broad-shouldered, but now that he was nearing his fiftieth summer he had begun to stoop a little. The perspective of the picture disguised this, by looking up at the baron as though the artist was at a lower level. Thus the painting's viewer would always seem to be gazing up at a natural superior. Baldemar's dark, bearded face and deliberately stern expression reinforced this impression with a look of disdain that Rebecca knew all too well. Kedar had imbued the heavy-set grey eyes and the mane of coarse hair, now flecked with silver, with a cold, almost regal authority, reinforced by contrasting the strong lighting of the central figure against the almost total darkness of the background. It was as though lightning was flashing overhead, but had chosen to illuminate only the baron. Even though Old Growler and the mysterious trunk in the bottom left-hand corner were in the foreground, they seemed dim by comparison.

Rebecca glanced again at the brass-bound chest, still hoping to find some clue, some proof, that the painting lived. She had never seen the chest before – but it looked strong and secure, with the promise of great riches within. She suddenly realized what Kedar had done, and laughed aloud at this latest irony. Just as the sword and hound were meant to imply active virility, so the chest represented supposed wealth. Perhaps Kedar had not known of the baron's debts to many of his noble neighbours, or of the relative poverty of his lands, but Rebecca doubted it. Her father's situation was common knowledge, and while he kept up appearances as best he could, Rebecca was unhappily aware of his inner desperation. It was the central fact of her existence.

It's no use brooding, she told herself, shaking off a growing gloom, and deliberately returning her attention to the painting. *Just keep looking*, a small voice whispered inside her head.

There was no doubt that Kedar had done a remarkable job, and the portrait had been greeted with almost universal approval. Only Rebecca had been disappointed because there was no magic in it.

She had entertained high hopes for Kedar. There had been a spark in the artist's green eyes, and his voice had been warm and friendly despite the slight stutter which afflicted him when he talked of anything other than his work. The sketches he had done to demonstrate his talent had been lively and intuitive, hinting at secret subtleties beneath the practised shapes. Rebecca had longed to be able to keep some, but Kedar had carefully gathered them all, stowing them away in the satchel which contained his chalks and crayons as well as his precious sheets of paper. However, as soon as Baldemar had commissioned him to add yet another portrait to the ancestral gallery, Kedar had seemed to lose some of his sparkle. He had become a professional craftsman, producing what his customer wanted, and accepting his fee graciously as his due.

After the portrait was complete, Kedar had left immediately, not even waiting to see the painting hung in the spot chosen for it in the gallery. Rebecca had no chance to talk to him – or to show him the other painting, *her* painting. The magic painting.

*   *   *

Rebecca had been ten summers old when she had found the picture of the robed man, who, from his garb and his strangely cut hair, looked as though he must have been a monk. It had scared her badly then; now, nearly eight years later, it still frightened her – a little. And yet it also fascinated her. A bond had grown betwen her and the man in the painting.

The reason for her fascination was simple. Every time she looked at it, the picture had *changed*.

The man was seated at a plain wooden table, in a stone-walled room whose dim recesses were lined with shelves full of books. Only the upper half of the monk's body was visible, but Rebecca knew – without understanding how – that he was tall and had large feet on which he wore rope sandals. His hands were placed on the table, palms down, on either side of a square board. This board was divided into small squares, alternately black and white, and on the squares were placed a number of curiously carved pieces, some black, some red. It was obviously a game of some sort, but nothing like the simple chequers that Rebecca knew. The pieces varied in size and shape from the smallest, which were simple representations of soldiers, to the largest, which was a giant by comparison. This last figure wore a crown and was holding up a perfect sphere. In between were armed men mounted on rearing horses, the slender, curved figure of a woman, several beasts – including a bear and what might be a dragon – and others which Rebecca did not recognize.

The monk was obviously playing with the red pieces, and his dark brown eyes gazed at an unseen opponent on the other, invisible side of the table – the side out of the picture. Rebecca had wondered about this arrangement. Had the artist been the original opponent? Or was it intended that the onlooker should be the player of the black pieces? She had found out much about the picture and its contents since first discovering it, but had still not found the answer to those questions.

All this would have been interesting but hardly remarkable had it not been for two incredible facts. Firstly, while the man always gazed out of the picture, his expression varied constantly. He usually wore a slightly quizzical smile, as if weighing up his adversary, but Rebecca had also seen his plain, pleasant features creased in a delighted, white-toothed grin, and, on occasion, frowning angrily. She had witnessed a fierce look of concentration, and also a soft, dreamy vagueness, as though his thoughts were far away. These changes never took place in her sight, but each time she returned to the picture, it was the monk's face Rebecca looked at first. She no longer found the changes unusual, and had come to think of it as just finding out what sort of mood he was in.

There had been a few occasions when, after glancing away from the painting, she returned her gaze to find that his expression had changed in just those few moments. The first time this happened, during her very first encounter with the monk, Rebecca had run from the room,

11

screaming and afraid, needing the comfort of her bemused nurse. It had taken her some time before she could summon up enough courage to return to the dusty room in the castle's unused East Tower, but once she had done so, curiosity soon overcame terror. This time, the man smiled benignly throughout, as if to reassure the young girl. After that, each approach was accompanied by both a tremor of fear and a mounting excitement. Here at last was something truly magical in an otherwise barren life.

The mystery of the changing expressions would have been enough in itself to frighten and fascinate Rebecca, but the second extraordinary fact, which came to her attention some time later, was even more amazing. The game pieces had always been lined up in four rows, two each on opposite sides of the board. But one day Rebecca saw that a red soldier had been moved forward, and that the monk now seemed to be waiting for a response. Thereafter, the positions of both black and red pieces changed frequently, and the game appeared to progress. Some pieces were even removed, and placed to one side of the table. A game, or perhaps several games, were being played out before her. And the strangest thing of all was that Rebecca sometimes felt as if she were playing too.

As soon as she had lost her initial fear of the unknown, Rebecca had tried to find out all she could about the subject of the picture. She went for this information to Radd, her tutor and her father's chamberlain. Baldemar would never have concerned himself with anything so trivial as monks or board games – or even little girls – but even if he had, Rebecca would still have approached the other man first. The chamberlain was her mentor as well as her teacher, and his attitude towards her had always been sympathetic and caring. Rebecca's mother had died when the little girl was only three, and since then, Radd had been the nearest thing to a true parent that she had.

She never revealed the reason behind her questions, however. For all his compassion and friendliness, Radd disapproved of the myths and legends which told of magical deeds and wizardry, and which so captivated

Rebecca. Instead, she simply quizzed him about the life of monks, and about the game she had seen; he took all this as natural childish curiosity.

Thus, Rebecca learnt that communities of monks tended to live either in the remote areas of their country, on the rugged parts of the southern coastline, or in the mountains to the west and north. The inhabitants of these isolated monasteries chose to dedicate their lives to the gods of the Web, foregoing personal power and wealth, and living quiet lives of contemplation and humility. Although this did not seem to fit in with Rebecca's observations of the character in the painting – some of his expressions had seemed anything but humble – she accepted her tutor's words, and kept any doubts to herself.

'Are their robes always brown?' she asked.

'Most, but not all,' Radd answered. 'Brown is the simplest cloth to make, but I've seen pictures of some dressed in white.'

'Where?' Rebecca demanded eagerly. 'Show me!'

The chamberlain smiled and rummaged around in his small, disorganized library until he found the book he was looking for.

'Here we are,' he remarked, blowing the dust from the tome's cover and coughing. 'Let me see.' He began to leaf through the heavy pages, with Rebecca peering over his shoulder. Inside were hundreds of lines of delicate script, handwritten in black ink. Some of the letters had been decorated with red and gold, and were quite beautiful. Every so often there was a page devoted to a particular drawing or to a painting of some important event. Radd eventually found the one he wanted.

'There. You see?'

Rebecca nodded, both intrigued and disappointed. The men in the picture wore robes like those of the man in the painting – except that these were white – and their hoods had been pulled up so that the monks' heads were hidden. The picture was competently done, depicting a procession of some sort, but it did not have the life of her picture. There was no magic in it.

'Can I borrow the book?' she asked.

13

'No, Rebecca, I'm sorry. It's very valuable.' Radd's tone was such that she knew protest to be useless. He was her friend, but he could be firm when he wanted to. 'I'll read you part of it if you like.'

Rebecca accepted readily, but soon regretted her curiosity. The words were as dry as the dust that had recently covered them, and made little sense. Her tutor soon observed that her attention was wandering, and stopped reading.

'When you're older,' he said, 'I'll tell you more about the Web, and then you'll understand this.'

Rebecca nodded resignedly, and Radd smiled to see her so uncharacteristically solemn. *She hasn't had much of a life,* he thought, *but she's usually more lively than this. Perhaps she's beginning to grow up.* The idea saddened him rather, and he was happy that the next question was more in her normal manner.

'Do they all cut their hair funny?' she asked.

'As far as I know.'

'Why?'

'I've no idea.'

Rebecca stared at him suspiciously.

'But you're supposed to know everything,' she stated accusingly.

'Well, I'm afraid I don't.' He fought to keep a smile from his face, thinking that it was high time this particular delusion of Rebecca's was corrected, and scolding himself for not having realized it before now. 'There is far too much in this world for any man to know it all,' he added. '*Even me.*' After a pause, he went on, 'If I *did*, I'd know why you've developed this sudden interest in monks.' He looked at her expectantly, but Rebecca did not meet his gaze, and remained silent.

'Well?' he prompted.

'I . . . I heard someone talking . . . about them.'

'Who?'

'Scuttle,' she replied, regaining some of her confidence. 'You know how he talks to himself all the time?'

Radd nodded, keeping his face determinedly neutral. Scuttle was one of Baldemar's longest-serving and most senior household servants – and a notorious drunkard.

'I don't think you should take *too* much notice of what Scuttle says,' he told Rebecca seriously.

'I don't,' she replied brightly. 'Especially when he talks about you.'

'What! What does he say?'

But Rebecca only smiled sweetly, and said nothing. Eventually, Radd realized that he was being teased, and laughed. Rebecca joined him, glad that she had managed to divert his attention from an awkward question, and remembering occasions when Scuttle *had* made some rather interesting references to her tutor.

CHAPTER TWO

Rebecca pursued another line of research, concerning the game played by the enigmatic monk and his invisible opponent. Once again, Radd was her main source of information, and he taught her the rudiments of a game called chess, which, according to references in his library, had been played for centuries. He even arranged for a new set of pieces to be carved for Rebecca, but somehow, this was not enough. Although a few of the pieces were similar to those in the painting, most seemed much less interesting – and nothing like the more exotic designs used by the monk.

Nevertheless, Rebecca became a diligent student of the game and surprised her tutor with her instinctive grasp of strategy and her rapid progress. Before long, she began to enjoy these miniature battles for their own sake, never forgetting, however, that her primary purpose was to try to understand the movement of the monk's pieces. She tried many times to analyse the positions of the strangely shaped red and black combatants, and sometimes even drew their alignments, so that she could compare them with their placings on her next visit. She often thought a pattern was emerging, but her hopes were always dashed by a change that fitted none of her preconceived ideas. Each sequence of moves contained yet another mystery.

Rebecca would frequently try to imagine herself in the place of the monk's opponent, endeavouring to work out which black piece to move next. She even tried to *move* her chosen player by closing her eyes and picturing her hand stretching out into the painting. On one occasion, her wish had actually come true and she had stared at the picture with her heart thumping wildly, hardly daring to breathe. Nothing else had happened, though, and when she next came to the secret room the pieces were all in completely different positions.

Her move had been to advance one of the lowly soldiers forward by one square. She tried to repeat this many times, and also tried to think the more powerful pieces into new positions, but after the first occasion nothing ever changed as she envisaged it. Rebecca did not know whether this was because she was ignorant of the way in which these strange players were supposed to move, or whether the monk's games were set on a preordained path. She came to the conclusion that her being able to move the soldier had just been a lucky coincidence.

She tried to prise more information out of Radd about other versions of chess, but with no luck. He told her that over the years there had no doubt been many variations of the game, but that he knew nothing of them.

'Were there ever animals as pieces of a chess set?' she asked once.

'Not that I'm aware of,' he replied. 'Why?'

'Well, men use animals in battles, don't they,' she replied. 'As well as the knights' horses, I mean. Dogs and bears, for instance.'

'I suppose so. But we haven't had war here for many, many years. Thank goodness.'

'I know, but I've read about them in old stories,' Rebecca told him. 'There were even *dragons* then,' she added unwisely.

'Dragons are only mythical creatures,' Radd insisted tersely. 'They never existed. Why do you fill your pretty head with such nonsense?'

Rebecca realized her mistake, and held her tongue.

'Do you want to finish this game or not?' he demanded, still sounding rather cross.

She nodded, and after thinking for a little while, made a move which she knew would eventually lead to her defeat.

*   *   *

17

Rebecca was older and wiser now, and still something of a diplomat. She stood in front of her father's portrait, though in fact she was lost in her memories, and had not taken any notice of the picture for some time.

There's no chance of this painting ever changing, she thought ruefully, and was seized by a desire to visit the monk again. In recent years, the picture's fascination had worn off a little, and she had visited the East Tower less frequently. This had been due in part to her continued frustration that, even after all this time, she was still no nearer to finding the key to the painting's magic. The monk and his game remained an insoluble riddle. The other reason was her growing conviction that if she was ever to find some meaning to her life, it would have to be through her own personal efforts, in her own time, and not because of an ancient painting.

Now, however, the young artist's visit and her subsequent disappointment with his work had rekindled old longings. She turned on her heels and walked along the balcony which ran around all four sides of the Gallery, until she came to the stairs. In doing so, she passed several generations of her ancestors – barons, their wives and children – as well as many depictions of famous events in her family's history – battles, weddings, visits from the emissaries of royalty. Rebecca hardly noticed these, and hurried down to the ground level, where she slipped through the large wooden door into the South Tower, glancing around all the while to make sure that she was not observed.

The lower reaches of the South Tower housed the castle's main armoury, and were dark and cold. Faint light from above made the racks of swords, shields and spears gleam dully, but Rebecca knew her way well, and needed little illumination. She went quickly to the stone staircase that ran in a spiral from top to bottom of the square tower, and began to climb.

The higher levels were more or less empty, and she paid these haunts of spiders, bats and owls no attention. About two-thirds of the way up, she opened a door cautiously, knowing that its hinges always squeaked. When she was sure the coast was clear, Rebecca stepped out on to the battlements atop the east wing of the castle's southern wall. She hurried along, grateful for the protection of stone on either side which made the long drop seem much less alarming. Although the walls were worn in places, they were still sound, and the inner rampart made it unlikely that anyone inside the castle would notice her. Especially if, as now, she resisted the temptation to look over to her left at her father's quarters, and down at the kitchen gardens which separated the East Tower from the rest of the castle.

Rebecca reached the corner of the battlement, turned left, and was immediately faced with the iron-studded door into the tower. She quickly checked that no one else had been this way since her last visit. No, the thread was still intact across the top of the door and the lintel. Her secret place remained secure. She untied the thread and went inside, the gloom swallowing her as the door swung closed. She did not hesitate. Walking carefully up two flights of steep wooden stairs, she reached the topmost room in the tower. Here there was light from several narrow windows and a hole in the roof. There was also a musty smell that Rebecca knew well.

The floorboards creaked ominously as she crossed the room, threading her way through piles of forgotten debris, but she knew that she was safe as long as she avoided the spot beneath the hole in the roof, where rain had rotted the wood. Dust and cobwebs had reclaimed their territory, as always, but most of the items about her were easily recognizable. Rebecca had spent much time cleaning and identifying the contents of this chamber, and although she had never found anything else as interesting as the painting, each object told a story of its own. There were old clothes, slowly turning to dust and mildew, a wooden sword, and a rocking horse, lovingly crafted and painted but fading now. There was a basket full of wax candles which had proved invaluable to Rebecca, though she used them sparingly, knowing that a light in here would cause suspicion. A huge pile of broken furniture filled one corner, while another corner revealed a selection of shards of pottery, some of which had been inexpertly glued together. Rebecca's most exciting discovery had been two leather-bound books, but these had proved to be a great disappointment; they had been so wet and so badly decayed that she could hardly separate their pages, let alone read any of the contents. Even their titles were unintelligible. There was also an odd collection of wooden pipes which she thought might be a musical instrument, two small bells, and several glass jars containing different coloured powders. Her list of finds was long – but insignificant compared to that first discovery.

The painting stood in the driest corner of the room, propped against the wall on a wooden box and covered by a black cloth. Even with the sun's rays falling directly on it, as they did now, there was no indication that there was anything unusual in the room.

As always, Rebecca felt a twinge of excitement and fear as she knelt down and stretched out her hand to remove the covering. The monk stared back at her, his habitual smile of enquiry on his face, but it was the board, brilliantly lit by the mid-morning sunlight, which made her gasp aloud. Not only were the pieces in an entirely new alignment, one which she had never witnessed before, but the board itself had changed. Every other row had moved sideways half a square, so that the familiar chequer-board effect was lost. Black and white now ran in crooked diagonal lines, and the sides of the board were crenellated, like battlements turned on their side.

'What does *that* mean?' Rebecca whispered aloud, trying to make sense of this new layout. She could find no answer, and the monk's enigmatic smile soon began to irritate her considerably.

'I don't know what *you're* looking so smug about,' she told him. 'I'm sure I could beat you if I knew the rules, but *you* won't tell me, will you! You enjoy tormenting me, you cruel . . . ' Several impolite names occurred to her but even here, alone, she did not speak them aloud.

Suddenly feeling rather foolish, Rebecca closed her eyes and tried to calm herself. *It's no use shouting at a picture. What am I doing here anyway?*

She opened her eyes again – and only half stifled the scream which rose in her throat. For a moment her heart seemed to stop beating, then it began thumping madly.

The monk was gone. In his place sat a hideous, misshapen being whose skin glistened red, and whose arms ended in cruel talons. Its mouth was open, displaying pointed teeth and a long blackened tongue; its yellow eyes, just above a long, rat-like snout, were fixed on Rebecca's.

The crooked board was empty. All the pieces lay on the table, most of them on their sides, as if they had been roughly swept aside.

The creature's expression was half-mocking smile, half-human malice. *What rules?* it seemed to sneer.

With a shaking hand, Rebecca reached out for the cloth. She meant only to hide the hideous image from her view, but fright made her clumsy, and the picture fell forward on to the box with a loud bang. As Rebecca gazed in horror at the back of the frame, she experienced a sinking feeling of utter dread. Her muscles were frozen and useless, but she felt as though she was falling – falling as if the dark tower below was swallowing her whole.

She fought desperately to keep herself from fainting. As she struggled to draw breath, a voice from behind her said, 'I might have known I'd find you in this rat-hole. Why *do* you persist in making life so difficult for me?'

CHAPTER THREE

The spell was broken, and Rebecca felt her bones turn to jelly in relief.

'Come on!' the newcomer insisted. 'Don't just sit there. I need your help!'

And I need yours, Rebecca thought, her mind still in a daze. Aloud she said, 'Emer, I am *so* glad to see you.'

Something in her voice must have given away her need, because her friend hurried over to her side.

'What's the matter, Becky? Are you all right?' Emer's voice was gentle and concerned as she put her arm round her friend's shoulder.

'Get me away . . . from that,' Rebecca said weakly.

With Emer's help, she got shakily to her feet, and the two girls stumbled across to the far side of the room, where they sat down on the remains of an old bed.

'From the first time you dragged me up to this room, I knew coming here was a mistake,' Emer remarked. 'All this dust and darkness – it's no *wonder* you imagine things!' Although her words were typically forthright, the tone was kind.

'I don't,' Rebecca whispered. 'It's real.'

'Tell me about it.'

It was a demand, not a request. Rebecca turned to meet her friend's gaze, then lowered her eyes and looked away. Emer's face bore that set look which Rebecca recognized as her I'm-not-going-to-let-you-get-away-with-this-nonsense expression. Rebecca knew that Emer's reaction could be either to laugh uproariously, make a sarcastic remark, or talk non-stop in deadly earnest but, for now, the baron's daughter had no choice but to do as she was told.

'The picture changed again,' she explained.

'I'd never have guessed!'

'It was different this time,' Rebecca went on, rallying herself and allowing a little indignation to colour her voice. Emer smiled.

'How?' she demanded.

Rebecca described in quiet words the misshapen board, and the hideous, malevolent creature which had taken the monk's place. The conviction in her voice was enough to silence Emer – but only for a few moments.

'Gods, Becky! Has Nursey been putting powders in your bedtime milk again?'

'It's nothing like that, and you know it!' Rebecca exclaimed, but she could not help smiling. Emer always made her laugh, whatever the situation – and they had shared both laughter and pain as they grew up together in the ancient castle that was their home.

'Maybe not,' Emer said thoughtfully. 'You're much too nice a girl to *imagine* anything like that – even under the influence of Nursey's tender care. I'd better have a look at it myself.'

'No!' Rebecca made a grab for her friend's arm, but Emer was too quick for her. Rebecca shut her eyes, not wanting to glimpse that hideous image again, even from across the room.

'Did you know there's a name on the back?' Emer asked a moment later.

'No.' Rebecca opened her eyes, intrigued in spite of her misgivings.

'It's pretty faint. Looks like . . . K.A.V.A.N. Kavan. I wonder why he didn't sign it on the front.'

'Perhaps it's not the artist's name . . . ' Rebecca suggested, then shut her eyes again quickly as Emer raised the picture and propped it against the wall.

'Looks just the same to me,' Emer said, sounding almost disappointed. 'Come and see.'

Rebecca opened her eyes a fraction, daring a quick glance at where her friend was pointing. The sun's rays still fell on the picture, and even across the width of the tower room it was obvious that the monk was back in his place, as benign as ever. Even the game-board was back to normal, a square once more, with the pieces lined up for the start of a new game.

But what game is it? Rebecca thought helplessly. *Am I a player – or merely one of the pieces?* She shuddered and looked away.

Emer was the only person with whom she had shared her secret, but the other girl had not been impressed, and was sceptical about the painting's magical nature. She had studied it closely when the mood took her, and even admitted that, on occasions, it *perhaps* appeared a little different from the last time, but she remained untouched by the feelings that haunted Rebecca. Emer's argument was that, even if it *did* change, so what? It was still only a painting. It couldn't do anything, or affect anything in the real world. So why worry about it? Life was full of more immediate and interesting challenges.

'Are you all right, Becky?' she asked now as she returned to her friend's side.

'It's changed back,' Rebecca said weakly.

'And a good thing too,' Emer replied. 'I didn't like the sound of that new fellow.'

'You don't believe me, do you?' There was a suspicion of tears in Rebecca's large blue eyes.

'Of course I do,' Emer stated firmly. 'But it's gone now. So forget about it.' She paused. 'This place isn't good for you. Look at it – full of all this ancient rubbish. It's no wonder . . . '

'But it's full of memories, hopes . . . and dreams,' Rebecca said softly. 'I can feel them sometimes.'

Emer rolled her eyes in exasperation.

'That's just what I mean,' she said loudly. 'Dreams and *nightmares*. I wish you wouldn't come up here alone, Becky. I swear, if it weren't for me keeping you down to earth, you'd have floated off into the sky long ago.'

'Like an angel?' Rebecca asked innocently, smiling at the images her friend's words conjured up.

'Hah! More like a blonde chicken,' Emer retorted. 'You're almost as empty-headed.' She was glad to see

Rebecca recovering her good humour, and her grin widened. 'Besides,' she went on, 'I've got a bit of a problem – and I need your help.'

'Not again! What have you done *this* time?'

'You needn't sound quite so long-suffering,' Emer replied. 'You know I only do these things to add a bit of adventure to your poor, dull life.' She was doing her best to sound self-righteous and annoyed, but the twinkle in her green eyes gave her away.

'Tell me about it then,' Rebecca said mildly.

*   *   *

Emer was Radd's daughter, his only child. She was a month younger than Rebecca, and was like the sister that Rebecca had never known. The two girls had grown up together in the enclosed community of Edgefield Castle, sharing in each other's happiness and sorrows. There were some similarities between them, but even more differences.

They both had blonde hair, worn at shoulder length or just longer, but whereas Rebecca's was golden, with a gentle natural wave, Emer's was paler and quite straight. They were both of medium height and slim, although Emer's figure was more rounded in places – a fact which she counted a curse or a blessing depending on her mood. Both had naturally pale skin, and in Rebecca's case the delicate textures of her heart-shaped face contrasted strongly with her uncannily large, cornflower blue eyes. Emer's eyes were green, deep-set, and seemed always to sparkle on the brink of laughter. In short, Rebecca was possessed of a stunning, almost unreal beauty, so lovely that she had more than once provoked comparisons with the angels, while Emer, by her own admission, was plainer but still undeniably attractive. And it was she, not Rebecca, who could boast of the conquests to prove it.

However, the contrasts between the two girls went beyond their physical appearance. Indeed, their characters seemed at times to be diametrically opposed. Even as small children they had been categorized by the castle staff by the simple terms of 'nice' and 'naughty'. This division was surviving as they grew into womanhood. Rebecca was – to outside eyes at least – quiet, cautious and conventional, tending to view things in a serious manner. She laughed as loudly as any at tales of the absurdities of life, and at Emer's wild jokes, but Rebecca rarely placed herself in the role of storyteller. Within her slender frame, she was often shaken by strong emotions, but she always kept them to herself. Emer, on the other hand, held little back. She was strong-willed and reckless, determined to extract every possible pleasure from each moment, and more than willing to see the funny side of any event – even at her own expense.

The relationship between the two young women was thus one of opposites attracting. This was even true of their social positions, as heir to the baron's realm and servant respectively, and the varying degrees of personal freedom that this entailed. They often annoyed each other to the point of distraction, and had had many a flaming row, but their friendship was stronger than any words, and each would have sacrificed everything for the other's happiness.

There were, perhaps, two main reasons for the intensity of the link between the two girls. They both shared a keen intelligence – something considered an unnecessary encumbrance for most women in Ahrenia, especially for members of the nobility – and each could appreciate the other's point of view, once they had stopped to think about it. The fact that they applied their intelligence to widely differing ends was indisputable, but this did not prevent them from valuing each other's minds.

The second – and the most important – reason for their closeness was that both girls had lost their mothers while they were still very young, and they had grown up in the care of fathers who, for quite different reasons, had entirely failed to understand their daughters. It was in the fire of this sad predicament that their friendship had been forged into an unshakeable bond.

And it was that bond which allowed them to talk to each other as they talked to no one else.

*   *   *

'Tell me about it then,' Rebecca said mildly. She grinned at her friend, feeling the shock and horror of the morning begin to fade. Being with Emer always made the world seem more immediate somehow, reduced problems to a manageable state, and usually brought a smile to her face – a smile which came from deep inside. 'What have you done *this* time?'

'Nothing! I swear!' Emer replied. 'Nothing that I'm ashamed of, anyway,' she added more quietly.

'But?'

'But some people might not see it that way.'

'Like your father, for instance.'

'As always, your judgement of the situation is impeccable,' Emer stated pompously, mocking her friend with a supposedly reverent bow.

'So what did you *do*?' Rebecca exclaimed, caught between laughter and exasperation.

'I went with Galen to the Salt Cellar last night,' Emer started, a touch of pride in her voice. The Salt Cellar was the best – or the most disreputable – tavern, depending on who you believed, in the town of Edgefield.

'Is that all?' Rebecca asked. From her friend's manner, she had expected something rather more dramatic. 'He's taken you there before, hasn't he?'

'Yes, but Father doesn't know that.'

'You've come up with excuses enough before now for an evening's outing,' Rebecca went on. 'And besides, I thought your father liked Galen.'

'He does, sort of,' Emer agreed quietly.

'Then what's your problem? I know he's only a stable lad, but . . . '

'I haven't been home since,' her friend interrupted.

For a moment, Rebecca's mind failed to register the significance of this fact, then—

'You were out *all night*?' she half shouted.

'Yes,' Emer replied defiantly, her eyes gleaming.

For the first time, Rebecca noticed the somewhat dishevelled state of her friend's clothes, and realized

27

that Emer was indeed wearing her outfit of the previous day. She felt shocked by the way Emer took advantage of her relative freedom, and envious at the same time. But Rebecca knew in her heart that she would never behave that way, even if she had the opportunity to do so.

The silence stretched awkwardly.

'What were you doing?' Rebecca asked finally – immediately regretting the question. She blushed furiously.

'Becky, *please*,' Emer said. 'I'm nearly eighteen. We'll be old before you know it!'

Rebecca was relieved by her friend's avoidance of a direct answer but felt at the same time frustrated and intensely curious. She knew, or thought she knew, what had happened between Emer and Galen the night before, but that only made matters worse. What had it been like? Did it really change you for ever? Confused images swirled in her head, making her blush even more, but she was unable to make the connection between them and the girl beside her. She had often been envious of Emer's easy friendships, and of her shameless flirtations with all manner of young men, but it had never seemed at all serious. Their own friendship would always come first. She had been quite sure of that – until now.

'What's the matter, Becky? *Say* something.'

'You will still be my friend, won't you?' Her voice sounded small and pathetic, and she winced at the sound of her own words.

'Of course,' Emer replied, both mystified and concerned. 'Why ever not?'

'Well, now that . . . you . . . and Galen . . . '

Emer finally caught on and laughed softly. She moved closer and put her arm round Rebecca's shoulder, hugging her tight.

'Oh, little one,' she said fondly. 'You have so much to learn. Did you really think that last night was the first time?'

Mixed emotions welled up in Rebecca. She felt resentment at the fact that Emer had had such a secret, and not shared it with her, but also relief and joy that even those momentous events had not harmed their friendship. A new curiosity burned within her.

'Galen?' she asked, turning to look into her friend's eyes.

'Yes.'

From the way Emer said it, Rebecca knew that this was not the whole story, but she could not bring herself to ask about the others. Then her friend grinned, and Rebecca had to follow suit, even though a small part of her felt like crying.

'I don't know why I put up with you,' she said, trying to sound stern but failing miserably.

'Oh yes you do. You'd be bored to death without me,' Emer responded. 'Admit it. *And* I make you laugh. Remember the marrow?'

Rebecca giggled. She would never forget the morning when they had watched the cook, Silberry, standing over the space in the vegetable plot where his prize marrow should have been. He had been nurturing it with single-minded and overbearing determination for Baldemar's name-day feast, only to find that the huge vegetable had disappeared during the night. He had first looked all around, as if to make sure that he was searching in the right spot, then had glanced up towards the sky, as though suspecting that the marrow had been spirited away by a giant bird – or some supernatural force. At this point, the two girls, who were watching from Rebecca's bedroom window, had had to stifle the laughter which was threatening to get out of control.

When Silberry at last noticed the piece of parchment under a stone and bent down to retrieve it, they could contain themselves no longer, and had to turn away, thus missing the incredulity with which Silberry read the note. It informed him that the marrow had been confiscated by order of the Guild of the Friends of the Marrow, who considered its presence to be unseemly so close to such common vegetables as potatoes and leeks. The message was signed 'Zucca Gourd'.

Silberry stomped off to complain to Radd, who found the whole matter incomprehensible – and said so. The cook threatened to resign on the spot, but was dissuaded by promises of future marrows and increased vigilance on the part of the castle guards.

The marrow, of course, was subsequently discovered in one of the kitchen pantries, none the worse for its nocturnal adventure.

'All right, all right, I admit it,' Rebecca laughed, then grew serious again. 'But how do you expect me to get you out of this one?'

'That's easy,' Emer answered confidently. 'Just tell Father that I slept in your chamber. He always believes anything you tell him – it must be those big blue eyes of yours.'

'But Nursey knows you weren't there when I went to bed,' Rebecca objected, 'and if you'd come in later, Pickle would have started yowling and woken her up.'

'Didn't she take any of her *medicines* last night?' Emer asked.

'No.'

'Typical!' Emer grimaced briefly. 'In that case, we'll have to say I climbed in through your bedroom window.'

'Why?'

'Because Nursey had locked the door and I didn't want to wake the whole castle up by hammering on it.'

'But if everyone else was asleep, that means you were out late and you'll still be in trouble!'

'A bit,' Emer admitted. 'Father will grumble and complain, but he'll soon get over it. Besides, if you confess to a little crime, they'll never suspect that you're concealing something much more *wicked*.' She rolled her eyes and cackled insanely.

'Stop it!' Rebecca laughed. 'Your story still doesn't make sense. Nursey knows you weren't in my room this morning.'

'Ah, but I left by the window again,' Emer responded instantly.

'Why?'

'Because I was feeling guilty,' she answered, lowering her eyes in a picture of mock remorse, 'and I was trying to sneak home before my father got up.'

'But he beat you to it?'

30

'Exactly. And so I came to find you.'

'You're a genius.'

'Thank you. Now, do you think you could possibly come with me now and explain all that to my father? I rather suspect he's going to be calling me something *else* just at the moment!'

CHAPTER FOUR

The worst was over, much to Rebecca's relief. Emer had played her part to perfection, all contrition and guilty remorse, eyes demurely downcast. Rebecca had kept her own role to a minimum, just saying what was necessary to confirm her friend's tale. She surprised herself at the steadfast manner with which she was able to blend a few facts into the main fiction, thus making it sound more convincing. After the shocks of that morning, her self-assurance was all the more amazing, and she managed to push aside her guilt at the deception with one simple thought. The truth would have hurt Radd even more.

As Emer had predicted, Radd did not consider the possibility of a more serious misdemeanour when the lesser wrong-doing was openly admitted. Emer submitted to her father's subsequent lecture on responsibility and tact with convincing humility, and it was only when she was at the door of his study, on the way to her bedchamber, whence she had been banished for the day as punishment, that the contrite façade crumbled momentarily. From behind her father's back, she grinned at Rebecca and winked in an exaggerated fashion, before disappearing from sight. Rebecca found it difficult to keep a straight face, but she managed it somehow.

Radd sighed as the door closed behind his daughter.

'I sometimes wish she could be more like you,' he said wistfully.

'Well, *I* wish I could be more like *her*,' Rebecca replied emphatically, determined to continue the defence of her friend.

'Don't say that,' he groaned. 'One of Emer is enough for

any father.'

'But you're not my father,' Rebecca pointed out.

'More's the pity,' Radd answered. He slumped into a chair and waved Rebecca to another, obviously intent on talking. She complied happily, feeling more comfortable now that the deception was over, and having something of her own to discuss. But first, her tutor had more to say about his daughter.

'I sometimes think the two of you must have been mixed up at birth,' he said, smiling ruefully. 'You are so much closer to my own temperament, while Emer has all of the baron's wilfulness.'

Teacher and pupil had long since come to an understanding about Baldemar. They knew his strengths and weaknesses, and spoke of both with equal candour. Each had suffered – and would suffer more – because of the baron's single-minded obstinacy, and this was one of the reasons that they had grown to be so fond of each other.

Rebecca saw the core of truth in his statement, but also its sweeping injustice.

'Our mothers may have had *something* to do with it,' she said lightly, then wished the words back as a spasm of pain passed over Radd's face. His wife's death, though many years in the past, haunted him still. *Unlike my father*, she reflected bitterly, then determinedly put that thought away.

'The baron has few ideas in his head,' she went on quickly. 'And you know how boring that gets. You could never say that of Emer – she has more life in her than a dozen normal people.'

'I know it,' he admitted slowly, nodding. 'I gave up any pretence of being able to control her long ago.' He sighed again. 'There's nothing wrong with her mind. I . . . we gave her that at least. I just wish she would apply herself to something other than flirting with stable boys.'

'She's not a little girl any more,' Rebecca said quietly, knowing the full truth of her words. 'She has enough sense to find her own path, and she'll learn from her mistakes.' *Perhaps*, she added silently.

Radd eyed her thoughtfully.

'I hope you're right,' he said.

'As long as she's happy,' Rebecca replied. 'That's the main thing, isn't it?'

'You are wise beyond your years, young lady.'

'Thank you, kind sir,' she responded, with a little bow of her head. As golden locks of hair bounced around her face, Radd smiled.

'I sometimes wonder which of us is the teacher,' he said.

'Don't get sentimental,' she teased. 'I have a serious question to ask you.'

'Good,' he said, obviously glad to have changed subjects, and rubbing his hands together with exaggerated enthusiasm. 'I like nothing better than to play the role of knowledgeable ancient.'

'You're hardly ancient,' Rebecca responded. 'Not yet, anyway.'

'Any more remarks like that,' he replied, 'and I shall have to thrash you with my walking stick.'

'If you can catch me first.'

'Oh, cruel youth!' he declaimed. 'Mocking the aged and infirm.'

They laughed together. This was a game they often played. For a man who had been born in the castle, and who had seen more than half a century of life there, Radd was remarkably fit. His wiry frame held no excess fat, and he often displayed more energy in his role as the baron's chamberlain than men half his age. The only sign of his advancing years was the fact that his brown hair was thinning now, and flecked with grey. If not for that, his sharp, hawk-like features and clear blue eyes could easily have been mistaken for those of a much younger man.

'What was it you wanted to talk about?' he asked eventually.

'Is it possible . . . ' Rebecca began, picking her words with care, ' . . . to dream, and yet be awake at the same time?'

Radd frowned in puzzlement.

'Not a daydream,' she went on hesitantly, 'but to see something that is really inside your head . . . like a dream . . . or a nightmare?'

'I'm not sure,' her mentor replied slowly. 'That's quite a deep question.' He paused, gazing at the ceiling and collecting his thoughts. 'The human mind is capable of far more than we ask of it during the course of our everyday lives,' he said. 'But dreams are the product of our sleeping minds. I don't think they can intrude when we are conscious. Unless we're drunk, perhaps!' He chuckled. 'And I trust that was not the case with you.'

He grew serious again then, as if realizing what he had said.

'Why do you want to know?' he asked. 'Have you been disturbed by your dreams?' His concern for her was obvious.

'No,' she answered, smiling. 'I sleep well enough . . . '

'When my daughter lets you,' he put in.

Rebecca let that pass.

'It's just that I . . . imagine . . . things sometimes,' she finished lamely.

'We all do that,' Radd said, trying to reassure her. 'Half-seen movement in the corner of your eye, reflections on a window-pane. The sound of the wind in the battlements.' He stopped abruptly. 'The Web preserve me,' he breathed. 'What ideas am I putting into your head?'

'You could have been a poet,' Rebecca commented, charmed by her tutor's imagery.

'Leave poetry to the wordsmiths,' he replied quickly. 'My business is the running of this castle – and that is neither poetic, nor a dream. It's too prosaic for either. Don't worry about your imagination, child. You'd be poorer without it.'

'Have you ever heard of a man called Kavan?' she asked, glad in her turn to be changing the subject.

Radd was silent for a while, rubbing his chin with finger and thumb while he ransacked his prodigious memory. 'Kavan,' he murmured. 'Kavan. The name rings a bell.' A few moments passed as he thought, then he exclaimed, 'Ah, yes, I've got it. My goodness, you are coming up with some tricky questions today.'

'Tell me,' Rebeca said, the usual mixture of fear and excitement pulsing through her.

'He was an artist,' Radd began. 'Quite a good one.'

Rebecca's heart was pounding now. 'He had quite a reputation around these parts, I understand,' her tutor went on. 'But that was centuries ago. Way back before the keeping of any proper records.'

'How do you know of him then?'

'There are old stories, of course. Not that you can put much faith in those,' he added with typical scepticism. 'And a few of his pictures have survived the years. Your father has one, in fact.'

'He *has*?' Rebecca nearly jumped out of her seat. *Surely Radd doesn't know.*

'Yes, up in the Gallery. It's one of your ancient ancestors,' Emer's father went on. 'Do you want to see it now?'

Rebecca nodded dumbly, not knowing whether to be relieved or sorry.

'Come on then.'

They left the chamberlain's quarters, and crossed the main courtyard.

'What made you ask about Kavan?' Radd enquired.

This time, Rebecca had her answer ready. 'I dreamt about his name,' she said. 'The letters were whirling round, then they came together to spell his name.'

It sounded far-fetched and unconvincing to her, but Radd accepted the explanation with a nod. They entered the Great Hall from the north door, and walked along its length to the entrance to the Gallery. Once inside, Radd led her to the upper level and stopped in front of a portrait of a knight in shining black armour, his vizor raised to reveal a bearded, smiling face.

'Oh, *him!*'

'Yes, *him*,' Radd agreed. 'I gather you've heard some of the stories.'

'I'm not a child,' she objected. 'Cadell was famous, wasn't he? For one reason or another.'

'I think this conversation has gone quite far enough,' her tutor replied, with forced severity. 'We were supposed to be discussing the artist, not his subject. Look. There's his signature.'

The small letters were hiding in the corner of the canvas, barely visible.

'You must have seen it without realizing, and that's where your dream came from,' Radd said confidently.

Rebecca nodded, glad that he believed this simple explanation. Her own thoughts were much less certain. *There's no magic in this painting, even though it is well done. Why did he sign this one on the front but not the other? I must be missing something – but what?*

She stared at the picture as if she could prise out its secrets by the force of her will alone. But nothing was revealed.

'Come on,' Radd said. 'I've got work to do, and it's a lovely day outside. Why don't you go and get some fresh air – the sunshine will do you good.'

They walked down to the lower level together, then went their separate ways.

'And Rebecca,' Radd called over his shoulder. 'Don't worry about dreams. They can't hurt you.'

* * *

Deprived of Emer's company, Rebecca wandered aimlessly through the castle. Radd had been right about the weather; a gentle southerly breeze blew from the salt flats and, even in late summer, this meant that the day would be warm and dry. Yet Rebecca shivered, trapped in a cycle of uncomfortable thoughts. She had so often wished that her life could be more like the romantic old stories – which Radd derisively called 'those ridiculous myths' – which had captivated her ever since she had first learnt to read. Magic had been commonplace then. No, that was wrong. True magic could *never* be commonplace, but it had been an accepted part of life, as real as the wind, or sunlight, or the music of songbirds – all those things whose existence was undoubted but intangible. And yet, here she was, having faced a dramatic demonstration that magic *was* present in her world, and her overriding sensation was one of fear. Fear of the unknown, of the inexplicable; fear that the terrible nightmares of her childhood might be returning to haunt her; fear that her own rampant curiosity might lead her down avenues she would rather not explore.

37

Deliberately, Rebecca pushed her anxious thoughts aside, deciding to concentrate instead on an entirely trivial task. She began a game that she and Emer had played many times, ever since they had been old enough to count. The game was called Rooms, and it entailed walking through the castle and counting the number of rooms contained within. This childish pastime had resulted in many arguments, about such desperately important matters as whether the stables were really one big room, or whether each stall should be counted separately with the walkway as another – like bedchambers and a hallway – or whether pantries and cupboards were eligible if you could walk into them without ducking your head. It had got the girls into trouble on more than one occasion, when their enthusiasm for the truth had led to them being rather more inquisitive than was welcome in the servants' quarters, or the baron's. Nevertheless, Rebecca held fond memories of their various attempts.

Needless to say, they had come up with a different total each time, producing answers that varied from sixty-five to over a hundred. Today, she did not really care about the result of her investigations, but needed the security of a familiar and essentially meaningless task.

Eventually, she found herself atop the massive West Tower, having reached the record number of 122 rooms. From her vantage point, Rebecca could have looked out over most of the town and the leagues of flat farmland beyond, as well as the vast salt-flats to the south, but she chose instead to look inwards, preserving the cosy feeling induced by her game, and seeing her home laid out before her like a plan.

As a small child, Rebecca had accepted the intricacies of Baldemar's castle, blithely assuming that everybody's home was the same. After all, she had never known anything else. Later, she formed the opinion that whoever had built the ridiculous structure must have been stark, staring mad. Nothing fitted together as it should have done, and much of the design was plainly absurd – even to her young eyes. Further observation and her own growing understanding of the castle's history led her to accept that many of the architectural eccentricities had come about because countless barons – and their families – had had a hand in the construction, seemingly adding and amending at random, in a bewildering variety of styles and material. Finally, she decided that although the multiplicity of builders could account for some of the oddities, most of them must have been mad anyway.

Dating the older sections had proved impossible, even with the help of Radd's archives. It could be safely assumed, however, that, apart from the massive base-stones, anything that was genuinely ancient would have fallen down by now. Therefore, the enclosed community spread out below her must be of comparatively recent origins. It was quite apparent, for instance, that the Great Hall, which stood near the centre of the square formed by the outer walls, had been rebuilt several times. There were at least six different strata in its wall, varying in colour from sandy red to pale grey, and its windows were all shapes and sizes. The tiled roof was mud-coloured, except where roosting birds had stained it white, and was showing signs of decay in many places, revealing the heavy roof timbers beneath. The baron's lack of money meant that urgently needed repairs could not be undertaken.

The ancestral gallery adjoined the northern end of the Great Hall, and ran in turn into the South Tower. Holding the castle armoury, this was one of three huge, square-built towers which were joined by the crooked southern wall. The West Tower, where Rebecca was standing now, was the tallest of the three, and the only one whose upper levels were in good repair. It stood at the south-western corner of the castle walls, and housed various store rooms and servants' quarters. From the base of this tower, along the inner side of the western wall, were a variety of stone or wooden structures which housed most of the castle staff. The row ended in the 'house' shared by Radd and Emer. Across from these dwellings, and built on to the sides of the Great Hall and the Gallery, were the kitchens, main pantries and store-rooms. This arrangement gave the western side of the castle the look – and often the atmosphere – of a town street.

By contrast, the eastern half of the interior was more open. Baldemar's quarters, and Rebecca's adjoining but separate apartments, were attached to the Gallery and the Great Hall respectively. The designer of these apartments had obviously had a taste for the grotesque; the roof was a conglomeration of gargoyles, miniature turrets and intricately carved arches and buttresses. Subsequent residents had thankfully refurbished the interiors in relatively comfortable style but outside, unseen by most, the peculiar structures remained, now the province of birds and moss.

The kitchen gardens lay beyond, isolating the third tower from the rest of the castle. The East Tower had been abandoned – by all but Rebecca – and had fallen into disrepair. For some reason it had not been built on the corner of the castle, but just north of it.

In the far corner, the north-east, stood the stables. These ran from the main gate at the centre of the northern wall to one of the lesser towers that marked the northern corners of the castle. These towers were circular, more ornamental than defensive, and, as their name implied, were much smaller than the three huge southern structures. Next to the stables, built in a sort of square, were more living quarters, occupied by the stable master and his staff, gardeners, and the legally required number of soldiers.

The baron's soldiers were something of a joke; few had had any proper training, none had ever fought in earnest, and their duties were non-existent. Edgefield Castle was indefensible anyway. No one in their right mind would attack from the south, where the towers and massive battlements provided ample defence, because the north side was little higher than a garden wall which even small boys had no difficulty in conquering. Moreover, the main 'gate' was not a gate at all. It was just a large gap, open to the town beyond, and defended by only two guard-houses. Great metal hinges were slowly rusting in the stonework on either side, but whatever gates had once hung there had long since been removed or rotted away. The position of Commander of the Castle Guard was a sinecure, carrying the responsibility only of collecting a meagre monthly wage, and of wearing a gaudy but threadbare uniform if anyone important chose to visit Edge – an event so unlikely that no one ever took the possibility seriously. The present incumbent did not even live within the castle walls, requiring the comfort of a constant supply of ale close at hand.

One day, all of this will be mine, Rebecca thought ironically. *All one hundred and twenty-two useless rooms of it.*

A white salt-rook landed on the battlements nearby and regarded her solemnly, its head on one side.

'Although, to be strictly accurate,' Rebecca told it, 'all of this will be my *husband's* – if Father has his way.' She desired neither the ownership of the castle nor the husband, but knew that both were more or less inevitable.

'Caw,' said the bird, and flew away.

'My thoughts exactly,' Rebecca answered.

CHAPTER FIVE

Rebecca was in the Gallery once more, but this time *she* was trapped within the gilded frame, stretched out on display for the men who had once been merely paint on canvas, but who were now living creatures. Her father stared at her with hostility in his eyes, his expression as cold as the steel of his war-sword. One booted foot was raised, resting upon the lid of the mysterious chest.

It's full of memories, hopes . . . and dreams.

The lid sprang open, releasing a mass of letters which whirled round in an insane dance. Rebecca tried desperately to read the words they spelt out, but could not do so. As she watched, the letters began to lose their shape; they took the forms of wriggling snakes and worms.

Dreams and nightmares.

Cadell was in front of her now, smirking evilly within his black helmet. With a flick of his gauntleted hand, he produced a table out of thin air. On it stood a chessboard, set ready for play. He gave Rebecca a grotesque wink, then his vizor fell, hiding his face.

I could beat you if I knew the rules.

The pieces started to move. One of them was a salt-rook, its head on one side – but the bird was blood-red in colour. It flew away, leaving a gap which the other players rushed to exploit.

You're much too nice a girl to imagine anything like that.

The table began to dissolve. Suddenly, it was no longer Cadell inside the black metal; Rebecca screamed as the vizor rose to reveal yellow eyes and a glistening red snout.

And the black queen was falling, falling into darkness.

'What is it, my pet? What's the matter? There now, it's all right. Nursey's here.'

But the residue of the nightmare still clung.

Don't worry about dreams. They can't hurt you.

Rebecca had woken with a sob, her chest heaving. Soft hands fluttered ineffectually over her hair and shoulders, and she sat up and hugged the old woman. Nursey returned her embrace, murmuring softly, and, for once, Rebecca did not mind the fussing of her guardian.

'There now. It's all right,' Nursey repeated, patting her charge's back as if she was a baby again, surprised but pleased by the fierceness with which Rebecca clung to her. 'Do you want to talk about it, my pet? You haven't had dreams like this for such a long time.' She pulled back a little, and saw the tears on Rebecca's cheeks. 'Dry your eyes, pretty one, or you'll crinkle up like me.' It was her standard response to tears, and was always accompanied, as now, by a fumbling in the voluminous folds of her clothes for a handkerchief. Eventually the search was successful, and she dabbed at the girl's face.

'Why so sad?' she asked softly.

Some of the details of the dream were already fading, but one image stayed dreadfully clear in Rebecca's mind's eye – the black queen falling, and her own hopeless efforts to save her.

'I dreamt about my mother,' Rebecca whispered at last.

Nursey did not respond for a moment. Then she said, 'She was a fine lady, but she's part of the Web now. That was a long time ago,' she added quietly.

'I still miss her.'

'Of course you do. Of course you do.'

They were silent for a while, both lost in thought.

'Try to go back to sleep,' the old nurse said eventually. 'It's still more than an hour to daybreak. Shall I get you a powder?'

'No, thank you. I'll be all right now.'

Rebecca allowed herself to be tucked in.

'Thank you,' she whispered.

43

'Sleep tight, my pet. Remember, Nursey's always here.'

Alone again in the darkened chamber, Rebecca knew that sleep was impossible. Too many memories had been stirred up, and she would have to lay them to rest before she could risk the realm of dreams once more.

* * *

Rebecca had been five when her mother became pregnant for the second time. At first, this was a time of great excitement for them all, because the baron – who was then in his early thirties and already a large, domineering figure – was convinced that this time he would get the son he so desperately wanted. Celebrations were planned, a suite of rooms prepared for the future heir, and a rota of attendance for nurses and midwives arranged, ensuring constant attention for the baroness. Nursey had been one of these midwives; even then Rebecca had not known her real name. She was a capable woman, who had borne eight children of her own. Now that they were grown, she had decided to care for other women's babies, and used any spare time to perfect her home-made herbal remedies.

Rebecca enjoyed all the activity, and shared in the anticipation. She was fascinated by the thought that the baby was inside her beautiful mother, but found it difficult to understand why they had to wait so long for her little brother to come out. She was too young to realize just how the new arrival would affect her own position, but she somehow sensed that she was receiving less attention from both her parents. Rebecca and Emer, already firm friends, looked forward to the arrival of a new playmate but, as time went by and the baroness grew larger, these feelings of expectation were tinged ever more with an unnameable anxiety.

It was from Nursey that Rebecca first learnt that all was not well, and from that moment on, her worries began to take form, turning slowly into dread. Her mother now spent all her time in her bedchamber and, all of a sudden, she was not so beautiful any more. Rebecca visited her often, which made the baroness smile, but the little girl was never allowed to stay too long.

One night, however, as Rebecca arrived for her customary visit before going to her own bed, she was met at the door by the nurse.

'Not tonight, my pet. Your mother's asleep.'

There was something in the woman's face that didn't seem quite right to Rebecca, who had recently become aware that grown-ups did not always tell the truth.

'Is she all right?' she asked quickly.

Nursey sighed wearily, then caught herself and forced a smile.

'She's very tired, my pretty. Making a baby is hard work.'

'Is it very heavy?' Rebecca asked, still suspicious. Her mother's belly had become so swollen recently that she thought the baby must be huge.

'Yes,' was the reply. 'Too heavy.'

'What do you mean?' the child demanded, sudden fear making her shrill.

'Nothing, pet. Come on, let's get you to bed.' The midwife gave Rebecca a gentle push, but she was not to be diverted.

'Why is it too heavy?' she insisted, as they walked slowly along the corridor. There was no immediate answer, and Rebecca's companion appeared to be deep in thought. The little girl was about to speak again, but as they reached the door to the girl's room, Nursey appeared to reach a decision.

'Get into bed quickly!' she said. 'I'll fetch you a nice drink, and then we'll have a talk. All right?'

Rebecca nodded meekly and hurried to do as she was told. She was changed and sitting up in bed when the midwife returned with a mug of hot, sweet milk.

'Sip it gently,' she advised, 'or you'll burn your tongue.'

The child obeyed, wondering what was coming next.

'Your mother is not very well, Rebecca,' Nursey began. 'And that's what is making her so tired.'

'Is it because of the baby?' Rebecca asked quickly, her drink forgotten.

'Yes.'

'Then why don't you take it out?'

45

'Babies have to come at their own time. If it comes too soon it could hurt your mother, and we wouldn't want that, would we?'

Rebecca shook her head solemnly, her huge blue eyes wide with fright.

'The baby is taking a lot of mummy's strength,' Nursey went on, 'and she isn't able to eat enough to stay strong. *That's* why she needs to sleep more now.'

'Does that mean I can't go to see her any more?' Rebecca asked, remembering her mother's pale face and the nasty smells that were sometimes in her room.

'No, of course not,' the nurse exclaimed with a smile. 'She likes seeing you. And she needs all the love she can get. But you will have to go in the daytime, when she's awake.'

Rebecca nodded, feeling slightly reassured.

'Drink some more milk, there's a good girl.' Nursey watched as her charge took a few more sips. 'You mustn't talk about this to anyone, Rebecca. It'll be our secret. Do you understand?'

'Yes.'

'Your mother wants you to be happy. It's very important that you show her that you *are*. Can you do that?'

Rebecca nodded again, feeling very grown up at having been given this responsibility.

'She *will* be all right, won't she?' she asked quietly.

'Of course, my pet. Now drink the rest of your milk, and go to sleep.'

There was something in the woman's voice which made Rebecca feel uneasy again, but she obediently swallowed the rest of her drink and slid down beneath her sheets. Nursey took the empty mug and went out.

'Sleep well, little one,' she said as she closed the door.

For a little while, Rebecca lay and stared at the ceiling. It was lit by the flickering glow of her night-candle, but her eyes were unseeing, her mind full of other images.

Years later, she understood how it was that she had managed to sleep so soundly that night; by then she was more than familiar with the effects of the nurse's various powders.

46

She awoke the next morning to find Emer sitting on the edge of the bed.

'Wake up, sleepyhead!' her friend remarked when she saw Rebecca's eyelids flutter. 'It's nearly lunch-time.'

'What are you doing here?' Rebecca asked, rubbing her eyes.

'Nursey said I could come in,' Emer replied. 'She said you'd need someone to talk to.'

The conversation of the previous night came back to Rebecca in a rush. With a sinking feeling in her stomach, she scrambled out of bed. Still in her nightgown, she ran across the room and opened the door.

'Where are you going?' Emer cried.

'To see Mummy.'

'You can't!'

Rebecca stopped in her tracks.

'Why not?'

'Because the baby's coming.'

'No, it isn't!' Rebecca said angrily. 'It's too soon! Babies have to come at their own time.'

'Yes, it is,' Emer retorted. 'I heard your father shouting about it.'

Her vehemence made Rebecca hesitate.

'What did he say?' she asked quietly.

'He said, "Early or not, just make sure that he's all right. Understand?" Then he came out of the room all red in the face and went away.' Emer was still indignant at having had her word doubted, and didn't notice that her friend's face had gone white with fear.

'I want to see my mother,' Rebecca said softly, and ran off down the corridor. After a moment's hesitation, Emer followed, and the two girls arrived at the baroness's door at the same time. A scream of pain from inside the room brought them both to an abrupt halt. As they listened, hardly daring to breathe, they could hear mumbled words of reassurance mingled with the clink of glass. Then Nursey's voice said, 'Drink this.' This was followed by sounds they could not identify, then another scream. The little girls both jumped, and Rebecca began to cry. Emer was soon sobbing too and someone within must

47

have heard them. The door opened a fraction and the midwife's head appeared. She looked tired and pale.

'Rebecca, go and fetch your father here quickly,' she ordered. 'Emer, you go with her.'

The girls stared at her for a moment, then Rebecca turned and fled, with her friend close behind. They found the baron in his study, wreathed in the smell of brandy, a goblet in his hand. He looked angrily at the two breathless, tear-stained girls, but said nothing. Rebecca could not bring herself to speak, and began to weep quietly, so Emer had to deliver the message.

'Nursey wants you quickly,' she gasped. 'The baby's coming.'

'I know that!' he snapped. 'I've been up half the night already.' He drained the goblet and threw it into a corner, where it landed with a clatter, startling Rebecca. Baldemar laughed mirthlessly. 'Wants you *quickly*,' he muttered, then strode from the room, staggering slightly and bouncing off the side of the door. The girls made to follow, but were brought to a halt by the baron's voice.

'Stay here, you two!' he roared, adding in an undertone, 'Too many damn women already!'

For a little while, they stood in the baron's study, not daring to look at each other. Then Rebecca's longing for her mother grew too fierce, and she ran out. Emer followed, in spite of her fear.

When Rebecca reached her mother's bedchamber, the door stood wide open. Inside, the three midwives were standing beside the bed; on it, her mother lay quite still. Her face was pale and translucent, like the most delicate porcelain. Baldemar was standing at the foot of the bed, his back to the door, hands on hips.

'Well?' he demanded, his voice loud and harsh in the stillness of the room.

'She is alive, but weak,' one of the nurses answered.

'Not her. The boy!' Baldemar shouted. '*How is the boy?*'

'The baby is a girl,' Nursey told him quietly.

There was an awful pause. Then, 'Gods!' the baron growled between clenched teeth. 'What a waste of time.'

Rebecca's gasp was the only sound to break the ensuing

silence.

'Can she bear another?' Baldemar demanded.

'We don't know yet,' the third midwife began, but the baron did not wait for her to finish. He turned and stormed from the room, his face mottled with rage.

'But sir, your wife . . . !' The midwife's words had no effect on the retreating figure.

In that moment, Rebecca understood what Nursey had meant when she had said that her mother needed all the love she could get. It would be years before the girl would be able to put what she had learnt into words – but inside she knew.

She ran into the room, hardly noticing the sickly, cloying smell that filled the air, and went straight to her mother's side. The baroness's eyes were open, but only stared sightlessly at the bed-canopy above; her breathing was shallow and hoarse.

'I love you, Mummy,' the little girl cried, flinging her arms around the unmoving figure. 'I love you!'

But her mother did not react.

The baroness died two days later. Her illness, combined with the difficult birth, had weakened her to the point of exhaustion – but it was her mind that eventually gave up the struggle. In spite of all her daughter's desperate efforts, she simply lost the will to live. The midwives did their best, muttering darkly about the baron's callousness, and shedding a few tears of their own over the hopeless devotion of the little girl, but in the end they were equally helpless. Nothing could restore their patient's spirit.

Nursey took charge of the distraught child then, beginning a task that was to last for the rest of her life; the baby, who was very weak, was passed to a wet-nurse. Rebecca hated the infant with a searing intensity, and was glad to see it go, blaming it for taking her mother away. She hoped it would die. Her wish was to be granted within a month.

The last time Rebecca saw her mother, the baroness was laid out in a wooden box, clothed in magnificent black ceremonial robes, her face and folded hands white against the dark cloth, and a silver circlet resting in her hair.

Rebecca and Emer stared at her with awe.

'She doesn't look real,' Emer whispered.

'She isn't,' Rebecca replied.

'She's part of the Web now,' Emer said, repeating words she did not really understand, but trying to bring her friend some comfort. 'Only magic could bring her back.'

'She's beautiful,' Rebecca breathed, not listening to her friend. 'Like a queen.'

* * *

Rebecca lay awake still, though the first light of the day was filtering through the window coverings. *Why did that stupid dream have to bring it all back so vividly?* she wondered sadly.

Years later, she had learnt that her father had tried to marry again soon after her mother's death. However, there had been several unpleasant rumours prevalent at the time, and no respectable family would allow their daughter to wed a man whose neglect – it was believed – may have driven his first wife to relinquish her hold on life. In some quarters, he was even suspected of murder, though no action was ever taken. Had Edge been a rich land, Baldemar would undoubtedly have been able to acquire another bride, but that was not the case. And so the baron had grown older and more bitter, alone.

Which is all he deserved, Rebecca thought. *After all, he made my mother's life a misery.* Theirs had obviously not been a love-match.

This was all very well, except that it left Rebecca with a major problem. She was Baldemar's sole heir, his last hope of salvaging his family's succession, his fortune and his land.

Two days from now, I'll be eighteen summers old, she thought grimly. *How much longer can I stave off the inevitable?*

Worn out by her memories, and by unanswerable questions, Rebecca turned on her side and went back to sleep.

CHAPTER SIX

Emer was the first to visit Rebecca next morning. She burst into her friend's room, only a moment after knocking, and practically skipped over to the bedside.

'Happy name-day!' she exclaimed, beaming.

'What?' Rebecca replied, sitting up slowly. Her mind was still foggy from her disturbed night, and she wondered how long she had actually slept. 'I'm not eighteen for two days yet!'

For an instant – but only for an instant – Emer looked disconcerted. She recovered her poise immediately.

'Just practising,' she remarked with a casual wave of her hand.

Rebecca burst out laughing, an action which afforded her considerable relief. After the traumas of recent days, laughter was an important – and much needed – release from tension.

Emer could never keep a straight face for long, and they were soon giggling together.

'And there was I,' Emer said, trying hard to assume a serious expression once more, 'thinking that you were at last a fully fledged, grown-up *woman*. I was quite prepared to be meek and deferential . . . and to take your advice on needlework and other such womanly topics.' She paused to glare at her friend, whose laughter had redoubled at this idea. 'I'm serious!' she exclaimed, in blatant contradiction of the truth. 'But now I find you're just an immature girl like me. Pah!'

'Not exactly like you,' Rebecca protested when she could find the breath. 'There are womanly topics I shall certainly need *your* advice on.'

'Go ahead,' Emer suggested. 'My advice may be defective, even downright misleading, possibly even dangerous . . . but at least it's free.' She assumed a sage-like expression, her fingers steepled and eyebrows raised in expectation.

Rebecca hesitated, not wanting to break the atmosphere of good humour, but in the end she could not resist the question.

'Do you love Galen?' she asked.

Emer's ridiculous façade fell away, and for a moment she seemed nonplussed.

'Yes . . . probably . . . I don't know. Good grief, I said advice, not philosophy! You need an ancient buzzard like my father for that – someone who's past anything else.'

'But he's fun to be with?' Rebecca persisted. 'Galen, I mean.'

'I didn't think you meant my father,' Emer retorted. 'And yes, Galen is definitely fun to be with. I can vouch for that *personally*.'

'Don't you ever worry about having a baby?' Rebecca wanted to know.

'I'm shocked!' Emer exclaimed, her eyes wide in mock surprise. 'What sort of girl do you think I am?'

'But . . .'

'Besides,' Emer went on, ignoring her friend's sudden bright confusion, 'there are *ways*, you know. Ask Nursey.'

'You didn't ask her!'

'Of course not! I'm not completely stupid. Besides, the old dear would probably end up giving you something to clear your sinuses or stop you going bald.'

'Not much use in the circumstances,' Rebecca agreed, trying hard to appear nonchalant.

'You *do* need some advice,' Emer said thoughtfully, serious now. 'I can see I'll have to take you in hand.'

Rebecca was suddenly filled with excitement – and a sort of nervous dread. She had never thought of herself as a woman before, and the prospect seemed full of contradictory promises. *In two days' time I'll be eighteen. And I don't really know anything about life. Thanks to Father.*

'Especially as the baron undoubtedly has plans for

you,' Emer went on, eerily echoing her friend's thoughts. 'And he's not going to wait much longer – unless you can act first.'

'What do you mean? What *can* I do?'

'We'll think of something,' Emer replied, 'but we'll have to be quick. Your name-day may well be his deadline.'

The same thought had occurred to Rebecca.

'He won't tell me who's coming to the feast,' she admitted.

'Well, at least we have a bit more time than I thought,' Emer replied jovially. 'I'd reckoned it was tonight.' She paused. 'Come to think of it, I *thought* the preparations were a bit behind schedule.'

'I hope your memory's better as far as *other* dates are concerned.' Rebecca grinned, surprising herself by her boldness.

'Phew!' Emer breathed. 'At least I won't have to explain *everything* to you.' She pretended to wipe the sweat from her brow.

Rebecca laughed, feeling slightly self-conscious; she was saved any further discussion of this embarrassing subject by a timid knock on the door.

'Come in!' she yelled, knowing that Nursey was partially deaf – a deafness that rather depended on whether the old woman was interested in hearing what was being said.

Her aged guardian peeked round the door, then came into the room once she saw that her charge was awake.

'It's a pretty morning, my pet, Mistress Emer,' she said, nodding in greeting as she shuffled across the room. 'Did you manage to get back to sleep?' she added.

Emer glanced at her friend, eyebrows raised, but Rebecca shook her head slightly. Nursey mistook the gesture as an answer to her question, and sighed.

'Promonious things, dreams,' she stated solemnly. Words had never been Nursey's strong point, and her language was growing more eccentric as she got older. She often confused one word for another, and sometimes used expressions whose existence had hitherto been known only to herself. Rebecca had learnt to sift the meaning from these occasionally obscure utterances, but other people, including Emer, found the old woman either amusing or incomprehensible. As far as anyone knew, Nursey was approximately sixty summers old – a prodigious age indeed – but some thought her even older.

She patted Rebecca's shoulder.

'Never you mind,' she said consolingly. 'I'll give you one of my special powders tonight.' Behind her, Emer raised her eyes heavenward.

'Don't fuss, Nursey,' Rebecca said kindly, though she knew that this was like asking a river to stop flowing downhill. 'I slept like a baby.'

'Well, babies cry and need feeding,' the old woman replied knowingly. Although her memory of recent events could occasionally be haphazard, Nursey could remember details from long ago with absolute clarity. The days when she had brought up her own children and acted as midwife to others were among her favourite recollections.

'That's not what I meant, and you know it,' Rebecca said, smiling fondly. 'I slept well.'

'No more dreams?'

'No.'

Nursey nodded slowly. She appeared to be deep in thought.

'You should get dressed,' she said finally.

'On the other hand, you could always stay in bed all day and catch up on your sleep,' Emer suggested.

Nursey ignored the interruption.

'I'll get your blue dress,' she mumbled, moving towards the large wooden wardrobe.

'It's too hot for that,' Rebecca said hastily, clambering out of bed. 'I'll wear my skirt and blouse, like yesterday.'

'Can't,' Nursey replied shortly.

'Why not?'

Obviously puzzled, the old woman frowned. 'Didn't I tell you?'

'Tell me what?' Rebecca asked, becoming a little irritated.

'The baron wants to see you in his study,' Nursey replied. 'And you must wear the blue dress. You know how he likes you to look soporificated.'

'Oh.' Rebecca could think of nothing else to say, and

Emer's grin had disappeared. This was too close to their recent discussion for comfort.

'What does he want?' Emer asked eventually. A summons such as this was rare enough, and the timing of this one seemed particularly ominous.

'That's not for me to say, or for you to ask,' Nursey answered officiously. Then her tone became conspiratorial, and she added, 'But a little whisper told me there are to be guests at my pet's name-day feast. Men,' she concluded with a satisfied smile. Her expression implied that this news should be both eagerly anticipated and welcome, and she failed to notice the worried glances exchanged by the two girls. Their worst fear was a step nearer to becoming a reality.

'Who?' Emer asked, unable to stop herself in spite of Rebecca's continued silence.

'Just guests,' Nursey replied smugly. She smiled to herself as she laid out the heavy blue dress, and began humming an unrecognizable tune.

Rebecca donned her clothes in silence, then followed Nursey from the room.

'I'll wait for you here,' Emer told her.

Rebecca nodded. We'll think of something, Emer had said. *Whatever it is, we'd better think of it quickly!*

* * *

'Come in, daughter.'

For once, Baldemar sounded almost affable, a state normally only reached after his consumption of a good deal of drink. He and Radd were seated in the baron's study, and the chamberlain rose as Rebecca came in. His expression was serious.

'You look beautiful,' Baldemar said approvingly. 'A dish fit to set before any man.'

Rebecca's heart sank even further.

'I am not food to be eaten, Father,' she said quietly.

Normally, such insolence would have brought an angry rebuke, but the baron was in determinedly good humour this morning.

'Of course not,' he boomed jovially. 'We have important matters to discuss. Leave us, Radd. I'll call you when I need you.'

'Yes, my lord.' The chamberlain walked quickly from the room, as if he were glad to leave. As he passed Rebecca, his back to the baron, he mouthed, *Stay calm*, with the merest hint of an accompanying smile. She knew his advice to be good – whatever it was that her father wanted to discuss – but if the topic was what she dreaded, then staying calm would be easier said than done. She had no wish to risk the baron's violent temper, but . . .

'Sit down, Rebecca,' Baldemar said as the door shut behind Radd. She obeyed, placing her hands demurely in her lap; keeping her expression neutral, she waited.

'I have good news for you,' he began.

For you perhaps, she thought bitterly. *Not for me.*

'In two days, you will be eighteen,' the baron went on, beaming. 'Accordingly, I have agreed to your betrothal. It will be announced publicly at your name-day feast.'

Rebecca could not keep her dismay from showing in her face. This was worse than she had thought! That possible suitors were to be guests in the castle was predictable – after all, it had happened before – but the fact that the betrothal had already been agreed was much more serious. Judging by the smug look on her father's face, the agreement must be so profitable that she would have no chance to change it.

She swallowed hard, and spoke with as calm a voice as she could muster.

'Am I to have no choice in the matter, Father?'

The first tiny flash of annoyance showed in the baron's eyes, but he kept his smile.

'It is my choice, daughter. As is my right, and my duty. Your duty is to obey me.'

'Yes, Father. But you have not even told me who it is I am to marry!'

'That need not concern you,' was his calm reply.

Rebecca was too astonished to respond. *My future husband? Not concern me?*

'You will meet him soon enough,' Baldemar continued.

'He is young and of noble birth, the second son of a baron.'

Even as her brain reeled in bewildered horror, Rebecca noted cynically that her father had evidently lowered his sights. The offspring of higher-ranking nobles had obviously proved beyond his reach; he had had to settle for one of his own level – and a second son at that. Which made it surprising that he was so pleased with the arrangement.

He's hiding something, she realized with growing conviction.

'You can stop looking so amazed,' the baron remarked testily. 'You are a full-grown woman now, and it's time you put childish things behind you once and for all. You must dress and act according to your age and position. I shall expect you to be a credit to my House. Is that understood?' There was ice in his voice now.

Rebecca struggled to find her next words.

'May I not know even his name?' she asked shakily.

'Cranne,' he replied shortly.

The name meant nothing to her.

'How can you expect me to love a man I do not know?' she burst out, unable to contain her misery any longer.

'Love?' Baldemar roared, his face suddenly contorted with anger. 'Love? What has *that* to do with anything?' He rose to his feet, towering over his daughter who shrank back in fear. Rebecca wanted to protest, to cry out that her mother had died because *she* had not been loved, but even if she could have found her voice, Baldemar would not have heard her. His lecture became a tirade.

'How can you be so stupid? Have I taught you nothing about the necessities of position, of the responsibilities of nobility? The House of Edge? *Those* are the things you should be heeding, not some childish fantasy about love and *romance*.' He sneered, making the words sound obscene. 'You sound just like a common serving girl.' He paused for a moment and when he next spoke, his voice had returned to a relatively normal tone. 'I've been lax with you for too long,' he stated. 'You have spent too much time with your inferiors. From now on, you will see less of Emer – she is clearly a bad influence. I shall speak to Radd.'

57

The baron turned away, as Rebecca gulped convulsively. For an instant, she thought she might be able to make her escape, but her father rounded on her once more, evidently intent on giving her another piece of his mind.

'You should be grateful!' he shouted. 'The Web knows I've done all I can to find you a good husband, but *you* . . . you had to be so high and mighty . . . so unwomanly . . . it's no wonder the best men were put off.' Baldemar almost choked with self-righteous indignation. 'We could have been part of one of the *great* Houses if only you hadn't been so confoundedly stubborn!'

The complete injustice of this latest outburst was more than obvious to Rebecca, but she knew better than to argue with her father in his current mood. There *had* been several possible suitors – some of them high-ranking – but every one of them had been put off the possible match by factors other than Rebecca's habitual coolness. The obvious poverty of Baldemar's estate and his widespread debts, coupled with the man's transparent ambition and dubious reputation had been more than enough to prevent any betrothal contract.

Some of her suitors had actually seemed quite pleasant – though others had been quite nauseating – but Rebecca had never had a chance to try to get to know any of them. Sickened by her father's obsequious behaviour, she had had to distance herself from the proceedings. How could the baron be so blind to his own sheer awfulness?

'Would it have hurt you to have smiled at them – just once?' Baldemar continued, his anger unabated. 'To have worn something pretty, made your suitors feel welcome? Oh no, not you. You had to slump around like a rag doll in the rain, wearing an expression to match. Who could want a woman like that?' He paused for breath, then went on with malicious satisfaction. 'Well, *this* time, young lady, it's going to be very different. Everything has already been decided, and you are going to welcome your future husband with open arms and warm smiles. If you don't, it will be the worse for you! Now get out of here!'

He waved an arm in dismissal, and Rebecca fled.

CHAPTER SEVEN

Emer provided the shoulder to cry on that Rebecca so desperately needed. As Rebecca related her sorry tale, her sobs of misery turned to tears of rage.

'He can't do this to me. He can't!' she breathed, shaking her head in disbelief. 'Marry me off to a man I've never met, never even heard of?'

Emer tried her best to console her friend, but there was little she could really do except listen – and grow angry in her turn.

'We could run away,' she suggested without much conviction.

'You might be able to,' Rebecca answered. 'You have the freedom to do more or less as you choose.' There was a hint of envy in her voice. 'But he'll have me watched now, I know he will. Besides, I'm not even supposed to see you any more.'

'Why?'

'Because you're a bad influence!'

'Well, you can't really argue with that, can you?' Emer smiled, but Rebecca was not to be comforted.

'What am I going to do?' she wailed.

'We'll think of something,' Emer replied. *We must!* she added silently.

*   *   *

Baldemar's penury and his consequent desperate efforts to lift himself from that state had its roots in events many centuries earlier. When the great salt flats were formed, almost half of the barony had been covered, rendering the land lifeless and without worth. If the old legends were to be believed, the capital city of the time had also been submerged. Derith had reputedly been quite close to Edge's southern border, and this proximity to the centre of both royal government and trade had naturally led to considerable prosperity for Baldemar's ancestors. But with Derith gone and Ahrenia's capital now Garadun, far to the north, Edge's prominence had declined rapidly. Not only was it too far from the seat of power to hold any influence, but the vast extent of the treacherous salt-flats meant that Edge was no longer on the country's main trade routes between the coastal ports to the south and the northern cities. It was a rare businessman who would entrust his precious cargo to the tender care of the notorious 'Archaeologists' who, for a fee, would undertake to guide travellers across the salt. Most people preferred the much longer – but infinitely more secure – trek round the eastern side of the salt.

As a consequence, Edge's trade had suffered badly, and baronial revenue from transit taxes had fallen to almost nothing. The House of Edge could do nothing but watch as the lands to the east, between the salt and the Fire-dart Swamps, prospered.

It was believed nowadays that Edge was so called because it bordered the salt flats, but this was not the case. Centuries before, rich deposits of iron ore and other minerals had been discovered in the area, and its people had subsequently learned the dangerous arts of smelting, forging and shaping metal. The best smiths had become famed weapon-masters, and their blades were prized by warriors all over the country. The ancient barons had harnessed these skills to their own advantage, promoting their subject's wares until the phrase 'the sharpest edge' had become synonymous with their swords – and then with the land itself.

In the years that followed, the mines had mostly been worked out, meaning that ores and metals had to be imported. Later, through the countless decades of peace, the fall in demand for weaponry meant that the smiths who still worked had to turn their talents to more mundane items. Baldemar still found it hard to swallow the fact that he now ruled over the realm's primary producer of cutlery – and this had been another reason for his insistence that his sword be included in the portrait.

Edge had had little else with which to replace the declining industry. Its agricultural land was of poor quality, for obvious reasons. In fact, the farmers waged a constant battle against the salt which threatened to destroy their crops altogether. A vast array of banks, ditches and silt-channels held it at bay, but the defences were in need of constant repair. Every year the destructive white crystals crept forward, and one more farmer gave up the unequal struggle and fled to more hospitable pastures.

Much of the peasantry now lived at little more than subsistence level, and those that were driven from their land into the town found themselves no better off. Beggars were a common sight on the streets of Edgefield.

A few scraped a living from the export of salt, but that was a meagre business; salt was such a common commodity that dealing in small quantities was almost worthless.

Even so, the barons of Edge could have fared well enough had they not squandered what remained of their fortunes on follies and absurd schemes. Baldemar's grandfather, for instance, had been convinced that gold was to be found beneath blackthorn trees, and had offered massive rewards for information about their location. For a short time, various enterprising characters had done a roaring trade in saplings. These could be planted, then conveniently 'discovered' and reported to the baron's representatives – many of whom turned a blind eye to the newly dug earth in return for a cut of the proceeds. Needless to say, no gold was ever discovered, but by the time the baron had been persuaded of the error of his ways, the coffers in Edgefield Castle were emptier by a considerable amount.

Baldemar had inherited an already bankrupt barony while only in his teens, and his constant struggle to borrow money and find ways of restoring his House to its former glory had soured him early in life. Now, his self-imposed task had become an obsession, and his chances of success had finally dwindled to one last hope. Rebecca.

Scuttle had a way of dealing with hangovers. He took his own head off.

The procedure was simple enough. First, he undid the imaginary knots which secured it to his neck and then, very carefully, with one hand on either side, he removed his head and laid it gently on his pillow. He had performed this delicate operation so many times now that it took little effort to ensure that the unpleasant after-effects of excessive alcohol intake stayed in his bed. Gone were the days of thumping headaches, the shooting pains whenever he looked at anything brighter than a shaded candle, and the rooms that spun round, making him feel extremely sick. The flesh and bone which remained on his shoulders, incapable of feeling pain or nausea, was a simple receptacle for sight, sound and smell; its only purpose to guide him through the early part of the day.

Later, when he knew it would be safe, Scuttle could return to his room and gingerly replace his head, securing the knots tightly. Now he would be complete again, happily facing the rest of the day and ready to appreciate the magic of alcohol once more. He never worried about leaving his head un-attended because few people were foolish enough to venture into his private room, and the few that did were miraculously unable to see his head as it lay on the pillow. Anyone who *did* visit his room met with a torrent of abuse if Scuttle was at home, and were soon driven away by the overpowering odours of brandy spillage, smoke and stale air if he was not.

But this morning was to prove different.

The previous night had been an especially festive one. The baron had received private and final confirmation of the details of Rebecca's betrothal, and he had been in gleeful mood, ordering a plentiful supply of wine and stronger spirits with which to celebrate. As Baldemar's butler and personal servant of many years, Scuttle knew better than to ask for a reason for the celebration, but took full advantage of it, sampling the rare liquid delicacies from the castle cellars, and ensuring that any unfinished bottles found their way to his room. The baron and his butler had grown drunk together in long-accepted fashion, enjoying a cameraderie which none the less never quite breached the gulf in rank between them.

Scuttle had woken early, despite his late night, and realized immediately that he was in dire need of his special technique. Leaving his head on the pillow, he walked automaton-like to the kitchens to check that all was well. He was given the news that although Baldemar had risen, he wanted neither breakfast nor any other service, as he was currently in conference with Radd and would shortly be visited by his daughter. Satisfied, Scuttle returned to his room and sat down gratefully in his only chair. Within moments, he was fast asleep.

Some time later, he was rudely awakened from a dream – about gigantic barrels of ale – by what appeared to be a small tornado invading his room. As he struggled awake, the whirlwind vision spoke.

'Gods, it's stuffy in here! How can you *stand* it?'

Scuttle's eyes forced themselves into focus; he recognized Emer, and groaned. His real head still lay on the pillow, and without it, he felt incapable of dealing with this outrageous invasion of his privacy. He watched her sourly as she completed a last circle of inspection, then winced as she plumped herself down on his bed, rattling the teeth in his abstract skull.

'It's good manners to knock, you know,' he grated peevishly.

'I did,' his tormentor replied breezily. 'You didn't answer.'

'Go away,' Scuttle said. 'I'm busy.'

'Rubbish! You were asleep,' she responded.

He scowled, wishing he could replace his head, but knowing it was too soon for that – his hangover still held sway.

'*You're* in a good mood,' Emer commented, her voice sounding obscenely loud and cheerful in the cluttered chamber. 'All right, I'll go – so long as you answer me one simple question.'

Scuttle regarded her in sullen silence.

'Who's Cranne, and what's he like?'

'That's two,' the butler objected grumpily.

'What?'

'Two questions.'

'Who is he?' Emer exclaimed, almost shouting.

Scuttle shrank back, feeling his delicately balanced and self-made protection begin to crumble. He swore under his breath as he felt the headache thump once more.

'Baron's son from up north someways,' he muttered. 'Don't know any more.'

'But you must!'

'Don't.'

'Then who does?' Emer insisted.

'Go away,' the butler responded.

'You're hopeless!' she exclaimed, exasperated. 'There must be someone apart from Baldemar who knows of him.'

Scuttle said nothing, and just stared at her accusingly; eventually, much to his relief, Emer rose and went to the door. She paused there, and gave him one last, hopeful look.

'I'm sorry I disturbed you,' she said gently.

Scuttle nodded, immediately regretting his action.

'Try Cluny,' he whispered.

Emer smiled. 'Thank you,' she replied gratefully. The door closed very softly behind her.

* * *

'Cluny?' Rebecca exclaimed. 'Loony Cluny?' That was the inevitable name by which the alchemist had become known to all the children of Edgefield. 'How could he possibly help?'

'He's a good source of information,' Emer replied. 'Know your enemy. That's the first rule of battle.'

'What's the use?' her friend asked gloomily. 'When we've already lost the war.' Her earlier anger had turned to a deep depression as the certainty of her fate sank in. But Emer was having none of it.

'You're becoming a serious disappointment to me,' she announced hectoringly. 'You can't just take this lying down.' She refrained from adding that if Rebecca did not put up some resistance, that was exactly what she would be doing.

'Don't you ever listen?' the other girl retorted. 'It's all agreed. Baron to baron. Man to man.' Her beautiful face contorted with bitterness. 'Who am I to try and change things?'

'Well, you may be giving up,' Emer announced, 'but I'm not.'

'What else can I do?' Rebecca asked limply, as if uncaring of her friend's concern.

'Kill yourself?' Emer snapped.

The two girls stared at each other in shocked silence for a few moments, then Rebecca began to cry softly. Emer took her in her arms, whispering words of encouragement.

'I didn't mean it, you idiot! We haven't even started yet. You *mustn't* give up!'

Slowly, Rebecca's weeping subsided.

'What should I do?' she asked. Her voice was small, but this time she sounded more positive.

'That's better!' Emer drew back and gave her friend's shoulders a gentle shake. 'I didn't expend all my time and energy on bringing you up properly just so that you could throw yourself at the first man who comes along.'

Rebecca smiled through her tears.

'Go and talk to my father,' Emer went on. 'He must know something about the agreement, and he'll tell you just what's going on.'

'He won't act against my father though.'

'Not directly,' Emer admitted, 'but we may find ways . . . '

'Are you really going to see Cluny?' Rebecca asked, wiping her eyes.

'No. I'm going to send Galen,' her friend replied. 'That boy has his uses.'

Emer grinned, and, for the first time, Rebecca felt a tiny spark of hope. Perhaps she had more allies than she'd thought.

CHAPTER EIGHT

Galen knew he had come to the right place when he heard a muffled roar from the basement. As he waited, not knowing what to expect next, the door flew open and dense green smoke billowed out.

He threw himself to the ground, hoping to avoid any flying missiles; when nothing else happened, he stood up, dusted himself down, and approached the building with some caution. The street had been quite crowded only moments before, but now it was suspiciously empty. That didn't make him feel any better.

'You all right in there?' he called, peering in through the smoke.

He was answered by a racking cough. Then a man and a woman emerged from the green smog, and staggered up the steps to the street, their arms about each other.

'Are you all right?' he asked, looking from one to the other. The man was wearing a purple doublet with a silver thread running through it, blue hose, and a close-fitting skull cap. It was an amazing outfit – Galen had never seen anything like it. The woman wore a simple brown dress; her hair was long and straight, the colour of moonlight on water. Their faces were both stained green, and they grimaced with their efforts to breathe.

Their choking eventually stopped, and the couple turned to face each other, ignoring their visitor completely.

'I *told* you you'd put in too much walking ink,' the woman said accusingly.

'But it was such a little pinch,' the man whined defensively.

'Pinch? Pinch? You call that a pinch? More like a

handful, you great oaf!'

'I'm sorry, my love. I only thought . . . '

'Don't try to soft soap me, Clue. You *don't* think. That's your trouble. You know the experiments are delicate . . . '

The man caught sight of Galen just then, and he suddenly began to cough loudly, gesturing with his head. The woman looked round, saw the stable-lad and was silenced, her mouth still open in mid-recrimination.

Now that he could see them better, Galen realized that they were younger than he'd first supposed, perhaps only ten years older than his own two decades. They both had piercingly coloured eyes – one set green, one set blue – that seemed to stare right through him.

'Are you Cluny?' he asked hesitantly.

'I am,' the man replied. 'Alchemist, historian and practitioner of the higher arts.' His voice had become louder as he spoke, and infinitely more confident, almost pompous. 'What can I do for you?'

Galen was somewhat taken aback by this introduction, and glanced at the woman, who had withdrawn a little.

'This is Anselma, my wife and my assistant,' Cluny added. The woman nodded curtly in response to Galen's slight bow.

'I've come from the Castle,' he said. 'With a message for you – and some questions.'

At these words, Cluny was instantly attentive.

'Then come in, come in,' he said. 'Er . . . it should have cleared by now.' Anselma led the way down the steps. As he followed, Galen noted that, above ground, the building was more or less a ruin. He had not noticed this until now, but it wasn't hard to imagine why.

'What was the smoke?' he enquired.

'That? Oh, just a little experiment,' Cluny replied jovially. 'I am in the forefront of research into weapons which will make swords, bows and arrows and such like totally obsolete. One day, Edge will be as famous for my discoveries as it once was for its blades. Would you like to see?'

'No! No, thank you,' Galen said quickly. 'I seek advice on very different matters.'

67

They were inside by now, and Cluny spread his arms wide, to indicate the large cluttered room before them.

'My kingdom,' he explained. 'Containing all the wonders of the world.'

By now, Galen was half-way to believing that his host's reputation for insanity was actually well deserved, but he was too busy trying to make sense of the room and its contents to take the thought any further. In one corner, tendrils of green smoke still rose from a grubby sink, and the shards of broken pottery and glass were strewn about. But somehow, the air inside seemed clearer than that outside. A number of tables were laden with pieces of mysterious equipment, together with bottles, jars, and pieces of paper that were covered with an illegible scrawl. A human skeleton stood stiffly to attention in a corner of the room; beside it was a rack containing an extraordinary variety of pliers, hammers, knives, and other implements which Galen could not identify. He wondered whether he had stumbled into a torture chamber, but then he saw the large, rumpled bed, the endless shelves of books, the fish swimming in glass bowls and the numerous plants which flourished in their pots. The room began to take on a different aspect.

'You had a message?' Cluny prompted. 'From the baron?'

'Actually, it's from Radd, the baron's chamberlain,' Galen replied, recovering some of his natural poise. *Actually, it's from his daughter*, he thought, *which almost amounts to the same thing*.

'You're forgetting your manners, Clue,' Anselma put in.

'Of course, of course. Would you care to sit down? Can I get you a drink?' The self-styled alchemist began to clear a heap of jars and books from a chair.

'Don't bother,' Galen said. 'I'll sit here.' He hoisted himself on to a clear space on the edge of one of the tables. Anselma looked nervous, but Cluny just smiled.

'Make yourself at home,' he beamed. He perched on the arm of the chair.

'The chamberlain wanted me to tell you that the baron appreciates the worth of what you are doing,' Galen improvised, 'and hopes to be able to invite you and your lady wife to the castle in the near future.'

'Well, this is *most* gratifying,' Cluny began. 'I had no idea . . . ' He paused modestly.

'Your exploits and experiments are well known.' Galen went on, beginning to enjoy himself. *Especially to every small child in Edgefield*, he added silently. 'And with your help, the baron looks forward to restoring Edge to its rightful pre-eminence.'

Cluny bowed in acknowledgement, though Galen could not help but notice that the alchemist's pleased reaction was not matched by that of his wife. Anselma looked altogether more sceptical.

'Pretty words from someone dressed like a stable-lad,' she muttered.

'Please, my love!' Cluny exclaimed, looking troubled.

'It's true that I work in the stables,' Galen admitted. 'But I do have some learning. That is why E . . . Radd uses me as an envoy.'

'Of course. Now what about those questions of yours?' Cluny was glad to change the subject.

'There is to be a wedding in the castle,' Galen began.

'You don't want love potions, do you?' Cluny interrupted, leaning forward and squinting suspiciously from beneath furrowed brows. 'Because they don't work.'

'We've proved it,' Anselma added emphatically.

'Besides,' her husband went on, 'you're a handsome enough lad – I'm sure you're not in need of any artificial help. Ha ha!'

'No,' Galen said, smiling in spite of himself. 'You've got the wrong idea. It's not for me . . . '

'A *friend* is it?' Cluny asked, winking significantly.

'No . . . I mean . . . I don't want any love potions!' Galen half shouted. 'I want some *information*.'

'Ah,' the alchemist said. He leaned back again, knocking a pile of books to the floor and raising a cloud of dust. He fussed about for a few moments, then waved a dismissive hand and returned his attention to his guest. Anselma watched her husband in long-suffering silence, but he seemed quite unperturbed.

'Who is getting married then?' he asked.

'Rebecca, the baron's daughter.'

'She's a pretty thing,' Cluny mused. 'I'm surprised some fellow hasn't snapped her up before now.'

Anselma clicked her tongue and glanced up at the ceiling; Cluny, noting her disapproval, looked shamefaced.

'I think the baron may have had something to do with that,' Galen commented, grinning.

'Of course. Quite. Not my place to . . . ' The alchemist smiled gratefully and waited for Galen to continue.

'Rebecca is to be betrothed at the feast for her eighteenth name-day, in two days' time. Everything seems to have been arranged in some haste and secrecy, and in order to set Rebecca's mind at rest, the chamberlain has suggested that you – as a renowned historian – might be best placed to ensure that her suitor is . . . er . . . suitable.'

'Suitor . . . suitable. Ha, ha. Very good!' Cluny exclaimed.

'Surely the baron will have seen to such an important matter,' Anselma said, looking very serious.

Galen nodded and turned to face her. 'Of course, my lady, but . . . ' He paused, seeing the hint of a smile on her face. 'This is a matter of some delicacy, as I'm sure you'll understand.'

'Of course,' Cluny whispered eagerly, leaning forward again. By now, Galen had their undivided attention, and he began to feel confident that they had accepted his tale. *My talents have been wasted*, he decided, making sure that he kept a straight face. *If they swallow this lot . . .*

'The baron is quite satisfied,' he began in confidential tones, 'but, as chamberlain, Radd is responsible for many things within Edge – things that are perhaps not best suited to the baron's undoubted strengths and qualities. I'm sure you take my point.'

Cluny looked mystified, but Anselma nodded vigorously and her husband followed her cue.

'Of course,' he said again.

'Then you'll help me?' Galen asked hopefully.

'If I can, dear boy. If I can,' Cluny replied jovially. 'What's the fellow's name?'

'Cranne. He's the second son of one of the northern barons.'

'Do you know anything else of him?' Anselma asked.

'That's all the information I'm allowed to impart,' Galen replied solemnly, hoping he sounded convincing. *It's all I know.*

'Come back in an hour,' she said decisively.

'We shall have to consult our references,' Cluny explained pompously. As he stood up, a jar fell from the chair, spilling a fine blue powder all over the floor. Galen slipped gingerly off the table and made for the door.

'Thank you,' he said. 'I'll be back later then.'

He turned and ran up the steps to the street, which was busy once more, and strode quickly away. He managed to keep from laughing until he was out of earshot.

*   *   *

At first, Radd would not meet Rebecca's eyes, and her small hopes receded. If *he* was going to hide the truth from her, then it must be worse than she had imagined.

'Couldn't you have warned me?'

'I didn't *know*,' the chamberlain protested, looking hurt by the accusation in her voice. 'The baron kept the whole thing to himself. I only found out about it this morning, just before you did.'

Rebecca knew that while his words were obviously sincere, they were not the whole truth.

'Tell me about Cranne,' she ordered.

'He's the second son of Farrand—'

'I know that!' she snapped. 'Tell me about *him*. How old is he? What does he look like? What kind of man is he?'

Radd spread his hands wide.

'I don't know, Rebecca.'

'Why is Father so keen to marry me off to him? And in such a hurry!'

Radd looked at his feet, saying nothing.

'I thought you were my friend,' Rebecca whispered sadly.

He looked up then, and she saw the pain in his eyes.

'I am,' he said quietly. 'As the Web is my witness.'

'But?' she prompted.

'I can't tell you what I don't know,' Radd said miserably,

71

'and it is all settled, Rebecca. There's nothing I can do. Baldemar and Farrand made the arrangements between themselves, and have exchanged signed agreements. I've seen the betrothal contract, and the terms are all clearly laid out. All that's left is the public announcement.'

'How much am I being sold for?' she asked, unable to keep the bitterness from her voice.

'Please . . . '

'How much?' she demanded.

'Ten thousand crowns, plus a good deal more in goods and promises of future aid.'

For a moment, Rebecca was stunned into silence. It was a colossal sum.

'Well, I only hope I'm worth it,' she breathed. 'There must be *cheaper* ways of buying a woman.'

Radd winced.

'Farrand must be terribly anxious to get rid of his son,' she went on. 'What is he? A hunchback? Or a dribbling idiot?' Her voice was shrill now, close to hysteria.

'He's nothing like that!' Radd exclaimed.

'But you said you don't know anything about him!'

'It's in the contract,' he replied, shamefaced. 'One of the conditions was that Cranne must be of sound body and mind.'

'Well, that's a big relief!' Rebecca laughed humourlessly. 'So what's in it for them?'

'Cranne becomes baron on your father's death,' he replied. 'One of the king's men will be here on your name-day, to ratify the change of succession.'

'Edge is hardly the richest prize in the country,' she retorted. 'Why, you could buy half of it for ten thousand crowns!'

Radd shrugged, and shook his head. For a while they stood in silence, each lost in their own thoughts.

'When is the marriage to take place?' Rebecca asked eventually.

'Within a month of the announcement,' Radd replied quietly. 'The date is to be fixed while Cranne and his father are here.'

A month! Rebecca's mind went blank with horror. A

72

month. Maybe less. What am I going to do?

She turned on her heels and walked from the room without looking back.

'I'm sorry!' Radd called as she went out.

But Rebecca did not hear him. She was deaf to all but the helpless, silent screaming inside her head.

*   *   *

Galen spent the hour wandering around the run-down district of Edgefield where Cluny had his home. After seeing the state of the alchemist's house, he found it easy to understand why Cluny chose to live in that particular section of town. A more prosperous and 'respectable' neighbourhood would have been unlikely to tolerate his eccentric presence and unpredictable 'experiments'; here, most of the locals regarded Cluny as peculiar, possibly mad, but essentially harmless – provided you didn't get too close! Emer had described him as 'interesting – because he's interested in everything', and Galen was beginning to see what she meant. Everyone he spoke to had a tale to tell of how the alchemist had helped someone with a long-lost remedy, or had predicted strange phenomena such as an eclipse of the sun. Others told of the explosion which had wrecked the upper floors of his home, and of the various unaccountable noises and fumes which issued forth from his basement. But the one thing everyone agreed about was the scope of Cluny's knowledge. He was recognized as an authority on a bewildering variety of subjects, ranging from medicine and metallurgy to magic and mythology; 'the knowing of the hills' as one old man put it.

Galen retraced his footsteps to the alchemist's home, feeling more optimistic. He had known of Cluny by reputation for a long time, but had never before realized just how highly regarded he was. Talking to the man's neighbours had been an enlightening and enjoyable exercise.

Conversation came easily to Galen and he was familiar with enough of the life of Edgefield's lanes to feel at ease with most of the denizens of those dilapidated alleys. They in turn saw beneath his veneer of castle-bred respectability, and recognized one of their own. On the surface, Galen was a handsome lad, with sharp features and brown hair cut short and spiky, and he was dressed well enough to show that he had a regular, if modest, income. His movements were lithe, with a stride that told of confidence, and his blue eyes were always alert, missing nothing and smiling at the little dramas of the streets. The knife at his belt was not the fancy weapon of a braggart, but a comfortable, purposeful part of his clothing. He was, in short, someone with whom almost everyone felt comfortable, and who only the most reckless would provoke in all but jest.

During the course of his wanderings, he was offered food by travelling pie-sellers, drink by innkeepers enjoying the sun in their doorways, and other services by ladies of the oldest profession. He refused them all, pleading both a lack of appetite – which led to several humorous exchanges – and a scarcity of money – which brought forth expressions of incredulity. Yet during all the banter he gave as good as he got, and he was able to turn the conversations politely to other topics.

A group of children included him in their game of tag, and he played his part with a complete lack of self-consciousness appreciated by the onlookers, who showed no hint of mockery. A crippled beggar pleaded for alms, but Galen could tell that the man was a fraud, and a few quiet words saw the supposedly legless pauper walking away as fast as he could, much to the amusement of several bystanders.

So the hour passed quickly and pleasurably, and Galen enjoyed the time, free from stable chores, responsible for once only to his own whims. However, he was in a serious frame of mind again when he knocked at the alchemist's door. He knew how important his mission was to Emer and Rebecca.

He entered the basement room in answer to a shout from within, and found the place transformed. Every available surface was now covered with open books and loose leaves of paper and parchment. The whole place looked to be in such chaos that Galen doubted whether any sense could possibly be gleaned from such a mess, but Cluny rose from amid the debris with a broad smile on his green-tinged face.

'Success!' he exclaimed, waving a book in the air and then casually throwing it over his shoulder. 'I think we have all you need, young man. Am I right, my dear?'

Anselma nodded, unsmiling, and handed her husband a piece of paper on which a neat list had been written. Cluny laid it on the table before him and began to read out the various points, ticking them off on his fingers.

'Cranne is twenty-two years old, and is the second son of Farrand, Baron of Rockwool. Their home is in the far north-west of the country, where the Ringwall and Eagle mountains meet.' The alchemist looked up at Galen as if expecting some sort of confirmation. Galen nodded obligingly, and the list resumed. 'His elder brother, Glanville, is already married and will of course inherit the barony. My latest information is that Glanville's wife was expecting a child, but we haven't had any news of the birth yet. Sorry about that.'

'It doesn't matter,' Galen told him. 'Tell me about Cranne.'

Cluny smiled gratefully and continued.

'His family is very powerful. Their lands became rich centuries ago both through the wool trade and through gold mining, and the Baron of Rockwool has traditionally always been one of the king's closest advisers.' The alchemist paused and Galen nodded encouragingly, wondering if he would ever learn anything about the man himself.

'Cranne is reported to be handsome and immensely strong,' Cluny went on. 'We have no likeness of him, but he is reported to resemble his father closely. That's Farrand – there.' He pointed to a drawing in a book on the table between them. Galen saw a square-jawed man, with pale eyes and thin lips. 'Like father, like son,' Cluny continued. 'Cranne has won several tournaments and jousts, and his skill with lance and sword is unparalleled. Not someone to pick a fight with. Ha ha!'

Galen wondered with some foreboding just what it was that Emer was planning.

'Anything else?' he asked, half hoping that there was not.

'Well . . . ' Cluny hesitated 'There are some unsubstantiated rumours, but I hardly think—'

'Tell him!' Anselma said abruptly, startling both men. 'If I'm the judge of anything, it's more than gossip.'

'What rumours?' Galen asked, his unease deepening.

'He has . . . er . . . a reputation for violence,' Cluny said quietly, nervously waving a hand as if to indicate that this was of no consequence. 'There are tales of killings that have been hushed up . . . '

'Oh.' Galen could not hide his growing concern.

'It's all hearsay, of course,' the alchemist put in. 'I'm quite sure that the baron would have looked into all this much more thoroughly—'

'The only thing that interests the baron is the bride-gift,' Anselma interrupted with some irritation.

'Really, my dear!' Cluny remonstrated. 'I'm sure it's not our—'

His wife silenced him with a glance, and turned to Galen.

'I mean no offence,' she stated firmly. 'Do you want the truth or not?'

'Yes. Of course.'

'Then you should know that Cranne has almost certainly killed at least two men in fights, and possibly a young woman as well. The circumstances of *that* have been kept very quiet – as you can imagine. While there's no proof – his father made sure of that – the rumours are too strong and too consistent to be ignored. He was betrothed once before but the wedding was called off for no apparent reason.'

'It's a complete mystery,' Cluny put in, shrugging his shoulders.

'But one which doesn't take too much imagination to understand,' Galen said quietly.

'Exactly,' Anselma concluded. 'I would not wish to be in Mistress Rebecca's shoes.'

The room was silent as Galen considered the implications of what he had just learned. From outside came the faint, incongruous sound of children laughing as they played.

Eventually, Cluny cleared his throat and forced a smile.

'Even if all these stories are true,' he said, 'I'm sure they were only the indiscretions of youth. Marriage and a family will settle him down.' When there was no response from either his wife or his guest, he made another effort to restore some good cheer. 'In any case, she will be joining one of the richest and most powerful clans in Ahrenia. She'll want for nothing, and Edge will benefit greatly from the connection. Think of the possibilities for trade.'

The alchemist rattled on, picturing aloud the festivities to come, and fishing unashamedly for an invitation. He failed in this, because Galen was no longer listening. He was wondering instead just how he was supposed to break this news to Emer. He loved Radd's daughter for a variety of reasons, and took great pleasure in her intimate companionship; he also knew how much her friendship with Rebecca meant to her. *Oh gods, how am I going to tell her?* he groaned inwardly. *She was upset enough without this.* He was beginning to wish he had never agreed to visit the alchemist, when something in Cluny's rambling monologue caught his attention.

'What did you say?'

'That the wedding will be a great day for the people of Edgefield,' Cluny replied. 'It's not often they have an excuse for a celebration.'

'No, after that.'

Cluny hesitated, trying to recall his words.

' "It's not every day that someone comes to capture the People's Queen"?' he said.

'Capture the People's Queen?' Galen queried. 'What do you mean?'

'It's an old saying,' Cluny replied, happy to be on safer ground. 'Have you never heard it?'

Galen shook his head.

'It's a very old tradition which serves as a public entertainment on the occasion of the wedding of the baron's daughter, and as a test of sorts for the groom. We found a reference to it while we were—'

'Tell me about it,' Galen interrupted.

Cluny was only too happy to oblige.

CHAPTER NINE

In the early evening of that same day, another discussion was taking place which was to have far-reaching effects on the future of Edge. Two men sat in a village tavern talking quietly, while the landlord, who had not seen such well-to-do trade in many a month, scurried eagerly to meet the needs of the travellers and their company. Twelve riders from the city meant that his rooms and stables were full, and his takings for one night's food, wine and ale would equal what he normally received in a week. The innkeeper gave no thought to who the men were or where they were headed in such a large party, preferring to dwell instead on his unexpected profit. Had he been more observant, he might have noted that the men who led the party passed most of their meat to others and drank only sparingly. They seemed preoccupied, intent on their half-whispered conversation.

'How far from here then?' the younger man asked.

'Ten leagues, no more,' the other replied. His full beard and rugged face, scarred forearms and calm, iron-grey eyes told of many years of service in his profession. 'If we'd pushed on, we could have been there tonight.' There was a faint note of accusation in his tone.

'I'm in no hurry to meet them face to face,' his companion responded. 'The gods know, I wish this whole business was over.'

The older man shrugged, his face neutral. He respected his commander's courage and intelligence, but he did not understand the young man's occasional qualms of conscience.

'If a job's got to be done,' he remarked gruffly, 'best do it right. That's why he sent us.'

'I wish there was a way to avoid bloodshed,' the other said

softly. The expression on his clean-shaven face showed his distaste.

'Perhaps there is,' the soldier replied. 'And if so, I'd wager all I have on you finding it. If not . . . ' He fell silent, and completed his thought by patting the hilt of the knife sheathed on his belt.

'I know,' the young man replied. 'If it comes to a fight, there's no one else I'd rather have by my side. But you know it's more complicated than that.'

'Aye.'

'Timing is crucial – get it wrong, and we'll be in a worse mess than before.'

The veteran nodded, smiling.

'Not to mention the fact that we might also be dead,' he remarked.

His commander grinned.

'I know you better than that,' he said. 'We'll do what has to be done, but if the look of the thing isn't right . . . '

'We've handled tougher jobs,' the older man stated.

'All the same, we need to get the lie of the land. The whole thing happens the day after tomorrow.'

'An early start in the morning, then,' his companion decided. 'We'd better see that this lot don't drink too much.' He a jerked thumb towards a group of their fellows who were becoming a little boisterous.

'I'll leave them in your tender care,' the younger man replied. 'Personally, the way I feel about this mission, I can think of no better occupation than getting blind drunk right now.' He grinned ruefully, then picked up his own goblet and took a careful sip.

*　　*　　*

In a day which had already seen Rebecca's mood swing violently in many directions, she had now reached a plateau of emotion. Emer had done her best to keep her friend's despair at bay and Galen's return had allowed a little hope to filter through. In their subsequent discussions, a plan of sorts – incomplete but no less satisfying for that – had been formed. Some of its less important aspects had already been put in motion, and now everything depended on Rebecca herself. Elation turned to fear at the thought of what she must attempt, and the possible consequences – should she miraculously succeed – unnerved her.

As she stood outside the door to her father's study, dressed in her most feminine finery, she accepted her fear, and channelled it into her new-found determination. She *would* succeed! In the past, Emer's exploits had exercised Rebecca's theatrical talents to the full, but now the baron's daughter was preparing to play the greatest part of her young life.

Slowly, she raised her hand, then knocked as loudly as she dared. The sound echoed ominously in the silent corridor. There was no response at first, and she was about to knock again when she heard an incoherent grunt and took this for permission to enter.

She opened the door and stepped inside, making sure that her inner turmoil did not show in her calm expression. She clasped her hands behind her back in case they should shake and give away her nervousness.

Baldemar sat in one of his deep leather armchairs, and a single glance told Rebecca that her father was drunk. His face was red, and his eyes narrowed, and there was a half-empty bottle of brandy at his elbow. She had almost expected him to be in this state, and was not sure whether to be relieved or afraid. The drink could affect him in different ways; it could make him more amenable to persuasion, or more belligerent – even violent.

She stood demurely just inside the room, her eyes downcast. Baldemar did not move.

'What do you want?' he asked eventually, scowling.

'I've come to apologize, Father.'

The baron's eyes widened slightly at this, but he said nothing. Taking a deep breath, Rebecca launched into the speech that she had prepared.

'I was wrong to question your decision this morning. I'm truly sorry, and I beg your forgiveness.' She looked up hopefully, and Baldemar nodded. 'I am still young, Father,' she continued. 'My words were the foolishness of youth, but in future, I will do everything in my power to be a credit to you and to our House.'

The baron remained silent, but he watched her like a hawk, and the intensity of his gaze unnerved her. *I will succeed*, she insisted inwardly, and steeled herself to go on.

'It will be my duty and my pleasure to accept Cranne as my husband, and I will abide by any conditions you see fit to set down.'

'Good,' Baldemar growled. 'Good. I'm glad you've come to your senses.'

'In return,' Rebecca began hopefully, and saw her father stiffen, 'I have a favour to ask.'

'You seek to *bargain* with me, child?' His voice was dangerously quiet, and the room took on the atmosphere of heavy menace that precedes a storm.

'No, Father, I would not dare. I only ask a favour, which is yours to grant or deny as you please. It is a matter of pride, Father. Family pride.'

'Explain yourself,' he growled, showing no sign of softening.

'It hurts me to think that my future husband and his family may see me as someone who is theirs by *right*, with no effort on their part. I would like Cranne to feel that I was worth fighting for, and I would like the people of Edge – *your* people – to see that I was viewed in that way. Am I foolish to have pride in myself and my House?'

'Of course not!' Baldemar spluttered. 'Just how do you propose to achieve this?' His face was now an even deeper shade of red.

'By public test, a competition. Something that will demonstrate to the world that Cranne is worthy of me, and which will allow me to retain my self-respect. A sort of game, if you like.'

'What!' Baldemar exclaimed. 'You think this is a *game*? Don't be so ridiculous. Where do you get such ideas?' He got slowly to his feet as he spoke, and now seemed to tower over his daughter. A vein pulsed in his red-mottled neck.

'But it's a custom of Edge, Father,' Rebecca said quickly, frightened in case he rejected her out of hand before she had even had a chance to explain. 'It's been part of our heritage for centuries, but so many of the old traditions have been forgotten. This is one I would like to revive.'

'Since when have you been so interested in your heritage?' the baron demanded suspiciously.

'I have *always* been interested in our family history, you know that,' she replied, as vehemently as she dared. 'The glories of the past should never be forgotten.'

Baldemar raised his glass and drained it in one gulp, then stared at her unsteadily.

'So what is this *game*?' he asked abruptly.

'It's chess, Father, played on a giant board in the town square, with real people taking the part of the pieces.'

'What?' The baron was bemused.

'Cranne would play one side, while I would be the opposing queen,' Rebecca went on, her words coming in a rush as she tried to explain. 'All he has to do is capture me!'

Baldemar shook his head in brandy-fogged confusion.

'Again, girl!' he snapped. 'Slowly.'

Rebecca repeated her explanation, adding that it had once been a traditional part of the betrothal ceremonies of the daughters of the House of Edge, and had been regarded as an occasion of great good humour and festiveness, with citizens vying for the opportunity to take the place of the chess pieces. Baldemar eventually grasped the principle, and voiced the obvious question.

'What if Cranne doesn't play chess?'

'Then he can be provided with all the advisers he wants,' Rebecca replied. 'Anyway, he can't lose. It's only for show – though of course the audience won't know that. Part of the tradition is that Edge's side is played by someone from "below the salt" – one of the servants. They wouldn't stand a chance.'

Rebecca paused while her father took this in.

'That's why it's called "capturing the People's Queen"', she added helpfully. 'Oh, Father, it would be such fun, and this means so much to me. *Please* say yes.'

A few moments passed in agonizing silence.

'In the square, you say?' Baldemar said eventually.

'Yes,' Rebecca replied, her spirits leaping. 'Just outside the castle gates. Cranne and his opponent will sit in tall chairs to play, and so will the judge. You would preside, of course.'

She watched as that idea sank in, and noted his slight smile with delight. *The idea of lording it over such a show appeals to him,* she thought triumphantly.

Baldemar sat down again, and his expression grew thoughtful. He poured himself another generous measure of brandy, and sipped it slowly. Then he frowned, and Rebecca tensed, fearing a last moment refusal.

'Perhaps I could offer the position of judge to Montfort's envoy,' he mused.

Rebecca was so stunned by this statement that it took a few moments for its implication to sink in. *I have succeeded,* she thought jubilantly. Then she expressed her amazement aloud.

'The King is sending an envoy to my betrothal?' she asked, astonished, then recalled that Radd had said something similar. She had been too distraught to take much notice then.

'Of course,' Baldemar replied pompously. 'He has to be here to ratify the change of succession. You didn't think Montfort would let the sole heir of one of his most important barons marry without the crown being represented, did you?' He smiled over the rim of his glass. 'We'll give him quite a show.'

'Thank you, Father!' Rebecca exclaimed. She went over to his chair, leant forward and kissed his cheek. 'It'll be a wonderful celebration. Everyone will see how happy I am – and what a wonderful father I have.'

'See that you play your part with dignity, Rebecca,' he responded gruffly. 'You are a child no longer.'

'Of course, Father,' she replied solemnly.

He waved her away then with a slight, drunken smile, and Rebecca forced herself to walk slowly to the door.

'Goodnight, Father.'

'Goodnight.'

She closed the door quietly behind her, took two sedate steps down the corridor – and then *skipped* back to her own apartment. Once within the privacy of her own bedchamber, she laughed aloud, danced a little jig on the spot and shouted, 'I did it! I did it!'

'Did what, my pretty?' Nursey enquired as she emerged from behind the closet door.

Rebecca did not reply, but ran to her companion, folded her well-padded bulk in her arms and whirled her about the room. When she stopped, they were both dizzy and laughing.

'Well I never!' Nursey exclaimed breathlessly. 'What's brought on all this extraneous behaviour?'

*　　*　　*

The next morning saw a great deal of activity in the castle, even before a somewhat hung-over Baldemar had risen from his bed. If, in the cold light of morning, the baron regretted his agreement to Rebecca's request, this was something only he would ever know. By then it was out of his hands.

Nursey believed Rebecca's glee to have been caused by her imminent marriage, and approved of the idea of the chess game immediately. She even dredged up an ancient memory from the depths of her mind, in which she recalled her grandmother telling of such an event. 'What fun!' she had chuckled. 'And all for my little girl.'

Before the night was out, the news had spread throughout the castle, and many of the servants willingly volunteered to help with the preparations. Rebecca enlisted Radd's help, being careful to stress the playful nature of the event, but also making quite sure that he saw that her pride was at stake. The chamberlain was soon leafing through his ancient books, and checking old inventories to see if he could find any record of the participants' chairs and costumes. The historical references confirmed what Cluny had told Galen, and Radd grew quite enthusiastic, delighted that Rebecca had been diverted by this light-hearted project.

'It's strange,' he commented. 'Perhaps *this* is why you were so fascinated by chess as a child.'

'I was just practising, you mean?'

'Not quite,' her tutor replied. 'Because this time you have to lose.'

'Lose *myself*,' Rebecca agreed cheerfully as she left him to it.

Radd's search for clues to the whereabouts of the game's equipment was not very successful. Although they were mentioned in several accounts, even with a couple of old pictures, the only inventory in which they were actually listed was over 150 years old. There was no indication of where the items were stored, or what might have happened to them.

'Still,' he mused aloud, 'there can't be many places where something as big as those chairs can be hidden. If they're here, we'll find them.' He gathered his staff together, and organized a search.

Meanwhile, following instructions given to them by Rebecca, a group of soldiers were already marking out the giant chess board in the open area just outside the castle gates. One of the men had been a bricklayer in the days when he had worked for a living, and it was he who organized the measurement of a giant square, eight paces to a side, which would then be divided into sixty-four smaller squares. This was accomplished with much ceremony and displays of self-importance towards the curious onlookers. Wooden pegs were driven into the hard-packed earth, then connected at ground level with lengths of twine. It took several attempts and many arguments before the grid thus constructed met with the soldiers' approval, but eventually it did, and their attention turned then to the colouring of the alternate squares. The white was easy. Salt was a commodity always in plentiful supply; by using the coarsest grade and sprinkling it with water so that it formed a crust, half of the squares were soon completed.

By this time, quite a crowd had gathered, drawn by gossip about the strange goings-on, and most of the soldiers became engaged in keeping the spectators – especially the children – from trampling over their handiwork. At the same time, they took great pleasure in telling the crowd about the human chess game, emphasizing that the really important roles – except for that of the People's Queen, of course – would be played by soldiers, eight on each side. Public curiosity was further enhanced by a proclamation about the celebrations planned to accompany the game. The prospect of a free meal and a drink or two, together with the thought that they would see various members of the nobility make fools of themselves, was something to be savoured. It was soon obvious that most of Edgefield's population would be present to see Rebecca 'captured'.

Eventually, even the captain of the castle guard was prised from his habitual seat in a favourite tavern, and he came to see what his men were up to. It was he, together with the ex-bricklayer, who finally decided on the material that would be used for the black squares. Coal-dust and peat had already been ruled out – they would be too messy – and, for a time, no other ideas had been put forward. Then came the brainwave. On the outskirts of the town was an irregular hillock, formed by waste deposits from the time when iron and silver had been mined in the area. This slag-heap was overgrown now with grass and weeds, but there were rich seams of clinker and gravel beneath the surface, formed by the night-black rock known as torgrist. The hill was soon covered with eager explorers digging in search of this unthought-of treasure.

There was a similar ferment of activity inside the castle. Radd's search had produced results as far as the costumes were concerned. He had guessed, logically enough, that they might be stored in the armoury with the other ceremonial outfits, objects of ritual, and outdated suits of armour. His hunch proved correct when several trunks which had lain unnoticed and unopened for decades proved to contain the dusty remnants of the necessary costumes. The garments were in urgent need of repair, so Nursey was summoned and given the task of organizing a team of seamstresses.

'Don't bother with costumes for the soldiers,' Radd told her. 'Their own uniforms will do just as well. But we'll need all the other pieces.'

Nursey revelled in the importance of the task, and the work was soon progressing apace, needles and thread working overtime as the ancient designs took shape once more.

'Such fun!' she exclaimed. 'And all for my little girl.'

Radd had hoped to locate the chairs in the armoury tower as well, but they were nowhere to be found. So before long, every large room in the castle – anywhere big enough to accommodate such structures – had been searched. It began to look increasingly as though the chairs had been destroyed, perhaps dismantled to make more practical furniture, or broken up for firewood. Radd's thoughts were turning to the idea of constructing new ones from scratch – even at such short notice, they could surely produce *something* – when it occurred to him that no one had yet looked in the East Tower.

The chamberlain led a procession across the castle gardens to the base of the tower. The door was locked, and it took some time to draw the rusty bolts back, but after that, the rotted hinges proved no hindrance. At the first solid push from Radd's band of helpers, the door collapsed inwards; the wood had obviously long since succumbed to worms and rot.

Inside, the tower was dark and dirty. The air was musty and cold, but when lamps were fetched, their light revealed three high seats mounted on travelling frames. It took a little while to manoeuvre them into the sunlight, but the results proved more than satisfactory. The basic structures were still sound. A few minor repairs and a cleaning, and they would be almost as good as new. Radd's men set about the work in good humour, while he returned to his quarters feeling very pleased with himself.

Shortly before noon, as the last of the torgrist chippings were being stamped into place, a group of horsemen trotted into the town square. The two men at their head, a clean-shaven youngster and a grizzled veteran, looked at the chessboard, the soldiers, and the jovial crowd with amazement. They received a few puzzled glances of their own, but no one paid them much attention. The horsemen turned and rode in through the castle gates.

CHAPTER TEN

After visiting Radd, Rebecca spent the rest of the morning closeted in her apartments with Emer and Galen. The young man's presence in her rooms would have been regarded as outrageous by many of their elders, but they decided that it was worth the risk. Rebecca had expressed a wish for complete privacy to prepare for her big day, so Galen was unlikely to be discovered. In any case, most of the castle staff – including Nursey – were too busy with other tasks. Emer had always enjoyed a free run in her friend's rooms, and Baldemar had apparently forgotten his threat to separate the two girls. The risk of having Galen with them was more than justified by their desperate need to take their hastily made plans a stage further.

Rebecca's earlier euphoria had long since evaporated. She was in deadly earnest now, fully realizing the fateful nature of what she was about to undertake. If they did succeed in thwarting the baron's intentions, the consequences could be more than unpleasant. The alternative was even worse, however, and her mind baulked at the prospect of yielding herself to her father and the unknown Cranne.

'The feast will start at noon,' Rebecca began, 'and the game will be played after the meal.'

'Try and make sure that Cranne has plenty to drink,' Emer suggested, then turned to Galen. 'And you stay sober!' she commanded imperiously.

'Yes, miss,' he replied, looking down and pretending to pull on a non-existent forelock. Emer grinned at him.

'The formal betrothal announcement will be made after the game,' Rebecca said, and her friend looked serious once more.

'Not if we can help it,' Emer stated, her jaw set.

'Er . . . listen . . . my . . . ' Galen hesitated as the two girls looked at him. He still felt a little awkward in Rebecca's company – especially here in her private quarters – and in spite of her friendly instructions to the contrary, found it difficult to address her by name. 'We're all assuming that I'm going to be Cranne's opponent, but how can you be sure that someone else won't be chosen?'

For a few moments, the girls were taken aback. They had been taking Galen's willingness to play for granted, ever since he had suggested the idea of the game, but this problem – obvious though it was – had not occurred to them. Emer recovered first.

'That's easy!' she exclaimed. 'We just have to make sure that Rebecca is the one who does the choosing.'

'Is that part of the tradition?' he asked.

'Who cares?' she retorted. 'No one's going to quibble with that, are they?' She turned to Rebecca. 'You can say it's the bride's prerogative.'

'I suppose so.'

Emer frowned at her.

'Yes!' Rebecca responded emphatically.

'That's better,' Emer commented approvingly.

'All right,' Galen put in. 'Let's assume you can choose me.' He felt a little more at ease now, having witnessed the easy way that Emer behaved with the baron's daughter. 'How can we be sure that I'll win? I mean, I know the moves of chess, but I'm not *that* good a player.'

'You'll win,' Emer replied. 'Or I'll . . . ' For once her imagination failed her. 'Besides, we're going to cheat.' She glanced from one to the other. 'Aren't we?' she added uncertainly.

'How?' Galen persisted. 'Rebecca's the only one of us who's an expert, and she'll be on the board. I can hardly nip down to ask the queen's advice all the time, can I.'

Rebecca had been thinking hard, and her friends gave her their full attention now as she re-entered the conversation.

'I can give you some lessons,' she began. 'I know we haven't got much time, but there *are* a few tricks we

89

could use that are easy enough, and which could give the enemy some problems.' The others refrained from commenting on her terminology. 'However, it's more complicated than that. For a start, even if Cranne isn't a chess-player, he'll have advisers who *are* – and good ones, too. Even if someone in his own party isn't a good tactician, my father will make sure that he gets help.

'You'll get advice too, Galen, from the crowd – but that's not likely to be of much use. We can't risk letting anyone else know what we're doing, so there's no chance of planting someone in the crowd to help you. Everyone must think that the game is just for show.'

The difficulties of their undertaking were becoming more and more apparent as she spoke, but Rebecca had still not finished. Her voice remained calm as she explained the rest of her reasoning.

'I *had* thought of enlisting Radd's help, but that would be crazy. No one else must know.'

'Especially not him!' Emer put in.

'Besides,' Rebecca went on, 'even if you were a chess-master, it wouldn't do us any good. If you won too easily, they'd know that something was wrong, and they'd stop the whole thing.'

'So what *am* I supposed to do?' Galen asked.

'We shall have to seem to win almost by mistake,' she answered, then went on, ignoring their puzzled looks. 'Ideally, it should be a really long game, with pieces all over the place, so that no one can tell exactly what's happening . . . until it's too late.'

Rebecca's face had taken on an expression of dreamlike concentration, as if she were seeing the movements of soldiers, knights and kings in her mind's eye.

'Wait a moment!' Emer exclaimed. 'Galen has his talents, but how do you expect him to pull *that* off? He's already told you he's no chess-master!'

'As you said,' Rebecca replied, grinning. 'We cheat.'

'Thank the Web for that,' Emer breathed. 'For a moment there, I thought you were suffering from an attack of honesty!'

'But how?' Galen asked. '*How* can we cheat – and how

can we keep them from noticing?'

'We have one big advantage,' Rebecca answered. 'Cranne is going to be expecting to win. The idea that he might lose probably won't even enter his head.'

'What we need is a system of signals,' Emer put in suddenly. 'That way, you can show Galen what he's supposed to do next.'

Rebecca nodded.

'That's right.'

'But we'll be surrounded by people,' Galen objected. 'Someone's *bound* to notice.'

'But they could be natural movements, things she'd be doing anyway,' Emer said. 'It shouldn't be too difficult to work something out.'

'There'll be a lot of movement all around, I hope,' Rebecca agreed. 'And the crowd will want to join in. If the old reports are anything to go by, they always enjoy getting involved – and that's something we'll encourage.'

'That'll be my job!' Emer said delightedly.

'The signals will have to be in two parts,' Galen decided. 'One to indicate which piece to move, then the second to indicate where it should go.'

Rebecca nodded eagerly.

'Exactly!' she said. 'I've got some ideas about that. Let me show you.'

An hour later, they were all laughing.

'So what does this mean?' Rebecca asked.

Galen watched carefully, then looked down at the chess board in front of him, and moved one of the white knights.

'Yes!' Rebecca exclaimed, clapping her hands.

Galen beamed. This was easier than he had thought it would be, and for the first time, he allowed himself to think ahead.

'Right,' he said. 'We can do it.'

Emer let out a whoop of glee and leaned over to embrace her friend. But Galen's next question silenced the celebration.

'If I win,' he said, 'what happens then?'

'They'll have to cancel the betrothal,' Rebecca said eventually.

'Are you sure?'

'Of course!' she responded. 'That's part of the tradition.' Even as she spoke, doubts were forming in her mind.

'They wouldn't dare not to,' Emer decided. 'With so many witnesses, there'd be a riot.' But even she sounded a little uncertain.

'Well, let's hope you're right,' Galen said, his expression serious. 'It wouldn't be the first time tradition has given way to expediency.'

Emer looked at him in surprise.

'Just because my father wasn't a lord or a chamberlain,' he said, slightly on the defensive, 'doesn't mean that I can't keep my eyes and ears open.'

'At the very least, they'd have to delay the betrothal,' Rebecca said hopefully. 'And that would be better than nothing.'

'It would give us time to think of something else,' Emer agreed.

'You may not *have* to,' Galen said. 'If there's any disagreement, things could get very nasty for a while.'

Rebecca nodded.

'I know,' she said quietly. 'My father's going to be absolutely furious.'

'His guests wouldn't be too pleased either,' Emer added.

'If they believe they've been made to look foolish, they might postpone the betrothal indefinitely,' Galen suggested. 'Or even cancel it altogether.'

'So we should try to make sure their arguments are nice and violent,' Emer said, grinning. 'That shouldn't be too hard. They'll already be so angry . . . ' She stopped, noticing Rebecca's expression. 'What's the matter?'

'You'll be in danger,' she said, looking at Galen. She had been so intent on devising a plan, and on her own fate, that she had not stopped to consider the risk to Galen, until now. What was being asked of him suddenly seemed unreasonable.

'I know,' he said. And grinned.

In the silence that followed, they could hear the sound of several pairs of boots tramping across the gardens.

'They might decide to take their anger out on you,' Emer said. Both girls were worried now, but Galen still seemed unperturbed.

'I'll have won by mistake, remember,' he pointed out. 'And I'll have a few friends in the crowd. I should be safe enough. Just make sure they get mad with each other, not me!'

'But you may not be able to come back to the castle,' Rebecca said, sounding distressed by this realization.

'I know,' he repeated. 'But I wasn't going to be a stable-lad all my life anyway. And it's time I saw a bit of the world.'

'Are you quite sure you want to go through with this?' Rebecca insisted. His bravado had not convinced her.

'Yes,' he replied firmly, avoiding Emer's eyes.

A shout of triumph from outside halted their discussion. Rebecca and Emer went to the window, and saw a group of men clustered around the base of the East Tower. The door at its base had been demolished, leaving a large black hole into which most of the men subsequently vanished.

'What are they doing in there?' Emer wondered aloud.

Rebecca was silent, trying to remember whether the tower's staircase was intact from the bottom floor to the uppermost room – the room with the magic picture. She wondered what would happen if anyone found it. Would it change for them? She found herself hoping desperately that it would not be discovered, for no other reason than that it was a secret, her secret.

Her fears proved groundless when, a short while later, the first of the tall chairs was manoeuvred out into the open, amid much shouting, cursing and hilarity.

'So that's what they're doing,' Emer exclaimed. 'Looks as if everybody's getting in on the act.' They watched as the other two chairs emerged and then followed Radd's progress as he walked back to their quarters, a smile on his face. Only when Emer turned back into the room did the import of what Galen had said sink in. *It's time I saw a bit of the world.* For once in her life, Emer found that her voice failed her.

'What's going on?' Galen asked. He had stayed away from the window, to avoid the possibility of being seen.

'They've found the chairs for the game,' Rebecca replied.

'Good,' he said. 'I'll have a decent view then.'

With those words, he confirmed their agreement and they resumed his lesson. Emer stayed on, mentally rehearsing the part she would play the next day, but she said little, and seemed subdued.

Galen called a halt at noon.

'I can't take in any more just at the moment,' he said, his head buzzing with moves and counter-moves. 'And I've got work to do. The other lads will have covered for me so far, but there's a limit.'

Rebecca looked disappointed – she would have been happy to practise all day.

'Don't look so worried,' Emer advised her, making an effort to sound cheerful. 'After all, there's a chance that this might not be necessary.'

Rebecca looked at her, frowning.

'Cranne may turn out to be the man of your dreams,' her friend explained.

'I'll let you know,' Rebecca replied, forcing a smile. 'But I wouldn't count on it.'

At that moment, Nursey's voice was heard calling from the corridor.

'Becky, my pet. Where are you, little one?'

'Get out of sight, you two,' Rebecca whispered urgently, pointing towards the bedroom. 'And make sure Galen isn't seen when you leave.'

'Have no fear,' Emer replied, with a grin. 'Concealing men in bedchambers is my speciality.' They went out, closing the door quietly behind them.

'I'm in here, Nursey!' Rebecca called.

The outer door opened and the old nurse's head appeared round the edge. Her face was flushed, and she was a little breathless.

'Mercy me!' she gasped. 'I'm all of a palpability.'

Rebecca waited for Nursey to catch her breath, then asked, 'What is it? I've got a lot to do to get ready for tomorrow.'

'That's just it,' the old woman answered. 'You've to come now. Your young man is just arriving!'

CHAPTER ELEVEN

Farrand's entourage approached the town square from the west. The riders who flanked the heavily laden baggage horses were functionally dressed in black, their swords and light helms fastened to their saddles. They rode without speaking, their ease of movement and watchful eyes evidence of their training and experience. By contrast, the two men who rode at the head of the party were dressed flamboyantly in silks and leather, and the harnesses of their mounts were decorated with a noble crest showing three stars, yellow, red and orange, over a white wolf's head surrounded by midnight black. The Baron of Rockwool and his son were much alike. Both held themselves upright on their massive chargers, riding easily and confidently, smiling and talking as they went. They were both tall and broad-shouldered, and while Cranne's arms had the smooth muscularity of youth, his father's strength was still apparent. They also shared the same facial appearance, square-jawed and thin-lipped, and the same shock of straight black hair. At first glance, even their eyes looked alike, but closer inspection revealed the difference in those pale grey orbs. Farrand's were shrewd and calculating, as if they constantly weighed the value of everything he saw. They were cold and precise. His son's gaze was less measured, shifting restlessly, always seeking amusement. His eyes were also cold, but this time with the chill of a cruel nature; few men could meet his gaze without flinching.

The imperious bearing and obvious wealth of the two men prompted whispered conversations among the local people, who found the visiting nobles both impressive and frightening. No one was in any doubt that these were the guests for whom their own baron was making such elaborate preparations.

For their own part, Farrand and Cranne ignored the onlookers, concentrating their gaze on the town itself. They had already noted the poverty of much of Baldemar's lands, and his home town only served to confirm their initial impressions.

'No wonder he was so desperate for our money,' Cranne remarked, laughing. 'Look at this place!'

'Don't judge too quickly,' his father advised. 'The surface may appear to be crumbling, but the people here have many skills, and we can make use of them. After all, if they can survive and keep an incompetent leader like Baldemar from total ruin, just think what they'll achieve under our rule.'

'Under *my* rule,' Cranne gloated, and his father glanced at him sharply. 'But half these buildings are falling down.'

'The homes of peasants have never given you cause for concern before now,' Farrand commented drily.

'Besides,' the older man went on, 'you won't be baron here until Baldemar dies.'

'Ah, but Father, that unhappy event can surely not be too far away.' Cranne's smile broadened. 'After all, his health is *very* poor.'

They laughed together, provoking further comments from the nearby spectators.

'That young lord seems in a merry mood.'

'So would you be if you were about to wed Rebecca.'

'Aye, there's many a man would like to be *her* bedfellow.'

'I heard that!' a woman's voice shrilled from the window behind them. 'Aren't I good enough for you?'

'I worship at your feet, my love,' the man replied. 'You should know that.'

'That's not *all* you worship at,' she retorted in good humour, closing the window with an extravagant bang that left her husband's companions in fits of laughter. Echoes of their merriment reached the departing horsemen.

'They'd better not be laughing at me,' Cranne declared, twisting round in his saddle, his eyes flashing. 'I'll teach them a lesson they won't forget!'

'Peace!' Farrand said. 'Peasant ribaldry is no concern of yours. We have business to attend to – concentrate your mind on *that*.'

Cranne relaxed slowly, though he still scowled, and they rode on into the crowded square.

'Gods! What's all this?'

Father and son looked at the milling throng, the giant chess board and the soldiers guarding it, and shook their heads in amazement. Then they looked beyond the spectacle and to the right, and saw Baldemar's castle for the first time. They stared in disbelief, taking in the dilapidated entrance, the mismatched towers and the ludicrous mixture of architectural styles. Farrand's expression grew coldly furious, but Cranne only burst out laughing.

'We'll have to make sure he spends some of the bride-price on new fortifications,' he commented.

'It's no laughing matter,' his father retorted. 'He lied to us.'

'Not really. He *does* have a castle. Of a sort,' Cranne replied, still chuckling. Then his face fell as he considered another possibility. 'I shudder to think what his guest quarters are like.'

'Let's go and find out,' Farrand said sourly. 'By the look of it, we might have been better off staying at one of those taverns.'

They spurred their mounts on, and began to push their way through the crowd. Their gaudy appearance, their implacable retinue, and Cranne's impatient yells at those who were slow to get out of his way meant that their party became the focus of attention for everyone in the square. The nobles accepted this as their due; their guards remained stony-faced, ignoring the whispers and the curious stares.

They eventually entered what passed for a gateway, and rode on into the relative calm of the castle courtyard. A look-out in the guard house had obviously given warning of their approach, because Baldemar was already waiting to welcome them. He was flanked on one side by his chamberlain, and on the other by a young man whom he introduced as Tarrant, the King's special envoy.

While greetings were being exchanged, the newcomers' mounts were led away to the stables, and arrangements made for their baggage to be taken indoors. The lad who took Cranne's mount noted with distaste that the horse's flanks were badly scarred where spurs had ripped the stallion's skin. He patted the animal's neck, murmuring wordlessly. *I don't envy you your job, old mate,* he thought, but knew better than to voice his opinion to anyone.

Meanwhile, Radd was detailing a number of servants and castle guards to guide Farrand's soldiers to their quarters. These instructions were listened to intently by Tarrant. Then all conversation ceased abruptly, and everyone in the courtyard turned to look at the newly opened outer door of the Great Hall. A figure stepped out, and the silence intensified.

'My friends,' Baldemar announced proudly. 'This is my daughter.'

Rebecca stepped forward into the sunlight, and her golden hair became almost radiant. Her dress was simply cut yet elegant, and clung to the delicate curves of her body. Whispers of appreciation filled the air, and Cranne's eyes lit up. Although he had understood Baldemar's daughter to be pretty, nothing had prepared him to expect such exquisite beauty. Still gazing at Rebecca, he lent close to his father's ear.

'Perhaps we haven't made such a bad deal after all,' he whispered.

'Curb your impatience, my boy!' Farrand said loudly, making a point of appearing jovial. 'You're not married yet!' He knew his son well; Cranne's ability to wait for something he wanted was not one of his better points. They could not afford to make any mistakes at this late stage. Cranne took the hint and stayed silent, smiling.

The two barons laughed together, apparently enjoying the impatience of youth.

'Come forward, my dear!' Baldemar called. 'Come and meet your husband-to-be.'

Rebecca walked towards them slowly, her eyes demurely downcast. She curtseyed, then looked up at the man she already knew to be her adversary. For a moment, his predatory gaze made her falter, and cast a chill over her heart, but she recovered quickly.

'Welcome to Edgefield Castle,' she said. 'May it be as loving a home for you as it has always been for me.'

Her father beamed with pride. Rebecca had never looked lovelier, and her words of welcome were all he could have wished for.

'Your beauty surpasses my greatest expectations, my lady,' Cranne responded. 'And I count myself at home already.' His smile remained constant, but his eyes told of his true feelings.

'And you, sir, are as handsome as your words,' she replied, forcing herself to smile at him in turn as the exchange of ritual flattery was completed.

'You must be hungry after your journey,' Baldemar said then. 'A meal has been prepared.'

The two fathers fell into step, and led the way into the Great Hall, deep in conversation. Cranne and Rebecca followed side by side, exchanging pleasantries. Throughout the meal, Cranne remained a model of courtesy, smiling and agreeing with his host as arrangements were made and the future discussed. The only time his affable façade showed the slightest sign of cracking was when the chess game was mentioned. However, Baldemar reassured him that it was merely a formality, an entertainment for the townsfolk who would eventually be Cranne's own subjects. He stressed that it was a festive occasion only, and not a genuine contest.

'I count myself a good player,' Cranne told him.

'Then you need have no worries,' the baron replied.

To Rebecca, that meal seemed endless. While she could not point to anything specific in the friendly and polite behaviour of Cranne and Farrand, she knew instinctively that the two men were not to be trusted. The father struck her as secretive and devious, while her suitor was like a loaded crossbow, tense and ready to spring, balanced on a hair-trigger – and potentially as deadly. Her determination to avoid the marriage intensified. In fact, the only one of her near neighbours that she warmed to at all was

Tarrant. He said little, and appeared serious, but his quiet demeanour and watchful eyes carried none of the sinister overtones of the other guests' behaviour.

At last, everyone had eaten and drunk their fill – Rebecca was glad to notice Cranne's considerable intake of wine – and Baldemar suggested that the travellers repair to their quarters to rest before the evening's entertainment. Farrand agreed readily, and the guests went their various ways.

Baldemar had given up a part of his own suite of rooms for the visiting baron and his son; on reaching his quarters, Farrand drew Cranne aside and spoke softly.

'Watch Tarrant carefully,' he advised. 'Montfort had to send someone, but I've never heard of this man – and that makes me nervous.'

'Of course, Father.' Cranne nodded, though his thoughts were elsewhere.

'Their lodgings are decent enough, after all,' Farrand added, glancing into his room. 'I'll see you later.'

The door closed behind him, and a servant beckoned to Cranne.

'This way, sir.'

'Not yet,' he answered quietly. 'I must return to the Great Hall for a moment.' He strode away without waiting for an acknowledgement.

Baldemar and Radd were sitting alone when Cranne reached the hall. The chamberlain excused himself, seeing that the visitor obviously wanted a private conversation with his future father-in-law.

'I have a favour to ask,' Cranne said.

'Anything. Anything at all.' Baldemar's cheeks were flushed with too much wine. He felt pleased that the young man was taking him into his confidence so soon, and agreed readily to Cranne's request.

'Of course. Of course. It's a good idea. I'll arrange it. Shall we say in two hours' time?'

Cranne nodded, smiling.

'And if there's anything else you want, just ask.'

'I'll do that. Thank you, sir.'

Cranne retraced his steps, and followed the servant

to his rooms. He was still smiling as the door closed behind him.

* * *

'Alone, Father? But surely I should have a chaperone?'

'You're not a girl any more, Rebecca,' Baldemar replied irritably. 'Cranne merely wants to get to know you better. After all, you *are* to be man and wife. A certain amount of privacy seems appropriate at this stage, don't you think?'

'But we're not formally betrothed yet,' she objected.

'Don't argue with me!' the Baron snapped. 'I thought you had got over this ridiculous timidity. You can have nothing to fear from him – he seemed a thoroughly pleasant and courteous young man.'

You didn't see the look in his eyes, Rebecca thought, but knew that her father would not accept such flimsy evidence.

'He has invited you to join him for a drink and to discuss your future together,' Baldemar concluded. 'You will accept – and that is the end of the matter.'

'As you wish, Father.'

* * *

Rebecca forced herself to knock boldly on Cranne's door, though in truth she felt anything but courageous. She was glad when the door was opened by young Davi, one of Scuttle's underlings. Cranne was standing on the far side of the room with his back to her, looking out of the window. He turned as she came in, and smiled wolfishly.

'Welcome, Rebecca,' he said smoothly. 'I hope you did not object to me inviting you here like this.'

'Of course not—'

'Good!' Cranne interrupted. 'You must get used to doing what I tell you.' His smile never faltered.

Davi cleared his throat then, and Cranne glanced at the servant as if he had forgotten his existence.

'Pour us some wine, boy. Then get out.'

Davi did as he was bid, but before he had filled the

second glass, Cranne snatched it from the table. The dark red liquid splashed on to the cloth and on to Cranne's hand, and Rebecca watched in horrified silence as her suitor's face became a rigid mask. He set the glass down with exaggerated care, then turned to face Davi. So fast that it brought to mind a snake striking, Cranne's arm flashed out, catching the serving boy a vicious blow across his face with the back of his hand. Davi sprawled backwards and crashed into the empty fireplace. The bottle of wine shattered on the stone grate, leaving a slowly spreading blood-red stain.

'Be more careful next time, you clumsy oaf,' Cranne said, his voice quiet and controlled. 'Now get out of here – and send someone more competent with another bottle.'

Davi scrambled to his feet, one hand held to his bleeding nose and hurried from the room after casting a pitying glance at Rebecca. Cranne raised his hand to his mouth, and sucked the wine from his fingers, then turned, picked up both glasses, and offered one to Rebecca.

She made no move to take it, feeling cold and sick to the pit of her stomach.

'Was that really necessary?' she asked, fear and anger mixed in her voice.

'Servants have to be taught respect,' he answered smoothly. 'And incompetence must always be punished.'

It's hopeless, Rebecca thought. *I could argue with him all afternoon, but I know that my only reward would be to be treated the same way. Just get through this! We'll deal with him tomorrow.*

So she accepted the proffered wine, and Cranne smiled.

'That's better,' he said, and took a gulp from his own glass. Then, placing it on the table, he took a step towards her and reached out a hand. Rebecca stiffened, but did not flinch as it came to rest on her shoulder.

'Respect is also something a *wife* must learn,' he said softly. 'Don't you agree?'

Rebecca did not reply, but her revulsion must have showed in her eyes, because Cranne abruptly pulled her towards him. As his other hand grabbed the front of her dress, she shouted incoherently and flung herself away, dropping her glass and staggering towards the door.

'Playing hard to get, are we?' he remarked nastily, advancing on her once more. 'Just wait until we're married – there'll be none of this nonsense then.'

At that moment, there was a timid knock at the door, and Rebecca, her heart pounding, waited to see what Cranne would do.

'What is it?' he roared angrily.

'Your wine, sir,' came the barely audible response.

'About time too,' he muttered. 'Bring it in.'

One of the chambermaids came in, looking understandably scared. Rebecca regained a little of her composure, and wondered whether she could make her escape.

'Over there,' Cranne commanded, waving a hand at the table. 'And clear up that mess.'

The maid hurried to obey, but when she straightened up from the fireplace, Cranne – who had been watching both women in silence – caught her unawares. One hand caught and held her chin as he kissed her roughly, while the other fondled her breast. Then he pushed her away and turned to Rebecca with a look of triumph on his face.

'You see, other girls are not so *timid*,' he said. 'I'll find them soon enough.' He turned back to the terrified maid. 'One word of this to anyone, and I'll slit you from throat to . . . ' He made a slicing motion with one forefinger down the length of her torso.

'No . . . no, sir,' the girl stammered.

'You'll all know your place when I'm baron here,' Cranne stated smugly. Then he laughed. 'Now get out of here, both of you.'

Neither woman needed a second telling. As they fled in opposite directions down the corridor, Cranne's laughter followed them. It was the most horrifying sound that Rebecca had ever heard.

CHAPTER TWELVE

Rebecca endured that evening's meal in the relative safety of company. Baldemar was obviously making an effort to impress his guests, so the food and drink were good, and the musical entertainment was adequate – but not the best. That was being kept for the name-day feast.

Throughout the evening, Cranne was a model of courtesy and polite good humour, and Baldemar was clearly impressed by the young man's manner and bearing. At times, Rebecca found it hard to believe that this was the same brutish man who had so disgusted and terrorized her earlier – but then he would glance at her and smile, and the vile creature within was revealed in his eyes.

Rebecca left the table early, glad of the excuse that she had much to prepare for the morrow. As previously arranged, she went to find Emer and Galen. Fear had lent her a desperate determination that was obvious to her friends as soon as she joined them.

'I take it he's not the man of your dreams then?' Emer enquired.

'He's a monster,' Rebecca replied. 'From my very worst nightmares.'

'That bad?' Galen asked softly.

'I don't even want to talk about it,' she answered. 'We *must* win tomorrow – there is absolutely no alternative. The thought of marrying that . . . that . . . *thing* makes me shudder. Just knowing that he's under the same roof is bad enough.'

Her friends did not press her for an explanation, but accepted her judgement. They turned their attention to the task ahead.

'We need more practice,' Rebecca began. 'The system's not infallible, and it will get more difficult as the game progresses. I'll show you.' A chess set had already been laid out. 'Emer, you know what you have to do.'

'Yes. My part's not exactly going to be too difficult, is it,' she answered. She grinned, but Rebecca remained deadly serious.

'Good,' she said. 'Let's begin.'

They worked solidly for three hours. By that time they were all exhausted, so Rebecca called a halt. They had proved that they would be able to cope with most eventualities, but there were still possible combinations where they would have to rely on luck or direct – and therefore risky – intervention.

It was well after midnight now.

'You'll be late home again,' Rebecca said to Emer, smiling weakly.

'No one's going to notice me with all this fuss going on,' her friend replied. 'There'll be plenty of empty beds tonight.'

Rebecca turned to Galen.

'Thank you,' she said simply. 'Good luck tomorrow.'

'I won't need luck,' he replied confidently. 'We can do it!'

'Together,' Emer completed.

'Together,' Rebecca repeated, nodding.

*   *   *

In her dream, the only noise was a faint, constant rustling – like dry salt slithering beneath bare feet. All colours drained away, leaving only the faintest of hues amid the starkness of black, white and grey.

Rebecca felt herself drifting helplessly, weightless within this bleached, empty world, driven by a gentle, unearthly wind. Then the figures began to form; at first little more than ghostly silhouettes, they soon became real – pale imitations of their wordly counterparts, but no less frightening for that. The monk was first, his enigmatic smile and tonsured head the colour of clouds on a summer's day. Next to him was Cadell, his dark features

105

sharp against the frosted nether-sky. Her father was beyond him, smaller than his real self. On his other side, an unknown juggler tossed white letters into the air, where they floated in a meaningless jumble. The line continued with an artist, his back to her, his canvas and palette completely empty. As Rebecca floated past, the painter turned, displaying eyes blinded by a milky glaze. Cranne was next, as she had expected him to be, sadistic insanity mixed with cunning on his handsome face. Last but one in the parade was the monster from her painting, its hideous wet redness muted to a pale, glistening pink. But the ultimate horror was saved until the end – a being of flame and crystal, rising up from nothing, then towering over her, the ravening demon that had haunted Rebecca's nightmares since she was an infant.

Her screams were nothing more than half-heard whispers in the void.

And then she was held fast, captive in an upright web of steel, forced to look down upon a giant chess-board. Facing her on the other side were the eight phantasms. *I can't fight them all.* Yet they did not give the impression of waiting to oppose her moves; instead, they seemed to be sitting in judgement on her. She glanced at the other pieces on the board, recognizing none of their outlandish shapes, and felt a wave of helplessness. She knew that she had to make a move, yet was unable to decide what or where – or even how. The numbness of defeat crept through her limbs. Soon it would reach her head, and then it would all be over. It would almost be a relief. *No!* She struggled testing her bonds, and her perspective changed abruptly.

Rebecca no longer sat aloof and imprisoned, looking down upon the weird characters of the game. She was among them now, one of them – and ranged against her, beyond a line of ghastly, half-human soldiers, were the eight etiolated men.

In that instant, the silence evaporated and the air was filled with cries and laughter, shouts and howls. A huge crowd surrounded the board, invisible yet palpable. Rebecca felt the pressure of their eyes upon her, heard their conflicting advice. Still she could not decide what move to make.

The enemy advanced, pressing forward on every side. *I can't fight them all.*

Some of her own pieces disappeared, swallowed up by the board itself, and the clamour of the unseen audience increased, adding to her confusion. *I must move.* She glanced down at herself for the first time. She was dressed in bridal white, her shoes stark against the black square on which she stood. *Safe*, she thought, but then was filled with terror as her feet moved forward of their own accord. Salt crunched beneath her as she moved on to the white square ahead.

Salt that shifted, squirmed, and then became a whirlpool, sucking her down, down into the darkness beneath.

The board here went on *for ever* – black and white squares offset in endless diagonal rows, stretching to four distant horizons. Shapes and patterns danced before her eyes. Triangles, diamonds, parallel lines. And it was empty. Cold and lifeless. *Alone. Inside the Web.*

In that instant, Galen and Emer appeared, some way off, equidistant from her, and linked by a line of their own. The noise of the crowd returned, their overlapping voices urging her to action.

Together.

Signals passed between them, all three, and Rebecca felt a glow of warmth and hope.

The voices from the unseen throng changed. Melded. Became one. Now there was no mistaking their unified message, but it faded from her memory as soon as the words were spoken.

Rebecca woke, grasping at quicksilver. Moments later, even the feeling of the dream had deserted her. She could make no sense of it at all.

*   *   *

In the early morning of Rebecca's eighteenth name-day, two men met to discuss just how the festivities might be turned to their purpose. Tarrant, the king's envoy, and his trusted lieutenant, a grizzled veteran named Pike, talked quietly as the sun rose in the eastern sky, producing a dull glow through the heavy drapes at the room's only window.

'You've seen the layout of the hall and the tables, then?' the younger man asked.

'Aye. We've got several options, but the timing will be difficult,' Pike answered. He went on to outline the various alternatives he envisaged, comparing them with Tarrant's own ideas.

'What about outside, in the square?'

'The game, you mean—'

Tarrant nodded.

'The gods know what *that's* all about,' he said, with a slight shrug. 'I always knew this place was behind the times, but I hadn't realized they were quite so primitive.'

'It's an old custom, or so I've heard,' Pike remarked, eyeing his captain thoughtfully. 'It's a *tradition*. The suitor must prove that he is worthy of winning the baron's daughter.' There was the hint of a question in his words.

'Yes,' Tarrant replied. 'But it's not a real contest. It's just for show.'

'So what would happen if Cranne *were* to lose?' Pike asked quietly.

'He can't,' the envoy began, then grew silent, thinking.

'We could always arrange for his opponent to have a little help,' Pike suggested.

'No. It won't wash,' Tarrant said eventually. 'We don't even know who it'll be yet, and besides, it's too risky. We can't afford to be involved in something as suspicious as that would seem.'

Pike nodded, though he looked disappointed.

'I don't suppose Baldemar and Farrand would accept a decision against them anyway,' he said gruffly. 'They'd just dismiss the whole thing as a piece of frippery and go ahead regardless.'

'You're probably right,' Tarrant agreed. 'We'll stick to our original plan. Let's not count on any miracles.'

'We might be able to use the game to get something started, though,' the lieutenant suggested. 'If things were to get a bit heated . . . '

'Perhaps,' the other responded, after a moment's thought. 'The formal betrothal won't be announced until after the conclusion of the contest, so we can wait and see. Don't make a move until I give the signal.'

'Of course,' Pike answered, annoyed that Tarrant should feel the need to give such an instruction. 'It could get very messy, though. There'll be an awful lot of people about.'

'I've thought of that,' the envoy replied heavily. 'I don't like it, but it *will* create a lot of confusion, and with luck no one will know who started it.' He paused. 'It has to be final, though. There can't be any chance of them kissing and making up later.'

'We'll make sure of that,' Pike responded. 'Though from the look of the girl, there'd be little enough kissing.'

'You noticed that too?' Tarrant said. 'She's not as keen on this marriage as her father.'

'*She* isn't getting the money,' Pike commented cynically.

'Baldemar wouldn't keep it for long anyway,' Tarrant said.

'It's a wicked world,' the older man remarked with a twisted grin.

'It is that,' Tarrant replied. 'And we're part of it.'

'Aye. Because it's what we're good at.'

'Let's hope so,' the envoy said, his expression serious. 'You know how important this is. And beyond the main objective, there's only one other thing we have to ensure.'

'Aye.' Pike patted the hilt of his sword, his eyes agleam at the thought of action.

CHAPTER THIRTEEN

Rebecca's name-day feast began at noon. The Great Hall
became hot and noisy as large numbers of people crowded
in. Baldemar sat at the centre of the top table, which was
raised on a platform at the southern end of the room, so
that he could look down upon his assembled guests and
subjects. He was joined by Farrand, his son and the king's
envoy. They were all dressed in their finest attire, and
made an imposing tableau for the multitudes below.

The other tables were laid out in two sections, with a
large aisle in the centre to allow room for the various
entertainments. The first section, just below the baron's
group, consisted of sets of three tables. Seated there were
his senior staff, including Radd and Emer, members of
Farrand's and Tarrant's parties, and a selection of the
more eminent townspeople – those merchants, smiths and
other tradesmen who had sufficient standing in the community, and sufficient money, to make the baron treat them
favourably. Invitations had been eagerly sought after, as
much for the status they implied as for the benefits which
the patronage of the baron's newly arrived successor might
bring. Every seat was filled as curiosity – and the prospect
of a free meal – added to the event's attraction.

Each section of those assembled had congregated with
their peers, merchants with others of their trade, craftsmen
in their guilds, the castle staff clustered about Radd, and
soldiers with their colleagues. Only one band was
scattered, and Tarrant smiled to see the way in which Pike
had deployed his men. There was little the old soldier did
not know about the ways of subterfuge.

The second section of tables was divided into two rows

at the far end of the hall, and held the castle staff not involved in either preparing or serving the meal. Places had been reserved for the kitchen servants and those who had been pressed into service as waiters, but they would not be permitted to sit down and eat until the higher tables and their fellows below the salt had all been attended to. Rebecca tried to catch sight of Galen as she made her entrance – accompanied by a burst of music and a thunderous roar of applause – but she could not see him. A sudden doubt crossed her mind, and she almost panicked, terrified in case he had lost his nerve at the last moment. She glanced at Emer, hoping for reassurance, and found it in her friend's broad smile and brief nod of acknowledgement. If Emer was worried, she gave no sign of it.

There was food, wine and ale in plenty. Silberry had surpassed himself in the preparation of extravagant dishes, and no one went hungry. Before long, the drink had added its own heat to the general atmosphere; conversations grew louder and merrier. Scuttle's staff rushed hither and yon, bearing vast platters and bowls, refilling glasses and mugs, and clearing away debris. While all this was going on, a constant stream of entertainments was presented. Acrobats, musicians and singers, a fire-eater, jugglers – even a man whose trained doves danced in the air to his commands – paraded their talents before the assembled company.

Mercifully, the constant supply of food and the various spectacles meant that the need for conversation was kept to a minimum. Rebecca was thankful that her father was sitting between her and Cranne. Farrand, on her other side, said very little during the meal, not bothering to hide his boredom. Although she pretended to be engrossed in the proceedings, the only act which genuinely caught Rebecca's attention was the jugglers. As she watched the flight of their balls and skittles, she felt a tremor of recognition. *They're too fast,* she thought, *and they should be juggling with something else.* This idea nagged at her but refused to make itself clear, and her mind eventually reverted to more immediate matters. Where was Galen? She peered down the hall, but still could not see him. *What will I do if he's not there?*

At last the meal was over. Even the serving maids had eaten their fill, and there was an expectant hush as Baldemar rose to his feet, pounding his fist on the table to gain their attention.

'As you know,' he began, 'today is the eighteenth name-day of my daughter Rebecca.' His voice rang loudly in the crowded hall. 'On this day, she joins the ranks of woman-hood, and we are here to celebrate this fact with her. It has been my pleasure to gather you all here to join in our festivities. I consider myself blessed – no man could wish for a lovelier daughter.' Applause and yells of agreement greeted this statement, and Rebecca looked up at her father in amazement. His hypocrisy astonished her – there were actually tears of emotion in his eyes as he raised his goblet.

'A toast!' he cried. 'To Rebecca!'

The whole company rose to salute her, intoning her name, then drinking deeply and raising a ragged cheer.

'But this is a momentous day for yet *another* reason,' Baldemar went on, raising his voice and silencing the hubbub. 'I have an important announcement to make, but first . . . ' He paused theatrically. 'We have another entertainment for you. In accordance with our ancient custom, a suitor for the daughter of the House of Edge must prove his worthiness by capturing the People's Queen.' The noise level rose, and there was some movement towards the doors.

'Wait!' Rebecca exclaimed, afraid that events were moving too fast. 'Father, I must choose my champion first.' She forced herself to smile, as if this was merely part of the fun.

'What?' Baldemar looked puzzled.

'I have to choose my champion from below the salt. To play against Cranne,' Rebecca explained. 'That's right isn't it, Radd?' she called down to the chamberlain.

He looked startled by the sudden question from the top table, and stuttered, 'Eh? Er . . . '

'You remember, Father. It was in the book,' Emer hissed in his ear.

'Oh, yes. Of course.' Radd nodded gratefully, and the baron smiled and gave his assent.

112

Rebecca rose, glanced once at Emer, then made her stately progress down the centre of the hall to the servants' tables. All eyes were upon her; she heard whispered comments about her beauty, but paid them no attention. *Where is he?*

There were four long tables in the lower section, each flanked by wooden benches. Rebecca began a circuit of the first one and – at last – saw Galen among the throng. He gave her a brief, lop-sided grin, then returned his attention to his mug. As relief flooded through her, she smiled, and this brought the assembled servants to life. Some laughed nervously, others pointed to themselves in the hope of being chosen, while others offered advice about their neighbours.

'The only thing *he's* champion of is the ale-barrel, my lady!'

'He can't even stir hisself, let alone move other people.'

Rebecca was grateful for this show of friendliness. Her father had always insisted that she remain aloof from the servants, but she had treated those she came into contact with with kindness. This was in marked contrast to her father's behaviour, and had endeared the girl to all but the sourest of the staff. Now they were repaying her in kind, making plain their friendly regard, and thoroughly enjoying themselves at the same time.

Rebecca entered into the spirit of the occasion, stopping several times as she considered the choice of the person before her. The different reactions she got – varying from over-eager smiles to a rapid dive under the table – drew further laughter from the spectators. The ordeal ahead of her somehow seemed more bearable now.

At last she completed her turn about the tables, having gone full circle. She looked at Galen properly for the first time, and had to struggle to keep from laughing. She understood now why she had not been able to recognize him from afar. The stable-lad was wearing a hideously coloured, ill-fitting jerkin whose sleeves were far too long and had been folded back. His hair had been partially slicked down with some sort of grease, but a few spikes had escaped and were sticking up at all angles. He had an unidentifiable dark smear on one cheek, and beer stains down his front. All that was missing, Rebecca reflected, was the straw in his hair.

The room erupted into laughter once again as she stopped behind him, and she received further advice from her audience.

'Not him!'

'You'll have to slop him out first.'

'He's as drunk as a fly in a cider press!'

Galen twisted round to face her, rolling his eyes. For a moment she wondered if he really *was* drunk, but then his eyes met hers and she knew it was all part of the act. *Why do I keep doubting you?* she wondered.

'Your healf, milady,' he slurred, grinning.

'I have chosen,' Rebecca announced grandly. 'You shall be my champion.'

Her statement was greeted with a roar of hilarity which doubled when Galen tried to stand up, and in the process knocked over a plate, spilling gravy and scraps of food over his breeches. His bumbling efforts to retrieve the offending crockery only made the situation worse. Eventually he straightened up and the expression he wore – a gormless mixture of pride mingled with embarrassment – was a picture to behold.

'Don't overdo it!' Rebecca whispered amid the clamour.

He nodded almost imperceptibly and straightened up, standing to attention. The effect was spoilt when his sleeves flapped down, enveloping his hands. By now the Great Hall was in an uproar.

'Let the game begin!' Baldemar yelled from the far end of the hall.

Those members of the gathering who had volunteered or been pressed into taking the parts of chess-pieces left the room, and went to change into their costumes. Then everyone else filed outside, crossed the courtyard and entered the town square.

The two barons walked side by side. Farrand's demeanour was serious and he said little, but Baldemar failed to notice his guest's distraction and kept up a non-stop monologue. He was in high spirits, buoyed up both by alcohol and by the thought of a brighter, solvent future. Behind them came Cranne and Tarrant. While Farrand's son was slightly drunk, the envoy was cold sober, and their conversation was stilted.

'Not much opposition there,' Tarrant remarked, indicating Galen who was walking – a little unsteadily – several paces ahead of them, surrounded by a group of laughing companions.

'No,' Cranne replied, sounding disgusted. 'It's almost an insult. This is a complete farce, and I don't know why my father agreed to it.' He looked round at the gathering crowd and snorted derisively. 'Gods! Look at them.' He shook his head. 'I'll just have to get it over with quickly.'

A sizeable area around the chess-board had been roped off for the principal guests; within this, the high seats had been placed on three sides. There was a large number of people already in the square, and their numbers were being swollen by the newcomers from the feast. Spectators were peering out of nearby windows and standing on the roofs of the surrounding buildings. The castle walls were also well populated.

The air was filled with the tumultuous noise which accompanies any large gathering, and the sound level rose even higher as Galen and Cranne climbed to their chairs on opposite sides of the board. Tarrant took his place as adjudicator. A great deal of good-natured heckling was directed at Galen, and he played up to the crowd, waving and bowing from his precarious perch.

'Don't fall off, lad. You'll have lost before you start.' Then attention switched to the arrival of the costumed pieces, which took their turn as the butt of the communal wit. The sixteen soldiers who formed the front ranks of the opposing forces wore their own uniforms, but were distinguished by black or white cloth cuirasses. Most of these men were members of the castle guard, but a few of Farrand's group had been co-opted – albeit unwillingly – and there were also two of Pike's men, one on each side.

But it was the other players who caused the most comment. They were all known to their audience, and the

115

hurried repairs and alterations had produced some rather interesting costumes.

The two kings – played by a large blacksmith whose muscular arms threatened to split his sleeves at any moment, and by a short, rotund senior merchant – sported gaudy uniforms and ill-fitting crowns. The knights wore stylized horses' heads which rendered them almost unrecognizable, and obscured their vision so that they were forced to walk rather gingerly, arms outstretched before them. The captain of the castle guard was beneath one of the pair of black headpieces, having decided that 'knight' was the rightful title for one of his rank; the other was worn by the owner of a tavern called The Black Nag. He was pointing out this fact and advertising his establishment at every opportunity. The two white knights remained anonymous, but caused considerable hilarity with their neighing, and by threatening to nuzzle anyone who came too close. Finally, they put on a lewd display, pretending to mount one another before being forcibly separated and led to their respective stations on the board.

The costumes for the castle pieces were made of cloth divided into squares, which was supposed to represent stone, and their hats were bordered by miniature 'battlements'. They looked quite ridiculous. The traders who had unwisely agreed to take these parts were embarrassed at first, but they mellowed in the general atmosphere of good humour, and soon all but one – whose overdeveloped sense of dignity left him isolated and irate – were laughing and responding happily to the jibes.

The most successful costumes were those of the four monks. These consisted of cowled robes of black and white, each criss-crossed by a spider's web pattern in red, which was meant to represent the greater Web – the spiritual network of their world. The simplicity of these garments, and the fact that they hid almost everything beneath them, meant that the players who wore them were able to make a stylish and dramatic entrance. The fact that at least two of these religious characters were being portrayed by the most disreputable citizens of Edgefield was not lost on the watching crowd.

'It'd take more than robes to turn *you* into a monk!' one wit called.

'Monks?' another cried. 'Demons, more like!'

'Slippery characters, monks,' a third voice claimed. 'They only travel sideways.'

'Aye, there's nothing straightforward about *them*!'

In the long procession of pieces, the last but one to arrive was the black queen. She was played by one of the castle cooks, her ample form accentuated by a padded dress and a tall crown that seemed in permanent danger of toppling over. Her arrival was greeted with whistles and obscene suggestions which she ignored majestically.

And then Rebecca made her appearance. The crowd grew silent as she walked slowly into their midst. The skirt of her white dress spread wide above a multitude of petticoats, and her shoulders were padded, giving an impression of regal authority. The gown was covered with beads of pearl and glass; on her head she wore a delicate circlet which served as her crown. The effect was one of light and glitter, heightened by the afternoon sun, and though her shape had been altered to that of an unnatural doll, Rebecca still looked beautiful. The silence was replaced by a hearty round of applause.

'A fairy princess,' one old woman whispered as the baron's daughter entered the square. Even Cranne watched her approach with rapt attention, though the gleam in his eye was that of a fox as the chicken draws near.

The organization of the pieces on the board had been progressing haphazardly, especially as no one could remember in which order the kings and queens were supposed to go. Rebecca's arrival changed all that, and soon everyone was in position. The heckling died down, for a while at least, and the pieces stopped waving to their friends and stood still. Baldemar and Farrand, with their respective parties, gathered around Cranne's chair, while most of the other important guests congregated on the empty side, opposite Tarrant. Rebecca, who had only managed one brief glance in Galen's direction, was glad to see that Emer was already in the forefront of this group. She knew that they could both see her clearly.

Tarrant had been briefed on his duties, and now he held up his hands for silence before making his announcement. As he spoke, he looked towards Pike, who had stationed himself on the far corner beside Cranne's castle, and received the signal which meant 'all is ready'.

'The normal rules of chess apply,' the envoy began. 'To prove his worthiness, the suitor must either win in the usual manner, or capture the People's Queen.' He did not mention the possibility of any other outcome. 'In the case of dispute, I am the final arbiter. White will move first.' He waited for a few moments, to let the suspense build. Then, 'Let play begin!'

'Malrick! Two squares forward!' Galen shouted immediately. The soldier in front of the white king moved obediently, and the crowd cheered. Galen waved and bowed, accepting their applause as if he had just completed a masterful ploy.

So much for the easy bit, Rebecca thought. *From now on, it's up to me.*

'King's Knight to King's Monk Three!' Cranne called. This caused some confusion, as nobody had thought to familiarize the pieces with the game's terminology and the innkeeper had not expected to move until some of the soldiers had cleared his path. Eventually, after a good deal of argument, and advice from all sides, the move was completed.

Let him take the soldier if he wants to, Rebecca thought. *Easy targets will gain him little.* She glanced over at Emer, waited, saw her friend move, and set in motion her own reply, hoping that Galen was paying attention. When he did not react, she began to worry, and took advantage of the fact that all the other pieces were turning round to look at him to do the same. She immediately saw the spark in his eyes and was reassured, in spite of his otherwise bewildered appearance.

Galen was enjoying himself, playing the role of bumbling ignorance to perfection. He looked puzzled, scratching his head, then stood up in his chair as if to see better.

'The horse,' he said, pointing. 'Over there. Move up the side, halfway.'

Roars of laughter greeted his decision. Even Cranne smiled. The knight indicated held up his hands in mute question.

'Can't I do that?' Galen asked Tarrant.

'No,' the envoy answered. 'The knight can go to the side, but only to the third square.'

'That's no good then,' the people's champion responded, amid fresh waves of heckling and laughter. He paused, studying the board.

'You'd better play, judge!' someone called. 'We'll be here all night at this rate.'

'Don't try to think too much, lad,' another spectator advised. 'You might pull a muscle.'

'The soldier in front of the horse,' Galen decided eventually. 'Yes, the fat one. One square forward.'

Rebecca breathed a sigh of relief. For all his feigned incompetence, Galen had made the move she had wanted. *It's working!*

True to form, Cranne took the defenceless soldier with his knight. The man walked disconsolately off to the side, muttering to himself.

'*You* didn't last long, Malrick,' someone jeered.

Now it's going to get interesting, Rebecca thought.

Battle was well and truly joined.

CHAPTER FOURTEEN

Several moves later, Galen had lost another soldier, but that was all. Pieces were scattered around the board, making it much harder for Rebecca to follow what was happening. She felt elated, none the less. Galen had responded perfectly to her prompting, and her concentration, while fierce, seemed almost effortless. *We can do it! Together.*

By this time, Galen had gained even more support from amongst the crowd, who had not expected such prolonged entertainment. It seemed to them now as though *anything* could happen. At the same time, Cranne was becoming more than a little frustrated. He could see the apparently easy ways to win the game, only to find himself thwarted almost by accident. The afternoon sun had made him hot and sweaty inside his heavy, formal clothes, and this had not improved his temper. Farrand and other members of their entourage had tried to give him advice on several occasions, but he had ignored them, sure that he knew how to beat his incompetent opponent. Now, as the game grew more complicated, his pride made him continue to reject their help; he was also increasingly annoyed by the constant barrage of shouted suggestions and jokes from the crowd. Although most of this was still directed at Galen, and most of the advice was either absurd or contradictory, the noise still affected Cranne's nerves.

In fact, Galen had begun to make use of the hecklers to help him with his moves. Once Rebecca indicated what she wanted him to do, he listened to the crowd and if anyone suggested what she had indicated, he would address the like-thinking spectator.

'What was that?'

The suggestion would be repeated, and after a moment – in which he appeared to be considering the possibility of success – Galen would accept the proffered advice.

'All right. I'll try that.'

Rebecca admired his quick thinking, but she had little time to dwell on such considerations. The game was at a crucial stage, and any lapse of concentration on her part could prove disastrous. She waited as Cranne made his next move, feeling sticky and hot beneath the layers of her costume.

'King's Castle to King's Knight Four!' Cranne called. 'One square to the left, you fool!' he added with some irritation when the chosen piece did not respond immediately.

He's left the castle open to my monk, Rebecca thought. *Is it a trap?* Try as she might, she could see no pitfall, so after glancing at Emer, she decided that the time had come for Galen to start being a little more aggressive. She fidgeted, adjusting her right shoulder pad, then smoothing the waistline of her dress with her left hand. Then her crown was bothersome, so she pushed it straight. Galen gave a small yelp of excitement.

'Take the castle! Take the castle!' he yelled. 'Come on, monk, move!'

The man playing the white monk realized what he should do, and set off diagonally across the board. He was halted by a scream of rage from Cranne.

'You can't do that! The castle isn't in his path.'

Various comments greeted this obvious contradiction of the truth.

'The castle's in the wrong place!' Cranne yelled furiously. 'I said two places to the left, you imbecile!'

The merchant who was playing the endangered black castle glanced round at Cranne first, then at Tarrant. When he received no further instruction, he edged into the adjacent square – and out of danger. The white monk returned to his original place, completely confused. The crowd was in an uproar, shouting abuse and booing. Rebecca glanced up at Tarrant, but the envoy made no move to reverse the miscarriage of justice.

121

He's going to let him get away with it! She realized with horror that Cranne might not be her only opponent this day. At least the noise and confusion gave her time to reconsider her next move. She checked on Emer, pushed her right shoulder pad into place again, then wiped the perspiration from her brow. As she adjusted her other shoulder, she noticed Tarrant watching her closely, and her stomach sank at the thought that their subterfuge might be discovered. She looked away, but as she did so she caught the discreet signal passing between the envoy and his lieutenant, Pike. *What's going on? Does he know?*

'You again. The monk,' Galen called. 'Go in the same direction, but only move two squares this time.'

The robed figure obeyed the instruction. As Rebecca had hoped, her move provoked Cranne into taking one of her advanced soldiers. This in turn led to the exchange of several pieces – and this time her opponent put up no objections. He was probably glad, like Rebecca, to clear the board a little and simplify the puzzle, provided he lost no ground in the process. The dismissed pieces wandered off the board, and stood gossiping around Tarrant's chair.

The crowd was now completely involved in the game. What had begun as a spectacle, a humorous entertainment, had become a real contest – and one in which they felt they had a genuine stake. The People's Champion had become a reality, and most of the spectators hoped that he would win, in spite of the odds against him, and the possible consequences. As a result, they were vociferous in their attempts to help the stable-lad who had ridden his luck so far and who was, when all was said and done, one of them. Unlike the arrogant foreigner on the other side.

These feelings were to intensify when Cranne bent the rules once again. His latest move had left his own king in check, but instead of returning to the original position, he insisted on another piece being moved to block the threat. The costumed players were not sure what to do, and Cranne became abusive; he had to be physically restrained from leaping down from his chair and enforcing his will personally. In the ensuing muddle, the game came close to being abandoned. Both Farrand and Baldemar were very worried now. The game was showing every sign of turning ugly. Soldiers of every party began to stir, and the tension grew almost unbearable as Cranne continued to denigrate the intelligence of the players and of Edge's people in general. His father managed to quieten him eventually, but the damage had already been done. Almost to a man, the throng in Edgefield Square now fervently wished for the baron's son to lose.

To Rebecca's astonishment, Tarrant once more backed Cranne, and the game resumed from the changed position. The crowd registered its protest with angry shouts, then grew dangerously quiet.

End it now! Rebecca ordered herself. *They'll never be more on your side.* After a nervous glance at Emer, she adjusted her crown first with her right hand, then her left, and finished by hooking her left thumb into her belt. After a few moments, Galen called for his queen to move forward and to the left one square. *I've got you now!* she rejoiced inwardly. Victory would be especially sweet when she, as queen, would be the one to strike the final blow.

Cranne's response was swift and predictable. Encouraged by Tarrant's leniency, he moved his own queen forward, intent on crushing the white opposition. Then he sat back, smiling with renewed confidence.

There were mutterings in the crowd as they saw the black queen advance threateningly, but Rebecca was jubilant. He had given her the very opportunity she wanted. *Three moves!* she thought. *He can't stop me.* She fidgeted again, adjusting her clothing, and waited for Galen to call the next move. Long moments passed and nothing happened.

'Come on!' Cranne roared.

Rebecca looked round for Emer, and her heart fell into the pit of her stomach. Her friend was being led away by Radd, his hand on her arm. Although Emer was resisting, her father was resolute and all she could do was give one last despairing look back as she disappeared into the crowd. Fighting panic, Rebecca repeated her instructions, hoping Galen would be able to interpret them correctly.

'Do you resign?' Cranne shouted.

Galen's voice broke the silence, calling his move.

No! Rebecca wailed inwardly. *The knight, not the monk!* She could not understand how he could have misread her signals, but was forced to abandon the mystery as Cranne reacted quickly, moving in for the kill. The crowd became vocal once more, bombarding their champion with conflicting advice. Suddenly, Rebecca realized what was wrong. Her last move had placed the large bulk of the white king between Galen and herself. *He can't see me properly. I'll have to move.* She studied her options and despaired. To move the queen now was to invite disaster. She *had* to move the knight. But with Emer gone and Galen's view obscured . . . *The system is not infallible.*

It's hopeless, she thought numbly. *We're going to lose.* She glanced up at Cranne. He sat gloating in his chair, watching her with a vicious smile upon his face.

Sickened, Rebecca looked away, hanging her head in defeat.

CHAPTER FIFTEEN

The numbness of defeat began to creep through Rebecca's limbs. She stared down at the ground, unable to face the world. Salt whispered beneath her feet.

The noise of the crowd faded, becoming a spectral echo of its former tumult; colour no longer existed in this world of despair – the very idea of it seemed absurd. The pearly whiteness of the rustling crystals dominated everything.

The salt began to shift. Then squirmed. It was a whirl-pool now, and Rebecca fell into the realms of nightmare.

When she finally looked up, she saw two worlds both frozen in time. One was the scene in Edgefield Square, the fateful game stilled, hundreds of pairs of eyes peering, mouths agape in mid-shout. The other was cold and con-stricting, superimposed on the real world of warmth and sunlight like a gossamer web of darkness. In that realm the black king was a glistening monster, the knight a blind painter; a castle juggled black letters, and the queen was a crystal demon of black flame.

I can't fight them all.

The monk wore his usual enigmatic smile.

I must move.

The chessboard went on forever, its pattern dancing before her eyes.

Alone. Inside the Web.

Terror held her in its frosty grip. Ironically, the way in which she could win the game had become as clear and logical as the spelling of her own name. Cranne's last move had been a serious mistake. A more subtle approach would have guaranteed him victory, but he had been hasty and grasping, and had rushed to pick off an easier target.

125

Rebecca's response was obvious now, but she could not move. Trapped within this dual world and robbed of her allies, she gave up all thought of signalling. Emer was gone, and Galen could not see her. It would be over – and it would almost be a relief.

No!

A new determination filled Rebecca, and she struggled, testing the bonds of fear. In an instant, Galen and Emer appeared, remote and invisible yet more real than anything else in this strange world. The link between the three friends was like a thread, faint but unbreakable, a triangle of hope. Signals passed between them, and the crowd regained its voice. The air was filled with shouts and laughter, and with the sound came movement and life. The wheels of time were turning again. Rebecca still faced both worlds, and in her own she was still held immobile. But in her dream . . .

She heard every voice in the crowd, from the faintest whisper to the loudest bellow. Heard them all as strands of sound. Listened. Picked out the one she wanted. Concentrated.

And began to weave.

* * *

Galen was in a cold sweat. Earlier in the game he had actually enjoyed his role, using his wits and playing to the audience. But now the endless concentration was beginning to take its toll. Although Rebecca's signals were easy enough to read, his memory was faltering under the pressure, and he began to long for her to finish it. He could not take much more.

There were also distractions outside the game. Galen was aware of shifting undercurrents in the atmosphere, but forced himself to push these to the back of his mind. The game was demanding his complete attention.

Cranne made a move which left his own king in check. Galen saw the mistake immediately, as did many of the observers. Cries echoed in his ears.

'You can't do that!'

126

'Forfeit!'

'That's check! That's check!'

Galen looked at Tarrant, saw him hesitate, but was then distracted by a torrent of foul language from his opponent. Cranne had finally realized his error, but instead of admitting it, he insisted that one of his few remaining soldiers was in the wrong column, and should be blocking the threat to his king.

'Get back there, you miserable piece of horse-shit!' he roared. 'Is *everyone* in this place a complete moron?' Fists clenched, he made as if to climb down from his chair, but was restrained by his father. Farrand looked angry and worried.

The pandemonium continued for some time. Insults and accusations filled the air, then Tarrant eventually upheld Cranne's claim and the soldier moved. Galen, like the suddenly quiet crowd, could not believe it.

That's twice! he thought incredulously. *What is he trying to do?* Then he saw Rebecca move, and hurriedly switched his attention back to her. *Good,* he thought when he realized what she wanted. *It's about time you got into the action yourself.*

'The People's Queen,' he called. 'Forward and to the left one square.'

Cranne responded by moving his own queen forward.

Galen glanced between Emer and Rebecca in what was by now a familiar routine. To his horror, he saw that Rebecca was partially obscured by the white king; to complete the nightmare, he saw Radd take Emer's arm and drag the protesting girl away. Her last despairing look back flickered to the crowd behind him, and he hoped that he interpreted that correctly.

'Come on!' Cranne yelled.

Galen looked at Rebecca. She was moving again, but . . . Had she touched her shoulder or her waist? The People's Champion was perspiring heavily. *Decide!* he ordered himself.

'Do you resign?' his opponent roared.

Galen shook his head, and instructed his remaining monk to move. Cranne's response was swift, and the crowd found its voice once more. An avalanche of conflicting advice crashed over Galen, but the only person whose opinion he sought was out of reach. With Emer gone too, the prospect looked bleak, and for the first time, Galen felt completely at a loss. He looked up at Cranne and saw his opponent's cruel eyes fixed on the unmoving figure of Rebecca, He was reminded of a wolf gloating over its crippled, helpless prey.

Wake up! he told himself. *You'll have to do it on your own.* The pieces on the board seemed like statues to him as he considered his possible moves. The noise of the crowd receded, and he became lost in the intricacies of threat and counter-threat. He tried to analyse several possible moves, but each seemed fraught with danger. Indecision haunted him and he glanced at Tarrant, wondering how much time he would be allowed. The king's envoy sat still, his eyes missing nothing.

Perhaps I should move Rebecca, Galen thought. *Yes, that's it! Then I'll be able to see her properly again. But where to?* As his mind ran frantically through the options, a strange sensation crept over him. Suddenly, and very strongly, he felt Emer's presence – even though he could no longer see her. She was trying to tell him something . . .

For a moment, he saw Rebecca's face as clearly as if she was standing right in front of him. She was talking to him, but he could make no sense of her words.

What is it? he pleaded with them. *What am I supposed to do?* Then the girls disappeared, and the noise of the crowd swept over him again. But this time the sound was very different. Not only could he hear each individual with perfect clarity, but one of the voices was amplified, speaking clearly over the rest. With a growing sense of wonder, Galen realized that this voice was telling him not to move the queen, but the knight . . . and he knew he must take the advice. He did not stop to consider what was happening – or even *how* it was happening – but somehow realized that he had no choice. As he moved the knight, he saw a slight movement behind the white king. Rebecca had raised her head.

Thereafter, the game progressed at almost breakneck speed. Cranne's plan was obvious. He was attacking recklessly, pushing forward to crush all opposition. Galen played in a trance. Whenever it was his turn, an unknown voice from within the throng – a different voice on each occasion – would rise above the tumult. He accepted their counsel gratefully and without question. His conviction that he was following the right course of action grew ever stronger, in spite of the fact that the white pieces appeared to be in constant retreat. Having moved Rebecca on several occasions, he could see her clearly again now, but she no longer attempted to signal moves to him. The sunlight was glittering on her costume and her golden hair. Her head was held high, and she seemed to glow with exultation. This more than anything, convinced Galen that he was doing the right thing.

Nevertheless, Cranne still pressed forward, marshalling his forces for a final onslaught. The black queen moved closer.

'I have you now,' Cranne exclaimed. 'You little scum-rat.'

Around the square, the tension was almost at boiling point. Soldiers looked to their superiors, waiting for any sudden order. Tarrant sat perfectly still, his face a frozen mask that hid the furious calculations in his mind. He teetered on the brink of allowing the seemingly inevitable conflict to take place. Farrand, his face mottled with rage at his son's ineptitude, and at the unbearably long, drawn-out game, looked as though he was about to explode; Baldemar was practically white with horror. Only Galen seemed calm. He moved a white soldier forward one square – a seemingly innocuous move, but one that opened up a new avenue of space for his queen.

Cranne pounced gleefully, taking the last white monk.

This time, Galen knew what to do even before the insistent voice from the crowd confirmed it.

'Queen to the right-hand side, in front of the knight,' he announced, trying hard to remain outwardly unexcited.

His audience had no such inhibitions.

'That's check!' several voices shouted. A few moments later, their judgement was amended.

'That's checkmate!'

'I'm not your mate,' Galen responded, playing his part to the last, barely able to contain the joy which welled within him, and which threatened to overpower his supposed ignorance.

Others took up the cry.

'Checkmate. Checkmate.'

'You've won, son! You've won.'

Galen did his best to look surprised as the square exploded with noise.

Cranne was on his feet now, a look of total disbelief on his face. About him, several hands strayed to the hilts of their swords.

'No!' Cranne screamed. 'Play on! It's not over! It's not!' He sounded like a petulant child, and was rewarded by a vast roar of laughter from the crowd. They were already celebrating their victory, yelling and hugging each other.

'I'll kill him!' Cranne bellowed, his voice raw and hysterical. He leapt down from his chair, grabbed a sword from one of the soldiers, and strode furiously across the board. The remaining players scattered before his berserk fury. All except Rebecca.

She stepped into his path, her eyes blazing, her delicate jaw set firm.

'Out of my way, woman!'

She did not move, even when he raised his sword as if to strike her.

'Hold!'

Tarrant's voice cut through the din, and within moments all was silent, the whole bizarre scene freezing at the sound of authority.

The king's envoy was standing now, high above the crowd. He spoke again, and his words carried easily to every part of the square.

'In accordance with the custom of this land,' he announced solemnly, 'the suitor has been found unworthy of the People's Queen.' Cranne's jaw dropped as cheering filled the arena. 'As envoy to the king, my judgement is final. My lord Cranne, withdraw. Your behaviour is less than seemly in one of your rank.'

The public jubilation that followed drowned any protests from within the central area. At a signal from Tarrant, Pike and another soldier moved forward, disarmed Cranne and led him away, stunned and rigid with disbelief.

Galen could contain himself no longer, and dived full length from the back of his chair into the crowd below. They welcomed him in a sea of eager arms and he disappeared without trace amid the jubilation. As a consequence, he did not see how the last piece on the board finally succumbed to the turmoil of the day.

Rebecca fainted clean away, her gown spreading on the black and white squares of the battleground. An instant later, a figure erupted from the edge of the crowd like an avenging fury. Nothing and nobody could have kept Emer from her friend's side at that moment.

CHAPTER SIXTEEN

The two barons were waiting for Tarrant in stony silence, each with a strong drink in his hand. Cranne had been banished to his own quarters until his temper cooled. Judging by the crashing sounds of splintering furniture which reached them through the wall, this would be a lengthy process. Baldemar winced as something heavy and obviously breakable smashed in the adjoining room, followed by screamed obscenities.

Tarrant entered Farrand's room without knocking, his young face serious but calm. The barons had been glaring at each other, but turned to him as he came in.

'Surely you're not going to let this ridiculous fiasco stand?' Farrand demanded.

'Cranne was supposed to *win*,' Baldemar added pathetically.

'I had no choice,' Tarrant replied coolly. 'You saw how the crowd reacted.'

'But it's outrageous!' Farrand burst out. 'Since when have we allowed *games* to interfere with affairs of state?'

Tarrant refrained from stating that in Edge at least, such had been the case for centuries. The temptation to do so was great, but he knew that such a reply would not be well received. Though the envoy's expression remained grave, inside he was smiling.

'My duty was to preserve the peace,' he said firmly. 'At all costs. If I hadn't confirmed the result, there would have been a riot, and people could have been hurt. Our land has been at peace for a long time, but today's events could have been disastrous for you both.' Turning to Farrand, he went on. 'I doubt if your troops and mine would have

132

been able to protect you and Cranne from the mob.' He paused, letting the implication of his words sink in, then emphasized the point by adding, 'How do you think Glanville would have reacted to the news that his father and brother had been killed in Edge? At a betrothal celebration!'

Farrand opened his mouth to make an angry retort, but remained silent in the face of Tarrant's calm gaze.

'Under the circumstances,' the envoy went on, 'I have no option but to refuse the proposed new succession in Edge—'

'You insolent puppy! How dare you?' Farrand exclaimed. 'By what right?'

'My *right* comes from the very highest authority in the land,' Tarrant snapped back, his voice icy. 'And you would do well to remember that.'

The northern baron did not respond; his face had turned white with shock.

'But our agreement?' Baldemar pleaded. 'What about Edge?'

'Montfort's first concern is for the whole country,' the younger man replied. 'Your agreement must take second place to the nation's interest.'

'But—' Farrand began, but Tarrant cut him off.

'I am bound to say, Baron, that your son was less than helpful today,' he said, with heavy sarcasm. 'Had he been more diplomatic in his language and behaviour, concentrating on the game instead of displaying his arrogance and stupidity, then he would have won easily, and this *unnecessary* unpleasantness could have been avoided.' The envoy noted with satisfaction that Baldemar was nodding in agreement. 'I know for a fact that he refused good advice – and what is worse, he cheated.'

'And you let him!' Farrand responded defensively.

'I had to, or he would have started a riot *personally*,' Tarrant replied. 'Besides, I still believed that the result of the game would be a foregone conclusion!'

'It was supposed to be!' Farrand snarled, glaring at his host.

'Can I help it if my stable-lads are more intelligent

than your son?' Baldemar half-shouted. 'Cranne acted like an imbecile!'

'He was betrayed!' Farrand lashed out, furious now. His hands were balled into white-knuckled fists at his side.

'Oh, yes? How?' Baldemar retorted, equally enraged.

'My lords—' Tarrant began, trying half-heartedly to intervene, but his effort was brushed aside. He observed the two old men as they glared at one another, and wondered whether to risk provoking them even further. *It would be easy enough,* he thought. *And then they might even murder each other. But perhaps that would be taking things too far,* he decided.

'And as for threatening to attack my daughter,' Baldemar went on, his rage increasing at the thought, 'I should have killed him myself for that.'

'You? Ha! You couldn't even lift his sword.'

'My lords!' the envoy tried again, but the fury which had been smouldering for so long was aflame now, and would not be dampened until it had run its course. Tarrant stiffened, expecting to have to intervene physically – but enjoying the war of words none the less.

'This whole charade was your idea anyway,' Farrand accused. 'This mess is *your* fault. I had no idea Edge had such ridiculous customs.'

'That's rich, coming from a northerner!' Bigotry was never far from the surface with Baldemar.

'At least I *am* rich!' the other shot back, lunging for his adversary's weak spot.

Baldemar gulped, seeing clearly for the first time just what a dreadful catastrophe had befallen him. Until a few hours ago, his future had seemed assured. Now, it was once more as bleak as the endless salt flats. Indignation had lent him stature, but now he grew old and bent in just a few short moments. Bile rose in his throat.

'*Your* son was the one who fouled things up,' he said spitefully. '*He* was the problem.'

'Well, it's *your* problem now,' Farrand retorted. 'If the betrothal is cancelled, so is our agreement. You have had a great deal of money in advance – and I want it all back.'

'No!' Baldemar was desperate now. 'That money was

given in good faith. I've already spent most of it on entertainment for you and your idiot thug of a son!'

'You will return the money, or I'll take it by force,' the other threatened, his voice little more than a deadly hiss. 'I could take this whole place with no more than ten of my men.'

'My lords, my lords!' Tarrant interrupted loudly. *This has gone far enough.* 'I am sure that some arrangement could be reached that would satisfy you both.'

The barons turned to stare at him silently, the anger in their eyes slowly being replaced by hope and greed.

'The king will repay you both for any losses you have sustained. If you will let me have your accounts, I will arrange for payment as soon as possible. Montfort would want you to receive some recompense for the unfortunate events of this day. And it will be a small price to pay for the continued peace of his realm.'

He watched the two barons cynically as they weighed up this opportunity. Their honour would be satisfied, their coffers refilled, but a lasting grudge would remain. It could not have been more perfect.

A small price to pay for peace, he thought. *And a smaller price for a bloodless success.*

* * *

Rebecca opened her eyes to find Emer watching her; there was a strange mixture of emotions on her friend's face.

'Are you all right?' Emer asked quickly.

'Yes,' Rebecca croaked.

'I'll get you a drink.' Emer left the bedside and returned quickly with a cup of water. 'You've been asleep for two hours. Nursey and I were getting worried.'

Rebecca sipped gratefully.

'I'm exhausted, but I feel wonderful!' she said hoarsely, and smiled. 'We won.'

'Of course,' Emer replied. 'Did you ever doubt that we would?'

'At one time I was sure of it!'

'No faith. That's the problem with the younger generation

135

today,' Emer pronounced, grinning widely.

'How did my father take it?'

'He was stunned, I think. Farrand was livid, but the king's envoy managed to calm him down a bit. The three of them have been sorting things out while you've been asleep.'

'The betrothal *is* definitely off, isn't it?' Rebecca asked anxiously.

'Yes. Quite definitely.'

The baron's daughter breathed a long sigh of relief. She felt utterly drained, but very contented. Even the prospect of having to face her father could not dispel her feeling of well-being.

After fainting on the board, she had recovered consciousness as she was carried into the castle, but had still been groggy when they tucked her into bed. In no time at all, she had fallen into a deep, dreamless sleep.

'What *I* want to know,' Emer said, 'is how you managed those moves at the end without me.'

'I don't *know* how,' Rebecca told her. 'Everything had gone dreadfully wrong . . . then . . . why did Radd take you away?'

'He could see trouble coming.'

'He wasn't far wrong.'

'I could have *killed* him!' Emer exclaimed. 'But then, in the crowd . . . I could *see* you and Galen . . . Only I couldn't *really* see you. But I could. If you know what I mean.'

'Yes, I know. I felt it too,' Rebecca said, remembering. 'It was like that in my dream.'

'What?' Emer looked more puzzled than ever. 'What dream?'

Her friend was prevented from answering when the door opened and Nursey shuffled in, carrying a tray.

'I've brought you something to eat, my pet,' she announced.

'I'm not hungry,' Rebecca told her.

'She needs to sleep,' Emer added, hoping the old woman would take the hint.

'Then why are *you* here, Mistress Emer? Gossiping and keeping her awake?' Nursey was not to be put off. 'You need food, my pretty, to keep up the nutriments in your fluids. After a day like today . . . ' She clucked her tongue, shaking her head in dismay. 'Such a to-do . . . you need your strength.'

Rebecca eyed the food suspiciously.

'There's nothing in it, is there?' she asked.

'Only what will do you good,' Nursey replied primly. 'Eat a little.'

So Rebecca obliged, picking at a few morsels, and sipping the mug of milk. Although she could taste nothing unusual, she did not want to take the chance of being sent to sleep too early by one of Nursey's powders. There was too much she had to discuss with Emer, now that the frightening events of the afternoon were fresh in her memory.

'I don't want any more. Really,' she said. 'Please take it away.'

Nursey picked up the tray with great reluctance.

'Drink the milk,' she insisted. 'It'll help you sleep.'

The two girls glanced at each other at this admission, but Nursey was unabashed.

'Come along, Mistress Emer,' she ordered. 'We'll leave her to rest. '

'I'll stay for just a little while,' Emer replied quickly.

'We want to talk,' Rebecca added. 'I'll make her go as soon as I get tired.'

Nursey had to be happy with that, but looked from one to the other sternly.

'Very well,' she conceded. 'But not for too long, mind.' She went to the door. 'And don't think I don't know that you two are up to something,' she added as she left. 'You're acting very conspitorial.'

They burst out laughing as soon as the door closed.

'Conspitorial?' Emer said. 'Sounds disgusting.'

Then they grew serious once more.

'Tell me about it,' Emer demanded. 'And for pity's sake, don't drink any milk.'

'Last night,' Rebecca began, 'I had a very strange, unpleasant dream.' She described the sights and sensations of her nightmare, then told her friend how some elements from it had been superimposed on the real world when the game had started to go wrong. Emer listened patiently, astonished and worried all at the same time, but when Rebecca went on to describe how she had influenced the shouts of the crowd, she was openly sceptical.

'You told Galen how to move by singling out a particular voice from the crowd?'

'I don't know how else to describe it,' Rebecca replied, feeling rather frightened now as she realized just what she had done. 'I knew the move that was needed . . . and because of the dream I knew that the three of us were linked – and that the noise of the crowd was there to be used. And somehow Galen always did what I wanted him to. How else can you explain it?'

They were quiet for a while as Emer digested these strange ideas.

'So you see,' Rebecca went on eventually, 'we didn't manage without you at all. *You* were there too.'

Emer nodded. The one thing keeping her doubts at bay was the peculiar sensation she had experienced as Radd led her away. That link had felt real enough in her mind. *The three of us were linked.* And it fitted in exactly with Rebecca's description of events. Somehow, it seemed to make perfect sense.

'This is fantastic,' she breathed.

Rebecca smiled.

'I didn't think you'd believe me,' she said.

'But it's . . . it's like . . . '

'Magic.' Rebecca completed the thought for her. 'Scary, isn't it?'

Emer nodded, her eyes shining.

'And it's linked to that old picture of yours,' she said thoughtfully. 'The monk and the monster. Perhaps you're not as crazy as I've always thought.'

'The demon goes back to my childhood, though,' Rebecca said quietly. 'You remember the nightmares I had, after . . . '

'I remember,' Emer replied.

'I thought they'd gone for ever. I wish they had.'

'Promonious things, dreams,' Emer intoned solemnly.

138

Rebecca grinned.

'I'm beginning to think so,' she said. 'At least *this* time I was able to put them to good use.'

'True.' Emer was still struggling to make sense of it all.

'But I needed your help,' Rebecca added. 'Help from *both* of you.'

Emer nodded.

'Is Galen all right?' Rebecca asked. She felt guilty because she was only now considering his fate. 'What happened to him?'

'He did a swallow dive into the crowd,' Emer answered. 'And I haven't seen him since. There's a huge party going on in the town, and he's probably in the middle of it. He'll be having the time of his life!'

'Do you want to go and look for him?' Rebecca asked, seeing the faint worry in her friend's eyes.

'No. I'd never find him. And in any case, I don't think my father would think too kindly of the idea.'

'That's never stopped you before.'

'Galen will turn up again if he wants to,' Emer said, keeping her tone determinedly light. 'He knows where I am.'

Rebecca, on the edge of sleep once more, did not notice the longing in her friend's voice. 'I hope he's all right,' she whispered.

CHAPTER SEVENTEEN

At that moment, Galen lay fast asleep in a rumpled bed in a run-down part of Edgefield. From the other side of the cluttered basement room, Cluny and Anselma sat watching him, talking in low voices.

'I feel responsible,' the alchemist whispered. 'After all, if we hadn't told him about the old tradition, none of this would have happened.'

'He certainly got more than he bargained for,' his wife agreed. 'But I don't think he was an unwilling participant. And the results were quite remarkable.'

The couple had been among the crowd watching the chess game, and had been surprised to see the messenger boy from the previous day playing the role of 'the People's Champion'. This was too much of a coincidence, and they had watched attentively, wondering what was afoot.

'They were cheating, of course,' Cluny said.

'Yes. Though it wasn't obvious,' Anselma replied. 'The girl's movements looked quite natural unless you were actually watching for signals.'

'But late in the game . . . there was something else,' her husband went on.

'Yes.' Anselma nodded, looking thoughtful. 'I felt it too.'

'Magic?' he asked quietly.

'It must have been. And yet it's been such a long time,' she answered.

They sat in silence for a while.

'It's obvious Rebecca didn't want to marry the man,' Anselma said eventually.

'Can't say I blame her,' her husband remarked. 'Unpleasant fellow.'

'Yes, but why did she go to such lengths?' Anselma went on. 'And did anybody else know what she was doing? Apart from him, of course.' She indicated the young man asleep in their bed.

'Perhaps he can tell us when he wakes up,' Cluny suggested.

'That might not be for some time yet,' Anselma commented. 'The poor lad was absolutely exhausted.'

After diving from the high chair, Galen had been swept along by a jubilant crowd, all of them intent on making him the focus of their celebrations. All manner of drinks had been pressed upon him as the festivities became a victory parade through the streets of Edgefield. Galen had joined in happily while the delirious excitement of the game still buoyed him up, but eventually that febrile energy had drained away, and the exertions of the day had caught up with him.

Cluny and Anselma had fought their way close to him when he showed signs of exhaustion, and Cluny took charge in his most authoritative manner. The revellers all knew and respected the alchemist, and obeyed him out of habit; they carried Galen to Cluny's home, then returned to the streets to continue their revels. Galen had fallen asleep as soon as his head touched the pillow.

'We certainly need to talk to him,' Anselma said.

'Of course, my love,' Cluny replied. 'But in the meantime,' he went on, sounding slightly worried, 'where do *we* sleep?'

* * *

It was late in the evening when Tarrant and Pike finally managed to meet in private. The envoy rose from his seat as his deputy came into the room. Both men grinned. Wordlessly, they raised their right arms and slapped their palms together, clasping hands in a salute to their success.

'You handled that well,' Pike said as they settled into their chairs.

'I did very little,' Tarrant replied. 'They did all our work

141

for us. Who'd have believed . . . ?'

'We've seen stranger things,' the older man put in.

'Not many.'

'Even so, you interceded perfectly,' Pike went on. 'You left it long enough to make sure that the match will never be made, but still managed to stop things getting out of hand. My lads were ready, right enough, but it would have been a messy solution.'

'That's an understatement,' the envoy replied. 'And I almost left it too late. We want her unharmed, remember.'

'Aye.' Pike looked almost chastened for a moment. 'We nearly slipped up there. I never expected him to move so quick.'

'Perhaps we are fallible, after all,' Tarrant suggested, smiling.

'Everyone needs a little luck,' his lieutenant countered.

'We cannot afford to rely on luck. Next time—'

'Let next time take care of itself,' Pike interrupted. 'We did everything we could. You got them all warmed up nicely. Even if the lad hadn't won the game, we could have started a nice, convincing fight. Perhaps even killed Cranne.'

'He's a nasty piece of work, sure enough,' Tarrant said, regretting for just a moment that the game had not ended in violence. 'But it's better this way. We're not implicated, and there's little chance of a reconciliation between Baldemar and Farrand after the conversation they've just had.' He smiled.

'Let's hope not!' Pike laughed happily. 'I never expected that boy to put up much of a show. He didn't look the brightest of characters.'

'He surprised a lot of people,' Tarrant replied. He watched Pike carefully, but the veteran obviously had no suspicions about the stable-lad's unexpected prowess.

'I'll tell you this though,' Pike went on. 'Rebecca was certainly plucky at the end.'

'Yes, she was,' Tarrant agreed. 'I'll have to talk to her before we leave.' *About a lot of things.*

*   *   *

Farrand, Cranne and their men left at first light the next day. Tarrant was there to wish them farewell, but Baldemar had pointedly remained in his bed, leaving the organization of the departure to Radd. The chamberlain breathed a long sigh of relief as the last of the horsemen left the castle.

They took with them the gifts and money they had brought as part of Rebecca's bride-price; Farrand also carried a letter, signed by the king's envoy on behalf of the royal treasury, promising to make good his earlier losses.

Edgefield was very quiet that morning. Most people were still recovering from the excesses of the previous night; as a result, the streets were almost empty. Farrand rode stiffly, looking straight in front, his temper not improved by the prospect of the long and tiresome journey ahead. By contrast, Cranne's gaze was everywhere, scowling at the deserted streets.

'I'd like to burn this place to the ground,' he muttered.

'Perhaps we will, one day,' Farrand replied, not looking at his son. 'But I'd like to give the job to someone more competent than you. Judging by your recent efforts, I couldn't even trust you to organize a bonfire.'

Cranne opened his mouth to protest, then saw the expression on his father's face, and wisely decided to remain quiet.

They rode out of the town in grim silence.

*　　*　　*

Rebecca did not get out of bed until mid-morning. She was greeted by Nursey, who had obviously been waiting in the next room.

'How are you feeling, my pretty?' the old woman asked as she bustled into the bedchamber. 'Have you recovered? What a terrible business! Such a shock!'

'I'm hungry,' Rebecca said, surprised by this fact. Food had been low on her list of priorities during the last two days.

'Good!' Nursey exclaimed, clapping her hands in delight.

'That's a good sign. You must forget all about that horrid young man, my dear. I'm sure there'll be another suitor along soon.'

Is that supposed to cheer me up? Rebecca thought sleepily.

'Get dressed, and I'll bring you some breakfast in the other room,' the old nurse went on. 'Do you feel up to having a visitor?'

'Who?'

'The king's envoy,' Nursey replied importantly. 'He asked if he could talk to you.'

'All right,' Rebecca answered. 'What does he want?'

'As if he'd be telling *me* that!' Nursey exclaimed. 'I'll tell him to come in when you've finished eating.'

Rebecca's appetite suddenly drained away. *What does he want?* she wondered.

An hour later, she sat facing Tarrant; he had greeted her warmly, yet his expression gave nothing away.

'You won't go back on your word, will you?' she blurted out.

'No,' he replied evenly. 'I speak for Montfort, and the king's word is not to be questioned.'

'I just wondered . . . ' she began, then held her tongue.

'They've gone,' Tarrant said. 'Cranne will not bother you again.'

Rebecca heaved a sigh of relief. 'Good riddance,' she said with feeling.

'You did not care for your suitor then?'

'He was a monster. I would have died rather than marry him!' Her face reddening, she faltered, realizing that she had said too much to a man she hardly knew. And yet there was something about Tarrant which had made the admission easy. The envoy smiled.

'Whose idea was the chess-game?' he asked.

Rebecca hesitated before replying.

'Mine,' she admitted eventually. 'It was a matter of pride.'

'Only that?' he asked, all innocence.

'I did not wish to appear as an object that could be sold without my consent,' she answered fiercely. 'I was forced

144

to accept my father's decision . . . ' Tarrant let that pass without comment, ' . . . but I wanted the world to see me as someone worth fighting for, not just a helpless piece in the barons' game of strategy.'

'Affairs of state make demands on all of us,' he said mildly.

'Was your wife chosen for you?' she retorted.

'I'm not married.'

'Oh.' Her expression lost some of its anger. 'Perhaps I'd better ask Nursey to sit with us, then. I don't usually entertain single men in my private chambers.'

'You're safe enough with me,' he responded, knowing that he was being teased. 'I travel too much to have need of a wife.'

'Am I supposed to feel sorry for you?' she asked caustically.

'Oh no. I am content with my life. It allows me to travel and to see many beautiful sights – such as yourself, for instance. That makes up for my abject loneliness. ' Putting a hand over his heart, he gazed up at the ceiling and sighed heavily.

'Are you *sure* I shouldn't call Nursey?' she laughed. 'She has powders for that sort of thing.'

'Er . . . no, thank you.'

'Why did you let Cranne get away with his cheating?' Rebecca asked suddenly, catching him off guard.

'Your man had some help too,' he said, not answering her directly. He watched her closely.

There was a prolonged silence; a mixture of emotions appeared on Rebecca's face.

'You knew?' Her voice was small.

'I guessed.'

'Why didn't you stop us then?'

'Because I wanted to see what would happen.'

'You won't tell Father, will you? He might . . . '

Tarrant shook his head.

'What's done is done,' he said.

'Did anyone else notice?'

'Not that I'm aware of. You were very clever. I still don't know how you managed it.'

Rebecca's pride got the better of her caution, and she jumped to her feet.

'I'll show you,' she said, sounding now like an impulsive child. 'I'd have my back to you, of course.' She turned away and spoke over her shoulder. 'There are eight columns on the board, so by moving my hands to one of these eight places . . . ' She touched her thigh with her left arm straight, then her waist, her left shoulder and her head, repeating the sequence in reverse order with her right hand, ' . . . I identify the piece which started in that column. For example, this,' she touched her right shoulder, 'is the monk from the right side of the board.'

'Why couldn't that be the soldier from the same column?' Tarrant asked, enjoying her eagerness.

'That's where E . . . my friend . . . came in,' Rebecca replied. 'She was at the side of the board and I only moved when she was in the right position. If she looked forward that meant a soldier, if back, then the other piece.'

'But you still had to tell . . . your champion . . . where the designated piece was to go.'

'I used the same method,' she told him. 'The square it was to go to could also be identified by a column and a row. You've seen how a column was signalled. All that was left was to give the row, and I used the same eight movements.' She demonstrated again, counting from one to eight, then turned round and sat down again, looking pleased with herself.

'I am amazed,' Tarrant said truthfully. 'It's a simple system, but it must have taken an amazing amount of concentration – especially once the pieces were spread about the board.'

'It was hard work,' Rebecca admitted, 'but a lot of combinations weren't possible, so that reduced the likelihood of a mistake.'

'Remind me never to play you at chess, young lady,' he remarked. 'I wouldn't stand a chance.'

'You were doing some signalling of your own,' Rebecca pointed out.

Tarrant raised his eyebrows, giving her an appraising look.

'I'm surprised you had time to notice that,' he said. 'I was making sure my men were prepared to keep things from getting out of hand. You were playing a dangerous game, you know.'

Rebecca nodded, accepting his explanation readily, and remembering Cranne's sword raised above her.

'You weren't signalling towards the end of the game,' Tarrant went on. 'Why not?'

'Ga . . . my champion was playing on his own by then.' This sounded weak, even to her. Tarrant said nothing.

'The crowd helped him,' she added, shamefaced.

The envoy still did not speak, and just watched her calmly.

'There *was* something else,' she admitted eventually. 'But I didn't understand it.'

'Something between you and the lad?'

'Sort of.'

'Between you and your other friend?'

'I . . . I suppose so. And with the crowd, too. I was able to influence them somehow, so that Galen heard what I wanted, without me having to show him. It sounds silly now.' She shook her head doubtfully.

'Not to me,' Tarrant said. 'I've seen too much that's strange in this world – I don't dismiss such things just because I can't explain them. You may have a rare talent, Rebecca. It would be a shame to waste it.' He had noted the name of her fellow conspirator, but saw no point in alerting her to her slip.

'Dreams can't hurt me,' Rebecca said quietly.

'Dreams?' Tarrant was intrigued.

'That's where the influence came from,' she replied, then looked up, suddenly hopeful. 'Can you tell me what it means? Do you know what I did?'

'No, Rebecca, I'm sorry. And I won't tempt fate by guessing.'

'That's not fair!' she exploded. 'Leading me on like that—' She stopped abruptly, astonished by her latest realization. 'You didn't *want* me to marry Cranne! Did you?'

'What makes you think that?' he asked carefully.

'Do you always answer awkward questions with more questions?' she responded. 'That's why you let the result stand. What would you have done if I'd lost?'

'There are some things it's better for you not to know,' he said. She looked frightened for a moment, then grew angry again.

'That's typical! Just because I'm not a man . . . ' She stopped, suddenly feeling tired once more.

'We'll meet again, Rebecca,' Tarrant said with conviction. 'And the time will come when you'll see I was right.'

'And what do I do in the meantime?' she demanded wearily.

'Live your life,' he replied.

'Oh, that's very helpful!' She sat brooding for a while. Tarrant showed no sign of being in a hurry to leave. 'How's Father taken it?' she asked eventually.

'He's like a bear with a sore head,' the envoy replied, 'but he'll get over it. The king is easing his debts a little to make amends.'

'That'll help,' Rebecca said bitterly.

'He's very proud of you, you know,' Tarrant added.

'Me?'

'I didn't see too many others rushing to stand in front of Cranne when he grabbed that sword.'

'Perhaps, if I'd been a boy . . . ' Rebecca did not finish the thought.

'You have a spirit more than equal to any man's,' the envoy said.

They looked at each other, aware – without the need of words – of each other's worth. Respect was added to their mutual admiration.

'I don't feel terribly spirited now,' Rebecca said, yawning. 'I'm still so tired.'

'I'll leave you,' he said, but was stopped by her next words.

'Montfort . . . I mean the king . . . is he . . . is he well?'

'Yes. He's well. And he has fond memories of you.'

'Don't lie just to please me,' she retorted. 'He won't remember . . . '

'You're wrong,' Tarrant interrupted. 'He recognized your worth long ago. Now I see that he was right.' Tarrant rose, bowed, and walked to the door. 'Farewell, my lady.'

'Goodbye,' she responded weakly. She stared at the door for a long time after it had closed.

He has fond memories of you.

In that instant, Rebecca was a little girl again, lost in memories of her own.

CHAPTER EIGHTEEN

Rebecca had only met Montfort on three occasions; the first of these had led to one of the most terrifying experiences of her young life.

The prince, who had then been sixteen years old, was accompanying his father, King Ralf, on a royal tour. Baldemar had been thrown into a frenzy as soon as he learnt of their proposed trip to Edge. Ralf rarely travelled, and even when he did, it was unusual for him to visit the less important parts of his realm. The baron had therefore hurried to make the most of the opportunity presented by this rare honour, spending money he could ill afford on a lavish feast, and hiring as many entertainers for the evening as could be found at such short notice.

One of these performers was 'Zadok the Wizard' who – as good fortune would have it – was passing through Edgefield at the time. His conjuring and trickery were reckoned by most to be both entertaining and amusing, and Baldemar was delighted that he would be able to offer his sovereign something a little more interesting than the usual parade of musicians, jugglers and storytellers.

Rebecca, who was at that time a melancholy little girl of six, grew most excited about the forthcoming performance. The idea that someone was coming who could perform magic seemed much more important to her than the arrival of the king and his son. This attitude outraged her father, who lectured her on respect, loyalty and allegiance to the crown, and on the nobility of the house of Edge. He added that while entertainers were all very well – after all, they were an important part of her land's culture – they had to be put in perspective.

She must get her priorities right.

Even at that age, Rebecca had known that she must listen politely, nod where appropriate, and say all the right things when prompted to do so. Inside, however, she remained stubbornly indifferent to the approach of the royal party, and longed only to meet Zadok. She was not given the opportunity to do so before the banquet began, because Nursey – all of a flutter at the thought of their royal visitors – kept the child under her watchful eye. Bathing and dressing for the evening took up much of the afternoon, much to Rebecca's disgust.

'You'll see him at the dinner,' was the only response to her insistent enquiries about the wizard.

'Will he do *real* magic?'

'Of course, my pet,' Nursey replied, only half listening as she concentrated on making minute adjustments to Rebecca's dress.

At last all was ready, and the child joined Baldemar in the Great Hall. The baron was visibly nervous, and his eyes rapidly checked his daughter's appearance, before he moved off to take care of something else. He did not acknowledge her presence at all until Ralf and Montfort actually made their entrance. Then she was made to join in his effusive welcome; Rebecca curtsied as she had been taught, keeping her eyes lowered.

After an exchange of pleasantries, the meal began, with a constant stream of servants bringing various courses first to the top table, then to the guests on the lower level. Ralf and Montfort sat on Baldemar's right, while Rebecca sat at his left. Other noblemen from the royal party made up the rest of the table. The atmosphere was formal; the baron was desperate that all should be done correctly and Ralf made it painfully clear that he was only there out of duty. Montfort behaved in a more genial manner, trying unsuccessfully to enliven the conversation. Rebecca decided that she liked the young man, but that his father was as cold as a dead fish. She wondered whether being a king made you like that. In any case, she paid them little attention as she waited impatiently for Zadok to appear. She would normally have enjoyed the procession

151

of entertainments, but tonight she was too preoccupied with the thought of magic. The various diversions were greeted with muted applause, with the other diners following Ralf's lead. He ate sparingly, talked little, and grimaced openly at the standard of some of the acts. Baldemar, taking his cue from his sovereign, dismissed some of the players before they had finished, hoping each time that the next act would meet with royal approval.

Finally, after what seemed like a lifetime to Rebecca, the meal was almost over, the goblets filled once more, and the main attraction of the evening strode into the performer's area. Zadok was a tall man, with night-black hair, a handsome face and delicate, long-fingered hands. His black cloak, lined with red, swirled about him as he walked, and gave him a slightly sinister air. He was accompanied by an attractive young woman who was his opposite in appearance. She was fair-haired, small, with a well-rounded figure and a pretty, smiling face. She pushed a sort of table on wheels before her. Together, the pair made an imposing sight, and Rebecca could hardly contain her excitement.

'I am Zadok the Wizard!' the magician intoned, his deep voice filling the hall. 'Humble greetings to your majesty, to Prince Montfort and to Baron Baldemar.' He and his assistant bowed low. Straightening up, Zadok continued. 'My lords, ladies and gentlemen, I bring magic and wonder into your gathering.'

So saying, he swept his arms wide with a flourish, and red flowers suddenly appeared in each hand. There were a few gasps from the audience and a ripple of applause as Zadok began his act. A stream of coloured hand-kerchiefs appeared from his closed fist, balls floated unsupported in the air, objects borrowed from the guests disappeared and reappeared on his assistant's table, and more flowers were produced from out of the air and distributed to various ladies in the audience. These tricks were all accompanied by extravagant movements from both performers, and by constant loud exclamations from Zadok. This annoyed Rebecca intensely, as it prevented her from concentrating on the magic. It did not seem very impressive

152

to her; this was not at all what she had expected.

'And now!' Zadok announced. 'I shall produce living creatures from out of nowhere!' He stepped to one side of the table and waved his arm in the air with a familiar gesture. The young woman twirled about in similarly dramatic style, but Rebecca ignored these flourishes. She was much more interested in what was happening with Zadok's *other* hand – the one which was inside his cloak. She caught a small movement and a flash of white; when the dove emerged as if from thin air, fluttering softly in Zadok's hands, she knew where it had really come from. Everyone else applauded as they watched the bird fly up towards the rafters and then return to the wizard's assistant. Rebecca had kept her eyes firmly on the wizard, though, and had seen another tell-tale movement. When the second dove appeared, she could no longer keep her suspicions to herself.

'It was under the table,' she whispered.

'Hush, child,' Baldemar hissed.

'I saw it!' Rebecca insisted more loudly.

Several people glanced at her, and the baron glared with anger.

'Be quiet!' he snapped.

Rebecca subsided, unaware of the embarrassment her intervention had caused.

Zadok hesitated briefly, but continued his act at a signal from Baldemar. Exchanging a glance with his assistant, he let the second dove fly free. Most eyes followed its curving flight, but Rebecca's did not – and the wizard knew it. His fingers fumbled with the third dove, and its hiding place became obvious.

Rebecca leapt to her feet and pointed triumphantly.

'There!' she cried. 'He keeps moving things so we won't watch his hands!'

Zadok froze, his face a picture of alarm, as a stricken silence fell upon the Hall.

'Sit down and be quiet,' hissed the lord on her left, but Rebecca was too indignant, and took no notice of him. This was not what she wanted. She had been tricked!

'Do some *real* magic!' she exclaimed. 'Bring my mother back!'

'You stupid child!' Baldemar growled, keeping his voice under control with difficulty. He grabbed her arm roughly, and almost threw her to Nursey, who had hurried up to the table, her homely face distraught. 'Take her away,' the baron ordered through gritted teeth, his face almost purple with rage and embarrassment. 'I never want to see the wretched child again!'

Crying now, Rebecca was hustled from the room. Baldemar apologized gruffly, and motioned Zadok to carry on. As she left, Rebecca belatedly realized that she was in disgrace, and suddenly wanted to hide from all those prying eyes. She noticed, none the less, that the young prince's gaze had followed her rather more kindly than the others.

Then she was in the dark corridor leading to her quarters, and the pain of unfulfilled expectations redoubled her anger and her sorrow. She heard Emer's words once again, words which had meant little at the time, but which were now deeply embedded in her subconscious. *She's part of the Web now. Only magic could bring her back.* Her weeping grew more violent.

'There, there, my pet,' Nursey said. 'It's all right now.' She had been horrified by her charge's outburst, but now all that mattered was the child's well-being.

'He's not a *real* wizard,' Rebecca gasped. 'Why does he *say* he is?'

'It's just a name, little one. He's an entertainer – it's all part of a long tradition.' Nursey's voice was full of concern, but the little girl was not to be consoled.

'You said he'd do *real* magic,' she sobbed accusingly.

'I didn't know what you meant,' Nursey replied, distressed by her own part in the confusion. 'You know what a silly old thing I am.'

'If he'd been a proper wizard, he could have brought my mother back,' Rebecca stated miserably.

'I don't think so, dear. Your mother's part of the Web now.' Nursey was silently berating herself for not having explained the Web – and the things that went with it – to the child.

'Why didn't Father explain?' Rebecca demanded

154

suddenly. 'He never tells me anything.' Her tears had stopped now, but her lovely little face was mottled with fury. 'I *hate* him!'

'You mustn't say that,' Nursey exclaimed, genuinely shocked by the vehemence in the child's voice. 'He didn't mean what he said.'

In order to placate her aged guardian, Rebecca kept her thoughts to herself, but a new idea was beginning to form in her head.

By now they had reached her bedchamber and Nursey began fussing with her clothes.

'We'll tuck you up in bed, and I'll get you a nice drink,' she said, happy to be back in familiar surroundings. 'Would you like that?'

'Yes, please,' Rebecca replied quietly. 'I can change myself,' she added.

'All right,' Nursey said. 'I'll get us both something hot and cheering, and I'll be back as soon as I can.' She was glad that the baron's daughter seemed calmer now. 'Tuck yourself in, and we'll have a little talk.'

A soft yowl of greeting told them that they were not alone. Pickle, Rebecca's pet beek, padded silently into the room through the still open door, and came to rub round her mistress's ankles.

'There,' Nursey said delightedly. 'Pickle will keep you company until I get back.'

Beeks were similar to the young of that rare and semi-mythical creature, the cat. For the most part, they all had white fur, though some had rings of grey or orange on their tails. All beeks had huge, batlike ears, attuned to the quietest sounds and to those high-pitched noises inaudible to humans. Their eyes were large, and usually grey or green in colour. Retractable claws and tough, padded paws – which spread out when weight was put on them, and which looked too large for their slim legs – meant that beeks could move swiftly and quietly over most surfaces. The little animals also shared another unique ability, which made them valuable for more than their pest-controlling abilities, and the fact that – in some cases – they made good pets.

Pickle had originally belonged to one of the kitchen maids, but Rebecca had become so infatuated with the tiny white bundle – in spite of the animal's fiery temper and sharp claws – that the maid had given the beek to her. This had to be kept secret for a while, because Baldemar had forbidden his daughter to keep pets in her quarters, but Pickle eventually became accepted as her own, and now roamed freely throughout the castle.

Rebecca knelt down to rub the soft fur under the creature's chin and behind her ears, and Nursey departed with a relieved smile. Her expression was very different when she returned later to find both the bed and Rebecca's nightclothes untouched. There was no sign of the girl or her pet anywhere.

CHAPTER NINETEEN

The rest of that night was a terrifying ordeal for Nursey, although Rebecca did not hear of this until much later. At first, the old woman had assumed that Rebecca was playing a trick on her and hiding, or had retreated into a dark corner to sulk. She checked the apartments carefully, but found no trace of the little girl, and began to get a little worried. Finding other servants to help her search proved something of a problem, as they were nearly all occupied with the banquet in the Great Hall. She eventually rounded up some assistance, but the ever-widening search revealed no trace of Rebecca and, at last, breathless and afraid, Nursey decided to tell the baron that his daughter was missing.

This proved less than easy. When she returned to the dining hall, Baldemar told her in no uncertain terms that he did not wish to hear anything about his daughter while he was with such important guests. Shivering with fear, Nursey withdrew, and waited helplessly for the carousing to end.

When the baron at last accompanied Ralf and Montfort from the hall, Nursey tried again, but she was dismissed with violent threats. Horrified, and rigid with shock, her terrified mind conceived the notion that no one could help her but Baldemar. As a result, she huddled in the shadows outside the baron's room, hoping that the royal audience would soon end. Unfortunately, her master was intent on making the most of this rare opportunity, and the private meeting went on for over an hour. Eventually, however, servants were summoned to escort Ralf and Montfort to their own chambers.

Nursey hid until they were out of earshot.

'I thought he'd never let us get away,' she heard the king mutter. 'The necessity of being polite to men like that is a strain I could well do without.'

His son did not reply.

Nursey crept to the baron's door, and knocked timidly. There was no answer and so, her heart thumping wildly, she opened it and looked inside. Baldemar stood facing the window, his head tipped back as he drained his glass. The brandy bottle was in his other hand.

'My lord . . . ' Nursey began tentatively, but got no further. Baldemar staggered unsteadily as he swung round, and the bitter malice in his eyes made her tremble. His face was contorted with rage.

'*You* again!' he roared. 'Get out! Get out before I tear you apart!' She backed out of the door in the face of this furious onslaught. 'As if the visit hadn't gone badly enough . . . ' Baldemar spluttered, 'but you have to come and plague me with your miserable concerns. Get out! If I hear one word about that disgusting runt of a girl, I'll have you both boiled alive. Do you hear me?'

Nursey stood frozen to the spot, unable to speak or move.

'What are you waiting for?' he bellowed, red-faced. Without waiting for an answer, he flung the half-empty bottle at his tormentor. Glass splintered as it hit the door frame and Nursey fled, the aroma of the strong spirit filling her nostrils. A moment later, the door slammed shut behind her with a crash that shook the walls of the corridor.

Nursey came to a stumbling halt, her chest heaving and her mind in turmoil. What was she to do? The baron clearly would not listen to her. Who *would* he take notice of? When the idea came to her, it was terrifying – and yet so obvious. Baldemar would have to listen to the king!

She made her way quickly to Ralf's chamber, and stood outside for a moment, waiting to catch her breath, and wondering whether she actually had the nerve to carry out her plan. She became aware that a conversation was taking place inside, and could not help but hear what was being said.

'Such behaviour had to be punished,' Ralf said. 'If you had acted that way at her age, I'd have done exactly the same.'

'Even so,' Montfort said, sounding defensive, 'it's easy to understand her outburst. We've all heard the rumours about her mother.'

'Rumours are not our concern,' the king snapped. 'What can you expect from these people? They're not even civilized! It's bad enough that we had to spend time in this Web-forsaken place, but having to put up with that boor and his brat of a daughter has been almost more than I can stand! If it were not for the greater alliance, I'd have nothing to do with either of them.'

'You're too harsh, Father,' the boy answered.

'Wait until you're in my place,' the king replied angrily. 'See how *harsh* it seems then. Enough of this! If I hear one more word about those two, I shall go mad. Now, go to bed.'

'Goodnight, Father.'

Footsteps receded; a door opened and closed quietly.

Nursey felt her legs grow weak, and knew that she did not have the courage to face her sovereign. She turned and shuffled away.

At the first dark corner, her legs gave way altogether and she collapsed in a heap, unable to do anything but cry softly.

* * *

Rebecca knew that taking Pickle with her on this journey was absolutely necessary, though she did not understand exactly why. She remembered that all travellers on the salt – including the notorious Archaeologists – were accompanied by beeks. And that was where she was headed – to the salt!

He won't be able to find me there, she thought, her anger still fierce.

Getting out of the castle had proved simple enough, even with Pickle struggling occasionally in her arms. She had worked her way through the deeper shadows at the foot of the East Wall, skirted the stables, then picked her moment to slip past the single guard on the gate. There were few people about, and the evening, though warm, was cloudy, dimming the moonlight.

Then Rebecca had walked right around the outside of

the castle, and headed south. The flat, semi-barren fields between Edgefield and the salt-flats made for easy walking, even in the poor light. After a while, however, the silence and loneliness began to unnerve Rebecca, and she talked softly to Pickle, who was a soft white blur in the darkness.

Rebecca's hurt and outrage, coupled with the sheer obstinacy of childhood, kept her going. She thought many times of things she would have liked to have brought with her, but knew she could never go back. All she had managed to gather in her hurried departure were a woollen cloak and a few scraps of food left over from her midday meal.

'I wish Emer was with us,' she told Pickle, though she knew that too was impossible.

Deep into the night, when her legs were beginning to stumble and her eyelids were drooping, Rebecca came upon a series of large banks and ditches. She forced herself to go on, sure that this must be the edge of the salt, but found the climbs ever harder and the down slopes ever more treacherous. Finally, she and her beek crested the last ridge and looked out over the awe-inspiring vastness of the salt-flats. The faint moonlight made it shimmer; it was unreal and beautiful and terrifying all at the same time.

'We're here, Pickle,' she told her tiny companion. 'We'll go across tomorrow.'

By now, Rebecca was completely worn out and she practically fell down the slope back into the dry ditch. She was not hungry, but fed Pickle a few titbits before wrapping the cloak around them both and falling into a light, restless sleep.

She awoke at dawn, cold and scared, but still determined. *Perhaps I'll die, and then he'll be sorry,* she thought bitterly; she remembered her mother, whom she still missed terribly, and she realized that her father was probably incapable of any such emotion. 'I will not cry!' she exclaimed aloud.

Pickle yowled her agreement, and the two travellers clambered up the slope above their resting place.

In daylight, the salt-flats looked less mysterious, but just as huge. Rebecca could see that the ground shimmered because of its crystalline nature – it was almost blinding in the sunlight.

They set off together, heading south still, straight into the heart of this great white desert. Pickle was entranced, and the little creature ran around in circles, sniffing delightedly and darting about with boundless curiosity. Rebecca smiled at her antics, but could no longer hide the fact that she was now feeling rather nervous. She had not realized that there was so much salt – it stretched as far as she could see, to the east, west and south. The white crystals crunched under her shoes and seemed to float in the air, making her eyes and nose tingle.

By mid-morning, Rebecca was tired, thirsty and hot. She decided to stop for a rest.

We should get to the other side soon, she thought hopefully. *Or at least find the Archaeologists.* There was nothing but salt and sky in her world now.

Pickle bounded up to her and nuzzled her ankles. The beek seemed full of energy, and was obviously quite at home in this strange land. Rebecca felt a twinge of jealousy, but then noticed something very strange.

The little creature was turning pink!

It was only the faintest flush, but compared to her normal pure white it was quite unmistakable, especially as her fur now contrasted with the salt beneath her paws.

'What's happening to you? Are you all right?'

The beek yowled in response, not sounding at all distressed; in fact, she gave every indication of being perfectly happy. She rubbed around Rebecca's legs, and responded affectionately to her stroking and tickling. This soothed the tired child, and she dozed off for a while, waking cramped and sore-eyed.

The first thing she saw on awakening was that Pickle had turned several shades darker. Her fur was almost red now, but the creature still showed no signs of discomfort.

Then the skin crawled on the back of Rebecca's neck as she heard the sound of animals howling in the distance. It seemed as though they were encircling her, and in those bleak, unworldly surroundings, the sound took on an eerie,

161

threatening aspect. A few moments later, the first of them began to appear, white shadows half-seen against the brightness of the salt. They terrified Rebecca with their blood-curdling cries. Pickle raised her own voice in answer, but sounded soft and weak by comparison.

The other beeks closed in, all seeming larger and infinitely more fierce than her beloved pet. Pickle appeared unconcerned, however, and just walked around her mistress – almost as if she was on parade. Eventually, Rebecca could stand it no longer.

'I'll protect you,' she whispered, snatching up the pink beek and hugging her to her chest.

The other animals responded by yowling and hissing, but this cacophony faded as the salt itself began to scream.

Beneath her feet, Rebecca felt the crystals shift, and a grating, slippery noise was added to the supernatural howling. Too frightened to move, she did not resist when Pickle struggled violently and leapt to the ground. Rebecca stared helplessly as her last friend streaked away over the salt, heading back to Edgefield.

'Come back!' she yelled, but her words had no effect. She just had time to realize that the other beeks had also disappeared, and was glancing back and forth in hopeless indecision, when the ground below her lurched even more sickeningly, and the unearthly screaming reached a crescendo. As Rebecca turned to face south again, impossible blue-white flames leapt up from the salt, flickering like sunlight on moving water. Before her petrified gaze, the flames sifted, writhed and slowly took form, until the grotesque image of a giant wavered above her, its eyes blazing fury. For a moment, the apparition seemed a creature of irredeemable malice, but then its aspect changed. The eyes grew softer, the tendril-like hands beckoned; there was even a hint of a welcoming smile on its inhuman face.

Rebecca felt her heart start beating again. She stood mesmerized, all thought banished from her mind, as the demon continued to beckon to her.

In a dream she took a step forward. The salt slipped beneath her feet, and in that moment, her fear returned in full measure. Rebecca turned and ran – back in the direction of the only home she had ever known.

She did not stop running until she was right off the salt. There, exhausted and sobbing hysterically, she had been found by the search party belatedly organized by Radd, after he had found the distraught Nursey and made sense of her garbled story.

Baldemar punished his daughter severely for her 'foolishness', and her description of the demon was dismissed as complete nonsense. Rebecca soon learned that trying to convince people that she was telling the truth only made matters worse – but the nightmares in which she relived that frightful confrontation plagued her for years.

Pickle had returned to the castle alone and, within a few days, was completely white once more. Much later, Rebecca discovered that the reason for the animal's change in colour had been because she was on heat; this was what had attracted the wild males who lived along the borders of the salt-flats. However, the shifting of the salt, or quicksalt as it was known, had frightened them away. Pickle had also obeyed the instincts of all beeks, in being able to predict and then flee from the quicksalt. It was this ability which made the little animals so valuable to travellers and to the Archaeologists.

Pickle had died when Rebecca was fourteen, and was buried in the castle grounds. A new pet had since replaced her, and assumed her name.

* * *

He has fond memories of you.

Tarrant's words still lingered in Rebecca's mind as the memories of her childhood faded.

He can hardly have fond memories of me from that time! she thought. *I was an embarrassment to everyone.*

Her next meeting with Montfort had taken place when she was ten summers old. That was in Garadun, Ahrenia's capital, and was not nearly so traumatic an occasion. Even so, Rebecca had almost found herself in trouble again.

Ralf had called a formal gathering of all his nobles,

something which only happened once or twice in a decade. To her great surprise and excited pleasure, Baldemar agreed to let Rebecca accompany him on the journey. Once within the vast palace complex, the baron had left his daughter to her own devices while he attended to 'affairs of state'.

Needless to say, Rebecca could not resist the temptation to explore a little – even though she was trying her hardest to behave impeccably – and inevitably, she became lost. One evening, she had found herself in one of the small, square gardens within the grounds, for what seemed like the tenth time – and she still could not find the way back to her own quarters. As she was looking about uncertainly, on the verge of tears, a young man strode purposefully into the quadrangle. He noticed her at once, and diagnosed the reason for her confusion with one glance.

'You're Rebecca, aren't you?' he asked, smiling as he came up to her.

She nodded, feeling tongue-tied and awkward as she curtseyed.

'Everyone gets lost on their first visit,' he reassured her, and she was grateful for the kindness in his voice. 'It puzzles me sometimes – and I've lived here all my life!'

Rebecca could not help staring at him, thinking that he had the most striking brown eyes she had ever seen. He was tall and well-built, despite his relative youth, and his clean-shaven, strong-featured face was framed by dark brown, close-cropped hair. Abruptly, she realized what she was doing and looked away quickly, hoping in vain that she would not blush.

'You're staying in the Falcon Wing, aren't you?' he asked.

'Yes,' she whispered.

'Shall I take you there now?'

Rebecca nodded. He was a hero to her already.

'I'd be very grateful,' she managed to say.

'Well, the quickest way would be through there,' he remarked, pointing, 'but we might run into your father and the other barons, so I think we'll find another way.'

He held out a hand and Rebecca took it, not quite

believing her luck. She allowed herself to be led through the labyrinth.

'This *is* your first visit here?' he asked, after giving her advice about the route they were taking – which Rebecca promptly forgot.

'Yes,' she replied timidly. 'It's such a long way from Edge.'

'I know,' he agreed amiably. 'I remember the journey back from there.'

'You've been to Edge?' Rebecca found this hard to believe.

'Yes. Don't you remember? Your father gave a dinner for the king – and you didn't think much of the wizard, if I remember correctly.'

'You were there then?'

'He wasn't very good, was he.'

Rebecca was too astonished to reply; before she realized it, they were outside her room.

'I was glad that they found you unharmed,' he said quietly, releasing her hand. Rebecca blushed, and could not meet his gaze.

'Well, here you are,' he said cheerfully. 'Can you remember the way back for next time?'

She nodded, though of course this was not the case.

'Thank you,' she breathed.

'It was a pleasure, my lady. I hope we shall meet again before you leave.'

With that, he was gone, leaving Rebecca in a daze.

The young man's hope was not to be fulfilled. The only time Rebecca saw him again during that visit was from a distance, in a large ceremonial gathering. It was only then that she realized her guide had been Prince Montfort.

* * *

And now he's king, Rebecca thought. *What are my worries compared to his?*

Her mind returned to the present, and she considered her recent conversation with Tarrant. Montfort's envoy had not given much away, but she had liked him, and

165

hoped that she had been right to trust him. Somehow, she did not think he would reveal her secrets to Baldemar.

What's done is done.

What is happening in Ahrenia? she wondered. *And why should my marriage concern the king?*

These were questions she had no way of answering.

CHAPTER TWENTY

Galen woke late the next morning, worn out by his efforts as the People's Champion. A night of wild dreams, together with the confused memories of the previous day, reinforced his feeling of disorientation as he looked around the strange room. Cluny and Anselma were already awake, having spent a cramped night on their makeshift beds. They saw their guest blinking drowsily, and went to see how he was. Galen looked surprised to see them, but then remembered their kindness of the night before, and recovered rapidly.

'How are you feeling?' Cluny asked.

'Fine.. . . I think,' he replied. 'I'll give you a proper answer when I'm really awake.'

'You slept for eighteen hours,' Anselma told him. 'You must have been absolutely exhausted.'

Galen nodded slowly.

'Would you care for some breakfast?' the alchemist enquired. 'It's a long time since you last ate.'

To Galen's surprise, he found that he was indeed hungry, and he accepted the offer promptly. His hosts bustled about, obviously in some confusion as to where things were; he began to wonder exactly what kind of meal he was to be presented with. It eventually turned out to be a simple but very satisfactory collection of bread, cheese and fruit. Galen ate with relish, though he thought that the food – good though it was – hardly warranted the fuss that had preceded its arrival. He began to get the feeling that the alchemist and his wife gave a rather low priority to mundane matters such as feeding themselves. By the time he finished, Galen was feeling wonderful, especially when he remembered the amazing success of the previous day's adventure.

'Thank you,' he said gratefully, after swallowing the last morsel. 'That was just what I needed. You've been very kind.'

Anselma had been sitting patiently, watching him eat, while her husband had pottered about the room on mysterious missions of his own.

'Will you repay us by answering a few questions?' she asked.

Galen did not respond immediately, and Cluny came to join them.

'What really happened yesterday?' the alchemist asked.

'I just got lucky, I suppose,' Galen replied, on his guard. *What did happen yesterday?* he wondered, trying to make sense of it all.

'Please,' Cluny went on, serious now. 'Ignore my reputation. This could prove to be very important.'

'And you must admit,' Anselma added, 'that your learning of the game from us, and then appearing as Rebecca's champion, was just a bit suspicious.'

'Were you in league with her?' Cluny asked.

Galen thought of denying it, but in the face of those uncanny eyes he faltered, then gave up and admitted the truth.

'You were doing it just to help Rebecca?' Anselma wanted to know.

'Yes. Why?' Galen's puzzlement increased.

'Who else knew what you were doing?' the alchemist responded.

'No one.'

Cluny and his wife exchanged glances.

'There had to be at least one other,' Anselma said to her husband. 'For the signalling.'

Cluny nodded, looking down at his cupped hands. Galen was aghast. Had *everyone* seen what they were doing?

'All right,' he admitted. 'There *was* someone else . . . a friend.'

'And that was all?' Anselma persisted.

'Yes!' Galen was beginning to get annoyed. 'What's

168

this all about?'

'The political situation in Ahrenia is extremely volatile at the moment,' Anselma replied. 'Though people here in Edge seem to be unaware of this. Obviously, the alliance by marriage of two noble families could affect that. We thought that you might have been working on behalf of some outside party.'

What in the Web have I got myself into? Galen wondered. The ripples of their actions seemed to be spreading ever wider.

'No. It's just that Rebecca didn't want to marry Cranne,' he said defensively.

'Can't blame her for that,' Cluny mumbled, still looking down at his hands.

'Is he telling the truth?' Anselma suddenly asked her husband.

Galen's indignation was curbed by a new fear.

'Yes,' the alchemist replied.

'What *is* that?' Galen asked. 'What have you got there?'

'Just a feather,' Cluny answered, holding up his right hand, palm uppermost. In it, a small grey feather was standing upright, balanced impossibly on its pointed end. Galen stared at it, intrigued; then, acting on impulse, he blew sharply. The feather fluttered gently, but stayed in Cluny's palm, almost as if it was rooted to his skin.

'How do you do that?'

'Practice!' Cluny seemed very pleased with himself.

'What does that feather have to do with whether I'm telling the truth or not?' Galen asked, thoroughly mystified.

'Did you love your mother?' Anselma asked him.

'What? My parents are dead.'

'Just answer the question.'

'Yes. Of course.'

The feather remained quite still on Cluny's palm.

'Did you love your father?' Anselma continued.

'Yes. What . . . ?'

Galen stopped as he saw the delicate fronds begin to quiver, and then watched in amazement as the feather began to revolve slowly. Two pairs of piercing eyes stared at him accusingly.

'I never knew my father,' he admitted quietly. 'I never even knew what he looked like.' Long moments passed in silence.

'I'm sorry,' Anselma said eventually.

Galen shrugged.

'How did you do that?' he repeated.

'There are links in the Web which can be used for many purposes if you know how,' Cluny answered.

'And if you can find them in the first place,' Anselma added, smiling fondly at her husband.

'I used one such link to read the emanations of your aura,' he went on.

'What?'

'If the emotions attached to something you say are strong enough,' Anselma explained, 'then the aura will vibrate in a certain way, depending on whether or not you're telling the truth. As an adept, Cluny is able to transmute those vibrations into an object.'

'That's incredible,' Galen said, his eyes fixed on the feather.

'It's actually a very delicate procedure,' Cluny said enthusiastically, but subsided at a warning glance from his wife.

'How did you know about my father?' Galen asked.

'I didn't,' Anselma replied. 'But everyone has strong emotional ties to their family, one way or another – and they also tend to lie about them sooner or later, even to themselves.'

'Do you realize— ' Galen began.

'Yes, of course we do,' Anselma interrupted. 'But if this became common knowledge, we'd have no peace at all.'

'But— '

'Trust me,' she insisted. 'It must remain a secret. We've taken an enormous risk telling you this much.'

'Then why tell me at all?'

'Because of what happened yesterday. It could be very important,' Cluny said. 'And you were part of it.'

'What happened at the end of the game?' Anselma asked before Galen had a chance to respond.

'I don't really know,' he began, eyes still riveted on the tell-tale feather. 'It was as if the crowd was telling me what to do.' He went on to explain the uncanny three-way link he had experienced, and described the way he had heard the voices in his head. Cluny and Anselma listened with rapt attention, letting him take his time when something was not clear. It was only when he finished his explanation that Galen realized Cluny was no longer holding the feather.

'Have you had any experience of magic before?' the alchemist asked.

'No.'

'Nothing at all?' He sounded disappointed.

Galen shook his head.

'Then it's Rebecca,' Anselma said.

'Or possibly the third party, whose name Galen has been at such pains to conceal,' Cluny remarked.

'It won't be her,' Galen said, sure of this without knowing why.

'Rebecca then,' Anselma decided, and Cluny nodded his agreement.

'What *are* you talking about?' Galen asked.

Anselma ignored him, and addressed her husband.

'But the other two must have been receptive, or they couldn't have been involved.'

Cluny nodded again.

'If you don't explain this to me,' Galen exclaimed, 'I'm going to strangle the pair of you!'

That got their attention, and they stared at him in amazement. Galen laughed nervously.

'I was joking,' he said. 'Just tell me . . . '

'The tide of magic is rising,' Cluny began. 'It has lain dormant for ages, but something is happening now, and it's growing stronger every day.' The alchemist's words sounded absurdly dramatic, but – for once – he did not sound the least bit pompous. Galen did not doubt his host's sincerity. Anselma took up the story.

'It was just little things at first,' she said, 'and we could easily have missed them, but the signs are there if you know what to look for. Eventually, if the old legends are to be believed . . . '

'You think the game was part of all this?' Galen interrupted unable to hide his scepticism.

'Possibly.'

'But what *is* it? What's happening?'

'We don't know for sure,' Cluny answered. 'The old stories tell of a conflict that will recur throughout history.'

'We thought we had been lucky enough to be born in safer times,' Anselma put in.

'But we—' Galen began, feeling less and less sure of his ground.

'We may be mistaken,' Cluny said quickly.

'I'm not sure I believe in all those tales anyway,' Galen stated, almost defiantly.

'Some of them are undoubtedly apocryphal, while others are pure fancy,' Anselma responded, 'but *all* mythology contains a core of truth.'

'Whatever it is, it's got nothing to do with me,' Galen said, trying to convince himself.

'If we're right, *everybody* will be affected,' she said.

'I'll show you something,' Cluny said, and stood up, beckoning Galen to follow. Still in a daze, the lad did so, and joined the alchemist in a small side-room. It was dark, and Cluny lit a lamp. The sudden glow illuminated a cluttered, windowless chamber, filled with dozens of pieces of glittering white marble. Each piece had been shaped and decorated, though many were broken, and the carvings were all worn smooth. Galen had never seen anything like them. He stared at the swirling veins of delicate crystal, and wondered what relevance the beautiful stone had to their conversation.

'This is snow-cluster marble,' Cluny said, waving a hand at the contents of the room. 'It's been unobtainable now for several centuries. Quite valuable stuff, in fact . . . '

'But what's carved on it is more valuable still,' Anselma put in, joining them. 'You see, these pieces came from beneath the salt.'

'The salt-flats?'

'Yes. The Archaeologists find them every so often, together with other items that they deem more valuable.' Cluny shrugged. 'They're ignorant men for the most part, and don't know the true worth of these objects – but they've always been eager enough to accept my money.'

'These pieces all date from before the time when the land

172

was inundated and the salt-flats formed,' Anselma added. 'Eight hundred years ago.'

'I thought that was just an old wives' tale,' Galen said.

'Even *they* contain elements of truth,' Cluny commented.

'There's no known source of snow-cluster marble anywhere now,' his wife went on. 'So we can only assume the quarry must have been buried along with everything else.'

'Derith?'

'There was definitely a great city of that name once,' she answered. 'And it would explain a lot if it really *was* buried beneath the salt.'

'Then these could be from . . . ' Galen bent closer to examine some of the stones, and ran his finger gently over the worn carvings. He was lost in wonder at the thought of touching something from a city that had previously only existed in legend.

'Possibly,' the alchemist agreed.

'What do the carvings show?' Galen asked. 'I can't make anything out.'

'This one might interest you,' Cluny replied, indicating one of the largest slabs. 'It's only a faint impression, but it was obviously done with great skill.' Galen stared hard, but could not decipher the markings. 'The light's not very good in here,' Cluny went on, 'and it's too heavy to move easily, so I made a tracing.' He led the way back into the main room. 'We never realized just what it meant until now,' he remarked, drawing forth a large sheet of paper and laying it carefully on a table.

Galen peered at the tracing, and gasped in disbelief. Even as a two-dimensional copy, the scene depicted was remarkably lifelike. It showed a crowd surrounding a human-sized chess board. On the otherwise empty squares, a man threatened a costumed girl with a sword, but she stood firm, upright and unafraid. On a raised chair at the side of the board a man stood, his arms held aloft as if calling for quiet.

And from the remaining high chair, a young man was caught in mid dive – into the welcoming arms of the crowd below.

'Still think the old tales have nothing to do with you?' Anselma asked quietly.

173

CHAPTER TWENTY-ONE

'Is this really eight hundred years old?' Galen breathed, still studying the tracing.

'Possibly more,' Cluny said, watching the stable-lad's face. 'We don't know how old it was *before* it disappeared beneath the salt.'

Galen's face was a picture of amazement.

'You see now why your performance yesterday so impressed us?' Anselma asked.

'You knew!' Galen exclaimed, looking up at last. 'You knew about this when you told me about the game.' His hosts did not respond. 'Why didn't you tell me?'

'We thought it better not to,' Cluny replied.

'It would have altered your whole attitude to the game,' Anselma added. 'And the outcome could have been very different. We would have been interfering in things that we do not understand.'

'*You* don't understand!' Galen said, more bewildered than ever.

'Now that the game is in the past again,' she went on, 'we decided that it was safe to show you. Until yesterday, we didn't even know that it was relevant to this time.'

In the past again! Galen thought. *What kind of a riddle is that?* 'Surely telling me about the contest in the first place was meddling?' he persisted.

'In a sense, yes,' Cluny answered. 'But the risk was very small. If subsequent events hadn't matched this . . . ' he waved a hand at the tracing, ' . . . so exactly, then we would have been proved wrong.'

A lengthy silence ensued.

'What does it all mean?' Galen asked eventually.

'We were hoping that you might be able to help us there,' Anselma replied, smiling.

'Not a chance,' he answered emphatically. 'The more I hear, the more confused I get.'

'You won't want to see what's on the other stones then,' Cluny remarked.

Galen was about to protest when he saw the twinkle in the alchemist's eyes.

'Show me,' he said, grinning. 'I'll put up with the confusion.'

'To tell the truth,' Cluny replied, 'there's not much to see. Certainly nothing as detailed as this. Most of them are so faint that they can hardly be seen at all.'

'Show him the letter circle,' Anselma suggested.

'That's certainly the clearest,' her husband agreed, 'but it's not as interesting as the pictures. We have no idea what it means, although we've been puzzling over it for years.'

He went back into the stone room and returned with a flat piece of marble which was roughly circular and about as wide as his outstretched fingers. Galen took it and held it carefully, studying the carvings and tracing them with a finger. Inside a perfectly drawn circle was a jumble of deeply incised letters.

```
A R T S S
P E O I
S O I F X
F W T A
E H T E C
```

'Mean anything?' Anselma asked hopefully.

'Not a thing,' Galen replied, turning the marble from side to side. Cluny and his wife managed not to look too disappointed – they had not been expecting miracles, after all.

'Doesn't make much sense, does it,' the alchemist remarked cheerfully.

'Could it be a code?' Galen suggested. 'Or a foreign language?'

'A code's the more obvious solution,' Anselma replied,

'though we haven't been able to break it. It certainly isn't any language we've ever come across.'

'Perhaps you have to mix the letters up and rearrange them,' he said.

'Like an anagram, you mean,' Cluny responded.

'If you say so.'

'We've tried that too,' Anselma told Galen. 'In all sorts of combinations, but nothing makes sense.'

'Maybe there is no answer,' her husband remarked. 'Our friend the ancient stonemason may have put it there as a joke – he's probably laughing at us now from somewhere in the Web.'

They all smiled at this idea, but knew that it was not a theory to be taken seriously. There had to be a solution – if only they could find the key.

Galen put the piece of marble aside, knowing that if the efforts of his hosts had produced no results, then he was unlikely to be able to help them now.

'Show me the others,' he said. 'Are they all pictures?'

'As far as we can tell, yes,' Cluny replied. 'I've got tracings of them all, but if you want to see the originals, just ask.'

The next two hours were frustrating, but passed swiftly. It was difficult even to be sure what the insubstantial images represented. One looked like a man on a horse, another was a castle with flames leaping from its towers, and a third seemed to depict a group of musicians. It was impossible to make any sense at all of the rest – and detailed scrutiny only made things worse. Only the chess game scene held any relevance for Galen and at last he sat back and sighed despondently.

'I give up,' he said. 'It's hopeless.'

'We'll find out what they mean one day,' Cluny announced, sounding pompous once more. 'The search for knowledge never ceases – and is never wasted.'

'I just hope we find out in time,' Anselma added softly.

Galen was about to ask her exactly what she meant by that when there was a loud knock at the door. He tensed, ready to flee, while Cluny and Anselma quickly put the tracings away. Then a sound from outside the rear windows made Galen more nervous still. Unless he was very much mistaken, the building was being surrounded – and he was trapped. There was no other way out.

'In there!' Anselma whispered, pointing to the marble room. Galen slipped inside, and she shut the door quietly just as the knocking sounded again. 'Go and answer the door, Clue,' she said loudly.

The alchemist adjusted his tunic, strode purposefully to the door and opened it wide. Tarrant stood, alone and apparently quite relaxed, on the steps.

'My lord,' Cluny exclaimed, bowing low. 'To what do we owe this unexpected pleasure?'

'I would talk with you, alchemist,' the envoy responded, echoing Cluny's effusive manner.

'Come in, come in. May I present my wife, Anselma.'

Tarrant entered the room, smiled in acknowledgement of the woman's nod of greeting, then glanced around.

'You are alone?' he asked.

'Yes, my lord.'

Tarrant paused before speaking again.

'I am sure you are doing it for the best of motives,' he remarked eventually, 'but I am afraid that you are lying.'

Cluny began to protest, but the envoy silenced him with a gesture.

'Please, I know that Galen is here, and you have my word as the king's envoy that I wish him no harm. Ask the young man to come out from wherever he is hiding – I have a proposition to put to him, and time is of the essence.'

Tarrant waited patiently as Cluny and Anselma looked at each other, suspicion clearly written on their faces. However, before they had a chance to respond, Galen took the decision out of their hands and came out of the store-room. He closed the door carefully behind him and stood facing the envoy squarely.

'How did you find me?' he asked.

'I have a man in my service who excels in these matters,' Tarrant replied, smiling. 'Your trail was easy enough to follow!'

'So what's this proposition you have for me?' Galen asked. He was surprised to find that it had been the envoy rather than Baldemar or Cranne who had come looking for him, but while there were obviously armed men all around the building, he saw no harm in cooperating – for the moment, at least.

'I'd like you to work for me,' the envoy stated.

'Doing what?' Galen asked, trying hard not to look astonished.

'Travelling around the country, gathering information, carrying messages and the like.'

'Spying, you mean. Why me?'

'Because I was impressed both by your nerve and by your quick thinking yesterday,' Tarrant replied. 'Not many stable-lads could have won that game.' He paused, measuring the young man before him and liking what he found. 'Besides, you can't go back to the castle just now, can you. So what have you got to lose?'

'You must have plenty of men on your staff already,' Galen retorted. 'A little nerve and a bit of quick thinking can't be *that* rare – even in soldiers.'

Tarrant laughed heartily. 'Well said!' he responded. 'Though I'm glad Pike didn't hear you! The king's soldiers do have a little of these attributes, but my problem is that I need someone with no previous connection to the king, his army, or to me. You fit those criteria, *and* you have the perfect reason for wanting to leave Edgefield.'

'To go where?' Galen asked.

'I'd like you to join a certain group of Archaeologists,' the envoy told him. 'Cross the salt with them and make contact with some people to the south. You'll be helping your king, and you might even make some money out of it – apart from your fee, of course.'

'That's all?'

'That's all. Will you do it?'

Galen was assailed by a number of conflicting thoughts. He knew that he would miss Emer, but he also knew that he would be less than welcome at the castle just now. On the surface, this was an incredible opportunity – and something he had always wanted. He would be travelling as he'd always longed to do, and the thought of joining up with the Archaeologists, who had always held a kind of fascination for him, was very exciting. Their adventures were legendary – and he might even uncover some more snow-cluster marble from below the salt. But that was taking Tarrant's words at face value. Could he really trust the envoy? Was it really as simple as he had suggested? And why such haste?

Galen glanced at Cluny and Anselma. The couple had been mute witnesses to the conversation, and their expressions were serious, giving nothing away. He was on his own.

'I need a bit more information—' Galen began.

'But you'll go?' Tarrant put in.

At that moment, instinct took over. *You either trust this man or you don't,* Galen told himself.

'I'll go,' he decided.

'Excellent! Pike will explain everything to you, but you *must* leave immediately. He's just outside. You will be provided with everything you need. Get going – and good luck!' Tarrant waved a hand towards the entrance.

After a moment's hesitation, Galen strode to the door. There he paused, and turned back to his hosts.

'Thank you for everything,' he said. 'I'll let you know if I find anything interesting. Goodbye.'

'Farewell,' Cluny called.

'Good luck,' Anselma added, as Galen ran up the steps outside and disappeared from sight. Events had moved so quickly that the couple were almost dazed. They did not know what to think.

'Thank you for keeping him safe,' Tarrant said, smiling.

'Was it *absolutely* necessary to surround our home in that way?' Anselma asked, her face deadly serious.

'Galen was obviously nervous,' the envoy replied. 'And while that was perfectly understandable, I did not want to run the risk of him slipping away. If he had tried to escape, no harm would have come to him.'

'We only have your word for that,' she retorted.

'That is all I can offer,' he answered smoothly. 'And it has obviously been good enough for Galen. I apologize for any offence my actions have caused.'

Anselma's indignation subsided a little, and Tarrant took

the opportunity to change the subject.

'I have been informed that you are developing a new type of weapon,' he remarked.

Cluny brightened at this, though his wife still looked solemn.

'It's still only in the experimental stage,' he told the envoy, unable to disguise his enthusiasm.

'Montfort would be interested to learn more,' Tarrant said. 'Will you show me? I'm afraid I have very little time – I must leave this afternoon.'

'Do you have any proof that you are indeed the king's envoy?' Anselma asked suddenly.

'Baldemar and Farrand accepted me as such without the need of proof,' he replied, though without rancour. 'But I have the king's seal here.' He patted his jerkin pocket. 'But I suppose I could have stolen it.'

'My love, I'm sure—' Cluny began.

'It would be dangerous knowledge in the wrong hands,' she went on, ignoring the interruption.

'Your secrets will be safe with me,' Tarrant assured them. 'Montfort is a good man and my master, and I am merely carrying out his orders in investigating reports of this nature. If you do not wish to tell me anything then I will respect that and go on my way.'

Anselma and Cluny, like Rebecca and Galen before them – and many others before them – found the envoy could be very persuasive – and they were soon talking animatedly about chemical reactions, propellants and explosives. Although some of their terms made little sense to Tarrant, he got the general idea.

'At the moment,' the alchemist concluded, 'we can put on a pretty display, but the power of these things, while undeniable, is still random. If we can learn to harness them, we could revolutionize the art of war.'

'Or the art of preventing it,' Tarrant commented, and the others glanced at him in surprise. 'Thank you for your time, and for sharing your knowledge. I hope you succeed in harnessing these forces – it would be a great accomplishment. And now I must go. I have already delayed my departure too long. Thank you again.' He paused. 'May

I ask you not to tell anyone of Galen's new . . . career . . . or where he is heading? It's vitally important that this remains secret.'

Cluny and Anselma thought about this for a few moments. They knew, as the whole town did, that Galen and Emer were close friends, and Anselma especially wondered what effect the stable-lad's departure would have on the young girl. Then she nodded.

'We'll say nothing.'

With that assurance, Tarrant turned and strode quickly from the room, taking the steps two at a time. At the top he drew a handkerchief from the pocket of his jerkin, and examined the plain white cloth. *My goodness!* he thought facetiously. *It must have faded. This looks just like an ordinary handkerchief to me. It's a good job they didn't insist on seeing the seal!* He replaced the cloth, and set off down the street, smiling to himself.

Back inside the basement room, Cluny and Anselma stood in silence for a while, trying to make sense of what had happened. Then they hugged each other tightly.

'Do you trust him?' Anselma asked softly.

'Yes, I think so,' Cluny replied. 'And if we *can* help Montfort, then it will be work well done.'

'I hope Galen will be all right,' she said. 'It might just have been a ruse to get him away somewhere quiet and kill him.'

Cluny drew back in surprise.

'Why?' he asked. 'What would be the use of that? The game is over now.'

'Revenge,' his wife replied. 'That's the way of the world – and certainly the way of men like Farrand and his son!'

Cluny stepped back from their embrace, nodding thoughtfully.

'Yes,' he said seriously. 'We must be very careful.'

He turned, and accidentally knocked several lengths of glass tubing from the table, sending them crashing to the floor. Anselma sighed, and began to gather together the broken pieces.

CHAPTER TWENTY-TWO

As Galen was leaving Edgefield, bemused by the speed with which his life was changing, Rebecca was venturing outside her apartments for the first time since the fateful game. Tarrant's words – and the hints behind them – had left her unable to relax, and the obvious person to turn to was Radd. He might be able to help her make sense of it all.

Rebecca walked slowly through the castle, still feeling weak in spite of her long sleep and the food Nursey had made her eat. To her relief, the chamberlain was at home – and his concern for her was immediate and obvious.

'I thought you were still in bed,' he said, ushering her in. 'Are you all right, my dear? This whole business must have been a terrible ordeal for you.'

'It was,' she admitted, 'but I'm all right now. A bit tired, that's all.' She sat down gratefully, and Radd moved his own chair next to hers. 'I'm worried about Father, though.'

The baron's chamberlain hesitated for a moment before replying.

'He was in a murderous mood for a while,' he said eventually, 'but Tarrant seems to have smoothed things over. For such a young man, he makes a remarkable diplomat.'

'Yes, he does,' Rebecca agreed. *In more ways than one!*

'I'm sure he couldn't have expected to have to deal with something like this,' Radd went on.

Rebecca grinned mischievously.

'No, he probably thought it would just be a matter of being wined and dined, and making a formal announcement,' she remarked, not believing a word of what she said.

'You seem remarkably cheerful about it all,' Radd said, surprised but glad to see her smiling again.

'Well, I *am* glad, in a way,' she admitted. 'In spite of the difficulties it may cause Father. Cranne was not my idea of a suitable husband.' *And that's putting it mildly!* she added silently.

'No. He behaved abominably,' Radd said thoughtfully. 'And you were very brave. Though he'll never admit it, I think your father was very proud of you.'

'Really?' Rebecca still found this hard to believe – though Radd was the second person to tell her so.

'Of course. You proved to him that his pride in his family was justified. You restored his faith in the House of Edge.'

'But I haven't restored his fortunes!' she responded cynically. 'I thought the money was all that mattered to him.'

'Tarrant has helped out there too,' Radd answered. 'The baron won't get as much as he'd have liked, but it'll be enough to cushion the blow.'

'So Father has accepted the cancellation of the marriage?'

'If I know him, he'll sulk about it for a few days,' the chamberlain replied. 'He'll stay in his rooms, get drunk and bemoan his fate, but yes, he *has* accepted it. In the end, he had no choice.'

'I wonder how long it will be before he comes up with another suitor?' Rebecca was fishing, trying to discover whether there were any other candidates waiting in the wings, but Radd's next words reassured her.

'This setback will force him to reflect, at least,' he said with a shrug. 'And perhaps he'll consult us next time.'

'That would be nice,' she commented.

They smiled at each other ruefully.

'Of course, I would accept my father's decision,' Rebecca said, choosing her words carefully, 'but . . . '

'But you'll make sure they can play chess first,' Radd interrupted.

'Only if I like them,' she retorted, grinning. 'What I was going to say was that it's difficult to keep my own feelings out of it. It's hard to look upon my marriage as an affair of state.'

'Of course,' he said, serious again now. 'That's only natural. But we can't always do what we want in this life.'

'Affairs of state make many demands on all of us,' she quoted. Radd nodded thoughtfully.

'You didn't have anything to do with Galen winning, then?' he asked offhandedly.

Rebecca had been half expecting this question and was able to answer quite calmly.

'No. I picked him because I thought he'd be fun, and because the crowd would enjoy watching him. I mean . . . he seems nice enough . . . and he's a stable-lad, one of them. But I had no idea that he was such a good player.'

Rebecca hoped that Radd would take her obvious embarrassment to be because of his daughter's association with Galen.

'He was lucky too,' her mentor replied, apparently accepting her words at face value. 'Cranne made some stupid mistakes, and refused any advice.'

'I couldn't really tell what was happening,' Rebecca said.

'Really?' Radd was watching her closely, and she began to feel uncomfortable.

'Being on the board changed the whole perspective,' she explained.

'Mmm. So you're not upset at having to remain a maid for a while longer?'

'No,' she replied, glad of the opportunity to change the subject. 'Anyway, you haven't completed my education yet.'

'Recently it seems to have been you teaching me,' he remarked.

Rebecca was not sure how to take this, so she ploughed on regardless.

'I mean, you've told me so much about the history of our land – about the kings and queens, about how the traditions of travelling artists grew up, and how the salt-flats were formed by a freak storm, and so on – but I don't understand what relevance the past has to me. Why should Montfort be concerned with my marriage, for instance?' she concluded, probing for information.

'That's politics, not history,' Radd answered.

'Don't they amount to the same thing?'

'In some ways, I suppose so,' he replied. 'History is our

record of change, and politics often determine the rate – and the effects – of change.' He paused, smiling. 'I rather like that. I'll have to quote it next time I'm talking to someone important.'

'Any more comments like that,' she warned him, grinning back, 'and I'll have Father fire you.'

'Ungrateful youth,' he muttered.

'Tell me what's happening with the rate of change now,' she demanded, pretending petulance. 'Or I'll have you fired anyway!'

'Your wish is my command, my lady,' Radd responded deferentially. He got to his feet and paced the room for a few moments, gathering his thoughts. When he turned to face Rebecca again, his expression was serious.

'At the moment,' he began, 'the rate is slow, as is normal in times of long established peace. But if Montfort gets his way, it could speed up – rather *too* much for some.'

'But he's the king,' Rebecca said. 'Why *shouldn't* he get his way?'

'Montfort has some radical ideas about government,' the chamberlain replied, 'but one man – even a king – can't do everything. He needs allies, and is anxious that his nobles don't oppose him.'

'Yes, but—'

'So he keeps a watchful eye on any alliances – for instance, on that proposed between Baldemar and Farrand,' Radd went on.

'Oh.' Rebecca had plenty to think about now. *So Farrand must be opposed to Montfort. This whole thing is more serious than I realized . . . No, wait a moment. Why does that follow? Even if he's against Montfort, why should the king want to stop Cranne from marrying me? Edge isn't important any more.*

'What are you thinking about?' Radd asked curiously, interrupting her reverie.

'I'm confused,' she answered truthfully. 'What *are* these ideas of Montfort's? Do you agree with them?'

'For the most part, yes. He's trying to loosen the grip of the aristocracy on the common people. Some of the folk here in Edge have a hard enough life, but it's much worse in other places. If Montfort can replace the worst elements of the old feudal system with something just and humane, then he will be regarded as a great man by me and by many others.'

'But not by the nobility?' Rebecca had rarely seen her tutor so animated.

'That's the point,' he replied. 'So many of them have vested interests in keeping things just as they are that the task of persudading them to change their minds will be a difficult one – especially for a king who's half the average age of his nobles.'

'Might it come to fighting?' she asked softly.

'I doubt it. Montfort won't push *that* hard,' Radd answered confidently. 'Civil war would be the last thing he wants. *Everyone* would suffer then.'

'Is Farrand opposed to the changes?' she asked, hoping to clarify her earlier thoughts.

'That I don't know,' Radd replied frustratingly. 'We're out of the political mainstream here in Edge, and he certainly didn't confide in *me* while he was here!'

'What about Father?'

'Oh, he's too wrapped up in his own problems to concern himself with what Montfort is trying to do. In principle, I'm sure he'd detest it, but . . . ' and he smiled conspiratorially, ' . . . he might eventually be persuaded otherwise.'

'I wish *you* were baron here,' Rebecca stated wistfully.

'Oh, no!' he exclaimed. 'It's bad enough being a chamberlain.'

They sat in silence for a while, Rebecca berating herself for not having prised more information out of Tarrant, and Radd wondering at his pupil's sudden interest in politics. He had never hidden anything from her on the grounds of her youth or sex, and he wasn't about to start now, but she had always seemed more interested in the past, with its intrigue and romance – and its remoteness. It appeared that the problems of the present-day world had been brought into focus by the abortive plans for her betrothal. It had made them more personal.

'You've led a privileged life, Rebecca,' he said eventually. 'So have I, come to that.'

'I know,' she said, her blue eyes solemn.

'And Montfort is trying to reform the system that made those privileges possible.'

She nodded but said nothing, realizing now that her life might be changing whether she married or not.

'Do you remember, when you were about twelve,' Radd went on, 'how I told you about the peasants who were caught in a vicious trap? The value of their land lessened as they had to divide it among their children, and at the same time they were faced with an increase in taxes and the reduction in the value of their crops. And the situation was being made worse because the essentials they needed but couldn't grow for themselves were getting ever more expensive?'

Rebecca nodded slowly.

'Most of them became virtual slaves to the land-owners,' she said quietly.

'And do you remember what you said?'

'No.'

'You said, "But that's wrong!" And you spoke the truth,' he continued. 'It was a disgrace then, and it's still unjust. There is much in the world that is wrong, but if Montfort succeeds, then at least we'll be moving in the right direction.'

* * *

After the panic and excitement of the three days which had threatened to turn Rebecca's world upside down, the next few months passed in a haze of boredom and frustration. There was no one left to ask about the political situation in Ahrenia, and how it might affect her own life. Edge, it seemed, was the last place to hear of any developments in the current power struggle.

Radd's predictions about Baldemar's behaviour proved accurate. The baron had aged visibly, and seemed quieter than before, but at least he did not seem unhappy. The promised money arrived from Tarrant, and no further threats were heard from Farrand. Before long, it was as if the whole incident had never taken place.

Summer turned to autumn, and the chess-board in the

town square was gradually worn away. For all but a few, the contest soon became a forgotten memory.

* * *

Only Cluny and Anselma thought often of the game and its implications. They kept their word to Tarrant, and pretended to have no knowledge of Galen or his whereabouts, but found it difficult to keep from contacting Rebecca. They knew that she had done something to help her champion, and that the help she had provided had been extremely unusual. It was frustrating for them to know this and not be able to do anything about it. They knew, however, that they must not interfere – in spite of their intense curiosity and desire to help – and eventually decided that they must play a waiting game. Events would take their own course.

* * *

Castle life once more resumed its tedious, unchanging pace, leaving Rebecca and Emer bored and restless. Emer was also depressed by Galen's disappearance. No one knew where he had gone, and neither she nor Rebecca had Pike's skill at following a trail. Her efforts to find an amorous replacement among the local young men were half-hearted and short-lived. After a while, Emer seemed reluctant to discuss Galen at all, and Rebecca was at a loss to know how to comfort her friend.

Rebecca's unease was intensified by her reborn sense of social guilt. *You've led a privileged life.* Nothing seemed to have much meaning any more, and she could not see how to change things. Even her long search for magic was at a standstill. She experienced nothing even remotely like the waking dream-images or the three-way communication which had made the chess game so extraordinary, and Radd still would not take her enquiries on this esoteric subject seriously. The picture in the East Tower remained a mystery – but one which held little attraction for her any more. Even her dreams were unremarkable, until one evening when Nursey unwittingly prompted a sequence of images which carried over into Rebecca's sleep.

She opened the door to her bedchamber to find the old woman dusting the room. She was about to tell her not to bother, but stopped when Nursey, completely unaware of her audience, began to sing a nursery rhyme that Rebecca knew well but had not heard for years.

'White earth, white earth, crunching on the floor,
Push hard, push hard, push it out the door.
Big broom, big broom, sweep it all away,
White sky, white sky, filling up the day.'

Throughout the verse, Nursey matched her actions to the words as a child would – Rebecca remembered doing the same thing during her own childhood. First, the old woman scraped her feet on the floor, then she pretended to wield a broom, and finished by looking up and waving her duster in the air above her head, as if she were looking up at an imaginary sky.

Then came the chorus.

'Pickle hollow, pickle hollow,
A little goes, but more will follow.
Pickle hollow, pickle hollow,
We will all lie down tomorrow.'

'Not doing that bit at *my* age,' Nursey muttered, and Rebecca remembered that the last line had been a signal for each singer to fling themselves to the ground and lie still.

Although the words were set to a simple, jolly tune, they sent a chill through Rebecca's heart. She had realized for the first time just what they meant. The seemingly innocent rhyme told of how the falling salt had inundated people's homes, and of their desperate, futile attempts to stem the dry, white tide. *A little goes, but more will follow.* The last line, once a source of so much fun, was the most chilling of all. *We will all lie down tomorrow.*

How terrible it must have been, she thought, shivering.

Rebecca stepped forward into the room then. Nursey showed no sign of embarrassment over the fact that her performance may have been witnessed.

'Nearly finished,' she remarked cheerfully. 'What have you been doing this afternoon?'

'Nothing much.' Rebecca was still held by the spell of the song.

'Apostrophe,' Nursey admonished her. 'That's what you'll do if you don't keep active. Wither away before your time.'

'I'll remember that, Nursey,' Rebecca said, smiling wanly.

'Always keep busy,' the old woman went on. 'It'll keep you from brooding.' She went to the door. 'Sleep well, little one.'

Alone once more, Rebecca could not get the images out of her head, and she lay awake for a long time that night.

* * *

The salt was pouring into her room from every direction. It crept in through the cracks around the doors, trickled steadily down from the ceiling, poured in through the open window, and erupted in white fountains from the floor. She tried frantically to clear it away, but for every handful she scooped up, six more flooded in. Then the door gave way, the window shattered and floorboards sprang loose as the deluge became unstoppable. Rebecca scrabbled helplessly, but to no avail. Slowly, she was enveloped by the dreadful white crystals until she could no longer move. Only her head was free – and still the salt poured in. *No!* She was suffocating, choking. *Help me!*

Then the woman appeared, tall and graceful, moving through the salt as if through pure, clear air. She plucked unseen letters from out of the all-consuming whiteness, and used them like magical building blocks.

A R T S S

Meaningless jumbles of letters, words that were not words, were built into walls of safety within the dream.

P E O I

What does it mean?

S O I F X

How can this protect me?

F W T A

The woman did not answer, but went on calmly producing letters from out of nothing like a proficient wizard.

E H T E C

And the salt was gone. Rebecca was safe again, and she felt such an overwhelming surge of gratitude that she stepped forward to hug her saviour. But the woman faded away, leaving only the light from her eyes behind – and words, accompanied by sweet, sad music, that held Rebecca in thrall.

For you, my child, the light will never fade.

* * *

She awoke in the middle of the night, imprisoned by twisted bedclothes. Nightmares were nothing new to Rebecca, but this one had left her strangely uplifted. The horror had turned to happiness – and the music was with her still.

CHAPTER TWENTY-THREE

The next morning, Emer brought news which – at least temporarily – took Rebecca's mind off the mystery of her latest dream.

'There's a fair coming to Edgefield,' she announced enthusiastically. 'It'll get here about midday tomorrow.'

The approach of a fair always signalled a good deal of excitement for the town and castle, but Rebecca had never fully shared in this. Her previous experience of such delight had usually been second-hand, in the form of exploits described by Emer and others. On the rare occasions when she *had* been allowed to visit a fair, her father had ensured that her enjoyment of it was spoiled by the chaperones and guards who had prevented the child from falling under its spell. Even when permitted to sample the various festivities, it had been a frustratingly bland experience. Most of the travellers were hardly likely to perform their best when faced with a little girl whose importance was emphasized by the presence of armed soldiers, watching them like hawks.

The tradition of travelling artists – musicians, painters, storytellers and the like – had remained strong in Ahrenia for centuries. It had originally stemmed from the belief that such people were somehow closer to the Web, in touch with matters of the spirit, and that this was displayed in their varying gifts of artistry. In an earlier age this may even have been true, but in Rebecca's time many of the entertainers were barely proficient, so the idea of such a link seemed absurd. And yet the tradition persisted, with many itinerant artists – of widely varying abilities – making a precarious living by offering their services to the castles of the nobility and the homes of the rich.

Fairs were something different. Although they were also constantly on the move, rarely staying in one place for more than a few days, the similarity ended there. Fair people travelled in one large group; they inhabited a mobile village, made up of dozens of brightly painted caravans. They did not seek out patrons for their services in castles or mansions, but set up camp on the outskirts of towns, letting the people come to them. Nevertheless, individuals who made up a fair worked as a team, and were a genuine community; as such, their combined resources could offer experiences beyond the scope of most peripatetic entertainers. Moreover, the fair deliberately set out to appeal to all manner of tastes and appetites, rather than the more refined artistry demanded by both merchants and nobility. To enter such a pleasure-ground was to enter a new and mysterious world.

Most towns anticipated the arrival of such a treat eagerly; an advance party would usually arrive a day or two ahead of the rest, to publicize the various attractions and to generate an air of excitement. Edgefield was no different from most places in this respect, though, as elsewhere, the more sober-minded citizens disapproved of such festivities, considering them corrupt – and corrupting.

There was an element of truth in this attitude; travelling fairs did attract characters who might be considered undesirable by any self-respecting community, but the fairs were usually self-governing as well. The livelihood of all their members depended on being welcomed back to venues again and again, so any of their number who went too far were soon dealt with by a form of rough and ready justice. Nevertheless, rumour and a reputation for lawlessness did keep some people away.

Baldemar, for instance, had never regarded denizens of the fairs as proper artists, and would never consider inviting any of them into his home. However, he was shrewd enough to know that he would be extremely unpopular if he tried to refuse them permission to pass through his land, or to make camp near Edgefield. Equally, he did not dare to ban his servants or subjects from attending. He reserved his disapproval for those closest to him and, as a consequence, Rebecca's visits had been few and far between.

Radd had not placed the same restrictions on his own daughter. Emer was a veteran of many fairs, and was adamant that she was going again this time, even though she knew it would not be quite the same: Galen had accompanied her on the last few occasions, and his absence made her all the more determined to persuade Rebecca to come.

'It'll be fun!' she exclaimed. 'The Web knows there's been little enough of that round here recently . We've been bored rigid for months!'

Rebecca hesitated. 'I'll never get permission,' she said.

'Don't be silly,' Emer retorted. 'Your father's bound to say you can't go. Even if he *does* agree, you'll be lumbered with all sorts of cretins who've got orders to "look after you". '

'What then?'

'Sneak out,' Emer replied, amazed that her friend should need to question anything so obvious. She half expected Rebecca to refuse, and was preparing to exercise her considerable persuasive talents, but the baron's daughter surprised her by taking the suggestion in her stride.

'Won't it be dangerous?' she asked. 'If we're all alone?'

'We're both eighteen now,' Emer answered, laughing. 'Full grown women!' Her name-day had been half a month ago – and had passed less eventfully than Rebecca's. 'We can look after ourselves.'

'*You* can, maybe.'

'All right, I'll look after you too.'

'But won't people recognize me?'

'We'll go in the evening,' Emer replied promptly. 'It'll be dark. And that's the best time, anyway. You can disguise yourself – use a little of that amazing imagination of yours.'

Her confidence and enthusiasm were contagious, and Rebecca began to feel both excited and nervous at the prospect. She had only ever visited a fair in daylight before, and the thought of wandering freely through its

194

forbidden zones after dark was intoxicating.

'How could we get out of the castle without anyone noticing?' she asked. 'Nursey practically lives in my pocket these days.'

'Oh, we can handle *her* between us,' Emer replied scornfully. 'And anyone else for that matter. With your brains and my cunning, we're a match for anyone.'

'Even for our fathers?'

'Mine has never been able to stop me doing something I really wanted to,' Emer answered with a grin. 'And the baron spends so much time in his rooms these days that I doubt whether he'd notice if you were here or not. Anyway, what could he do, short of locking you up?'

'I wouldn't put that past him,' Rebecca said sombrely.

'Don't be ridiculous,' Emer ordered amiably. 'Look, the fair may only be here for one night, two at the most. Edgefield isn't big enough to keep it here for longer. So you can't spend weeks making up your mind. Are you coming with me or not?'

Faced with her friend's defiant stare, Rebecca could not keep silent for long.

'Can we get everything ready by tomorrow night?'

'Of course,' Emer replied, smiling. 'All you'll need is some money. You've got a bit hidden away, haven't you?'

'What do we need money for?' Rebecca asked.

Emer rolled her eyes. 'You *have* led a sheltered life,' she said, exasperated. 'What's the point of going at all if we can't sample what's on offer? A baron's daughter might have gifts pressed upon her, but ordinary girls need to pay for their fun!'

'Oh.' Rebecca felt stupid and ashamed.

'Unless, of course, we can find some young men who'd be willing to pay *for* us,' Emer went on with a mischievous grin. 'That's not beyond the bounds of possibility.'

Rebecca was taken aback by this idea, and for a moment, she began to doubt the wisdom of this adventure. Her thoughts must have showed in her face, much to Emer's disgust.

'Good grief!' she exploded. 'It was a joke! And I'll be with you.' Annoyance made her cruel and she could not resist adding, 'Are you going to let Baldemar pick *all* your boyfriends?'

Rebecca's eyes snapped up, angry and hurt. She had been stung by the accusation in her friend's words, but when she spoke, her voice was calm and determined.

'All right,' she said. 'We'll go.'

'That's better,' Emer remarked, happy again. 'Now, let's get your escape plan sorted out!'

* * *

Slipping out of the castle proved to be simplicity itself, and did not even involve Rebecca in any direct untruths. She had merely told Nursey that she was going to spend the evening with Emer, and not to wait up for her. Her friend told the same story in reverse to her father, reckoning that if their ruse *was* discovered, it would be too late for either of their guardians to do anything about it.

They met outside the kitchens, as arranged, and donned their disguises before walking boldly across the courtyard and out through the gate. Rebecca's dark cloak and hood covered her from head to foot and left her face in shadow, while Emer's rough coat and maid's cap, with her hair pinned up inside, hid both her identity and her natural charms. Her eyes were glowing with excitement as they passed the solitary sentry who sat on the guard-house steps.

'Goodnight, girls!' he called after them. 'Don't do anything you'd be ashamed of, unless you come back here and do it with me as well!' He laughed at his own witticism, but made no move to get up.

'I doubt if you could keep up with us,' Emer yelled back, without turning round. 'We're looking for *younger* talent.'

The sentry laughed again, though not so smugly this time. He stared after the retreating figures and tried to place the scornful voice. He gave up after a few moments, and leant back against the steps. He was soon snoring peacefully.

Emer and Rebecca walked on through the gathering gloom, and plunged into the nearly empty streets of

Edgefield.

'Looks like most of the town's already there,' Emer remarked.

It was a cloudy night, with a damp promise of rain in the air, and there were few stars visible, but nothing could quench Emer's spirits as they approached their goal. Lamplight and the flickering of dozens of fires illuminated the scene. The noises and smells of the fair reached them long before they entered its invisible boundary. Music, the confident cries of showmen and vendors, the clatter of hammers and other tools, animal noises and a welter of human voices filled the night, and added to the smells of food, smoke, mud, animals and humanity to create a jumble of chaotic but wonderful sensations. Emer was in her element as she strode forward.

The girls were swallowed up by the milling crowds, and suddenly the chaos began to take shape. Invitations to try this, buy that, or to witness something else filled the air, and Rebecca found herself not knowing where to look next. The wonders of the night gradually overcame her self-consciousness, and she began to point things out to Emer as they threaded their way between the colourfully painted wagons and caravans. The temporary stalls, tents and stages had been set up in seemingly haphazard fashion, but none the less drew the spectators in, towards the heart of the fair.

Rebecca found it hard to keep track of all she was seeing. There was so much, compressed into such a small space, that she was totally bewildered. First to take her eye were the various games, competitions, and trials of strength. There was a target shy, where contestants hurled wooden balls at painted skittles. Another challenged you to throw hoops around the various prizes that were spread invitingly on a table only a few paces away. There were weight-lifting stalls, and a huge man who offered a reward to anyone who dared to wrestle with him and who could stay in the ring for a count of more than twenty. Success in these enterprises usually resulted in the awarding of a prize, but some pandered to baser instincts. Hitting the centre of the target on another stall resulted, via an ingenious apparatus, in a dog being dropped from his platform into a tank of water, where it then thrashed and scrabbled to get out. Its only reward was to be put back on its original perch. The animal looked bedraggled and miserable, but made no attempt to get away. Contestants egged each other on, placing bets on the possibility of the dog drowning through sheer exhaustion should enough of them score direct hits. Such casual cruelty sickened Rebecca, and she quickly turned away to more palatable sights.

Foremost among these were the multitude of food and drink stalls. Exotic sweets, warming brews bubbling over fires and braziers, all kinds of pies – their crusts still hot from the baking – and much more besides was on offer to tempt the hungry. There were also a variety of potent liquors for those foolhardy or unwary enough to risk them.

In another area was a group of people who were taking advantage of the fair to offer their labour – or in some cases, that of their children – to prospective employers. They called out their skills and strengths in the hope of landing a lucrative position, whether it was short- or long-term. Some of them, especially the children, looked thin and tired, and Rebecca found their dejection pitiful.

Another group was putting forward their skills in an altogether more self-reliant fashion. These were the men and women who made their living by buying and selling cutlery, crockery, and 'precious' stones and jewellery; they included knife-sharpening in their services, as well as pottery-mending that was 'invisible to the naked eye'.

There were animal traders too, with beeks, dogs and horses offered for sale. One man claimed to be able to break any horse, however wild, in just a few hours. Others sold furs and pelts, as well as leather – which they claimed to be the result of hunting in the open wilds, but which had probably been obtained by their skill at poaching. There was even a man peddling a selection of elixirs which he claimed would cure anything from a common cold to gout, from impotence to an ingrowing toenail. He was obviously a trickster, but his patter was so amusing and enthusiastic that many people, including the two girls, stopped to listen. Those who bought his brightly coloured wares obviously believed in their efficacy – and few felt cheated afterwards.

While they were listening to the 'doctor', Rebecca noticed a detail of her father's soldiers marching raggedly between nearby stalls. She nudged Emer, but her friend just shrugged, determined to ignore the newcomers.

'It's just a regular patrol,' she whispered. 'They're not looking for us.'

'How do you know?'

'Because if they were, they'd be making a lot more effort,' Emer replied. 'At the moment, all they're doing is pretending to be important.' Rebecca watched as the guards marched on, chests puffed out and eyes looking about with disdain. They were regarded by fair-folk and locals alike with barely concealed amusement. 'Look at them!' Emer chuckled. 'Who do they think they're fooling?'

Rebecca took her friend's point. If the patrol was meant to strike mortal fear into those who saw them, then it was failing dismally.

'Come on,' Emer said. 'Let's go and see something else. I think my ingrowing toenails can take care of themselves.'

The two girls strolled on, and found themselves in a slightly quieter area, where several highly decorated wooden caravans were drawn up close together. Each one advertised the talents of the owner within, both with written notices, and, for any potential customers who had not mastered the art of reading, with simple pictures. Rebecca was immediately fascinated, though Emer remained unimpressed. Each wagon was apparently occupied by a fortune-teller of some description. Some claimed to read the future with cards, others used mirrors or crystal, and there were several palmists. There was even one clairvoyant who claimed to be able to predict a person's life from a single strand of their hair – from any part of the body!

'I'll wager she's had a few interesting readings,' Emer remarked sardonically.

'But there are so many of them,' Rebecca whispered, trying hard to match her friend's indifferent attitude but

199

failing miserably. The idea of being able to see into the unknown fascinated her.

'They're all charlatans,' Emer said. 'Let's go and find the theatre.'

'But . . . ' Rebecca began.

'Don't waste your money,' her friend insisted. 'You'd only hear what they think you *want* to hear.' With that, she strode away, but Rebecca lingered for a few moments, watching customers entering and leaving various caravans, and hoping she could learn something from their expressions. Then she turned and hurried after Emer, who was making her way towards a large stage. There, actors were calling out to passers-by, advertising a performance which was to 'combine the finest traditions of storytelling with thespian artistry beyond compare' and 'music fit for the gods, with settings more realistic than your own homes'. There was some good-natured heckling from the crowd below, but Rebecca was entranced. The actors' words, their graceful movements and ready smiles, the artfully displayed scenery which was lit to dazzling effect, and the brief bursts of melody which emerged from dark, hidden places beneath the boards all held her attention. She had never before seen such a combination of talent, all put together to create a harmonious whole. The possibility of such a thing had never occurred to her. Once suggested, however, it seemed an entirely logical – and quite wonderful – extension of the artists' skills.

'Can we go to the play?' she asked breathlessly.

'Of course,' Emer replied, smiling at her companion's rapture. 'It's one of the best things here, but it doesn't start until later. We've plenty of time to see something else first. What would you like to try?'

'I don't know,' Rebecca answered. 'There's so much!'

'All right. Let's keep wandering then,' Emer responded, sympathizing with her friend's indecision. She had felt just the same when first confronted with the fair's bewildering array of choices.

They came to a small open space, where a man was addressing a shifting crowd of onlookers. He wore a long robe, which was patterned with a spider's web, just like those of the monks in the chess game. There were a number of people there, but most only stayed a few moments before drifting away again.

'Oh-oh, it's a webby,' Emer warned.

'A what?'

'A webby, a preacher,' she explained. 'Come on, let's go. This is boring.'

But Rebecca did not agree. She had caught some of the preacher's impassioned words, and felt compelled to hear more. She shook her head and stood firm, so Emer stayed with her, albeit reluctantly. She knew that the webbies were tolerated by the other fair people because they sometimes helped smooth their path in the more 'respectable' townships. However, most people found their religious hectoring both tedious and irrelevant, and, like Emer, felt that they had heard it all before. Not so Rebecca! She was mesmerized by the fervour in the preacher's eyes.

'Repent!' he cried. 'Give your allegiance to the Web, from whence all life stems. The Web is vast, immeasurable, infinite. All things are within the Web – gods, demons and angels. One day you too will be part of this wonderful creation, but whether you live there in everlasting peace or eternal torment and damnation is up to you. Repent your sins, give your allegiance! The price of failure is high. Remember Derith, that city of evil. Where is it now? Buried beneath the weight of its own sin.'

The preacher stared into his audience, but no one would hold his gaze, and he turned abruptly and disappeared into his caravan. The remaining onlookers moved slowly away, and Emer let out a sigh of relief.

'Can we go now?' she enquired, but Rebecca did not hear her. She was lost in the memories of another person's teachings about the Web. The subject had arisen some years ago, in connection with the topic of artists and their supposed closeness to the Web.

'Of course, there's nothing like that now,' the chamberlain had concluded.

'Why not?' Rebecca wanted to know. 'Wasn't that why some of the artists were magical?'

'I refuse to fill your head with such nonsense,' he had

replied irritably. 'If magic ever did exist, it doesn't any more.'

'What is the Web exactly?' she had asked, recognizing that she would get no further with her favourite subject.

'I'm no expert,' he began slowly, 'but, in essence, the Web is the spirit of our entire world, a universal mind if you like. All life contributes to it, but the whole thing is a mystery, too big and too strange for anyone to understand properly. I certainly don't.'

'But is it good or bad?' she persisted.

'Of course, the Web is held to be good,' Radd answered carefully, 'but because everything is contained within it, the capacity must exist for evil.'

Rebecca blinked, coming back to the present as Emer tapped her on the shoulder. *Gods, demons and angels.*

'Wake up,' Emer said sternly. 'Where have you been?'

'Just thinking,' Rebecca replied. 'Let's go.'

They walked on, entering an area filled with the clamour of competing attractions.

'Do you want to try something?' Emer asked. 'How about something to eat?' She waited, but Rebecca did not answer. 'Well, what are we going to do?'

'I'm going to see the dream-weaver,' Rebecca answered, staring intently into the distance.

'What are you talking about?' Emer was mystified. 'There's no dream-weaver here, whatever that is.'

'Yes, there is,' her friend insisted. 'Down there.' She pointed to an alley between two stalls, leading to a group of caravans which were a little distance away from the bustle of the public shows. Screened lamps bathed them in a dull red glow.

'We can't go down there!' Emer exclaimed.

'Why not?'

'Only men go to those wagons.'

Rebecca glanced at her friend, eyebrows raised.

'Do I have to spell it out?' Emer asked, adding in a lowered voice, 'Those are the whores' caravans. Someone might take us for—'

'I don't care,' Rebecca interrupted determinedly. 'The dream-weaver is there, and I'm going to see her. I've been waiting for this for a long time.'

'How do you know there's a dream-weaver down there?' Emer asked, astonished by her friend's behaviour.

'That sign,' Rebecca replied, pointing into the alley.

'What sign?' Emer was getting worried now. 'There's nothing there, Becky!' All she could see were the caravans, and a shifting pattern of lights playing across their wheels.

'Can't you see it?' Rebecca asked, looking at her companion in surprise.

'No. All I can see is a narrow path into one of the most dangerous parts of the fair,' Emer insisted.

'It says "Visit the dream-weaver",' Rebecca went on, turning back to the alleyway. ' "Your dreams explained". And underneath that, it says, "Follow the red lights".'

She marched away without further ado, threading her way between the stalls. After a moment's hesitation, Emer followed, having to hurry to keep up. *I'm supposed to be protecting her!* she thought, worried and confused.

'Have you been taking Nursey's powders again?' she asked.

'It was there!' Rebecca retorted defiantly. 'I saw it.'

'Well, it's not there now,' Emer pointed out.

'I know,' her friend replied, but kept on walking through the dull red glow.

There were few people here, and those they met hurried away with eyes lowered. Peculiar noises came from some of the caravans, and one of them was rocking gently as they passed. Rebecca would normally have been embarrassed by all this, but tonight she did not give it a second thought. Emer just laughed.

Rebecca seemed to know exactly where she was going. Eventually, they reached a drab, unmarked caravan, set well away from the bustle of the fair.

'This is it,' Rebecca said. Her voice was quiet, but filled with excitement.

Emer looked doubtful. There was nothing to distinguish this wagon from the others around it – and their intrusion into *those* would be less than welcome.

'Are you sure about this, Becky?' she asked anxiously.

'Yes.'

Rebecca climbed up the three high wooden steps and knocked boldly on the door. It swung back noiselessly, and from the gloom inside a cracked and ancient voice emerged, startling both girls.

'Only one of you should be here. Send the unbeliever away.'

Rebecca turned to look at Emer.

'I'm not leaving you here alone,' her friend whispered, thoroughly frightened now.

'Send her away if you wish to learn anything,' the voice said.

'I'll be all right,' Rebecca said, her face aglow. 'Go on. I'll meet you at the theatre in an hour.'

'No.'

'Please, Emer. This is something I must do.'

Long moments passed in silence.

'All right,' Emer agreed reluctantly. 'I only hope you know what you're doing. If you're not there in an hour, I'm coming back for you – and I'll be bringing the guards with me.'

'Thank you,' Rebecca smiled, nodding.

Emer turned and hurried away, worried, but glad to get back to the main part of the fair.

'Come in,' the voice instructed from the gloomy interior. 'And shut the door behind you.'

CHAPTER TWENTY-FOUR

Rebecca stepped into the caravan, and closed the door behind her. Her eyes slowly adjusted to the gloom, and she began to make out details of the cluttered interior, which was lit by a single lamp, burning low. Yet it was only when the old woman moved that Rebecca caught sight of the wagon's occupant.

'Why have you come here?' The voice was harsh, little more than a croak.

'I thought—' Rebecca began.

'You thought I'd explain everything and make it easy for you.' The ancient crone sounded distinctly testy.

'No. I *do* need to understand, but I'm not expecting it to be easy.'

'Good. Because it won't be,' the old woman said.

Now that her eyes were used to the poor light, Rebecca studied her hostess, who was seated at the far end of the caravan. Her face was wrinkled, with deepset eyes, and her grey hair was straggling and wispy. She wore a shapeless dress, whose only adornment was a circular pendant engraved with an angular pattern.

'Sit down. We'll talk,' the old woman instructed. Rebecca obeyed, perching on the edge of a padded couch. 'It's lucky for you that I'm celebrating tonight,' her hostess went on. 'Otherwise I might not be so amenable. My name is Sancia, by the way, not that it's of much significance.'

'I'm Rebecca. What are you celebrating?'

Sancia leaned back and produced a glass from one of the caravan's many recesses. She filled this with wine, then leaned forward and handed the glass to Rebecca.

'An anniversary,' she said eventually.

'Of what?'

'How would I know?' the old woman snapped. 'It hasn't happened yet.' She sipped her wine appreciatively.

Rebecca tasted her own drink, feeling thoroughly confused, and with no idea of what to expect next. The silence stretched. Sancia showed no sign of wanting to speak, and Rebecca eventually felt compelled to say something.

'Can you really explain dreams?' she ventured timidly.

Sancia chuckled, a dry, papery sound.

'That's the easy part,' she said. 'I thought you wanted more than that.'

'I don't know *what* I want,' Rebecca admitted.

'Magic?'

'Is there really such a thing?' the girl asked eagerly.

'Is there such a thing as air?' Sancia responded. 'Magic is every bit as necessary – and just as common.'

'Tell me!' Rebecca exclaimed.

'It's not as easy as that,' the old woman answered. 'True magic reveals itself. Why do you want to know about such things?'

Although Rebecca had come here to listen, and hopefully to learn, she now found that she had no choice but to tell her own tale. Her whole life was laid bare: the death of her mother and the unfocused longings which had followed that tragic event; the confrontation with the demon from the salt and her childhood nightmares; the discovery of Kavan's painting, her subsequent investigations and the peculiar dreams which had followed; and much, much more.

As she talked, time ceased to have any meaning. Sancia did not interrupt, and just nodded occasionally. She sipped her wine, and refilled both glasses as the young woman's words flowed on.

Finally, Rebecca described the events leading up to the fateful chess game, and the dream-images that had been superimposed on her personal reality. She explained as best she could the extraordinary way in which the game had ended.

'That was a month and a half ago,' she concluded.

'And now you're here,' Sancia said.

'I saw your sign,' Rebecca explained. 'I hoped . . . '

Sancia held up her hands. Unseen jewellery rattled gently inside her voluminous sleeves. She smiled, and when she spoke, her voice was softer, kinder than before.

'Now it's my turn. Listen carefully. I haven't the energy to repeat myself these days.'

Rebecca nodded, her wine forgotten. She was at ease now, but all her senses were alert; she could see tiny motes of dust floating in the lamplight, smelt the slightly musty odour of the room, and noted the dark, mottled patches on Sancia's skin, the fine hairs on her incredibly wrinkled hands. Everything was observed with absolute clarity. Faint noises from the outside world filtered in, as if from a dream, but they disappeared as the old woman began to speak. Soon, her voice was the only thing that existed.

'Magic is a complex web. Most people call it the Web. It pervades everything, and within it, there is the potential for both good and evil. Everyone can tap into the Web, though they don't always know that they're doing it. Some of the people here . . .' she waved a dismissive hand to indicate the fair outside, ' . . . the fortune-tellers and the like, feel it sometimes. Enough to convince the gullible, at least. Most people are completely unaware of the Web, however, and of their potential within it. You have avoided that at least! But there are some – call them wizards, if you like – who are not only able to link up with it consciously, but who can wield the results of this in a way that other people call magic. Magic is all around us, but it's only when it becomes noticeable that it is called that.'

'No one's ever explained this to me before,' Rebecca said quietly.

'Hardly surprising,' Sancia responded. 'Most people aren't aware of it, and even more don't want to be. But accept the Web, and all things are possible.'

'It sounds almost too simple,' Rebecca commented.

'Not really.' Sancia smiled. 'Think about what you were telling me earlier.'

Rebecca paused, deep in thought. She had so many questions that she did not know where to start.

'Was Kavan a wizard?' she asked eventually.

'In a sense, yes. Artists of all kinds have a particular affinity with the creative strands of the Web – whether conscious or unconscious – which allows them to communicate with others by acting directly on their senses or emotions. Provided, of course, that the observers' minds are receptive and not closed to such things. Receptiveness varies, but nobody is *completely* shut off. It's a question of degree, and of willingness.'

'And he was able to put all that into his pictures?' It seemed incredible to Rebecca that something so insubstantial could have lasted through the centuries.

'When he wanted to,' Sancia replied. 'He must have had some special purpose in mind when he painted your monk.'

'But what?'.

'That's for *you* to find out,' she replied. 'It wasn't an accident that you were the one to discover the painting.'

'I've been trying—' Rebecca began.

'Have patience,' Sancia put in, her voice kind but firm. 'It'll come.'

After another pause, Rebecca asked, 'And the demon?'

'The Web contains many beings which do not fit into the usual pattern of life,' the old woman replied. 'If they're perceived as good, we call them gods or angels. If they're evil, then we say they're demons or devils. The human mind can only comprehend the Web by picking out one small part of it at a time, and concentrating on *that*. The totality is beyond comprehension.'

'But it *is* real?

'Oh yes. As real as the world we see and touch about us every day. More real, in fact. When all this is gone, the Web will remain. When we are all dead and buried, the part of us that lives on – our emanations, if you like – will be part of the Web.'

'Ghosts?'

'That's one way of putting it,' Sancia replied. 'There are many things that men call supernatural, which are facets of the universal Web. The links within it are infinite. Ghosts, telepathy, absent healing, curses . . . even fortune-telling. You're an intelligent girl. You could provide explanations for all those things if you wanted to. Magic is only a mystery if you want it to be.'

'But where do I fit in?' Rebecca asked, almost pleading. 'I've been searching . . . for something . . . Why did you call me?'

'I didn't,' the old woman said. 'You called to me. The sign only appears to those who need to see it.'

Suddenly, Rebecca remembered her appointment with Emer, and was immediately stricken. The hour must surely be up by now! Sancia read the thoughts revealed by her worried expression.

'Don't worry,' she reassured her. 'Your friend has forgotten where you are. She is not fretting, and will not disturb us. We'll finish our talk, and then you can go to meet her at the play.'

Rebecca stared at her new mentor, fresh wonder in her eyes. She knew that the old woman was speaking the truth.

'What is a dream-weaver?' she asked quietly.

'Many things.'

'Is dream-weaving magical?'

'Not in itself,' Sancia replied. 'Though some might call it that. It can be used as a link to enhance the powers of true wizards, but there are not many of those nowadays. So we have to use our talents for more modest ends.'

'We?'

'You're a dream-weaver too. You told me as much yourself.'

Rebecca was speechless, shaking her head in instinctive denial.

'Come, child! Why do you think you are here?' Sancia asked, some of the old sharpness back in her voice. Then she smiled again, and reached for the wine bottle. 'Forgive my impatience,' she said as she poured. 'I have little time left, and there is no one to take my place. I have been very lonely – and growing old has not agreed with me!'

Rebecca sensed her companion's frustration, and felt sad for her.

'Let me explain,' Sancia went on, and sipped her drink before continuing. 'Dream-weaving is normally viewed as a craft which has four stages of development. It is like working on a loom, bringing different strands of the process together to create something solid, useful, and – hopefully – harmonious. The first and simplest stage is that of interpreting dreams. Almost anyone can do that if they put their minds to it, though you'd be surprised at the nonsense some people spout on the subject. The second is of being able to see the truth in dreams, accepting both their relevance to everyday things, and the knowledge they impart.'

'Isn't that the same as interpreting them?' Rebecca asked.

'No. You can interpret lies as well as truth. Each is just as revealing, but only one has universal meaning.'

Rebecca was not sure she understood this completely, but was reluctant to interrupt again.

'The third stage,' the old woman went on, 'is to see both the past and the future in dreams. Many people experience flashes of this but remain unaware of it.'

'You mean like when you go somewhere and feel you've been there before, but know that you haven't?' Rebecca was almost gabbling in her eagerness.

'That's right,' Sancia replied, smiling at her pupil's enthusiasm. 'But a dream-weaver learns to recognize these signs immediately.'

'I understand how you can see the past,' Rebecca said thoughtfully, speaking slowly now as she concentrated. 'Everything is recorded in the Web, after all . . . ' She looked up and received a confirming nod. 'But how can you see something that hasn't happened yet?'

'Time is not constant in dreams, and has no meaning within the Web,' Sancia answered.

Rebecca was confused again, believing what the old woman said, but unable to work out exactly what it meant.

'Don't worry. You'll understand when you need to.' Sancia's voice was hoarse now. 'I'm not used to all this talking,' she remarked, taking a gulp of wine. 'Where was I?'

'The fourth stage?' Rebecca prompted.

'Ah, yes. The fourth stage.' She paused as if considering the best way of explaining it. 'A genuine dream-weaver can shape their own dreams to their own ends. They can use them to ask questions, or to influence events in the waking world . . . which is what you did in that chess game of yours.'

Rebecca was staggered by this. Although it seemed so obvious when Sancia explained it, was it *really* like that in the world outside this caravan?

'Normally, you'd have needed to master all the earlier stages before you could tackle that,' the old woman went on. 'But you seem to have jumped straight to the end. It must have been very confusing for you.'

Rebecca nodded vigorously.

'Being able to master the fourth stage is the mark of a true dream-weaver, though, so you must have been doing something right!' Sancia continued. 'Once you've mastered all four stages, you will have both knowledge and control. The knowledge usually comes first, and is necessary for the control, but you seem to have reversed the process.' She paused, then added, 'Your talent is unquestionable, but you have much to learn.'

'Teach me!' Rebecca implored her.

'Only the years can teach you genuine truth,' the old woman replied.

'But . . . '

'What was the last dream you had before coming here today?' Sancia asked abruptly, forestalling any protest.

After a moment's thought, Rebecca related the story of the deluge of salt, of how she had nearly suffocated, but had been saved by the woman who built a protective barrier of letters.

'Do you remember what the letters were?' Sancia wanted to know.

'No. They didn't make any sense.'

'You'll learn to remember things like that in future.' The ancient dream-weaver was silent for a time, apparently deep in thought. 'Weren't there letters in some of your earlier dreams?'

'Yes,' Rebecca answered, remembering the juggler and the worms wriggling away. 'But they were all jumbled up. Nothing that I could read.'

'But this time the letters saved you from the salt?'

'The lady did.'

'Next time, remember the letters . . . ' Sancia's voice

211

trailed away and when she spoke again there was a sense of finality in her words. 'I must sleep now, and your friend will be waiting.'

The abrupt dismissal shook Rebecca, but she stood without protest. The meeting was over, but there was one last question she could not help but ask.

'Why do you live here?' she said quietly. 'Among all these . . . ?'

'They have dreams too,' Sancia replied, her voice little more than a whisper now. 'They're human . . . and I protect them.'

'How?'

'The same way I helped your friend not to worry,' the old woman answered enigmatically.

Rebecca waited uncertainly, not wanting to go, but knowing that she must.

'Farewell, Rebecca. And thank you,' Sancia said. 'Now I know what the anniversary celebration was for.'

'Farewell, Sancia,' the girl responded, happy in the knowledge that their meeting had obviously been pre-ordained. 'I'll never forget you.'

She opened the door and stepped outside, then turned back for one last look. Afterwards, she could never be sure whether it was just the reflection from the solitary lamp – or whether there was something gleaming in the old woman's eyes.

For you, my child, Rebecca thought as she closed the door behind her, *the light will never fade.*

CHAPTER TWENTY-FIVE

Rebecca walked in a daze. *So many things . . .*

When she reached the open space in front of the theatre, it was crowded, and she had to search for a while before she found Emer. Eventually she saw her friend talking and laughing with a young man. He looked appreciatively at Rebecca as she approached.

'You didn't tell me you were with someone,' he said.

'This is Annie. She's pretty, but a bit simple.' Emer grinned at Rebecca as she spoke. 'Annie, this is Iven. He's an actor.'

'Hello, Annie. I hope you're going to stay for the show?'

Rebecca nodded, her golden tresses bouncing. She was happy to play the part Emer had provided for her, if it meant that her identity would not be revealed.

'Put your hood up,' Emer hissed. 'People can see you.'

Rebecca hastened to do so. She had forgotten that her disguise was no longer in place, and looked around guardedly.

'I have to go now,' Iven said, apparently seeing nothing odd in this exchange. 'I'll see you later.' He and Emer exchanged smiles.

'Good looking, isn't he?' Emer remarked, her eyes following the actor as he made his way backstage. Rebecca did not respond.

Emer was puzzled by her friend's lack of animation, but decided to blame it on the lateness of the hour and the anxiety of their escapade. She turned back to face the stage.

'Look! The play's about to begin.'

Rebecca found her voice at last.

'Don't you want to know what I've been doing?' she asked quietly.

213

'I know what you've been doing,' Emer replied. 'Talking to one of those fortune-tellers!' Her gaze remained fixed upon the stage, where painted scenery was now being put into place, and where multi-coloured lamps illuminated the set. The effect this produced was that of a fantasy woodland glade – where only moments ago, there had just been pieces of wood, iron and cloth. The crowd gave this an appreciative round of applause.

'Did she tell you anything interesting?' Emer went on. Again there was no response. 'Tall, dark, handsome stranger . . . that sort of thing?' When even this provoked no reaction, she glanced at Rebecca, momentarily worried by her friend's solemn expression. 'You can't take them seriously, Becky. Don't you want to see the play? Iven says it's very good.' Unseen musicians began to play, conjuring up images of running water and wind in the trees, adding their own special contribution to the radiant scene. Actors in flamboyant costumes began to appear on stage. 'There he is!' Emer exclaimed.

Suddenly, Rebecca knew that she could not explain what had happened to her. She would not know where to start, and Emer would probably find the whole thing ridiculous.

So she pretended to watch the play, but noticed little. Emer, on the other hand, was enthralled, and did not notice her friend's preoccupation. Rebecca spent the time trying to put her thoughts in order.

Sancia can do so much! She knows what dreams mean, and can see the truth in them; she can foretell the future, protect the whores – even make Emer forget her promise! And all because she's a dream-weaver. And yet she says I'm one too! But I can't do anything, not really. Even in the game, I needed the help of others. So how can it be?

She went over the conversation in her head again and again, remembering its revelations, its mysteries – recalling every word. She did not notice the play, though the audience reacted enthusiastically to the sights and sounds, laughing and applauding.

I believe her explanation of the Web, but what else did she really tell me? She didn't interpret any of my dreams, after all. Am I better off now – should I go back?

214

In her heart, Rebecca knew that she could not return. *What would be the use?* Sancia's dismissal had been unmistakeable. *Your talent is unquestionable, but you have much to learn.*

Rebecca told herself that although it would be a long time before she could call herself a dream-weaver, at least the ancient woman had given her one definite purpose.

Next time, remember the letters.

As a tumult of applause erupted about her, Rebecca realized that the play was over. The actors smiled, waved and bowed from the stage, and their associates took round leather pouches to accept the audience's coins. Emer was jumping up and down, clapping wildly.

'Wasn't it wonderful!' she enthused. 'So funny, and so sad at the same time. It was almost real!' She was bubbling over, tears brimming in her eyes, but then she caught sight of Rebecca's sombre expression and turned to face her, hands on hips. Adopting a ridiculously pompous tone of voice, she added, 'Of course it may not have had the depth and subtlety of the time-worn classics, or the refined wit of Ellerian poetry, nor yet the ultimate inner truth of the great mysteries . . . but I thought it was ace!'

Rebecca could not help but smile.

'She's alive!' Emer exclaimed turning heads. 'I saw her move. Can she speak?'

'Stop it,' Rebecca whispered urgently. 'You'll have everyone looking at us.'

'And why not?' the irrepressible Emer retorted, her spirits still elated by the drama. 'A finer pair of beauties have rarely been seen . . . and yours aren't too bad either.'

'Be quiet!' Rebecca said, laughing.

'What did you think of the play?' Emer asked more soberly.

'I don't know.'

'Seen one, seen 'em all, eh?' Emer shrugged.

'I—' Rebecca began, but stopped when it became obvious that her companion's attention was focused elsewhere. Iven and another young man were approaching.

'Hello, Emer. Good?'

'Very,' she replied, her eyes still shining.

'Annie, this is Laval,' Iven went on.

Laval was fresh-faced, with trace of recently removed make-up clinging to his eyes; he seemed only a year or two older than Rebecca. Smiling, he bowed in elaborate fashion.

'We would be most honoured, dear ladies,' Iven said smoothly, 'if you would accompany us to a refreshment stall.'

'We'd be glad to,' Emer replied.

'No,' Rebecca said.

'Oh, come on!' Emer pleaded. 'It's early yet.'

'I can't . . . I have to . . . ' Abruptly, Rebecca turned and fled, her dark cape flapping about her legs as she threaded her way through the crowd.

'I'm sorry!' Emer told the young men, her hands spread wide in apology. 'I told you she was a bit simple.' She ran off in pursuit, and the bemused actors stared after her in disappointment, then shrugged and went in search of other amusement.

Emer eventually caught up with Rebecca and fell into step beside her. They left the domain of the fair and began walking back through the deserted streets of Edgefield.

'I don't understand you,' Emer said. 'First you stick so close to me I thought you were sewn to my petticoat, then you go dashing off on your own to see a fortune-teller. And then you go all timid again and run away!'

'She wasn't a fortune-teller,' Rebecca stated.

'What then?'

'A dream-weaver.'

'A what!'

Rebecca explained as best she could, the words rushing out in a breathless torrent as they walked home. Emer listened, puzzled and openly sceptical. She did not know what to believe, and the abrupt end to a promising evening had left her feeling irritable and lonely.

They marched back into the castle, not caring who saw them, and went their separate ways when they reached the courtyard. It was an acrimonious parting, and they both said stupid, hurtful things that they knew they would regret later.

'I just want to go to sleep,' was Rebecca's last comment before they went to their respective homes.

But sleep was a long time coming that night, and when it did, there were no dreams for her to remember – no dreams to weave. She awoke feeling drained and desolate.

*   *   *

Mid-morning found Rebecca standing on top of the West Tower, feeling more frustrated than ever, and shivering in the damp northerly wind. She was watching the wagons of the fair roll away to the north-west, the mass of colour and humanity made drab and impersonal by the distance.

She heard someone else clamber up out of the trap-door and knew that she had been joined by Emer. A few moments passed in awkward silence.

'I'm sorry about what I said last night,' Emer volunteered.

'I'm sorry too,' Rebecca said meekly. 'I don't suppose I was making much sense, and it must have seemed very strange to you. I'm not sure I believe it myself now.' The memory of the night was already taking on the mercurial, half-forgotten aspect of a dream. 'And I'm sorry I spoilt your evening.'

'Oh, easy come, easy go,' Emer replied philosophically, looking down at the retreating caravans.

'Wouldn't it be wonderful to be able to live like that,' Rebecca said wistfully. 'Always on the move, always seeing something new.'

'Of course it would,' Emer replied. 'How could a secure, dry room, with a quilted bed and servants to look after you possibly compare with sleeping on old boards on the mud under a rickety old cart?' The sarcasm in her voice was softened by fondness for her friend, and an understanding of the other girl's longing to escape the restrictions of her life.

'There are other things to life than comfort,' Rebecca said defensively.

'You'd not survive a week living in a fair,' her friend responded. 'Half the people in them are crooks – though I'll admit some of the men *did* look quite interesting.' They smiled at each other.

217

'They must have thought I was a complete idiot.'

'Quite mad,' Emer agreed.

'Do you still think I'm mad?' Rebecca asked.

'Only sometimes. Tell me again about this dream-weaving stuff.' It was Emer's peace offering, the final healing of the temporary rift between them.

So Rebecca repeated her tale; this time Emer listened seriously and did not interrupt. She could make no more sense of the mysteries than her friend, but did agree that Sancia's general principles seemed reasonable. In any case, it was a great comfort for Rebecca to have a sympathetic ear at last.

Eventually, the weather grew too inhospitable for them to remain on the tower, and they made their way back down the long winding staircase, crossed the narrow western courtyard, and passed through the store-rooms into the Gallery by its seldom-used side entrance. From there, they made for Rebecca's apartments. This route took them past Baldemar's study. As they drew level with his door, they could hear the baron arguing with his chamberlain. Emer stopped immediately, with a warning hand on Rebecca's arm, and put a finger to her lips. The idea of eavesdropping on their fathers horrified Rebecca, and she tried to move on. Emer held her fast.

'Listening at keyholes is wrong,' Rebecca whispered.

'Don't be ridiculous,' her companion replied softly. 'You're the one who complains that they never discuss anything important with us. Now's our chance to learn something interesting.'

At that moment, Rebecca was forced to agree. She had just overheard Montfort's name in the conversation, and this was all the encouragement she needed. They crept closer, and listened.

*　　*　　*

'Am I to hand my castle over to riff-raff from the fields?' Baldemar roared, brandishing the offending letter.

'Of course not, my lord,' Radd answered. 'Montfort is not suggesting anything of the sort.'

218

'Seems like it to me,' the baron retorted.

'If you read the message carefully,' the chamberlain went on patiently, 'you'll see that all he is asking for is your support for some law reforms, designed to alleviate some of the land's worst suffering. He merely seeks to curb the excesses of the more unscrupulous nobles, not to rob those such as yourself of their rightful position.'

'They should take care of their own peasants,' Baldemar stated loudly. 'Those people are their property – why shouldn't they do what they like with them?'

'Because there is such a thing as humanity, my lord,' Radd said mildly.

The baron paused, as if considering this novel idea.

'And what's this ridiculous nonsense about the people electing representatives?' he went on. 'Anyone who'd suggested that in his father's time would have been strung up for treason.' *And quite right too,* his tone implied.

'The king merely wishes—' Radd began.

'*Merely?*' Baldemar interrupted. 'Merely this, merely that. He's too merely by half. And so are you. Merely mouthed!'

The baron laughed at his own joke, then stared at his chamberlain as if daring him to say anything further.

Radd took up the challenge. It was not often he felt capable of standing firm against his master, but this was a subject close to his own heart. *I wish you were baron here.*

'Montfort wishes the common man to have a mouthpiece,' he said steadily, 'through which he can obtain justice. After all, the nobility can't be expected to have to listen to the needs of every peasant—'

'Quite right,' Baldemar interrupted.

'—but there should be a civilized form of communication that would be to the benefit of all. Just think, if your subjects are contented and work well, then that means more revenue and less trouble for you.'

'I still don't hold with it – and there's plenty who agree with me,' the baron stated flatly. 'We can't have *peasants* telling us what to do! It's no wonder there are so many rumours flying about.' He snorted derisively. 'It wouldn't be so bad if young Montfort showed any signs of being responsible. How old is he now? Twenty-eight? He's been king now for five years, and he still hasn't married – let alone produced an heir! It's madness.'

'I can only assume that he considers his planned reforms to be of more immediate importance,' Radd replied. He knew, but did not add, that even Montfort's staunchest allies doubted his wisdom in this matter. A kingdom without a clear line of succession was always likely to be heading for turmoil.

'More important than the throne?' Baldemar shouted. 'Remember what happened the last time a king died without an heir.'

The terrible civil war which followed the death of King Tyrrell many centuries earlier was a part of Ahrenia's history that was familiar to everyone.

'There's no reason to think Montfort will die childless,' the chamberlain answered. 'He is young, and in good health.'

'What about accidents?' Baldemar demanded. 'And even – the gods forbid – treason. What then?'

Radd was shocked that his master should be talking about such a matter, even in private.

'It's true that the nobility are divided over the issue of the king's marriage,' he said firmly. 'But surely it would not come to that.'

'You've heard the rumours,' the baron snapped back. 'Treason is the least of it.'

'You should not give credence to such wild gossip, my lord.'

'There have been too many ill omens,' Baldemar said darkly. 'Something is happening.'

'Omens, as you call them, and other such far-fetched ideas, are superstitious nonsense,' Radd said pompously. 'And have no relevance to rational men such as ourselves.'

'I hope you can still be as *rational* when this unrest turns to open rebellion,' Baldemar sneered.

'I hope so too,' the chamberlain replied, outwardly calm. 'Though I devoutly hope that such a situation will not arise.'

He waited in silence for a few moments, wondering what the baron would see fit to rail against next. In the event, he was surprised.

'How am I to answer this then?' Baldemar asked, suddenly mild, waving the letter about once more.

'You must answer as your conscience dictates,' Radd answered quietly.

'Pah! Conscience and politics rarely mix well.'

More's the pity, Radd thought. Aloud, he said, 'Shall I draft a possible response for you?'

'Do that,' Baldemar commanded, handing over the letter. 'I need a drink.'

Radd turned to leave, smoothing the paper between his fingers, feeling the broken halves of the royal seal.

'And Radd,' the baron added. 'Make sure that he realizes I'm aware of our strategic importance here. I don't want him taking me for granted.'

'Yes, my lord.'

Outside in the corridor, the girls fled in opposite directions as Radd moved towards the door.

CHAPTER TWENTY-SIX

Rebecca had been thirteen when she had seen Montfort for the third time. But on this occasion, unlike their earlier encounters, he had been a remote figure, the principal character in a grand play in which she was onlooker. The pomp and circumstance of the new king's coronation had been awe-inspiring, and Rebecca, accompanying her father on her second trip to Garadun, could only look on in wonder.

At one point during the subsequent celebrations, she thought that perhaps Montfort had looked at her, possibly even winked, but it was a fleeting moment, and she later decided that it had only been her imagination.

The festivities had gone on for days, with seemingly endless feasting, music, dancing and storytelling. An army of artists was on hand to paint the official portraits that would commemorate the event, and scribes busily noted the words of the king and other important nobles for posterity. Rebecca was shy and withdrawn at first, awed by so much finery, but she eventually got to know some of the young visitors, and was soon having the time of her life. The palace, the other magnificent buildings of the capital, indeed the city itself, were like an enchanted playground, with fresh wonders around every corner. The crowds of joyful people, the soldiers in their impeccable uniforms and the festival atmosphere all contributed to this spellbinding time – which ended abruptly when Rebecca and her father returned to Edge.

* * *

Was that really five years ago? Rebecca wondered now. She could recall some scenes as if they had taken place only yesterday.

Deliberately, she put her memories aside, and turned her thoughts to the conversation overheard earlier that day. She and Emer had escaped undetected, but had not seen each other since. Rebecca badly needed to talk to someone about it. She had been alone with her thoughts now for several hours, and was glad when the door opened and Emer's face appeared.

'Can I come in?' her friend asked, looking serious.

Rebecca beckoned, but before Emer was halfway across the room, the door opened again and Nursey bustled in. She greeted the girls and shuffled purposefully over to Rebecca, a steaming mug held before her.

'Drink this,' she commanded, handing it over. 'It'll make you feel better.'

Rebecca looked suspiciously at the thick brew, then back at her nurse.

'I don't need to feel better,' she said. 'There's nothing wrong with me.'

'Yes, there is,' Nursey replied defiantly. 'You told me so yourself. You know you should have been in your nice warm room this morning, not standing about on nasty, cold battlements. If I had the breath in me I'd have climbed up there to fetch you down myself.' She paused for an instant and Rebecca seized the chance to get a word in edgeways.

'What did I tell you?' she asked, mystified by this turn of events. 'I don't remember any of this!'

Behind Nursey's back, Emer whispered, 'Just let her cure you. Then she'll go.'

'Last night,' the old woman went on. 'You told me you had a sore throat.'

'I didn't. I was late home last night,' Rebecca protested, 'and I went straight to bed. I didn't even *see* you.'

'You must have dreamt it, Nursey,' Emer remarked, smiling.

Nursey hesitated, her earlier certainty wavering.

'Well, it's come to a pretty pass when a body can't even sleep in peace,' she complained. 'Whatever next?'

Rebecca and Emer exchanged glances, willing the old woman to leave. She showed no signs of doing so, however, but stood her ground, shaking her head slowly.

'There's one of the king's men here,' she said eventually. 'From Garadun. He's being fed in the kitchens right this moment.' Her original mission had evidently been forgotten, and she was now intent on having a good chatter. 'He brought a letter from Montfort himself, they say.'

The girls did their best to look surprised.

'What about?' Emer asked.

'There's all sorts of gossip, of course,' Nursey replied. 'Not that I take any heed of that, mind,' she added self-righteously. 'That's for idle, frivolsome minds that have nothing better to do.' She paused, then went on in a sly tone, 'Perhaps he's heard you're free again, my pet. Maybe he wants to marry you himself.'

'Don't be ridiculous, Nursey!' Rebecca exclaimed as Emer laughed.

'He's a tight-lipped one, though,' her guardian went on.

'Who is?'

'The messenger,' Nursey answered. 'Still, you can't help wondering what it's all about.'

To the girls' dismay, she plumped herself down into a chair, obviously intending not to take any heed of the gossip for some time. However, she stood up again almost immediately as a fourth person entered the room.

It was Scuttle, dressed in formal attire and carrying a small metal tray, which he was balancing on the fingertips of his right hand. There was absolutely nothing on the tray, but he nevertheless kept it perfectly level as he walked slowly into the room. This feat was made all the more remarkable because the rest of his body seemed to be moving in all directions, swaying and leaning at unnatural angles. His feet appeared to be permanently at right angles to each other. This, together with the fact that his face was flushed and his eyes fixed in a glassy stare, indicated that Scuttle had drunk a particularly good lunch. He came to an uncertain halt in the centre of the room, keeping the tray perfectly still while everything else about him continued to waver as if in an invisible wind. Had there been an array of full glasses on that tray, not a drop would have been spilled.

Scuttle looked around, and became aware for the first time of the three women, who were staring at him with unnerving curiosity. The butler drew himself up to his full height, opened his mouth to speak . . . and shut it again. He had completely forgotten why he was here.

'What is it, Scuttle?' Rebecca asked.

He began fishing in the murky depths of his memory, lowering hooks and lines in the hope of making a catch. *Brandy*, he thought. *More brandy*. No. That wasn't it. He'd done that already. His recent life began flashing before his eyes, something he had always thought would only happen when he was about to die. He was touched by a moment's fear. *I need a drink . . . The letter! Was it the letter?* Baldemar has greeted its contents with anger. No. That wasn't it either. Radd was looking after that. *A message! That was it. Message to . . . about . . .* His mind went blank again.

'Was it me you wanted?' Rebecca prompted, trying not to laugh. Emer had turned away, and was looking out of the window, her shoulders shaking.

Rebecca. A hidden fish impaled itself on a hook, and was dragged, thrashing, to the surface.

'Message,' Scuttle said abruptly. 'Your father . . . wants you . . . dinner tonight . . . his chambers. My lady,' he added as an afterthought.

'Thank you,' she replied. 'Was that all?'

'Yes, my lady,' he answered, hoping he was right.

'You may go now, Scuttle,' Rebecca said, glancing at Emer who had turned round again, speculation already written on her face.

Scuttle executed a sort of pirouette and took one long step forward. This brought him face to face with a cupboard door. He considered this for a few moments, then decided against making his exit that way, and turned again. Several attempts and a few bruises later he eventually made his escape – his tray still held perfectly level.

When in this state, Scuttle tended to leave a room using the same method as a demented bumble bee. That is, by flying – or in his case, stumbling – into every available object until, by the laws of random probability, he eventually hit upon the right doorway and disappeared through it.

'Go and see that he's all right, will you, Nursey?' Rebecca suggested. 'He could hurt himself like that.' A muffled crash from the corridor underlined her words.

'What can you expect when he sups all the leavings of others,' Nursey grumbled as she shuffled out.

'Especially when *you've* had anything to do with their preparation,' Rebecca remarked, glancing at the mug her guardian had brought in.

Nursey chose not to hear this comment, and left, closing the door behind her.

'Well done,' Emer said. 'Those two make quite a double act, don't they.'

There was a pause then, as they remembered the purpose of their meeting.

'What did you make of what we heard?' Emer began.

'Your father had already told me about the proposed reforms,' Rebecca replied. 'So *that* didn't surprise me.'

'He'd mentioned them to me too,' her friend said. 'But I hadn't paid much attention.'

'I had no idea that they might be leading to treason – or even civil war,' Rebecca continued. 'It's madness to let it go that far.'

'Perhaps they're getting bored,' Emer suggested.

'Who?'

'The nobles. They've had peace for such a long time now – it must be getting on their nerves.'

'You mean this could all be just an excuse?' Rebecca asked, horrified.

'Why not? They can only get so much satisfaction from *hunting*,' Emer responded. 'Some men need their games to be a little more exciting.'

'Civil war isn't a *game!*' Rebecca was frightened just thinking about it.

'I know that. You know that,' Emer replied. 'But would someone like Cranne know it?'

Rebecca stared at her friend in horror, grateful for her narrow escape yet again – and imagining the terrible consequences had she not avoided the betrothal.

'Well, Tarrant – and therefore presumably Montfort –

didn't want you to marry Cranne, did he?' Emer went on. 'Which probably means that they're on opposite sides.'

'I suppose so,' Rebecca replied. The same thing had occurred to her. 'But why should it matter? Edge is not exactly the most powerful barony in Ahrenia.'

'But if your father is to be believed,' Emer said, 'it *does* have strategic importance.'

'*What* importance, though?' Rebecca had been puzzling over Baldemar's remark, and was still mystified. Was her father bluffing? Or were they just empty words?

'I have no idea,' Emer admitted. 'I think I'd prefer Edge to remain an insignificant backwater.'

'It would certainly be safer,' the baron's daughter agreed. At the same time, she felt that it was rather cowardly and treacherous of her to be harbouring such thoughts. 'I wonder why Montfort has never married?' she said, changing the subject.

Emer gave her a look which she could not interpret.

'He probably hasn't had time,' she said. 'It sounds as if he's a bit obsessive, if you ask me.'

'There must have been plenty of prospective brides,' Rebecca pointed out.

'Perhaps he prefers horses,' Emer suggested, grinning. 'Or dogs. He wouldn't be the first man whose animals took priority over his wife.'

'He's not like that,' Rebecca protested.

'Then maybe he's still searching for the *perfect woman*,' Emer said, fluttering her eyelashes wildly. 'Let's face it, Becky, we've no idea why he hasn't married. I'm more interested in all those wild rumours and ill omens my father didn't want to talk about.'

'Have you heard anything else?' Rebecca wanted to know.

'That's for idle, frivolsome minds that have nothing better to do!' Emer quoted.

'Yes, but . . . '

'If I *have*,' Emer went on, 'I've forgotten it. My taste is for gossip of a different kind.'

'We seem to be coming up with more questions than answers,' Rebecca said glumly.

'Well, we can hardly go and *ask*, can we?' Emer responded.

'It would be an admission of our appallingly deceitful conduct this morning.' She paused. 'Fun, though, wasn't it?'

They grinned at each other.

'But frustrating,' Rebecca added. 'There's so much going on in the world – and we know nothing about it!'

'So what's new?' Emer remarked. Her voice took on a false tone of humility. 'It has always been thus. We women tend the hearths and homes, light fires, make beds and cook meals, provide a sympathetic ear and raise children when required. In short, we nurture the life and spirit of this land . . . ' She paused dramatically. 'While the men plot ways to f . . . foul it up.'

'Not *all* of them,' Rebecca said, laughing.

'Oh, you eternal optimist,' her friend commented.

'I hope Montfort wins!'

'You're infatuated,' Emer accused. 'Ever since he held your hand when you were a little girl.'

'He's a good man, and kind too,' Rebecca retorted. 'Your father knows that.'

'He may be good and kind,' Emer replied, 'but he's fifty leagues away. You're as bad as Nursey! Stop day-dreaming – you're so starry-eyed, it's embarrassing. As if he'd really look at you.'

'I never said—'

'But you thought it!' Emer was grinning, but she meant what she said. 'Forget him. There are plenty of other men much nearer home.'

'Like Galen?'

It was a cruel blow, instantly regretted. Emer's face fell.

'I'm sorry,' Rebecca whispered. 'I didn't mean . . . '

'It doesn't matter,' her friend replied quietly.

Although recent events had placed their friendship under some strain, the relationship had been a long time in the making, and any setback would be temporary. Emer recovered quickly.

'I was only joking,' she said, smiling bravely. 'You've got more sense than to think you could ever become queen.'

'A girl can dream, can't she?' Rebecca asked, grinning.

'In your case, yes,' Emer replied. 'Rather too much.'

Rebecca's dinner with her father that night proved to be a frustratingly uninformative occasion – in all but one respect. Baldemar refused to discuss the contents of the king's letter, in spite of her persistent probing, and refused to be drawn into a discussion of the various rumours he had mentioned earlier. Politics, he felt, were of no concern to women. Marriage, on the other hand, was. And although he said nothing on the subject to Rebecca, he was already planning to use recent developments to further his aims in that direction.

'I may have to go to the capital soon, to see Montfort,' he remarked casually. 'And I'd like you to come with me. I trust this meets with your approval.'

'Yes, Father. I'd love to come.' Rebecca could hardly believe her luck. Surely there she would be able to find answers to at least some of her questions.

'Good.' The baron began to compile a mental list of eligible young nobles who made their homes in or near Garadun.

Father and daughter parted some time later and went to their respective bedchambers more than satisfied with the results of the evening. As Rebecca got into bed, she realized that her throat was beginning to feel a little sore.

* * *

She saw the city as if through a white haze, the colours bleached and pale. Her father stretched out a hand to her.

'I'd like you to come with me,' he said.

'This isn't Garadun,' she replied, finding it hard to breathe the thick white air. At the end of the road, a black pyramid rose towards the sky.

'No, but it's the capital,' he answered, then disappeared, leaving Rebecca alone in the empty, whispering streets.

She began to move towards the pyramid, walking slowly at first, then more quickly, until she was running, running as fast as she could. And yet the pale buildings on either side of the road barely seemed to move. The faster she ran,

229

and the harder she tried, the less she seemed to achieve. The pyramid mocked her with its continued remoteness.

Suddenly, it was night, the milky haze making the shadows deeper. *Time is not constant in dreams.*

Rebecca stopped running, her breath harsh in her throat and looked around fearfully.

A ghost appeared from one of the silent buildings, and glided towards her. She tried to scream but could not. The phantom-shape solidified, became a walking skeleton; dessicated skin and sinew stretched tight over brittle bones; bleached hair and eyes shrivelled to the size of peas.

The apparition stopped in front of Rebecca, and stretched forth an emaciated hand. In it was a circular tablet of white stone. Rebecca took it, and the ghost vanished. She looked down and saw that she was holding two tablets now, one in each hand. They were both covered with deeply incised letters, but neither made any sense. It was as if the letters had been deliberately jumbled up, and she almost flung the stones away in disgust.

Then the ground beneath her feet heaved, and she staggered, trying to keep her balance. Great cracks appeared in the surface of the road and the walls of the buildings, and Rebecca felt the cobbles push up against the soles of her shoes. Suddenly, the whole street was filled with a jostling throng of hideous dead people, all craning their necks, bony fingers pointing towards the sky. And every shrunken eye was turned upwards, as if they longed to rise up into the heavens.

Rebecca was engulfed by a wave of longing, so desperate that it tore at her throat. Then the voices came, at first only faraway echoes, then gradually becoming louder as the scene about her faded. She felt relief at her escape, and knew that the dream was coming to an end, but still an obstinate memory nagged at her brain.

Next time, remember the letters . . .

Hastily, she looked down at the stones in her palms. They too were fading, and she fought to commit the letters to memory before it was too late.

```
T  H  E  D  R
D  L  N  E
F  L  O  A  U
I  O  M  C
W  E  H  T  T
```

The other one. Quickly! she urged herself. All around, the long-dead voices rose to a crescendo.

```
W  T  H  E  S
```

The dream was fading now, flowing away like sunlit water.

```
O  D  O  A
```

Wait! I can't read it all.

```
T  L  W  L  O
O  E  T . . .
```

The last line vanished and Rebecca was in her own bed again, the taste of salt filling her mouth. Tears ran down the side of her nose and between her lips. Wracked by another sob, she sat up, searched for a handkerchief, and wiped her face.

'I tried, Sancia,' she whispered aloud. 'I tried.'

Her throat was very sore.

CHAPTER TWENTY-SEVEN

'I must be getting physic in my old age,' Nursey remarked as she handed the mug to her patient.

'Thank you.' Rebecca sipped gratefully. *At least this time I waited until you were awake.*

Nursey bustled about the room, tidying things out of habit, while Rebecca appreciated the soothing drink and tried to untangle her thoughts.

'Did you dream anything last night, Nursey?' she asked eventually.

'Nothing that I remember,' the old woman replied.

Next time, remember the letters . . .

Rebecca started to get out of bed, but was halted by her guardian's indignant words.

'And just where do you think you're going, young lady?'

'I have to write something down,' she replied.

'You stay where you are,' Nursey ordered. Then, seeing the expression on the girl's face, she added, 'I'll bring you pen and paper.' She rummaged around in Rebecca's desk, found the items she wanted and handed them over.

'Thank you.' Rebecca was feeling distinctly groggy, and was glad not to have to move.

'Mind you don't spill ink on the sheets,' Nursey warned.

'I'll be careful.'

Rebecca hurriedly noted down the letters she could remember from her dream, annoyed with herself for not being able to complete the second set. Nursey watched as she wrote.

'What's that, then?' she asked.

'A sort of puzzle,' Rebecca answered. 'A riddle, if you like.'

'Looks like nonsense to me,' Nursey commented dismissively as she removed the pen and ink to a safer place.

Looks like nonsense to me too, Rebecca thought. *But it's important nonsense. It has to be.* Try as she might, she could not decipher any hidden message in the letters.

The morning passed in a haze as Nursey's potion took effect. Rebecca dozed, thought about her latest dream, and stared in vain at the jumble of letters.

Shortly before noon, Emer came to visit her friend.

'That'll teach you to stand about on nasty wet battlements,' she remarked.

'I'm feeling much better now,' Rebecca responded truthfully. The half day of warmth and rest had restored her spirits considerably.

'Good,' her friend replied. 'Because you're getting up now.'

'Why?'

'I've found something that might interest you,' Emer answered.

'What? Why didn't you tell me earlier?'

'Nursey wouldn't let me near you till now,' Emer replied. 'I had to exercise my *considerable* powers of persuasion to get in here at all.'

Rebecca grinned. She had experienced her friend's powers before. 'What did you do?' she asked.

'I told her Silberry was ill and asking for her,' Emer admitted shamelessly. 'By the time she finds out he's perfectly all right, we'll be well away – as long as you don't take all day getting up.'

'What have you found?' Rebecca asked eagerly as she scrambled out of bed and began dressing hastily.

'A book.'

'About dream-weaving?'

'No. About history.'

'Oh.' Rebecca felt vaguely disappointed.

'After you told me about the jumbled-up letters in your dreams, and that Sancia had told you to remember them next time,' Emer explained, 'something started nagging away up here.' She tapped her head with a forefinger. 'I knew I'd seen *something,* but I couldn't remember what – or where. I found it yesterday afternoon.'

'In the book?'

'Yes. Come on, let's go.' Emer opened the door and peered into the corridor. 'All clear,' she reported.

Rebecca snatched up the piece of paper and stuffed it into her pocket before following her friend. They hurried down to Radd's house, talking as they went.

'Is it in your father's library?' Rebecca asked.

'Yes. In the special cupboard that's always locked,' Emer replied.

'Then how . . . ?'

'Oh, I found the key ages ago,' the chamberlain's daughter answered, unabashed. 'I always thought the books I wasn't allowed to see must be the most interesting.'

'And were they?'

'Not really. Some of the drawings in the medical books were quite entertaining . . . but they were mostly very boring. Just history.'

'So what prompted you to read this one?' Rebecca asked.

'I wasn't *reading* it,' Emer replied. 'Just looking at the pictures.'

As they reached the house, Rebecca was suddenly worried.

'Where's your father?' she whispered.

'With Baldemar, discussing accounts,' Emer answered. 'They'll be hours – they always are. Come on.'

So they entered the chamberlain's study, and went through to his library. Rebecca was familiar with the small rectangular room, whose walls were covered with shelves of books. She had been inside on countless occasions, always enjoying her excursions into that realm of words, but, unlike Emer, she had never thought to wonder what was in the sturdy wooden cupboard at the far end of the room. For the first time ever, she felt nervous about being in there.

Meanwhile, Emer was checking along one of the rows of books. Finding the one she was looking for, she lifted it out, then reached into the space behind it and drew out a brass key. Quickly, she unlocked the cupboard, and took out one of the volumes inside. Rebecca could not help glancing anxiously at the door to the study.

'This is it,' Emer stated, and handed the book to her friend. At the touch of the heavy tome, a strange thrill of excitement ran through Rebecca, and she forgot her nervousness. Perhaps here, at last, she would find some answers to the questions which were multiplying in her head. The book was bound in black leather; the title *Beneath the Salt* was stamped in silver on the front.

Rebecca sat down at the table, opened the book at its first page and read aloud: ' "Beneath the Salt. Archivist Alomar. Being a discourse on various objects recovered from the Great Salt Flats, and of the legends pertaining to them." '

'Try page 256,' Emer suggested.

Rebecca carefully turned the heavy pages until she came to the one she wanted . . . and froze, as she found herself staring at the tablets from her dream.

```
T  H  E  D  R        W  T  H  E  S
D  L  N  E           O  D  O  A
F  L  O  A  U        T  L  W  L  O
I  O  M  C           O  E  T  D
W  E  H  T  T        F  O  B  E  W
```

For an instant she saw Sancia's face again, mouthing *True magic reveals itself*. Then her own tongue began working again.

'That's it!' she exclaimed. 'That's what I saw in the tablets!'

'What tablets? I thought the letters were a sort of barrier, protecting you,' Emer said, pleased by her friend's reaction, but still puzzled.

'That was the dream *before*,' Rebecca said, as if Emer should have realized this automatically. 'I had another dream last night, and a dead man handed me two tablets with writing on. These! It's incredible.'

'It certainly is,' Emer remarked and the scepticism in her voice made Rebecca look up for the first time. Wordlessly, she pulled the crumpled piece of paper from her pocket and smoothed it out on the table, next to the book. Emer glanced back and forth between the two, her expression growing steadily more amazed. She refrained from any further comment, however, and Rebecca turned back to the book, eagerly scanning the text for an explanation.

'Illustrated here,' she read, 'are the so-called Okran Stones, named after their discoverer. The original tablets have since been lost, but are believed to have been of snow-cluster marble, with the letters deeply incised. Many attempts have been made to decipher the coded messages, but without success.' Rebecca's hopes were dashed. 'It has been suggested that these stones may form part of a larger message, and that reading them will be a simple matter when all have been found. However, although rumours of others persist, these two are the only tablets whose existence has been proven. It hardly needs stating that these enigmatic discs are very old, but exact dating is not possible. It may be that other examples (if any did in fact exist) have been destroyed or eroded beyond recognition.'

There's at least one more! Rebecca thought, remembering the dream of the salt invading her bedchamber. *If only I could remember the letters!* Although she was frustrated because the book did not unravel the mystery, she felt glad that at least now she had a complete transcript of the tablets from last night's dream. Emer handed her a pen, anticipating her need, and she wrote the missing letters down on her piece of paper before turning back to the book.

'Many legends and superstitions are attached to the Okran Stones. The following list details the more colourful:

—The fate of the land will depend upon the nature of the person who first reads them.
—Anyone who deciphers the message will be able to command demons.
—The tablets give a secret code to the location of fabulous treasure.
—A curse will fall upon anyone who reads them.
—The decoding of the tablets will portend a great natural disaster – such as an earthquake, flood or volcanic eruption.

'Other suggestions about the stones vary from their being an elaborate practical joke, to a depiction of arcane symbols (the shape of the letters can be seen either as a perversion of a pentagram, or as a crown on its side), and from clandestine communications of lovers to an obscure form of poetry. Only one thing seems certain now, and that is that none of the dire predictions given above is likely to occur, as the riddle is almost certain to remain unsolved – unless the theoretical existence of the other tablets is proven.'

Rebecca did not care for the sound of the various legends, but she did not share Archivist Alomar's view that the riddle was insoluble. *Accept the Web, and all things are possible.* It just might take a little time . . .

'What do they mean then?' Emer asked, breaking into her friend's reverie.

'I don't know. I was hoping the book would tell me.' Rebecca was engrossed with this new source of wonder, so Emer left her to get on with it. She got other books down from the shelves and glanced idly through them.

'The Okran Stones were discovered in the year Brion 27,' Rebecca read. 'They were found at a point ten leagues west-south-west of Blackator, the torgrist mountain which is the only natural edifice to protrude from the Salt Flats. This spot coincides almost exactly with the point where speculation has always placed the site of the mythical city of Derith (reputed to have been Ahrenia's capital in a former age), and it is popularly supposed that the Okran Stones originate from there. However, there is no proof that this is in fact the case.'

And with that, the book left the subject. This was most frustrating, especially as Rebecca's hopes had initially been raised so high. *It's almost worse than knowing nothing,* she thought, then changed her mind. *No, it's not.* This was proof, if it should ever be needed, that her dreams were more than just the fanciful imaginings of her subconscious. *Your talent is unquestionable, but you still have much to learn.*

Rebecca began to skim through the rest of the book, stopping every so often to examine the details of another artifact that had been retrieved from the salt. There was nothing remotely as interesting as the tablets. The finds were mostly of stone, pottery or glass, with some precious metals, but there were also pieces of wood which had become almost fossilized by the all-enveloping crystals, as well as bones, both human and animal. These discoveries had been scattered all over the flats, but the majority were clustered in a relatively small area around the supposed location of Derith.

A picture of an engraving caught Rebecca's eye. It showed a city of elegant white buildings, dominated by a huge black pyramid. The caption underneath read, 'A copy of a mural sculpture most commonly assumed to depict the city of Derith and the Tomb of King Tyrrell.' Rebecca read this through twice, her eyes wide with renewed wonder.

'I've seen it!' she exclaimed aloud. 'That's where it was!'

Emer looked up. 'What?'

'Derith,' Rebecca replied. 'That's where I was in the dream. It wasn't *today's* capital, but the capital as it used to be.'

Emer looked at the picture over her shoulder.

'Until the salt buried it?' she said.

'Yes.' Rebecca shuddered, recalling the dessicated ghosts and her own horror at nearly suffocating in the salt.

'You're even spookier than I'd thought,' Emer remarked. 'That was centuries ago! Everyone knows that.' In spite of her casual tone, Emer was obviously impressed.

'And they were all looking upwards . . . ' Rebecca whispered, her thoughts far away, ' . . . as if they were longing to see the sky.'

'It was just a dream, Becky.'

'How can you say that to *me*?' Rebecca demanded. 'It was real. They're waking up. Derith is waking up!' She was almost shouting now, half-crazed with her imaginings.

'Shh. Be quiet!' Emer hisses urgently. 'The whole castle will hear you.'

Though Rebecca calmed down, the manic intensity was still in her eyes. She returned to the book, and read what little had been conjectured about the existence of the city of Derith. Emer watched her anxiously, glancing towards the door every so often. Rebecca paid her friend no attention – she was once more engrossed in the revelations from *Beneath the Salt*.

'The myths and legends that surround Derith far outnumber the known facts, and are almost too numerous to catalogue here. One of the most common, which exists in

238

several versions, is that the city was banished by angry gods – many ages ago – to languish beneath the sea. Its people lived the cold-blooded lives of underwater creatures until a great battle restored it to the open air. Central to this battle was . . . ' Rebecca turned the page, ' . . . the conflict between opposite sides of the magical spectrum within the Web. The opposing forces were, to put it simply, good and evil, and they remained deadlocked until the intercession of a character known variously as the Child of the Web, the Seeress of Night and the Tears of the World. All the chronicles agree that she lived by the edge of the sea, and most versions state that she was the only child of a cruel, widower baron. Several give her name as Rebecka, though the spelling of this varies, and it was her death . . . '

'Quick,' Emer hissed in panic. 'Father's coming.' She grabbed the book from the table as noises came from the study outside.

'No!' Rebecca cried, jumping up from her chair and trying to snatch the book back. She tumbled, and Emer pushed her roughly back down before diving over to the cupboard, shoving the book back inside and pushing the door shut. She just had time to sit down herself when Radd appeared in the doorway. Emer pretended to be reading, but Rebecca sat frozen, numbed and quite unable to think.

'Hello, girls,' the chamberlain said brightly. 'What are you up to?'

'Just browsing, Father,' Emer replied.

'It's not often that I see *you* in here,' he replied, looking at his daughter. 'What are you reading?'

Emer, who had chosen her book at random and was not quite sure what it was, held it up for him to see. It was a weighty tome concerning the geography of the northern mountains.

'Hmm,' Radd commented, looking surprised. 'And you, Rebecca?'

The baron's daughter could not speak. Her mind was almost at breaking point. The eerie parallels between the ancient Rebecka and herself, combined with the abrupt, untimely end to her reading, had left her stunned and fearful. Emer looked at her friend pleadingly.

'Are you all right?' Radd asked solicitously.

There was no answer.

'Becky?' Emer began, but then their attention was drawn elsewhere. Slowly, agonizingly, and with a long, drawn-out creak of its hinges, the cupboard door swung open.

Radd's face was like stone. Emer closed her eyes in horror while Rebecca stared, mesmerized. For a few moments, the very air in the library seemed frozen. No sound, no movement disturbed the petrified atmosphere. Then the chamberlain came back to life and stormed over to the cupboard.

'Why is this open?' he demanded. His eyes scanned the shelves, finding that nothing was missing. 'Have you been reading something from in here? Have you?' He saw that *Beneath the Salt* was upside down, and plucked it out. 'Have you?' he shouted, shaking the book at the two girls.

'No,' Emer responded quietly, looking down at the table.

'Yes,' Rebecca whispered, gazing at the leather-bound volume as if hypnotized.

'Give me the key,' Radd commanded, compressed fury in his voice. Nervously, Emer handed it over. 'Now get out of my sight,' he ordered. 'Go!'

Emer gave one last glance at her friend, who still had not moved, then fled, white-faced and trembling. She had never seen her father this angry before.

'Rebecca, have you been reading this book?' Radd asked, controlling his voice with a visible effort. His hands were shaking.

'Yes,' she whispered, cowering before his prodigious fury.

'Which part?' he demanded.

'Derith,' she breathed.

A flicker of fear passed over Radd's face.

'Derith is a mythical city,' he stated icily. 'If it ever existed, it's lost for ever now. *For ever*. Do you understand me?'

'I've been there,' she said softly.

'Don't be absurd, child!' he exclaimed. Only the quiet conviction in Rebecca's voice kept him from screaming at her.

'In my dream,' she explained desperately. 'I knew about the tablets and the black pyramid.'

'Superstitious nonsense!' he spat. 'You probably saw a

reference to them somewhere, and turned that into a dream.'

'You never let me read those books,' she retorted defensively. 'So how could I?' Rebecca was angry herself now.

'And a good thing too!' he exclaimed. 'Filling your mind with such rubbish is bound to be harmful. You're still young, Rebecca . . .'

'I'm a dream-weaver.' She would never have dared make such a claim except in desperate self-defence.

'There's no such thing!' he shot back. 'Where did you get this ridiculous idea?' His anger burned white hot.

After a moment's hesitation, Rebecca confessed her visit to the fair. At first she spoke reluctantly, relating only the bare facts, but as the memories returned, her voice grew in conviction. Radd listened in silence, and his fury turned gradually to sorrow.

'I'm disappointed in you, Rebecca,' he told her sadly when she had finished. 'I hadn't thought you capable of such deceit. Emer yes, but not you. First the fair, and then this.' He waved the fateful book in front of her.

'I'm sorry,' she said in a small voice.

'Some charlatan fills your head with ridiculous ideas . . .' Radd spluttered to a stop, his indignation getting the better of him.

'She told me to remember the letters and . . .' Rebecca began, but he silenced her with a gesture.

'If you have *any* sense, you'll forget all about them – and about everything else you read in here.'

'But there's something about . . .'

'What you read in here is ancient history,' he interrupted once more. 'And *legend*. It has absolutely no relevance to today.'

'But . . .'

'I refuse to discuss the matter further,' he stated firmly, then replaced the book and locked the cupboard. Pocketing the key, he turned back to Rebecca. 'You will no longer be allowed in here unless I am with you. Is that quite clear?'

'Yes.' *You can't do this to me!*

'Please leave now,' he said coldly.

Rebecca went without another word.

241

CHAPTER TWENTY-EIGHT

Rebecca walked, without knowing where she was going. When she came to her senses some time later, she found that she was in her secret room near the top of the East Tower. An instinct born of the need to hide away had taken her there.

Outside, the day had turned cold and wet. Rain dripped through the cracks in the roof, and draughts made the room chilly, but Rebecca was lost in misery, and noticed none of this. She knew that her prized relationship with Radd would never be the same again, and she also knew now why he had been so unwilling to teach her anything about the old legends and about magic. They had both learned unpalatable facts about the other today; Radd knew her to be capable of duplicity, and she had discovered that he had deliberately withheld knowledge which must surely have a bearing on her life.

Quotations from *Beneath the Salt* kept running through her mind.

The city of Derith and the Tomb of King Tyrrell. That place no longer existed just in the realms of myth. It was as real as her own home – she had *been* there. And, of course, Tyrrell was the notorious king of so long ago, whose death without an heir had precipitated a bitter, bloody civil war. Rebecca had not realized before that he had been buried in Derith – and wondered why none of the history books mentioned that fact. But she was more curious about *when* he had died. Had it been just before the salt claimed the city? Or at an earlier time?

. . . languish beneath the sea . . .

Only now Derith was below a different sea – a sea of salt.

. . . people lived the cold-blooded lives of underwater creatures . . .

The dessicated ghost-skeletons that she had seen lived in the salt as fish lived in water.

. . . a great battle restored it to the open air . . .

Could it rise again after centuries beneath the crushing weight of the flats? And, if so, how would the battle be fought?

. . . good and evil . . . deadlocked until . . .

the Child of the Web, the Seeress of Night and the Tears of the World . . .

The three titles all seemed doom-laden, but only the Seeress of Night could be interpreted in any way to match Rebecca's own situation. In one sense at least, a dream-weaver could be called a seeress of night.

. . . she lived by the edge of the sea . . .

Rebecca's home was on the edge of the salt-flats. Even the name of her father's land made the connection stronger, so that the next lines paralleled her own experience too closely for it to be a coincidence.

. . . the only child of a cruel, widower baron . . .

. . . Rebecka . . .

. . . her death . . .

Rebecca shuddered, feeling herself caught in a trap that was made even more terrifying because she could not see or touch it, something so nebulous that to oppose it was like trying to push back the wind. She wanted to deny her new knowledge, to confirm that it was not true, that it had nothing to do with her . . . but she could not.

Why me? she pleaded. *Why are my dreams showing me this if I'm not supposed to find out what it all means?*

Desperation welled up within her, like a palpable force. It felt as though her life was now entirely beyond her control. Opposing forces were pushing her this way and that; Baldemar with his greed and arrogance; Farrand and Cranne with their subterfuge and possible treason; Tarrant with his counterplots and veiled hints; Sancia with her double-edged advice; and Radd with his angry denials.

'What about *me*?' she asked aloud. 'Don't *I* get a say in

any of this?' Her voice cracked and she began to cough. There was no one answer to her questions. From the far side of the room, the monk stared benignly back at her, unmoving.

I have to see that book again! she decided, then trembled at the thought. *Do I really want to know? But I'll go mad if I don't.* She knew that there was no way in which she could achieve her purpose while Radd remained implacably opposed to her wishes. She dared not face him again so soon.

After a long time, during which her thoughts whirled round in endless circles, Rebecca remembered the other mystery in the book. The Okran Stones were an enigma, but one which was not so personal, and she was glad to turn her mind to a puzzle that made demands upon her intellect but not her emotions.

They must be important, she thought. *They came from Derith . . . and I saw them in my dreams. Perhaps if I could decipher them . . .*

She rummaged in her pockets in search of her transcription, but could find nothing. *I can't have lost it!* The last time she could remember seeing the piece of paper was when she had written down the missing letters.

Rebecca tried to recall the letters, but found to her horror that she could not. Her depression deepened. Outside, the day grew dark and the rain continued. Rebecca sat slumped in feverish dejection, hot and cold by turns. Her throat hurt, but she paid it no attention. She did not even look up when the door to the battlements opened and a bedraggled Emer came in, a lamp sheltered within her rain-soaked cape.

'Gods, Becky. What are you doing here in the dark?' She came over and peered at her friend. 'Are you all right? You don't look very well.'

Rebecca looked up then, and the hollow panic in her eyes made Emer's heart sink.

'What's the matter?' she asked, kneeling down and taking her friend's cold hands in her own. 'What happened?'

Slowly, falteringly, Rebecca told Emer what she had read in the book, and the point at which she had been interrupted. Though her voice was quiet and hoarse, her conviction was unmistakeable. Emer tried half-heartedly to allay Rebecca's terrible fears, but knew in her heart that it was a hopeless task.

'All that was only old stories,' she began. 'Just because . . .'

Rebecca cut her off.

'Don't try to explain it away, Emer. Your father tried, but I know he was frightened. I *have* to read the full story. Perhaps then I'll know what I'm supposed to do.'

After a long pause, Emer admitted defeat.

'If it's that important,' she said, 'I'll get it for you somehow.'

'How?'

'I don't know yet. Give me a day or so. Until he cools off.' She reached down inside her blouse. 'In the meantime,' she added, handing over a crumpled piece of paper, 'I thought you might like this.'

Rebecca took it and read the letters with relief. *One day,* she promised herself, *I'll be able to understand what this means.* A faint smile touched her lips at this thought.

'How did you get it?' she asked.

'I grabbed it when Father came in,' Emer replied. 'Even if he'd seen me, he's hardly likely to have searched in here.' She patted her bosom and grinned. 'It's lucky one of us was still thinking.'

'I don't think it would have fitted in mine anyway,' Rebecca commented, glancing down at her own less rounded chest.

Emer laughed, happy to see her friend regaining a little of her good humour. The sound was welcome and infectious, but when Rebecca's laughter turned to coughing, Emer was immediately concerned.

'Come on,' she ordered. 'You should be in your bed, not in this cold rat's nest.'

They walked together round the windswept walls, and into the shelter of the South Tower.

'How *is* Radd?' Rebecca asked softly.

'I don't know,' Emer replied. 'I haven't seen him since I ran out.'

Nursey took charge as soon as they reached Rebecca's apartments. She fussed and clucked her tongue, looked suspiciously at Emer's wet cloak, but said nothing. Emer left as soon as Rebecca was safely in bed, knowing that for once she needed exactly those qualities which Nursey possessed in abundance. The old woman stayed by her patient's bedside all night, occasionally dozing in her chair, but always ready to hold Rebecca's hand, talk soothingly to her, or prepare another drink or potion.

That night passed in the delirium of restless dreams, and the following morning found Rebecca suffering from a spiteful fever. She writhed and sweated, groaned and slept by turns. Nursey and two other maids stayed with her, and Emer paid frequent visits, but Rebecca showed no sign of recognizing any of them. Nursey decreed then that she was to be disturbed as little as possible. The baron's daughter was very ill, and her guardian was taking no chances. The old woman's vigil continued throughout the second night.

At times Rebecca cried out in her sleep, but her words made little sense and Nursey was unable to calm her.

'You have to see it!' Rebecca sat up, her eyes staring sightlessly. 'You have to see the letters. Remember the letters.'

She seemed to be pleading with someone only she could see, and did not settle until the early hours of the morning.

By the evening of the next day, the worst seemed to be over. Rebecca's fever had almost burnt itself out but she was still very weak, and racked with aches and pains in every part of her body. However, her mind was under her own control once more – and she had no memory of the previous nights and day – and the endless questions returned to plague her. She persuaded Nursey to let Emer visit her, and her friend took advantage of a few private moments to admit that she still had had no chance to get the book.

'I'm working on it, though,' she added confidently.

'Thank you,' Rebecca whispered.

'I do have some other news,' Emer went on. 'You're going to Garadun in three days' time – so get better!'

'I'll try,' Rebecca promised, buoyed up by this news. Perhaps in Garadun she would be able to find some of the answers she was seeking. And there was always the chance of meeting Montfort again . . .

'I wish I could come too,' Emer went on. 'Some girls get all the luck.'

'Why can't you?'

'Someone has to stay and make sure Edge doesn't go to rack and ruin while the baron's off gallivanting,' she replied.

'Your father.'

'Right. And that means I stay too.'

'How is he?'

'Quiet,' Emer answered shortly. 'We've hardly spoken to each other. I think he's trying to pretend it never happened.'

Rebecca smiled sadly.

'Poor Radd.'

The next three days passed slowly. Rebecca's health improved steadily, though not fast enough for her liking. Nursey took a positive pride in her charge's recovery, and treated her as if she were a five-year-old once more, congratulating her on cleaning her plate and scolding any attempt to leave her bedchamber. Emer came to see her often, but had no further developments to report. Even Baldemar paid his daughter a quick visit, to reassure himself that she would be fit to travel. Radd was noticeable by his absence, however – something which caused Rebecca both relief and sadness.

On the evening of the day before the journey to Garadun, Emer brought the news that she had been able to get inside the library cupboard again – Rebecca did not ask how – but that *Beneath the Salt* was no longer there.

'He must have hidden it somewhere else,' she concluded.

'Either that, or he's burnt it,' Rebecca replied, horrified by this thought.

The next morning, Baldemar, Rebecca and Nursey – who had made it quite plain that she was not leaving her charge's side – set off on the journey north, accompanied by four soldiers on horseback. The two women rode in a covered carriage which, although it was not very comfortable, and jolted over the uneven roads, at least had the virtue of protecting them from the elements. The day was dry but cool, and there was a strong wind blowing. Baldemar rode until they were beyond the boundaries of

Edgefield, then joined his daughter and Nursey in the relative warmth of the carriage.

Their progress was necessarily slow, with frequent stops for meals and to attend to the horses' needs, but Baldemar had arranged to stay with fellow barons for their two overnight stops, so their accommodation was more than adequate. Even so, it was a relief to all when, shortly before noon on the third day of their travels, the party entered the city of Garadun.

CHAPTER TWENTY-NINE

Garadun was, if anything, even busier than Rebecca remembered. The crowded streets were noisy and bustling, and the passage of Baldemar's carriage was slowed by the press of people and by other horses and vehicles. There was evidence everywhere of thriving trade, and the variety of goods on offer – even from the makeshift stalls of the street-markets – was much wider than anything seen in Edge.

They had to wait at one junction for a party of soldiers to cross their path; the men marched in strict time, their uniforms immaculate and their weapons gleaming. At the head of the column, a standard-bearer held their colours high. The contrast between their precision and purposeful bearing and the slapdash manner and appearance of the Edgefield Castle guard was painfully apparent, but Baldemar only watched them pass approvingly.

The city possessed buildings of every conceivable style and size, many of them very impressive, but the undoubted centrepiece was the royal palace. This structure, built over many centuries, was part castle, part governmental chambers, and part court community. It was indeed a city within a city, complete with its own guest houses, gardens, store-rooms, treasury, and all manner of accommodations and facilities. Several hundred people lived and worked within its grey stone walls, in capacities ranging from chief tax-collector to kitchen scullion, and from Commander of the Royal Guard to bakers, butchers and stable-lads.

As the carriage entered the arch of the main gate, they could see several colourful pennants flying from the turrets and walls. Before long, the baron and his party were comfortably installed in chambers in the Eagle Wing.

Baldemar immediately arranged for messages to be sent, organizing various audiences for the following day; Rebecca was grateful just to be in a room that was not swaying and rattling! The journey had tired her, and she was still suffering from the after-effects of her recent illness. Nursey felt weary too, and the two women were more than happy to spend the rest of the day quietly.

The next morning, Baldemar went about his own business, leaving his daughter to her own devices. She made enquiries with one of the servants assigned to care for them, and discovered the whereabouts of the Palace Archives, intending to make use of the library there as soon as she could. Nursey found this idea incomprehensible, and tried to persuade Rebecca that they should stay in their rooms until the baron called for them. When her charge insisted on going out, the old nurse fretted aloud about all the more interesting things they could be doing.

'Why do you want to shut yourself away with a lot of dusty old books?' she asked, 'when there's so much to see here?'

'You can learn a lot from books,' Rebecca replied, hoping that Nursey would lose interest and let her go alone.

'You can learn a lot more elsewhere,' the old woman muttered, but when she saw that Rebecca was not to be persuaded, she gave up – and the two set off together.

The archives were housed in an enormous building that was constructed of the same grey stone as the palace walls. The large double doors were closed, but a smaller inner door stood ajar so Rebecca opened this boldly and stepped inside. The interior was a vast hall, lit by seemingly endless rows of lamps, and by the slanting rays of sunlight coming through the high windows. In the central aisle, dozens of clerks and scribes sat busily working at large wooden desks. A few looked up when Rebecca came in, but soon returned to their chores. All round the walls, in row after row of shelves, were books of all shapes and sizes; above them was a balcony with yet more shelves between the high windows. The hall was cool and very quiet.

Rebecca stood silently, overawed by the almost religious atmosphere of calm study. She gazed at the endless lines of books, and despaired of ever being able to find what she wanted. Nursey crept in behind her, obviously ill-at-ease in such surroundings.

A man in a dark brown robe rose from the nearest table and approached them. His feet made no sound as he moved, and he seemed almost to glide over the stone floor. Although his hair was cut normally, he somehow reminded Rebecca of a monk.

'Can I help you, my lady?' he enquired, his voice barely more than a whisper.

'I'm . . . I'm looking for details about the history of my family,' she replied softly.

'Indeed. And you are?' His tone was courteous but cool, implying that she had better not waste his time with anything trifling.

'Rebecca, daughter of Baron Baldemar of Edge,' she answered.

He nodded, his face expressionless.

'Edge is to the south . . . ' Rebecca began.

'I am aware of its location, my lady,' he interrupted. 'What aspect of your family's history did you wish to research?'

'The . . . er . . . ancient legends . . . and such like,' she whispered, cursing herself for her inarticulate answer.

The man's eyebrows rose slightly.

'There's a particular book,' she went on, feeling more awkward by the moment. 'It's called *Beneath the Salt*. I was hoping you might have a copy.'

'Wait here,' he instructed, then turned and walked away.

'Friendly here, aren't they?' Nursey commented loudly, much to Rebecca's embarrassment. 'Let's go and find something else to do.'

'Shhh, Nursey,' Rebeca hissed. 'This is something I *must* do. You can wait outside for me if you prefer.'

The old woman hesitated, clearly torn between a desire to escape the oppressive hall and her duty to the baron's daughter. Eventually, as Rebecca had hoped, she gave in.

'See that you're not too long, then,' she grumbled. 'Can't see what you're going to learn from Master Stone-face there.' With that, she shuffled with relief out into the autumn sunshine, and began to look for somewhere to rest her weary legs.

Rebecca's thoughts returned to the robed man. *Has he gone to find me a copy of the book?* she wondered, hardly daring to hope. Stone-face had disappeared between two stacks of the innumerable volumes.

After a little while, he re-emerged, accompanied by another robed man.

'My lady Rebecca, this is Archivist Milden,' he said. 'He, if anyone, will be able to assist you.' The introduction made, he strode away without another word.

'Don't mind Humbold,' Milden remarked. 'He's like that with everyone. Come with me. It will be easier for us to talk in the outer section.' He smiled, his pleasant round face reassuringly normal.

Rebecca followed him in silence as he threaded his way between the vast shelves, eventually reaching another door. Milden opened it and ushered her into his own domain.

'The world of myths, legends and mystery,' he announced jovially as he closed the door behind them. 'Not many people show much interest in them any more.'

Rebecca stared at this second hall, smaller than the first, but still more than half the size of Edgefield Castle's Great Hall. This was also full to overflowing with books, but unlike the other room, was empty of scribes.

'There are so many!' she exclaimed, finding it difficult to take in.

'You're looking for legends concerning the family line of Edge, is that right?' Milden asked, smiling.

'Actually, there's one book I particularly want to see,' Rebecca explained eagerly, turning back to her guide. 'It's called *Beneath the Salt*.' She gave a brief description of the book's contents.

Milden scratched the side of his head, looking puzzled.

'I must confess, I've never heard of it,' he admitted eventually.

Rebecca's hopes plummeted.

'It was by a man called Alomar,' she added hopefully.

'Really?' Milden's interest grew. 'Have you ever seen this book?'

'No. Just references to it,' she lied. 'Have you heard of him?'

'He was one of the ancient Heretics,' he told her. 'They were a small sect of renegade monks who had some very confusing – and confused – theories about the Web being a circle.' His obvious pleasure at being able to display and share his knowledge shone in his eyes. 'They thought that our world's history travels around and around, repeating certain fixed patterns throughout eternity.'

Rebecca listened breathlessly; the relevance of this philosophy to what she had read, and to her own situation, was readily apparent.

'They tried to prove this by reference to old artifacts and mythology – which seems to fit in with what you know about this book – but almost all their ideas have long since been discredited. In fact, most scholars think they're complete nonsense.'

Rebecca was not sure whether she found this reassuring or not. There were too many coincidences to feel comfortable with the thought that they *were* merely coincidences.

'Of course,' Milden went on, 'the Heretics didn't help their own cause. In their later years, they behaved in a most eccentric way, doing things like burying live animals in salt, living on top of pinnacles of rock, and claiming to eat fresh air.' He shrugged, still smiling. 'I suppose most causes will attract *some* madmen, but the Heretics seemed to have more than their fair share! Then again, we know so little about their early years that it's difficult to judge them properly. I'd love to see this book of yours. It might fill a lot of the gaps in our knowledge.'

'Do you have *any* of their writings here?' she asked.

'Yes,' he replied, 'but there isn't much.'

He led Rebecca to one of the distant corners of the room, and showed her a tattered collection that contained only a few slim volumes. The books were clearly very old.

'We should really have had them copied,' Milden said ruefully. 'They're fading now, and some of the pages are dificult to handle. But there are always so many more important things for the scribes to do, and I'm the only one to have shown any interest in these volumes for years. I can only do so much,' he concluded sadly.

The archivist's love of his job was obvious, and Rebecca

253

regarded him with mixed feelings. No one man could possibly hope to care for all these books properly, and she pitied him for having to choose what to save for posterity. She was also envious. To have unlimited access to this almost infinite treasure-house of ancient knowledge was a privilege she would have given much to share.

'Were you looking for any particular aspect of their writings?' Milden asked.

'Legends connected with Derith,' she answered, 'and that might be linked to Edge, or to my ancestors.'

'Hmmm,' he responded, his eyes running swiftly along the shelves. 'There's nothing like that here. But there'll be plenty in other sections. The non-heretical stuff, if you like.' He chuckled, and added, 'Most authors seem to have got a little carried away when writing about Derith.'

'I'd like to look at these anyway,' Rebecca said politely.

'Of course. But please treat them carefully.'

'I will,' she promised.

'How long will you be in Garadun?' he asked.

'I don't know. Only a few days, I expect,' she answered regretfully.

'Can you come back tomorrow afternoon?'

'Yes.'

'Good. I'll dig out the best stuff on Derith for you.' Milden sounded eager, and Rebecca thought that the occasions when the archivist could share his passion must be rare.

'I'll start on it now,' he added. 'Let me know when you're ready to leave.'

'Thank you,' she said quietly. 'You've been very kind.'

As she watched him walk away, a new purpose in his stride, she guessed that he must spend the majority of his waking hours within these four walls – he had the pale skin of a city dweller who rarely saw the sun. She judged his age to be between thirty and thirty-five. Milden's life had clearly been a solitary one for the most part, and Rebecca wondered what had brought him to this hall of petrified myths.

She turned back to the writings of the Heretics, and picked out a book at random. For the next two hours she struggled through the obscure ramblings of long dead men, turning the fragile pages gingerly. The semi-insane texts covered several subjects, ranging from visions, theology and the theory of time, to philosophy, embalming fluids, the patterns of the stars – and vegetables, one member of the sect having apparently concluded that carrots were symbols of irredeemable vileness. Rebecca could find nothing even vaguely relevant to her own situation, nor did she find any books written by Alomar. However, she did come across a couple of brief references to his work in the recovery and interpretation of ancient relics.

Eventually she gave up and called out softly to Milden, reluctant to make any loud noise in that dusty quiet room. At first, she was not sure that he had heard her, but just as she was nerving herself to shout again, he appeared, a book in each hand.

'Find anything?' he asked hopefully.

Rebecca shook her head.

'Odd lot, weren't they?' The archivist smiled.

'That's putting it mildly,' she replied, grinning back. 'How have you been getting on?'

'Slowly,' he said cheerfully. 'I'll be better organized by tomorrow, though.'

'I don't know how to thank you,' she said. 'Going to so much trouble . . .'

'It's a pleasure,' he answered, his smile broadening. 'I don't get many visitors – and certainly none as attractive as you.'

'I'll come back tomorrow, then,' she said, blushing slightly.

'I'll look forward to it,' Milden replied. 'It might be wise for you to go now. I think your companion may be getting rather bored . . .'

Rebecca had forgotten all about Nursey, and hurried outside once Milden had led her back through the main hall. The old woman was sleeping on a stone bench, but woke as if by instinct when her charge approached.

'Had enough of that dusty old place at last?' she asked, then tried to get up, only to find that her ancient limbs were cramped and stiff. Rebecca took the old woman's hands and helped her to her feet, then they slowly walked back to the Eagle Wing.

'What you need,' Rebecca remarked, smiling at the reversal of their usual roles, 'is a nice hot drink with something in it.'

Nursey muttered something inaudible about her knees then added, 'Perhaps I won't go dancing tonight after all.'

CHAPTER THIRTY

Baldemar was in good humour that evening; his discussions that day had obviously been successful.

'We are invited to dine with the king tomorrow night,' he announced happily.

'Me too?' Rebecca was delighted.

'He asked for you especially,' the baron replied. 'This is a great honour for you – I shall introduce you to some very important people.'

At this, warning bells began to ring in Rebecca's head, but they could not dispel her pleasurable anticipation.

'And how did you spend *your* day?' Baldemar asked.

'Nursey and I saw a few of the sights,' his daughter replied. 'And I read for a while.'

* * *

That night, Rebecca's dream began in eerie silence, as brief images which she remembered from her recent fever flashed by, unrecognizable but vaguely threatening. She struggled, trying to swim through a whirlpool of visions.

Then the music began, rising slowly from the silence, and growing steadily in power and beauty. It was like nothing she had heard before and it soon grew to dominate the frenetic activity that swirled all about her. The whirlpool slowed down, and was replaced by a scene of great beauty – a gently flowing river, trees blowing lightly in the wind, and a feeling of utter peace as Rebecca found herself surrounded by lovely countryside.

Sancia appeared. She was smiling, her eyes aglow, but when she spoke it was with another's voice.

'Have patience, little one. Don't fret. In time, you will understand.' The well-remembered tones were as sweet to Rebecca as the music which still enveloped her. 'True magic reveals itself, and truth cannot stay hidden for ever.'

Then the image of the dream-weaver faded; moments later, the music had gone too. When Rebecca awoke, she felt happier and with more peace of mind than she had for many days. The advice had been welcome, and she accepted it without question, intending to obey the instructions as best she could.

Rebecca still accepted that her mother was dead in the way that humanity understood it, but also knew that she was not gone completely. It had been her voice which Sancia had used in the dream, rendering the healing nature of the message all the more effective.

She's part of the Web now, Rebecca thought. *But magic has brought her back.*

* * *

That morning, Nursey allowed Rebecca to escape from her quite easily; the old woman was still suffering from the effects of the journey and her outdoor nap of the day before. Baldemar left early on business of his own, so Rebecca was left to do as she pleased. However, she had no firm plans until her appointment with Milden later that day, and consequently spent much of the morning wandering aimlessly through the city streets.

Although she was distracted by thoughts of the archives, she could not help noticing that there were large numbers of soldiers and cavalry on the move. This military activity was watched by the citizens of Garadun with wary eyes, and there was a general mood of uncertainty. The streets grew quiet as the soldiers passed by, then filled with whispers after they had gone. The rumours which had spread as far as Edge were obviously prevalent here, and Rebecca began to share in the common unease.

Otherwise the city appeared normal enough, with the endless demands of commerce fuelling the activity of its people. Although Rebecca was the object of several appraising glances, she was not approached, and was thus left to her own thoughts.

She returned to the archives at noon. Much to her relief, Milden was waiting for her at the main entrance, and his welcome was warm as he led her quickly to his own territory. There, he showed her a huge number of books, spread out over his desk and two additional tables. Many were already open at the relevant pages.

'All these?' Rebecca exclaimed. *Where do I start?*

'Quite a few of them appear to be more or less identical,' he replied cheerfully 'I've tried to mark the ones which seem most closely connected to Edge, but as you can see, Derith was a popular subject for legends.'

'You must have been up all night!'

'Most of it,' he admitted happily. 'And I enjoyed myself immensely. Let me run through what's here, then you can decide what to concentrate on.'

The next few hours passed quickly in a fascinating discussion of the mythology and history of the fabled city of Derith. Milden did most of the talking, referring frequently to various volumes, while Rebecca listened and asked an occasional question. She was so absorbed by their conversation that she almost forgot her original purpose, but eventually remembered to ask about the legend which placed an earlier Derith under the sea. She told Milden everything she could remember, but omitted any mention of the name Rebecka. The archivist shook his head.

'There's nothing like that that I know of,' he said.

'But it was supposed to be a common myth!' Rebecca exclaimed. 'There were several versions of it.'

'How do you know?'

'Er . . . the reference said . . . ' She faltered, lost for words.

'You're not telling me everything, are you?' he said, eyeing her thoughtfully.

'No,' she answered, smiling. 'Perhaps I'm a Heretic – in disguise!'

'All right,' he said, laughing. 'I suppose a lady is entitled to a few secrets.' Privately, Milden was speculating not only on the reasons for her interest, but also on the possible ways in which such a 'common' myth might disappear completely. Even direct censorship was unlikely to have been wholly successful in eradicating something so widely known. And yet he was positive that Rebecca was not making it up. *Perhaps*, he thought, *all the Heretics really were mad and it was just a story invented to pass the time!* He did not believe that idea either.

'I'll leave you to read,' he said. 'Call me if you want any help.'

'Thank you.' Rebecca wanted to say more, but the words would not come, and Milden disappeared into his maze of shelves.

She went on to read fuller versions of the tales already outlined for her by the archivist. As well as those familiar to her – of the city's burial by the salt – there were also a vast array of possible suggestions as to the cause of the catastrophe. These varied from the mundane through the improbable, to the positively absurd. The most plausible was a theory which combined the drying out of a distant inland sea with a change in climate – this was supposed to have precipitated a huge number of storms and high winds which transported the salt in great crystalline clouds. The most ridiculous suggestion concerned pieces of the moon breaking off and falling to the earth as salt-dust.

Then there were the stories about Tyrrell's death and his formal burial. Much to Rebecca's disappointment, no mention was made of the black pyramid. The civil war was also referred to, but she skipped through most of that, being already familiar with the history of the struggle for the vacant throne.

Of more interest were the other, less weighty legends concerning the former capital. One told of a great bell which hung in a tower at the city's centre; the bell could not be rung except in times of dire peril, when it could reputedly be heard in every part of the kingdom, tolling the doom of the hour. Yet another described a crystal bridge which spanned the city's unnamed river. To cross this was reported to be like 'walking on solid air, amid a confusion of rainbows', and anyone who did so was certain to return to the city. There were many more, all containing fascinating snippets, but there was nothing which brought Rebecca any closer to solving her own personal dilemma.

She took this philosophically, accepting for the time being her mother's – or was it Sancia's? – advice, and taking pleasure in the reading of such wonderful tales. When her eyes started to blur after the hours of continuous study, she had to stop. Her head ached dully, but she counted this a small price to pay. Milden appeared without her having to call for him

'It's almost dark,' he told her. 'You should be on your way.'

Rebecca rose and stretched.

'Thank you,' she said gratefully. 'I'll help you put these away before I go.'

'No,' he replied. 'I'll leave them out. You've whetted my appetite, and I might do some reading of my own. In any case, I was hoping you might pay me another visit before you leave the city.'

'I will if I can,' she promised.

* * *

When Rebecca returned to her room, she found Nursey in a panic. Although there was still more than an hour before dinner, she had been having nightmares about her charge not being ready on time. However, all was well, and Rebecca was pronounced to be perfectly attired and adorned a few moments before a page arrived to conduct her and the baron to the royal quarters.

The dinner that night completed an extraordinary day for Rebecca. It was the first time she had been universally treated as an adult, especially in such exalted company.

Montfort met each of his guests personally as they entered the royal chambers. An usher stood at his shoulder, ready to prompt the young king should he need reminding of anyone's name, but his skills were almost never needed. Montfort greeted Baldemar with a firm handshake, then turned to Rebecca and smiled appreciatively. She curtseyed and he bowed slightly in response.

'You're welcome here, my lady.'

'Thank you, your majesty,' she responded quietly.

'Tarrant did not exaggerate when he described your beauty,' Montfort went on. Rebecca blushed, lowering her eyes in some confusion. 'I trust that unfortunate matter is truly behind you. I understand that you behaved impeccably and with great bravery.'

How much does he know? Rebecca wondered, still not daring to look up. She was amazed at his ability to recall such matters, when he was obviously burdened by affairs of state.

'You have a daughter to be proud of, Baldemar,' the king concluded.

Her father beamed, nodding in acknowledgement, and Montfort moved on to the waiting guests.

Altogether, there were twenty-four people around the large circular table when they sat down to eat. Rebecca and her father were side by side, directly opposite the king. A young nobleman had been placed on Rebecca's other side; he introduced himself as Callan, and informed her that he was the son of a baron who was sitting further round the table. There were a few women present; Rebecca was easily the youngest, and she felt plain and awkward beside their finery.

The meal – which was excellent – was presented by silent, efficient servants. Conversation flowed freely but only rarely across the width of the table, so Rebecca heard little of what the king was saying. Most conversation was in small groups of close neighbours. Baldemar soon found himself involved in a discussion with two fellow nobles about trade and taxes. Rebecca tried to listen to what Montfort was saying – he was deep in discussion with the two barons on either side of him – but she was distracted by Callan, who was intent on monopolizing her attention. He seemed pleasant enough, but Rebecca could not help wishing – though knowing full well that this would have been impossible – that it was the king beside her. She found herself thinking that he was even more handsome than she remembered, and she recalled Emer's joking accusation of infatuation. She told herself firmly that her interest in the man stemmed only from wanting to learn about his political ideas.

'Have you been to Garadun before?' Callan asked, interrupting her train of thought.

'Yes. Twice,' she replied. 'When I was younger.'

'It's a wonderful city,' he enthused. 'It would be a pleasure to show it to you.'

'I think my father has other plans,' she responded.

'Really?' Callan tried hard not to show his surprise. He happened to know that Baldemar's plans were for Callan to spend as much time with Rebecca as possible! Tonight's seating arrangements had been no accident. He was under orders from his father to be attentive to the girl; although initially reluctant, he had grown much more willing when he had seen how attractive she was. It made up for the fact that she came from a run-down barony. Callan was not aware that Baldemar had several other prospective escorts lined up should he fail.

'There's so much to see,' the young man persisted. 'And the entertainments here are unsurpassed in all Ahrenia. We live close to the city, and I have been here many times. I know *all* the best places.'

Rebecca smiled politely and tried to listen as he went on to describe his home, which lay a few leagues to the east, and the lands which went with it. He added that his father was sitting next to Montfort. When Rebecca remained unimpressed, Callan tried to coax her into talking about herself and her home. She was not forthcoming, however, and tried to steer the conversation towards the king's proposed reforms. Callan claimed not to concern himself with such matters and expressed surprise that Rebecca should do so.

'I leave all that to my father and older brother,' he said.

'And what do *they* think?' she asked then, becoming irritated with her enforced companion.

'Oh, they never tell me anything!' he exclaimed, laughing to show that this was meant as a joke.

I know the feeling, she thought, choosing not to share his humour.

Distinctly discouraged now, Callan made one last effort.

'Are you sure I can't show you around tomorrow?' he asked, a note of pleading in his voice.

'No, thank you. I shall be busy,' she replied without even looking at him.

So Callan gave up, for a while at least, and left Rebecca in peace to pick up fragments of more interesting conversations. The meal ended and the room grew quiet as Montfort rapped on the table for his guests' attention.

'My friends,' he began, his eyes scanning the faces before him. 'As you know, I firmly believe that we stand upon the brink of a new era, a new age of enlightenment and justice. I am sure that I can count on all of you to lend me your support in this great undertaking.'

How much of what he says is wishful thinking? Rebecca wondered. *And how much is a subtle form of pressure?* She too found herself looking round the assembled faces, trying to read their expressions.

'A toast,' the king continued. He stood up, and raised his glass. 'To a new age of justice for all.' His guests rose, and drank. As they did so, Rebecca thought that Montfort's eyes met her own over the rims of their glasses.

Soon after that, the dinner party broke up into smaller groups, who went to continue their conversations in the adjoining rooms. Callan left Rebecca's side and joined his father, declaring indignantly that Baldemar's daughter was a cold fish, for all her pretty looks. However, Rebecca was not left alone for long. She soon had two other young men competing for her attention, and she was relieved when her father approached and told her that it was time for them to go.

Some of the other guests had already left, and Montfort made a point of bidding them farewell personally. He repeated this courtesy for Baldemar and his daughter.

'I hope we will meet again during your stay,' he told Rebecca.

She smiled and nodded, wondering whether he really meant what he said.

'I hope you are managing to find your way about this time,' Montfort went on, returning her smile.

Once again, Rebecca was astonished by his memory.

'I believe so, your majesty,' she replied bashfully. 'And it seems I now have several willing escorts, should I

264

feel in need of them.'

'I am bound to say that that does not surprise me in the least,' he said. 'It would be a blind man indeed who did not relish such a task. You must inform them that they are under my instructions to make sure you enjoy your stay here.' He turned to the baron. 'Goodnight, Baldemar. I shall welcome your contributions to tomorrow's conference.'

'I shall be honoured, sire,' was the reply. 'Goodnight.'

The two men exchanged bows, then father and daughter departed, both in good humour.

'I shall be busy all day tomorrow,' Baldemar remarked. 'You are free to spend your time with an escort of your own choice.'

'Thank you, Father.'

'I'm sure you will find ways to enjoy yourself,' he added meaningfully.

'I'm sure I will,' she replied.

CHAPTER THIRTY-ONE

Rebecca rose early the next morning, and decided to sneak out before Nursey woke up. Although they were sharing a bedchamber, the old woman did not stir as her charge slipped out of bed and dressed. As Rebecca donned her cloak and left, Nursey was still snoring.

Outside it was cold, with a thin mist hanging in the still air, and Rebecca was soon glad of her warm clothes. She decided to go for a walk and set off through the maze of gardens and courtyards, keeping a mental note of where she was going. She still recalled with embarrassment the occasion when such an expedition had left her completely lost. As she walked, she became aware of some faint, melancholy music coming from one of the deeper recesses of the formal gardens. Intrigued, she followed the sound, drawn by such unexpected beauty. She had finally tracked down its source, although the musician was still invisible behind a high green hedge, when the music changed. Now it was a jaunty, cheerful tune, as though the player had been seized with the urge to dance.

For a moment, Rebecca wondered whether she should retreat, not wanting to disturb what was obviously a private moment. Her curiosity eventually got the better of her, however, and she crept forward, rounding the corner of the hedge. There she stopped, suddenly feeling extremely awkward. A few paces in front of her, Montfort sat alone on a bench, playing a sort of flute. He was lost in the music, his foot tapping out the lively rhythm. Then, without a break, the tune grew sad once more.

Rebecca decided to leave, but a slight sound must have alerted the king because he stopped playing and turned to her in surprise. When he saw who it was, he smiled.

'I . . . I'm sorry,' Rebecca stuttered, on the point of fleeing.

'There's no need to be,' Montfort replied, standing up. 'You are more than welcome.'

She still hesitated, her cheeks reddening with the shame of having been caught eavesdropping.

'This is the only time of day when I am allowed to put affairs of state aside,' the king went on quickly, aware of her discomfort. 'I would be glad of your company – it will be a pleasure to talk to someone who doesn't want me to do something, agree to something else, sign this or decree that.' He paused, watching her closely. 'Come and sit with me for a few moments.'

'Yes, your majesty.' Rebecca curtseyed and came forward slowly.

Montfort grimaced.

'Please leave all that for more formal occasions,' he entreated her. 'In this garden, my name is Montfort, as yours is Rebecca.'

They sat down together on the bench.

'Tell me about your chess game with Cranne,' he said.

Rebecca told him of the events surrounding her abortive betrothal, nervous at first, and stumbling over her words, but growing in confidence as the moments passed and the king showed every sign of being engrossed by her tale.

'I wish I could have seen that,' he remarked when she had finished. Rebecca wondered whether she dared ask him the questions Tarrant had refused to answer. 'Still,' Montfort went on, 'I'm sure you'll not lack for suitors.'

'If I wanted them,' she responded.

He looked at her enquiringly.

'Perhaps I have more important things to do . . . ' she added without thinking.

'Are you teasing me, Rebecca?' he asked, his smile returning. 'The Web knows enough people have been trying to marry me off. Why can't they see—' He stopped abruptly and the frown which had begun to form disappeared.

Rebecca took her chance, and changed the subject.

'Are Farrand and Cranne . . . sympathetic to your ideas?' she asked.

'Now, young lady, I thought we'd agreed not to talk about politics.'

'Why? Because I'm a woman?' It was an instinctive reaction and Rebecca was appalled by her own boldness as soon as the words were out.

'No,' he replied, in a tone which, though serious, did not sound at all offended. 'Because as king I am bound by more restrictions than my subjects – and besides, I have enough of that during the rest of the day. Even when I'm alone, my thoughts are never far from what lies ahead, from what I must do. Can you blame me for wanting to enjoy this distraction?'

Rebecca looked down at her hands, folded demurely in her lap. She felt chastised, though his words had not been unkind.

'Let's just say that I was not displeased by your champion's victory,' Montfort went on unexpectedly.

Rebecca glanced up at him.

'Is Edge really that important?' she asked quietly.

'It could be,' he replied, equally softly, then returned her look and added, 'In any case, it produced you – so it *must* be important!' He laughed as Rebecca blushed.

'I . . . I just wanted you to know . . . ' she said awkwardly, looking away again, 'that I support what you're doing . . . and I'm not alone in that.'

'I count that as a blessing,' he said, serious once more. 'And can I count on your father to feel the same way?'

'I'm not really sure,' she answered. 'He's so set in his ways. But I'll work on him!'

'Then the battle is already won,' Montfort said, grinning.

'Hardly – he doesn't take much notice of me. I'm only his *daughter*.'

'Most of us seem to have to battle against our parents,' he commented ruefully. A few moments passed in silence. The king gave every sign of being at ease, but Rebecca was not.

'You play very well,' she ventured, indicating his flute.

'Not really,' he replied dismissively. 'If I have any talents, they lie elsewhere. However, there are some musicians in

268

the city who you must hear before you leave. Have you arranged escorts for the rest of your stay?'

'No. It seems I am perverse – I prefer my own company.'

He did not respond to that, and Rebecca wondered anxiously whether she had offended him.

'Your honesty is refreshing,' he commented eventually. There was a weary note in his voice. 'What have you been doing with your time here?'

At this, Rebecca saw an opportunity to attempt to repay Milden for his kindness. She told Montfort about her visit to the Archives, the fascinating reading she had done and the help she had been given. She was enthusiastic in her praise of Archivist Milden, in the hope of persuading the king that he was someone worth supporting. Montfort listened politely, but his attention was obviously not wholehearted.

'I don't know half of what goes on in there,' he admitted when she finished. 'Humbold doesn't exactly encourage . . .'

'I noticed,' Rebecca said. 'But Mil—'

'I have little time for such matters,' he interrupted. 'There is always something more immediate to be dealt with.' Then, seeing the effect his words had had on her, he added in a kinder tone, 'I'll see. Why are you so interested in mythology?'

'Because legends can sometimes tell us more about the present than the past.'

'Meaning?'

'That perhaps history repeats itself.'

'Only if we let it,' he stated firmly. 'And I have no intention of doing that.' He grinned suddenly. 'You'll be telling me next that I face magical foes as well as worldly ones, and that I should keep a wizard at court, and look out for omens.' Though his words were light-hearted, there was a serious core beneath their surface.

Rebecca decided not to pursue the subject. *If I start talking about dream-weaving and the Heretics, he'll think I'm completely mad!* She found it difficult to believe that she was actually sitting there talking to the king. *I wish Emer could see me now!*

'I'd better be going,' she said reluctantly.

'Not yet,' he responded quickly. 'Do you sing?'

'No.' She smiled weakly. 'If I have any talents, they lie elsewhere.'

'Like playing chess?' he asked, all innocence, as he put the flute down on the bench between them.

'Among other things,' she replied, recovering her composure rapidly.

'I daren't ask.'

'Surely a king may dare anything,' she responded. *What am I saying?*

'If I were only a king perhaps,' he answered, smiling. 'But I hope I am also a civilized man, and thus bound by the laws of courtesy.'

They sat in silence once more, but this time they were both at ease. By now the sun had risen above the line of the hedge, and the early-morning dew sparkled on grass, flowers and leaves.

'Beautiful, isn't it?' Montfort remarked, indicating the garden.

Rebecca nodded.

'But it's so tame,' he went on. 'I so often wish that I lived in the mountains, or by the sea. The wildness and freedom, that's real beauty. This needs too much tending – the hand of man is in every blade, every leaf.'

The longing in his voice touched a chord in Rebecca's heart, and she realized that this man was trapped more effectively than any prisoner, bound by the awesome responsibilities of a position he had no choice but to accept.

A thrush flew into the garden, settled on a nearby bush and began to sing.

'Now you have someone to accompany you,' Rebecca said quietly.

'No,' he replied softly. 'I can't match that.'

They both listened to the liquid song for a while, then Montfort clapped his hands sharply and the startled bird flew away. Rebecca looked at the king in surprise.

'It didn't belong here,' he said. 'It was too beautiful.' He stood up and smiled again, but the tension within him was apparent once more. 'Perhaps we should go our separate ways now,' he suggested. 'If we stay here much longer, there'll be rumours about our relationship! And I think we could both do without that.'

They laughed half-heartedly, exchanged brief farewells, and left the garden, heading in different directions.

* * *

Rebecca did not return to the Eagle Wing. Her conversation with Montfort had left her restless, so she resumed her interrupted walk as the day gradually warmed up. Part of her route took her along the battlements of the palace walls; from there she was able to watch the city as it came to life. It seemed hard to believe that all these people owed their allegiance to the young man whose early morning vigil she had shared.

Eventually, her steps led her back to the Archives, as she had known they would. Milden was glad to see her, and was even happier when she gave him another line of research to pursue. It had occurred to Rebecca that if two sets of mysterious letters had been recorded in *Beneath the Salt*, then there might be more in other books. When she mentioned this possibility, the archivist reacted promptly.

'You mean the Okran Stones,' he said. 'I've wondered about that myself. But we definitely don't have any others here, although they're mentioned in several volumes. I'll get them out for you.'

During the ensuing hours of reading and discussion, Rebecca learnt nothing new but, once again, Milden's company was a pleasure in itself. When he suggested that they have lunch together, she accepted gladly, taking literally her father's advice that she was free to do as she liked for the whole day. And she was indeed very hungry, having missed breakfast altogether.

'It may not be quite the style you're used to,' Milden warned her.

'Baron Baldemar's home does not have the facilities of Garadun's palace,' she replied. 'I'm sure I'll survive!'

They went out together through the main hall, prompting whispered speculation among the scribes, and Milden led

271

Rebecca to a large room filled with trestle tables which adjoined the palace kitchens. It was here that many of the palace staff came to eat, and it was a noisy, bustling place, with people coming and going constantly amid the clatter of plates and cutlery. Milden was greeted by several people, and his guest was the subject of interested scrutiny.

They collected food from the refectory, and sat down at one of the tables. Milden apologized for the noise, but Rebecca reassured him that she did not mind – indeed, the cheerful atmosphere was a powerful antidote to the morning's introspection.

As they ate, Rebecca told her companion about her early morning encounter with Montfort, and the fact that she had mentioned Milden's work to the king. Her companion looked surprised, then vaguely alarmed.

'Montfort doesn't have much time for the sort of thing I do,' he commented. 'He's much too pragmatic to be bothered with history and legends. And when I consider the problems he is faced with, his attitude doesn't surprise me.'

Rebecca and Milden went on to discuss the political situation, and then, their meal over, returned to the Archives. Rebecca spent the afternoon reading the wonderful tales that Milden picked out for her – simply because they were his favourites. She learnt nothing new about her own situation, but eventually came away, after fond farewells, with her head full of marvellous images of bearded giants, castles built of clouds, music which could transport the listener to any part of the world, and a boat of beaten silver floating serenely on a mist-enshrouded lake.

Returning to her own apartments brought her down to earth with a bump.

'And where have you been?' Nursey wanted to know. 'There have been young men calling for you all day, and I couldn't even tell them when you'd be back.'

'Well, I didn't want to see them,' Rebecca said wearily.

'Why should you be so high and mighty?' the old woman grumbled. 'Some of them had gone to a great deal of trouble making plans for your entertainment. You've been most incommodious – to them, and to me.'

'I'm sorry, Nursey, but I really didn't feel like being

entertained.'

'Well, don't count on getting any more gentlemen callers,' her guardian said peevishly, as if this should be seen as a punishment. 'They'll have given up by now, and we'll have to spend the evening here on our own.'

Much to Rebecca's relief, that turned out to be the case, and the two women ate a quiet meal in their rooms. Just when Rebecca was considering going to bed, Baldemar returned – in a foul temper. He did not explain what had made him so angry, and confined himself to a terse announcement that they would be leaving Garadun at first light. Then he went straight to his own room, leaving Rebecca to wonder whether the conference had gone badly – or whether her own uncooperative behaviour with the queue of prospective suitors was to blame for her father's mood.

'Now you won't get to see anything at all, will you, young miss!' was Nursey's only comment as they made ready for bed.

* * *

Although Rebecca was caught in a whirlpool of quicksalt, she was somehow not affected by it; her fear was that of an observer.

A hand, black and scarred, rose from the swirling whiteness and threw something towards her. The flat object sailed slowly through the air, turning languidly. One side was plain, the other had markings on it – and she knew exactly what it was.

Then the whirlpool was gone and the tablet fell to the ground, letters side down. Pickle, her fur bright red, sniffed at the stone suspiciously. She looked up at Rebecca, who still floated above the scene, and yowled. The sound echoed faintly all around.

'Turn it over, Pickle,' Rebecca urged. 'Turn the stone over!'

The beek prodded the tablet uncertainly with one outsize paw, then, with a last cry, she turned and fled.

A heavy boot crunched down upon the stone.

'I have little time for such matters.'

273

Rebecca could not see the owner of the boot, but she recognized his voice, and wondered why the man she had always warmed to was behaving in such an unpleasant way.

'This is the present, not the past,' she pleaded. 'I have to read it.'

'Only if I let you,' he replied. 'And I have no intention of doing that.'

'Please.'

'You'll be telling me next that I face magical foes.'

'Yes.'

'That I should keep a wizard at court.'

'Yes!'

'And to look out for omens.'

'I'm a dream-weaver.'

'You're mad.'

I wish Emer was here.

His foot stirred, pushing the tablet into the dirt.

And Galen too, came the response from far away.

The boot disappeared and the stone flipped over of its own accord. The incisions had been filled with dark earth, and the letters stood out clearly.

```
A G I C F
M S N A
F E I T V
I N E E
L R O R R
```

Rebecca committed them to memory before waking up.

CHAPTER THIRTY-TWO

Baldemar and his party made an early start the following morning. The baron drove his horses hard, and as a result, they arrived home in the late evening of the second day, having spent only one night on the road. Throughout the journey, the baron had been morose and irritable, and any attempt to talk to him had proved futile. He had spent most of his time in the saddle, eschewing the comfort of the carriage for the open air, which freed him from any attempt at conversation. On reaching the castle, he had gone straight to his rooms after giving his chamberlain a few terse instructions.

Rebecca was tired, and saddened by their abrupt departure from Garadun, but she cheered up when Emer came to see her, demanding a full account of her visit to the city. It was well past midnight by the time they finished talking, defeated at last by sheer fatigue. Emer's reaction to all she had heard was fairly typical.

'You wouldn't be making all this up, would you?' she asked.

'It's true. I swear,' Rebecca insisted sleepily. 'I even dreamt about Montfort after our meeting in the garden – and I persuaded him to show me another tablet. Look.'

'Now I *know* you're crazy,' Emer said as Rebecca took out the piece of paper, which now had three sets of letters written on it. She peered at it curiously, none the less.

'I'll find out what they mean if it *kills* me,' Rebecca told her friend dramatically.

'Let's not get carried away,' Emer replied. 'I'd miss you.' She stood up, and yawned. 'I'm off to bed now.'

'Goodnight, Emer.'

' 'Night, Becky. Sweet dreams.'

* * *

As tradition demanded, Radd had organized a celebration to mark the baron's return to his realm. Although on this occasion the gathering was to be a relatively modest one, the chamberlain had still engaged a group of musicians to provide entertainment. His arrangements had been thrown into some confusion by Baldemar's unexpectedly early return, but all was now organized, and the event set for the early afternoon of the following day.

Rebecca was dreading the occasion, knowing that her father was in no mood for such festivities, and also realizing that sooner or later she was going to have to face Radd. The acrimony of their previous meeting still remained, and everything that she had learnt since then had only served to make her even more certain of her own position – and consequently more resentful of his. And yet she still longed to resume their friendship, and if there was to be a reconciliation, they had to start somewhere.

There were only about forty guests at the banquet, arranged both around the top table, where Baldemar and Rebecca were joined by the most important local merchants, and at two other tables set nearby. This left plenty of room for the eight musicians, who were using traditional woodwind instruments, drums and lutes. As the meal got underway they played a medley of old songs – which were hardly noticed by the guests. Rebecca was probably the only one paying them any attention; her grim, silent father was less than good company. The musicians were good, she decided, but nothing special, and she wondered what she had missed by not hearing those in Garadun.

Just as she was beginning to lose interest, the group's leader stepped forward to announce that their youngest member, a lad who looked no older than Rebecca, was going to play something new for them. The young man came to the front while his colleagues sat down and relaxed, watching him with indulgent smiles. He carried a stringed instrument which looked rather like a misshapen

276

lute but, instead of plucking the strings, he placed the base of the strange wooden object under his chin, holding the neck with one hand. He began to play very softly, drawing a long, stick-like bow across the strings in smooth, controlled movements. Although most of the guests ignored him. Rebecca was instantly fascinated. The music he was producing was strange and beautiful, like nothing she had ever heard before.

The sounds of eating and conversation faded away, and Rebecca's companions suddenly seemed to be trapped behind a gauze screen. The young girl closed her eyes and let the music sweep through her, enraptured by its insistent beauty and astonishing resonance. Then it changed, becoming louder and more passionate. New notes filled the air, cascading over the slow stately bass rhythms in a graceful cataract of sound. Rebecca opened her eyes and stared at the young man. He was now playing a flute, perfectly oblivious to everything around him. And yet the strange stringed instrument still played!

Layer upon layer, the music grew and developed, full of heartache and longing, and yet charged also with the joy of creation. Her heart full, Rebecca watched, totally unaware of her surroundings, knowing only that she was witnessing the creation of true magic.

There were no words to these songs, but none was needed. Love, romance, battle and betrayal, intrigue and mystery – all these and much more were conjured up by the magical sounds. Rebecca saw sparkling waterfalls, heard thunder in a dark sky, and blinked at sunlight in a new morning's snow. Forests and mountains passed by; the flash of red as a fox went to ground; seagulls white against threatening black clouds; the blue-green shimmer of a diving kingfisher . . .

And then it was over. As the music came to an end, utter silence settled over the hall – even the wind in the castle's towers was still for a moment. Rebecca met the musician's eyes – and, for an instant, the two young people understood each other perfectly.

Then the clatter of the hall resumed and the spell was broken. For a moment, hurt showed in the young man's eyes, but then the professional entertainer within him took over. He joined his fellows in more of the old ballads – but his smile was like a mask, frozen on his face.

The audience – with one exception – obviously approved of the change.

'Nasty, screechy thing,' one guest commented.

'This is much better,' someone else agreed.

Rebecca gazed about her in disbelief. No one else seemed aware of what had happened, of the enchantment that had held them all for a few brief moments. They had returned immediately to the mundane, the vulgar world of her father's court, with its drunkenness and gluttony, and its mean spirit. Rebecca was left with an indefinable feeling of loss, and began even to doubt her own memory. She felt emotionally drained, her appetite gone, and the ordinary music that now played sounded thin and hollow in her ears.

The wind moaned in the towers once more, and Rebecca knew that whenever she heard that desolate noise, she would see the young man's face, hear snatches of his enchanted music, and feel the emotional longing, the yearning for faraway places, that had welled up within her.

It was all that she could do to stop herself from going to him immediately. But she knew such a thing was impossible, and instead made mental plans for when the meal was over. As soon as she could, she excused herself and went to find Emer, who was sitting at one of the other tables. Her friend looked surprised and excited by the whispered message she was given. Rebecca returned to her seat, saw Emer pass on her communication, then waited impatiently for the music to finish. As the last notes died away, she stood up and left the hall – as if heading for her rooms. Baldemar was already quite drunk and did not give her a second glance.

Instead of going to her own apartments, Rebecca doubled back and made her way up to the balcony in the Long Gallery. She positioned herself so that she could see the door which led to the store-rooms and servants' quarters, and waited. And waited. As time passed, she grew more and more nervous. Where was he? Surely he would come!

When the waiting became intolerable, she decided to take

278

matters into her own hands. Although she took the risk of being seen by the servants – and of her father's fury – she was desperate now, and ran to the two small rooms near the kitchens where the musicians were quartered. She knocked on the door, and the group's leader opened it with a smile – which disappeared as soon as he saw who their visitor was.

'My lady?' he said, bowing awkwardly.

'The musician who played the solo instrument tonight,' Rebecca gasped. 'I must talk to him.'

He looked at her for a moment, then turned back to the room. 'Boomer, the lady Rebecca wants to talk to you.'

She heard whispers from inside as the young man came to the door.

'Will you come with me to the Gallery?' she asked breathlessly.

'Why?' he asked, surprised by this unlooked-for attention.

'Get along, lad. Where's your manners?' his leader said. 'The baron's daughter wants to talk to you.' And with that, he pushed the younger player forward.

Boomer stood before her, looking sullen and tired. He glanced from side to side, as if looking for an escape route.

'Please!' Rebecca tried again. 'I heard your music. I heard it.'

At first he did not react, but then a spark flamed in his eyes.

'It was you,' he said. 'On the top table!'

'Yes. Don't you recognize me?'

'My eyesight's bad, unless things are close to me,' he told her.

'Will you come with me – please?'

He nodded, and Rebecca retraced her steps to the relative privacy of the gallery.

'Is Boomer your real name?' she asked as she led him towards the balcony.

'No – my real name's Newell,' he answered, peering intently at the pictures as they passed. 'Boomer's just a nickname the band gave me.'

'I've never heard anything like your music before,' she said as they came to a halt. 'Where does it come from?'

279

There was a moment's silence.

'There are stories in the air,' he told her. 'I just borrow them.'

'Stories here? In Edge?'

'*Especially* in a place like this. You have so much history.' He waved a hand at the portraits. 'It must be wonderful to live here.'

Rebecca was astonished. *If only you knew!* she thought.

'All the past of this place, all the people,' he went on. 'Their loves and hates, joys and sorrows . . .'

He stopped abruptly, as if suddenly realizing who he was talking to. Colour rose in his cheeks and he made as if to leave, mumbling an apology.

'Don't go,' Rebecca pleaded. 'I have no illusions about my ancestors.'

He hesitated, obviously reluctant to linger, but trapped by the need in her voice.

'How do you find all the stories?' she asked, needing to keep him talking.

'I don't,' he said simply. 'I let the music find them.'

'Through the Web?'

'I suppose so – if that's what you want to call it.'

'But it was so beautiful!'

'Perhaps I save the bad bits for when I'm on my own,' he replied, no longer smiling.

'Well , with my family, there'd be plenty of those,' Rebecca commented. 'I'll show you some of them.'

So they walked together down the endless row of portraits, and Rebecca gave the musician a running commentary. Newell looked around, but said little.

'That's Uncle Egwin,' she said. 'He went mad, and decided that he would only drink milk from virgin cows.'

'But . . .'

'I know!' she laughed. 'To this day, no one knows how they managed to fool him. That's Edriana,' Rebecca went on. 'She had fourteen children, but only two of them survived.'

'I bet her husband was pleased with her!' Newell commented sarcastically.

'He had to be quite pleased with her in the first place

to have had fourteen babies,' Rebecca replied.

The musician's reticence was gradually worn away. In spite of his earlier misgivings, he found himself warming to the baron's daughter.

'Who's this?' he asked.

'My father,' she replied. 'I hope what you played didn't come from his stories!'

'He looks bigger here.'

'He's supposed to,' Rebecca said dismissively, moving on down the Gallery. Newell stayed where he was, peering short-sightedly at the Baron's painting. He seemed particularly interested for some reason in the depiction of Baldemar's hound, Old Growler.

'When was this painted?' he asked. 'And who by?'

'Just a few months ago. The artist's name was Kedar.'

'Is the dog still here?'

'Old Growler? Yes, of course.'

'Can we see him?'

'Not now. It's feeding time, and the kennels will be in uproar. Why's he so special?'

'No reason. I just like dogs,' Newell replied.

They moved on.

'This is one of my favourites,' Rebecca said. 'My great-grandfather, Derward.' She told Newell of her ancestor's misguided attempts to find gold under blackthorn trees. By the end of her tale, they were both laughing.

'You're not like most of them,' Newell remarked, sounding rather surprised.

'You're not exactly ordinary yourself,' Rebecca replied. 'Your talent . . . '

'Is useless!' he exclaimed, suddenly fierce.

'No!'

'No one hears – not even my fellow musicians.' He spat the words out contemptuously.

'I heard!'

For a few moments, they stared at each other in silence. They felt a bond between them, but knew that a greater barrier still remained.

'Do you want to see any more?' she asked quietly.

He nodded, and they went on.

281

'This is one of the oldest,' Rebecca said. 'His name's Cadell.'

'He's an evil-looking bastard,' Newell said.

'Aptly put,' she replied. 'Apparently, he was nothing like his father, and so there were some ugly rumours at the time. But we're not supposed to tell visitors things like that!'

'Kavan,' Newell read. 'Does that *really* say Kavan?' There was a strange tremor in his voice as he pointed to the artist's signature.

'That's right,' she confirmed. Then she felt as though she had been struck by a thunderbolt. Newell's music was magical – like Kavan's *other* painting. Perhaps he could explain it to her.

'I have another painting by him,' she said tentatively. 'One that changes.'

His eyes grew round.

'Really?'

'I'll show you—' she began, then stopped suddenly as the lower door into the Great Hall creaked open. Radd hurried across the room and looked towards the balcony.

'Rebecca, are you up there?' he called, sounding worried and angry. 'Who's that with you?'

'I have to see the picture,' Newell whispered urgently, ignoring the interruption. 'Go and get it.'

'What about . . . ?' Rebecca began, as Radd started up the stairs.

'I'll take care of him,' he insisted. 'Where shall I meet you?'

'My apartment,' she whispered. 'We won't be disturbed there.' She gave him hurried directions.

'Right. Now go!'

Radd was on the balcony now, almost running towards them.

'Rebecca, please!' he called breathlessly. 'I *must* talk to you.'

'Don't hurt him,' she whispered, rooted to the spot.

'Of course not,' Newell replied. 'I'll just make him forget he saw us.'

The musician reached inside his shirt and pulled out a tiny flute. As he began to play, Radd came to an abrupt halt. Newell walked slowly towards the chamberlain, the music weaving all about him. Rebecca felt a touch of its hypnotic power but knew that it was directed at Radd and not at her. As she ran past the unmoving figure, she noticed that his eyes were glazed and unseeing.

Rebecca made the familiar journey to her secret room in the East Tower in a breathless state of excitement and fear. The sun was setting as she returned along the southern battlements with the picture wrapped in a cloth under her arm. From there she made her way through her father's apartments, knowing that he would still be drinking in the hall, and reached her own rooms without being seen. She hid the picture in a wardrobe and waited.

*   *   *

Newell led the unresisting chamberlain into the storerooms, and left him there peacefully asleep. Although he had stopped playing now, the music continued inside Radd's head. This hynoptic effect was a facet of the musician's talent that he rarely used, but he smiled with satisfaction now, knowing that the effort was justified in this case. If Rebecca really *did* have such a picture . . .

However, he did not go immediately to her apartment but first made his way to the kitchens and asked for directions to the kennels. Once there, he found Old Growler and approached the dog, making small welcoming noises with his tongue. The hound came to him readily and allowed his ears to be fondled.

But it was the dog's collar that Newell had really come to see. It was black leather, studded with metal – exactly as Kedar had painted it – except that in the portrait it had been adorned with a metal tag marked with a circular device. Newell smiled, reached within his shirt and drew forth a pendant. Engraved on the metal was the same device.

He stood up and went back into the courtyard. It seemed busier than before, but he was too intent on his purpose to take much notice.

*   *   *

Rebecca had been in her room only a few moments when she was almost startled out of her wits by Emer's head appearing round the door of the adjoining bedroom. Her friend was grinning widely.

'Well, where is he?' she demanded.

'What are you doing in here?' Rebecca gasped, her heart thumping.

'Snooping,' Emer replied happily. 'What's he like? Is he coming?'

Rebecca laughed nervously as she realized that Emer had planned to eavesdrop on what she assumed was a romantic assignation.

'He is coming here,' she said, her excitement returning as she waved her friend into the room. 'But it's not what you think.'

Emer raised her eyebrows.

'He's a wizard!' Rebecca explained. 'A real one! He's going to tell me about the magical picture.'

'A wizard?' Emer exclaimed.

'Yes. Didn't you hear his music? That was magic, just like the artists in the old legends.'

For once, her friend was speechless.

'Don't you see?' Rebecca went on breathlessly. 'He's going to explain magic to me. This is wonderful! Everything's going to be just as I want it to be from now on.'

At that moment, the outer door opened, and the two girls turned to look expectantly at the newcomer.

'I wouldn't be too sure of that if I were you,' he said.

It was a voice Rebecca had hoped never to hear again. As the man stepped into the room, she stood petrified with horror. He mocked them with a slight bow.

'Good evening, ladies,' Cranne said.

Part Two
BENEATH THE SALT

CHAPTER THIRTY-THREE

'Put these on,' Pike instructed, tossing Galen a woollen hat and a simple black cloak. 'You're too much of a celebrity round here just at the moment, and I don't want anybody to see you leaving.' With that, the grizzled soldier turned and walked away, giving Galen no chance to respond.

So the young man quickly donned the extra clothing, cast one last glance at the entrance to Cluny's basement home, and hurried after Pike.

'Where are we going?'

'North first. Can you ride?'

'I was a stable-lad, for Web's sake,' Galen replied. 'What do you think?'

'Being able to shovel horse manure doesn't necessarily mean you can ride,' Pike responded testily.

'I can ride,' Galen insisted.

Pike led him into the back alleys. They were hurrying, and Galen was soon sweating beneath his extra layers. Tarrant's lieutenant was not in uniform, and carried a dagger but no sword. Few people gave the pair a second glance. They were met outside a tavern on the northern outskirts of the town by two more soldiers, also out of uniform. The soldiers eyed Galen curiously, but did not speak to him. They had two horses waiting for the travellers, who rode away with only a few words being exchanged.

Pike set their pace at a steady trot along the main road which led north from the town. However, once they were well out of sight of Edgefield's last buildings, he slowed to a walk, and they turned on to a track heading east.

'You can take those off now,' he said gruffly, and Galen removed the hat and cape.

'We can be in Cutover by nightfall,' Pike remarked. 'That is, if you're capable of staying in the saddle at anything more than a trot.'

Galen did his best to ignore the scorn in the soldier's voice – he was more interested in the news of their destination. Cutover was a small town just over the border into Quarry, the adjoining barony, and, like Edgefield, was less than a league from the salt-flats. He had been there on a handful of occasions, but remembered little of the place.

'Is that where we'll meet the Archaeologists?' he asked.

'Yes. But before we get there, there are a few things I need to tell you.'

'Go ahead.' Galen was eager to learn what was expected of him.

'This isn't a game,' Pike said, glancing at him. 'There are lives at stake, including yours, so listen carefully. Can you do that and ride at the same time?'

Galen reined in his mount. Pike went on for a few paces, then stopped and twisted in the saddle to look back, his expression carefully neutral.

'Listen!' Galen began, his temper frayed by the events of the day and by the needling of the older man. 'Do you want me or not? Tarrant seemed quite keen for me to join you . . . and no matter what you think of me, I'm willing to try. I'm not stupid and I'm not afraid. I'll ride and listen and remember.' He faltered as a slow smile spread across Pike's face. 'If you don't think I'm good enough for you, I can turn back now,' he finished quietly.

'You could turn back now, though I wouldn't advise it,' the veteran replied. 'Later, when you're better informed, you won't have that option. You'd be dead before you went a hundred paces.' His voice remained soft but boldly assured. 'Make your choice.'

The two men stared at each other, measuring and being measured. Galen knew that he was being tested.

'I'm going on,' he said firmly. 'Tell me.'

'Good,' Pike responded, as Galen brought his horse alongside. 'When we get to Cutover, you'll meet a man named Redfern. He's your contact, and your link back to us. He's an innkeeper, so you shouldn't have any difficulty in thinking up an excuse to meet him.' This time Pike's comment was not a jibe but a simple statement of fact.

'Which tavern?' Galen asked.

'The Raven. On the salt-side. Know it?'

Galen shook his head.

'You won't forget it once you've been there,' Pike said, grinning. 'Or Redfern for that matter. And if he tells you to do something, you do it. All right?'

'Yes.'

'After that, you'll be introduced to the Archaeologists,' Pike went on. 'This particular group is led by a man named Peyton.'

'I know them,' Galen said. 'Or rather I know *of* them.' Peyton's group was notorious, and had visited Edgefield on several occasions.

'Do they know you?' Pike asked quickly.

'I doubt it,' he replied. 'No. I'm sure they don't.'

Pike looked thoughtful. 'In any case,' he said, 'news of your recent exploits won't have spread that far yet. At least, let's hope so.'

'How do I join the group?' Galen asked.

'They're always looking for new members,' the soldier told him. 'Someone to do the dirty work.' He grinned. 'You know how they live?'

'I've a fair idea.'

'You'll have to look out for yourself,' Pike added.

'I've been doing that all my life,' Galen said, on the defensive again.

'Anyway,' the older man went on, 'buy them a few drinks and clink a few coins in your pocket, and you'll be their friend for life – or at least until the inn shuts!'

'I don't have much money,' Galen pointed out.

'You'll have enough.' Pike tapped his jerkin. 'I'll have to trust you to spend it wisely.'

'Where am I supposed to have got the money from? I don't exactly look like a wealthy merchant.'

'How much do you think I'm going to give you?' Pike asked, laughing.

'I just want to get my story straight,' Galen replied seriously.

'There's hope for you yet,' the soldier commented. 'Use your imagination. Don't admit to anything, but imply that you *acquired* it.'

'And why do I want to join the Archaeologists?'

'Tell them you came between a man and his bride-to-be,' Pike answered, grinning. 'They'll appreciate that.'

'But don't tell them the real story?'

'Absolutely not. They'd expect you to lie about it, and we don't want anyone connecting you with Rebecca.' Pike was pleased that his pupil was thinking things through.

'Then what?' Galen asked.

'You go south with them – probably in the next day or so.'

'How do you know?' The behaviour of Archaeologists was generally regarded as completely unpredictable.

'Two reasons,' Pike replied promptly. 'The first is that they're running out of money, which means no more drink – and the girls won't be so interested any more. Your arrival might rectify the drink situation temporarily, but I may arrange some gambling losses to speed the process up a bit. The second is the merchant Shahan, who's been waiting to cross the salt for two days now. He'll be getting impatient, and as their money runs low, his gold will seem even more attractive.'

Galen nodded. It did not even occur to him to ask how Pike knew all this.

'Where will we be headed?' he asked.

'Riano – that's Shahan's destination. And it's where we want you to go.'

'That's Baron Jarlath's place, isn't it?'

'Yes.' Pike looked at the young man in surprise.

'Friend or foe?' Galen asked flippantly.

'This is not a joking matter, boy!' Pike snapped fiercely. Galen's smile disappeared. 'Sorry,' he muttered.

'Jarlath is not a man to be trifled with,' Pike went on. 'Where he stands politically is no concern of yours.'

'If lives are at stake, *including mine*,' Galen shot back, angry with himself now, 'I have a right to know.'

'Very well,' Pike replied, relenting slightly. 'It's no secret that Jarlath is one of the foremost opponents of Montfort's ideas. Whether he takes his opposition any further is another matter – and that's what we're trying to find out.'

Galen knew a little of the king's proposed reforms, but the implication of his companion's words was obvious. *Foe, then,* he thought. 'What am I to do there?'

'We have a man in Riano, inside Jarlath's court. Davin. You're to contact him – discreetly, mind you – give him a message, and get any report from him back to Redfern.'

'How will Davin know me?'

'By code. When you contact him, use a sentence with the words "fire" and "business" in it. He'll reply with one containing "smoke" and "money". If he says anything else, you've either got the wrong man, or an exchange is impossible at that time. If his reply uses the word "water", it means danger, either to him or you – or both. If that happens, get away fast. If his reply is as expected, then you answer with the word "journey". After that, it's up to him. Got all that?'

Galen repeated the code words, fixing them in his memory.

'Think you can handle that?' Pike asked.

'I don't see why not,' Galen said. 'What does Davin look like?'

'Small, clean-shaven, black hair, green eyes, delicate hands,' the veteran replied. 'He's a scribe to Jarlath's chief treasurer, and that places him close to a lot of interesting information. Don't let his appearance fool you – he's one of the bravest, smartest men I've ever known.'

'Anything else I should know?'

'Yes. Keep an eye on Shahan,' Pike said. 'He may not be exactly what he seems. He's a merchant all right, but we're sure that's not the whole story, and it will be interesting to know what he gets up to in Riano.'

'I'll keep my eyes open,' Galen promised.

'Do that,' the soldier advised. 'And not just with Shahan.'

Galen nodded, fear, excitement and anticipation knotting in his stomach.

'One last word of advice,' Pike said sternly, 'and I mean this. No heroics. Do what you have to, no more. You're new to this game, so don't try to run before you can walk. Any more questions?'

'Not for now.'

'Let's ride then, or we'll be out all night.' Pike spurred his horse into action and Galen followed, intoxicated by the speed and power of the sleek animal, and relishing the thunder of the hooves and the rush of wind in his face. Until the last few days his life had proceeded at a sedate trot. He was galloping towards a very different future now.

*   *   *

They slowed their pace as dusk closed in and let their horses walk for a while, the moist breath of the animals white in the cooling air. It was dark by the time they reached Cutover, but Pike led them through the streets confidently.

The Raven was a large, timber-built inn with a cobbled yard; a warm yellow light spilled invitingly from its windows. As they drew up, a young lad appeared and led their mounts to the stables. Pike and Galen went inside. The bar seemed more like a barn than anything else, with an enormously high roof crossed by massive beams. The furniture was simple and functional, and the floor was spotlessly clean. Although there were a few customers, most leaning against the long bar, conversation seemed subdued. The reason for this was not hard to find. Behind the counter stood the biggest man Galen had ever seen. He was at least a head and shoulders taller than Galen, himself slightly taller than average, and his arms were heavily muscled, and covered with thick red-brown hair – which also covered his head and most of his face. What you could see of his expression revealed a wary eye and a vague look of disapproval. He was not a man you would approach carelessly, much less annoy.

'That's Redfern?' Galen whispered.

'Yes,' Pike replied. 'The most sober man I know.' He led his young recruit to the bar, and ordered two mugs of beer.

Redfern put them down with a bang.

'It's not good for you,' he remarked in a deep, lugubrious voice. 'Are you sure you want it?'

'Yes,' Pike answered firmly.

'I just wanted you to know,' the innkeeper said, as Galen

stared at him curiously. He had never come across a landlord quite like this before!

'Redfern, my old friend, this is Galen,' Pike said loudly. The hum of conversation did not waver at this announcement, and the veteran smiled.

'Glad to meet you.' Redfern extended a huge hand which Galen took with some trepidation. In the event, the barkeeper's grip was firm, but failed to crush any bones.

'We could do with a meal,' Pike said, sipping his beer appreciatively.

'Go round the back,' Redfern replied. 'Take your drinks with you, if you still want them.'

'I wouldn't waste this,' the soldier replied. 'Come on,' he told Galen, and led the way past the end of the bar into a corridor. Picking one of several doors, Pike entered a cosy room furnished with a table and several well-upholstered chairs.

'This is for Redfern's *special* guests,' he remarked, sitting down and motioning Galen to do the same.

'Why do people come here at all?' the young man asked. 'He's not exactly welcoming, is he? It's as though he resents you drinking anything at all.'

'That's just his habit,' Pike replied. 'People come because he serves the best beer in Cutover. Try it.'

Galen took a sip from his mug, swallowed, then took a larger mouthful. 'I see what you mean,' he said.

'Being considered eccentric can have its advantages,' Pike explained. 'It means that people don't look for anything else odd about you.'

'Such as acting as go-between for special messengers?' Galen suggested.

'Exactly.' Pike produced a small leather bag from his jerkin and passed it across the table. 'Don't spend it all at once.'

Galen loosened the draw-string and peered inside.

'Think that'll be enough?' Pike asked, smiling.

'It's more than I've ever had before,' was the quiet answer.

'Don't let Peyton and his lot know how much you've got,' Pike advised.

'I'm not stupid!' Galen exclaimed.

'So you keep telling me,' the veteran replied. He drew a

folded sheet of paper from his pocket and gave it to his companion. 'This needs to get to Davin,' he said. 'You should try and hand it over personally, but if for some reason that's impossible, then make sure the means you use are secure. Don't go handing it to a servant and assuming it'll get to him.'

Galen nodded, unfolding the paper and glancing at the contents.

'What is it?' he asked. 'A receipt?'

'Yes,' Pike replied 'The sort of thing treasury scribes have about them all the time.'

'In code?'

Pike nodded. 'Keep it safe. Burn it if you can't get it to Davin.'

Galen stowed it away. 'What do I say if anyone else sees it?' he asked.

'Pretend you can't read it. Make up some story . . . you found it, it looked important. Play dumb. You've got the looks for the part.'

'But it'll be difficult for me to hide my natural intelligence,' Galen responded.

'Just try,' Pike answered. They grinned at each other.

Redfern came in, carrying a large tray.

'This is good,' he commented enthusiastically. 'Eat well.'

He put the heavily laden tray down, and enticing savoury smells filled the room.

'Redfern, Galen is one of us,' Pike told him. 'He will be needing your help at some time in the future.'

'No problem,' the innkeeper replied, a vast smile displaying two rows of sound white teeth. 'As always.' He left, closing the door behind him.

'That's it?' Galen asked.

'That's it. Redfern never forgets a face,' Pike replied. 'Or a name.'

'I'm glad he's on our side,' the young man said with feeling. They turned to their food and ate in companionable silence, doing justice to the excellent cooking and huge portions.

'Right. Pretend I'm Davin,' Pike said as he belched and patted his stomach with satisfaction.

'What? Oh.'

'I'm busy,' Pike said, changing his voice and pretending to write. 'What do you want?'

'Er . . . my master wants to know about the recent fire in the business district,' Galen replied.

'I hate to think of all that money going up in smoke,' Pike replied. 'What does he want to know?'

'He's just returned from a journey and needs to find out what his losses are,' Galen improvised.

Pike sat back and relaxed. 'Not bad,' he said, and Galen grinned.

'Can you use that thing?' Pike asked, indicating the dagger in Galen's belt.

'If I have to.'

'Let's hope you don't.' He paused, studying the young man. 'Tarrant may have been right about you, after all.'

'There's nothing like praise for instilling confidence in your colleagues,' Galen remarked.

Pike laughed, then grew serious again.

'There are times,' he said, 'when it's right to be afraid. Remember that. Mess this up, and you may not get a second chance.'

'I'll remember,' Galen promised.

'Why are you doing this?' the veteran asked quietly.

'Because I know Montfort's a good man,' Galen began. 'And if he's opposed to the conditions that killed my mother, then he deserves supporting.'

'I see,' Pike said thoughtfully.

'Besides, I didn't want to be a stable-lad for ever.'

'Fair enough.' The soldier drained his mug. 'Sorry, Redfern,' he remarked, then stood up. 'Ready to meet your new colleagues?'

They went out into the bar again, and asked the inn-keeper where the Archaeologists were most likely to be. They had apparently last been seen at The Shepherd, but had probably moved on by now. Redfern's diagnosis proved correct. The Shepherd was much too quiet, so Pike and Galen moved on to The Quarryman. Just as they were approaching the tavern, a large, bearded man flew out of the doors backwards, and crashed to the floor. He lay there for a moment, then groaned, got gingerly to his feet and staggered back towards the tavern's entrance.

'My money's good, you scumrat!' he bellowed. 'Why don't you . . .'

The rest of his question was lost in a rush of sound as he wrenched open the door. The noise of fighting and splintering furniture came from within.

'Oh, good,' Pike remarked. 'We've found them.'

CHAPTER THIRTY-FOUR

Galen started forward, but was halted by Pike's hand on his arm.

'Wait till it's a bit quieter,' the old soldier advised.

'No,' Galen replied determinedly. 'This is a good opportunity.'

Pike held his gaze for a few moments, then shrugged and let him past. Galen ran lightly to the doorway and slipped inside – to be greeted by a scene of absolute mayhem. Tables had been overturned, broken chairs lay against the walls, and shards of glass littered the floor. There were several fights in progress, fists were flying, and a wrestling match was taking place on top of the bar. Galen hesitated, glancing wildly around the room, and wondering desperately how to identify the men he had come to find.

In the centre of the room, two antagonists circled each other warily. One, a tall thin character with straggly black hair, held a knife, while the other, shorter and rounder in stature, was unarmed.

'You Archaeologists are all the same!' the tall man shouted. 'Cheats, liars and thieves!'

'Let's talk about this over a drink,' the other suggested, his eyes never leaving the threatening blade. But his opponent only laughed nastily.

'I'm going to cut your gizzards out,' he announced. 'Then we'll see if you still want a drink!' He lunged, but the other man dodged out of the way. However, in avoiding the thrust, he stumbled, tried to catch at a lop-sided table, and ended up sprawled on the floor. His assailant closed in, grinning.

Galen quickly stepped between the two men, his own knife held in an unwavering hand, his expression calm.

'Out of my way, boy!' the dark man growled, but Galen didn't move, though his heart was beating wildly. The other occupants of the tavern grew suddenly quiet, aware of this new, and unexpected confrontation. Their own personal battles were put aside in favour of the intriguing spectacle.

'Say please,' Galen reprimanded the knife-fighter.

'What's your game?' The tall man's gaze darted around, looking for help, but he found none, and suddenly had the air of a cruel bully who had just been confronted with the elder brother of his intended victim.

'I don't like to see a knife used on an unarmed man,' Galen replied evenly. 'This . . . ' he waved his own dagger slightly, ' . . . makes it even.'

'But they're scum!' the other replied. 'Why side with them?'

'Any man deserves a fair hearing. Carving him up first is not my idea of justice.'

'Aye,' came the comment from the floor. 'My gizzards deserve better than that!'

There were a few bursts of laughter around the room at this remark, and one of the onlookers added that he'd not noticed much honour among knife-fighters before now.

'He was cheating!' the tall man exclaimed shrilly, and waved his free hand at the playing cards now strewn across the floor. Several bystanders muttered their agreement.

'And he was playing with money he owed me!' the barman added. He had emerged from his hiding place behind the bar, and was surveying the wreckage with dismay. 'This one was threatening me, trying to get more!' He pointed to the man who had been temporarily ejected, but the broad-shouldered, bearded man just grinned nonchalantly at the innkeeper's indignation.

'Keep the money,' the prostrate Archaeologist said. 'All of it. You're—'

'That seems a reasonable offer,' Galen put in firmly. 'Are you going to take it?' His hand was still steady, and his eyes had not left his opponent, who hesitated, not knowing how to react.

'But what about . . . ?' the barman began.

'Shut up!' the dark man snapped. 'Get out – all of you! Before I change my mind.'

'And take those disgusting animals with you,' the innkeeper added.

In the ensuing silence, the fallen man got slowly to his feet, dusted himself off, then turned and walked out into the street. Five other men detached themselves from their stilled fights and followed, some of them picking up small boxes on the way. Knives were sheathed, and Galen turned to leave.

'You'd better not show your pretty face in here again,' the dark man warned. 'Unless you want it rearranging.' Now that he knew he was not going to have to fight, he was regaining his bravado.

'Thanks for the advice,' Galen replied. 'I certainly wouldn't want to end up looking like you.' He closed the door behind him with exaggerated care, and looked round at his new companions.

'There's *nothing* left?' one of the younger ones demanded. It was half-question, half-accusation.

'No,' the barrel-like man replied cheerfully. 'Looks like we'll have to go back to work, lads,' He spotted Galen then, and beckoned him to join them. 'I am in your debt, sir. Unfortunately I have no money with which to repay you.'

'You're Peyton, aren't you?' Galen said.

'Indeed I am.' A smile spread over the round face.

*   *   *

Half an hour later, Galen was sitting with the six Archaeologists in the main bar of The Raven. They were each sipping carefully at the beer bought for them by Galen; they knew that it might be their last for some time. The offer of hospitality by their new acquaintance had been readily accepted, and his suggestion of Redfern's tavern was also agreed upon – Peyton pointing out that they had already outstayed their welcome in each of Cutover's other establishments. The landlord watched over them from behind the bar, having served the round with his habitual

298

bad grace. Pike was an unnoticed observer, having entered the bar a few moments after the Archaeologists and their new companion.

Peyton introduced his comrades to Galen. Holmes was the man who had been thrown out of The Quarryman, and Milner was a sharp-faced, grey-bearded man with keen blue eyes. The three younger members of the group were Kibble, who was tall and wiry with ever-shifting eyes, Flank, who was short, solid and morose, and Drain, the youngest at sixteen years or so, whose hair was forever falling into his eyes. Galen introduced himself as Grant, hoping that no one in the tavern would remember his earlier introduction, and told them that he came from a small village in Edge. They listened willingly enough – Galen had bought the drinks, after all – and showed little surprise when he expressed an interest in joining them.

'It's the only life,' Holmes remarked, peering into his tankard.

'We know that,' Peyton replied, 'but it's an uncertain sort of existence. Why do you want to enlist in the glorious ranks of Archaeology?'

'It's a bit tricky for me at home just now,' Galen replied.

'Yes?' Peyton prompted, scenting a story.

'There was a little trouble . . . with a girl . . . and her betrothed.'

'Where have we heard *that* story before,' Milner remarked.

'I thought it would be best,' Galen continued, 'to make myself scarce for a while. And where else could I look for a bit of adventure in this dull world?'

'A man after my own heart!' Holmes commented.

'And I've heard the stories of the treasure, of course,' Galen concluded.

'You'll be picking last,' Drain said quickly.

'What?'

'If we find anything in the salt,' Peyton explained, 'we pick out what we want in order of seniority. Me first, then Milner here, then Holmes, Kibble, Flank and Drain. And then you.'

'What if we only find six items?'

'Tough,' the other replied. 'Those are the terms. You still want to join?'

Galen nodded.

'How do I move up?' he asked.

'You wait for one of us to get pickled,' Holmes told him, laughing.

'Or until someone leaves for other reasons,' Peyton added. 'If anyone joins after you, *they* go to the bottom of the pile.'

'Of course you could always start your own band,' Milner put in, grinning. 'Then you'd be picking first—'

'But you wouldn't last long,' Peyton completed. 'Not as a rookie. You ever been across the salt?'

'No.'

'Have you got a beek?'

'No.'

'Then you'd better stick close to us unless you've got the money to buy one,' Peyton advised.

'Maybe he can catch a wild one!' Kibble put in. They all laughed at this ludicrous idea.

'You answer to me at all times when we're on the salt,' Peyton went on. 'On solid land you're free to do as you please, but we generally stick together, good times and bad. Clear?'

Galen nodded.

'*Still* want to join us?'

'Yes.'

'So now we are seven,' Peyton said, sounding pleased. 'Nice round number.'

Each man raised their tankard to toast their new recruit. *So far, so good,* Galen thought, resisting the temptation to glance in Pike's direction.

'You'll have an easy ride to start with,' Holmes told him cheerfully. 'We'll have lubbers with us.'

'Lubbers?'

'Passengers,' the big man explained. 'Off-salt travellers.'

'In this case, a merchant and his playmates,' Peyton added. 'They pay us to see them safely across the salt.'

'Playmates?'

'Bodyguards. Two of them.' Peyton spread his hands wide in mock surprise. 'Anyone would think he didn't trust us!'

'But we could surely take on three men between us,' Galen said.

'Oh-oh!' Milner exclaimed, raising his eyebrows. 'We'll have to watch our backs with this one.'

Galen wondered whether he had gone too far. He had been trying to impress his new colleagues, but he did not want to lose their trust.

'We could,' Peyton replied. 'But it would not be good for us in the long run. In our business, it's better to be trustworthy. If you want to try anything like that, you'd better make sure the prize is worth it. News like that travels fast round the salt, and we need the lubbers' money. We can't just rely on finding treasure.'

'You can starve that way, unless you get lucky,' Milner added.

'Not to mention the fact that digging it out can get a little *too* exciting sometimes,' Holmes put in.

This comment was the signal for the older Archaeologists to launch into tales of their various adventures. Galen listened attentively as they told of narrow escapes and dramatic moments, and of discoveries that ranged from the valuable to the worthless, from the mundane to the downright bizarre. There was no mention of stone sculptures or obscure coded messages, and Galen did not like to ask about them specifically. He was content to listen and accept the oft-told, probably exaggerated stories, and wonder how many of the former colleagues mentioned had retired to a peaceful old age. His guess was not many, and the way his companions joked about being pickled made him wonder about the fate that several earlier 'rookies' must have suffered. What was it Pike had said? *Someone to do their dirty work.* Galen smiled inwardly. *It's too late now, in any case,* he told himself. *And I want to do this!*

Galen was fascinated by his new companions, in spite of his misgivings about their way of life. Their humorous, though sometimes ill-tempered cameraderie was easy to identify with, and he found their tales wonderfully entertaining. Apparently, this was not the case with the younger Archaeologists, who had obviously heard it all before. They contributed very little to the conversation. Kibble and Drain looked openly bored, and gazed continuously round the room in search of something more interesting. Flank merely stared into the diminishing depths of his beer.

Peyton lifted his tankard one last time, drained it, then stared into the empty vessel meaningfully.

'I don't suppose . . . ' he began, glancing at Galen.

The new apprentice shook his head.

'I'll need what little I have left for provisions,' he said.

'Oh, well. It's late anyway, and we have to be up early tomorrow,' Peyton said resignedly. 'Go and find Shahan. Tell him we'll leave in the morning. Early.'

'Why me?' Flank complained, having been roused from his morose stupor.

''Because I said so,' his leader replied. 'Or does Grant move up a rung?'

Flank heaved himself to his feet and went off, grumbling to himself.

'Half the money before we go!' Peyton called after the retreating figure. He was about to shout further instructions, but subsided after a stern look from Redfern.

A few moments later, Pike rose from his seat and went out into the night.

'What does Shahan deal in?' Galen asked.

'Furs, spices, jewels,' Peyton replied quietly. 'Pretty much anything that's light and valuable.'

'That's not all, though,' Drain said knowingly.

'Drain is our very own political expert,' Holmes commented derisively. 'He reckons Shahan's a *spy*,' he added dramatically.

'He *is*,' the youngest Archaeologist retorted. 'Stands to reason. He's always got letters and such on him.'

'You've read them, have you?' Peyton enquired mildly.

'Don't need to,' Drain responded. 'He's as tight as *that* with Jarlath.' He held up a fist clenched round his other thumb.

'With Jarlath's *wife*, maybe,' Holmes replied, mimicking Drain's hands with a rather more crude gesture of his own.

'You're stupid, you are!' Drain said disgustedly as the others laughed. 'There are things I know . . . ' He brushed back his errant hair.

'Whoa!' Holmes exclaimed, mocking the lad's fervour.

'Secrets yet?'

Drain refused to rise to the bait and sat back, his cheeks flushed. Galen made a mental note to check whether there was anything susbstantial behind these seemingly facile claims.

'It's Shahan's gold that interests me,' Milner said. 'Not his letters.'

Galen was following this exchange intently, though trying not to appear too interested.

'Where are we going then?' he asked.

'Riano,' Peyton replied. 'City of a thousand vices.'

'Well, three anyway,' Holmes amended.

'Mae, Selia . . . ' Milner hesitated, looking puzzled. 'Who's the third?'

'Este, of course.'

'Right. How could I forget her?'

'I can think of better ways of wasting my money,' Kibble remarked sourly.

'That's only because you wouldn't know what to do with them when you got there,' Holmes replied, grinning. 'Perhaps you'd better ask Grant here to give you some lessons.'

'So that some angry suitor can chase me out of town?' the younger man sneered.

Holmes turned to Galen with a resigned expression, his hands outspread.

'You see what I have to put up with?' he remarked plaintively. 'Archaeologists used to be moral degenerates.' He shook his head sadly. 'Those were the days.'

Galen grinned, while Kibble and Drain exchanged glances, then gazed up at the rafters in long-suffering silence. Galen, not knowing exactly how he would fit in to the group, but wanting to gain the confidence of both divisions, said nothing for a while. The beer had long since run out and the only sound came from the intermittent scuffling of the beeks in their boxes under the table.

Redfern came out from behind the bar, and the Archaeologists watched his approach in wary silence. He placed a wicker basket piled high with chunks of bread on the table.

'Eat,' the giant of a man instructed. 'You should soak up that stuff! The bread is on the house.' With that, he turned and strode away. There was a moment of astonished silence.

'We should come here more often!' Holmes said. Soon they were all chewing vigorously; it was plain fare, but welcome none the less.

'You realize that this is a fiendish plot to sober us up,' Holmes remarked between mouthfuls.

'Sober?' Peyton exclaimed. 'We've not had enough to get drunk in the first place!'

'Just looking at that man is enough to sober anyone up,' Milner added. 'No wonder this place is always half-empty.'

While they were eating, Pike came back in and took his place at the bar.

'How long will it take to get to Riano?' Galen asked.

'Depends on the quicksalt,' Peyton answered. 'Shahan won't want too many stops . . . Four, five days maybe.'

'You used to walking?' Milner asked.

'I'll manage,' Galen replied. 'Why don't we use horses?'

'You got one?' Holmes asked immediately.

'No.' Galen saw Pike smile.

'Pity.'

'Horses are useless on the salt,' Peyton explained. 'Even when it's stable, their hooves can go through the crust, and they'll break a leg if you're going too fast. And they get spooked when the quicksalt shifts.'

'They need too much water,' Milner added. 'Most of what they'd have to carry would be their own supplies, so we'd probably end up walking anyway. They're just too heavy.'

'What about the goods we have to transport?'

'As our junior member, you get to carry it,' Holmes replied. Just as Galen was about to object, the bearded face split into a grin.

'You'll get used to Holmes' juvenile humour eventually,' Drain advised Galen. He was obviously relieved that he would no longer be the older man's target.

'Shahan will have a sledge and dogs to pull it,' Peyton said. 'We take only what we can carry comfortably.'

'Salt by night, travel light,' Milner and Holmes recited together, then slapped themselves on the side of the head with the palms of their hands. They burst out laughing as the younger members of the group looked on in disgust.

'You'd think they'd be able to remember something

simple without it having to rhyme,' Kibble remarked sarcastically. 'At *their* age!'

His comment only served to redouble the others' enjoyment of their joke.

'That's the trouble with the younger generation today,' Milner gasped. 'No sense of tradition.'

'Better than no sense at all,' Drain responded, though he too was smiling now, infected at last by their absurdity. Only Kibble remained stony-faced.

'Now that you know the Archaeologists' motto,' Peyton told Galen, 'your education is complete. From tomorrow, you're one of us.'

'What do I need to take?'

'A blanket, food, and water. Get a leather bottle – Redfern will fix you up, if you've any coin left. The rest we take care of together.'

'Where are we sleeping tonight?' Kibble wanted to know.

'At Pia's,' Peyton replied.

'Hold on!' Holmes responded. 'She's a very obliging girl, I'll admit, but it'll be a bit overcrowded, with seven of us.'

'There's plenty of room,' their leader stated.

Holmes looked distinctly unhappy.

'If you're worried about privacy,' Milner said, 'it's a warm night. You can take her up to the roof.'

'Thanks very much!'

'Watch out for bats though,' Drain added.

'And owls,' Kibble put in, enjoying himself. 'They might mistake your rump for a fat, juicy rat!'

'Laugh if you want,' Holmes said. 'Jealousy is a terrible thing in one so young.'

Galen got the feeling that this exchange would have continued happily for some time, but Flank entered the tavern then, and rejoined the group.

'Dawn tomorrow,' he reported sullenly. 'Outside The Flagon.'

'Where's the money?' Peyton asked hopefully.

'He wouldn't give me any,' Flank replied. 'He'll give us half as we set off. Said that was his best offer.'

'Cheek!' Peyton began.

'Anyone would think he didn't trust us!' the others completed for him in unison.

CHAPTER THIRTY-FIVE

Pia reacted philosophically when the seven men arrived at her small home – it was obviously not the first time this had happened. She and Holmes disappeared, ignoring the various comments that accompanied their departure, leaving the others to spend a cramped and uncomfortable night wherever they could. Peyton and Milner naturally claimed the best sleeping places, and were soon snoring contentedly.

Galen was less fortunate, and curled up on the floor in his blanket, using his leather bottle as a pillow. These two items had been his only purchases, Peyton having advised him that everything else would be taken care of in the morning. During the transaction, Galen had been able to let Redfern – and Pike, who was seated nearby – know of the proposed journey. Although Pike had not spoken, he had acknowledged the news with a slight nod, and did not follow when Peyton's group left The Raven. Galen had taken this to mean that he was on his own now.

The Archaeologists rose at first light and gathered together their few belongings. These consisted of cloth backpacks, a few items of clothing, water bottles, and special lightweight digging implements, together with the beeks. Holmes and Pia emerged from their hideaway and bid each other a fond farewell, to the accompaniment of bleary-eyed laughter and a few ribald remarks.

'Throw a bucket of water over them,' Peyton suggested. 'Otherwise we'll never get away.'

'It'll take more than that to cool their ardour,' Milner replied. 'Look at them. You can almost see smoke!'

'Ignore them, my love,' Holmes responded, 'They are old and jealous, and *all* their parts are cold.'

306

Eventually, however, all was ready and the seven set off for The Flagon. Shahan was already there, pacing impatiently. Galen looked carefully at the merchant, and saw a tall, thin man, with black hair and sharp eyes in an angular, humourless face. His clothes were of rich fabrics, and showed little sign of wear, but his boots were solid and practical and had obviously covered a good few leagues in their time.

Behind him, standing quite still and staring suspiciously at the newcomers, were his two bodyguards. They were both large, muscular men. One was completely bald, his skin almost grey in colour, while the other's hair was blond and cut so close to his head that it looked like the bristles of a brush. They both had short swords attached to their belts. Galen thought they looked a sinister pair. Beside the guards was the merchant's sledge. His cargo was covered with a tarpaulin, and Galen eyed this speculatively, wondering whether it would be worth the risk of trying to see what it covered. Pike's words came back to him. *No heroics. Do what you have to, no more.* The sledge itself was made of strong, light wood, and was carried for the time being on detachable wheels. Behind them were the flat wooden runners which would be used when crossing the salt. Four large hounds were harnessed to a miniature pole at the front of the sledge. As the dogs and caged beeks scented each other, there was an exchange of growling and hissing.

'I'm so pleased you have decided to honour me with your presence at last,' Shahan snapped, his voice dripping with sarcasm.

'Always glad to be of service,' Peyton returned easily, bowing to the merchant and smiling.

'Then let's get started before any more of the day is wasted.'

'The money?' Peyton put in quickly, his tone still amiable. 'Half before we go, as we agreed . . . '

Shahan took out his purse, counted out several coins and handed them over with ill-concealed distaste.

'Now let's go!' he ordered.

'I regret to say that there will be a short delay,' Peyton said calmly, 'while my colleague here goes to buy some provisions.' He flipped a coin to Milner, who caught it deftly and turned to go. He was stopped by the merchant's command.

'No!' Shahan exclaimed. 'We leave immediately. I've waited long enough – I could be halfway round the eastern rim by now.'

'But we won't get far without food,' Peyton pointed out.

'I had anticipated that,' the merchant retorted contemptuously, 'and I have food enough for all.' He pointed to the sledge.

'May I see?'

'Show him,' Shahan ordered, and the bald guard lifted a corner of the canopy. Peyton inspected the stores, then nodded in approval.

'May we proceed now?' the angry merchant enquired.

'Of course.' The Archaeologist smiled at this unexpected bonus, and the party set off through the quiet early morning streets. As they left the town, they paused only to fill their waterskins at a pump, then followed a farm trail towards the salt. The dogs stepped out purposefully, and pulled their load with ease. Before long, they were manoeuvring the sleigh over the protective banks and ditches, and were soon at the edge of the salt.

Galen stared at the vast white expanse, feeling suddenly overawed – and a little lost. The flats glittered in the early morning sun, blinding and apparently endless.

'Your new home,' Peyton remarked, noticing the young man's rapt expression. 'Beautiful, isn't it?'

'Yes.' The reply was hardly more than a whisper.

'But not kind,' the other added. 'You have to earn anything you take from the salt. And it can be deadly hard work.' He paused before adding, 'Last chance. You still want to come with us?'

'Yes,' Galen replied promptly, his voice firm now.

'Good,' Peyton said approvingly. 'Then you can start by carrying this.' He handed over his well-worn spade. 'You'll need your own soon, and you might as well get used to carrying one.'

They grinned at each other in understanding as Galen slung the tool over his shoulder with the strap provided.

By now the cart wheels had been removed and stowed away, and the sledge sat square upon the crystals. Peyton, who seemed to have grown in stature as soon as they reached the salt, made sure that all was ready, and then led them southward. The barrel-like man was on home ground now, and his authority was unquestioned. He set the pace, steady but unhurried, and walked at the head of the group with Milner. Shahan came next, striding beside the sledge with his bodyguards close behind. After them came the ebullient Holmes and the almost silent Flank. These two could hardly have been more different in temperament or physique, but they seemed content to trudge along together.

Galen joined Kibble and Drain at the rear. He had been out on to the salt while at Edge, but this time, he was seeing everything anew. The crunch of their footsteps, the whispering rasp of the sledge, the tang in the air – all combined to enhance his feeling of being fully alive.

After they had travelled a short distance, Peyton, Holmes and Drain each released their beeks from their cages. They had acted at the same time, as if by some unspoken agreement, and Galen had seen no signal pass between them. The three little creatures delighted in their new freedom, and darted about inquisitively, sniffing the air, circling the entire party, and staring at the placid hounds. For a short time their plaintive yowls – and those of their still confined companions – filled the air, then they quietened and spread out like scouts as the caravan headed deeper on to the salt. Galen watched their antics and took advantage of their release to start up a conversation with his new colleagues. In spite of the wonder of the morning, he was anxious to learn all he could about his new profession, and about their 'lubber'. He was determined to prove that Tarrant's trust had not been misplaced, and his own age and inexperience made Kibble and Drain the most obvious place to start.

'Do you all have beeks, then?' he asked.

'Yes,' Kibble replied shortly, his eyes flicking from side to side as always.

'But we don't let them all out at once,' Drain added.

'Why not?'

'They get tired, and they fight sometimes,' the youngster explained. 'This way we always have some that are rested and alert.'

'And they can be a bit of a problem when they're on heat,' Kibble added. 'Takes their minds off their work.'

'But we can tell when that's going to happen,' Drain muttered, flicking his hair from his eyes.

'How?' Galen asked.

Kibble laughed, a malicious glint in his eyes.

'Their fur turns pink, then red,' he replied. 'Rather like Drain's face now.'

The youngest of the group was indeed blushing furiously, but Galen refrained from smiling at the young man's discomfort.

'Is three enough to give us proper warning then?' he asked.

'Plenty.'

'So why do you carry so many?'

'Because some of them are less reliable than others,' Drain answered pointedly. 'Kibble's is quite capable of running away at any time.'

'Rubbish!'

'Then why don't you ever let her go near the rim?' Drain insisted, sensing his advantage and intent on exacting revenge. 'Eh?'

'I'd back mine in a crisis any time,' Kibble said defensively.

Drain spat his derision.

'In any case, we each have one,' Kibble went on, 'because they'd *all* be needed if we had to split up for any reason.'

'Yeah,' Drain agreed. 'The salt's not a good place to be left without a beek.' He shuddered at the idea.

'I'd better get one for myself, then,' Galen said.

'You'll need money,' Kibble remarked. 'Beeks aren't cheap.'

'I'll manage,' Galen said confidently. Ignoring the speculative glances of his companions, he went on, 'Why don't merchants like him get one?' He gestured towards Shahan. 'It would save them a lot of money.'

'Nah,' Drain replied. 'Takes time to gain their trust and train 'em properly. And if they're away from the salt for too long they lose the knack, and you have to start all over again.'

Kibble nodded.

'Ours are trained to warn us of quicksalt and get us clear,' he explained. 'But a wild one would just run away.'

'Anyway, we're worth it to people like him,' Drain went on. 'We know the best routes, make sure they don't get lost, and save them time and distance.'

'Not to mention taxes,' Kibble put in. 'Some of the barons round the eastern rim are a lot more organized than Quarry and Edge!'

'You can say that again,' Drain agreed, laughing.

'That doesn't surprise me,' Galen said. 'If Baldemar's anything to go by, they could hardly be *less* organized.' They laughed together.

'Know him well, do you?' Kibble asked suddenly.

Galen gulped inwardly and cursed his carelessness.

'Of course,' he replied, grinning, determined to brazen it out. 'I moved in the very best circles, you know.'

'Fancy!' Kibble exclaimed. 'We've been joined by one of the nobs!'

Drain looked uncertain for a moment, then realized that he was being teased, and chuckled.

'Everyone knows Baldemar couldn't organize a drinking contest in an ale-house,' Galen said. 'Let alone collect taxes properly.'

'I've heard his daughter's a tasty morsel,' Kibble remarked.

Careful, Galen cautioned himself. *Change the subject!* Aloud he said, 'Never seen her,' and shrugged dismissively.

'She's going to marry some baron from up north,' Drain said knowledgeably.

'Lucky bastard,' Kibble commented sourly. Galen kept his mouth firmly shut.

They trudged on in silence for a while. The day grew warmer, and the sun became a white glare in a pale blue dome. Galen squinted into the shimmering distance and began to understand the stories of men who had gone blind amid such unrelenting brightness. He unstoppered his bottle and swallowed some warm water.

'Don't have too much,' Drain advised. 'That's got to last you a few days.'

'Listen to the fount of all knowledge,' Kibble mocked, then added, 'He's right on this occasion, though.'

'Ha, ha. Very funny,' Drain retorted. 'Just because you don't understand my theories—'

'Oh, come on!' Kibble interrupted. 'You've got to admit that some of your *theories* make the idea that the moon is made of salt seem almost likely!'

Drain glared at Kibble, but said nothing, and Galen took his chance.

'What makes you think Shahan's a spy?' he asked quietly.

'Oh, don't start him off!' Kibble exclaimed, but Drain ignored his companion.

'You hear things,' he said mysteriously.

'Such as?'

'Just things.'

'*What* things?' Galen persisted.

'Careful. He might hear us,' Drain whispered, glancing ahead. 'Besides, I don't know you. Perhaps you're a spy too.'

Kibble burst out laughing at this, and Galen did his best to join in.

'*Keep quiet,*' Drain hissed.

'Then tell us some of your wonderful theories,' Kibble demanded, still laughing. 'Astound us with your wisdom.'

The object of this derision glanced nervously at his two associates, then at the men walking ahead. No one seemed to be paying any attention to their laughter, but he still hesitated.

'What have you come to spy on, Galen?' Kibble went on, obviously intent on exacting the maximum revenge for the earlier jibes about his beek. 'What the Archaeologists eat for lunch? The dark secrets of Drain's pack? Does he *really* own a second pair of socks? Vital stuff, eh! Certain parties would pay a fortune for information like that.'

'Why don't you let him speak for himself?' Galen put in tersely. He was finding this line of conversation uncomfortable – even in jest.

'Suit yourself,' Kibble replied, looking rather put out. 'Don't say I didn't warn you.' He lapsed into a sullen silence.

Drain said nothing, but his expression showed a measure of relief and gratitude.

'Well?' Galen prompted softly.

'No one ever sees what he's trading,' Drain began quietly. 'Lots of people will tell you what it is, but no one ever *sees* it. There could be anything under that cover. He's always trading somewhere else, and if anyone asks him, he just says it's all tied up elsewhere – even if he's got a sledge full of stuff. Does that sound like a normal merchant to you?'

Galen shook his head slowly.

'Yet he's always got plenty of money,' Drain continued, still in an undertone, but warming to his subject now. 'And he's always carrying *letters* in that pouch of his. It never leaves his side – even when he's asleep!'

Galen said nothing, and Drain went on. 'Not many merchants have bodyguards like *them* either. They could be dreekers.'

'What!' Kibble exploded, unable to keep up his feigned indifference. 'Are you crazy?' He looked at Drain in disbelief. 'Where do you *get* this stuff?'

'What are dreekers?' Galen asked, in more measured tones.

'Don't ask!' Kibble put in. 'He's quite mad.'

'They're creatures made from parts of dead bodies – of people who have been buried in the salt,' Drain answered, ignoring the interruption. 'They have superhuman strength, and can only be created by wizards.'

Galen could not help smiling, but Drain appeared to be in earnest and was watching the bodyguards intently. Kibble raised his eyes, and spread his hands in mute apology.

'And another thing,' Drain said abruptly, returning to Galen's original question. 'Shahan is in tight with Jarlath, the baron in Riano – and everyone knows *he's* a weird one.'

'Why don't you shut up,' Kibble moaned, but he made no move to leave their company.

'How weird?' Galen asked.

'He keeps having visitors from *overseas*,' Drain answered, spitting out the word as though it might poison him. 'And he keeps company with those monks – and *they* make human sacrifices. You want to watch yourself there,' he added significantly.

'I'll be careful,' Galen promised.

'Don't encourage him,' Kibble groaned.

'How do you know all this?' Galen asked, ignoring the advice.

'You hear things,' Drain replied, and would say no more.

Galen walked on in silence, watching and thinking. *Is he making it all up?* On the face of it, Drain's stories seemed preposterous, but Galen doubted that the young man had the imagination to dream up such wild tales. He must surely be elaborating on overheard gossip, and gossip, however far-fetched, often had a core of truth. *Besides,* Galen concluded, *Drain is right about Shahan – at least in part.*

Peyton called a halt shortly before noon, and the party rested during the hottest part of the day. Shahan did not object to the delay – even his lean frame was damp with sweat, and in this waterless tract they could not afford to drink too much. They ate a frugal meal from the merchant's stores, and sipped at their water bottles. Before they set off again, Galen was given further proof of his junior status. Under Peyton's watchful eye, he was set to digging a pit for their refuse. The salt yielded to his blade easily enough, but it was still hard work. The hole had to be 'hip-deep, and wide enough for easy digging'.

As Galen laboured, Peyton told him that it was a tradition among Archaeologists that the salt's surface should be left clean and unsullied. *Admirable sentiments,* Galen thought. *Especially with someone else doing the work!*

As they broke camp, all their debris was thrown into the pit, and the salt shovelled back on top. Several pairs of boots helped stamp it flat, then Peyton removed a small flask from his bag, and let a couple of drops fall from it on to the newly packed salt. They left a small, round blue mark.

'What's that for?' Galen asked.

'We make our living from recovering stuff from beneath the salt, boy,' Peyton replied.

'We wouldn't want to dig up our own rubbish, now would we,' Holmes added, grinning.

The convoy set off again, in the same formation. Galen said little, and listened to Kibble and Drain grumbling about Peyton, Milner and Holmes. It became clear that they resented the older members' domination of the group, and found their attitudes to life contemptible. They were determined not to 'end up like them', and talked eagerly about an unspecified time in the future when they would be able to set up on their own. Galen was happy to leave them to their daydreams, and settled into a numbing routine of walking, watching, and trying to ignore his increasing thirst. The landscape was unchanging; only the creeping movement of their own shadows told of the passing of time.

They made camp at dusk, and Galen had the pleasure of digging another pit. Simple tents were erected and a rota of guards – two at a time, together with their beeks – was agreed. Galen was glad to be resting, and wrapped himself in his blanket with relief. As his first day as an Archaeologist came to an end, he laid his head on a makeshift pillow and was soon fast asleep.

He dreamt of a dull booming sound rising up from below the salt – and woke to find that the noise was not confined to his dreams.

CHAPTER THIRTY-SIX

'What's that?' Galen asked groggily.

Flank, who had just come in from his spell on guard duty, replied in a weary mumble.

'Deep shifts. It's no problem . . . leagues away. Go back to sleep.' Within moments he had followed his own advice, but Galen found it difficult to relax again. He lay in the darkness, listening to the faraway thunder, and wondering what it meant. Eventually, though, he fell asleep, and did not wake again until Peyton roused them all at first light.

Galen was stiff from the unaccustomed exercise of the previous day, and was glad when their chores were completed and they were able to move off. He had at least been spared the nocturnal sentry duties. Some of the Archaeologists had grumbled about his exclusion, but Peyton pointed out that the rookie had no beek, and that he himself would ensure that Galen made up for it in other ways. The young man resigned himself to the thought of digging two deep pits a day.

Peyton led the way once more, but this time he called Galen up to walk beside him. The leader set a brisk pace, determined to make the most of the cool of the early morning.

'Your feet all right?' he asked, noticing that the rookie was walking rather gingerly.

'They're fine,' Galen replied. 'But my legs are stiff.'

'That'll go,' Peyton stated cheerfully. 'But you've got to watch your feet. I've known men beg us to leave them behind just because their boots were too tight.'

'I'll be careful.'

'I believe you will,' Peyton said thoughtfully 'If I'm any

judge, you've got a bit of sense in your head – not like some of *this* lot.' He jerked a thumb at the party behind them. 'But don't think that you'll know it all after a few days. It takes years to become part of the salt, to know how it lives and breathes. Oh yes,' he added, seeing Galen's surprised expression. 'It may look flat and unchanging to you now, but the salt guards its secrets. Don't underestimate it.'

Galen looked about him. The flats stretched away to the horizon in every direction, featureless and arid. Yet Peyton had set off that morning with no hesitation.

'How do you know which way to go?' Galen asked. 'By the sun?'

'Partly,' the group leader replied. 'And by the moon and stars at night if you need to. Though I don't recommend that – moonlight plays strange tricks on the salt. But mainly it's experience and intuition. Some routes are easy, like this one. I've done it so many times . . . you'll learn when something's right or wrong.'

'I hope so,' Galen said earnestly. 'I'd hate to be lost out here.'

'Aye, the salt is unforgiving,' Peyton agreed. 'And what she takes for her own, she keeps.'

There was a mixture of admiration and another, deeper, emotion in the Archaeologist's voice. Galen noted his use of the feminine pronoun without surprise.

'You love it here, don't you?' he said quietly.

'It's the nearest thing to a home I have,' Peyton answered. 'It gets in your blood.'

They were silent for a little while, lost in their own thoughts. When Peyton spoke again, his voice had lost its reverential tone and the spell was broken.

'See there,' he said, pointing. 'Scrape marks. There are plenty of signs on the common routes if you know how to look for them.' Galen could hardly make out the marks amid the sunlit glare, but he nodded obediently.

'And there's the blue marks from the pits,' he suggested.

'Those too,' Peyton agreed. 'Mind you, they fade soon enough, but by then the salt has claimed the contents.'

From then on, Galen kept a sharp eye out, trying to pick up any signs of earlier crossings. He was pleased when

317

he began to notice that the surface was not uniform. There were subtle differences in texture and colour, and even the sound of their footsteps varied from place to place. Every so often he noticed faint scrape marks or the indentations of boot or spade. Peyton smiled when he pointed them out, glad to see his latest apprentice so enthusiastic.

The morning passed quickly. The air grew warm about them, and the breeze began to shimmer in the heat. Shahan and his silent bodyguards kept to themselves, and Galen did not even consider approaching them. *Don't run before you can walk.*

After the midday break, Galen found that his legs had stiffened up again but, knowing he had no choice, he forced them into painful submission and tried to forget about the necessity of motion. Instead, he concentrated on navigation, and occasionally watched the antics of the different beeks. He was familiar with the little animals, but until now had never seen them in what seemed to be their natural element.

The rest of the day passed uneventfully until, about an hour before sunset, the subterranean booming began again. The entire party stopped to listen. Even the dogs were still.

'What makes that noise?' Galen asked quietly.

'Deep shifts ahead,' Milner answered softly. He had been walking beside Galen for some time but now, even though he turned his face to his companion, his blue eyes were unfocused, his whole body concentrating on the mysterious sounds. Galen waited until the others started moving again before speaking.

'Quicksalt?' he asked.

'It may not reach the surface,' Milner replied. 'We'll find out tomorrow,' he added ominously.

They went on until dusk, then pitched camp for the night. Throughout the hours of darkness the booming of the salt came and went, keeping them all on edge and making sleep difficult. The loudest reverberations were accompanied by yelps and howls from the beeks.

Galen noticed that Shahan looked very worried. The Archaeologists were more phlegmatic, but nevertheless they watched the beeks carefully, and were obviously tense, in spite of their ready humour.

'The salt's welcoming you, rookie,' Holmes remarked. 'It doesn't put on a show like this for everyone.'

'I'm honoured,' Galen returned, grinning.

'Don't be,' the big man replied. 'We might all be pickled by the morning. Eh, Flank?'

'Shut up!' the younger man snapped. 'How close is it now?' His voice, normally dull and slow, sounded shrill in the evening gloom.

'Three, four leagues,' Peyton answered calmly. 'Not close enough to worry about.'

'It's big though, isn't it?' Kibble said.

'Aye,' their leader agreed. 'Big enough.'

* * *

All was quiet in the morning, and Galen made the mistake of assuming that the salt was safe. When he made a comment to this effect, Peyton pointed out that the booming was a signal of large movements deep below the surface, which, in itself, was no danger to the travellers.

'But when there's movement down below,' he went on, 'sooner or later it'll come to the surface – and as silently as the footsteps of a spider. The beeks are the only way we'll ever know when it's going to happen.'

'Why doesn't it happen straight away?' Galen wanted to know.

'Sometimes it does,' the older man replied. 'At other times, we don't get quicksalt until three or four days later. The salt doesn't make it easy for us, rookie!'

Galen nodded thoughtfully.

'It usually gets to the top within a day or so of the deep shifts, though,' Peyton added. 'So you'd best stay alert.' He laughed cheerfully, striding across the salt in his usual confident manner.

After that, Galen found that he watched the beeks very carefully. He soon realized that most of the others were doing the same. Every sudden movement or piercing yowl sent ripples of unease through the party, but their southward trek continued. There was no telling where the quicksalt might strike; moving on was no more dangerous than staying put.

In the early afternoon, the three beeks suddenly stiffened, ears twitching, their long tails erect. This time even Peyton stopped to watch them, and Galen felt his heart begin to pound. The little creatures were all facing south-west, their muscles tense as if ready to pounce upon an invisible prey. A new sound filled the air, a throaty gurgling that Galen had never heard before. The threefold voice twisted eerily in the still air, and even those who had heard it many times before felt the hair rise on the back of their necks. No one spoke; each man was alone with his thoughts and un-answered questions.

The beeks held their ground, staring fixedly across the white plain. Then one of them turned and ran a few steps before coming to a skidding, splay-legged halt. This action almost prompted some of the party to turn and flee, but the other two animals stood still, and Peyton raised a hand.

'Hold fast!' he cried, and there was more authority in those two words than in anything Galen had ever heard him say before. Even Shahan froze, as if rooted to the spot.

Time ceased to have any meaning. The only sound which broke the crystal silence was the continued growling of the beeks.

Do we just stand here for ever? Galen wondered. *What's happening?* He peered into the distance, following the direction of the beeks' gaze, but could see nothing out of the ordinary. The air began to dance before his eyes, and he suddenly understood the tales of mirages and dreams coming to life which had formed part of the Archaeologists' repertoire. *While the beeks stay still, we're all right,* he told himself, hoping it was as simple as that. *But if they run . . .*

Silence. *They've stopped growling.* And Galen felt the tension drain out of the air. The beeks began to move normally once more, and someone laughed nervously. Soon, everyone was moving again, looking round and smiling at each other.

'Show's over,' Peyton announced, and set off without further ado. The rest followed automatically. It was not long before Galen, still paying close attention to his leader's navigation, realized that Peyton was gradually changing direction. Whereas before they had been heading slightly east of south, now they were going south-west. This puzzled and frightened him a little, but he said nothing. No one else gave any sign of noticing anything out of the ordinary.

It was Holmes who saw it first.

'There!' he exclaimed, pointing.

Peyton looked, nodded and, with a satisfied smile on his round face, turned further to the west.

'What's going on?' Shahan demanded, striding up to join them.

Wordlessly, Peyton pointed ahead to a large circular patch of salt, perhaps forty paces across, which stood out from the surrounding plain. Its surface was jagged and rough, and seemed darker than usual.

'I'm not paying you to go scrabbling about for buried trash!' the merchant said angrily. 'I insist that we continue south.'

'We can't pass up an opportunity like this,' Peyton replied calmly. 'It won't take long . . .'

'I don't care *how* long it takes,' Shahan retorted. 'I am in a hurry, or I would have gone round the salt. Your delays have inconvenienced me enough already.'

The Archaeologist kept walking, his eyes still fixed on the jagged surface ahead. Shahan reached out a hand, intending to grab Peyton's shoulder, then obviously thought better of it. Holmes grinned at the merchant's exasperation.

'Of course, you could always go on alone,' Peyton remarked mildly.

'This is outrageous!' Shahan spluttered, his face red. 'I will not pay you another crown if we do not go on immediately.'

'That would not be wise,' the other replied. 'That is, if you ever want any Archaeologist to help you cross the salt again.'

'Accidents *can* happen,' Holmes added helpfully.

'You dare to threaten me?' The merchant looked fit to explode. 'Let me tell you, I have some very powerful friends . . .'

'We'll take our chances on land,' Peyton replied. 'But at the moment you're on the salt. We're the only friends you have *here*.'

They had reached the rough patch now. Shahan turned away in disgust and went to sit with his bodyguards by the sledge, some distance away. The Archaeologists surveyed the salt before them. Close to, its crystalline nature was emphasized, with angular shapes, some as big as a fist, protruding from the surface. Elsewhere, the salt was as fine as powder, swirling in any slight movement of the air.

'Perfect!' Peyton declared. He turned to Galen. 'Time to learn your trade, rookie.'

'What do I do?' Galen tried to ignore the faintly malicious grins that were being directed at him by his companions.

'Dig,' Peyton replied. 'You've had a little practice, now you're ready for the real thing. Why do you think I've allowed you to carry my spade all this time?'

Galen unstrapped the tool, while the others relieved themselves of their own burdens. Holmes took a rope from his pack and began coiling it round his forearm.

'Is this quicksalt?' Galen asked, trying not to reveal his nervousness.

'Not now,' Peyton answered. 'It *was*, a while ago, but it should be safe now.'

Should be? Galen gulped, and glanced at the beeks. They were pacing daintily round the edge of the roughness, apparently unafraid but still not willing to venture inside.

'If you find anything, chuck it out,' Peyton went on. 'If the salt moves, get *yourself* out!' He smiled encouragingly.

'By the sound of it last night,' Milner added, 'this stuff could have come from way deep. There could be some good finds.'

'Where do I start?'

'In the middle,' Peyton replied. 'It'll be softest there.'

Galen trod gingerly at first. The crystals crunched and settled under his boots, making him feel dreadfully insecure. But he persevered, and when he reached the centre, turned back to look at his colleagues. Receiving a nod from Peyton, he began to dig. The salt was indeed soft, and he was soon knee-deep in a wide hole. His confidence grew as the salt continued to behave normally, and his thoughts turned to the possibilities of what he might unearth. Or rather, *unsalt*, he corrected himself. *I'm getting quite good at this*, he decided as the pit grew deeper and wider. He hardly noticed that the others had now also braved the circle, and Flank, Drain and Milner were all engaged in digging separate holes of their own. He did notice when one of the beeks also entered the rough area and came to inspect his work. The little creature sat on its haunches, its tail curled round its legs, ears and whiskers twitching. Galen took comfort from the animal's presence and went on with his digging.

An hour passed but nothing was found. The silence was broken only by Shahan's periodic complaints, and some coughing from the young men as the powdery salt made breathing difficult. Then, at last, a shout went up. Drain had hit something solid. Moments later, the excitement turned to disgust and then laughter when it became clear that his find consisted only of some ancient, bleached bones.

'Give them to the dogs,' Holmes suggested, but even the hounds showed little interest in the long-dead remains.

As the excavations were resumed, Galen wondered whether all the effort was worthwhile.

'Come on!' Shahan burst out. 'We've wasted enough time.'

'A little patience,' Peyton replied, as he surveyed the workers. 'We don't like to waste a dig.'

'But there's nothing here!' the merchant persisted. 'Any idiot can see that.'

Galen lifted his spade again, feeling that Shahan might well have a point. He was now almost shoulder deep, his throat was sore, and he was being constantly harassed by the salt that fell back into the hole from around the rim. He had removed nothing except the endless white crystals, and frustration suddenly made him bring the blade down harder than usual. There was a loud crack – and Galen felt the salt shift beneath his feet. Panic-stricken, he uttered a strangled cry as he fell. Darkness enveloped him, and he landed with a thump. *Get me out! Get me out!* He fought the salt, and was rewarded only with slithering sounds. *I'm going to die.* A little light filtered into his prison, and with it a measure of calm. Perhaps his career would not be over before it began, after all. He became aware of the fact that he was still breathing – albeit painfully – and that there was solid ground beneath him. *Why wasn't there any warning from the beeks?*

He wiped the salt from his face, looked up, and saw the hole he had fallen through. Above, in the remote sunshine, faces stared down at him. A rope was lowered, and he caught it gratefully.

'You all right?' Holmes called.

'I think so.' Galen's voice shook.

'It was just an air pocket, not quicksalt.'

His heartbeat was beginning to return to normal. Salt slipped and fell into the cavern, and Peyton yelled angrily.

'Step back from the edge!' he ordered. 'Do you want to kick half the flats in on top of him?'

Several faces moved away.

'Anything down there?' Peyton called.

Galen's eyes were gradually adjusting to the gloom, and now that he had recovered a little from the shock of the fall, he began to look round, sifting eagerly through the loose salt which carpeted the cave. His fingers closed upon some solid items, and he quickly dug them out. As he felt smooth stone, and perhaps metal, his hopes rose.

'There's stuff here!' he called, 'but I can't see it properly. Throw me a bag.'

It landed beside him – accompanied by more salt.

'Stand back, you idiots,' Galen heard Holmes say. 'We don't want a collapse.' Some of his fears returned, so he quickly stuffed his finds into the bag, made a cursory search for more, then looped the rope under his shoulders.

'There's nothing else!' he shouted. 'Pull me up.'

His invisible companions obeyed and Galen soon found himself back in the world of daylight – much to his relief. He handed the bag to Peyton, and brushed the salt from his clothes.

'Like a ghost from the deep,' Milner commented.

They left the rough area, and everyone watched as Peyton emptied the bag. Shards of broken pottery, a piece of half-fossilized wood, a pitted, corroded knife-blade and a small, greenish coin tumbled out. Even Galen could see immediately that it was a worthless collection. It seemed a poor reward for his frightening experience.

'Rubbish,' Flank said mournfully, as he and the others turned away.

Peyton threw all but the coin into the nearest pit.

'The wind'll soon fill them in while the salt is still loose,' he explained, then flicked the green circle to Galen. 'A souvenir, rookie. Your first find!'

Galen caught it deftly, inspected the unrecognizable coin with a rueful smile, then pocketed it.

'Can we go now?' Shahan demanded impatiently.

Peyton nodded, and the convoy reassembled and set off. Galen found himself walking next to Holmes.

'Hardly worth it, eh?' the big man remarked.

'Are air-pockets common?'

'Common enough.'

'You might have warned me,' Galen complained. 'I thought it was quicksalt.'

'Oh, no,' Holmes replied cheerfully. 'If it had been, we probably wouldn't have been able to get a rope to you!'

CHAPTER THIRTY-SEVEN

They made camp as soon as darkness fell. Although the salt remained quiet throughout the night, a warm wind rose, keening eerily through the tent ropes, and Galen was greeted the next morning by the most spectacular sunrise he had ever seen. As he stared in wonder, a huge salt-storm rose into the sky many leagues to the east. The whirlwind writhed and twisted in a slow, sinister dance, rising ever higher in a futile attempt to blot out the sun. While the edges of the crystalline storm sparkled with an astonishing rainbow of colours, there was an ominous pillar of darkness at its heart.

'It's beautiful,' Galen breathed, mesmerized by the awe-inspiring sight.

'From a distance, yes,' Holmes commented drily.

'It's moving away,' Peyton pronounced. 'In any case, it'll blow itself out by nightfall.'

No one questioned his statement, but Galen was not the only one who glanced frequently to the east that day. Indeed, Drain started to see shapes in the cloud, and naturally took them for omens. Galen found it difficult to tell whether his young colleague was being serious or not, but was intrigued none the less. Others reacted differently.

'See that!' Drain exclaimed. 'Demon's claws. Reaching out to the left. There!'

'You and your stupid theories!' Kibble said, rolling his eyes. 'I've never heard anything so ridiculous.'

'That means someone's going to die on the salt,' Drain went on, ignoring his companion's scorn. 'It's a sure sign.'

'See what I mean?' Kibble commented, looking to Galen for support. 'Hopeless!'

Galen shrugged, not knowing how to react. Drain's ideas appeared ludicrous, but he had seen the fear in Flank's eyes.

'The salt produces a lot of omens, does it?' Galen asked.

'You're as bad as he is!' Kibble exclaimed, and stalked away in disgust.

Drain then launched into a series of tales about ghosts, demons and other apparitions, about men disappearing without trace, and about the unearthly sounds that some-times issued from Blackator. Whenever the salt was restive, he claimed, calamities were sure to follow. Flank, who had stayed with them as they trudged along, listened in silence, his sad eyes displaying a mixture of unwilling fascination and mute terror. Galen remained interested but sceptical.

'You've seen all this yourself, have you?' he asked.

'Most of it,' Drain answered defensively. A few moments later, he added, 'You hear things, anyway . . . '

'If you keep your ears open,' Flank completed for him, surprising both his companions.

'Yeah!' Drain said defiantly. 'Not like some.' He nodded towards Kibble and Holmes, then flicked his wayward hair out of his eyes.

The rest of that day passed uneventfully, but was en-livened by the periodic appearance of salt-sprites, tiny swirls of white crystals that sped across the flats in the warm breeze. They seemed to play with the travellers, and made the dogs sneeze, but were otherwise quite harmless. The beeks appeared to regard them as amusing toys. It was only when Galen thought of them as miniature versions of the vast storm, now behind them to the north-east, that he suffered any disquiet.

The next morning was the last they would spend on the salt on this voyage, so Galen made a belated attempt to engage Shahan's bodyguards in conversation. They regarded him suspiciously at first, but when he showed no interest in their master or his cargo, the heavily muscled men relaxed a little. Galen asked them about their own travels, gradually bringing the discussion round to the city of Riano. It transpired that the two men often worked for merchants who traded there, and so they knew it well. They were especially pleased to be hired by Shahan; they knew that, as his servants, they would spend two or three nights in the unaccustomed luxury of the guest quarters in Jarlath's castle. Galen gleaned as much information as he could from their laudatory reports of these accommodations.

'I'd like to stay there myself,' he remarked.

'You'll be lucky!' The bodyguards laughed at the idea.

Then the conversation turned to a more general description of Riano's amenities. It sounded very much like a larger version of Edgefield, and Galen felt confident that he would be able to find his way round easily enough – especially with his fellow Archaeologists as his guides!

The party reached the southern rim of the salt about two hours after noon. Peyton's navigation had been so accurate that they emerged from the flats within a hundred paces of the land-road that would lead them direct to Riano. As his men made the necessary adjustments to the cart, Shahan counted out the second half of the Archaeologists' fee, and handed it over with bad grace. Peyton was unconcerned, and simply divided the proceeds, giving each member of his team their portion. Their reactions varied from Holmes' exaggerated glee to a slight lifting of Flank's habitual gloom. Galen was paid last, as tradition demanded, and he assumed that his share would be the smallest. Even so, he was pleasantly surprised at the amount he pocketed; the services of the Archaeologists obviously did not come cheap.

Now that they were off the salt, Shahan set the pace, and he and his burly companions were soon well ahead of the others. Although Galen's colleagues did not dawdle, they were content to walk the two leagues to the city in a state of pleasurable anticipation. Holmes, speaking to no one in particular, gave a detailed account of exactly how his money was going to be spent. It sounded an exhausting and very expensive programme, but Galen had no doubts that Holmes was not exaggerating. He began to understand why Archaeologists rarely had any money for very long. The others appeared more circumspect, and Kibble and Drain revealed nothing of their plans. However, it soon became clear that the first evening was to be spent together, on a tour of Riano's taverns. All his companions, even the younger members, seemed to accept this arrangement without question. Some customs, it appeared, were sacrosanct.

Galen would have preferred to follow the merchant to Jarlath's castle, but realized that this would probably do him no good. In any case, to desert his companions on their first night off-salt – when they all had money in their pockets – would obviously cause great offence. He had no wish to lose his means of travel, his livelihood and his only friends this side of the salt all in one go.

They reached Riano in the late afternoon, and Shahan soon disappeared into the maze of streets. The outlying areas of the town consisted mainly of poor, miserable dwellings, where hard-eyed women and half-naked children watched their progress with curiosity and suspicion. Galen felt uncomfortable under this intense scrutiny, but his companions were obviously used to it, and took no notice.

Just as Galen was beginning to think that Riano was a rather unpleasant place, they reached a large gate, and Peyton led them into what was evidently a much smaller, and older walled town at the heart of the city. The huge wooden doors stood open, but there were soldiers on guard, and watchful sentries on the towers to either side. Galen wondered what criterion was used to determine who should enter and who should not, but Peyton's group passed through without comment.

Inside, the contrast between the two sections of Riano was immediate and striking. Although the streets here were narrow and not particularly clean, the buildings were generally in good repair, the people seemed well dressed, and trade of all kinds flourished around them. Even so, there was a strange atmosphere about the place that Galen could not identify, but which none the less made him uneasy. His earlier confidence began to evaporate; Riano was clearly not simply a larger version of Edgefield. A new set of rules applied in these streets, and he was glad to be in the company of experienced travellers.

By an unspoken agreement, the Archaeologists headed directly for the very centre of the city, emerging eventually into a large square. This was bounded on one side by an imposing castle, obviously the baron's stronghold. Its grey stone battlements and towers looked down imposingly on to the people below. The main gate was shut fast, and although Galen scanned the area quickly, he could see no sign of Shahan, so presumed the merchant to be already inside. The other three sides of the square were formed by a variety of prosperous-looking establishments, but at the centre stood a simple, solid wooden platform which seemed incongruous in such surroundings. When they got closer, Galen saw the dark stains upon the surface, and realized with horror its grim purpose. His blood ran cold at the thought of a ruler who would leave such a harsh reminder of his justice in such a prominent place, and he recalled Pike's prophetic words. *Jarlath is not a man to be trifled with.*

His companions were obviously not bothered by such thoughts, and were heading directly towards a large, thriving tavern on the far side of the square. Peyton led the invasion and marched purposefully up to the bar. His colleagues, their conversation now loud with anticipation, were close behind. The landlord and several members of his staff looked rather alarmed at this incursion, and three large men rose from their seats in the darker corners of the room. The confidence of the Archaeologists never wavered, however. Indeed, Peyton appeared to be enjoying the effect that they were creating, and banged several coins loudly on the bar. The innkeeper's eyes flicked uneasily from his face to the money – and back.

'Feel better now?' Peyton enquired pleasantly.

The landlord nodded, forced a smile, and made a slight gesture with his plump, white hands. The three men returned to their seats, although they seemed reluctant to do so.

'What can I get you, gentlemen?'

'Seven measures of your best ale,' Peyton replied. 'And not the watered-down version you serve to those who don't know any better.'

'I assure you . . . ' the innkeeper began, then thought better of it, and signalled for two barmaids to draw the ale. He slid several coins off the bar, returned a few smaller ones as change, then hurried away to attend to other customers.

While the Archaeologists arranged themselves around a large table near the bar, and stowed their few belongings beneath, the serving women brought their drinks across.

One of them seemed petrified, but the other grinned knowingly at Holmes.

'Welcome back,' she said, winking.

'Join us later,' he told her.

'*These* won't last long,' Peyton added, picking up his tankard. 'Make sure—'

'Don't worry,' she interrupted. 'I'll see that all your requirements are taken care of.' She walked away, swinging her empty tray – and her hips.

'Who's that?' Milner asked Holmes.

'I have no idea,' the other replied, watching the receding form. 'Welcome back to land.' He raised his glass at the toast, and the others followed suit.

A few moments passed with only swallowing noises and sighs of satisfaction breaking the silence. The rest of the clientele, who had been eyeing the newcomers warily, gradually resumed their conversations. From the next table, a woman was heard to comment about the unpleasant smell of their animals. Holmes swivelled in his chair to face her.

'I'm afraid you are mistaken, my lady,' he remarked in a comically refined tone. 'Beeks are in fact the cleanest of creatures.' With a broad, beatific smile, he added, 'We're the ones who stink!'

* * *

Much later – when time had ceased to have any meaning – the night's events merged into a happy blur. Even Galen, who had more reasons than most for wanting to stay sober, found that task beyond him. Several establishments had come and gone, each less salubrious than the last, and he had no idea where they were at present. This tavern was very different from the first – though strangely enough the beer tasted just as good – and was taking the noisy presence of the Archaeologists in its stride.

Galen vaguely recalled that there had been music and singing at various points during the evening, even a session of hilarious dancing. Their party had been periodically enlarged by other people, mainly women, but also a few men on the look-out for a free drink. It seemed that half the town's population knew this particular group of Archaeologists; they were revelling in their new-found celebrity and the comfort of money in their pockets.

Galen struggled to focus on each of them in turn. Peyton was red-faced and sweating as he held court over an ever-changing audience with stories that had been tall to start with and were now reaching up into the clouds. Holmes, with the latest of a succession of girls cradled in his lap, had become ever more rowdy, singing, impersonating his companions, and making fun of anyone and anything about him. His uncannily accurate version of one of Flank's slow-eyed double-takes and dolorous speech had been especially hilarious, for all its unintended cruelty. Some of his efforts had met with rather less approval – especially when those being mocked were outside his group of colleagues. They had left some taverns in a hurry rather than let the violence which simmered just below his amiable surface spoil their entertainment.

Milner was less demonstrative, but he too had talked virtually non-stop once he had downed a few tankards. He continued even when no one was listening, apparently content with the sound of his own voice. Concentrating furiously in order to hear what was being said now, Galen concluded that Milner was either speaking in a foreign language, or was spouting gibberish. It amounted to the same thing, really. He lost interest and turned to Kibble, who had long since lost his habitually condescending manner; even his tall, angular frame seemed to have softened. His face flushed and his normally restless eyes glazed, he was draped gracefully over a large chair, looking up at the dimly lit rafters.

Flank, by contrast, sat silent and unmoving, his face white and his hands clenched around his mug. Galen wondered, without concern, when his companion was going to be ill. Drain sat next to Galen. He had been quiet at first, 'keeping his ears open' no doubt, but as the night progressed, the youngest Archaeologist had become more voluble, and happily joined in the general flow of talk adding his own embellishments to Peyton's tales. There was only one subject that shut him up – and that was the feminine sex. At the mere mention of the topic he became secretive and silent, and no amount of teasing could produce any response.

Fortunately for Galen, he had not been called upon to take a leading role in the night's activities or conversation, and so a small part of his brain had been able to keep him from revealing his real reasons for joining the Archaeologists. However, when the talk next turned to women – as it seemed to be doing with increasing regularity – and Drain once more proved uncommunicative, Galen found that it was his turn to be interrogated.

'Wha' abou' the rookie?' Milner slurred. ''E lookslike one for the girls.'

'Yeah,' Kibble said, apparently talking to the ceiling. 'Lots of them, I should think.'

Galen shrugged, trying to appear nonchalant. 'A few,' he agreed.

'This issa man who came between a woman and her fiansay, remember!' Holmes laughed. 'A true d'gen'rate,' he added admiringly.

'Tell us 'bout it, rookie,' Peyton commanded.

Galen had no intention of telling them the real story, and was trying to work out a suitably adapted version when he was overwhelmed by a vision of Emer. Pangs of guilt coursed through him as he realized that this was the first time he had thought of her since leaving Edge. He had left no message for her – and even Tarrant's insistence on haste seemed a poor excuse for that now. Images of their intimate moments filled his mind. He closed his eyes and swallowed hard, feeling his body stir in spite of his drunken state. Emotions heightened by alcohol insisted that he missed her, and everything else was confusion. He found himself quite speechless.

'Gods,' Holmes commented, as the others laughed at his obvious discomfort. 'If she wass *that* good, you should've stayed an' fought.'

'Or brought 'er with you,' Milner suggested. 'Getslonely onasalt.'

'Leave him 'lone!' Drain said with unexpected fierceness. ''S'private.'

The others looked at him curiously, registered slowly that he was serious, and were then distracted by the arrival of a serving maid with yet another round.

'I know how you feel,' Drain whispered to Galen during the commotion. 'They're all pigs!'

Galen nodded, still tongue-tied and bemused. He resolved not to say another word until he was sober again. In three or four days perhaps.

CHAPTER THIRTY-EIGHT

While the Archaeologists were celebrating their new-found prosperity and return to land in time-honoured fashion, Shahan had wasted no time in reporting to the castle. He made rapid arrangements for accommodation for himself and his guards, and for the storage of his goods, then made his way to the audience chamber.

The baron was already there, waiting alone. Jarlath stood facing the door, thick legs slightly apart, leathery hands on his hips, and his dark face set. Shahan strode forward with all the confidence he could muster, and bowed in greeting. Jarlath was an unpredictable master, with a violent temper, and the merchant knew better than to speak first.

'You're late,' the baron stated flatly.

'Dealing with the Archaeololgists is never easy,' Shahan began. 'As it was, I had to pay an outrageous fee, and . . . '

'Never mind that now,' Jarlath cut in. 'I assume you have some news for me?'

Shahan nodded. 'I do, my lord.'

'Then you'd better sit down to tell it,' the Baron responded. 'I'm sure you need the rest!'

Though Shahan was thrown into some discomfort by this remark – he knew that his master was capable of great sarcasm – he said nothing, and followed the other to his table.

The Baron of Riano was a short man, with incredibly broad shoulders, a feature he liked to emphasize by wearing padded leather jerkins, reinforced with mail. The result made him look almost as broad as he was tall and this, combined with wire-thick black hair and beard, had given rise to comparisons with various mythical creatures, such as trolls, dwarves and goblins. However, these comparisons were not made aloud in the baron's presence; anyone foolish enough to do such a thing would have found it the last thing they ever said. It is an easily proven fact that talking is impossible when one lacks a tongue.

The baron's sinister reputation was enhanced by the cross-hatching of scars upon his face. Rumour had it that some of these wounds had been self-inflicted, but no one had chosen to enquire into the truth of the matter.

'All is ready,' Shahan began, once they were seated. 'One way or another, Edge will be secure within two months. We can proceed as planned.'

Jarlath grunted, pouring wine from a jug into two silver goblets.

'Farrand and Cranne are there now?' he asked, pushing one in his guest's direction.

'When I left, everything was set for the betrothal,' Shahan replied, leaving his drink untouched. 'But I would not put my trust in that. Cranne is capable of fouling up any scheme that requires anything other than brute strength.'

The baron nodded in agreement. 'He is even more stupid than his father,' he said contemptuously. 'So?'

'Such a failure would not be *too* significant,' the merchant went on. 'A betrothal would be convenient, but even if it doesn't come off, they will have given themselves a perfect excuse to return to Edge without arousing undue suspicion. At worst, they will have seen the lie of the land.' He went on to detail alternative plans and concluded, 'There are more ways than one of skinning a rabbit.'

'Baldemar's flesh would be stringy and tough, even after you'd skinned him,' Jarlath chuckled. 'His daughter sounds like softer meat.'

Shahan hid his distaste for such sentiments, and took a sip of his wine.

'If our plans call for direct action,' he went on, 'we can time things so that Montfort has no chance to react before our other schemes are in operation. And by then it will be too late.'

Jarlath smiled slowly. It was not a pleasant sight.

'Then we can begin to move in earnest,' he said.

'Yes. At last!' Shahan replied, relieved that his report had been accepted at face value. He would have been hard pressed to justify all his claims. 'What news from the south?'

The discussion carried on deep into the night, and by the time he left, Shahan was feeling much happier about their prospects. He also had the details of his next assignment, and knew that he could afford to spend two days in Riano before leaving again. He intended to use the time well – both in trading to keep up his merchant's disguise, and indulging in the varied pleasures that the city offered a man of his means.

Alone once more, Jarlath drained his cup, then refilled it with the last of the wine and sat back with a satisfied smile. However, his good mood did not last long. Almost immediately, he felt a silent crackling in the air, and his skin crawled. He fought to keep his expression calm as the space above a third chair began to waver, but there was a hint of fear in his dark eyes.

A robed figure materialized from out of thin air. When it was fully formed, a thin hand rose to sweep back its hood, and an uncannily pale pair of eyes stared at the baron.

How long has he been there? Jarlath wondered irritably. *I do not like to be spied upon!*

Unknown to Jarlath, Hakon was one of only two of the brethren who could perform such feats in safety. The first chamberlain's privileged position gave him access to sources of power which only he and his abbot dared use, and in the crucial days to come, even they would have need of care. The rest of the brethren had been conserving their sorcerous reserves for some time. All their power would be needed for the climax of their generations-long struggle.

Hakon spoke then, in his familiar dry rasp, and his first words did nothing to allay the baron's sudden unease.

'Do you trust the merchant?' the newcomer asked.

* * *

Eventually, the victory of alcohol over both bodily and mental functions was conceded by the Archaeologists. Galen realized suddenly that Holmes and Kibble were no longer with the group; when he looked around for them, he saw that daylight had come to the world outside. Peyton and Milner were engaged in the thankless task of trying to lift the comatose form of Flank from his most recent resting place – the floor beneath their table. Galen studied their rate of progress, and decided that it would be a lot easier if all three of them gave in and slept where they were.

He swore as an elbow jabbed him painfully in the ribs.

'Come on!' Drain hissed loudly. 'We'll leave them to it. Get your stuff.'

They gathered their packs and Drain's beek, and staggered uncertainly into the pale early sunlight, wincing at the brightness.

And so the seven went their separate ways. No arrangements had been made to meet up again; this was obviously something that would just happen naturally. Drain was not the companion that Galen would have chosen, but he was in no state to argue.

'Where're we goin'?' he mumbled.

'The castle,' Drain replied, a touch of pride in his voice. 'I've got a girl who works there. Don't mind tellin' you. You're all right. But don't tell *them* . . . all wan' to come.'

They stumbled onwards. Galen's thoughts jumped around, leapfrogging over one another so that he could make sense of none of them. A tiny voice in his head told him that he had just received an enormous piece of good fortune, but he couldn't quite work out how. Another voice wondered idly if this was how Drain got so much strange information. However, Galen's main concern was finding somewhere to go to sleep. If his guide's plans included that, then he was all for it. He realized belatedly that Drain was speaking to him.

'. . . a chance to earn some money while we wait for them.'

'Them?' Galen asked, thoroughly confused.

'The others.'

'What will they be doing?'

'Holmes will be with his women for days,' Drain answered. 'Peyton and Milner will stay drunk as long as their money lasts. The gods know what Kibble does, and I think Flank just sleeps.' The fresh air was obviously reviving the youngest Archaeologist; to Galen's befuddled brain, he sounded positively lively.

'Girl. Wasser name?' he asked.

'I *told* you,' Drain replied. 'It's Beth. Works in the kitchen – she'll find a place for us.'

By now, Galen felt as though he were sleep-walking, and kept up with his companion with difficulty. Then someone was putting his hands on to the rungs of a ladder, and a female voice was saying, 'Up there! Quick!' He began to climb mechanically, aware of a comforting, familiar smell. At the top of the ladder he swayed and fell, bracing himself for a crash that never came. He landed softly in a mass of straw and was fast asleep by the time Drain joined him a few moments later.

* * *

When Galen woke, it was dark, and he had absolutely no idea where he was. He lay still, and tried to ignore the small man who was apparently trying to tunnel through his skull from the inside with a sledge-hammer. His tongue felt as though it had sprouted fur, and every muscle in his body ached intolerably. Movement was out of the question.

He stared into the darkness, seeing nothing, but his other senses gradually took over. The warm air held many recognizable scents – hay, manure, and an animal musk. Faint snuffling sounds came from below, together with the small clink of iron on stone as a sleepy horse shifted position. At first, Galen thought he was back in Edgefield, but the events of the last few days slowly came back to him, and he realized that, although he was indeed lying in a stable loft, it was in a castle far to the south of his old home.

He tried to sit up, but a wave of nausea swept over him, so he lay down again and waited for the redoubled hammering to subside. *Never again,* he vowed, thinking back to the night before. *Gods, I hope I didn't let anything slip.* He was heartily glad that Pike had not been there to witness his performance. *But I am inside the castle!* This was a greater piece of luck than he could have hoped for. *At least I think I am,* he added doubtfully. The memories of his reaching his present position were vague, to say the least. He could not summon the strength of purpose to risk moving again, so lay there for a while, feeling useless and miserable. However, it was not long before other considerations made it essential for him to stir. His bladder was close to bursting, and he desperately needed some water to soothe his aching throat.

He clambered gingerly to his knees, then waited for the world to stop swaying, hoping he was not going to be sick. At last he was able to move again, and felt about him with tentative hands. Finding the smooth wood of the top of the ladder, he manoeuvred himself round and climbed down. His bones jarred each time his boot hit one of the rungs, and by the time he reached the ground he was shivering and covered in a cold sweat.

A dull lamp burned at one end of the long stable, but it was instinct and his sense of smell that led Galen to the dung-heap. He relieved himself, then looked around for the first time. Huge walls reared up on two sides of the empty, starlit courtyard, and on the far side, the internal structures of Riano's castle rose in a staggering mass of arches, towers and vast, featureless walls. Galen stood in awe for a few moments, trying to relate this gargantuan edifice to his former home. He failed; the word 'castle' had suddenly taken on a new meaning.

Then something much more homely caught his eye. To one side of the yard was a well, and beside that, a trough, its contents glinting in the faint silver rays. He glanced around but saw no one, and realizing that his desperate thirst outweighed the dangers of being observed, walked very slowly towards the water. He drank, then ducked his entire head beneath the surface, and emerged spluttering and dripping. The chill relieved his nausea and soothed his throat, but his head and limbs still hurt. He climbed back up to the stable loft, burrowed into the straw, and thankfully fell back to sleep.

* * *

The chess game was in progress, and the human pieces moved across the giant board, their faces hidden by masks of black and white. But on this occasion, the battle ground was painted upon a wooden stage in Riano's central square, and the colours shifted as blood ran red across the surface, smearing the squares with death. This time, Galen dived from the high chair in fear, not in triumph, and instead of welcoming arms, he fell headlong into a dark void.

His hands and feet turned to stone, then his arms and legs. Soon, only his head remained flesh and blood. Just before his ears became lifeless, he heard a woman's voice say, *Still think the old tales have nothing to do with you?*

Then all was black, and as silent as the grave.

CHAPTER THIRTY-NINE

'Gods!' his torment complained. 'You're harder to wake than a rock.' Galen was firmly shaken again.

'What?' he mumbled, still enmeshed in the dread of his nightmare.

'You turned to stone or something?' Drain asked peevishly. 'You've been asleep for a whole day and a night.'

'What!' *How could it have been so long?*

'Time to get moving! Leave your stuff here – it'll be safe enough.'

Galen sat up and looked around. There was not much to see.

'If we go now,' Drain persisted, 'Beth will be able to get us some breakfast. Aren't you hungry?'

Galen thought about this and found, to his surprise, that he was ravenous. He no longer felt sick, his limbs were stiff but not painful, and his headache had receded to a manageable dull throb. He followed Drain down the ladder and out into the courtyard. There were several stable-lads already at work but they showed no surprise at the appearance of the newcomers. Two of them exchanged greetings with Drain, who then strode purposefully towards the main buildings. As they crossed the courtyard, Galen heard the murmur of a large gathering in the distance, and glimpsed a crowd through the castle's main gate.

'What's going on out there?' he asked curiously.

'There's an execution this morning,' Drain replied.

'Oh. Who?'

'Just some farmer who couldn't pay his taxes,' Drain answered dismissively. 'Come on.'

Galen's step faltered, remembering the blood in his

dreams, but his companion strode on, and he was forced to follow. A ragged cheer sounded from the square as Drain led him into the castle kitchens.

'There you are! I'd almost given up on you.' The speaker was a young girl. Her face and figure were pleasantly rounded, but her pert voice radiated indignation and her cheeks were rosy with the heat of the ovens. Drain looked sheepish, and Galen mumbled an apology.

'Food's over there,' she said tartly. 'Make the most of it – there's not much left.'

Some time later, Beth joined them at the table. By then all the bread and meat had gone, and they were picking through some half-rotted pieces of fruit. She sat down on the bench close to Drain.

'How long're you staying this time?' she asked, her voice gentler now. 'Gilgamer should have plenty for you to do. There's no end happening nowadays.'

'I know,' Drain replied. 'I've already seen him.' He put his arm round her shoulders, and they smiled at each other.

'Who's Gilgamer?' Galen asked.

Beth glared at him, obviously not welcoming his intrusion.

'He's third chamberlain to Baron Jarlath,' she replied.

'I usually do some work for him while I'm here,' Drain added.

'Drain can read and write,' Beth said proudly. 'So he gets important jobs.' She stared at the straw still sticking in Galen's hair, and remarked, 'What will you do? Muck out the horses?'

'I've worked with animals,' he admitted, 'but I can read and write too, and I'd rather do that. It sounds like an easier life.' He tried hard not to sound too eager.

'You can?' Beth appeared crestfallen.

'That's great!' Drain responded. 'I'll take you along. Let's go.' He kissed Beth lightly on the lips and stood up. 'See you later,' he said meaningfully. She said nothing, but her eyes glowed as she watched the two young men leave.

Galen followed Drain, hardly able to believe his luck. Finding Davin was going to be almost too easy.

'Nice girl,' he commented when they were out of earshot.

'She has her uses,' Drain replied, laughing. Then he grew

serious. 'Listen,' he said. 'Gilgamer's a lazy old sot, and drunk most of the time. He always has a few coins for someone who can save him from a bit of trouble. But he's not stupid – or gullible.' He paused, looking worried. 'You *can* read and write, can't you?'

'Yes.'

'I thought you might have been bragging.'

'Not in my nature,' Galen remarked, grinning.

'Good.' Drain smiled uncertainly. 'I've got a nice set-up here . . . '

'I won't spoil it for you,' Galen reassured him. 'What will we have to do?'

'All sorts. Write letters, copy accounts, run errands, that sort of stuff. Boring, mostly.'

'Mostly?'

'Sometimes you get to *know* things,' Drain said mysteriously.

'Like what?'

'You'll find out.'

They had been walking along a series of corridors and up some stairs, but now they came out on to an open stone bridge which traversed a gap between two buildings. At the far end was a soldier, fully armed and watchful. As they approached, he held up a hand and regarded them closely.

'Where are you off to, my pretty lads?' he said slowly.

'We're working for Gilgamer,' Drain replied promptly. 'I have his commission here.' He handed over a scrap of paper, and the guard stared at it without comprehension. Galen watched as he silently mouthed some letters.

'That's his signature,' Drain said, pointing to the bottom of the letter.

'I see that!' the sentry snapped. 'Let's have your weapons, then. You know the rules.'

'We don't have any,' Drain protested.

'What's that then?' the soldier asked, pointing to the knife at Galen's belt.

'A letter-opener?' Galen suggested, but the guard did not seem to share the joke.

'Leave it here, or you don't get in.'

Galen gave in gracefully, and unbuckled the sheath.

'How do I get it back?' he asked.

'You ask me nicely,' the soldier replied, with a nasty smile. They entered the building, and eventually reached Gilgamer's office. Drain knocked on the door and went in without waiting for a response. The air inside was warm and stuffy, and with a pungent aroma of strong liquor that made Galen's stomach lurch uncomfortably. From his companion's earlier comments, he had expected Gilgamer to be an ancient, crusty retainer whose descent into dotage had been accelerated by alcohol. But the sole occupant of the room was a beardless, blond man in his early twenties. Dressed in colourful, ornately embroidered clothes, he was draped languidly across a well-padded settle, a glass in his hand.

'About time too!' he remarked faintly. 'I have a great deal of work to do.' He waved a pale hand in the direction of a large desk on which were several untidy piles of documents. 'Who's this?' he added, noticing Galen for the first time.

Drain introduced his colleague, and explained that he had come to help. Gilgamer looked doubtful, then stood up reluctantly and went over to the desk. He selected a piece of paper from one of the piles and beckoned to Galen.

'Copy that,' he commanded.

Galen sat down, gathered pen, ink and a blank sheet of paper, then glanced at the document. It was written in an untidy scrawl.

'Exactly like this?' he asked. 'Or so that it's easier to read?'

Drain winced at these words, but Gilgamer only laughed.

'Don't you like my handwriting?' he enquired pleasantly.

'You were obviously in a hurry, sir,' Galen replied.

'Naturally. Baronial chamberlains rarely have time to dawdle. Just copy it as neatly as you are able.' Gilgamer sounded amused.

Galen did as he was told, producing a neat version in a short space of time.

'You'll do,' the chamberlain pronounced. If he was impressed, he gave no sign of it. 'All these need copying, so you may as well start now. Drain, that pile needs distributing. Come back here when you've finished – I have some important reading to do.' So saying, he returned to the couch, poured himself another glass of wine, picked up a book and arranged himself decoratively.

Galen glanced at his departing colleague, wondering whether any of the deliveries were for Davin, and wishing their roles could have been reversed. He shrugged mentally. *Don't try to run before you can walk.* He had been amazingly lucky to get this far so quickly. He settled down to his task, which turned out to be easy but extremely boring – copying documents which were lists of goods or taxes due or paid. There were a few letters, but nothing remotely interesting. Third chamberlains obviously dealt only with menial tasks.

Behind him, Gilgamer was silent, and Galen began to wonder whether he had fallen asleep. However, Drain returned before he had summoned up the nerve to glance round, and the chamberlain was immediately attentive, assigning him to the sorting and copying of another pile of papers. Occasionally, either Galen or Drain would come across something they did not know how to deal with. When they asked Gilgamer for advice, his answer was always the same.

'Put it to one side. I'll deal with it later.'

The morning passed slowly. The chamberlain inspected their progress at midday, but made no comment, and sent them off to the kitchens for a meal.

'Don't be more than half an hour,' he ordered. 'Ask Vine for my tray, and bring it here as soon as you've eaten.'

The two young men escaped gratefully, determined to make the most of their free time. Beth was nowhere to be seen, but the cooks served them without question. After eating their fill, they went out into the courtyard for some fresh air.

'Is it always so tedious?' Galen asked as they sat down on a step.

'No. Sometimes there's secret stuff, in code,' Drain replied, then shut his mouth firmly and looked away.

'Code? What for?'

'How should I know?' his companion answered shortly.

'Aren't you curious, though?'

'Doesn't pay to be too curious,' Drain said sullenly. 'I shouldn't have told you anything.'

'Perhaps Gilgamer's writing love letters to the wife of

346

someone important,' Galen suggested with a grin.

For a moment, Drain looked quite shocked, then he recovered and smiled weakly. 'Probably,' he agreed unconvincingly. 'We'd better get back.'

They collected Gilgamer's tray, retraced their steps, and were checked once again at the bridge – this time by a different soldier.

'Where's my knife?' Galen asked.

'Try the armoury,' the sentry replied with an indifferent smile that implied he did not give much for the young man's chances.

'That blade's important to me,' Galen protested quietly as they walked on.

'You'll get it back,' Drain reassured him.

'I hope this is all worth it,' Galen said doubtfully, feeling that he should be entering more into the spirit of his new role. 'How much do we get paid?'

'Depends on his mood,' the young Archaeologist replied. 'But it's more than enough, believe me. You could buy another *three* knives if you wanted to.'

'You must have a tidy sum stashed away then?'

'Enough,' Drain said, suddenly wary.

'Why bother trekking about with Peyton then?' Galen asked.

'Because I like it!'

'Fair enough. I didn't mean to pry.' His conciliatory tone had the desired effect; Galen had no wish to alienate his most useful contact.

The afternoon passed dreadfully slowly. Once again, Galen was confined to Gilgamer's office, while any errands were entrusted to Drain.

'Can't *I* take that?' he asked on one occasion. 'If I'm going to be as useful as I can, then I should start finding my way around.'

'I'll decide what you do,' the third chamberlain retorted. 'Just keep writing.'

At the end of another long and tedious session, Galen's brain felt dull and foggy, and his hand was suffering from cramp. Gilgamer inspected their work briefly, then dismissed them and nonchalantly flicked a coin to each.

347

'Tomorrow,' he said. 'Don't be late.'

The two young men departed gratefully.

'You see,' Drain remarked once they were outside, holding up the coin in the lamplight. It was a silver quarter-crown – a generous reward indeed for a single day's work.

'Not bad,' Galen admitted. 'Now what do we do?'

'You're on your own,' Drain replied happily. 'I'm going to find Beth. I can't arrange *everything* for you.'

'Fair enough.'

'You can sleep in the stables again – if you don't get lucky,' Drain added. 'See you in the morning.'

'Enjoy yourself.' Galen grinned. 'And thanks.'

Drain nodded, and they went their separate ways.

Galen returned to the hayloft to check on his few belongings, then found the armoury and talked the guards into returning his knife, ate his supper in the kitchens, and spent the remainder of the evening wandering around the outer buildings of the castle. The place was so vast that he got only a vague idea of its full extent; even then, it was quite obvious that anything of importance was in the central keep – and those entrances were all securely guarded. He talked to several servants, but Davin's name did not crop up, and Galen did not dare to mention it. He retired to the stables as darkness fell, and reviewed what he had learnt before falling into a dreamless sleep.

The following morning passed in a similarly frustrating manner. Galen was determined to make something happen after the midday break, but the chamberlain obviously meant to make the most of his unexpected help, and insisted that he stay at the desk. Although he protested, Galen sat and stewed – ignoring Drain's anxious glances.

Finally, he decided to take matters into his own hands. The desk was less cluttered now, and there was no telling how long his services would be required, so he felt justified in taking the risk. An opportunity presented itself when he picked up his next assignment and saw that it was a table of figures relating to the accounts of one of Jarlath's outlying estates. At the bottom, in Gilgamer's untidy scrawl, was the message: 'an extra copy for Waldo in Treasury'. Galen copied this faithfully, and added it to the pile for distribution. Then he shifted the pile and let some of the papers fall to the floor.

'Clumsy oaf!' Gilgamer yelled angrily, but made no effort to rise from his comfortable position.

'I'll get them,' Galen said quickly, and dived beneath the table. When he returned to his seat, the copy of Jarlath's accounts was nestling inside his shirt. He moved very carefully for the rest of the afternoon, afraid that the rustling of the paper would give him away.

The table was almost clear by the time dusk fell, and Galen's last problem was solved for him when Drain was dispatched with some deliveries.

'Don't bother coming back,' Gilgamer said, flipping him another coin. 'Grant can finish up here.'

Drain left, and his colleague completed his tasks with renewed vigour. Gilgamer glanced at his progress, and nodded.

'You've done well,' he remarked grudgingly. 'I should be clear by noon tomorrow.' He tossed a coin on to the desk, and turned away without further comment. Galen picked it up and left, closing the door quietly behind him.

Alone in the corridor, he hesitated, then turned and walked boldly into the unknown territory beyond Gilgamer's chamber. When he was sufficiently far away, he took the copy from inside his shirt, smoothed it out, then knocked on the nearest door. There was no answer, so he tried another. At the shouted response, he entered the room and found himself facing an immensely fat man behind a vast wooden desk.

'Well?' the man demanded, scowling.

'I'm looking for Waldo,' Galen began, holding up the paper. 'I've got—'

'Treasury's down the corridor. Turn left, then take the second on the right. Then it's the third door along,' the fat man interrupted, and returned to his work.

Galen let himself out and followed the directions. He rapped on the door, his stomach churning with a mixture of nervousness and excitement. The door swung open and a pale, dark-haired man stared out at him.

'Waldo?'

'Yes. What do you want?' There was suspicion and a little fear in the thin voice.

'I have this for you,' Galen answered, holding out the copy. 'Gilgamer forgot to give it to the usual messenger.'

Waldo took the paper and glanced at its contents.

'I wondered where this had got to,' he muttered irritably. 'That idiot would forget his own clothes if he didn't have servants to dress him in the morning.' He glanced up at Galen. 'You can go now.'

'Do you know where I can find Davin?' Galen asked quickly. 'I have something for him too.'

Waldo grunted at this further proof of the third chamberlain's incompetence, and pointed wordlessly across the corridor, then closed his door. Galen turned. *Here goes*, he thought, finding that his confidence was growing with each small step closer to his goal. He knocked boldly, and walked in.

The man sitting behind the desk matched Pike's description exactly. He was busy writing, and his position matched that taken by the veteran soldier at the trial run in Redfern's parlour. In spite of the obvious physical differences between the two, Galen felt an uncanny similarity.

Davin glanced up briefly, then returned to his writing.

'What can I do for you?' he asked coolly.

'Please, I need your help,' Galen began with a rush. He had rehearsed the words in his mind so often that they hardly made any sense any more. 'If I don't attend to my master's business, he'll probably roast me over a slow fire.'

Davin looked up again. This time, there was more than bored indifference in his green eyes.

'It would be a shame to see such a fine-looking lad reduced to ashes and smoke for the want of a little money,' he replied calmly. His voice was firm and resonant, and seemed somehow too large for his fine, sharp features.

'Then you'll make my journey worthwhile?' Galen said eagerly.

'I hope so,' Davin responded quietly. 'Do you have something for me?'

'Yes. A receipt.'

Davin took the proffered document, studied it, then

placed it in a desk drawer. He took a clean sheet of paper and wrote out a letter, while Galen stood waiting expectantly. The scribe folded the paper carefully, and sealed it. He addressed it to a merchant in Cutover, and handed it to Galen.

'You know where to go?'

Galen nodded and stowed the precious paper inside his jerkin.

'Good.' Davin went back to his work.

Galen hesitated at this apparent dismissal. *That's it?* he wondered. Davin looked up again, eyebrows raised in mute question.

'Isn't there anything else?' Galen asked falteringly. He was disappointed. It seemed almost too simple.

Davin frowned.

'Your master will be pleased at your work,' he said quietly, a hint of menace in his tone. 'But your position only entitles you to know what I wish to tell you.' The green eyes stared with an intensity which Galen interpreted as 'don't push your luck', and he turned to go. 'You would do well to realize that words rarely have only a single meaning,' Davin added softly, and Galen understood. The code-words that had been exchanged meant that he was trusted to carry messages but not to be directly involved with anything more sensitive. The scribe's words were as close to an explanation – and an apology – as he was going to get.

Galen nodded and turned towards the door once again, only to be halted a second time.

'Boy! For your trouble.' The words were spoken in a much louder voice this time, and Davin flicked a small copper coin through the air.

Galen caught and pocketed it.

'Thank you, sir,' he said, then left, feeling vaguely insulted.

Later that evening, alone once more, Galen debated what to do next. It was obvious that his employment in the chamberlain's office would not last much longer, but he could surely find another excuse to stay within the castle. That would be his only chance of finding out something useful, and he was sure that the Archaeologists would not leave Riano for a few days yet. On the other hand, he had completed the task assigned to him by Pike; by staying on, he might jeopardize not only himself but Davin as well. The scribe's warning had been clear enough. And then again, the stables were an awfully convenient and comfortingly familiar place to sleep. Duty and inclination warred within him; eventually, he decided to stay put for the night and see what the morning might bring.

In the late evening, after a couple of hours spent in the convivial but uninformative company of the kitchen staff, Galen crossed the courtyard on his way to the stables. However, before he had gone far, two hooded figures emerged, one of them leading a horse. At their sinister appearance, Galen slipped instinctively back into the shadows.

The two men passed quite close to him, their faces hidden beneath their dark coverings. They were speaking in low, hissing voices which set Galen's teeth on edge. He could hear only snatches of their conversation, and could make little sense of the odd words and phrases he did recognize. *Peninsula. Our time is near. The Seeress of Night.*

Galen shivered in spite of the warm night, and was greatly but inexplicably relieved when they moved away from him. One of the pair mounted the horse and rode out of the main gate, while the other turned back to the castle. As he passed beneath the lamps of the doorway, he glanced round and seemed, for a moment, to look directly at Galen. In that brief instant, the young man saw a face that seemed more like a long-dead skull than living flesh, its pale, luminous eyes radiating an almost palpable sense of dread. Even in the darkness, Galen felt exposed, naked and afraid, but the monk went inside, ignoring him completely.

Galen let out his breath in a rush. His decision had been made for him. He had no wish to stay within the castle now!

CHAPTER FORTY

Galen collected his few belongings and slipped out of Jarlath's stronghold without being challenged. He was still shaken from the sight of the macabre hooded figures, and even when he was outside the castle grounds, his unease remained. He began to lecture himself sternly, trying to restore his flagging self-confidence.

You've had it too easy so far! If Pike was here, he'd be saying that you've had a lot of good luck with this job. All you have to do now is stay calm!

About him the city waited indifferently. The flickering light of torches and lamps illuminated night-time scenes familiar in any town. The sound of voices and footsteps, the clatter of iron wheel-rims on cobblestones and snatches of singing mingled with the smells of smoke, decaying rubbish and food. Although the mixture should have been commonplace, Galen saw menace in every shadow, a threat in every footstep. He felt lost in an alien, hostile environment.

Get a grip on yourself! he ordered. *You've got plenty of money, and you're not weighed down by cumbersome possessions. You're not stupid, so this town should hold no terrors. After all, the others find temporary homes here easily enough – it shouldn't be beyond you!* he concluded emphatically and strode forth into the alleys of the night.

The further Galen got from the castle, the more his natural instincts took over. The monk's sinister face became less frightening as time and distance increased the gap between them, and Galen even began to wonder whether the whole thing had merely been a trick of the light. And as that memory faded, he looked around with

353

more confidence, taking the measure of his surroundings.

The taverns were the centres of most activity. Humanity would always find reasons for celebration, or the drowning of sorrows, and Riano obviously had plenty of both. Otherwise, the daily trade of the streets had been replaced by the nefarious dealings of the hours of darkness. Tricksters gathered crowds drawn by the prospect of an easy win, and musicians played, competing with ragged beggars for the small change of well-to-do citizens. Groups of men huddled in dark corners, talking in whispers and haggling over the price of the merchandise of illicit need and pleasure, while women of the night watched passers-by from lamplit corners or first floor windows, occasionally calling out their invitation. Some streets were crowded, others almost empty. Fires burned on waste ground, dogs howled at their own echoes, and patrols of soldiers marched through the night with a swagger, bringing with them a fearful silence that faded only gradually as they moved on.

Galen threaded his way through this mass of noisy people, watching and learning. Some places and some men were not to be approached – he knew this instinctively. Violence flared occasionally, but was easy to avoid. Nevertheless, he was glad of the knife in his belt.

He had thought of trying to find one or other of the Archaeologists, but it was getting late now, so he decided to postpone that search until the next day. A cheap room in a small, backstreet inn proved easy enough to find; Galen barred the door thankfully and fell into a deep, exhausted sleep.

On waking in the morning, his first reaction was to take another look at Davin's letter. It looked innocent enough – a message from one merchant to another – but Galen knew better, and was frustrated at not being able to read the contents. *Anyway, it'll be in code,* he told himself, and resisted the temptation to break the seal. Then he remembered the monks in the courtyard. What was it they had said? *Our time is near.* What did they mean by that? He decided to find out all he could about Jarlath's unexpected guests – but to do so in a circumspect manner. There would be plenty to tell Pike when he saw him next – and plenty of questions to ask.

Galen left the inn with the precious letter safely stowed inside his shirt, and set out to find his colleagues. His plan was simple; he intended to visit all the taverns in Riano. If reputation and Drain's information were in any way correct this should eventually lead him to Peyton. This was all very well in theory, but several weary hours later, all Galen had discovered was that Riano was larger than he had supposed, and that it contained a seemingly endless supply of drinking houses. Several of the landlords or their customers informed Galen that the Archaeologists had visited them in the past two days, but no one knew of their present whereabouts. Others grew angry at the mere mention of the group, forcing Galen to leave in a hurry. He consoled himself with the thought that at least he was becoming familiar with the layout of the city, and with the variety of its establishments.

In the end, the first familiar faces Galen saw belonged not to any of the Archaeologists but to the two men who had acted as Shahan's bodyguards. They were obviously drunk, and requested that he join them. He did so reluctantly, and listened while they boasted of their physical prowess and the life of luxury they were leading in the castle's guest-quarters. Galen did not reveal that he too had spent the last two days within Jarlath's walls, and his companions had obviously not even considered the possibility of such a thing. Before Galen made his escape, he managed to ask whether they were still working for Shahan. He was told – with a gleeful, drunken pride – that they were, and that the merchant's next trip was to be even more profitable.

'Where are you going?' Galen asked.

'Dunno. Somewhere down south,' the bald one replied.

'Who cares!' the other exclaimed. 'S'money's good anywhere. Have 'nother drink.'

That was all the information Galen could prise out of them, and by the time he left, it was almost dusk. His renewed search for his colleagues was rewarded an hour or so later when the sound of extravagant laughter guided him to a large, well-lit but dirty tavern in the northern part of the town. Inside, Peyton was holding court, with Milner and Flank nearby. A group of merry drinkers completed the audience for his outrageous tales. As Galen entered, the Archaeologist was in the middle of an oft-told story of how he had found the salt-pickled bodies of two lovers, their emaciated figures entwined for ever in a passionate embrace.

'What a way to go!' one of the listeners laughed.

'Aye,' Peyton agreed. 'The salt must have been pouring in, but they didn't care. They just kept on riding away until the roof fell in.'

'They'd been shrunk by the salt,' Milner put in. 'Eyeballs like dried peas, but still locked together.'

'Shrunk or not,' Peyton went on, grinning widely, 'he was still *that* long.' He held up his hands a considerable distance apart to cries of amazement and disbelief.

'It's no lie,' Milner added, prompting his colleague from long years of practice. 'That thing was a monster!'

'Aye. You could still see the smile on her face.' Peyton concluded, and was rewarded by a round of drunken laughter. At this point, he noticed Galen, and beckoned him over. 'The rookie returns!' he exclaimed as the young man approached. 'Where have you been hiding?'

'About,' Galen answered, smiling at the older man. He saw no reason to reveal his exploits within the castle, and knew that Drain would have kept his own involvement there a secret.

'I hope her husband didn't find you!' Milner remarked.

'No – I'm too quick for that to happen *twice*,' Galen replied, grinning.

'Aha!' Peyton exclaimed. 'I sense a story.' He stared expectantly, so Galen obliged, exercising his imagination. While his words were modest – as well as completely untrue – he managed to convey a picture of adventure and unfettered lust, and finished off with a narrow escape from a vengeful spouse. His tale obviously satisfied his audience.

'Bravo, rookie!' Peyton applauded. 'Holmes would be proud of you.'

'Let's hope the husband doesn't come looking for you,'

Flank commented in his dour way. 'One close shave should be enough for any man.'

'Flank has no sense of adventure,' the group's leader commented gravely. 'And yet, when you think about it, his life has often hung by the merest of threads.'

'What?' Flank seemed alarmed by this.

'Everyone's life – in fact everyone's very existence – has been within an *instant* of extinction,' Peyton went on, articulating his words with exaggerated care.

'What are you talking about?' Flank's bewilderment was plain.

'Consider,' his leader replied. 'You are the product of an endless line of ancestors.'

'All that breeding just to produce *him*,' Milner remarked. 'What a horrible thought.' Several people laughed, but Flank and Peyton ignored the interruption. The older man continued his line of argument, obviously enjoying this excursion into philosophy.

'It is certain,' he said, 'that someone in all those thousands of men and women – who later went on to father or bear a child who was *also* one of your ancestors – was once in deadly peril.' He paused while most of his slightly befuddled audience thought this through. 'They may have been suffering from a fatal disease, only for the cure to be found in the nick of time. They might have been condemned to death for the non-payment of a debt, to find an anonymous benefactor coming to their aid and winning them a last-moment reprieve. Everyone's heard of miraculous escapes from fires and natural disasters—'.

'Like old Redenelli,' Milner put in helpfully. 'We pulled him out of quicksalt expecting a corpse, but he'd been saved by the air in an empty water barrel.'

'Exactly!' Peyton said. 'Only the gods know why it didn't collapse, and knowing old Red, he'd have gone on to father at least one child after that.'

'What's all this got to do with *me*?' Flank asked, frowning.

'All this applies to *everybody*,' Peyton replied. 'You, me, everyone.' He waved an imperious hand at the company. 'We are all here against odds of millions to one!' His comment prompted the exchange of several puzzled glances, some muttering and a few larger than average swallows of beer. Peyton was enjoying himself, however, and was determined to pursue his train of thought. 'Of course, it wouldn't even have to be death that threatened,' he went on. 'What about the soldier who takes a sword thrust in his thigh? A handspan to the side and he'd be no good to a woman. In that instant, all his possible descendants disappear.'

Several of the listeners shifted uncomfortably at this idea, and one or two of them crossed their legs. Milner winced most noticeably, and Peyton pointed to him as proof.

'My friend here has actually experienced such a near miss,' he declared. 'I'd ask him to show you the scar, but he reserves that privilege for the ladies.' The assembled men laughed, but there was a touch of unease in their hilarity.

'What about couples who were supposed to meet but never did?' Galen suggested, entering into the spirit of the discussion. 'Because of some freak accident or something. All *their* descendants would disappear too.'

'The possibilities are endless,' Peyton agreed, then paused as a new idea occurred to him. 'Perhaps there are ghosts of the future as well as ghosts of the dead,' he said quietly. 'The spirits of people who might have been born, but who never were – because their parents never met or died too soon.'

'They say all things are possible within the Web,' one of the drinkers added, after a few moments' silence. Several of the others looked at him with suspicion, but Peyton nodded before looking up expectantly.

'Right now,' he stated loudly, 'the only possibility I'm interested in is someone refilling this mug!' He banged his tankard on the table, and the slight chill which had fallen over the company was soon dissipated by the glow of alcohol and the good-humoured, bawdy tavern conversation. Galen joined in happily enough, safe once more among friends – but he could not help thinking that there was more to the Archaeologists' leader than met the eye.

CHAPTER FORTY-ONE

The next morning, Drain rejoined the fold, and Peyton and the others greeted him like a long-lost brother. When they demanded an account of his doings, Drain answered vaguely, as Galen had expected, and gave nothing away. Later, when the two of them were alone, Drain looked at Galen curiously.

'Where did you get to yesterday?'

'It was too boring,' Galen replied. 'I couldn't take any more.'

'You missed the best pay,' Drain remarked smugly, flicking back his hair. 'And for just half a day's work too.'

'My loss,' was the indifferent reply.

'You missed some interesting letters, too.'

'What, more tax bills?' Galen suggested, trying to sound bored. He was getting annoyed by his companion's constant hints and self-important statements, and was ready to believe that it was all a product of Drain's fertile imagination. On the other hand, if he really *did* know something . . .

'I don't think I should say any more,' the young man said.

Galen swallowed his sarcastic response. Drain had been a great help to him in getting access to the castle, and could be so again in future visits. He could not afford to antagonize him.

'Suit yourself,' he said with a shrug, hoping that his seeming indifference would prompt further disclosures. Unfortunately, Drain stuck to his word, and did not elaborate. Galen brooded, infuriated by the possibility of secret information, and struck by the realization that he was already planning what to do on his next visit to Riano.

'Did you tell them where you'd been?' Drain asked anxiously.

'No. I made up some nonsense to keep them amused.'

'Good.' Drain smiled. 'Has Peyton said when we'll be leaving?'

'No.' This was something that Galen would like to know himself. The sooner he was able to deliver Davin's letter to Redfern, the happier he would be.

* * *

Kibble was the next to return. He arrived in the late afternoon, his gaunt face flushed, eyes bright with excitement.

'Web's teeth!' he exclaimed when he saw his colleagues. 'I thought I'd never find you.'

He explained breathlessly that he had heard of a rich merchant who wanted to take his cargo north. A large sum was being offered to the Archaeologists who took him across the salt.

'But only if we leave tomorrow,' Kibble concluded. 'We've got to hurry.'

'No problem,' Peyton replied calmly. 'As it happens, my funds have become sadly depleted these last three days. I can't think how . . . In any case, we'll be glad to take this lubber tomorrow. There's no need to get so excited.'

'There could be,' Kibble persisted.

'Why?'

'Because there's another group in town.'

'Oh.' Peyton paused, thinking. 'Who?'

'Jude and his crew.'

'They'll sniff this merchant out pretty soon,' Milner put in. 'They're good.'

'Not as good as us,' Peyton stated. 'Come on, Kibble. Let's go.'

The two men left quickly, leaving the others to rejoice at their good fortune. When they returned in the early evening, Peyton was in particularly good humour. The passage had been booked, fees agreed, and all the necessary stores arranged. He had even procured a down-payment as a guarantee of their services, and with the prospect of another lucrative payment only a few days away, he decided that whatever personal money he had left could be spent on the evening's entertainment. Long years of practice meant that Peyton could indulge himself and yet still be fit to lead his party on to the salt the next morning – and so he began to make a memorable farewell to Riano. Galen joined in cautiously, fully aware that he did not share the older man's capacity for alcohol.

'Where are we heading?' he asked.

'Back to Cutover,' Peyton replied. 'Money for old rope.' He chuckled happily, and Galen smiled. Luck was with him once again.

'It's the most common route across the salt,' Kibble explained. 'It's close to the shortest crossing, and yet it's in the middle of the long flats, so the lubbers have plenty to gain by going across instead of round to the east or west.'

'What about Holmes?' Galen asked. 'Where is he?'

'He'll be here,' Peyton replied confidently.

'How will he know?'

'He'll hear. He always does,' Milner said.

'Perhaps he trains those girls of his to be telepathic,' Peyton suggested.

'To be what?' Drain asked.

'Using their minds to send messages,' his leader explained.

'I shouldn't think Holmes' girls are chosen for their *minds*,' Kibble remarked sourly.

*   *   *

True to form, the last member of the group arrived early the next morning, just as the others were completing their preparations. Holmes looked tired, but was grinning as usual.

'Leaving so soon?' he exclaimed. 'Have you no respect for my reputation? Or for the substantial proportion of this city's fair sex who are being abandoned with such untimely haste?'

361

'Duty calls,' Peyton replied.

'And money,' Milner added. 'Lots of it.'

'Ah, well,' Holmes sighed. 'We all have to make sacrifices, I suppose.'

'You're not the only one leaving broken hearts behind,' Milner commented. 'Grant here is no slouch in that department. You have a rival, Holmes.'

'Rival? Never!' the big man returned, grinning at Galen. 'We're comrades! I insist upon hearing *all* the intimate details.'

Galen obliged reluctantly, hoping that he remembered enough of his earlier fabrication to sound convincing. By the time he had finished his tale, the party was already under way and approaching the merchant's ornate mansion. Cargo was stored on three carts, each pulled by six dogs, and the traveller was also accompanied by a secretary and three bodyguards. He lost no time in explaining to Peyton that speed was of the essence, as he must attend an important meeting in Garadun. He then informed the group that there would be a bonus for them if they completed the crossing in three days or less.

It was an uneventful passage – the salt was silent, and there were no storms. Overnight stops were limited strictly to the hours of full darkness, and they kept up a good pace during the day. Galen had the distinct feeling that travelling like this went against the grain as far as Peyton was concerned; their leader was mostly silent, and almost curt when he did speak, keeping his words to a minimum. Galen heard him muttering to himself on the third afternoon, and asked if everything was all right.

'Too quiet,' Peyton replied. 'Not a rumble, not a squeak. I don't like it.'

'But we're almost over now, aren't we?' Galen asked.

Peyton glanced at him, a little surprised.

'Yes,' he said. 'But there's always the next time. Sooner or later you pay for quiet times like this.' He sounded so tetchy that Galen took the hint, and left him to his own thoughts. He wondered whether anyone else shared Peyton's unsettling presentiment.

As dusk fell, the northern rim of the salt was in sight.

The other Archaeologists were in a good mood, knowing that they had earned their bonus, as well as a handsome fee. However, when they were no more than two hundred paces from land, the beeks began to act very strangely. This made the travellers nervous, but then Holmes pointed out the eagle flying away with something clutched in its talons.

'A wild beek,' he said. 'No wonder ours were twitchy.'

As they went on, a slight movement caught Galen's eye. When he went to investigate, he found a tiny, bedraggled infant beek, crawling slowly on the salt. Its fur was matted, its eyes were closed, and it was mewing piteously. Some of the others joined him as he knelt down to get a closer look.

'The eagle must have taken its mother,' Holmes said.

'It'll die,' Kibble decided. 'It's too weak.'

Galen gently prodded the tiny body with a finger. The beek hissed and struck out at him feebly.

'It'll die,' Kibble repeated. 'Leave it.'

'He's right,' Holmes agreed. 'Poor little bastard. Come on.'

Galen was left alone. He hesitated, logic decreeing that his more experienced companions were right, but something within him responded to the pitiful orphan creature. Very carefully, he tried to pick it up; the beek opened its eyes for a moment, and tried to bite his hand. Its teeth were like tiny needles, but the creature was so weak that its efforts only tickled.

'Come on, Spike,' Galen said, naming the beek on impulse. 'I'll see what I can do for you.' Even if his efforts were doomed to failure, there could be no harm in trying. The beek struggled for a moment, then gave up and went to sleep in Galen's hand. The young man checked every now and then that it was still alive by watching for the tiny rise and fall of its chest.

Peyton came over to have a look, and seemed impressed by the animal's docile nature.

'Either it'll be dead soon,' he pronounced, 'and it's given up, or you have a remarkable affinity with that little creature.'

An hour later, the Archaeologists entered The Raven, their new-found wealth burning a hole in their pockets. Galen had persuaded them to go there first, despite some initial opposition.

'It's the best beer in town, you know it is,' he argued. 'And later on, we might get a bit . . . noisy . . . for Redfern's liking. So it stands to reason that we should go there first. I'll even buy the first round myself!'

This generous offer obviously made an impression on his companions, even though Peyton insisted that the first round was his privilege, and agreement was quickly reached. Once inside, Galen went quickly to the bar, and enlisted Redfern's help in his attempt to save the beek. The huge man picked the animal up with such amazing gentleness that even the Archaeologists were impressed.

'Warmth, milk and later, a little ground meat,' the landlord decreed. 'Come with me.'

Galen went with Redfern to the kitchen, where they installed Spike in a basket near the ovens, a dish of milk nearby. He sniffed it suspiciously, then lapped a little before falling asleep again.

'Leave him here,' Redfern said. 'He must fight his own battle.' He beckoned for Galen to follow him, and led the way to one of the private parlours. There, Galen handed over Davin's letter, which was accepted without comment and placed in a huge pocket.

'Any news?' Galen asked.

'News?' Redfern replied, as if surprised by the question. 'No.'

'What do I do now?'

'Whatever you want. They'll contact you if they need you.'

That's all? Galen thought. *What am I supposed to do now?*

Redfern opened the door and went out. Galen followed him back to the bar. Slightly desperate now, he tried again.

'Hasn't Pike sent me any message?' he asked softly.

Redfern turned and looked down at him sternly. 'Who?' he asked. Although his voice was mild, his eyes were like steel.

A chill of confusion spread through Galen's body. He felt abandoned and useless.

Whatever you want.

When he returned to his companions, he found it almost impossible to join in their merriment.

CHAPTER FORTY-TWO

The Archaeologists' off-salt celebrations were relatively subdued that night. The fast pace of their trip had meant that the feeling of release on reaching land was not as intense, and, for once, Peyton's good humour seemed forced. He was still brooding about the salt and the drink only seemed to deepen his foreboding. The others recognized their leader's mood, and even the irrepressible Holmes soon gave up any attempt at celebrating in the usual style. Drain appeared especially preoccupied. He had been quiet on the journey, responding defensively to any questions. Galen, still upset and bewildered by his encounter with Redfern, was also lost in his own concerns, and played little part in the proceedings.

The party began to break up soon after midnight – an absurdly early hour – with various Archaeologists disappearing into the night. Kibble was the first to go, followed by Flank and then by the reluctant Holmes, who went in search of more amenable company. As soon as they had gone, Drain glanced around nervously, as if expecting ghosts to leap out at him from the tavern walls. The group had changed inns several times during the course of the evening, and the one they currently shared with the last of the hardened drinkers was called The Wagon and Horses. Galen noted his companion's nervousness, but said nothing. He was still trying to decide on his next move, and the beer he had drunk – though far less than he had consumed in Riano – had not helped his already uncertain thoughts.

Drain stood up abruptly, and glanced around once more.

'The moon's up, so I'm off to get some sleep,' he announced in a loud voice.

Galen was the only one to react to this peculiar statement. He looked up curiously as Drain waved a hand in farewell and walked quickly to the door, weaving between the empty tables with the swaying motion of someone who is slightly drunk but believes himself to be perfectly sober. Galen watched him go, a tremor of excitement fluttering in his chest. Drain's parting words had been so odd, and his departure so sudden, that Galen was intrigued. *Sometimes there's secret stuff, in code.* He heard his companion's words again and realization dawned. *You missed some interesting letters, too.* Obeying an impulse – which gave him a sense of purpose after floundering in depression for the last few hours – Galen got to his feet and waved goodbye to Peyton and Milner. The older Archaeologists hardly noticed his going.

Perhaps I'm not the only one carrying messages, Galen thought as he left the tavern and looked around for Drain. *That could be why he was so secretive on the journey!* He caught a glimpse of the retreating figure, and grinned as he set off in pursuit. *He couldn't resist dropping hints though, trying to impress me,* Galen thought smugly. *At least I know how to keep my mouth shut!*

His self-congratulatory mood intensified as Drain appeared not to notice that he was being followed. Galen kept to the deepest shadows, avoiding the few lamps which still burned, and staying well back until his quarry turned a corner. Then he would dash forward and peer round cautiously.

Eventually, Drain stopped and glanced about. Galen shrank back into a doorway and held his breath. Drain was no more than thirty paces away, and his quiet knock sounded loudly in the silent street. After a long pause, the door was opened, and a little light spilled out. A few whispered words were exchanged, then Drain handed over what looked like a parcel or a letter. He was given something in return, then the door closed once more. Drain scurried away, almost stumbling in his haste, but Galen did not move. Having been proved right about the young man's business, he now felt bold enough to investigate further. The package must surely have come from Gilgamer, but who was the recipient? That would be something to report to Redfern, and show that he could still be of use.

Galen waited until Drain was well away and the street was still once more, then crept forward. As he drew closer, he could see that a dull light still shone from the cracks around the door, and he wondered if he would be able to see anything through the keyhole. Three or four more paces and he'd be close enough . . .

Suddenly he was choking, a leather-clad arm clamped over his face. His right arm was bent behind his back and held there in a vice-like grip as he was dragged into a dark alley.

'Not a sound,' a voice hissed in his ear.

With his free hand, Galen fumbled for his knife – only to find that the scabbard was already empty. He was overwhelmed with panic, but as he began to struggle, someone hit him once just below the rib-cage. From then on, all his concentration was taken up with the apparent impossibility of breathing. His assailants dragged him into a small, dimly lit courtyard. His legs were kicked from under him and he fell to the flag-stones, gasping and heaving, too agonized now even to feel afraid.

Slowly, painfully, he regained the use of his lungs. He became aware of two pairs of boots, no more than a pace from his head. Their unmoving stance made the menacing presence of his assailants even more unnerving. Galen struggled to look up, and almost cried out in relief as he saw the stern faces looking down at him.

'I had high hopes for you,' Pike told him contemptuously.

'Rookies are all the same,' his unknown companion remarked. 'No sense at all – or too much.'

'I . . . I . . . ' Galen gasped, but could not get his voice to work.

'You'd done well up to now,' Pike went on. 'Even following your friend here showed initiative, but then you spoiled it all by trying to run before you could walk.'

'Leave spying through keyholes to those who are trained for it,' the other man said.

'No heroics,' Pike concluded. 'Remember?'

Galen nodded – feeling ashamed now, but angry too. What right had they to lecture him like this? He'd done everything that had been asked of him – and done a good job of it too – and then they'd abandoned him, left him high and dry! He swore as his indignation got the better of him, but all that passed his lips were a series of vitriolic hisses. Even that made him feel better.

'He's recovering,' Pike's companion remarked drily.

'Can you get up?' the veteran asked, but made no move to help.

Galen struggled to his feet, still bent double, then slowly straightened out and met the soldier's calm gaze.

'Better not give him his knife back yet, Covell,' Pike said. 'He has murder in his eyes.' There was no mistaking his amusement.

'Oh, I think we'll risk it,' the other replied. 'He's learnt his lesson.' He held out the dagger, blade first. Galen took his weapon with a shaking hand and returned it to its sheath.

'Why . . . didn't . . . you tell me?' he managed.

'Because we didn't know,' Pike answered. 'We suspected that one of them might be acting as a messenger, but we had no idea who it was, and no knowledge of his contacts.'

'Now we do,' Covell added. 'I'm surprised they couldn't do any better than Drain.'

'We also know who to watch here,' Pike said, 'which is even more interesting. You came close to messing all that up, young man.'

'I'm sorry.'

'No harm done this time,' Covell put in. 'Learn from it.'

'And another thing,' Pike went on. 'Never ever try something like that when you've been drinking. Ale can make you feel invincible, but unfortunately the real effect is exactly the reverse. You were making so much noise that even a deaf man would have heard you coming. I'm surprised Drain didn't.'

The reprimand over, Galen was led to a dingy house in a back street. There he was asked to recount everything that had happened on his trip. He obliged gladly, pleased to be able to report his successes, and to add to Pike's knowledge. There were three points that caused the most interest, but the veteran soldier would not elaborate. First, there was Gilgamer's role as Drain's contact in Riano, then the fact that

Shahan was now travelling even further south. The final point was the confirmation of the presence of the monks in Jarlath's castle. Galen tried to find out what was happening in Ahrenia, but Pike was tight-lipped on that subject.

'What's the news from Edge?' Galen asked.

'All quiet. Nothing much has changed,' Pike replied. 'Cranne and his lot have left.'

'Anyone looking for me?'

'Not that I know of.'

'So what do I do now?'

'Rejoin the Archaeologists. Sooner or later they're bound to go south again, and I'd like you to take another message to Davin.' He handed Galen a letter.

'What happens if we don't go to Riano?' Galen asked after a pause.

'Do what you can,' Pike replied simply.

'Should I still use the same code words?'

'He knows you now,' the soldier replied. 'Just use the word "business" to let him know you have a message. "Water" will still be the danger signal.'

Galen nodded, then yawned.

'Go back to The Raven,' Covell advised. 'You've a good excuse, after all.'

'You know about the beek?'

Pike nodded. 'I'm flattered that you should have named him after me,' he grinned.

* * *

Galen spent the next five nights in a tiny attic room at The Raven. He saw little of his fellow Archaeologists during that time, and in spite of his efforts, he could get no sensible answer from them as to when they would next go south. Peyton was still in a strange mood, and no one else seemed to care much. They were too busy enjoying the fruits of their labours. Galen found it difficult to face Drain when they next met, but the young man did not seem to notice anything unusual. There were no travellers wishing to cross the salt, so Galen was free to spend much of his time with Spike.

By the end of their stay at The Raven, the tiny beek had changed beyond all recognition. His white fur – with faint grey rings round his tail – was soft and silky now, his eyes were bright and alert, and his outsize ears twitched constantly at the faintest sound. He had almost doubled in weight, obviously thriving on the diet of warm milk, bread and a few slivers of raw meat, and had become increasingly adventurous. When he was sure the animal would survive, Galen had moved Spike's basket up to his own room. He spent hours watching the little creature's antics, which were all accompanied by a running commentary of yowls and hisses.

In spite of his size – he could still sit easily in the palm of Galen's hand – Spike did not seem to know the meaning of fear. He climbed up to the rafters and perched there, singing of his achievement, quite unconcerned by the long drop to the floor below. And the first time he saw a mouse – a creature not much smaller than himself – he attacked instantly. He appeared ready to follow his prey into its hole, but Galen scooped him up, fearing that he would be lost for ever.

At first, Spike was wary of his new master, spitting through bared fangs and lashing out with tiny claws whenever he came too close. He gradually grew to trust him, however, and soon their fights were only in play. Galen gladly submitted to being used as a climbing tree and took to putting Spike in his pocket when he went out. However, this restrictive mode of travel soon bored the animal, and he made determined efforts to escape until Galen hit upon the solution of allowing him to ride upon his shoulder. Spike was delighted with his new vantage point; he clung on tightly with his claws and wide feet, and protested loudly when anyone approached too close.

Redfern and his staff had all grown fond of the little adventurer, who became the object of much affection in spite of his defiant character. Galen did not have to pay for any of Spike's food, and one of the maids was even happy to wash his jerkin after the inevitable accidents.

On the afternoon of their fifth day at Cutover, Galen was in the bar, chatting idly to one of the customers. Spike sat on his shoulder, unusually silent but still observant. Then the door burst open and Peyton marched in, closely followed by Holmes, Kibble and Drain. They spotted Galen and came over to his table purposefully – only to be stopped in their tracks by a fierce hiss from Spike, who was positively bristling with indignation at their intrusion.

'What does he think he is?' Peyton exclaimed. 'A parrot?'

Galen had never even heard of a parrot, let alone seen one, so the question meant little to him.

'You've done well to keep him alive,' Holmes said, grinning.

'Where's his box?' Kibble asked.

'Doesn't need one,' Galen replied proudly.

'He'll run away as soon as we get near the salt,' the other predicted.

'I doubt it.'

'Well, you'll find out soon enough,' Peyton said, recovering from his surprise at the animal's progress. 'Can you leave first thing in the morning?'

'Of course. Where are we going?'

'Chasing the salt,' the senior Archaeologist replied. 'We've waited long enough.'

Galen looked puzzled, so Holmes explained.

'There'll be some big movements in the salt soon,' he said. 'Could throw up some useful stuff. We aim to get to it before anyone else.'

'How do you know?'

'I know,' Peyton stated flatly. 'I can feel it coming.'

'He's never been wrong before,' Holmes added. 'But chasing quicksalt is more dangerous than escorting lubbers. You still want to come?'

'Yes,' Galen answered and Spike yowled his agreement.

'That's settled then,' Holmes laughed. 'You're *both* in. Now, how about buying a thirsty man a drink?'

So the Archaeologists settled down, and Redfern served them with his usual bad grace.

'Where are the others?' Galen asked.

'Sleeping off last night's excesses,' Peyton replied. 'They'll be here tomorrow.'

'Which way will we go?'

'I'm not sure yet,' the leader answered, obviously not

371

wishing to give their plans away to Galen's earlier companion.

'Don't worry,' the man said quickly. 'You wouldn't get me on the salt at all – let alone chasing after quicksalt!'

Peyton regarded him for a few moments, then shrugged, apparently satisfied, and turned back to Galen.

'South-west.'

Galen did some mental calculations.

'That'll take us close to where Derith was buried, won't it?' he asked eagerly.

'So most people believe,' Peyton replied.

CHAPTER FORTY-THREE

The booming started during their second day on the salt. Spike, in his now customary position on Galen's shoulder, called out in response, and Peyton smiled to himself as the other Archaeologists exchanged glances.

Their departure from Cutover had been a shambolic affair, with each man infected by a kind of madness. With no outsiders to consider, their organization had somehow taken much longer than usual, and their high spirits carried over into practical jokes and arguments which delayed them even further.

Galen had been affected as much as anyone. He felt much more a part of the group, especially as he now carried his own spade and owned a beek – albeit a small, untested one. Although he was resigned to the fact that he was still a rookie in the eyes of the others, in his own mind, he was a real Archaeologist. Spike was holding his own too. One of the funniest sights during the chaos before their departure had been Spike nose to nose with one of the other beeks – an animal five times his own size – both growling and spitting. It had been the other beek who backed down, and after that, Spike had become an accepted member of the party, giving as good as he got in the interchanges between the animals.

Some of this initial excitement had worn off after nearly two days of uneventful walking, but a sense of anticipation remained none the less, and with the advent of the subterranean booming that feeling was intensified.

Peyton, whose senses were as always more finely attuned to the salt, advised them to set a 'fast' camp that night, one that could be abandoned swiftly should the need arise.

373

It was a night when the salt and the sky seemed to come closer together. Lightning flashed and thunder rolled above, but no rain fell and the flats replied with their own rumbling echoes. They reflected the splashes of light back with an eerie intensity – and at times it even appeared as if the salt was producing its own light. Vivid flares sprang up and died, bringing with them thoughts of ghosts and demons. The air rang with a barely audible music, which the beeks added to in their own inharmonious way. In the words of the old saying, it was 'a night when dreekers walk'. The Archaeologists were awestruck and a little scared, knowing that they had cast themselves adrift on an alien sea.

No one slept very much that night. When dawn came, their few possessions were soon packed away, but Peyton seemed uncharacteristically vague, almost as though he was in a trance. The six adult beeks had all been out overnight and they too were acting strangely, their normal fluid movements edgy and nervous.

The men all stood still, watching their leader uncertainly, and waiting for his signal to move off. The silence stretched, and Milner had opened his mouth to ask a question when he saw Peyton's eyes flash.

'Gods, it's big!' the leader breathed, then shouted in an odd voice, 'It's coming straight at us!'

At that moment, the beeks all began to run to the southeast.

'Run!' Milner yelled. 'This way!' He raced after the fleeing animals, and the others needed no further encouragement. As the beeks veered to the right, the Archaeologists changed direction as well, terrified by the trembling ground beneath their feet. Their mad flight continued for a few moments more, then the beeks veered again, some turning left, some right, and leaving their followers confused. At the same time, Galen felt a sharp pain in his left ear. Spike was biting it with all of his young strength. Still running, Galen swept up a hand to stop him, but in doing so, lost his balance and went crashing down to the salt. He lay stunned, feeling blood from his ear dripping on to his cheek and the earth beneath him shake. For a moment, his limbs refused to function, and when he did manage to look up, he stared in horror as the salt reared up no more than fifty paces away.

It was like a ghost ship rising into the sunshine after countless centuries on the sea bed. Even in its disintegration, it had a structure. Spars, masts, the boards of its spectral hull were glimpsed and lost as lights flared and the salt sprayed and foamed in fountains of spume. An explosive roaring filled the air, and only Spike's voice was raised in yowling defiance.

Kibble, who had been at the front of the rushing men, never stood a chance. He was engulfed in an instant, and swallowed whole by the welter of crystalline violence. Galen watched, numb with terror in the face of such primeval force, as the others made desperate attempts to avoid their colleague's fate. Peyton, Holmes and Flank swerved to the left and were rewarded with firmer ground, but Milner and Drain, following the instincts of their own beeks, ran to the right, only to have to turn again as the commotion spread in that direction.

Galen tried to get up but Spike bit his hand, more gently this time, and placed one furry paw on his arm. So he stayed where he was, hoping fervently that trusting in his tiny companion would not lead to his death.

Beneath him, the ground's shaking lessened to a constant shudder, and the volcano-like eruptions died away. Instead, the area affected spread gradually, almost calmly, away and to his right. Soon, a vast area was simmering gently, shifting and seething with a dry, rustling sound that filled his ears. Swirls of salt eddied on the surface, and slow waves rolled in all directions. Jagged crystals leapt up and fell back like dolphins at play in a white sea. But the salt beneath Galen remained stable, so eventually he stood up and gazed at the incredible scene about him. Spike cried out and, without thinking, Galen picked him up and put him on his shoulder. The beek immediately began to lick the blood from his master's injured ear.

'Ow!' Galen cried, wincing. 'That smarts.' And then he laughed. He looked sideways at the little creature and said, 'You knew, didn't you. You knew!' Spike yowled in apparent agreement.

Galen became aware of the voices urging him to move,

but he ignored them, knowing that he was safe where he was. Gradually, it became apparent that the salt's activity was lessening. The whirlpools were sluggish now, and the waves smaller. The normal quiet of the salt flats was slowly restored, but a vast area had been set anew. It made the circle where Galen had first dug for treasure seem like the tiniest, inconsequential ripple.

Slow footsteps sounded in the new-born silence as the Archaeologists joined him and gazed, as if mesmerized, at the aftermath of the explosion. For a long time, no one spoke.

'I've never seen it like that,' Peyton breathed eventually, breaking the silence.

Galen glanced around at the shocked faces – Holmes and Milner silent and pale, Flank still trembling, with the suspicion of tears in his eyes.

'Is it over?' Drain asked quietly.

'For now,' Peyton replied.

'What about Kibble?' Galen said.

'He's beyond our help,' Peyton answered with sad conviction. 'Even if we could find him in all that . . .' He waved a hand in a gesture of helplessness. 'He's a part of the salt now.'

No one doubted their leader's word – and there were no thoughts of recrimination. They all knew the dangers of their profession. It was Peyton's job to bring them to the places where the salt shifted – and no one could have predicted the incredible scene they had just witnessed.

The other beeks had joined them now. They had been scattered far and wide by the terror of something even their special senses had been powerless to escape. They seemed as stunned as the men. One of their number had been lost with his master, and they too had no words of farewell.

Milner laid a hand on Peyton's shoulder.

'Well, old friend,' he said slowly. 'You were right.'

'You can say that again,' Holmes added. 'This is the biggest shift I've ever seen!'

The words broke the horrible enchantment that held them all, and soon they were all talking as they gathered up their possessions – discarded in the panic of their flight.

'Did you see that spouter? Must have gone twenty paces

into the air!'

'There were flares in it, too. All colours.'

'If that lot didn't bring up something worth digging for, then we're in the wrong business.'

'We may not even have to dig much. It might just be lying there on the surface.'

Now that the immediate danger was over, their individual hopes and dreams were reasserting themselves. The story of this day would be told in many a tavern in days to come. And this time, exaggeration would hardly be necessary.

Once they were gathered together again, Peyton organized the work.

'We'll do this in pairs,' he said, his voice restored to its normal authority. 'We'll quarter the area first, to see if there's anything on the surface, and pinpoint any likely spots for digging. Go carefully. It'll be soft in places, and there may be slips. We'll leave all the beeks out. Keep them with you, and watch their movements. This may not be over yet.' He paused, then added, 'We'll divide up the stores. Leave some here and keep the rest with you. That way we won't lose everything if the quicksalt recurs.'

'We hope,' Holmes commented drily.

'When you've decided where to dig,' Peyton went on, 'let me know. If you find something big, call the others. This is a team effort.' He looked around to see if there were any questions, but none was forthcoming and they set about their tasks.

'Come on!' Drain called to Galen. 'We'll take this section.'

Peyton and Milner headed towards the centre, and the incongruous but no longer surprising pairing of Holmes and Flank made for the far end.

As he began, Galen thought back to his original reasons for joining the Archaeologists. He recalled the stone carving and the mysterious coded letters, and wondered whether he might uncover something like that. The idea excited him more than the thoughts of gold and jewels that dominated the day-dreams of his companions. However, he soon had little time for idle speculation – all his energies were focused on the job in hand. The rough salt slipped and settled under their boots, and they tested each foothold

377

before committing their weight. It was a time-consuming task, and they were all weary of it long before the end of the morning.

The quartering netted few finds; a handful of bleached bones, a selection of coloured pebbles and an uninspiring collection of worthless debris was all the Archaeologists had to show for a long morning's work. They took consolation from the fact that there had been no sign of the quicksalt recurring, and from the beeks' continued contentment. After all, as Peyton pointed out, they had brought enough food and water for several days – providing they were careful – so there was no immediate hurry. They rested through the hottest hours of the day, and resumed their search when the sun's glare was less oppressive.

Galen and Drain chose to dig at the spot where they had uncovered some old bones – their only contribution to the morning's haul. They collected their equipment and the portion of the stores assigned to them, and made their way to the marker they had left. They were able to move more quickly this time, knowing now where the possible soft spots lay. Spike and Drain's beek followed in their own manner, Spike bouncing and leaping, the other stepping daintily and observing the infant with disdain.

Under the watchful eyes of their animals, the two young men began to dig a wide circular pit. The salt was soft and uneven, easy to move but prone to collapse, and they had to keep expanding the hole's width in order to make any downward progress. It was hard and frustrating work, and all they found were more bones. One of these was a pure white human skull that sent a few shivers down their spines, but which was just as worthless as the rest. They finished as the sun set, disappointed and dog-tired.

The others had fared little better. Their combined efforts had produced only a few pieces of once-wood, some badly corroded metal, shards of pottery, and a pile of coloured beads. These had caused a stir at first, but had turned out to be just glass. There were also several half-fossilized lumps of *something*. Whatever these things had been originally, they were quite unrecognizable now, so no one paid them much attention – except Galen. He puzzled over them in the half light for some time, but was unable to identify anything even tentatively.

All in all, the day had produced enough to justify hope for future digging – after all, where there was iron there could be gold, and gems could lie among beads – but nothing more.

It was a subdued camp that night, pitched some distance from the edge of the rough area. Each man found himself thinking back to the tumult of dawn and the death of their companion, and the group ate their meagre rations in almost total silence. They were all tired and preoccupied, and there were some arguments over the duty rota for the night. This time Galen was included without question. It was a sign of his acceptance – and also of the fact that their number had now been reduced to six.

CHAPTER FORTY-FOUR

The next two days brought only an ever-increasing sense of frustration. The piles of their finds grew larger, but contained little of value or interest. A few coins and a gold ring – still attached to a skeletal finger – were the only rewards for their efforts. The hard, thirsty work, made worse by the strict rationing of water, left them all irritable. Even Spike was missing his home comforts. The little beek was living on a meagre diet of bread softened by a few drops of water, together with strips of dried meat, which he gnawed disconsolately. He voiced his disapproval frequently, and stared accusingly at Galen as if remonstrating with him for his failure to provide a decent standard of catering.

Galen and Drain had tried digging at several different sites, but had not found as much as a single coin. There were several mutterings that evening about whether this enterprise was worth continuing. Until then, their rare successes had been enough to keep everyone's hopes alive, but doubts were now beginning to creep in. The men's hair, clothes and nostrils were encrusted with salt, and the fine, acrid dust had made eyes and throats sore. To make matters worse, there were some ominously dark clouds moving in from the south. While rain was comparatively rare on the flats in the summer months, it was not unknown – and a single downpour could make the rough salt impossible to work, ending all hope of a major discovery. It would also make travelling much more difficult. On the other hand, it would give the Archaeologists a chance to replenish their dwindling water supplies, and put an end to the rationing.

'We'll stay one more day,' Peyton decided for them. 'Then we'll quit.'

'Unless it rains first,' Drain remarked, gazing up at the clouds as they blotted out more and more of the stars.

'Suits me,' Milner said.

'We'll go on to Fellran,' Peyton went on, taking the silence of the others for assent. 'That'll be quicker than going back.'

His companions nodded in agreement, then stiffened as they heard a booming noise deep beneath the salt.

'We can do without *that*,' Holmes commented, as everyone cast anxious glances at the beeks. The animals took little notice, however, and the tremor lasted only a few moments. Nevertheless, it was some time before those not on sentry duty were able to relax enough to get to sleep.

The rain held off overnight, but the last day of their excavation dawned grey and overcast, with heavy clouds streaming north. As they trudged off for one last effort, a warm, moist wind blew wisps of salt into the air.

'Where then?' Galen asked. 'Here?'

'Who cares?' Drain replied. 'One place is as bad as another.' He glanced up at the sky, and Galen knew that his companion was hoping for rain.

Spike had run on a few paces when they stopped. Now he let out an ear-piercing yowl and began scrabbling at the salt, even though his paws were quite unsuited to the task. The young men laughed.

'That's as good an omen as any,' Drain said.

They went to join Spike, and Galen scooped up the beek, tossing him gently to one side.

'Leave the digging to us,' he said as the little creature picked himself up and shook his fur, looking most affronted at this disrespectful treatment. 'That's our job.'

'Worse luck,' Drain moaned.

They settled into what was now an undemanding but tedious routine, digging a wide shallow hole and gradually spreading its limits. After an hour they had found nothing and were thinking of moving on when Galen's spade hit something so solid that the metal rang and he jarred his wrist. It soon became clear that he had reached stone, one of several large grey slabs which were bonded together to form a sort of pyramid. After that, the two young men dug with renewed enthusiasm and, concentrating on one of the four sides, quickly found that the stone continued, straight down, from where the pyramid ended.

'Are you thinking what I'm thinking?' Drain asked, grinning.

'It's a roof,' Galen replied.

'Yeah. And a solid one at that.'

'Can we get inside?'

'There's only one way to find out. Let's call the others.'

Drain went off to fetch his colleagues, while Galen continued digging. Before long, help had arrived. All six Archaeologists now worked together, clearing a way into what they hoped would be a treasure house.

'There must be a door somewhere,' Holmes remarked. 'All we have to do is find it.' This proved easier said than done, but eventually Drain made the breakthrough, finding the top of a rectangular hole in the solid wall. Concentrated effort soon cleared this completely.

'It's a window,' Peyton said.

'It's a way in,' Drain replied. 'That's all that matters.'

As he was the smallest of the group, he went first, crouching and tunnelling into the window space. Galen kept the passage clear, while the others removed the salt and checked it for anything that might be of interest.

The wall proved to be almost two paces thick, fuelling hopes that the building had been a stronghold of some kind. However, no iron bars stopped their progress and anything else that might have been guarding the window had long since disappeared.

A sudden fall of salt surrounded Drain, making it difficult for him to breathe – or see – for a moment, but when he recovered and more of the debris was cleared away, he cried out gleefully.

'I'm in! Get me a lamp!' This was duly passed in, and the others waited excitedly for his reaction. 'The roof looks solid enough,' he reported. 'I can't see anything else, though. The room's full of salt as high as the top of the window. There's an air pocket above that.'

'The roof must be sound then,' Peyton muttered. 'To have lasted this long . . . '

'Want someone to replace you for a spell?' Holmes asked.

'No!' Drain replied emphatically. 'This is fun. And it'll be a lot easier now I can stand up.'

'Let's go then!' Peyton called, as excited as the rest by this adventure.

The human chain continued to do its work, moving salt from inside the room, and shovelling it away. Much to the relief of his cramped limbs, Galen was soon able to join Drain inside, and thereafter the operation went even faster. And it was Galen – much to Drain's disappointment – who made the first real find when he came across a bracelet in among a collection of pieces of once-wood. He brought it out into the lamplight and drew in his breath, while his companion swore softly.

'It's gold,' Drain breathed.

'And those are real gems,' Galen added. 'I'd bet on it.'

They passed the precious armlet out, delighted by the exclamations and almost delirious laughter that accompanied its progress. Then they grinned at each other and set about their task with a vigour born of exhilaration. It was moments like this that an Archaeologist lived for – even a rookie knew that!

Soon the finds came thick and fast. Although nothing matched the fabulous bracelet, there were several other gold items, together with silver jewellery and pearls. After an hour or so, Galen and Drain were almost hysterical, and found it hard to keep themselves from laughing – definitely not advisable in that dust-filled room. Their mood was echoed outside – and their colleagues even dared to complain that some of the lesser items were not good enough.

'Precious metals only, please!' Holmes called, as he accepted a remarkably well-preserved brass candlestick. 'No more of this rubbish.'

Some of the wood in the room was obviously the shattered remains of furniture, and it was among some of this that two other extraordinary discoveries were made. The first was a book, its pages sealed together so that it could not be opened. No title was visible, but there was a geometrical design embossed on the spine. The second item very quickly restored Galen to a rational state. His heart thumped as he stood looking at the inscribed circle of snow-cluster marble,

383

and his thoughts went back to that fateful day in Cluny's basement room. The letters on this stone made no more sense than the ones he had seen then.

```
A  G  I  C  F
M  S  N  A  F
F  E  I  T  V
I  N  E  E
L  R  O  R  R
```

'What is it?' Drain asked.

'I don't know,' Galen replied truthfully. *I wish I did!*

'Don't waste any time on it, then,' his companion advised. 'We've plenty more salt to move.'

The book and stone were passed out.

'Do you really want to keep these?' Holmes asked, serious this time. 'They don't look worth bothering with.'

'Keep them!' Galen called. 'I want them.'

Gradually, the room was cleared. Although they found another window, there was no door, which seemed a very odd arrangement. One of the solid walls proved especially interesting to Galen – it was faced with marble, and was inscribed with carvings. He glanced at them as he worked, but had no time to study them properly. When the room was almost empty, Drain discovered a stairwell in the floor, with a spiral flight leading downwards.

'A cellar?' he wondered, and began scooping away some of the salt.

Galen did not answer. He was suddenly sure that they were in the top room of the tower. His imagination ran riot as he conjured up a vision of a tall, slender monolith reaching up to the sky. *What a view there must have been from these windows!* He tried to picture it in his mind's eye, but the images kept changing. *A view over what?* A royal palace? Farmland in the distance? A long-dead city?

'You still with us?' Holmes asked. He had joined them inside, and was looking at Galen curiously.

'What? Oh, yes.'

'Is that the lot then?'

'That's everything from in here. But look, there's a staircase,' Drain replied. 'Just think what we might find in the rooms below.' He carried on digging, and Holmes went to help him.

'Take it easy,' he said. 'We've already got more than enough to make this a very profitable trip. It could be dangerous down there.'

'It's survived this long,' Drain replied. 'Even the roof is perfect. I'm not going to miss an opportunity like this.' Greed rang in his voice, and his eyes shone like those of a fanatic.

'Go carefully, then,' Holmes warned, then glanced at Galen again. 'Are you all right, or would you rather go outside?'

'No. Not yet.' Galen was studying the marble carvings, knowing that even if they could be removed, they would be too big and heavy to carry. He was trying to memorize them all, tracing the lines with his fingers, blowing away salt-dust and studying the well-worn shapes – oblivious to the strange looks he was receiving from his companions. One of the carvings seemed to depict a battle, but the scene was very confused, and all the fine detail had vanished. Another depicted what Galen took to be a ship, though he had never seen one as big as this. Its sails were vast, towering over a row of long oars as it rode on the crests of stylized waves. The third panel looked like a building in flames, with a curious scene to one side. The details were not clear, but seemed to show a group of men doing the impossible – walking up the tall vertical wall of one of the burning towers. The final carving was the simplest – and yet the most enigmatic. Three men were portrayed in childlike fashion, their heads dwarfing sticklike bodies. They had been carved at differing angles, and the tops of their heads were joined by a simple triangle.

Peyton was squeezing himself through the window, and his arrival signalled the end of Galen's inconclusive study. Nothing here appeared to clarify the knowledge he had gained from the alchemist's collections of carvings.

Meanwhile, Drain was slowly descending the spiral stairs, working with his bare hands in the confined space. A familiar yowling sounded loudly in the chamber, startling those inside. Spike stood on the window ledge, surveying the scene before him.

'You've got a good one there,' Peyton remarked. 'Braver than most.'

Galen was about to reply when Drain gave a frightened yell. One of the stone steps had given way beneath him, and he had fallen out of sight. His shout was followed by a stream of curses.

'I'll get a rope,' Holmes said, leaping up and calling from the windows.

Galen moved quickly to the edge of the hole, and lay down at its edge, his arms reaching down into the darkness.

'You all right?' he called.

'I've hurt my leg,' Drain's disembodied voice echoed hollowly. 'But it's not too bad. I'm standing up now.' His head and shoulders came into sight, and he stretched up one arm. Their hands just met. 'Don't pull me up yet,' Drain said. 'There's hardly any salt in here. Pass the lamp down.'

Peyton handed this over, and when Drain received it he whistled in amazement.

'It's incredible!' he reported. 'The room's the same size, but it's empty except for this huge bell in the centre.' His voice was shrill with excitement. 'It looks like solid gold! Wait a moment.' He moved and Galen lost sight of him.

At that moment, the beeks started squealing.

'Quicksalt!' Peyton exclaimed. 'Get out of there, Drain!'

'It is gold,' Drain said in a dreamlike voice, oblivious to the danger of his situation.

'Come on!' Galen yelled.

A wave of salt poured through the second window, and Milner could be heard yelling from outside. Holmes was by the open window, a rope in his hands.

'Get out!' Peyton ordered.

Holmes threw him the rope, then did as he was told. Beneath them came the terrifying sound of stone grinding on stone and the ominous slithering of salt as it poured into the room below. Drain, suddenly aware of his peril, swore loudly and dropped the lamp. There was a brief flare of light, the darkness. Peyton dropped one end of the rope into the hole, and a hand appeared from the gloom. Galen grabbed it, but as he began to pull, salt surged into the lower room,

386

filling it in moments and cutting off Drain's terrified scream. More salt poured into the upper room, spreading over the newly cleared floor.

Peyton groaned as more shouts were heard from outside. 'Let's go,' he ordered. 'He's had it.'

'I can't!' Galen replied, fighting panic. 'He's got hold of my hand. I can't move it!' He was trapped by a vice-like grip that grew tighter by the moment. Peyton caught Galen under the arms and tried to pull him free, but to no avail. More salt flooded in.

'The window will be blocked soon!' Holmes yelled. 'Get out of there!'

'Go on!' Galen urged.

Peyton hesitated, his expression a mixture of horror and indecision, then he turned and scrambled out through the window. Galen, alone now with his doomed companion, fought with his free hand to keep his mouth and nose clear of the rising tide of salt. Drain's death-grip was so strong that Galen's hand was in agony, but that was of little concern. Neither of them could move. Galen felt the salt swirl around his body and raged inwardly at such an absurd fate as he fought to keep his face free.

Drain's hand began to shudder as he grasped his only contact with the living world even more desperately. Then, suddenly, it went limp. Galen wrenched his arm free and staggered to the window, feeling sick and afraid. *Not me too,* he pleaded silently.

The tunnel was partially blocked now, but desperation gave him strength and he scrambled through, emerging into the pit that he and Drain had dug a lifetime earlier. He climbed out, slipping and sliding on the treacherous surface, and ran towards his companions, who were standing beyond the edge of the rough salt. When they saw him, they began to yell their encouragement, and kept it up until he arrived, exhausted and trembling, in their midst. A loud crunch sounded from behind him.

'The roof's collapsed,' Frank said softly.

At this, Galen's legs gave way beneath him, and he slumped to the ground and began to cry quietly. The others left him to it, recognizing the symptoms of shock and knowing something of the horror of his ordeal. By the time he recovered his composure, the salt had stopped moving. It had only been a minor ripple, but had still been enough to kill Drain.

As Galen stood up and stared back at the scene, Holmes put an arm around his shoulders.

'He said there was a huge bell,' Galen said in a cracked voice. 'Made of gold.'

'Well, it's buried with him now,' Peyton remarked sadly.

The beeks were regathering now, their warning cries stilled. Galen looked round at them, a new fear rising.

'Where's Spike?' he asked.

CHAPTER FORTY-FIVE

Galen was suddenly dreadfully afraid for the tiny creature who had become so dear to him during their few days of partnership. After the horrible events of that day, he could not bear the thought of losing Spike as well.

'Where is he?' he repeated, still searching.

'Last time I saw him he was on the window ledge,' Peyton replied.

'I'm going to find him,' Galen stated determinedly.

'No.' Holmes tried to hold him back. 'It's too dangerous.' Galen reacted angrily, wrenching his arm free and pushing his colleague away. 'Let me go!' He turned and strode towards the rough salt.

'If he was in there, you won't find him now!' Holmes yelled. 'And if he wasn't, then *he'll* find *you.*'

Galen took no notice. Holmes looked to the group's leader, but Peyton just shrugged resignedly.

'You've been lucky so far, rookie!' Milner called. 'Don't spoil it now!'

But Galen marched on, ignoring their advice. Drain's death and his own narrow escape had left him in no mood to compromise. He knew that he would never forget the clasp of that hand, and he also felt – even though he realized that there was nothing he could have done – that he had somehow abandoned his former colleague. His rush to escape no longer seemed like the act of any sane man, but rather that of a heartless coward. He was determined not to abandon Spike in the same way.

Galen headed straight for the collapsed tower. When he was still a few paces from the edge of the pit, a small pile of loose salt exploded, and Spike leapt out. The little creature shot into the air and landed in a cloud of white dust, snarling, sneezing and shaking himself. It was almost as though he had been deliberately lying in wait for his master so that he could surprise him with his dramatics. Galen was delighted by his reappearance, and bent down to fondle the beek's soft fur and whiskers. Spike responded by yowling and pretending to bite his fingers. Galen picked him up and put him on his shoulder before walking back to join the others.

* * *

Spike's return restored a little of the group's normal good humour, but the mood in the camp that night was still subdued. Although all except Galen had witnessed deaths on the salt before, none of them had ever been on a trip where *two* men had been lost. It was accepted that the flats were a harsh environment, but the double blow would take some getting used to. Such feelings were offset by the knowledge that the treasure had all been saved. Their spoils were securely stowed in two sacks, and everyone knew that it was the richest haul they had ever seen. However, this was little compensation for Galen. The thought of monetary gain had not been his primary motivation in joining the Archaeologists, and he was too wrapped up in his own private nightmare even to think about the possible rewards of their ill-fated endeavour. He kept replaying the dreadful sequence in his mind's eye, and was still trying to reason out *why* it had happened. He ate his portion of their frugal meal, but tasted none of it.

'Why did it collapse?' he asked no one in particular. 'First the stairs, then the roof. Why now, when it's lasted so long?'

'The big shift had obviously weakened the structure,' Peyton replied soberly. 'And when we moved all the salt out, it must have altered the pressure on all the walls. Who knows what stresses that place was under.'

'If only— ' Galen began.

'Don't blame yourself,' Milner cut in. 'There was nothing you could have done'.

'Drain acted like a fool,' Peyton said, taking up the argument. 'If he'd taken the rope, or let you pull him up

390

earlier, then he would have been safe. As it was, his own imagination and greed got the better of him.'

'You think he imagined the bell?' Galen asked.

'I think he saw what he wanted to see,' the senior Archaeologist replied. 'If there *was* a bell down there, it was probably only brass. It would have been hard to tell in that light.'

'No one wastes gold on *bells*,' Frank commented dourly.

'Drain was always greedy,' Peyton said. His matter-of-fact tone made it clear that he was not speaking ill of the dead, but simply pointing out the truth. 'He'd approve of our saving this.' He waved a hand at the sacks.

'More for the rest of us', Milner added.

Galen found this remark callous, and his distaste must have shown in his expression, prompting Peyton's next words.

'That's our way, rookie,' he stated, his tone calm but not unkind. 'If you don't like it, you're under no obligation to stay with us. We'll mourn them in our own way when we reach land.'

Galen could think of nothing to say. He looked around at the solemn faces of his companions, and wondered what they had experienced in the past. *Who am I to judge?* he wondered. *If even half their stories are true . . .*

'Let's sort it out, then,' Holmes said. 'We'd have to divide it up for carrying in the morning anyway.'

Peyton nodded his agreement, and the contents of the two sacks were dumped on to the ground. Five pairs of eyes stared at the bounty speculatively, but Galen's thoughts were not of personal gain. It was only when he saw the inscribed stone again that a measure of his earlier excitement returned. Here was the first real proof that his private quest might not be in vain. Subsequent events had overshadowed its discovery, and that of the remarkable carvings on the tower room wall. *I must remember the pictures,* he thought now, running through them in his mind and fixing them in his memory. *But I'll be able to take the stone back to Cluny. Perhaps with two he'll be able to decipher the code.*

Peyton chose first, picking out the gem-studded bracelet, naturally enough. As the group's leader, he was entitled to the most valuable of the items. However, his words surprised them all.

'I'll share the proceeds of this,' he said, holding the circlet up so that the gold and precious stones winked in the lamplight. 'It'll be too much for me alone.'

This statement was greeted with a variety of wide grins. Their leader's gesture was as welcome as it was unexpected, and Galen saw yet another reason why the men who followed Peyton were so firm in their allegiance.

Milner and Holmes took other items of gold jewellery. Flank, after some deliberation, chose a heavy silver necklace rather than one of the smaller golden pieces. They all turned to Galen, but he had already made his decision, leaning forward and picking up the stone without hesitation. All but Peyton laughed at his choice.

'You'll be lucky to get much for that!' Milner exclaimed.

'Pick something else,' Peyton said, watching Galen closely. 'The stone will still be there at the end.'

'It's what I *want*, all right?' Galen snapped angrily. His emotions were running high, and he had realized too late that he had made a mistake. None of the others would have chosen the stone for several rounds – if at all – but now he had drawn attention to it by his obvious interest.

Peyton shrugged his acceptance. 'All right. It's your choice.'

'I hadn't realized you were a scholar of antiquities,' Holmes teased.

Galen did not trust himself to reply.

'Take the book as well,' Peyton said. 'If you're interested, that is.'

Galen accepted in silence.

The division of the spoils continued until all the items were claimed. When they had finished, each man stowed his tophies away and they began to prepare for the night.

'What about Drain's stuff?' Galen asked.

'Take what you want,' Peyton replied. 'He wouldn't begrudge it to you. We'll bury the rest in the morning.'

After the night's watches had been arranged, Galen went straight to his tent. Lying on his blanket in the dark, he traced the letters in the marble with his fingers, hoping for some inspiration, but they remained as meaningless as ever.

392

The book was similarly uninformative – he was unable even to open it.

He was alone in the tent that he had previously shared with Drain. Even Spike had deserted him temporarily. Drain's beek had run away, and was unlikely to be seen again. Galen turned to the possessions of his former colleague. A few items of clothing, a blanket, a water bottle and a bag to carry it all in – it seemed a pitiful collection, and Galen knew that everything else Drain had owned would either be in safe-keeping off-salt, perhaps with Beth, or had been lost with him. *Including the letter he was carrying*, Galen thought.

He lay back and tried to relax, but his mind was filled with the events of the day, and sleep would not come. He thought of the wall carvings again and again. A battle, a ship, and a fire. And then there was the last one, the three men joined by a triangle. That had been different from the rest, crudely executed, as though it had been chiselled out in a hurry. Had it been carved as the salt rose ever higher around the tower? A last desperate attempt to convey a message to the person who would find it? Galen shivered at the idea. If that was the case, then what was the message?

His train of thought was interrupted as Spike returned and proceeded to climb all over Galen's prostrate body, looking for a comfortable place to sleep. He settled down eventually, but Galen was still restless and could only doze fitfully. Spike, voicing his disapproval of this fidgeting, got up and moved over to lie on the pile of Drain's clothes. As the beek lay down, a slight crackling noise made Galen sit up quickly.

Surely not! he thought. *He couldn't have been so stupid.* He pushed Spike aside, ignoring the beek's protest, and picked up Drain's jerkin. It took only moments to find the letter, but it was sealed, and Galen hesitated. Should he open it and read the contents? Perhaps it would be in code. His brain refused to make any decision. He had just made up his mind to hide the letter away and think about it later when it began to rain. He finally fell asleep to the patter of water on the canvas.

393

* * *

The journey south was a nightmare of salt-slush and fatigue. The rain fell in intermittent bursts, and their clothes and the salt underfoot remained wet even during the dry spells. Galen kept both letters next to his skin, in an attempt to keep them dry. Every step became an effort, and their overnight camp was a horrendous mess. They were all determined to reach the southern rim before the following nightfall.

When the Archaeologists eventually reached solid ground, it was an occasion for rejoicing. Ironically, the clouds cleared away that same afternoon, so the spirits of the entire party, men and beeks alike, were doubly lifted.

By evening they had reached Fellran, a nondescript town about the size of Edgefield. Peyton led them straight to the best tavern, where he bartered one of his gold pieces for rooms for the entire party, together with as much beer as they could drink in a night. He was overpaying and everyone knew it – including the delighted landlord – but this was no time for half measures.

The gathering soon turned into an impromptu party, with several locals joining in. Each round of drinks was dedicated, with ever-increasing fervour – and ever-decreasing respect for the truth – to Drain and Kibble. The wake continued long into the night, with each of the travellers taking a turn in telling of their latest exploits.

Thus it was that the stories of the gigantic salt eruption, the fabulous golden bell, and Galen's encounter with the hand of death passed firmly into the lore of Archaeology.

CHAPTER FORTY-SIX

The wake lasted five days. During his more lucid moments, Galen realized that this may not have been the memorial that either Drain or Kibble would have chosen, but they were honoured and their deeds lionized none the less. For once, the Archaeologists confined themselves to a single venue. They were rich – at least temporarily – and cared nothing for the fact that the innkeeper was overcharging them outrageously. The cast of characters changed as sleep and other demands of nature took their periodic toll, but the ritual went on.

Galen existed in a semi-permanent daze, coherent only when he was caring for Spike, who had become a favourite with the tavern staff. For the rest of the time, he welcomed the near oblivion of drunkenness as he struggled to lay his own ghosts. Occasionally, he became vaguely aware that there was something he was supposed to do, and he kept trying to persuade Peyton to go to Riano – even though he could not remember why he wanted to go there. On each of his infrequent visits to his room, Galen blearily remembered to check that his possessions and the hidden letters were safe. But, somehow. when he returned to the noise and bustle of the wake, his mind grew confused once more.

Gradually almost all their valuables were used up. Only the bracelet was held back – there was no one in Fellran rich enough to pay a good price for such a fine piece of jewellery. The Archaeologists, secure in the knowledge of Peyton's promise, happily spent everything else they had, each contributing generously until only a few trinkets remained. Galen kept the stone and the fossilized book, but as Milner pointed out, no one wanted them anyway.

However, these esoteric finds were eventually mentioned during the course of one evening, and Galen made the mistake of showing the stone to the assembled gathering. It was passed from hand to hand amid much muttering and shaking of heads. Several of the observers would have been incapable of reading it even if it had been in plain language, but those who were less drunk – and literate – were also genuinely puzzled.

'Don't make no sense at all.'

'It's carved nice. Why would anyone bother with such?'

Most dismissed it as indecipherable nonsense, and the rest could offer no clues to the stone's meaning. Galen had expected nothing else. The artifact continued on its rounds until it came to Holmes, who took it in his left hand, stared at it with an expression of complete astonishment, and rose unsteadily to his feet. Flinging his right arm wide as if making an announcement, he stared round at his audience before making his proclamation in a loud voice.

'Agicfa messna feitiv, inee?' he asked, wide-eyed, ending with a comical bestial growl. 'L-roarr!'

While most of his audience thoroughly enjoyed this performance, Galen was furious and jumped to his own feet, almost falling over in the process.

'No!' he shouted indignantly. 'S'seriouss! Impordant!'

His interruption was ignored, and Holmes continued to bow and wave, milking the laughter for all it was worth. Galen tried to retrieve the stone, which was now being tossed from hand to hand around the table, and was further humiliated as he was led a merry dance. When his lunging chase finally ended in success, he took his prize back to his room, vowing never to show it to anyone again.

When their funds finally began to run low, Galen's repeated argument that they would be able to sell the bracelet in Riano began to make sense, and Peyton and the others agreed to set off the following day. It was a long and painful journey, lasting several days, but as their last few coins and trinkets dwindled even further, their destination became even more desirable. The gradual process of sobering up was made bearable by some of their stops in the villages along the way. Although many people gave the disreputable-looking band a wide berth, some inns were hospitable enough, and the Archaeologists reached Riano just over a month since their last visit.

Once inside the city walls, Peyton became businesslike, and began delicate negotiations to sell the bracelet. His companions waited anxiously, drinking the last of their worldly wealth. Galen very much wanted to go straight to the castle, but knew that he could not rely on the guards remembering him as a colleague of Drain. He decided that he would need money in order to gain admittance, so waited impatiently with the others.

When Peyton returned, his satisfied smile told its own story. Soon they all had coins in their pockets once more, and Galen made his excuses, leaving as quickly as he could.

'Don't be so impatient!' Holmes called after him. 'She'll wait for you!'

'Watch out for her husband this time,' Milner advised, laughing. 'We want you alive to tell the story.'

'Trust me!' Galen yelled back, waving farewell. 'Survival is my speciality.' Spike yowled his agreement, his tiny claws embedded in the shoulder of his master's jerkin.

Galen strode away in the opposite direction to the castle, then doubled back, making his way through side-streets to the main gate. He bribed the soldier on duty to let him in, on the pretence that he was courting Beth. The sentry grinned lasciviously.

'Beth, eh? She's a feisty one,' he said, pocketing the coin. 'You have a rival, my lad.'

Not any more, Galen thought grimly as he slipped inside.

He went to the kitchen entrance and asked for Beth, but was told by an officious cook that she was too busy and that he should come back later. So he made for the stables, where he reintroduced himself to a couple of the lads and helped them with their chores in return for a space to sleep in the hayloft. The familiar work was comforting, and allowed him to think through what he had to do.

Galen returned to the kitchen in the early evening. He spotted Beth hard at work on the far side, so settled down to wait. His presence was eventually pointed out to the girl by one of her work mates, but although she obviously recognized him, her face registered both surprise and disappointment. She had clearly been expecting someone else. At last her tasks were completed, and she came over to join him.

'Where's Drain?' she asked without preamble.

Galen could see no way of sparing her, so decided to come straight to the point.

'I'm sorry, Beth,' he said quietly. 'Drain's dead.'

'No!' Her face, flushed from the heat of the kitchens, turned white in an instant. Her expression was a mixture of denial and disbelief. 'You're lying!' She was half-pleading, half-shouting. 'You're just saying that to try and get his money from me.'

Galen shook his head, feeling both helpless and cruel.

'No, you can keep it,' he said, improvising as best he could. 'He would have wanted you to have it.'

'But he was coming back for me!' she wailed. Her evident misery was causing a sensation among the kitchen staff, increasing Galen's discomfort.

'I'm sorry,' he repeated wretchedly.

'You killed him!' Beth exclaimed shrilly, her eyes wide. She took a step back and raised a hand as if to protect herself from attack.

'No, Beth. No! Why would I do such a thing? He was my friend.' He had been prepared for her grief, but not for such hostility. 'The *salt* killed him. I tried to save him, but there was nothing we could do.'

'The salt?' she said in a small voice, her face falling.

'Yes.'

At this, Beth began to cry, all resistance leaving her small frame. The sight touched Galen's heart, and he stepped forward instinctively. She did not resist as he put his arms around her and held her as she sobbed. Several of the onlookers, who had been on the point of approaching them, relaxed at their embrace and smiled weakly. Galen stood there, not knowing what else to say or do. From what he knew of Drain, it was quite possible that the young man had just been using Beth as a convenient contact. He may have planned to abandon her once her usefulness had come to an end. On the other hand, he might have had a genuine regard for her. There was no way of knowing now, and Galen saw no point in revealing his cruel doubts. He held Beth tight, remembering the embrace of another young woman – in what seemed like a previous life.

'I loved him,' she whispered tearfully.

'He loved you too,' Galen replied promptly. 'He told me so.'

For a time, this redoubled her grief, but then she gradually regained her composure and drew back, looking up at Galen with red-rimmed eyes. Suspicion had been replaced by belief and, with it, a sadness that Galen found hard to face. He too needed to make use of Beth, and the urgency of his task made him swallow his distaste.

'I need your help,' he began hesitantly.

She stared at him, unspeaking.

'There is a letter that Drain was going to deliver,' he went on. 'I have it now. I think it's supposed to go to Gilgamer, but I don't know how to get to him. Can you arrange an appointment for me?' He waited, but she did not respond, and he began to wonder if she had heard anything he had said. 'If there's any reward for its delivery,' he added hopefully, 'you can have it. That's only right.'

Beth shook her head, but still said nothing.

'Will you help me?' he tried again.

'Yes. If I can.' Her voice was weak, little more than a whisper. 'Are you staying in the castle?'

'In the stables,' Galen replied.

She nodded and turned away, walking across the kitchen and into an adjoining room. Galen made no attempt to follow her, but just stood staring at the empty doorway. After a few moments, someone offered him food, which he accepted gladly. He gave an abbreviated account of Drain's death to a few of the kitchen staff, then returned to the hayloft and tried to sleep.

The next day crawled by. Although Galen kept a sharp eye out for any sign of Davin, Gilgamer or Beth, he saw none of them, so spent most of his time either helping with the horses or in restless inactivity. Brief investigations proved to him that it would be impossible to get into the inner part of the castle without help.

Help arrived during the darkness of the second night.

Galen was woken by a rustling noise in the hayloft, and for a moment he was on guard, fumbling for his knife and imagining all kinds of perils. Then his visitor spoke, and he relaxed.

'Grant, are you there?' Beth called softly.

'Over here,' he replied. She approached carefully, feeling her way in the darkness, then sat down next to him in the straw.

'I've got a note, signed by Gilgamer,' she said. Their hands met as the exchange was made.

'Thank you,' he replied.

There was a pause, then Galen felt an arm steal around his waist.

'Can I stay for a while?' Beth whispered.

So they comforted each other in the only way they knew how. For each of them their pleasure was mixed with guilt, and they were thankful for the unseeing darkness which enveloped them.

Beth left long before dawn.

* * *

Early the next morning, Galen set about the last stage of his task. Both letters were concealed next to his skin, but he hid his dagger with his other belongings, under a pile of straw. Gilgamer's signature proved enough to allow him inside the inner court, but instead of going to the third chamberlain's room, Galen went straight to Davin's office, hoping he had remembered the right door. This part of his responsibilities should prove relatively easy to discharge. He knocked and entered, but as soon as he opened the door he knew that something was wrong. The man seated behind the desk was a complete stranger.

'Oh,' Galen began, thinking fast. 'I beg your pardon. I thought this was Davin's room.'

'It is,' the man replied shortly. 'He's not here.'

'When will he be back?'

'Three, maybe four days,' the stranger replied, eyeing his visitor narrowly. 'What was it you wanted?'

Galen's heart sank. Davin must be leagues away.

'Just some business about the fire for my master,' he stammered, hoping forlornly that this might be another friend.

'What are you blathering about?' the man asked irritably. 'I can deal with anything Davin covers. What fire?'

'I'm sorry. It's a private matter,' Galen blurted out. He shut the door and bolted, cursing his own ineptitude and hoping it would not get Davin into trouble. After rounding two corners, he stopped to think. *Now I've got two letters that I don't know what to do with.* Drain's message carried no name, but only the small, single letter 'H' in one corner. Galen had been relying on Davin to advise him about its delivery. Now he could not decide whether to open it or not, or whether he should try to find its intended recipient. And it looked as though he was going to have to wait for several more days, each one increasing his risk of discovery.

Finally, he decided to go to Gilgamer and offer his services as before. At least that would maintain his alibi and give him a legitimate excuse to remain in Jarlath's lair.

The third chamberlain was delighted to see Galen, and quickly vacated his seat at the desk in order to allow him to start work immediately. Gilgamer showed no curiosity about Drain, and reacted indifferently to the news of his death.

'Your work is better than his, anyway,' he remarked nonchalantly. 'You'll just have to write quicker, that's all.'

So Galen settled down to another round of tedium, thinking that if Gilgamer had been expecting a letter from Drain, he was doing an exceedingly good job of disguising the fact. He tried to glean a little information, without mentioning Davin by name, but the third chamberlain was unforthcoming.

As he prepared to leave Gilamer's office that evening, Galen's frustration was such that he decided to try one last ploy. Standing up and stretching, he remarked, 'The moon's up, so I'm off to get some sleep.'

Gilgamer did not react, but simply carried on with his reading.

'Whatever you say,' he replied absent-mindedly, flicking a coin across the room. 'Same time tomorrow.'

Outside, Galen shrugged. *Oh well, it was worth a try.*

*　　*　　*

Three more days passed in similarly frustrating fashion. Galen continued to work as Gilgamer's secretary by day and sleep in the stables by night. Beth did not repeat her visit, something for which he was both sorry and grateful.

Despite his taking every opportunity to make discreet enquiries, there was no news of Davin. Without the scribe's advice, Galen dared not do anything more direct. At last, however, he caught sight of the familiar figure as he was leaving one evening. Davin was scurrying through the castle corridors, and Galen almost had to run to catch up with him. The spy disappeared into a chamber without looking back, but left the door ajar. Galen pushed it open without thinking, so great was his relief that his long wait was over. Then he stopped in his tracks. The scribe was searching through the drawers of a desk, but on hearing Galen's approach, his hand had gone to the knife at his belt.

Davin seemed terrified, but calmed down slightly when he saw who it was.

'Gods! What brings you here?'

'Business,' Galen replied, glad of this obvious opportunity to give the code word. He began to reach into his shirt for the letter, but stopped when Davin pointedly turned his back.

'I need a drink of water,' the scribe said loudly.

For an instant, Galen froze, recalling Pike's words. *'Water' means danger, either to him or you – or both. If that happens, get away fast.* He turned to go, his heart beating fast, only to be halted by Davin's whispered words.

'In the stables?' He glanced back at Galen, who nodded dumbly. 'Where's that *water*?' Davin added, turning away again and waving a hand at the door.

Galen left, walking as fast as he dared, and steeling himself against breaking into a run. He heaved a sigh of relief when he passed the inner court sentry without incident, and slowed his pace, though his heart was still pounding.

Now what do I do? he wondered. *Just wait?*

CHAPTER FORTY-SEVEN

That night, Galen waited in the hayloft with every nerve in his body tingling. Sleep was obviously out of the question. Startled every time one of the horses moved or snuffled, Galen constantly craned his neck to peer through the trap-door into the stables below. His vigil ended after some hours, when he spotted a dark figure slipping silently inside, a dim lamp sheltered by his cloak.

It was impossible to see the man's face, but something about his quick, delicate movements reassured Galen. He was certain that it was Davin. Nevertheless, he drew back into the shadows and slid his knife from its sheath. Hardly daring to breathe, he huddled in the darkness thinking that now – at last – he might get some answers.

The man walked the length of the stables and climbed the ladder, his soft-soled shoes making no sound on the wooden rungs. In the lamplight, Galen saw his face and breathed a sigh of relief.

'Here,' he whispered as Davin stared around.

Spike chose this moment to announce his presence, and leapt up, hissing ferociously at the intruder. Davin shied away from the miniature fury, and almost overbalanced, swearing under his breath in surprise and alarm.

'It's all right!' Galen whispered urgently. 'It's only my beek.' He had forgotten about Spike, who had until then been sleeping peacefully in the straw. As Galen moved forward to scoop the animal up, Davin recovered his composure.

'Gods!' he breathed. 'I could do without shocks like that just now.'

'I'm sorry,' Galen replied. 'I didn't think.' He tried to calm the beek, but when Spike continued to struggle in his hands, he tossed him gently into the straw a few paces away. His subsequent conversation with Davin was punctuated by unnoticed rustling noises and an occasional irate yowl as Spike fought his way back to his master.

Davin moved over to Galen, glancing about as if to make sure that they were alone – and that there would be no more surprise attacks. He set the lamp down on some empty boards, and turned the flame up a fraction before looking at Galen. There was fear and uncertainty in his eyes, and this made Galen uneasy. He recalled Pike's words. *Don't let his appearance fool you – he's one of the bravest, smartest men I've ever known.* Galen respected Pike's judgement – if a man like this was afraid, then there had to be a good reason for it.

'We haven't got long,' Davin said quietly. 'Why did you want to see me?'

'This is from Pike,' Galen replied, handing over the first letter.

Davin tore it open and quickly scanned its contents. When he looked up, he seemed even more worried than before.

'When did he give this to you?' he asked, handing the letter back.

Galen did some quick mental calculations.

'Less than a month ago,' he said. 'About twenty days, maybe twenty-three.'

Davin nodded, his expression giving nothing away.

'All right,' he said. 'When are you going north again?'

'I don't know. We've only just got here.'

'Make it soon,' Davin implored, reaching inside his shirt for another paper.

'There's something else,' Galen put in quickly. He explained about Drain's letter and how it had come into his possession, then passed it over.

Davin stared at the seal, his eyes wide.

'Gods!' he breathed. 'You haven't opened it?'

Galen shook his head.

'Good man.' Davin took a thin-bladed knife from his pocket and held it over the lamp for a few moments. Then he carefully slipped it under the wax seal, slicing it open. Gently unfolding the paper, he read the contents through twice, nodding to himself. Galen watched in fascinated silence. Finally, Davin held the knife in the flame once more, refolded the letter and resealed it perfectly with typically deft movements. It was as neat a trick as any Galen had ever seen. He was about to speak, but the expression on Davin's face kept him silent. The spy was perspiring, and his eyes were haunted.

'You've done well,' he said softly. 'But I'm in danger here. You mustn't be seen with me ever again. Don't even mention my name. Understood?'

'Yes.'

'Take this.' Davin shoved a folded piece of paper into Galen's hand. 'There was only time to put the first part in code, so you'll have to be extra careful. Things are moving too fast round here for my liking. Your turning up when you did was a lucky break. Make sure no one sees that report. Destroy it if necessary, and don't read it yourself until you're out of town.'

Galen nodded.

'Get it to Tarrant as soon as possible. It's a matter of life and death. And more.'

'I'll do it.' Galen said firmly. 'As fast as I can.'

'Good,' Davin said, smiling weakly. 'I must go now.'

'What's in the other letter?' Galen asked quickly. 'Who's H?'

'It told me nothing that I didn't already know,' the other replied. 'It confirms what's in here.' He tapped his own report. 'I had hoped that I was wrong . . . '

'What shall I do with it?'

'Destroy it, or leave it with Gilgamer to deliver to Hakon.'

'Hakon?'

'Jarlath's chamberlain,' Davin explained shortly. 'If you value your life, don't approach him directly.'

'Why not?'

'Just take my word for it!' the spy snapped, and made to get to his feet.

'Wait!' Galen hissed. 'Please. Just one more thing.' He scrabbled in his bag for the incised stone while Davin waited impatiently. 'Does this mean anything to you?'

Davin stared at the tablet. 'Not a thing. Jarlath has

something like it, though. Where did you get this?'

'From the salt.'

Davin shook his head, and shrugged.

'I have more important things to think about,' he said, then doused the lamp and left without another word.

Galen sat quite still, trying to work out whether the brief encounter had actually increased his knowledge at all. It had certainly increased his apprehension. His first instinct was to burn the first two letters and to leave the castle that very night with Davin's important – and dangerous – reply. However, after reflecting for a few moments, he decided to wait a little. Sneaking out very late at night would seem more suspicious than leaving in daylight – only a short time away now.

Once that decision was made, the next was much easier. It would surely be even less suspicious if he stayed the next day and worked with Gilgamer again. That way, he could stroll out at the end of the day as naturally as though he were making for a tavern. Galen had the sense to realize that he was being influenced by the newly acquired knowledge of another inscribed stone within Jarlath's castle. His thoughts kept returning to this, no matter how hard he tried to consider his situation rationally. He had to see it! If he could, then he would have a double reason for wanting to go north quickly. The more he thought about this, the more the idea appealed to him. He would hide the letters where no one would find them. Then, as long as he took great care, his plan could not do him any harm. After all, the Archaeologists would not be leaving for a few days, so he might as well take this opportunity to prove himself worthy of the trust that had been placed in him, and learn what he could. *Perhaps I can begin to run a little now*, he thought, remembering Pike's words, then lay back. He slept until dawn, when the clatter of hooves below roused him. Somehow, daylight made Davin's fears seem less important.

Gilgamer was delighted with his assistant's early appearance and piled the work in front of him before leaving to attend to business of his own. Galen was sorely tempted to investigate the other contents of the room – especially the bookshelves – but thought better of it, and set about his work with a will. He hoped that he would be able to find an excuse to leave and investigate other parts of the inner court. By noon he had finished all the copying and sorting, but Gilgamer had still not returned. So he began to doodle on a spare sheet of paper, and found himself writing out the letters from the stone he had found in the tower room, staring at the meaningless pattern.

```
A   G   I   C   F
M   S   N   A
F   E   I   T   V
I   N   E   E
L   R   O   R   R
```

He could only see one complete word: 'cater', in the fourth column. But that seemed innocuous, and he dismissed it. In any case, reading in columns made a nonsense of the letters on the far right. The top line intrigued him, though. By placing the first letter of the second line in front, and forgetting the last F, then the word 'magic' appeared – which seemed to Galen to hold much more potential than 'cater'. However, repeating this process with the other lines produced nothing that made any sense. Then again, he thought, perhaps the lay-out was irrelevant. Perhaps the code relied upon the substitution of completely *different* letters . . .

These musings were interrupted as Gilgamer returned. Without thinking, Galen tried to hide his scribblings. However, the third chamberlain was too fast for him.

'What's that?' he demanded, holding out a peremptory hand. 'You've not been wasting my time, I hope.'

'I've finished the work,' Galen protested.

'So you decided to do a little for yourself?' Gilgamer remarked, his hand still outstretched.

Galen gave in to the inevitable, and handed the paper over. His temporary master glanced at the letters, turned them this way and that, then shook his elegant head, obviously puzzled.

'What in the Web *is* this gibberish?' he asked.

'Those letters were cut into a stone tablet I found in the salt,' Galen replied, deciding that a carefully edited version of the truth could do no harm. 'One of the other Archaeologists told me that Lord Jarlath had one like it.' Gilgamer did not respond, and Galen pressed on hopefully. 'I was hoping he might like to buy it from me.'

'Buy it!' Gilgamer exclaimed, laughing. 'If Lord Jarlath wants something, you would be well advised to give it to him. If he so chooses, he may reward you – and then you would be suitably grateful.'

'Of course,' Galen replied, lowering his eyes.

'Anyway, it looks like complete rubbish to me,' the third chamberlain went on. 'I can't think why he *would* want it.'

'Have you seen the other tablet?' Galen asked.

'No.' Gilgamer tossed the paper back on the desk. He was obviously losing interest in the topic. 'Hakon's the one for that.'

'The chamberlain?'

'The *first* chamberlain,' Gilgamer replied, an odd inflection in his voice. 'It doesn't do to be too interested in *him*.'

You're the second person to warn me about that, Galen thought, perversely feeling more and more drawn to this mysterious character. All paths seemed to lead to him. But Gilgamer offered no further explanation, and instead dismissed his assistant.

'Shall I come back this afternoon?' Galen asked anxiously, not wanting to lose his method of access so soon.

'Of course,' Gilgamer replied. 'There'll be plenty more for you to do by then.'

During his break, Galen went to the stables, retrieved the letters from their hiding places, then collected his belongings and the now very restless Spike. He had made up his mind to return to the castle that afternoon to discover what he could, but after that he would stay well away. It seemed only sensible to move his few possessions – especially Davin's latest report – so that they at least were out of harm's way.

His heart was beating fast as he walked past the guards at the main gate, but they waved him through without a second glance. He walked quickly to the same squalid, backstreet tavern that he had patronized a month earlier, and took a room. After making arrangements for Spike's food, he hurried back to the castle. He had spent a little time finding a secure hiding place for Davin's report, which was now secreted below a loose floorboard under the bed in his room. As an afterthought, Galen had wrapped the paper in a piece of dirty cloth, together with most of his money. His other possessions, including the stone and the book, he left openly in the squalid room. The original letter had been safely burnt, but the one addressed to Hakon was nestling inside his shirt.

'You're late,' was Gilgamer's only comment when Galen represented himself. Another pile of papers and several thick ledgers lay on the desk, and Galen's heart sank.

'Shouldn't I deliver some of this morning's work first?' he asked, without much hope. Gilgamer just looked at him, and he subsided into his chair.

Working feverishly, Galen completed his tasks in a little over two hours. Gilgamer inspected the work sceptically but could not fault it. Not wanting to have the bother of preparing another batch, he decided to let Galen act as messenger. Various piles of documents were tied with string, the names of their intended recipients attached, then directions given as to their location.

'Think you can remember all that?' the chamberlain asked.

Galen nodded; Gilgamer flipped him a coin and instructed him to return at the same time tomorrow. As Galen set off with his first load, he hoped that he would not bump into Davin or the other official he had met yesterday. All went smoothly enough, and he made sure that the pile for the first chamberlain's office was left until his last trip. He was determined to make this chance count.

Finally, he was left with just one parcel, addressed to a man named Jarson, one of Hakon's assistants. Having made that delivery, he produced the sealed letter and asked, as boldly as he felt able, to deliver it in person. Jarson, a fat, pasty-faced scribe, looked first at the seal and then at the messenger with ill-concealed contempt. However, he told Galen to go in the next room and wait.

The chamber was small. It contained no furniture, but there were several lurid tapestries hanging on the walls. Although there were no windows, there were three doors other than the one Galen had come through. One of these stood ajar, and he could not resist peering through. The room on the other side was vast, a huge hall filled with an extraordinary variety of works of art. There were statues, paintings, tapestries and richly emblazoned shields. Swords and other ornate weapons hung from the walls, while smaller items were displayed on stands and tables. It was a veritable treasure trove, but Galen had eyes for only one item. He had seen the circle of snow-cluster marble almost immediately, and hesitated for only a moment before daring to enter the hall. With a quick glance around, he strode quickly towards the stone.

The letters were arrayed as before; three lines of five, interspersed with two lines of four. This set made as little sense as the others, but Galen stared at the deeply incised characters, memorizing them without thinking.

```
E   W   I   Z   A
E   N   N   R
O   R   N   D   E
O   H   S   E
B   H   T   I   R
```

The riddle still made no sense.
Now what? he thought.
With a shiver of fear, he became aware that he was being watched by someone standing behind him. He turned slowly, and came face to face with the chilling, mesmeric eyes of the skeletal monk.

'I am Hakon,' the apparition said. 'You have something for me?'

CHAPTER FORTY-EIGHT

Galen handed the letter over without a word, his fingers shaking slightly as he did so. All he could think about was the utter folly of his actions, and of all the warnings he had ignored. Face to face with such an implacable foe, his earlier boldness seemed stupid and unforgivable. Hakon radiated a cold, formidable power, and Galen realized at last that he was meddling in evil affairs. He promised himself silently that if he escaped from this encounter he would never again tempt fate in such a foolhardy manner. *No more heroics.* He would leave Riano that very night – if he was given the chance.

Hakon inspected the letter, checking the seal carefully, but made no move to open it.

'How did you come by this?' His voice was hoarse and rasping, and reminded Galen of the hissing of a snake. Pale, serpentine eyes reinforced the comparison.

Galen answered in faltering tones, hesitating often and trying not to meet the monk's hypnotic gaze for too long. He told of Drain's death, and elaborated slightly on what his former companion had told him of the messages he carried. To his own ears, his lies seemed transparent, but Hakon's cool expression never altered.

'Drain was a foolish young man,' he remarked disapprovingly when the stuttering explanation was over. 'On the other hand, you seem to have made the most of your colleague's misfortune. Such enterprise should not go unrewarded.' A bony hand disappeared into the folds of his robe and Galen heard the clink of coins.

'No . . . ' he said, without thinking.

Hakon's face stretched in a hideous smile.

411

'But surely you hoped—'

'I was just doing it for a friend,' Galen said quickly, feeling more awkward by the moment. 'I don't want—'

'Admirable sentiments, I am sure,' Hakon rasped, his death's-head grin never wavering. 'But, please, accept this for your trouble.' He stretched out a hand, and when Galen reluctantly did the same, a small blue gemstone was dropped into his palm. It shimmered in the fading light of the high windows, staining his skin with its cool luminescence. He felt a quiver of disquiet at the touch.

'Thank you, my lord,' he whispered.

'It is of little true value,' Hakon replied. 'But it may serve to impress a girl or two.'

What would you *know of such matters?* Galen wondered, then wrenched his thoughts away from this trivial irrelevance. He needed all his wits about him.

'How did you get in here?' Hakon asked suddenly, reinforcing Galen's concern.

'The door . . . was open,' he stammered. 'I saw all these wonderful . . . things.' He could not help himself from glancing at the incised stone, but quickly looked away. He cursed inwardly. 'I'm sorry. I . . . didn't mean to pry.'

'Curiosity is understandable,' the first chamberlain replied smoothly. 'But I hope you were not thinking of trying to steal anything. My master does not take kindly to the theft of his property.'

Galen protested his innocence. At that moment, all he wanted to do was to get away from the treasure house and its intimidating guardian. Hakon merely listened impassively.

'Darkness is falling,' the monk stated, after a long, uncomfortable pause. When Galen did not reply, he asked, 'Did your friend also tell you the correct response?'

'Er . . . the moon is rising . . . ' Galen answered unhappily. He could no longer tell whether his words were wise or not. 'So I'd better sleep . . . '

Hakon nodded.

'Go then,' he said quietly.

For a few moments, Galen did not react. Was the seemingly deadly game over? Could his adversary's instruction really be taken at face value? He found it difficult to believe that escape could be that simple.

Need overpowered uncertainty, so he bowed jerkily and walked from the room. Once outside, he fled into the labyrinth of corridors, intent only on distancing himself from the scene of his fear.

Hakon watched Galen's departure thoughtfully, then turned his attention to the letter the young man had brought. Opening it, he read the message slowly, nodding his approval, then folded it again and put it into one of the pockets concealed within his habit. His pale eyes turned to the white stone, scanning the letters, his face unmoving. Raising his right hand, Hakon clicked his fingers. A remote bell tolled languorously, as if in response. He picked up the tablet, weighing it in his hands, and measuring it with gimlet eyes. Another monk entered the hall and approached his master.

'Raliel, cast the aura of this disc for me,' Hakon commanded.

The newcomer took the stone reluctantly, distaste clear in his expression.

'I have never liked it, as you know,' he said. 'But now it seems quieter, less powerful.'

'It is different?' Hakon asked sharply.

'Yes, if memory serves.'

The tablet changed hands once more.

'Why such interest?' Hakon said, almost to himself. 'And by a simple messenger? It is not healthy. Of all the things in this room, why *this*?'

He held the offending article out at arm's length, then removed his hand. For a moment the stone hovered in mid air, trembling as though balanced between two tremendous forces. Then it smashed down on to the stone floor with such violence that it cracked into several pieces. Raliel jumped, dodging flying splinters, but Hakon was unmoved. 'I should have listened to your instincts earlier,' he snarled. 'Have the pieces destroyed – utterly.' He swept out an arm, and the widely scattered fragments regrouped, sliding across the floor as if they were alive. 'And find the boy!'

Raliel stopped in the process of picking up the shards, and looked up.

'What boy?'

'The messenger. He can't have gone far,' Hakon replied. 'And he carries a marker.'

Raliel hurried to obey his master's command.

* * *

Galen strode through the corridors as fast as he dared, forcing himself not to attract attention by running. He had almost become lost in his early panic-stricken flight, but he had regained his bearings now, and was thinking straight at last. He was praying silently that his own stupidity would not cause his downfall, and wondered what had made him think such a dangerous course of action was sensible – or even worthwhile. For the life of him, he could never have justified such an insane risk.

Just let me get past the inner court guards, he pleaded silently.

In the event, that boundary was crossed without alarm, and Galen's feeling of relief was almost overwhelming. He walked on, a little of his confidence returning, and came to the kitchens. He was so close to escape now . . .

A figure stepped out in front of him, calling his name. He was so intent on gaining the outer door that he only just stopped in time to avoid bumping into her.

'Did you pass the letter on?' Beth asked.

'Yes.' Galen glanced behind him, but saw no sign of pursuit.

'Do you want some food?'

'No. I must go.'

Beth looked disappointed but smiled bravely.

'What's that?' she asked, pointing to his fist.

Galen glanced at the blue gemstone, which was still clutched in his hand. He had forgotten it completely.

'It was my payment for delivering the letter,' he said quickly. 'It's for you.'

Beth's eyes lit up as he passed it over.

'It's beautiful!' she exclaimed. 'Is it really for me?'

'I keep my word,' Galen replied, looking over his shoulder again.

414

Beth threw her arms around his neck and kissed him, oblivious to the fact that he did not respond.

'I must go,' he repeated desperately.

'Why?' she asked, clinging tight.

'I *have* to.' Gently but firmly, he removed her arms, and manoeuvred past, all but running to the door and out into the courtyard. Beth watched him go, surprise and sadness mixed in her pretty face, then she looked down at the gem in her palm. It shimmered, colouring her fingers blue.

Galen crossed the yard, wishing with all his might that he had eyes in the back of his head. It was all he could do to keep from running – and a spot on his back, midway between his shoulder blades, itched intolerably. As usual, the main gates were closed, and several soldiers stood around the smaller door which opened to one side. Galen approached them, his heart thumping, hoping that the failing light of dusk would disguise his nervousness.

Suddenly a commotion broke out behind him. The sentries all stared in the direction of the noise, and Galen was forced to turn and look. To do anything else would have appeared unnatural. A group of soldiers had emerged from the castle buildings, and two of them were dragging the limp form of a man. Galen froze as they came towards the gate, but the sinister group paid him no attention, even when they passed close by. Their contempt for their burden was emphasized by the way they were carrying him, one man grasping each ankle, the victim's head bumping over the flagstones, his arms trailing. Davin was certainly dead, but the amount of blood which smeared his corpse and the expression on his lifeless face made it clear that his death had been neither quick nor painless. Galen watched him go by, feeling sick – and doubly desperate.

'Another one for the public platform,' one of the soldiers remarked.

'No fun left in him!' a sentry responded.

'We'll string him up anyway, and let them watch him rot,' the soldier replied indifferently.

The party went out through the small door, under the curious gaze of the guards. Galen stood stock still for a few moments, bathed in a cold sweat, and swallowing hard.

Eventually he regained a little of his composure and walked towards the door. He even managed to greet the sentries, who knew him by now, in a reasonably normal voice. They grinned and waved him on, just as more shouting came from behind.

'Hold the door!' The shout came from another group of soldiers, approaching at a run from the kitchens.

Galen tried to move quickly, and had reached the very threshold of freedom before a heavy hand fell on his shoulder.

'Not so fast, son. Someone wants word with you.'

* * *

The dungeon was pitch black. In the darkness, madness beckoned and imaginary terrors lurked. Damp stone and slime made exploration unwise. Galen could not tell how long he had been trapped in this forgotten hole. Time had ceased to have any meaning. There was no daylight, and few sounds.

Every so often, an unseen lamp illuminated the rim of the solid door which barred the only exit from his dismal cell. Then a small slot would be opened and bowls of food and water pushed in. Galen now lived for these moments, which were his only proof that he was still alive and had not gone blind. For some time he had shouted and screamed, pleaded with unseen gaolers, but there was never any response; eventually he merely accepted the sustenance and ate mechanically, oblivious to what was in the thin metal bowl.

During the early part of his incarceration, he had been interrogated by two men. They had shouted and beaten him, searching his clothes and the recesses of his body. They had been accompanied by a third shadowy figure, who had asked questions over and over again in a thin, hoarse voice that sent shivers down Galen's spine. He had kept his lies to a minimum, answering truthfully when he could about the letter he had delivered, Drain's death, his relationship with Gilgamer and the work he did for him, Beth, and the letters carved in the snow-cluster tablet. He claimed repeatedly that he had not known Davin, and was secretly very glad that he had obeyed the spy's last instructions and not read his report. In his fear and confusion, Galen was nearly caught out several times, but he managed to keep a precarious grip on his story – and on his sanity.

This process had been repeated twice, but then his tormentors seemed to have forgotten about him. He was left to dwell upon his pain and misery, the filth of his surroundings, and his own pent-up fury at his ineptitude. Days passed in the world above, but down below, nothing changed. Galen wondered how long it would be before his gaoler forgot about his existence and left him to starve. At times, this prospect seemed almost welcome.

His only escape was in sleep – and that would only come as the result of utter exhaustion. And sometimes this was worse than being awake. He dreamed of rotting corpses, of Davin's bloody, horror-stricken face saying, 'I'm in danger here.' Hands clasped his own so that he cried out with the pain. Then they went limp and turned cold, filling him with sorrow and desperation. He saw letters jumbled together, meaning nothing, but knew that he must remember them. Each time he tried to grasp the image, it changed, slipped away, and he heard a voice wailing, 'It's a matter of life and death – and more.' Another voice, calmer but no less urgent. *Next time, remember the letters* . . . He saw other sets of letters, three rows of five, two of four – but they were not the ones he had seen with his own eyes.

Inexplicably, he also saw visions of Rebecca mixed in with the other elements of his nightmare. Her eyes were glazed with delirium, and she appeared to be asking him questions, over and over again. But he could not hear her, and shied away from yet another interrogation. He sometimes had the uncanny notion that she was actually *directing* the purpose of his dreams, making him see images he would rather hide from – but he had no idea what it was she was seeking.

* * *

It had taken Hakon's messenger four days to reach the peninsula. It had been hard riding, but none of the brethren was afraid of work. Their time was near!

The rider guided his mount through the monastery gates, dismounted, and headed straight for the audience chamber. The abbot was already waiting there; nothing came as a surprise to their revered leader.

'Greeting, Ixor. You have news from Hakon?' The abbot's voice was thin and grating, and his skin pale, but there was a fierce intensity in his grey eyes.

Ixor bowed.

'Good news, my lord. Jarlath's arrangements are almost complete. The armies will march within two months.'

'And he still suspects nothing?'

'No. His greed drives him on. He accepts our aid with no thought of the price he will have to pay.'

The abbot nodded approvingly.

'And Montfort?

'He still believes that the threat to his kingdom is only political,' Ixor replied. 'That the conflict will be merely human.'

'Then they will both fall into our hands,' the abbot said. 'I have waited many lifetimes for this bargain to be fulfilled.'

Slow smiles spread over the two emaciated faces.

'Our time is near,' Ixor said quietly.

After centuries of waiting, their oft-repeated claim was taking on the ring of truth.

CHAPTER FORTY-NINE

The lamplight which shone tantalizingly through the cracks of the door frame seemed just the same, but this time, Galen sensed that something was different. Perhaps his hearing had become more acute now that his eyes were useless – and his ears had definitely registered a new beat to the approaching footsteps. Perhaps his nose had caught the faintest hint of a new scent. But he still found it impossible to rouse himself to hope. He sat, huddled in a corner, shivering and half-mad, waiting for the food which was his only link with the outside world.

The footsteps halted outside his door, and in the silence Galen could hear someone breathing deeply. Then came the sound of a bolt being drawn back gently, as if the person outside was trying to move the lock as quietly as possible. Galen's indifference was punctured at last, and he leapt to his feet, almost slipping on the slick floor as he lunged at the door.

'Talk to me!' he cried. 'Please! What's . . .'

He was interrupted by an angry hiss from outside.

'Shhh! Be quiet!'

Galen fell silent, shaking with a mixture of emotions, his palms resting flat upon the rough wooden surface. He listened as more bolts grated slowly – and then came the unbelievable sound of a key turning in the lock. The door opened and he almost fell through, blinded by the sudden glare of the lamp.

'Come on! Quick!' a voice whispered urgently.

Galen stumbled forward, and a blurred figure caught his arm and steadied him.

'What have they done to you?' the voice asked in shocked

tones. Galen's mind struggled towards recognition.

'Beth?' he croaked, still half-blind.

'Yes,' she replied curtly. 'We haven't got all day. Come on.' She tugged at his arm and led him along a dank corridor and up some steps. Another tunnel and more steps. When they were near the top, she doused her lamp and whispered, 'Quiet now.'

They crept on, Galen feeling his way, blind once more. Beth led him past the sleeping guard, through a door which creaked horribly, and out into the night-time courtyard. He breathed deeply, the air like heady wine, and gazed about – at the castle, at the stars above, and then back at the girl who still held his arm.

'The stables,' Beth breathed.

'But my things aren't there any more,' he replied, confused.

'I know,' she answered impatiently. 'I looked. Come on!'

She helped him across the moonlit yard, bracing him when he stumbled, and led him into an empty stall. There she stripped off his filthy clothes, and wiped him down as best she could with clean straw. She made him hold still while she drew a blade across his skin, shaving the youthful stubble from his face. He was too weak, too happy and bewildered to question her, but when she retrieved a maid's dress, made him put it on, and fastened a woman's cap to his head, he had to speak.

'What's this for?'

'You have to go in disguise – or they'll never let you out of here!' Beth snapped. 'Drink this!' She pushed a small flask into his hands, and Galen obeyed her command, swallowing a mouthful of fiery spirit. He choked, his eyes watering. For a moment, his head swam. 'That's enough,' Beth laughed, snatching it back and taking a gulp herself. Then she sprinkled some on their clothes.

She went to the stable door and peered out.

'All clear,' she said, beckoning for Galen to join her. He did so, and they linked arms.

'Now sing!' Beth ordered.

'What?'

'Sing. We're two young ladies heading for a night on the town.' She launched into a sentimental ballad and set off towards the main gates, dragging Galen with her. He saw that the sentries were already watching their staggering progress, and wondered briefly whether Beth was in fact quite mad. *Too late now*, he told himself – flight was obviously impossible. He would have to go along with her plan. He joined in with the half-remembered song, off-key.

'Higher!' Beth whispered in his ear.

'What?'

'You're supposed to be a girl!' she hissed.

Galen's subsequent falsetto attempts were cracked and comical, and the watching guards laughed as the 'girls' approached. Galen kept his face down as they drew near.

'Your friend's had too much already,' one the soldiers remarked.

'Aye,' Beth replied pertly. 'She'll make some man happy tonight. It's a pity you're on duty!'

'The watch changes in an hour,' he replied hopefully.

'Too late!' Beth cried. 'We'll have other fish to fry by then.' She pushed past the two men, dragging Galen with her, and suddenly they were outside. Freedom! He felt like dancing, and wanted to leap into the air with sudden exhilaration – but Beth kept him firmly anchored to the ground.

'Walk!' she ordered. 'We're not away yet.'

They crossed the square – the darkness mercifully hiding the central platform from their sight – and entered the shadows beyond. In the relative safety of an obscure alleyway, they collapsed laughing in each other's arms. Galen embraced his saviour joyously. He was only just beginning to realize the enormity of what had happened – and what she had risked for him.

'Thank you,' he said. The words seemed painfully inadequate, but they were all he had.

'I like you,' she replied simply. 'You were kind to me.' She reached up and kissed him. 'Though I think I prefer you dressed as a man! Goodness knows what people would make of us now.' They laughed, looking into each other's eyes.

'You took a terrible chance,' Galen said eventually.

Beth shrugged.

'I don't like those monks,' she said vehemently.

'Nor do I!' Galen replied with feeling.

'Just after you gave me the blue stone,' Beth went on, 'one of them burst into the kitchens with some of the Baron's soldiers. He pointed straight at me, then they grabbed me and started shouting, "Where is he? Where is he?" I said I didn't know.'

'Do you still have the stone?' Galen asked, suddenly apprehensive.

'No. They took it,' she replied bitterly. 'I hate them.'

Several heartbeats passed in silence.

'Thank you,' Galen repeated at last. 'How can I ever repay you?'

'By getting away,' she answered promptly, the pleasure of her accomplishment shining in her eyes. 'You *do* look a sight!' she added, dissolving into laughter. 'Where are your things?'

'At an inn called The Scabbard.'

Beth's eyebrows went up.

'Good.' she said. 'They won't look for you *there* in a hurry.'

'At least I *hope* they're still there,' Galen added worriedly. 'How long was I locked up?' He shuddered involuntarily.

'Six days, I think,' she replied. 'It took me ages to find out where you were. Come on. Let's get you to the inn.'

'Shouldn't you get back?'

'No – I'm enjoying this too much,' she said mischievously. 'And besides, I'll need the dress back!'

So they set off, Beth leading the way through the ill-lit back streets of her home town. Gradually, Galen felt himself coming back to life. It was only when he recognized some of his surroundings and realized that they were almost at their destination that he remembered Spike, and felt a pang of guilt. However, he soon had a more immediate problem to worry about.

Two men stepped out of a shadowy doorway and blocked their path.

'Don't fancy yours much,' one of them remarked, grinning.

'Why do you stick with her, darling?' the other asked, looking at Beth. 'We'll show you a much better time.' He made a grab for her, but Beth shied away, avoiding his clumsy assault with ease.

422

Galen, who had stood his ground, felt a sudden burst of rage. Putting all the weight of his pent-up fury behind the blow, he lashed out at the assailant. The punch caught the man squarely on the nose and he went down as though he'd been struck with a sledgehammer.

The first man looked aghast at his fallen companion, then glanced back at Galen.

'You want to be next?' the 'girl' asked gruffly.

The man turned tail and fled.

'It'll be a while before they try *that* again,' Beth commented, laughing.

* * *

At the tavern, Galen discovered with relief that his few belongings were still safe. They had obviously been searched, but had not been considered worth keeping, and had all been dumped in a corner of a dusty store-room. Even the stone tablet and the fossilized book were still there. All that was missing were the items he had hidden – and Spike!

Galen changed into his spare set of clothes, then set about finding them. His eccentric attire had caused some amusement on his arrival, and it was a relief to be in his own clothes again. Getting into his old room proved something of a problem as it was already occupied, but his insistence paid off and he was delighted to discover that the report – and his money – were still secure.

Finding Spike proved easier. As soon as Galen mentioned his beek, he was shown to the kitchens and greeted rapturously by his furry companion – who was larger, healthier and noisier than ever. His adoptive mistresses, the cooks, had obviously taken to the little creature, and though he protested vigorously at his earlier abandonment, Spike had clearly benefited from his sojourn. He resumed his place on Galen's shoulder amid much laughter. Whatever other abilities Spike could lay claim to, he was certainly a survivor.

Galen and Beth parted company in the early hours of the following morning. He had explained that he must leave Riano, and she admitted that she wanted to return to the castle now. It was a tender farewell, with few words spoken.

'Come back some day – if you can,' were Beth's parting words.

I was lucky to get into that castle, Galen thought as he watched her walk away. *And even luckier to get out! Thank you, Beth.*

He turned his mind to the task in hand. He had to go north immediately – too much time had already been lost. A few enquiries revealed that, as far as anyone knew, the Archaeologists were still in town. Galen was immensely relieved to hear this. He would have been prepared to brave the salt with only Spike for company, but it would obviously be safer and probably faster within a group. He began his search in time-honoured fashion, by visiting as many taverns as he could. He found his colleagues at dawn, by which time he was stumbling with fatigue. The whole group was already gathered.

'We thought we'd lost you!' Holmes exclaimed, with a welcoming smile.

'Impeccable timing,' Peyton commented. 'We're about to go north with a lubber this very morning.'

'Where to?' Galen asked, his flagging spirits buoyed by this news.

'Tybridge,' their leader replied.

It was a town well to the east of Cutover, but it was better than nothing. Galen set out with the others, trying to ignore the fact that his legs felt like lead and his eyelids had a distressing tendency to droop.

* * *

His companions naturally wanted to know what he had been up to, but they recognized his exhausted state and did not force the pace for the first day. That night, Galen slept so deeply from dusk to dawn that they could not rouse him to take his turn on watch.

'From the state of him,' Holmes commented, 'he must have left a number of jealous husbands in Riano!'

The following day saw Galen restored to something

424

approaching normal health, and he regaled the Archaeologists with a fanciful story, explaining how he had become so tired and had managed to lose most of his money and clothes. All the time, however, he was thinking about Davin's report and what it might contain – but he did not dare study it while the others were watching.

That night, he found the opportunity to be alone for a while and unfolded the paper carefully, reading it by the feeble lamplight. The first part looked like a set of accounts, and he assumed that this was in code, but the second half was written normally, in a hasty, small scribble – and its import was only too plain.

' "I have just seen proof. Mercenaries from the Southern Isles are to be used. An armada will bring them to our ports – possibly as soon as one month from now. They plan to march to Riano, then directly across the salt to Edge." '

Galen stared in disbelief. Across the salt? A whole army! That would be akin to mass suicide! He read on.

' "This way they think to reach Garadun before you have time to react and intercept them. You must act quickly!

' "In haste, D." '

Galen was stunned. Foreign mercenaries? Invasion? It was unthinkable. Yet these were the words of a man who had died horribly in the pursuit of such intelligence. Civil war was now a horrifying reality. *And the information has been entrusted to me!*

The rest of the journey across the salt was completed quickly, something which suited Galen even more than it did the merchant they were accompanying. The Archaeologists were in a relatively subdued mood, as this was their first crossing since losing two of their colleagues. No sounds came from the depths, and no storms or quicksalt slowed their progress. Indeed, the only event of note was their passing close by Blackator. This was an awe-inspiring black pinnacle of rock, the mighty tip of a once-mightier torgrist mountain. Wild music came from it as the wind played amid its whorls and crevasses, but otherwise there was an eerie stillness about the rock, something which was emphasized by the stark contrast in colour between the mountain and its surroundings.

425

It was early evening when Peyton and his troup arrived in Tybridge. The fee from the crossing had already been distributed, so they headed straight for the nearest tavern. Galen slipped away at the earliest opportunity, and went in search of a horse. He found one easily enough but was forced to overpay, using all the money left from Pike's initial outlay, together with his more recent earnings. His need was so urgent that he could not afford to waste time haggling. However, he knew that his purchase, a strong black stallion, was a fine animal that would serve him well on the journey.

He rode away immediately, feeling guilty about abandoning his companions, but knowing that he had no choice; explanations would have taken too long. He rode west throughout the night, and arrived in Cutover early the next morning, exhausted and clinging precariously to the horse's neck. In the pale early sunlight, The Raven's yard was a welcome sight indeed, but when he came to a halt, the stallion's hooves clacking on the cobbles, Galen felt almost numb and unable to move. He stirred when a giant of a man strode purposefully into the yard, and tried to dismount. In doing so, he overbalanced and all but fell into Redfern's arms.

CHAPTER FIFTY

Redfern looked up from Davin's letter.

'When did he give you this?'

'Eleven, maybe twelve days ago,' Galen replied. 'I think I was in the dungeon for about six days.' He shivered at the memory. Sitting here in a padded chair in The Raven's private room, that dark hell-hole seemed a lifetime away – and still too close for comfort.

'Then we have even less time than I thought,' the landlord said quietly, alarm registering on his normally passive face. 'And you're sure that Davin's dead?'

'Yes.' Galen saw again the bloody face and broken body that had been dragged past him. 'What are we going to do?'

'I don't know where Tarrant is,' Redfern replied thoughtfully. 'Or Pike for that matter. Let me think about this. You need to sleep.'

Galen did not argue. He was bone-weary, and ached all over. The innkeeper led him to a bedchamber, and promised to rouse him at noon. Galen collapsed on to the bed, still partly clothed, and was asleep as soon as his head touched the pillow. Spike curled up contentedly by his side.

Then someone was shaking Galen's shoulder.

'Go 'way,' he mumbled. Surely it couldn't be noon yet? Nevertheless, his tormentor persisted, so Galen opened his eyes reluctantly. A delicious smell filled the room, and helped him come to his senses.

'I've brought you some food,' Redfern said.

While Galen sat up and began to eat, Redfern talked.

'I can't leave here,' he began, 'and at the moment, there's no one else I can trust. You'll have to go to Garadun and take the news directly to Montfort.'

'To the king?' Galen spluttered, his mouth half full. 'Me?' He had hoped to be able to return to Edge, and this new instruction filled him with fresh doubts.

'Will you do it?' Redfern asked gravely.

'Of course. But how . . . ?'

'This will help you,' the innkeeper interrupted. He slid a ring from the middle finger of his left hand, and showed it to Galen. A small gold coin, of a type he had never seen before, had been mounted in a pale gold band. 'See here,' Redfern said, indicating a tiny catch in the recess beneath the coin. 'You press that, and . . .' One side of the coin became loose, and the landlord inserted a nail and prised it upwards. Inscribed on the metal beneath the coin was a tiny depiction of two hands clasped together. 'That is the symbol of Montfort's secret service. Any officer in the castle guard will recognize it, and it should be enough to get you in. So don't lose it!'

Galen nodded as Redfern closed the ring again with a tiny click.

'You'll also take Davin's report, of course,' the big man went on. 'And this letter from me. Don't show them to *anyone* unless they have a ring like this – unless it's the king himself!' He smiled at Galen's consternation.

'But he won't see me personally, will he?'

'Why not? You know more about these events than any mediator could. Montfort will have enough sense to realize that.'

From the floor, Spike yowled as if to emphasize Redfern's point. Both men looked at him and discovered that the beek was actually protesting over his now empty dish.

Redfern laughed. 'He has a healthier appetite than you,' he remarked, looking at Galen's plate. 'Eat up.' Galen resumed his meal, though his thoughts were far from food. 'Your horse is a good one,' the innkeeper continued. 'He should get you to Garadun without any problem. Do you need money?'

Galen nodded, and his host tossed a small bag on to the bed.

'I've packed you some supplies as well,' Redfern added. 'So you should only need to stop for sleep. Is there anything else you can think of?'

Galen shook his head, swallowing the last of his food.

'What's this?' Redfern asked then, holding up the stone tablet.

'I found it in the salt. Does it mean anything to you?'

'No. I've heard of such, though.' The big man put the stone back on top of Galen's bag. 'Now, are you fit to ride?' he asked.

* * *

Galen's horse carried him north all that afternoon and well into the evening. He slept for only a few hours that night, and set off again before sunrise, keeping up a steady pace all day. Galen knew better than to exhaust his mount by trying to gallop all the way to Garadun, but he also knew that time was vital. So he ate in the saddle, stopping only to feed and water his animal. By nightfall, both he and the stallion were very tired, and he was glad to reach a village and find a small but comfortable inn.

Before Galen fell asleep, he took out the inscribed stone and studied the letters. As before, enlightenment eluded him – and, to make matters worse, he found he could not recall the set of letters on the stone in Jarlath's castle. He had risked so much to see it – and now he couldn't even remember what it had said!

Annoyed with himself, he put the stone down and prepared to go to sleep. Spike jumped up on to the bed and prodded the tablet uncertainly with an outsize paw, as if suspecting it of having usurped his place at his master's side. Galen smiled, rubbing the fur on the beek's head and neck, and tickling him under his chin. Soon they had both settled down and were fast asleep.

* * *

The dream began with a whirling sensation that made Galen feel quite giddy. In the midst of this wild movement, Spike stood steady and unconcerned. The beek prodded ineffectively at a stone tablet which lay letters-down on the ground.

'Turn it over, Spike,' a familiar voice urged. 'Turn the stone over.'

429

Galen listened to the echoes of a half-heard conversation, but though he strained to listen to the dream-voices, he could not understand what they said. Until . . .

I wish Emer was here, Rebecca said plaintively.

And Galen too, a faraway voice responded.

'I am!' he cried. 'Look!'

He turned the stone over, the deeply incised letters now filled with dark earth.

There was a moment's silence, and then the dream began to fade. The unseen presences left him.

'There's another one!' he shouted desperately. 'I found another one!' The letters were clear to him now, but it was too late. There was no response to his impassioned plea.

Galen woke with the bedclothes twisted round him. Spike, fully awake, was staring at him with a very surprised expression.

* * *

It took Galen another day and a half to reach Garadun. It was his first trip to the capital, and he was astonished by its sheer size and remorseless vigour. He gazed about him wide-eyed, and had to ask directions to the castle several times. The locals obviously thought him rather stupid. *Everyone* knew where Montfort's palace was!

The huge walls of the royal castle came as yet another astounding sight in a long succession of such marvels. It took Galen some time to find an entrance – and when he did, the massive gates, flanked by imposing towers, made him feel insignificant, intensifying his nervousness. Nevertheless, he dismounted and approached his goal, knowing that his task was too important to delay. Two heavily armed guards eyed the bedraggled newcomer suspiciously as he halted before them.

'I'd like to see the Captain of the Castle Guard,' Galen said, as boldly as he was able.

'Would you now?' one of the sentries remarked.

'It's vitally important.'

'Want to join up, do you?' the other soldier asked.

'I have news from the south,' Galen persisted. 'Look.' He

fished the ring out from inside his shirt, where it hung on a thong round his neck. He pressed the catch and showed the hidden symbol to the guards. They exchanged glances, all amusement gone. 'Tarrant or Pike could vouch for me . . . ' Galen began.

'They're not here,' the first soldier cut in.

His colleague turned away and yelled an order. One of the gates began to swing open slowly.

'You'd better be right about the importance of your news, boy,' the first guard said quietly. 'Or you're in big trouble.'

Galen followed him inside while the other soldier took charge of his horse. He was taken to a room at the base of the adjacent tower, and his escort saluted the man who sat inside, raising his right fist to the centre of his chest.

'A messenger, sir,' he reported. 'He has one of the hand-clasp rings. Says he has news from the south.'

'Let me see,' the officer said, holding out his hand.

Galen removed the ring and handed it to him.

'What's your name?'

'Galen.'

'Where are you from?'

'Edgefield.'

At this, the soldier looked up in surprise.

'The chess player?' he asked.

'Yes. Tarrant recruited me after the game.'

'I'm Ellard, Captain of the Castle Guard. Where did you get this ring?'

Galen explained briefly, knowing that such answers were necessary, but itching to get to his real purpose.

'What is your news, then?' Ellard asked.

'Do *you* have a ring?' Galen asked, remembering Redfern's advice.

For answer, Ellard slid a ring from his finger and handed it over. The coin was different, but the symbol inside was the same. Galen sighed with relief and gave it back, then took out the two letters.

'This one's from Redfern,' he explained. 'The other is from Davin in Riano. He gave it to me just before he was killed.'

Ellard glanced up sharply at these words, but said

431

nothing, and read both messages. When he had finished, his expression was stern. He stood up abruptly.

'Come with me!' he commanded, striding out.

'Where are we going?' Galen asked as he hurried to follow.

'To see the king,' Ellard replied.

CHAPTER FIFTY-ONE

Montfort was alone in one of the state-rooms, studying maps, when they finally reached him. By using a mixture of expert diplomacy and stubborn forcefulness – a combination remarkable in a mere captain – Ellard had cut through the layers of protection that usually surrounded the king. He had brandished Galen's letters and emphasized how important their news was, but had given no explanation for the young man's presence. A succession of servants, adjutants and chamberlains had given way before his energetic persuasion, and they had now reached their goal.

'What is it, Captain Ellard?' Montfort asked, looking up from his work. 'Who is your companion?'

'Galen, sire,' the soldier replied. 'The People's Champion of Edge.'

Montfort won't know what he's talking about, Galen thought, feeling utterly ridiculous.

The king smiled. 'Ah, the victorious chess master,' he remarked. 'That was a commendable effort. Well met, Galen.'

The messenger bowed awkwardly, unable to hide his amazement and pleasure.

'Tarrant sent you south after that, didn't he?' Montfort went on.

'Yes, your majesty,' Galen managed.

'Galen brings grave tidings, sire,' Ellard put it, and passed the letters to his sovereign.

Montfort read in silence, his expression unchanging, while the tension in the room grew. When he had finished, he turned to Galen and asked several questions, filling in the gaps in his knowledge.

'It's worse than I imagined,' he concluded, looking at Ellard.

'Should I recall the northern detachments, sire?' the captain asked.

'No. It'll be too late, and unless I'm very much mistaken, they'll be needed where they are before long.' Montfort paused, obviously deep in thought, then came to a decision. 'Mobilize what units you can,' he commanded. 'We will march south the day after tomorrow.'

'Yes, sire,' Ellard responded. 'Could they *really* bring an entire army across the salt?' he added.

'If they are prepared to risk the lives of their soldiers, they can do anything,' the king replied. 'We can't assume that they will fail. We'll just have to hope that the northern detachments can handle the old guard without our assistance. No doubt the rebellion will be timed to try and divert our attention from the real threat. That damned conference should have shown me that it would have come to this!' Montfort was silent for a moment, glancing at Galen, then he turned back to his captain. 'Still, there's no way we can hide our intentions now,' he remarked philosophically. 'We will march with what we have.'

'And leave Garadun undefended, sire?' Ellard queried.

'We have no choice, Captain,' the king answered. 'If we do not succeed, this city will fall anyway. You know what to do?'

'Yes, sire.' Ellard bowed, and strode from the room. Galen heard him shouting orders as soon as he was outside.

'You've done well,' Montfort said. 'I am in your debt.'

Galen's uncertainty about what he should do next was increased by this unexpected statement. He stood his ground, feeling tongue-tied and awkward. Then a thought crossed his mind, comforting him for just a moment. *He's a man, just like me.*

'What will you do now?' the king asked.

'I'd like to return to Edge . . . sire,' he replied.

'Then ride with me,' Montfort suggested promptly. 'That is where all our fates will be decided.' Almost to himself, he added, 'One way or another . . . '

'Will they really use foreign mercenaries?' Galen asked, emboldened by the king's invitation.

'Why not?' Montfort replied. 'Foreigners are not devils,

you know – they're simply men like ourselves. And mercenaries of any race will fight for pay.'

'But *foreigners*, in Ahrenia?' To Galen, this was unthinkable.

'Is that worse than treason?' Montfort asked calmly.

'You *will* win!' Galen blurted out.

'In simple numbers, we can't even match Jarlath and his allies,' the king responded. 'And now we have to face mercenaries as well. I hadn't expected any of this to happen so quickly. But, Web-willing, we can still prevail.' He paused, and gave Galen a tired smile. 'And when we do, it will be due – in no small measure – to the People's Champion.'

Galen wanted to respond, but could not find the words. He knew, beyond a shadow of a doubt, that he would do everything he could to help the young man who stood before him.

'One of my adjutants will arrange somewhere for you to stay until we go south,' Montfort said, drawing the audience to a close.

As Galen left, the king returned to his maps, and began to study them anew.

* * *

The next day found Galen unoccupied, and left him feeling unbearably restless. The city was in turmoil, with soldiers everywhere, and the streets full of movement and shouting.

Galen tried to locate Ellard, in the hope of getting some news, but the captain was nowhere to be found, so he was left to flounder in the wave of rumours sweeping the city. One said that fighting had already started in the north; others said that it was the south that had seen the first skirmishes. But everyone agreed that conflict was inevitable now.

The word on everyone's lips was 'war'.

* * *

That same day, many leagues to the south, Ahrenia's two main ports were also in a state of panic-stricken dread. The reason was simple. Two vast armadas had sailed in, and were disembarking thousands of soldiers, together with

435

their horses and equipment. Members of the local nobility and their staff had obviously been forewarned, and were there to greet the mercenary's leaders, but the vast majority of the people were terrified. Even here, where the sight of foreigners was more commonplace than elsewhere, superstitions about them abounded, and the invasion – though bloodless – stirred up feelings of fear, resentment and uncertainty.

The local trading vessels and fishing boats were pushed aside by the naval craft, and many were damaged or even sunk in the process, but no one dared raise a voice in complaint. The foreign soldiers were pale-skinned, hard-eyed men, clad in leather and steel. At times they seemed to pay little attention to the control of their captains, but when they were organized, they were frighteningly efficient, unloading the stores from an entire vessel in a mere two hours.

While most of the local population cowered behind locked doors and shuttered windows, the twin armies from the Southern Isles marshalled themselves into travelling units. Within a day of landing, they began the march north towards Riano.

Everyone in their path either fled in terror or was brushed aside. The mercenary armies marched on, leaving a trail of devastation in their wake that appalled even some of the nobles at whose invitation they had come. The soldiers' songs were all of blood, death and glory. There was no mistaking their purpose.

Ahrenia trembled under the thunderous tread of their synchronized footsteps.

* * *

Still further to the south and many leagues to the west, on the peninsula which was their sole preserve, the brethren rejoiced.

The abbot lifted the chalice in both hands, and held it high above his head.

'The bargain is about to be fulfilled!' he cried.

The monks gathered in the great hall below the dais

looked up at their leader with rapture in their eyes.

'The time has come for us to leave our ancient home, and to witness the birth of a new city, a new land, a new life!' the abbot went on, his cracked voice ringing with triumphant emotion. 'Those who have stood in our way for so long will be swept aside. Nothing can stop us now. My brothers, we go forth to meet our destiny!'

He lowered the chalice and drank from its blood-red depths.

The massed ranks below him responded in unison, their grating roar shaking the monastery to its foundations.

'*Our time has come!*'

Part Three
DREAM-WEAVER

CHAPTER FIFTY-TWO

'Good evening, ladies.'

Cranne straightened up, the feral glint in his pale grey eyes making a mockery of his courteous manner. Farrand's son was clad in leather and mail, their family's wolf's-head crest emblazoned upon his chest. His square-jawed face was flushed with excitement, gleaming with perspiration, and his straight black hair was tied back. In his right hand was a sword, fresh blood glinting on its blade. For a few moments Rebecca and Emer stared at the intruder in horrified disbelief, unable to speak. Then Rebecca found her voice.

'Get out!' she demanded hysterically. 'Get out!'

'Why, Rebecca,' Cranne responded in mock surprise. 'Aren't you pleased to see your betrothed?'

'You are not my betrothed,' she shouted back. 'And never will be!'

'Ah. That's where you are wrong, my dear.' Cranne's smile did not reach his eyes. 'I think you will find that your father has handed over Edge only too willingly. I am baron here now . . . and you are my subject. My word is law.'

'What have you done to him?' Rebecca was pale now with shock and fear.

Cranne did not answer her immediately. He took a step forward, and she retreated automatically.

'I have not forgotten your treatment of me, *my love* . . . ' His smile had disappeared. 'I shall expect more amenable behaviour from you this time.'

The threat implicit in his words was unmistakable, and Rebecca's blood ran cold. She glanced around frantically, looking in vain for a possible weapon, then at Emer, who stood as though petrified. Her gaze returned to Cranne, whose cold inhuman certainty left her feeling helpless and terribly afraid. There seemed to be no hope; her mind was capable only of repeated, despairing denial, *No. Please, no!*

'Your beauty is as great as I remembered it,' Cranne remarked casually. 'It will give me great pleasure to see more of you.' He paused. 'And your friend's presence will only add spice to the game.' His gaze returned to Rebecca, and the grin which this last idea had provoked fell away. He moved towards her. 'You should not have denied me, Rebecca, or tried to embarrass me with that stupid game. It was both foolish and impolite. And yet in a way I am glad that you did. It will only serve to heighten my enjoyment of your submission now.'

Rebecca retreated another step, and found herself trapped against the wall beside the window. She thought briefly of flinging herself to the ground below, but knew that he would reach her before she could unfasten the latch. *No. No. No!* She cowered, then gathered herself and screamed.

'Get away from me!'

Emer chose that moment to attack. She snatched up an iron poker from the nearby fireplace and swung it at Cranne with all her might. So intent was he on his intended victim that he saw his peril only at the last moment. He ducked, trying to fend off the avenging fury. Though he took most of the weight of the attack on his arm, he also received a glancing blow to the side of his head. Cranne snarled as Emer struggled to keep her balance, then he swept the poker aside and raise his blood-stained sword.

'No!' Rebecca yelled, starting forward.

Emer stood her ground, tears of fury brimming in her eyes, almost daring Cranne to strike. He hesitated momentarily, then hit her with his left hand. It was a sharp, straight-armed blow with an iron-clad fist, and it caught Emer on the cheekbone below her right eye with stunning force. She crashed to the floor, overturning a chair as she fell, and lay still. Rebecca darted towards her friend. Cranne stared at the prostrate girl, contempt and spite contorting his dark features, then he turned back to Rebecca. She stopped in her tracks, a rabbit snared by the fox.

'She will pay for that,' Cranne grated, touching the side

of his head. 'I hope *you* have more sense.' There was no pretence of courtesy in his voice now.

'You bastard,' Rebecca breathed. 'You . . . '

Cranne laughed. 'Is that the best you can do?' he sneered.

Rebecca edged closer to Emer, only to be stopped once more.

'Leave her!' Cranne commanded. 'She has suffered nothing compared to what I am going to do to you. After . . . '

Despairing, Rebecca closed her eyes – just as a voice came through the open door from the corridor beyond, calling for Cranne. He hesitated, lust and fury warring in his eyes. Then a soldier appeared in the doorway, sword in hand.

'Farrand wants you, my lord,' he said breathlessly. 'Immediately.'

Cranne frowned, then turned abruptly and strode to the door.

'Until later then,' he said, returning to the mock civility of his earlier words. A humourless smile masked his face as he took the key from the lock. 'Just in case you have another key,' he remarked, 'the door will be guarded. And don't try the window. It's a long drop, and my men control the grounds below. Any stupidity on your part will only make things worse later, I promise you.' He bowed, then stepped outside, closing the door behind him. Rebecca listened to the key turn, thanking the gods for her temporary reprieve, then hurried to Emer's side.

Her friend was recovering consciousness, though her eyes were unfocused, their eyelids fluttering. She groaned and brought a trembling hand up to touch her cheek. It was already swollen, and there was a small cut where the skin had split over the bone.

'Are you all right?' Rebecca asked.

Emer grunted dismissively.

'Has he gone?' she croaked.

'For now. He'll be back, though.' Rebecca could not help trembling at the prospect.

'What's happening?' Emer asked, sitting up slowly and wincing as she moved.

From outside came the sounds of men shouting, the tramp of booted feet, and the occasional clash of swords. Rebecca helped her friend get to her feet, and together they went over to the window. Their vantage point on the first floor gave them a wide view over the gardens, the eastern wall and some of the servants' quarters. The scene below them was confused; there were soldiers everywhere, apparently moving at random in the gloom of dusk. A flickering red light added to the air of menace.

'Something's burning,' Emer commented softly.

The fact that their home had been invaded was beginning to sink in – with all the personal and wider consequences that implied. Rebecca was aghast, unable to accept the unthinkable, and at a loss as to how to deal with it.

'We can't stay here,' Emer said firmly, down-to-earth as usual, in spite of her groggy state.

'But where can we go?' Rebecca responded. 'And how? The door's locked and guarded, and we wouldn't get far down there.' She indicated the scene below.

'I'd rather take my chances outside than wait for the return of that *monster*,' Emer replied, squinting through her one good eye.

'But how?'

'Bedclothes,' Emer answered. 'You obviously haven't been reading the right sort of books. Come on!'

The two girls turned towards the adjoining bedchamber, but were stopped in their tracks by the sound of glass shattering in that room. Horrified, they imagined further terrors, but before they could move, a man in a tight-fitting hood burst in. Only his eyes and mouth were visible. The girls stared at him as if he was an apparition.

'Thank the Web, I've found you,' the man said, beckoning to them with the knife in his hand. 'Come on!'

'Who are you?' Rebecca exclaimed. His voice seemed familiar, but her brain was apparently refusing to function.

Wordlessly, the man pulled off his strange headgear. It was Tarrant.

'Come *on*!' he insisted, reaching forward and grasping Rebecca's arm. 'There isn't much time. We must get you out of here quickly.'

'But what about my father . . . and Radd . . . Nursey?' Rebecca hesitated, her mind reeling.

'You stupid . . . ' Emer called her friend a range of uncomplimentary names as she pushed her into the bedroom. Tarrant strode ahead of them, and went straight to the window – where most of the glass and much of the leading lay strewn upon the floor. The room smelled of smoke. A rope ladder dangled outside, swinging in the wind. Tarrant grabbed hold of this and beckoned.

'Climb!' he ordered, pointing upwards. 'Go!' He steadied the ladder while Emer found her footing and began to scramble towards the roof, cursing her long skirts as she went. Then he left Rebecca to hold the rope, while he barricaded the bedroom door with heavy furniture. He moved back to her side as crashing sounds came from the room they had just left.

'Quick!' he urged.

Rebecca climbed out, and grabbed the rungs tightly. As she started to climb, swaying in the smoke-filled air, she was assailed by vertigo and numbing confusion. She felt rather than saw Tarrant on the ladder below her, his weight steadying her climb and his voice urging her on. Then hands reached down and dragged her on to the roof. Tarrant followed, and one of his comrades slashed the ropes so that the ladder fell away into the darkness below.

There were three other men with Tarrant. As they moved off with the two girls, an arrow clanged into the stonework just below their feet.

Rebecca had often looked down upon the roof of her apartments from the castle towers, but she had never entered this haunt of moss and birds. It was the landscape of nightmares; gargoyles leered at them, miniature turrets of crumbling stone barred their way, and the intricately carved arches and buttresses made the roof seem like a maze built by a lunatic. It was full of hidden perils in the twilight, slippery surfaces and sudden drops, but somehow their progress continued.

They made their way towards the mud-covered sloping roof of the Great Hall. They were out of sight of the soldiers on the ground now, and could move along towards the South Tower in comparative safety.

The source of the red light was now visible. Flames were pouring from the upper windows of the West Tower, on the far side of the hall. Smoke drifted in dark swirls, and sparks flew into the evening sky. Shouts, screams and the barking of terrified dogs mingled with unidentifiable noises, adding to the horror and confusion of the night.

They crossed the roof of Baldemar's quarters, then scrambled over the sloping tiles of the Gallery to the great South Tower, where they were pulled in through a deeply recessed window by more helping hands. Once inside, they could hear sounds of fighting coming from the armoury below, but Tarrant led them quickly up some steps and round to the side door – which led on to the eastern wing of the south wall. Two ropes were uncoiled and secured to the battlements, then the free ends were thrown over. Rebecca glanced down at the huge drop, realization making her feel dizzy and sick. In the gloom below, a group of men and horses were waiting.

'They're friends,' Tarrant said, placing a reassuring hand on her shoulder. 'Think you can make it down?'

'Of course!' Emer answered for her friend.

Two soldiers were already on their way, sliding down the rope and using their feet to stop themselves from banging into the ancient stone walls. Emer hitched up her skirts, grabbed one of the ropes and followed, copying their movements as best she could. Rebecca watched, her heart in her mouth.

'It's easy enough,' Tarrant reassured her. 'Just hold on tight. We don't want to lose you now!'

Rebecca took one last look at the dreadful turmoil within the castle, then grasped the other rope and lowered herself over the edge of the precipice, desperately trying not to look down. Her arms soon began to ache and her hands to hurt from the friction on the rope, and her ankles jarred painfully on the stone. Though short, her downward journey seemed endless – and she almost fell the last few paces. Welcoming arms caught her as she stumbled to the ground, weeping silently.

Within moments, Tarrant and his remaining colleagues had reached the ground – and were in motion as soon as their boots hit the soil. Horses were gathered, then Tarrant moved towards Rebecca, his knife in his hand. She shrank away, not understanding, but he knelt down in front of her.

'Forgive me,' he said gently, and carefully slashed the material of her dress. 'So that you can ride easily,' he explained, then repeated the process for Emer. When the girls had been helped up on to their mounts, the whole party moved away eastwards, following a route between the town and the salt-flats to the south.

Rebecca had never ridden so fast before, and she clung on to the reins and the horse's neck with feverish desperation, not quite able to believe what was happening. The wind whipped her golden hair into a streaming banner and dried the tears on her face – tears that were a mixture of relief, shock, anger and dread. She rejoiced in her own escape but the violation of the only home she had ever known – and worry for those she had left behind – left her shaken and afraid.

After a while, Tarrant allowed the pace to slacken, though he glanced back over his shoulder from time to time. A little while later, they were joined by a lone rider.

'Any sign of pursuit?' Tarrant asked.

'Nothing so far,' Pike replied, grinning triumphantly. 'Cranne's going to be like a dog chasing his own tail for a while yet.'

* * *

'What do you mean, they got away?' Cranne stormed, his face mottled with fury.

The captain stood his ground, but there was fear in his eyes. 'They had help, my lord,' he replied as firmly as he was able. 'They climbed on to the roof, then went over the south wall.'

His explanation made little impression on Cranne.

'Incompetent morons!' he screamed. 'I told you to guard her!' He was almost choking with rage, and turned on the soldier again. 'Which way did they go?' he demanded.

Farrand entered the room as the captain replied.

'East. They had horses waiting outside.'

'Get my horse,' Cranne commanded. 'And gather Red Troop.'

'Yes, sir.' The captain turned to obey, but was halted by a gesture from Farrand.

'Let her go,' the baron said.

'No!' Cranne's white-hot desire for revenge overruled all else.

'She is not important,' his father replied calmly. 'What we're doing here *is*.'

'But . . . ' Cranne's fists were clenched, white-knuckled.

'You've already made enough of a mess of this business,' Farrand snapped, angry himself now. 'Do not even *think* of disobeying me.' There was steel in his voice.

Cranne glared at his father for a few moments, then turned away. 'Get out!' he yelled at the captain, who fled down the corridor. Cranne let out a long, slow breath.

'When I get my hands on that bitch,' he vowed, 'she'll regret the day she was born!'

CHAPTER FIFTY-THREE

Many other journeys were begun that day.

The mercenary armies, together with a few local adventurers and assorted hangers-on, left the southern ports for Riano. Further away, but headed for the same destination, the brethren rode out from the monastic peninsula which had been their home for so long. The euphoria of their final meeting within those ancient walls was still with them, and the thunder of their horses' hooves seemed to beat out the endlessly repeated phrase – *Our time has come.*

Their mounts were huge black beasts, specially bred and long used to the presence of the strange men who rode them. But every other living thing in their path, whether human or animal, shrank back in fear at the sight of the sinister figures. Only their hands and faces were visible beneath the monkish robes, but these were enough to mark the riders as no ordinary men. Their skin was stretched tight, the colour of ancient parchment on a skeletal frame – like corpses recovered from the salt. Yet each face held a spectral quality, and seemed hooded in mystery. There were fifty or so monks in the cavalcade, and the very air about them crackled, in a miasma of evil energy that made onlookers run and hide. The land emptied at their approach and was silent in their wake.

The oldest of them all rode at their head, his upright bearing and the ease with which he held himself in the saddle belying his frail appearance. The abbot's mind was filled with rejoicing; centuries of patience were at long last being rewarded.

He knew that his predecessors had foreseen this moment,

but now it seemed almost unthinkable that the ancient bargain with a long-dead king was about to be fulfilled. And yet it was so! The conditions – which had for so long proved impossibly evasive – would all be met in a few short days. War was coming, inevitable now; the presence of vast armies from overseas was guaranteed; the communal power of the brethren was coming to a peak; all reports indicated that the salt was in a state of perfect readiness – and Ahrenia was ruled by an heirless king. The Web was forming itself in their favour. Victory was guaranteed.

At last they would have the ultimate power – as the favoured coterie of a god-like king – and the ultimate gift. Immortality!

* * *

That same morning saw Montfort's army leave Garadun on the first leg of its journey to Edge. The city was quiet after they had gone, with an air of fearful expectancy hovering darkly over those who were left behind. Many fled from their homes, for what they hoped would be safer refuges elsewhere. Garadun became a city of whispers.

Galen rode with a troop of cavalry commanded by Ellard. The captain had taken the young man under his wing, and questioned him about Edge, the salt, and about his adventure with the Archaeologists. For his own part, Galen could only marvel at the vast size of Montfort's army. He watched the various divisions in their endless columns, and tried to estimate how many men made up this gigantic crawling animal. He soon gave up the task as hopeless.

Most of the force was on foot, so their progress was necessarily slow. The march was accompanied by clouds of dust and endless noise; villagers and country folk watched them pass in grim frightened silence, resentful of the inevitable damage that their passage caused, and Galen wondered how the people of his home town would react to the invasion.

The day wore on, and as the army's progress lost some of its novelty, Galen's thoughts turned to his own hopes and fears. It had been more than two months now since he had

450

seen Emer, and he longed to be with her again. He could not help worrying about her safety.

Galen was not the only one riding south who was thinking about Edge's womenfolk. Despite his many immediate concerns, Montfort's thoughts strayed to Rebecca, and he recalled their conversation in the palace garden. Why, he wondered, had he felt so refreshed by her company, so at ease by her side? What was it she had said? *Legends can sometimes tell us more about the present than the past.* The king smiled at the memory. *What nonsense!* he thought, yet wished that he had been able to retain that innocence of youth.

Now, heading for Rebecca's home – and for a war that would surely change her life for ever – Montfort hoped that he was right in believing her to be a young woman who was capable of taking care of herself. His faith in his own struggle did not waver, but he did not wish her to be a victim of it.

Throughout that day, Montfort received reports and news from several parts of his divided domain. But one important voice was missing, one message never came – the one he needed more than any other.

Tarrant, he thought, *if this help you've been promising doesn't arrive soon, it'll be too late. And I don't even know where you are!*

* * *

Tarrant's party consisted of nine men, including himself, plus the two girls. In spite of the youthful appearance of some of his men, all were veterans of many operations, and Tarrant would have trusted any of them with his life. Several had been present at Rebecca's chess game, and remembered her fondly. Tarrant had had little difficulty in persuading them that she was a prize worth rescuing.

When he was certain that it was safe for them to stop, Tarrant called a halt. Although he had lost no men during the raid on Edgefield Castle, there were wounds that needed tending – including the cut on Emer's cheek. Her face was badly swollen, and her eye was half-closed, the skin around

451

it already turning blue-black. Pike dabbed the injury with ointment, and Tarrant handed Emer a flask.

'Drink some of this,' he said. 'It'll help ease the pain. But don't have *too* much – we need you to stay on your horse!'

Emer took a swallow, and half-choked. She tried to hand the flask back, but Tarrant motioned for her to drink again. She smiled lopsidedly, wincing as the movement reawoke the pain in her cheek.

'You wouldn't be trying to get an innocent girl drunk, would you?' she asked.

'My intentions are strictly honourable!' he responded, glad to see that Rebecca's friend had a strong spirit. 'What happened to you?'

'Cranne!' Rebecca said in disgust.

'It could have been worse,' Emer commented. 'At least I'm still alive. Just not quite so pretty. In this state, my honour would be safe no matter *how* drunk I got!' she added ruefully.

'What's happening?' Rebecca asked Tarrant. She felt re-assured about Emer now, and her thoughts were turning to wider issues.

'It seems that your charms were not the only attraction of Edge for Farrand and Cranne,' Tarrant replied. Rebecca did not return his smile, and he went on quickly, 'They decided to take it by force, though I'm still not sure why. They were very clever about it. We'd have noticed any large movement of troops, so they had several small detachments travel separately, then link up for the attack. We were shadowing one of them, and only just realized what was happening at the last moment. It's lucky we arrived when we did.'

'You can say that again,' Emer muttered.

'It doesn't end here though, does it?' Rebecca asked seriously. 'They wouldn't have gone to such trouble if this wasn't just the first part of a larger campaign.'

Pike nodded. 'Such stealth is not Farrand's usual way,' he commented mildly.

'Do you know what happened to my father?' Rebecca asked.

'No. We can only assume he was captured,' Tarrant replied. 'None of us saw him, but his guards had put up more of a fight than I'd have expected.'

'I don't think they had much choice,' Pike put in. 'Cranne wanted blood. He'd have been *most* disappointed if the place had surrendered straight away!'

'Which means that, having got where they wanted, they don't mind being noticed now,' Tarrant said thoughtfully. 'Events must be moving fast, otherwise all their earlier stealth would have been wasted.'

'Either that, or Farrand couldn't keep Cranne on a leash any more,' Pike added drily.

'Let's hope that was the reason,' Tarrant replied. 'Either way, we'd better get the news back to Garadun.'

'Where are *we* going?' Emer asked.

Tarrant looked at Pike.

'Castlemane?' he suggested, and his deputy nodded. Turning back to the girls, he went on, 'It's a small barony to the north-east. You'll be safe there, and I'd like to get you there as soon as possible. Are you fit to ride?'

So the journey continued throughout the night, with only a few short stops to refresh themselves and their horses. The following day was much the same, a strangely uneventful trip after such a dramatic beginning. By the afternoon, both girls were suffering badly from fatigue, and Emer's face was causing her considerable pain. So their spirits rose when, at dusk, Tarrant pointed out the town of Castlemane only half a league distant. Their relief was quickly supplemented by a new excitement when they saw a fair on the outskirts of the town.

'Is it the same one?' Emer asked, squinting into the gloom.

'I think so,' Rebecca replied. 'But I can't be certain in this light.' Inside, however, she knew.

'They must have doubled back,' Emer remarked. 'I wonder why?'

Rebecca did not answer, but just stared at the distant gathering, her mind seething with possibilities. *I'll be able to talk to Sancia again,* she thought. *Get some explanations.* She remembered her fateful words to Emer, just before Cranne's unwelcome arrival. *Everything's going to be just as I want it to be from now on.* And she wondered whether it might be true after all. The shock of Cranne's appearance had been awful, but her rescue seemed in retrospect almost too good to be true. She felt as if fate had led her here to the new site of Sancia's fair, and she was eager to visit the dream-weaver. *I have so much to tell her.*

However, Tarrant insisted that she had more urgent needs to be attended to. Rebecca was too tired to argue for long, so the party made its way into the town and to the castle which stood at its centre. Once inside, Rebecca dismounted wearily and looked around. The castle was much smaller than her father's, but was in good repair – and its walls and towers were all built to the same scale. The place gave an impression of cleanliness and order – quite a contrast to her own home. She wondered suddenly what the man who ruled here was like. She found out soon enough.

Baron Locke appeared and warmly greeted Tarrant, who then introduced him to his two charges, and outlined what had happened in Edge. The baron was a small, rotund man, dressed in a manner which struck Rebecca as too ornate. He had a neatly trimmed beard and inquisitive blue eyes. He exclaimed over Farrand's outrageous behaviour, and fussed over the two girls, insisting that they go straight to their guest chambers and rest. Emer was more than happy with this arrangement. Her cut, though healing well, had left her with a thumping headache that had lasted a full day now. A soft bed and sleep were an inviting prospect. Rebecca was less sure, but acquiesced out of concern for her friend.

Locke found her desire to visit the fair curious and unimportant, assuming it to be the frivolous wish of a young girl, and Rebecca had neither the strength nor the patience to explain. Emer looked at her sympathetically, but was herself in no state to argue.

'The fair will still be there in the morning,' Locke reassured them jovially. 'Plenty of time to play then.'

Tarrant accompanied Rebecca and Emer to the chamber the two girls were to share, and took the opportunity of a quiet moment to explain.

'Locke is a fine man,' he whispered, 'but he has little understanding of women. His wife died many years ago, and all their children were sons.'

Rebecca felt ashamed of her uncharitable thoughts, and

454

said nothing. She was a guest in the baron's home, after all – and grateful for it.

'Anyone would think we were still five years old,' Emer grumbled quietly once they were alone. 'If he's like that all the time, we're going to need rescuing again!'

* * *

Morning brought the news of Montfort's march, and of the imminence of war. Though not unexpected, this nevertheless cast a pall of fear over everyone. To know that war was inevitable was one thing; to have its outbreak reported was quite another. Tarrant put a brave face on it, but Rebecca and Emer could both see the worry behind his intelligent blue eyes. They were seated in their room, bathed and dressed in borrowed clothes. Locke had sent them a note with the garments, apologizing for their quality, and explaining that the only items of a suitable size belonged to his servants.

'Will you go?' Rebecca asked.

'Yes,' Tarrant replied. 'Of course, I would much rather stay here in your company, but duty calls.' He grinned at Rebecca, and she smiled back sadly, wondering if she would ever see him again. That war could claim so vibrant a spirit seemed impossible and yet . . .

'Where will you join the army?' she asked, uncomfortable in the sudden silence.

'I don't know,' he answered. 'I have some other refugees from Edge to visit first.'

'Who?'

'Do you know where Galen is?' Emer asked before Tarrant had a chance to reply. He shook his head, and she relapsed into an uncharacteristic silence. A good night's sleep had restored her physically, her headache was gone, and even her cheek was on the mend – though her eye, in her own words, resembled 'a mad painter's version of sunset on a stormy night'. However, she was now sunk in a deep depression that even her own uncertain future – and that of her father – could not wholly explain.

'What are we to do?' Rebecca asked, after a moment's pause.

'Stay here,' Tarrant told her. 'Castlemane should be safe enough, and I'll get what news I can back to you.'

'If Locke lets us hear it,' Emer remarked sullenly.

'Don't be too hard on him,' Tarrant advised. 'He's a good man at heart. And alone – his sons are already with the army. He'll welcome your company.'

The girls exchanged glances.

'He musn't stop us going to the fair,' Rebecca said.

Tarrant laughed.

'I can't think why he should,' he said. 'Why is it so important?'

'It's a long story.'

'Then we must save it for another time. I have to go.'

He bowed then, and left, calling instructions as he went. The girls sat in silence for a few moments, trying to make sense of the momentous events that had overtaken their lives. Then they glanced at each other.

'To the fair,' they said simultaneously.

* * *

Getting out of the castle proved to be easier than they had expected. The courtyard was busy with men and horses as Tarrant and his group prepared to leave. In the midst of all this activity, Rebecca and Emer simply walked out of the main gate. Dressed as they were, no one paid them any attention, and they were soon heading through the un-usually quiet streets to the site of the fair.

'Everything feels different,' Rebecca said, looking about.

'They know about the war,' Emer replied. 'News like that travels fast.'

Castlemane was such a self-contained, peaceful town that thoughts of war seemed incongruous here, and yet the threat hung in the air like the heaviness that precedes a summer storm. One way or another, the lives of all who lived here would be changed by what was to come.

Rebecca crossed the invisible boundary that marked the confines of the fair, and felt her blood begin to race. She walked forward eagerly, staring at each passage between the stalls and wagons. She expected to see the special signs or

lights that would guide her to Sancia's caravan, but found
nothing. Rebecca was sure that it was the same fair – so
much of it seemed familiar – but she could not find the
dream-weaver. She began to feel a little frightened.

There were few people about, and those that had braved
the morning went about their own business, paying the
intruders no attention. Eventually, Rebecca decided that she
would have to ask for directions, and approached a pale-
faced woman who sat on the steps of her wagon.

'Excuse me,' she began, feeling unaccountably nervous.
'Could you show me the way to Sancia's caravan, please?'

The woman eyed her strangely but said nothing, and
Rebecca's unease intensified.

'The dream-weaver,' she added uncertainly.

'Sancia's dead,' the woman said flatly.

'No!'

Rebecca's hopes were dashed once more, and the world
suddenly seemed a cruel and vindictive place. *Why?* she
thought miserably. *She was alive only a few days ago. I need
her!*

The woman watched her distress through narrowed eyes.

'Are you Rebecca?' she asked abruptly.

'Yes.'

'Then come with me,' the woman said, a slow smile
spreading over her face. 'We've been expecting you.'

CHAPTER FIFTY-FOUR

Without further ado, the woman jumped down from the step and walked off. After a moment's hesitation, Rebecca and Emer followed.

'Why did you say you were expecting me?'

'You'll see. My name's Aleandra, by the way. I'm a whore.' She was totally matter-of-fact, announcing her profession with no sense of shame or false bravado. 'One of Sancia's girls,' she added. 'She used to protect us.'

'I know,' Rebecca said.

Aleandra led them deeper into the maze of wagons.

'When did she die?' Rebecca asked.

'Seven or eight days ago – though it seems much longer.'

'But you've kept her wagon?'

'Of course,' Aleandra replied. 'We knew that you'd need it.'

'I don't understand.'

'You will.'

They came to Sancia's caravan. Its drab, undistinguished exterior was just as Rebecca remembered it, and she felt strange seeing it again now.

'Go on in,' Aleandra urged. 'No one will bother you.'

She turned to leave but was stopped by the sound of Rebecca's voice.

'Wait! Please. There are so many questions . . .'

'Later,' the woman replied, smiling. 'Let Sancia answer you first.' She left them then, and the two girls watched her retreat, then turned to look at the wagon door.

Emer had been silent during the earlier exchange, feeling excluded and ignorant; she too was haunted by memories of their earlier visit.

'Do you want me to come in with you?' she asked quietly

458

'Of course!' Rebecca's surprise was obvious.

'Sancia didn't want me last time,' Emer pointed out.

'But she's dead!'

'Her influence is still here. I don't want to be in the way.'

'Don't be silly!' Rebecca exclaimed, hurt by the uncertainty in her friend's eyes. 'I *need* you.'

'If you're sure.'

'Of course I'm sure! I can't cope with all of this on my own.'

Suddenly Rebecca was seized by a memory so powerful that it seemed almost like a vision. 'Eight days ago,' she whispered, as though talking to herself. 'That's when I dreamed of Sancia in Garadun, only she spoke in my mother's voice.' *Have patience, little one. Don't fret. In time you will understand.* The words comforted her now as they had done earlier. 'I hope so,' Rebecca said aloud, while Emer looked at her strangely. *True magic reveals itself and truth cannot stay hidden for ever.*

Rebecca thought of that visitation as 'the healing dream', and it seemed even more important now that she knew it had been Sancia's final message to her. *She's part of the Web now.*

'Are we going to stand here all day?' Emer asked, rather irritably. 'Or are we going inside?'

Rebecca led the way up the wooden steps, and opened the door. It was gloomy inside, and the air was musty, but the sensation which assailed her was unmistakeable. *Welcome home.* It was so strong that she fancied she could hear Sancia's voice coming from the empty seat at the far end of the wagon. Rebecca moved forward, and went to stand between the narrow bed and the padded couch. Emer followed cautiously, nervously, as if expecting a ghost to leap out from the dark recesses of the room. While Rebecca simply stood and stared, Emer opened the shutters. As light flooded in, the mystery of the wagon flew away, and both girls saw the messages that Sancia had left.

In the narrow space in front of the chair was an upturned box, obviously used as a small table. It was covered with a plain cloth, on which were placed several cards laid out face down, a pendant, and a neatly folded piece of paper.

There was something written on the outside of the paper, and Rebecca knew, even before picking it up, that it was her own name. She unfolded the letter and read.

'Welcome, little one. Your friends are welcome too – I should have known that earlier.

'I learnt too late that you were my kin of the ages. Why some things remain hidden is still a mystery of the Web. But I will understand soon.

'Hold the dream, my child. It falls to you to follow the path laid down in ages past. Weave well!'

As she scanned the words, Rebecca heard the old woman's voice once more, and felt a lump in her throat. The message was signed with a simple 'S'.

'What does it say?' Emer asked, peering over her friend's shoulder.

Rebecca handed it over without a word and stood thinking while Emer read it. Her feeling of welcome had doubled, and it was obvious now why the fair people had been expecting her – but Sancia's letter contained no definite instructions, nothing specific to guide her actions. Rebecca felt as helpless as before.

'They're expecting you to stay,' Emer said, interrupting her troubled thoughts.

'What?'

'Aleandra and all the others. The fair people,' Emer explained. 'They're assuming you're going to stay here with them.'

'But—'

'Don't you see? You're Sancia's replacement.' Emer stared impatiently at her friend's blank face, but Rebecca was hearing another, older voice.

I have so little time and no one to take my place.

'I can't . . . I don't know what to do . . .' she stammered. *It falls to you.* 'Locke wouldn't allow me . . .' She was looking for excuses, and she knew it. *Have patience, little one. Don't fret.*

'How can he stop you?' Emer exclaimed. 'Even I can see that this was meant to happen. Why else are we here? Why all this?' She indicated the wagon and its contents with a sweep of her hand.

Rebecca's gaze was drawn back to the table. She picked up the pendant and studied the design engraved upon it. It consisted of two Xs between two horizontal lines that fitted neatly into the circular shape.

'Put it on,' Emer said softly.

Rebecca glanced at her friend, then obeyed, slipping the chain over her head. She half-expected some wonderful revelation, but there was no reaction save that of the metal resting snugly below her neck.

Then the cards drew her attention, and with a sudden jolt she realized that there were three rows of five interspersed with two of four – exactly the same layout as the letters on the Okran Stones! They had obviously been displaced a little by the movement of the wagon and some were crooked, but it took her only a moment to line them up properly. Her excitement grew as she did so; perhaps there was help here after all!

With Emer looking on curiously, having recognized what she was doing, Rebecca turned the cards over one by one – only to be terribly disappointed. If there was a message here, she could not read it. The cards came from a set known as 'The Emblems of Creation', which were often used by fortune-tellers, but only four of the many designs appeared on the table top. The top row consisted of four kings, two on each side of a card known as The Lovers; below that, two more kings flanked two queens. The middle row alternated three fire-demons with two lovers; the fourth row repeated the second, only in reverse – two kings between two queens – and the final row consisted of four queens with the lovers in the centre position.

The girls stared at the cards for ages, knowing that they must be significant, but unable to make any sense of them. There was a sort of pattern there, but in itself that was meaningless.

'Well?' Emer asked, without much hope.

'Nothing,' Rebecca admitted sadly.

'You wouldn't make much of a living as a fortune-teller,' her friend remarked cheerfully. She grinned, but Rebecca was too disappointed to respond. Every time she thought she was getting somewhere, all her hopes came to naught.

And yet . . . she still felt comfortable here, warm and secure. She sensed the place drawing closer about her – filled with unseen friendly faces, friendly thoughts, even love.

'Now what?' Emer asked.

'I *have* to stay here,' Rebecca exclaimed.

'Why?' Emer was surprised by the sudden change in her friend's attitude.

'To dream,' Rebecca replied confidently. 'That's the only way I can contact Sancia now.'

'It sounds crazy,' Emer commented. 'No, it *is* crazy, but I've learnt not to argue with you over something like this.' She laughed, ignoring a sudden stab of pain in her cheek. 'You always wanted to live in a fair. Now's your chance.'

'We'd better go and tell Locke,' Rebecca said.

'Do we have to?'

'Yes – or he'll send out search parties for us. We could get a lot of people into trouble. And that's no way to repay the help we've had from him and Tarrant.' She smiled, finding that Emer's return to her normal good humour had buoyed up her own spirits. 'Besides, I can persuade him. I know I can.' She felt more positive now than she had done in days. She had a purpose.

'Let's go!' Emer cried, opening the door which had closed behind them.

Rebecca stepped outside and stopped dead. Standing before her, packed into the space between Sancia's wagon and those opposite was a crowd of women, their faces up-turned as she appeared. Aleandra was standing at the front, and she, like the others, was smiling.

They're Sancia's girls, Rebecca thought. *My girls?* She swallowed hard.

Several of the women stepped forward, holding out food and drink.

'Your first meal in your new home,' Aleandra said, looking approvingly at the pendant at Rebecca's breast.

'Thank you,' was all Rebecca could say. She and Emer accepted the gifts, and quickly stowed them inside before re-emerging.

Another woman spoke. 'We have gathered here to welcome you. These are troubled times, Rebecca. We are glad to have Sancia's kin back among us.'

'She was our guardian,' another stated simply. 'And we loved her.'

'Will you take her place?' Aleandra asked.

'Yes, I will,' Rebecca answered firmly. 'As best I can – and I hope I prove worthy of your trust.' She knew now where the feeling of warm encirclement came from. 'I will do my best to keep Sancia's spirit alive.' Several of her audience nodded their approval, and there was a buzz of satisfied comment.

'But first . . . ' Rebecca began, and silence returned. 'I must return to the castle and let my host know what I am doing. I can't just disappear!'

'Then we will come with you!' someone called, and there were cries of agreement from all round. Having located their new guardian, the women were not going to let her out of their sight.

Rebecca glanced at Emer, who shrugged and smiled.

'Can you see the baron arguing with *all* of us?' she asked mischievously.

So the whole group went to the castle. Their progress was marked by their own high spirits and laughter, and by a variety of curious stares from the townsfolk. Some looked on with open disapproval, others with amusement or suspicion. The shame-faced blushes of former customers caused the most hilarity among the women, and several uncomplimentary comments were voiced concerning the men's prowess – or lack of it.

Rebecca was swept along in a wave of unexpected comradeship and earthy humour. A few hours earlier she would have been unable to envisage such a scene, but now it seemed wholly natural.

The group of women marched up to the castle gate and stopped in front of a bewildered sentry. Rebecca's followers fell silent, but she felt their support none the less.

'What's going on here?' the soldier asked, doing his best to sound in control of the situation. He was a young, beardless man with an attractive open face, and his attempts to look stern and powerful were less than successful. Several of the women nudged each other and

463

smiled, increasing his discomfiture. He had recognized Rebecca by now, and was looking to her for an explanation.

'I am Baron Locke's guest,' she said. 'I wish to speak with him.'

Other soldiers were appearing from the guardhouse now, watching the encounter curiously.

'Come in then, my lady,' the sentry replied.

'What, all of us?' she asked deliberately.

'No!' He looked so apprehensive at this prospect that some of the onlookers laughed, doubling his embarrassment.

'These are my friends,' Rebecca said. 'We travel together. Could you ask the baron to come out here?'

He hesitated, weighing all the options and finding none to his liking, then turned reluctantly and disappeared into the stronghold. A short time later, Locke emerged, and stared in horror at the assembled women.

'My dear . . .' he began. 'What . . . er . . . who?'

Rebecca came forward until she was close enough to converse with him privately.

'Baron, I have come to thank you for your generous hospitality, but Emer and I have found the perfect hiding place. These fair people . . . ' She smiled, aware of the double meaning of her words, ' . . . are my friends. They have been expecting me. I will stay with them.'

'But . . . ' Locke was at a loss for words, colour rising in his plump cheeks.

'What safer place could there be for me to hide?' she persisted. 'We all know that war is coming, and you and your men will likely soon depart. What would I do then?'

'But . . . '

'When you see Tarrant, please tell him of my plans. He would approve.' Rebecca smiled angelically, knowing she had won.

Locke glanced around as if searching for help.

'I see that you are quite decided, my dear. I hope . . . for one so young . . . ' He thought better of completing this sentiment, and made a practical suggestion instead. 'You must let me provide you with supplies, some clothes . . .'

'No, thank you,' Rebecca said firmly. 'I have all I need,

464

and I do not wish to be any more trouble to you.'

'No trouble, I assure you,' the baron blustered. 'Very well, Rebecca,' he went on, thinking with some relief of a return to his male-dominated calm. 'You must do as you think best. Go with my blessing.'

'Thank you, my lord,' she replied. 'Don't forget to give my message to Tarrant.'

'It will be done.'

'Farewell!' Rebecca called, already on her way.

Locke watched the retreating group of women for a few moments, then turned and walked back into the castle. 'What a strange turn of events,' he muttered to himself. 'Who *were* all those women?'

* * *

Rebecca and Emer spent the rest of that day getting acquainted with their new home, exploring its nooks and crannies. They found no more messages from Sancia; in fact there was remarkably little physical evidence left of the caravan's former occupant. However, their explorations did uncover some everyday tools and utensils, a few clothes and some jewellery, dusty trinkets and a painting of a mountain lake. The most remarkable find was a store of wine bottles, with most still full.

The girls received many visitors throughout the afternoon, both men and women; their welcome was universal and almost overwhelming. Whenever they found they were in need of something, one of the fair people would arrive to supply that need, without the girls ever having to ask. One woman came to tend Emer's eye, leaving her a salve to rub in before she went to bed.

The cards were left on the table, in the hope that inspiration would strike. They converted the couch into a second sleeping place, and then food was brought to them. They ate sitting on the wagon steps, watching the fair come to life as evening drew on.

Then they went for a stroll, savouring the old excitement of the fair but with a sense of belonging firmly woven in. This was their home now.

'Maybe you'll get to see your actor friend again after all!' Rebecca remarked.

'Perhaps,' Emer replied, her eyes sparkling. '*And* his friend.'

'But not tonight,' Rebecca warned. 'I need to sleep . . .'

'And dream,' Emer finished for her.

CHAPTER FIFTY-FIVE

Rebecca's dream that night was like none she had ever had before. Although she was asleep, she was still aware of the wagon and of her shell around her, providing protection but no barrier to her vision. The dream was unusual too, in that it possessed a sense of purpose, something linked to but not wholly controlled by Rebecca's will. She could direct her attention within the confined space to watch Emer, who shifted restlessly in her sleep, or to study the upturned cards which still lay on the table. But she wanted more! And knew that she was capable of it – if she could only find the courage.

Help me.

I'm here! Emer's dream-self replied, and a bond was formed between them.

Rebecca drew strength from this link, and cast her mind further out, becoming aware of the surrounding area, of the women's caravans. She felt a man's weight upon her, brutish in his need but easily manipulated; another was gentle and responsive, hoping in vain to give pleasure as well as receive it; yet another was tentative and unsure, pathetic in his eager misery, being guided patiently with well-concealed amusement. Experiencing these scenes, with all their varied emotions, saddened Rebecca – and yet she smiled. All was well with her girls.

Then a very different scene sprang up; a drunken man, sneering obscenities and threats, seen through the woman's terrified eyes as she was pressed against the side of a wagon in a dark passage. A bottle was smashed, its jagged edge raised, weaving patterns in the dark air. *I'm going to cut you, whore!* Fury rose in Rebecca and she flung all its force into her denial. *No! Leave her!* The man hesitated, scowling. *You're not worth it*, he spat, then tossed the broken bottle aside and staggered off into the night.

Thank you.

Rebecca's smile returned.

She dared to spread herself further afield, reaching out . . .

Other sections of the fair appeared, but distorted, as though she was seeing them under water; dizzying movement allowed her little time to glimpse the images as they flashed past; stalls, shows, animals and jugglers, food seller, a play in progress, more stalls, the press of people . . . The play drew her back. Actors on the stage in gaudy costumes; a comedy – but with dark undertones. Rebecca shuddered as the characters became people that she knew; her father, Radd and Tarrant in minor roles; at centre-stage, a night in gleaming armour faced a white wolf, a strange glow hovering over its ferocious head. Cranne's eyes looked out from the animal's face. A monk stood in the shadows at the rear, his bestial face flickering with a strange, unearthly light. The scenery shimmered, music played and words flowed – but Rebecca could make no sense of it, and swept it all aside in annoyance. She had had enough of meaningless symbols. *This* was not what she wanted!

Reaching out . . .

She was aware of the dangers of spreading herself too thin, of her growing weakness and the instability of the images which filled her mind. The infinite net was there, unattainable but real. *The Web.* Rebecca sensed that there was evil as well as knowledge within its imaginable scope, but her dream went on. She was driven by need, in spite of the risks involved. Searching.

Where are you?

Her call had been to Sancia, but it was Galen who answered.

I'm here too. Look! Look at this. He was anxious, eager, elated and fearful all at the same time. *I found another one.*

Letters materialized in mid-air, faint but recognizable, as though his memory of them was clear but somehow faraway.

```
E  W  I  Z  A
E  N  N  R
O  R  N  D  E
O  H  S  E
B  H  T  I  R
```

Remember the letters next time . . .

As Rebecca concentrated on committing the latest puzzle to her memory, she became aware that Emer was in some distress. Her attention faltered, the letters disappeared, and she felt her friend crying softly in her sleep, her hands raised to cover the disfiguring bruises around her eye.

What's the matter? Galen asked. *Why is she hiding?*

But the dream had a power of its own, and Rebecca could not answer him. Her vision grew vague, expanded and whirled. She sensed a multitude of others around Galen, and felt their mixture of dread and grim purpose as they waited.

The focus narrowed again – but not to Galen. Her whole perspective had changed, and the army was gone.

Montfort stood, resplendent in full armour, the royal crest emblazoned on his breast. His helmet was lodged under one arm, while his other hand rested proudly on the shoulder of his young son. The king looked calm but serious, but the child's expression could not be seen. The only part of his face which was not obscured by the miniature helmet – an almost perfect replica of his father's – were his eyes. They suddrenly widened in surprise at something Rebecca could not see. Then the small figure began to waver. He became misty, and faded, gradually disappearing altogether.

No! Rebecca was filled with enormous sorrow atmthe loss. Her anguish was mirrored by the stricken face of Montfort as he turned round and around, searching for the lost prince, his eyes forever returning to the spot where the boy had stood.

Behind the king, a massive demon rose, towering over him in fearful splendour, a being of fire and limitless power. And yet Montfort seemed unaware of his peril, and when Rebecca cried out to warn him, her voice was mute.

A golden bell tolled, signalling the doom of the land.

CHAPTER FIFTY-SIX

After a three-day march, Montfort's army had covered two-thirds of the distance between Garadun and the salt. They made camp that night on a barren upland heath, the temporary settlement sprawling over a vast area, and punctuated by hundreds of cooking fires. The warmth of the flames was welcome – the first chill winds of autumn had begun to blow from the east, whining through the tent ropes and swirling smoke into the starlit sky.

Within the boundaries patrolled by vigilant look-outs, there was constant activity. Messages were carried to and fro, meals were cooked, animals tended, and equipment maintained. Soldiers talked for hours, reminiscing about past deeds and speculating on the days to come. Old hands either slept or watched the younger ones work, and smiled at their eagerness. All was bathed in the flickering glow of the camp-fires, and imbued with the smells of smoke, dirt, and oil – the indefinable mixture unique to an army on the move.

Galen was working with the horses, as he usually did during the evenings, finding that the steady, familiar tasks helped calm his now fevered imagination. The horses seemed solid and dependable, and he was able to ease his worries by talking to them quietly as he worked.

Tonight, however, he was interrupted by one of Ellard's lieutenants. To his surprise, he was summoned to the king's command tent, where Montfort and his senior officers had gathered for a council of war. Galen hurried through the camp, was acknowledged by the guard, and stepped inside. Montfort and his companions were standing around a folding table, looking intently at the maps spread out upon it. They all looked up at the young man's entrance, and the king smiled in welcome. The other men all looked terribly stern; next to them, Montfort seemed very young. The only other person Galen recognized was Ellard.

'Gentlemen,' Montfort announced, 'this is Galen, a former resident of Edgefield Castle, and a man who has already proved his worth on several occasions. He brought me Davin's report – which as you all know is the reason for us being here.'

A number of the officers nodded in acknowledgement, and Galen, feeling extremely embarrassed, gave them an awkward bow.

'You are most welcome, Galen,' the king went on. 'We are glad of your help.' He beckoned, and his most recent recruit moved closer, glancing at the maps laid out before him. He could think of nothing to say, but was saved from having to speak by Montfort.

'I'm afraid that bad news was received this afternoon,' the king went on. 'Our scouts report that Edge has been taken by Farrand and his younger son Cranne, together with a sizeable contingent of men. Edgefield Castle is currently in their hands, and is being refortified.'

Galen had known that scouts had been active in all directions since they had left the capital, but until now he had not been privy to their news – although various rumours had of course spread throughout the camp. This news was the worst he could have imagined – and his horror showed on his face.

'We are more than strong enough to retake it,' the king reassured him. 'It was obviously not expected that we would respond so quickly. And we have you to thank for that. On the other hand, we *have* been taken somewhat by surprise. I had hoped to occupy Edgefield without having to fight – and we are not as well prepared as I'd like.'

'What this *does* do,' another commander explained, 'is confirm Davin's report. Edge is undoubtedly important to the enemy, and now we also know that the invasion from the south is imminent.'

'That's why it is imperative that we retake Edgefield soon,' Montfort went on. 'The enemy will be most vulnerable at the salt's edge, and we thus need time to prepare

471

a defence there. You know Edge and the surrounding area better than any of us. We need your help.'

Galen nodded dumbly. There was dread in his heart now – for his home, for Rebecca, but especially for Emer . . .

Montfort studied the young man carefully for a few moments. When he next spoke, it was as though he had read Galen's thoughts – at least in part.

'Our scouts don't know what's happened to Baldemar . . . or to Rebecca,' he explained gently. 'There are varying rumours about their capture or escape, but nothing definite.' Annoyance flickered across the king's face. 'Tarrant assured me recently that he would keep an eye on the baron's daughter.' The king was no longer talking just to Galen, but appeared to be addressing his thoughts to the canvas roof above them. 'I sometimes wonder whether that man actually works for me. I never know where he is!'

Galen's mind was in turmoil. The fact that they would be fighting soon did not alarm him. That had been expected by everyone. But knowing that it was Cranne and his father who had invaded Edgefield was a horrifying thought. His victory in the chess game seemed hollow now, and he could not help imagining the revenge that Cranne must have already taken upon his previous adversaries. He was sickened by the prospect.

Galen's thoughts were soon dragged back to his present situation as Montfort began to discuss their own invasion plans. Galen had already described the area in some detail to Ellard, but repeated what he knew for the benefit of those now present. It was all that he could do.

An hour passed in a detailed examination of Edgefield, the castle, approaches to the town and likely defensive positions. Galen did his best to answer everyone's questions, dredging obscure facts from the deep recesses of his memory, and grew in confidence as the older men responded to his information and ideas. At last the inquisition ground to a halt.

'That's it, I think,' Montfort concluded, looking round for confirmation. 'Anything else?'

'We must look further ahead, my lord,' Ellard replied. 'What we really need is intelligence from south of the salt.'

Montfort nodded. 'I'm still waiting to hear from our scouts. But our first priority has to be the recapture of Edge. Then we'll have time – and men to spare – for the rest.'

'I've been with some Archaeologists recently, sire,' Galen volunteered. 'I'm sure they would be willing to help.'

'You are indeed a man of many talents,' the king remarked, smiling. 'Where were they when you last saw them?'

'Tybridge.' Galen did a quick mental calculation. 'That was eight days ago. They were in pocket, so the chances are that they'll still be there.'

Montfort bent to study the map.

'It might be worth a try,' he decided. 'By nightfall tomorrow we'll be within Edge's boundaries. Would you be prepared to ride to Tybridge the next day?'

Galen hesitated for only a moment. He was torn between wanting to help his sovereign and his desire to return to Edgefield. In the end, though, he knew he could not refuse.

'Of course,' he answered quietly.

'He could go via Cutover,' Ellard suggested, 'and visit Redfern to see if he has any news. Who knows, he may even have some idea where Tarrant is!'

'Good idea,' Montfort responded. 'We'll send an escort with him.'

'I'd prefer to go alone, sire,' Galen put in quickly. 'It would seem less suspicious that way.'

'The Archaeologists are an unpredictable lot at the best of times,' another officer confirmed. 'They may not take kindly to being approached by a whole troop.'

'But you should have at least one other with you,' Montfort said. 'In case you need to stay with them but get a message back to me.'

'How about Arledge?' Ellard asked, naming one of his own men. 'He's a good scout – and he's the only one who can get close to Galen's beek.'

Spike had travelled with Galen the whole time, apparently revelling in this strange life-style and the precarious times spent on horseback. Arledge, a strong-minded thirty-year-old cavalry veteran, had taken a fancy to the beek, and had tempted the little creature with titbits. Spike had gradually been won over, and was now prepared to tolerate the soldier near his master and his master's possessions. Everyone else in the camp was warned off with a series of hissing threats and blood-curdling yowls.

'Does that meet with your approval, Galen?'

The young man nodded. Whatever happened, and whatever Arledge had in mind, he had every intention of heading straight back to Edgefield as soon as he had located the Archaeologists.

'Then, gentlemen,' Montfort decreed, 'to bed. We must be on our mettle tomorrow.'

Galen and Ellard walked back to their unit together, threading their way carefully between the fires, tents and guy-ropes.

'I know that Rebecca's important to you,' Ellard said carefully. 'You risked a lot for her in that chess game.'

'I suppose so,' Galen answered, nodding distractedly.

The captain had sensed Galen's earlier reluctance, and his horror at the news of Edgefield's capture, and sensed his half-heartedness now.

'Someone else?' he asked.

'Yes.'

'Tarrant said there was a third party involved. Who is she?'

Galen looked up from his study of the ground.

'Emer,' he said. 'The chamberlain's daughter.'

'I'll look out for her then,' Ellard promised. 'And try not to worry. Those men can't match our strength. They'll probably surrender without a fight.'

'That's not what I'm worrying about,' Galen stated flatly.

Ellard nodded, understanding.

'I'm sorry you have to go to Tybridge,' he said. 'But it *does* make sense.'

'I know.'

'Head for Edgefield afterwards, if you can,' the captain went on. 'We'll have it secure by then. And tell Arledge your plan. He'll enjoy the ride.'

Galen responded as cheerfully as he could, then headed for his tent. The only other current occupant was Spike, who greeted his master with great enthusiasm, as though he had been away for days. Arledge came in from look-out duty soon afterwards, and was delighted by Galen's news and the prospect of some immediate action. He was soon snoring, but Galen lay awake brooding for a long time. The night was half over when at last he fell asleep.

* * *

He lay in darkness, floating. His surroundings were so black that he could not even see his own hands, his own body. And he knew that something was missing. He felt incomplete. Yearning.

Into that endless darkness came a light. It was faraway at first, and faint, but it gradually spread wider. Searching. To Galen's dreaming mind it illuminated horrors as well as truths but he could not tell if any of them were real. It reminded him of starlight on the salt-flats – it was just as delicate, just as magical.

Where are you?

The voice and the light came from the same presence, which was weak but purposeful – and beyond her was another, fainter still, and reticent. He knew them both, and was filled with a mixture of emotions.

I'm here too, he called. *Look! Look at this.* He was determined not to repeat his earlier mistake. This time he was ready, and the letters were clear in his mind. *I found another one.*

He felt Rebecca absorb his message, and his anxiety lessened, but something else bothered him now. Emer was hurt. Why couldn't he 'see' her properly?

What's the matter? Why is she hiding?

There was no answer. He sensed tears, a wound, and his fears sprang up again. The link wavered and, as before, it left him too soon. Then it was gone, casting him adrift once more.

Wait! he called desperately. *Where are you? Are you all right?*

But the darkness and the silence mocked him.

He awoke feeling doubly frustrated – and found himself rubbing a sudden ache just below his right eye.

CHAPTER FIFTY-SEVEN

Rebecca was finally woken by the sounds of movement outside their caravan. In the shuttered gloom it took her a few moments to realize where she was. Emer was already awake, and the two girls looked at each other, the dream still reflected in their eyes. Neither spoke for some time.

'You heard him too, didn't you?' Emer whispered eventually.

'Yes. It was like the chess game,' Rebecca answered softly. 'The three of us together.'

'I didn't want him to see me like this,' her friend admitted quietly, raising a hand to her injured cheek. The skin was healing well, but was still mottled with various shades of black, purple and yellow.

'I never knew you were so vain,' Rebecca commented, trying to appear light-hearted. She wanted to raise her friend's spirits, even though the dream's terrible end had filled her with a nameless dread. 'In any case, it was only a dream,' she added, forcing a smile.

The irony of such a statement coming from her was not lost on either of them, but when Emer next spoke her voice was little more than a whisper, and filled with longing.

'He was so far away.'

'What else did you see?' Rebecca asked, hoping to take Emer's mind off her distress.

'I can't remember.'

Rebecca needed to share her own fears, and described the scene she had witnessed with Montfort.

'It was dreadful when his son disappeared,' she concluded. 'Montfort seemed so lost, so lonely. Then the demon . . . he didn't even see it! I tried to warn him, but

476

'. . . I felt as though there was a gaping hole inside me.'

'There was a bell,' Emer said quietly. It was all she remembered – everything else had slipped away.

'Yes.' Rebecca shivered involuntarily as she recalled the doom-laden reverberations. 'What does it all mean?' *Sancia would have known,* she added silently. Then something occurred to her, and she leapt out of bed. She had been so shaken by the nightmarish end to the dream that she had almost forgotten the earlier part.

'Galen showed me some more letters,' she explained as she opened the shutters, filling the caravan with morning light. Her friend joined her, and under Emer's curious gaze, Rebecca wrote down the latest puzzle and placed it alongside the three that she had carried with her. The two girls studied them, but their increased knowledge did not make the code any less impenetrable.

'Four sets now,' Emer said thoughtfully. She was no longer sceptical about the nature of the letters, and accepted that they were important. 'I wonder how many more there are.'

'At least one,' Rebecca replied. 'It was the first one I saw in my dreams, but I can't remember what the letters were.' She sounded disgusted with herself.

'Well, then,' Emer responded brightly. 'Set yourself a task for your dreams tonight. Remember the missing letters.' She grinned. 'Easy!'

Rebecca thought about this for a few moments, her expression serious. 'I'll try,' she said determinedly, then grinned. 'You believe me now?'

'I don't have any choice!' Emer exclaimed. 'When I said you were weird, it was obviously a serious understatement.'

'I'm so scared, Emer,' Rebecca whispered. ' I *am* a dream-weaver, but I don't know how to control it, how to weave in a pattern that will be of some use. The fair people expect so much of me, and what with the war and everything . . . ' She grew silent, and when Emer hugged her, she returned the embrace gratefully.

'We'll work it out, Becky,' her friend said softly. 'We've got this far, haven't we?'

'I'm glad we're together.'

'It'll take a lot more than a few last moment escapes from

477

certain death – and worse! – scaling castle walls, galloping through the night and running away with the fair to get rid of me!' Emer exclaimed. 'You've even got me believing in magic now, so you needn't bother trying to scare me away!'

A knock sounded on the door while they were dressing. Rebecca opened it to find Aleandra, with a tray of food. Outside, the fair was a hive of activity, with wagons being prepared for travel and the last of the equipment being packed away.

'We're leaving?' Rebecca asked as she accepted the tray.

'You're here now,' the woman said simply.

'You were waiting for me?'

Aleandra nodded.

'Where are we going?'

'All roads lead somewhere.'

Rebecca took the answer to mean that Aleandra neither knew nor cared where they were headed. She envied the woman her imperturbability.

'I'd rather this one didn't lead to Edge,' she said, and Aleandra laughed, a simple, carefree sound.

'Don't worry,' was her parting advice.

Shortly afterwards, men came to fix poles to the front of the wagon. They hitched a horse between them, and handed Rebecca the reins. Before they set off, however, they had another visitor. The woman carried a pile of clothes, and it was not until she was quite close that Rebecca recognized her, with a jolt, as the one she had 'saved' in the dream. The memory of that early part of the night's adventure had faded, but now it came back to her in full force. *Did I really do that?* She could not think how to ask.

The woman smiled. 'My name is Helice,' she began. 'We noticed that you didn't have any other clothes. Sancia's won't fit either of you, so we've gathered these from all of us. Take what you want and leave the rest.' She handed the pile to Rebecca, who was sitting beside Emer at the front of their wagon. 'The two things on top are mine,' Helice added.

Rebecca unfolded the black skirt and the green woollen jacket, and examined them. Helice's eyes followed the second item wistfully and it was obvious that this was a treasured item. Rebecca was doubly touched by the woman's generosity, and was not sure how she should react. Their new friend might be offended if her offerings were not accepted, but Rebecca had no wish to deprive her of such a precious possession. In the end she followed her instinct and compromised.

'The skirt will be fine for me,' she said. 'But this is too small for either of us. Thank you anyway.' She handed the jacket back, and was happy to see that Helice could not help smiling when she took it.

'I'm glad the skirt is all right,' the woman said. 'I must go now. Let me know about the rest later.' She gave them another smile, then returned to her own chores.

Emer, who had been silent during this encounter, gazed after the retreating figure.

'She looks familiar.'

'We saw her yesterday,' Rebecca answered. 'She came with us to the castle.'

'No, it's more than that . . . ' Emer said uncertainly.

'We helped her during the night.' Rebecca no longer doubted the truth of her statement.

'We?' Emer exclaimed. 'I'm supposed to be the *sane* one around here!'

'Then how did you know about Galen?'

'It's natural for me to dream about him,' Emer said defensively, not wanting to delve too deeply into her own involvement.

'What's the matter? Why is she hiding?' Rebecca quoted, and stared at her friend as if daring her to deny it.

'All right, all right,' Emer conceded. 'It must be the effect of this wagon!'

'You don't believe that. Think back – try and remember. There may have been other times when our dreams were shared.'

The idea excited Rebecca, but Emer was not so enthusiastic.

'My life is complicated enough without this,' she complained. 'You're the dream-weaver. I'm just the henchman!'

Their attention was distracted as the wagons began to move off.

'What do I do now?' Rebecca asked in sudden panic.

479

It soon became obvious that she would have to do very little. The horse started of its own accord, taking its accustomed place in the line, settling into a steady pace as it followed the wagon in front. The girls' caution was gradually replaced by confidence, and they took it in turns to hold the reins.

The long snake of caravans left Castlemane and moved into open country. Rebecca and Emer were left to themselves most of the time, but the few people who were on foot or on horseback made a point of greeting them as they passed. Everyone was warm but respectful towards the newcomers – even the children – and their ready acceptance made both girls feel at home. This was intensified at the midday break, when the entire mobile population ate from the communal pots of the cooks' fires. When they set off again, Emer was feeling noticeably happier. She now knew several of their companions and felt less self-conscious about her bruised face. When Rebecca remarked that she seemed to be settling into her new environment, Emer's reply surprised her.

'They've made me feel that I'm not just the dream-weaver's apprentice.'

* * *

That evening, the fair camped on open ground, with the wagons gathered in a compact group, almost as if huddled together for protection. Rebecca and Emer insisted on helping prepare their wagon and caring for their horse, not wanting to be seen as useless passengers. When they were finished, Helice came to collect the unwanted clothes.

'Annis is telling stories tonight,' she announced brightly. 'She never does it for townsfolk,' she added, 'only for us.' Helice paused, as though expecting some reaction to this, but none was forthcoming. 'Sancia always came,' she prompted hopefully.

'Of course we'll come,' Emer said, and Helice departed happily. Rebecca remained silent, her face suddenly pale in the early evening light.

'Are you all right?' Emer queried.

480

'I don't want to go,' her companion replied. Strands of an inexplicable fear were twisting within her, but Emer could not understand her reluctance.

'Don't be silly,' she said. 'Why ever not?'

Rebecca's fears remained, and when the time came to join the storyteller's audience, she still felt uneasy. Emer left, not bothering to hide her disgust at her friend's odd behaviour.

'I thought you *liked* this sort of thing,' was her parting comment.

Rebecca was fighting an inner battle against her reluctance. She knew that she ought to face her illogical fears, so she eventually steeled herself and followed Emer. She arrived just as Annis was beginning, but was still filled with misgivings, and hid where she could listen but not be seen.

'There once was a little girl who had read too many fairy tales,' Annis began. A smattering of laughter greeted her words, marking the relationship between narrator and audience as familiar and good-natured. The storyteller's voice was light, but carried easily. It was resonant, warm and inviting. She went on to tell of a girl who, while she was growing up, made a habit of kissing every frog she saw, in the hope of magically finding a handsome suitor. She was rewarded, eventually, but not by a prince. Instead, she was granted a unique gift. She was led by a huge gathering of frogs – who had come to love her – to a magic lake in the heart of a great forest. There, at the invitation of the Emperor Frog, she jumped into the muddy, reed-clogging water – and turned into a frog herself! Filled with happiness, she dived, jumped and swam in this magical world. Fish greeted her, insects fled at her approach, and she encountered creatures she could not recognize and whose very existence had previously been unknown to her. Underwater plants, even the mud and stones on the lake-bed, all became objects of wonder and mystery. She could not remember ever having had so much fun in her life, and she sat on a lily-pad and croaked her joy to all who would hear.

Then came a shrill warning, and there was a sudden panic as the frogs all swam and jumped for their lives. A pike, their deadly enemy, was approaching! The girl-frog swam as fast as she could, almost skimming over the water, and leapt out on to the bank. There she turned back into her human form, her heart beating like a drum, and listened to the outraged croaking of her friends as they tried to avoid the vicious fish.

'At that moment, she decided that she'd probably rather be a girl after all,' Annis concluded, 'but she made sure to tell her father – who was a keen fisherman – about the pike. And she never forgot the magic of that day – and her friends the frogs.'

The end of her performance was greeted with laughter and applause. Annis had enhanced the story by adapting her voice to suit each scene and character. Her tone had varied from the slight, delicate voice of the young girl – which had gained in strength as the story progressed – to the hilarious bass croak of the Emperor Frog.

Rebecca's fears had receded as she listened and found herself charmed by the storyteller's skill. *She's very good*, she thought, feeling quite foolish about her earlier misgivings.

As the ovation died down, someone called out from the audience.

'Did she ever find her prince?'

'That is the strangest, loveliest part of all,' Annis replied promptly, and her listeners were instantly quiet again, waiting for her to weave another imaginative spell.

'Before she had jumped into the lake, she had naturally removed her clothes. After all, frogs don't wear them! She hid them in the bushes beside the water, but in her terror when fleeing from the pike, she forgot where she had put them. And unknown to her a young forester was passing, and saw her emerge from the lake to sit naked on the bank. Fearing witchcraft, he hid behind a tree, but was so entranced by the magical nature of her appearance and by her glorious beauty that he could not help spying on her as she searched for her clothes. He fell in love with her there and then, and when she was dressed he followed her home.

'After that he courted her fervently, though at first she gave him no encouragement. He brought her flowers every day – rare and beautiful plants that he placed in her garden – and every kind of nut and berry that the bountiful forest could offer. He would do anything for her; no task was too big or too small . . . and, at last, his patience was rewarded and she returned his affection.

'Their love blossomed, and flowers to this day. It was soon the young forester who received all her kisses, and she no longer thought about her amphibian friends. But they did not forget her. On her wedding night, all the frogs of the forest gathered round the young wife's new home and sang of joy and the fulfilment of love. The girl and her forester listened, and smiled.

'Neither of them ever told the other of their part in the events of that magical night, but in their hearts they both knew what had happened. It was their secret, and it has bound them together in all the many happy years of their marriage.'

This time, her conclusion drew forth a gentle, satisfied murmuring. A few of the more sentimental members of the audience found themselves wiping away a few tears.

Annis was silent, seemingly content, until another of her audience requested one of the old tales. The gathering waited patiently while she decided which tale to tell. Eventually she stood up, pushed her chair away and looked down upon them from the small, improvised stage. Her voice changed yet again as she declaimed in melodramatic tones.

'An evil king once ruled this land!'

CHAPTER FIFTY-EIGHT

This beginning was greeted with murmurs of approval, and obviously signalled a familiar and well-loved tale. But Rebecca was shaken by a tremor of unease. However, this soon wore off as she was drawn into the tale, helped by Annis's sense of drama and comic invention. Before long, Rebecca was as rapt as the rest of the audience.

'He had everything that he could possibly want; a beautiful, gentle queen and many willing mistresses, riches beyond compare, a palace filled with beauty and comfort – and all attended to by an army of discreet and competent servants. He did nothing except what pleased him . . . and yet all this was not enough!

'The king was consumed by a fatal desire for the greatest gift of all, and he turned his frustrated anger upon everyone around him, constantly grumbling and complaining.'

Laughter greeted Annis's gestures and posture as she took the part of the king's fawning lackeys. Her demeanour and her voice had changed almost beyond recognition.

'But, sire,' she whined. 'You will be remembered for ever as the greatest of monarchs.'

Her voice boomed out as the irate king once more.

'I don't want to gain immortality by being *remembered*, you wheedling little worm!' she cried. 'I want to become immortal by *not dying*!'

Annis waited for the laughter to die down before returning to her own voice, soft now, and full of menace.

'His great obsession was immortality. He hunted out ancient tomes on the subject, reading all he could on how to achieve his goal. He consulted the oldest people he could find, hoping to steal their secrets. He even investigated the

484

myths surrounding the tree-that-lives-for-ever, sending out search parties to bring back its fruit. And finally he studied theories of the occult, learning what he could of the powers of the evil side of the Web. And there, at last, he found a way to achieve his dream.'

The word 'dream' prodded Rebecca into action, an irresistible impulse driving her forward. The power of the storyteller's skill had entranced her, and she left her hiding place, joining the ranks of the silent audience on their makeshift benches. Annis saw her as she stepped forward, and their eyes met briefly. The storyteller was pretty, but her face held a strange other-worldly quality, and this impression was reinforced by a shock of wavy hair which, in the lamplight, appeared to be salt-white.

A flicker of fear passed over Annis's delicate features, and she faltered in her tale for a moment, but then her voice grew in strength and the words began to flow once more.

The story took over, just as Newell's music had done. Rebecca was no longer in the fair; her new friends ceased to exist as she was transported into Annis's world; the realm of her imagination became real. The words took shape and life, and Rebecca actually *saw* what Annis described. She witnessed the great black pyramid that was to be the king's tomb; she saw the great labour of its construction, supervised by the evil wizards who had now joined forces with the king. Spells were wrought and potions brewed. Demons were summoned, and the agreement reached and sealed with blood.

Rebecca was there when the king 'died', and watched as his corpse was placed in the specially prepared chamber at the heart of the pyramid. And she knew that he would rise again – and that he would be immortal – and immeasurably terrible. But at the last moment, the land was saved by three good wizards who, at the cost of their own lives and those of countless others, brought about the destruction of the entire city. Derith and all its citizens, the tomb and its late king, wizards both good and evil – all were buried for ever beneath the cleansing deluge of salt.

Rebecca felt herself choking, salt filling her eyes, her mouth and her throat, burning her lungs. The whole world had turned white. She struggled, sure that she was about to die and be buried with the city.

But she still lived, and other elements slowly crept into her consciousness. Voices, full of concern. 'Are you all right?' 'Get her some water, quick!' 'Stand back – give her air.' Someone rubbed her hands and another patted her on the back as she coughed and spluttered, blinking as the real world gradually reasserted itself and she began to see again.

'Are you all right, Becky?' Emer asked anxiously, cradling her friend's hands in her own.

Rebecca nodded, and looked around. Many eyes were upon her, but there was only one pair whose gaze held under-standing as well as sympathy. Annis glanced away almost immediately, guilt and fear in her expression. The storyteller was still on the stage, a pale ghost against the backdrop of night.

'Becky?'

'I'm fine,' she whispered, her eyes fixed on Annis. She stood up, no longer aware of the press of people around her, the proffered cup of water. *It's happened again*, she thought. *Like the music. This is magic!*

She started forward, and people stepped aside to let her pass, concern and wonder still written on their faces. Annis saw her coming, however, and tried to leave, but Rebecca broke into a run and caught her before she could escape.

Their confrontation was watched by many of the fair people, but no one understood either Rebecca's garbled words or Annis's obvious fear.

'You have to tell me!' Rebecca began. 'You have to explain. I saw it . . . the city, and the salt . . . I was there!'

The storyteller looked terrified now. She glanced about, as if searching for an escape route, but remained silent.

'You made it real,' Rebecca persisted. 'I'd been there before in my dream . . . Where does it come from?'

But Annis only cowered, and could not or would not respond.

'The story took over, didn't it?' Rebecca cried, her frustration turning to anger now. '*Didn't it?*'

Annis spoke then.

'Are you one of us?' she whispered, white with fear.

'What?'

The storyteller looked confused, and twisted nervously at a ring on her finger.

'You can't have seen . . . ' she breathed, then clamped her mouth shut, turned away and ran into the darkness.

Rebecca started after her, but was held back. She turned angrily to face her assailant, recognizing him as the man who broke and trained wild horses. His grip was unrelenting, his eyes calm. Aleandra appeared beside him.

'Let her be,' she advised Rebecca. 'We have our own demons, and Annis's is her fear of strangers. When she gets used to you . . . ' Aleandra shrugged.

'But this is very important!' Rebecca complained.

'You'll get nothing from her now,' the man said. 'We all pay for our gifts, one way or another.' He released his grip as he felt her relax a little.

'The story was real!' Rebecca exclaimed, the exasperation of defeat in her voice. 'Didn't you see it?'

'She's very good,' Aleandra commented.

'No! It was more than that.'

'Perhaps you hear with different ears,' the man suggested.

Am I going mad? Rebecca wondered. *Why is it only me who responds like this?* Dejection gradually took the place of her indignation, and she subsided, suddenly feeling desper-ately tired. Emer took her arm and led her back to their wagon.

We each have our own demons, Rebecca thought bitterly. *We all pay for our gifts, one way or another.*

* * *

While Rebecca had been listening to Annis's story, Farrand and Cranne were talking in her former home at Edgefield Castle. Cranne was in self-congratulatory mood, still triumphant over their easy victory three days earlier. He had subsequently indulged himself in sufficient cruel pleasures to curb his wrath at Rebecca's escape, but now he was looking further ahead, and paced the room restlessly, his energy directionless.

'The first mercenaries should be in Riano by now,' he stated.

'If the latest report is correct,' Farrand replied coolly. The elder nobleman was by nature more cautious than his son. The risk they were taking made him nervous, even though they had taken every possible precaution, and he hated this slack time as they waited for their allies to arrive. He especially disliked having to wait in the company of his unpredictable son. There was no telling when Cranne might decide that he needed the diversion of even more bloodshed.

'Just a few days,' Cranne said, ignoring his father's remark, 'and they'll be here. Then we can begin in earnest.' His eyes gleamed at the prospect.

'Has Baldemar decided to cooperate yet?' Farrand asked.

'He's singing like a bird,' Cranne replied with a malevolent smile. 'But the stupid old bastard doesn't know much. It's obvious that his chamberlain ran this place.' He snorted derisively.

'And he?'

'Refuses to talk,' Cranne answered disgustedly, 'even after an unhealthy amount of persuasion.' He laughed suddenly. 'Anyway, he's half mad. What can you think of a man who lay sleeping in a store-room while his home was invaded? Didn't seem to be drunk, though he must have been. He just keeps mumbling about music, and it's impossible to get any sense out of him. Perhaps you could come and help me persuade him of the error of his ways.'

'I'll leave that sort of thing to you,' Farrand replied, his distaste obvious. 'I'm hardly likely to succeed where you have failed.'

A knock sounded at the door of the usurped baronial chamber, and at Farrand's response a messenger entered, clothes stained and his face flushed from riding hard.

'My lords . . . ' he exclaimed breathlessly. 'Montfort is at Edge's northern border. He has the whole strength of Garadun's army with him.'

A moment passed in petrified silence.

'That's impossible!' Cranne roared.

'How many units?' Farrand asked, his voice icy.

'At least six. Maybe eight.'

'Betrayed!' Cranne shouted. 'Who?' His face was mottled with rage and his hands clenched as if strangling an invisible traitor.

'That's all his strength,' Farrand said calmly, ignoring his son's ravings. 'Which means that the capital is undefended! Bring me my scouts.'

The messenger left quickly, glad to have escaped unscathed despite being the bearer of bad news. Cranne started to pace the room again, cursing loudly.

'If you hadn't been so *enthusiastic* in our attack on this place,' Farrand said caustically, 'we might be safe yet.'

Cranne stopped and stared venomously at his father.

'He wouldn't bring the whole army just against us!' he spat, proving that at least one corner of his seething brain was still functioning logically. 'We've been betrayed! Montfort knows what we're planning.'

'Then you'd better pray that our friends get here sooner than planned,' his father commented sourly.

*   *   *

However hard she tried, Rebecca's dream would not follow the pattern she wanted, and the lost letters were nowhere to be found. Nor was there any sign of Galen, or of Montfort. Instead, all she could see was an artist, at work on a vast canvas. He was painting feverishly, his brush flashing from palette to easel and back, but he occasionally turned around to look at her, his expression puzzled, before turning back to his work. She recognized him as Kedar, the young artist who had portrayed her father so effectively, and she called out to him. But he did not seem to hear her.

Abruptly, the dream shifted, and she was *inside* the painting, trapped in the living canvas. A black pyramid rose menacingly overhead; emaciated men stalked the streets of the lost white city; skeletal hands plucked at her clothes.

Are you one of us?

But Rebecca could not speak.

She awoke from the vision choking and terrified, just as she had emerged from Annis's story. One thought was pounding incessantly in her mind.

She got the ending wrong!

489

CHAPTER FIFTY-NINE

The second mercenary army reached Riano a day after the earlier arrivals, and joined their colleagues in the sprawling camp to the west of the city. However, they were not the only newcomers that day. More troops had been sent by Jarlath's various southern allies, and although their numbers were somewhat less than he had hoped for, there were still enough of them to fill the barracks in the town and require another camp. This straddled the road to the salt, north of Riano.

But the arrivals who caused the biggest stir were not soldiers at all in any conventional sense. When the monks rode into the city with the abbot at their head, even the fiercest of the mercenaries fell silent, and several people made superstitious signs as they passed, hoping to ward off evil. The citizens of Riano reacted by hiding behind closed doors. Few outside Jarlath's castle had ever seen Hakon, and his messengers had travelled mostly at night, when there were fewer witnesses. Such a huge number of skeletal creatures on massive black horses was bound to cause fear and revulsion. All who saw them shuddered, and most remained silent, not wanting to risk offending these dread visitors. But once the monks were installed in the sacred quarters, which has been kept in constant readiness by Hakon, the whispers began.

'Dead men riding to the war.'

'Don't look into their eyes. They'll turn you to salt.'

* * *

That evening, Jarlath called a council of war. They sat round a table in one of the most luxurious baronial chambers, but the mercenary leaders were singularly unimpressed by their surroundings, and were far more interested in the maps spread out before them. Jarlath surveyed his companions before speaking.

Olin, the most senior of the foreign generals, was much taller than the baron, but just as broad. His cold blue eyes stared from a face that resembled a slab of rock. Incongruously, his beard was wispy, and the colour of pale straw. Nur, the other foreigner, was also tall, but less solidly built. His dark hair and thick beard were matched by deep brown eyes, but his skin was almost white. Callouses on his hands marked the long hours of training.

I hope I am right to trust these barbarians, Jarlath thought, regretting the fact that the mercenary armies would outnumber his own men when they marched north. *This is a dangerous game.*

Also at the table were Hakon, whose spectral appearance had unnerved the southerners – a fact which had given Jarlath a flicker of cruel pleasure – and Sadir, the commander of the baron's own forces. Sadir was tall and thin, with a sharp angular face. He was older than his foreign counterparts, and could not have matched them in physical prowess, but he was nevertheless a shrewd man and an excellent tactician. The commander was ill at ease this evening, and eyed the outsiders with dislike. He was tainted with the bigotry common to Ahrenia, which regarded foreigners as less than human, creatures without a soul.

'We go north tomorrow,' Jarlath began. 'Across the salt. The entire force will travel on foot, carrying their own supplies. We will have access to horses on the far side, but they would be useless in the salt.' He looked around, but no one made any comment. The mercenaries were used to marching. 'In three days we will be here,' and the baron stabbed a finger at the map. 'Edge. Some colleagues of mine have already taken the town and the land surrounding it. Then we will go north to Garadun.'

'And will Montfort not meet us?' Olin asked.

'Not until it is too late. He knows nothing of your presence here, and it will take time to mobilize the forces left to him. Several of his detachments to the north will have their hands full. I have seen to that.' Jarlath smiled almost complacently.

'Even if he should bring his entire army – and I don't believe he will leave Garadun completely undefended – his force will still only be half the size of ours.' This was a slight exaggeration – but near enough to the truth to make little difference. 'Once we are over the salt, we will be invincible. This is why speed is essential. By crossing the salt, we waste none of our energy or supplies on too long a march, and with luck, we'll be on him almost before he's aware of the danger. We'll be fighting a disorganized rabble as well as an inferior force. Easy pickings!' he concluded triumphantly.

Nur was not impressed.

'Why must we cross the salt?' he asked flatly.

'Because Montfort would never expect us to go that way,' Jarlath explained. 'There is some movement in the salt. This is rare, but the gossip-mongers make it seem more dangerous than it really is. People are reluctant to make such a crossing.'

'Yet you expect us to march in to this . . . *movement*?' Olin asked, a touch of anger in his voice.

'I will be crossing with you,' Jarlath protested. 'Does the thought of such a small risk frighten you?'

Hakon entered the discussion for the first time, his rasping voice cutting through the growing tension.

'We will have escorts who are trained to give warning of any dangerous tremors,' he said. 'Should anything of that nature occur, my brethren have developed ways to control it.' *But not in the way you suppose!* he added to himself.

'Sorcery?' Nur asked, his eyes narrowed.

'If you like,' Hakon replied. 'The Web has been gracious enough to grant us some powers, and it would be foolish not to take advantage of that. Speed is of the utmost importance, and will lessen the chance of any movement affecting us. None the less, the brethren will march with you as a safeguard.'

Olin and Nur regarded him suspiciously. Olin was about to speak when Shahan burst into the room. All those seated round the table – except Hakon – jumped to their feet, hands instinctively going to their sword-hilts.

'There had better be a good reason for this!' Jarlath growled angrily.

'Montfort mobilized his army six days ago,' Shahan stated

defiantly. 'They could be in Edge by now!'

This shocked even Jarlath, and drew exclamations of anger and surprise from the others.

'How do you know this?' the baron demanded.

'My spies saw the army leave Garadun,' Shahan replied. 'Someone has betrayed us!'

'So much for your element of surprise,' Nur commented sarcastically.

'Is Edge secure?' Jarlath asked, ignoring the mercenary's remark.

'It was when I left,' Shahan said. 'But Farrand can't hope to hold it for long. Montfort has marshalled the entire royal force.' He paused for a moment, then added, 'My reports say that Cranne made a mess of the capture; there was a fire in the castle, and much bloodshed.' The merchant took a certain pleasure in reporting the shortcomings of others.

Acrimonious words followed, as Jarlath and his companions compared Farrand and his son to various unpleasant members of the animal kingdom.

'Cranne's foolish actions cannot have been the only reason for Montfort's reaction,' Jarlath spat. 'He could not possibly have reacted to that so quickly. He must have had other information.'

'Then you have a traitor in your ranks,' Olin stated coolly.

'Either that, or Montfort employs sorcerers too,' Nur added, grinning unpleasantly.

'Impossible!' Jarlath retorted. 'There was a traitor, but we weeded him out and disposed of him some time ago.'

The mercenary leaders just looked at him, their eyebrows raised in silent comment.

'If Montfort manages to establish defensive positions on the edge of the salt,' Sadir said, 'it will mean disaster. The barriers built to prevent the encroachments of the salt will provide him with natural fortifications, while we would have no cover at all. If we're caught on the salt, there will be no way of replenishing our supplies, and the danger of shifts will increase.'

'We could use another route,' Hakon interjected angrily. 'Montfort can't defend the whole rim.' His rage was such that his grating voice almost gave out altogether.

493

'You would have us march into a trap?' Olin demanded. The southern generals had already been unhappy with the thought of the salt and the monks' involvement; Shahan's news was the last straw. They saw little reason to trust the men who had hired them; there was too much that had obviously – and deliberately – been omitted from their earlier discussions.

Hakon tried to continue his argument, but Jarlath had already bowed to the inevitable and resigned himself to a delay. He ended the dissension by outlining his plan.

'The Archaeologists that we've retained as guides – I want some of them to go north now,' he instructed Sadir. 'Send someone reliable with them and get an *accurate* report of what's going on in Edge. We still have the vastly superior force, and while this delay is unfortunate, the ultimate outcome is not in doubt. Good day, gentlemen. I will call for you all when there is a need.'

So the council split up, and went their separate ways. Hakon was suppressing his anger with great difficulty, and went straight to inform the abbot of the latest developments. He almost quailed at the thought of the old man's fury and dismay.

*   *   *

To the north of the salt, Montfort and his men had spent the day preparing to rescue Edge. Scouts had reconnoitred the lie of the land and estimated the size of the force opposing them. The royal army was looking forward to some action now after the monotony of their march – especially when they realized that they would be facing vastly inferior numbers – but Montfort insisted that the usurpers be given the chance to surrender before the assault began. If they refused, then all was ready. The battle would be short, bloody, and utterly ruthless; there was no room for compromise. The king's only real concern was how to protect the civilian population of Edgefield from the onslaught. And Farrand was also sure to be holding hostages, who would suffer if events went against him. Montfort worried for the safety of Baldemar and Rebecca. But he had no choice; the future of the entire country was at stake.

Galen was not among those preparing for the morrow's fight. He had set off at first light for Tybridge, Arledge at his side.

* * *

Rebecca and Emer also spent the day on the move, and the fair had reached the small town of Merivale by early evening. Rebecca had been brooding all day; she had not seen Annis since the previous night, and her dreams had not solved anything. In fact, they had unnerved her even more.

The two girls wandered aimlessly through the streets as the fair was set up. Rumours of armies on the march and of war were on everyone's lips, reinforcing their sense of unease. They listened for news of Tarrant or Montfort, but heard nothing specific. Returning to their wagon, they sat on the steps, and wondered what was happening to their world. Some time later a stranger approached. Emer tensed, but the young man seemed familiar to Rebecca.

'I thought I m-might find you here,' he said, coming closer.

'Kedar!' Rebecca exclaimed.

'Why so surprised?' he asked, amusement shining in his bright green eyes.

'This is amazing! I dreamt about you last night.'

Kedar nodded, seemingly unmoved by Rebecca's statement.

'I knew it m-must have been something like that,' he said. 'I haven't been able to concentrate all day. You obviously weren't going to let me have any p-peace, so here I am.'

'But how did you find us?'

'I followed the signs.'

'What signs?' Emer asked, frowning.

Rebecca was silent, remembering the way Sancia had first led her to the caravan. *The sign only appears to those who need to see it.*

'The lights,' Kedar replied. 'Very p-pretty. What is it you want with me?'

He and Emer were both looking at Rebecca for enlightenment, but she hesitated.

'I don't know,' she admitted eventually. She knew the artist's arrival was important, but not *why* it was. As the others waited expectantly, she felt useless and wretched.

After an awkward pause, Kedar shrugged, put his satchel down and sat on an upturned box.

'You're Emer, aren't you?' he asked.

'Yes. How did you know?'

'I have a good m-memory for p-pretty girls,' he replied, smiling, not at all embarrassed by his slight stutter. 'What happened to your eye?'

'My enormous and colourful beauty spot, you mean!' Emer laughed. 'Don't you like it?'

'On you, anything would be lovely,' he replied gallantly, then turned to Rebecca. 'I can't say I b-blame you for running away.'

'We didn't,' she said defensively. 'Edge has been invaded by traitors, and we only just managed to escape. That's when Emer's face was hurt.'

'War is a m-messy b-business,' Kedar said gravely.

There was another pause, less strained this time, then the artist got to his feet.

'Listen,' he said. 'I'll be around for some time. A fair is a good p-place for me to find work. Sketches and so on. If you m-manage to work out what it is you want from me . . .'

His voice trailed away as another person approached, tiptoeing through the shadows between the wagons. Rebecca recognized Annis, and her heart lifted as a glimmer of understanding registered in her mind. *This is why he is here. The two of them belong together.* Anticipation built within her, together with a feeling of premonition that was just out of reach. *The search can begin.*

Annis emerged into the pool of yellow lamplight beneath the wagon steps, and looked anxiously at Kedar.

'Don't go,' she said quietly. 'I need you. I'm scared on my own.'

'Do *I* scare you?' Rebecca asked after a few moments.

'No. But what you're doing does.'

'I don't *know* what I'm doing!'

'You're searching,' Kedar said unexpectedly.

Rebecca stared at him, amazed.

'Yes!' Annis exclaimed. 'Me too.' She looked back at the dream-weaver. 'You wear the pendant. You are one of us, aren't you?'

Rebecca pulled the chain out from inside her blouse and studied the symbol it bore. Kedar smiled as she did so.

'This was Sancia's,' she said uncertainly. 'I don't know . . .'

Annis held out her hand, and showed them that the inscribed pattern on the pendant was repeated in miniature on the ring she wore. Kedar stooped to retrieve his satchel and held it up. Its metal clasp bore the same design.

'But what does it mean?' Emer asked, peering from one thing to the next.

'It's a secret society,' Annis replied.

'We call ourselves The Heretics,' Kedar added. 'This is our symbol.'

'Heretics!' Rebecca exclaimed. 'Then you know about the theory that history is repeating itself?'

'What?' Annis said, confused.

'The Heretics are an ancient sect, from the time before the salt,' Rebecca persisted, then faltered in the face of their puzzled expressions. 'The Web is an infinite circle . . . Alomar wrote a book . . . ' There was still no reaction.

'I know that we were p-persecuted once, but that was long ago,' Kedar said thoughtfully. 'Some p-people still have some very odd ideas about us . . .'

'But it's nothing like that nowadays,' Annis said, saddened by Rebecca's obvious disappointment.

'You don't know anything of your history?' she asked, without much hope.

'Not m-much,' Kedar admitted. 'We have our ceremonies, of course, and all m-members are p-pledged to help each other in time of need. B-but it's all innocent enough.'

'What ceremonies?' Rebecca demanded, clutching at straws now.

'We shouldn't really tell . . . ' Annis began.

'Please. It's very important.'

'We have special greetings, signs,' Kedar said. 'We even have our own song.'

'For those of us capable of holding a tune,' Annis put in.

'You have a wonderful voice,' Emer told her.

'But I can't sing.' The storyteller shrugged, grinning. 'At least not pleasantly!'

'And when at least three of us get together we drink a toast, promising to "uphold the m-magic of the elders".'

Rebecca pounced on the word.

'Magic?'

'All artists try to create m-magic,' Kedar replied. 'Though we rarely succeed.'

Rebecca was staring at Annis now, as realization dawned.

'But you did!' she exclaimed. 'You *did!*'

'That's what frightened me,' Annis said hesitantly. 'You saw . . . '

Kedar glanced at the storyteller sharply.

'You're a wizard?' he asked.

'No. Yes . . . I suppose so.' Annis was floundering in confusion. 'It doesn't happen often, and it scares me.'

'And you *saw?*' he went on, turning to Rebecca.

'Yes.' *At last – someone understands!*

Emer spoke next, beating Rebecca to it as she turned to look at Kedar.

'Are you a wizard too?' she asked.

CHAPTER SIXTY

Galen and Arledge arrived in Tybridge the following morning, having changed their plans and ridden there directly. This had gained them valuable time, and had enabled them to use a route far from any possible enemy positions. At least one of them would return via Cutover to see Redfern, as this town lay directly between Tybridge and Edgefield.

Finding the Archaeologists was remarkably easy. They made their first enquiries at the inn where Galen had left them eleven days earlier, and were told that the group was currently holed up at The Tar Pit. The landlord left Galen in no doubt that this was the cheapest, roughest tavern in town.

When Galen and Arledge reached the inn, they immediately knew that something was wrong. Holmes, Milner and Flank were slumped in their chairs, staring morosely at the tankards of untouched beer that stood on the table in front of them. It was still early, and the only other occupant of the room was a sleepy-looking barman. Galen approached the Archaeologists slowly, feeling guilty and apprehensive.

Flank saw him first and stared, slack-mouthed. Then Milner followed his comrade's gaze.

'Well, well . . . what do we have here?' he remarked derisively.

Holmes had been sitting with his back to the door. He turned as his colleague spoke, and saw Galen. Leaping to his feet, he lunged forward and grabbed the young man's collar. He stared malevolently into Galen's eyes, their faces so close they were almost touching.

'Where do you think you've been?' the big man spat.

Galen had not known what welcome he would receive,

499

but was none the less shocked by such venom, and was rendered speechless by it. Spike hissed and lashed out with a small paw, but Holmes ignored the attack. His intensity was such that he did not even blink.

'Let him go,' Arledge said quietly from his position behind Galen.

'And who might you be?' Milner asked, getting quickly to his feet. If there was going to be a fight then he wanted to be ready.

'A friend,' the soldier replied calmly. 'Don't judge Galen before you hear what he has to say.'

Holmes glanced at Arledge then, taking his eyes off Galen for the first time.

'Galen? This rat's name is Grant,' he said.

'What else have you lied to us about?' Milner asked bitterly.

Suddenly, Holmes shoved Galen backwards, and the young man stumbled and fell over a chair. Spike went flying, but made a safe, skidding landing on the floor, yowling with outrage. Galen slowly picked himself up, leaving the beek to fend for himself, and faced his former colleagues.

'I'm sorry for lying to you, but I had good enough reasons for what I did. Won't you let me explain?' He still did not understand the depths of their antagonism.

Milner and Holmes sat down again without a word. Galen righted the chair and joined them, while Arledge sat at another table a few paces away.

'Can I buy you a drink?' Galen asked, hoping to mollify them.

'We've got drinks,' Holmes said shortly.

'Is what I did so terrible?' Galen cried, distressed by their treatment and by his own lack of understanding.

Holmes leaned towards him, his face a grimacing mask of suppressed violence.

'Let me explain,' he said through clenched teeth. 'When we got here, as you know, we were feeling a bit low. Peyton especially. Losing Kibble and Drain like that hit him harder than he'll admit, and he always hated having to race across the salt for the benefit of lubbers. Then you . . . ' He pointed an accusing finger at Galen's face. ' . . . you desert us without even a word. Archaeologists don't do that! Understand?

500

Holmes was shouting now, red-faced, but calmed down a little before continuing. 'For some reason best known to himself, Peyton had high hopes for you. He was always ready to sing your praises – and you reward him like *that*!' He paused, almost strangling on his indignation. 'The man drank like a fish for three days, but since then all he's been able to do is talk about giving up. We haven't been near the salt for ten days.'

Galen began to understand the depths of their anger. Peyton had loved the salt, and had only come truly alive on the flats. If he was denying it now . . .

'He must be ill,' Flank said gravely. 'He hasn't had a drink for seven days.'

'He was the best,' Milner added. 'But he just isn't interested any more. He says there's no point.'

'Where is he now?'

'Upstairs, probably asleep,' Milner answered. 'He doesn't get up much nowadays.'

'Will you tell him I'm here?' Galen pleaded. 'I must talk to you – to *all* of you.'

'Tell him yourself,' Holmes said sourly.

'I'll go,' Flank volunteered, and lumbered off to the stairs.

'This'd better be good,' Milner told Galen.

There was an awkward silence. Then Flank returned, followed by a bleary-eyed Peyton. Galen stood to face him.

'I owe you all an apology,' he began. 'I'm here to make it now, and to ask for your help.'

Peyton blinked. 'Why?' he asked. There was no rancour in his voice, merely indifference.

'I need you to cross the salt,' Galen said.

'I'm too old for that sort of thing.' Peyton's eyes were glazed.

'I don't believe that!' Galen exclaimed. 'And this is vitally important. At least let me explain before you decide.'

So they all sat down again, and, as succinctly as possible, Galen told them the whole story. He began with his recruitment by Tarrant, and told of the messages he had carried, what had really happened in Riano during their two stays there, about Davin's death and what this meant. Then he explained the reasons for his desertion of their group. He told of his journey to Garadun, the meeting with Montfort and the subsequent mobilization of the army. Arledge joined in for the final part of the tale, helping to explain the current military situation.

Although the Archaeologists were at first openly sceptical, they listened patiently and their interest grew as more and more facts were revealed. Before long, Flank was wide-eyed, and Milner was beginning to make comments and ask questions. Even Holmes lost his hostility, albeit somewhat grudgingly. But it was Peyton that Galen watched most closely. The group's leader sat immobile, his expression almost unchanging, his eyes still blank.

Finally, Galen reached the specific reason for his visit.

'So you see, we desperately need someone to go south and find out what's happening in Riano. We need to know whether the mercenaries are there yet, and how many there are.'

'I've been told that you're the best,' Arledge put in. 'If anyone can help us now, it's you. And I'd like to come with you. Of course, I will make sure that you are well paid.'

Peyton's eyes suddenly blazed, and he leant forward, showing signs of animation for the first time.

'If we do this,' he declared, 'it'll be because it's worth doing. Not for money!' He slammed his fist on the table to emphasize his words, making the beer mugs jump and rattle.

'I meant no offence,' Arledge said, somewhat taken aback. 'Judge us by our cause. Galen has been open with you. I know he regrets not having been able to explain his motives before, but you must see that there were good reasons for his secrecy.'

'Please,' Galen added simply.

Peyton looked slowly from man to man.

'Well, lads, what do you say? One last trip before we end our days as milksop lubbers?'

The slowly growing smiles of the other Archaeologists gave him his answer.

'We leave at first light tomorrow,' Peyton said to Arledge, then turned to Galen. 'We still have your stuff . . . Galen.'

The young man swallowed hard and said, 'I won't be coming.'

There was a few moments' silence.

502

'I have to go to Edgefield,' he went on.

'Why?' Holmes asked, the edge back in his voice.

'Some people . . . I care about,' Galen replied. 'I have to find out what's happened to them.'

'Galen?' Milner said, looking thoughtful. 'Galen! I *knew* that name was familiar. You wouldn't be the one who played that chess game, would you? The People's Champion?'

Galen nodded.

'Gods!' Holmes shouted, laughing uproariously as only he could. 'You came between a man and his betrothed!' he quoted. 'I'll say you did. A baron's daughter, no less!' There was admiration in his voice now. 'You're famous, my lad.'

'No wonder you needed to leave town in a hurry,' Milner commented wryly.

'And now you're going back to her?' Peyton asked.

'And to another.'

'Lad, have you no shame?' Holmes exclaimed. '*Two* of them at once?'

Galen tried to explain, but found it impossible. He gave up, laughing and blushing at the same time, and threw his hands into the air in defeat.

'You'd never believe me,' he said, shaking his head amid the laughter.

Spike added his inimitable voice to the noise, and leapt up on to Galen's lap as the Archaeologists began to make their plans. Galen scooped the animal up, placed him on his shoulder and stood.

'I'll go now,' he said to Arledge. 'With luck, I'll be in Cutover by midnight.'

'Go carefully,' the soldier advised.

'You too.'

'I'll have help,' he replied, indicating the Archaeologists. 'And I have the feeling I'm in good hands.'

'You are indeed,' Galen confirmed, 'but your task is still dangerous. Good luck.' They clasped hands, then Galen spoke to the others. 'Farewell, my friends. We'll meet again.'

Their chorus of replies contrasted happily with the way they had greeted his arrival.

'I hope you find them both!' Holmes called as Galen went out.

503

'So do I,' he shouted back. *So do I.*

* * *

Montfort's advance through the barony of Edge had proceeded without a hitch. Farrand only had a few hundred
men at his command, and they either fell back or attempted
to escape once they realized that they were facing overwhelming odds. There was little fighting, and Edgefield
soon found itself caught in the grip of a well-planned pincer
movement.

Fearing carnage in the heavily populated streets, Montfort
tried to get a surrender demand through, but his envoy was
unable to reach the castle. The fighting began in earnest
then, with Cranne taking personal charge of the last ditch
defence. Every street, every building became part of the
battle arena, but the tide flowed only one way. Few of
Farrand's troops dared defy their baron's son, even though
they knew their cause was hopeless, and many met a bloody
and futile death as the unstoppable advance continued.
However, by late afternoon, word came from Farrand
himself that his men should withdraw to the castle – and
then even Cranne's threats and bluster could not prevent
the retreat.

Several buildings were set on fire, either out of spite or to
delay their pursuers, but other than that Edgefield was able
to breathe a collective sigh of relief as the fighting ceased.
Once the terrified populace realized what was happening,
Montfort's troops were greeted as liberators. Cranne and
his men had not made themselves popular during their brief
occupation of the town, and many citizens now ventured
outside to witness the final defeat of the usurpers.

Inside the castle, Farrand and his remaining soldiers
manned the gate, towers and battlements. They all knew that
the castle was effectively indefensible, in spite of the hurried
improvements they had made, but they still harboured slim
hopes of an improbable rescue.

Attempting one last bluff, Farrand sent a message to the
king, threatening to slaughter all hostages within the castle,
including Baldemar, unless he and his men were allowed

to go free. He did not mention Rebecca, assuming – incorrectly – that Montfort knew of her escape. The reply was prompt, and its contents not unexpected. The king entreated Farrand not to add cold-blooded murder to the crime of treason, and promised that if he and his men surrendered peacefully, then his soldiers would not suffer and the baron and his son would be given a fair trial. The message ended in uncompromising fashion.

'You cannot hope to withstand my forces, and should not think to bargain with me. I expect your decision within one hour. Montfort.'

Once this ultimatum had been delivered, a close watch was kept on the castle. Montfort fretted over the threat to the hostages, but knew that he had no choice. He had no time to waste on a long siege. The operation had to be quick; whether it would be clean was now up to Farrand. The king fervently wished for accurate intelligence about what was happening inside the castle; local opinion held that some of its inhabitants had escaped during the invasion, and Rebecca's name was mentioned, but no one could be sure. Montfort was firm in his resolve to do all that he must to protect his realm, but he was sickened by the thought of what she might suffer as a result. He also wished that Tarrant – damn the man! – was there to help him. His specialized skills might have provided them with an alternative to brute force.

Inside the castle, Farrand argued with his son. The baron had decided to surrender, but his decision had thrown Cranne into a violent fury.

'The alternative is death!' Farrand shouted. 'And what good will that do our cause?'

'If we surrender, we die!' Cranne roared. 'The penalty for treason is death.'

'There is always the hope that Jarlath will reach us before we stand trial,' Farrand stated.

'Trial?' his son yelled. 'Trial? Have you lost your wits? Montfort will execute us on the spot!'

'No – I believe that he has some honour,' the baron retorted. 'And so do I!'

'Then *yield* with honour,' Cranne spat contemptuously.

505

'If I am to die it will be with a sword in my hand.'

He stormed out then, and before anything could be done to prevent it, he gathered his own men together, ordered the recently built gates to be opened, and stormed out into the town square.

The charge caused panic as the besieging soldiers were hampered by groups of civilian onlookers. No one had expected such a suicidal foray, and Montfort's troops were taken by surprise, reacting too slowly to prevent the vicious attackers cutting a swathe of blood and terror through the square. Cranne led his men in a wide sweep, berserker fury wild in his eyes, before doubling back into a side street. There the mayhem continued as soldiers and unarmed citizens were cut down by the scything blades, or trampled under the flaying hooves of the war-horses.

However, once that initial shock was over, Montfort's troops rallied. Archers accounted for some of Cranne's cavalry, while others fell into ambushes hurriedly set up in the narrow streets. Cranne, together with a few of his men, made a break for the southern edge of the town, but their pursuers had the scent now, and only the baron's son survived to race across the fields towards the salt. It was the one route not guarded; there was no escape that way. Yet Cranne galloped on, with several of Montfort's horsemen, led by Ellard, a few hundred paces behind.

He flew over the mounds and barriers, and then, just as those behind were expecting him to turn left or right, Cranne kept going, galloping over the salt, the coat of his great stallion flecked with foam, its eyes wide with terror. His pursuers halted at the top of the final ridge, staring in disbelief at the retreating figure. They all knew that the horse could not survive such a race across the salt.

'Leave him,' Ellard decided. 'He is doomed.' They watched until Cranne was out of sight, then turned back to the town.

By some miracle, the salt supported Cranne and his mount for a full league before the inevitable happened and the crust gave way. One of the horse's legs shattered, and it fell, screaming, in a cartwheel of agony. Cranne was thrown clear, crashing and skidding on the salt.

After a few stunned moments, he picked himself up,

retrieved his sword and approached the crippled stallion with fury in his eyes. He slashed the animal's throat with one vicious, vengeful blow, then laughed insanely as the blood gushed forth staining the salt red.

As the last of the wretched animal's life bubbled away, Cranne turned and began walking south. As day turned to night, he was heading for the heart of the salt.

CHAPTER SIXTY-ONE

When Rebecca awoke the next morning, she glanced across at the other bed to see whether Emer was awake. But Kedar was lying in her friend's place, and she shuddered as the events of the previous evening came back to her. Emer had insisted on spending the night huddled under a blanket in Sancia's chair so that Kedar could get some proper rest, and as Rebecca looked across at her now, she could see that her friend was still fast asleep. Even in the dull light, her face was clearly visible; the skin on her cheek was perfectly smooth, with no sign of the cut or the discoloration that had marred her appearance for the last few days.

It was real! Rebecca wanted to rouse her companions instantly – there was so much to discuss! – but an inner voice told her to let them rest. Instead, she thought of the previous evening and the extraordinary way in which Kedar had answered Emer's question.

* * *

'Are you a wizard too?'

The young man did not reply, but instead he opened his satchel and drew out a sheet of paper, a slim brush, and a wooden box containing several small pots of paint. He clipped the paper to the firm back of his satchel, then sat down facing the three women, placing the bag on his lap like a portable easel. His brush flicked back and forth, gliding over the paper in a few simple, effortless strokes. Then Kedar looked up and grinned, and turned the painting around for his audience to see.

Emer gasped. At first it was as though she was looking

508

into a mirror. The image of her was so perfect that she almost fancied she could hear it echo her own laughter.

The women were all enthralled by the picture, but they each experienced something different as they gazed at it. Annis heard in her mind the story of a chamberlain's daughter, experienced her childhood and the pains and joys of growing, her friendships and adventures, successes and failures; the whole of Emer's past was there. Rebecca saw something less obvious, a promise for the future, a branching fan of possibilities; she felt love and trust but also pain and deception, and knew that Emer's future held all of these – and more.

Emer herself saw only happiness – and knew it now. She lifted her hand to her face and gave a small cry. Her injured skin was as smooth as it appeared in the painting. There was no cut, no swelling, and she knew without having to look that the ugly purple bruising had also vanished. Rebecca and Annis stared at her, wide-eyed, then looked back at the artist.

Kedar smiled. *The real Emer*, his eyes said, then turned to Rebecca. *Now you.*

He turned the satchel round, reversed the paper, and began again, with quick, deft strokes. The others waited breathlessly, anticipating new wonders, but Kedar suddenly faltered, and his rapt expression changed to a mask of anger, then horror.

'No!' he yelled. 'No!'

He stared transfixed at his work, his face ashen; his hands were clenched, white-knuckled, and his jaw clamped tight shut. Trembling, he dashed satchel and paper aside, then fell to the ground, twitching convulsively.

Emer and Annis sprang to his side while Rebecca grabbed the discarded satchel. The paper had torn loose, and had landed with Emer's perfect smile uppermost. Reluctantly, Rebecca turned it over, and stared in disbelief. On the left side of the sheet was a full-length portrait of herself, so lifelike that it almost seemed to move. It was a side view, and her arms were outstretched, pleading. On the other side of the paper, a small boy cried in anguish, in the grip of a fiery demon, its terrible claws rending his vulnerable flesh.

But even as she watched, the boy and the demon faded until no trace of them was left. Their disappearance left both Rebeccas feeling utterly bereft. Her image seemed to freeze in misery, and she turned to look at the artist, who now lay still.

'He's unconscious,' Emer said worriedly. 'Out cold. I can't rouse him.'

'Get him inside,' Annis said. 'He needs warmth and rest.'

They managed to pick the artist up, and started towards the wagon. As they were manoeuvring him up the steps they were startled by a sudden sound.

Whoomph.

The paper burst into flames where it lay and burnt fiercely for a few moments until only a few ashes remained. Then the breeze scattered the remnants of the ghastly painting until nothing remained.

* * *

They had taken turns to sit with Kedar for several hours, but there had been no change in his condition, the slow rise and fall of his chest the only sign of life. Eventually, Annis left, promising to return in the morning, and Rebecca and Emer finally gave in to their tiredness and fell asleep.

Now a new day had dawned – and Rebecca fervently wished that she was not the only one awake. She dressed quietly, and then moved to Kedar's side to continue her vigil. An hour or so later, Emer's eyes opened slowly – and her hand immediately went to her face.

'Nothing!' she breathed. 'It doesn't hurt any more. It's as if it had never happened. How . . . ?' She looked at Kedar.

'Still fast asleep,' Rebecca said.

Emer leaned forward, and gently nudged the artist's shoulder. There was absolutely no reaction.

'Typical man,' she remarked. 'One puny bit of magic and he's exhausted.'

* * *

When Kedar finally awoke, soon after midday, Annis had been with the two friends for some time, and had shared

510

their growing sense of frustration. The artist gazed at each of them in turn with bleary eyes.

'Three?' he commented. 'M-must be my lucky day. What happened?'

'Don't you remember?' Emer exclaimed. 'Last night? You healed my face.'

'I just p-painted it as it should be,' Kedar replied. 'The Web did the rest.' His smile faded as he looked at Rebecca, remembering. 'Gods!' he breathed. 'Did you see?'

'Part of it,' she replied. 'Can you tell me what it meant?'

'I don't know . . . something . . . something is looking for you.' His green eyes gazed at her as if begging for forgiveness. 'I tried to stop it, but . . . '

'What about the boy?' she asked.

'What b-boy?'

Rebecca described what she had seen, a hollow feeling in the pit of her stomach, but Kedar shook his head. He had no memory of the child, nor of the fire-demon. He just knew that something evil had stretched out towards Rebecca, testing the limits of its power.

'We're not the only ones searching, then,' Annis said quietly.

'That's obvious,' Kedar replied. 'B-but what are we searching *for*?'

They spent that afternoon and evening talking and arguing, and Annis and Kedar told a little of their own personal histories. Their stories were remarkably similar. Both had found, early in life, that their respective talents had been more of a curse than a blessing. Both had tried to suppress their gifts, tried to be more like other children, but had failed. They were driven by need, and had eventually left their homes and families in order to fulfil the demands of their craft.

It was obvious that they had both endured hardship since then, but neither could be drawn into talking about their early lives, preferring to relate their later experiences. Kedar had become an independent wanderer, while Annis had found much-needed security and contentment in the nomadic life of the fair. Both had learnt of the existence of the Heretics from fellow artists and had subsequently discovered their

511

own magical talent. But they had each reacted very differently.

Annis's revelation had frightened her, and had reinforced her instinctive fear of strangers. It had made her even more cautious and withdrawn, and ensured that she only told her stories when she was sure of her audience.

Kedar, on the other hand, had embraced his own 'wizardry' wholeheartedly, and had practised long and hard to master it, to control his tenuous link with the Web. He rarely had cause to use his talent, and knew better than to abuse it, but he always delighted in the few touches of magic in his life – until he had drawn Rebecca. The Web-link had been so strong, so terrifying, that it had taken all his strength to break it.

When it came to Emer's turn, she told the story of her life in three sentences.

'I'm only a chamberlain's daughter from Edge,' she stated impatiently. 'I've never done anything important, and I certainly don't have any talent or magic. Becky's the one you should listen to.'

Rebecca disagreed with all three statements, but confined herself to one brief denial.

'You're more important than you know.'

'Oh, get on with it!' Emer retorted.

So Rebecca told her tale. She skipped over most of her early life, concentrating on recent events; the chess game and the three-way link with Emer and Galen; her meeting with Sancia and the old woman's theories of dream-weaving; her discoveries in Garadun and the terrible, half-read passage in *Beneath the Salt*. She told them about Kavan's magical picture – and when he heard this, Kedar could hardly contain himself. He knew of the legendary Kavan, of course, but had only ever seen his lesser paintings. The 'dead' ones.

'If only I'd *known*,' he groaned. 'I was so close! He was one of the very first Heretics.'

Then they discussed in more detail the secret society, both from Kedar and Annis's point of view, and from a historical perspective.

'There are so few records left of their early years,' Rebecca concluded, 'that it seems almost deliberate – as if someone didn't want us to know their real purpose.'

'Our p-purpose,' Kedar amended.

That led to a discussion about the enigmatic sets of letters. Rebecca showed them all four, admitting shame-facedly that she'd been unable to remember the fifth. She told them about the legends surrounding the Okran Stones, and about her dreams. Both Heretics were fascinated by the puzzles but did not know how to unravel them.

Then Rebecca showed the artist and the storyteller the pattern of cards left by Sancia, laying them out again, and hoping that they might be able to provide some insight. However, none was forthcoming.

'It's obviously not another m-message,' Kedar said, shaking his head. 'P-perhaps it's supposed to tell you something about the ones you already have.'

'Yes, but what?' Rebecca had already come to the same conclusion.

'I don't know.'

They talked for hours, but only confused themselves even further. After an early evening meal – no one had even thought of food before then – their discussion turned to the current political situation and the coming war. Like most of the people of Ahrenia, they were ignorant of all but a few facts, and so their talk went round in endless speculative circles.

'It's connected to all this, though,' Rebecca said, pointing at the letters. 'I *know* it is.'

But she was at a loss to explain how, and the others could not enlighten her.

It was late at night before they finally decided to give up and get some rest. Annis and Kedar were about to leave when Emer asked one final question.

'Are all Heretics wizards?' she said. 'Do you *all* have magical abilities?'

'No,' Annis replied. 'In fact very few of us do.'

'So you two are special, then?' Emer persisted.

'Did you ever doubt it?' Kedar asked, with a broad grin.

* * *

513

There were no witnesses to Cranne's last moments; even if there had been, no sane man would have approached him. His legs moved mechanically as his eyes stared fixedly ahead at the dark horizon, his blood-stained sword still clenched within one powerful fist. The only sound was the regular crunch of the salt beneath his boots.

The last few strands connecting Cranne's mind to rationality had been irrevocably severed. Not even he could have described what passed for thought within his brain now. The baron's son walked towards his doom trapped in another world, a world that was entirely his own. A world that was completely and utterly insane.

Cranne's stride did not falter even when the salt-crust began to tremble. He was oblivious to all the danger signals; the slithering sounds, the way the salt ahead rippled in the starlight, and the sudden softness beneath his feet.

Finally he stumbled. One foot had sunk deep into the salt, preventing his forward progress. He tried to pull it out, but only slipped further down. For a brief moment, a tiny sliver of comprehension penetrated his lunacy, and the reality of his situation brought terror to his staring eyes. The salt began to churn all about him, whirling and rolling in slow waves. He struggled – and sank up to his waist in the crystal quagmire. So then he remained still, his sword discarded at last.

But the quicksalt did not relent. Slowly, and with an infinite cruelty that Cranne would once have appreciated, it drew him down into the darkness. Soon, only his head and arms were free, but Cranne no longer cared. He was laughing now. The manic sound added the final eerie touch to the desolate, starlit scene.

The echoes of his laughter seemed to resound long after the salt had filled his mouth, his nostrils and lungs, and choked him into silence. Only much later, when the quicksalt finally stopped flowing, did the flats reclaim their own alien quiet.

* * *

Galen arrived in Cutover in the middle of the night, and headed straight for The Raven to exchange news with Red

514

fern. The innkeeper was impressed with all that the young man had achieved, and said so, but Galen was sorely disappointed with the quality of Redfern's own information. Little had come from Edgefield except conflicting rumours. It was obvious that the castle had been captured and that there had been some bloodshed, but beyond that, nothing was clear. And no reports had been received from south of the salt.

Galen decided to sleep the rest of the night, and to ride on to Edgefield at first light. Redfern approved, noting the lad's weariness, and prepared food and a room for him. Spike had meanwhile re-introduced himself to those of the inn's staff who were still up. He was greeted fondly and fed royally, and it was this that prompted Galen to suggest that the beek remain at the inn while he went on to Edge.

'I don't want him with me if there's to be any fighting.'

'All right,' Redfern agreed hesitantly. 'But I doubt if he'll *let* you go alone.'

When Galen went to bed, Spike was close behind, curling up in the crook of his master's knees. Soon they were both sound asleep.

* * *

Rebecca saw the three men walking on the far side of a lake. Their figures wavered and shimmered; somehow their reflections in the water seemed more real.

She could not tell whether she was on the opposite shore, or whether she stood in a boat. Her own body was invisible.

The sun rose behind the men, a blue-white glare which all but obliterated the moving figures, making them even more insubstantial, mere shadows.

Then the scene faded abruptly, and she found herself face to face with a small beek. She flinched as it spat at her and yowled, its spiky fur making the tiny creature seem even more fierce. Was it protecting something – or someone?

'Who is it?' she asked. 'I won't hurt them.'

I doubt if he'll let you go alone.

She saw Galen in the beek's eyes, and felt a flood of relief. 'I thought I might find you here.'

515

'Follow the signs,' Emer added from the shadows.

'What signs?' the beek asked.

'The lights. You need to see the lights,' Rebecca answered.

'I don't know what I'm doing!' the animal hissed, baring its needle fangs.

'We all try to create magic,' the shadow-Emer said.

'Though we rarely succeed,' Rebecca added.

'I'm scared on my own,' Emer completed.

The scene changed again. This time, Rebecca saw the image of a square stone tower, built on top of an isolated hill. It was obviously ancient, and had once been part of a much larger, long-ruined building. A fire-beacon burned at the top, sending silver-red rays flashing into the distance. Rebecca had no idea where it was.

An unknown voice spoke to them all, its tone kind.

For you, my child, the light will never fade.

CHAPTER SIXTY-TWO

'I *did*!' Galen protested. 'I saw them!'

'It was a dream, boy,' Redfern growled. 'Use your head.'

'I am. They were trying to tell me something.'

The innkeeper shook his head. He clearly found his young guest's behaviour quite incomprehensible.

'You don't understand,' Galen said gently. 'This has happened before.'

'Are you serious, lad?'

'Yes. I don't know how it works, and I can't control it, but I really do hear them, and see them. I can even *talk* to them.' He paused as Redfern looked at him thoughtfully. 'Even Spike woke up yowling,' Galen added as an afterthought. 'He was in it too.'

Redfern laughed, a deep rumbling sound.

'Well, that settles it then,' he remarked. 'If you have a *beek* as a witness.'

'I'm serious!' Galen said earnestly.

'I know,' the landlord admitted. 'Maybe there's something in it, and maybe there isn't, but it's plain *you* believe it. What were they trying to to tell you?'

'Emer told me to follow the signs,' he replied. 'Lights, Rebecca called them.'

'That doesn't help much, does it?'

'No, but then I saw a tower on a hill, with a fire burning at the top.'

'A beacon?' Redfern regarded the young man calmly, his thoughts hidden.

'I suppose so. It was built of stone . . . and I got the feeling that it was all that was left of a much bigger building. Do you know of such a place?'

'Yes,' the innkeeper replied, and Galen's heart leapt.

'Where?' he demanded eagerly.

'There's a beacon like that above a town called Buckland,' Redfern answered. 'It used to guide travellers across the heath until the roads were built. It's kept burning now just as a tradition.'

'Then that's where they are!' Galen exclaimed, knowing he was right. 'Where is this place?'

'Due north from here, more or less. A day and a half's ride.'

'I'll be there tonight,' Galen vowed.

'Are you sure you know what you are doing?' Redfern asked, still not able to understand why this apparently sensible young man had become obsessed with such strange ideas.

'Yes!' Galen declared. 'Just tell me how to get there.'

Redfern did as he was asked without further hesitation.

* * *

Rebecca and Emer woke at the same time, and looked at each other with great excitement.

'He was here again, wasn't he,' Emer said, fighting to keep the dream from slipping away.

'Yes.'

'Do you think he'll find us?'

'I don't know.'

'Kedar did.' There was hope and longing in Emer's words. The two girls lay in silence for a few moments.

'What was that tower?' Emer asked. 'Do you know where it is?'

'I've no idea,' Rebecca said. 'I've never seen anything like it before.'

When Annis arrived with their breakfast, they told her of the dream and described the beacon tower.

'That's Buckland!' she exclaimed excitedly. 'It's quite near here.'

'Then we must go there,' Rebecca said quickly. 'Now.'

'All right,' Annis replied, accepting the dream-weaver's decision without question. 'I'll go and tell the wagon-

518

master.'

'I meant us, not the whole fair,' Rebecca said, taken aback.

'Where you go, we go,' Annis stated simply. 'It'll mean turning south, towards Edge. Are you sure you want that?'

'Yes.' Rebecca's conviction did not falter.

'Right.' Annis opened the door and started down the steps.

'Where's Kedar?' Rebecca called after her.

'Travelling with us,' the storyteller replied happily.

Within the hour, the fair was on the move again, heading just west of south, towards Buckland. Everyone knew that the wagon-master had chosen their destination on the advice of their dream-weaver, and were happy to do as she wished.

Rebecca sat on the driver's board, the reins held loosely in her hands, and wondered what they would find in the town beneath the beacon. After a while, the steady rhythm of the horse's pace reminded her of a couplet from the Heretic's song, sung to her by Kedar the evening before.

> 'Two parts shift and magic flows,
> The elders speak and power glows.'

Now what in the Web does that mean? she wondered.

CHAPTER SIXTY-THREE

'Well, we're here,' Emer said, gazing up at the hilltop beacon. '*Now* what do we do?'

Rebecca stared at the tower last seen in her dream. Its light shone brightly against the evening sky.

'I don't know,' she admitted. 'Wait, I suppose.'

All around them it was business as usual for the people of the fair. To them, one town was much like another, and the fact that they had arrived in Buckland on the whim of the dream-weaver made no special difference. The night was soon filled with the noise and colour and the special enchantment of the fair.

The two girls stayed close to their wagon, taking no notice of the bustle around them, talking quietly in the lamplight. Neither felt like eating; their stomachs were knotted with hope and an anticipation they dared not discuss.

Annis and Kedar, who had travelled together and who now showed every sign of becoming firm friends, came to visit the girls, and talk, but they left soon, knowing it was another's face the two friends wanted to see.

As midnight approached, Rebecca and Emer began to prepare for bed. Their shared disappointment made them unusually quiet, and neither voiced their thoughts about any dreams the night may bring. They slipped under their respective bedclothes, but Rebecca left the lamp burning low.

'He means a lot to you, doesn't he,' she said quietly.

'More than I ever knew,' Emer replied softly. 'It took the chess game for me to realize just how much . . . but then it was too late. Ever since then . . . ' She sighed eloquently. 'Listen to me!' she went on. 'I sound just like you when you're mooning on about whatsisname, you know, that king fellow.'

'I do not moon,' Rebecca insisted, laughing. 'I just think he's a good man, that's all.'

Emer looked at her sceptically.

'In any case,' Rebecca went on, 'it's different. I've only met him a few times. You and Galen had . . . been together a long time. It's only natural that you should love him.'

'You're an incurable romantic,' her friend announced.

'But you do miss him?'

'Yes,' Emer admitted. 'I miss him. And these dreams of yours have made it worse. I've had half a mind to go into business in one of the neighbouring wagons to help me forget!' She grinned at Rebecca's shocked expression. The dream-weaver had come to terms with the profession of the women whose lives had become part of her own, but it was really only a theoretical acceptance. Somehow, Emer's comment had made it seem too real.

'As least you look respectable again now,' Rebecca said, forcing a smile. 'And not as if you'd been brawling in some tavern!'

'Thanks to Kedar,' Emer replied, and touched her cheek. 'But I wouldn't exactly call our current environment respectable.'

Rebecca's thoughts returned to her 'girls', and her mind – or rather her dream-sense, as she was beginning to think of it – unconsciously scanned their caravans to check on their safety. All seemed well, but when an unearthly howling sound suddenly invaded her thoughts, she was instantly worried. *What have I missed?* But then she realized that the high-pitched cries were not connected with the women.

'What is it?' Emer asked anxiously.

'That noise,' Rebecca began. 'I don't . . . ' There was a strange stirring in her head. Anticipation seethed, and she could not speak. *You need to see the signs.*

When a knock sounded at the door, both girls froze. Their visitor knocked again, louder this time, and then, after a few breathless moments, the door was opened. An ear-splitting yowl filled the wagon.

Flinging her blankets aside, Emer sprang from her bed and flew into Galen's arms. Spike lost his footing under her whirlwind assault, and fell off, screeching indignantly as he landed lightly on the boards.

Rebecca sat up in bed, wide-eyed and filled with joy at seeing her friends together at last. In that moment, she began to believe that she really was a dream-weaver. *Shaping dreams and using them in the waking world.* There was a sense of fulfilment in the scheme, and also one of achievement. *We are woven together again,* she thought. *Together.*

Emer was laughing and crying all at the same time, and neither she nor Galen were able to speak sensibly. In the end, they gave up and kissed passionately. Rebecca lowered her eyes, but Spike was not so tactful. Already affronted, he now became insanely jealous, yowling constantly and literally climbing the walls in a frenzied scramble until the reunited couple drew apart.

The pandemonium gradually subsided. Rebecca got out of bed and stretched out her hands. Galen and Emer, still embracing, took one each. It was an instinctive action, but none of them expected the sensation that the linking produced. The caravan around them faded away, and they each felt as though they were floating, alone in a void where the other two were the only living souls. Everything else had simply ceased to exist – and yet there was no fear. They were secure in a cocoon of love and friendship.

Rebecca reluctantly released their hands, and the three stared at each other as the real world established itself around them once more. Even Spike was quiet, watching curiously from his perch on a high shelf. Still no one spoke. No one knew where to begin.

Galen and Emer sat down upon the dishevelled couch, their arms still around each other, while Rebecca sat facing them in her own bed. It was Spike who broke the silence at last.

'He's hungry,' Galen said. 'We've been riding since dawn.'

'We don't have any food here,' Rebecca told him apologetically.

'It doesn't matter,' he assured her gently. 'Let him out. He can forage for himself for once. He's grown lazy with all this pampering.'

Spike yowled in apparent disagreement, and they all

laughed. Rebecca got up and opened the door, and with one last disparaging glance at his master, the beek jumped down and went out.

'Where did you find him?' Rebecca asked, returning to her seat.

'On the salt. It's a long story!'

'Well, we're not going anywhere,' she prompted.

'What about you two?' he countered. 'What's been happening to you?'

'You first,' Rebecca insisted. She went to fetch a bottle from Sancia's wine-store, opened it and poured three glasses while Galen began his tale.

He began with the hours following the chess game, his retreat to Cluny's house and the remarkable discoveries there. When he described Cluny's stone, Rebecca realized that it bore the letters she had forgotten in her earlier dream. She made Galen spell them out, and added them to her list before he went on to describe his recruitment by Tarrant.

'Why didn't he tell us what he'd done with you?' Rebecca wondered aloud.

'I suppose he's been keeping secrets for so long that he's incapable of telling anyone *anything*,' Emer suggested wryly. Her words were caustic – if Tarrant could only have let them know what was happening, he would have saved them much worry.

'He doesn't waste words,' Galen agreed, then continued his story by recounting how he had joined the Archaeologists, and telling of his first journey across the salt and subsequent adventures in Riano. Then he told them of the deaths of his colleagues, and how he had found the tablet and book beneath the salt. At this point he went to pick up the bag which had fallen unnoticed to the floor during his initial welcome. He took out the stone and handed it to Rebecca. She stared at it in awe; this was the reality behind her dreams, a piece of the original puzzle. The letters floated before her eyes as her fingers explored the texture of the cold marble.

'Why are you so interested in these stones?' Galen asked.

'They're important,' was all she could manage to say.

'I've seen another one,' Galen added. 'Apart from Cluny's, I mean.'

'Where?' she asked eagerly, looking up.

'In Riano, in Jarlath's castle. But that's getting ahead of the story.'

'What were the letters on it?'

He told her, noting her disappointment.

'I've already shown you that one, haven't I?'

Rebecca nodded. Galen took the book out of his bag, and set it beside her on the bed, then returned to Emer's side. Close examination revealed nothing useful about the petrified volume, so Galen went on with his story. The second visit to Riano, with his brushes with death and imprisonment, made a frightening tale, especially when he got to the part where he finally learned what Davin's report contained. Then he told the girls of his subsequent journeyings, his meeting with Montfort at Garadun, his stormy reunion with the Archaeologists, and how he intended to return to Edgefield.

It was early morning now, but somehow no one was thinking of sleep. Rebecca and Emer had both been astonished and horrified by turns, but it was Rebecca who had asked the few questions and made any necessary responses. Emer had just been content to sit close to the storyteller.

Many of the elements of his tale were familiar to Rebecca, and she knew that some were linked to her dreams, although she did not know exactly how. The rest of Galen's story was completely new, however. The threat of civil war obviously loomed even larger now.

'Then, of course, I got your message about this place,' Galen concluded. 'I had quite a job convincing Redfern that I wasn't completely mad.'

'I know how he feels,' Emer mumbled.

'So here I am,' he ended. 'Now, what about you two? This . . . ' He waved his free hand at the wagon, '. . . is a bit of a change for you both, and if you don't tell me what's been happening, I really *will* go mad.'

Rebecca's mind was still filled with images from Galen's tale, but she could not ignore his plea, and so she dragged her mind back to the time when they had last seen each other.

'Nothing much happened after you disappeared,' she began hesitantly. 'But the last month has been a bit

. . . what you might call hectic!'

With an occasional contribution from Emer, Rebecca told him of their meeting with Sancia, the discovery of the fateful legend in *Beneath the Salt*, and of her illness and the delirious vision that had accompanied the fever.

'I'm afraid it must have been me who persuaded you to go back to Jarlath's castle to look for the stone,' she admitted.

'Don't be silly,' Galen began, then was silent, unwilling to admit the truth of her words.

'The sensible thing would have been for you to get away as soon as you got Davin's report, wouldn't it?' she continued. 'Why did you take such a risk?'

'It was my decision,' he said calmly.

'But I may have influenced you,' she persisted. 'I got you here, didn't I?'

Galen did not reply.

'I'm sorry,' Rebecca said. 'It was stupid of me. It could have got you killed – but I didn't know the danger you'd be facing.'

'Well, I wasn't killed.'

'No, but you ended up in the dungeons, didn't you. And because of that, Davin's report took longer than it should have done to get back,' she went on miserably. The dangers of her talent – as well as its advantages – were becoming painfully obvious.

'Forget it,' Galen said. 'In the end no great harm was done, and I *did* find the stone.'

Rebecca nodded, still unhappy.

'Besides,' Emer told her. 'You were ill. What could you expect? You're not entirely rational even when you're perfectly healthy!'

'What happened after that?' Galen prompted.

'My father and I went to Garadun,' Rebecca replied. 'We must have left the city just before you arrived.' She went on to tell of her discoveries in Milden's archives, and of her own meeting with Montfort. She glanced at Emer as she spoke, but her friend refrained from comment. The events after their return to Edgefield had taken on the blurred quality of a mirage, but Rebecca described the terrifying invasion and their miraculous escape as best she could.

'So here we are,' Rebecca concluded, relaxing at last.

'And now what do we do?' Emer asked yawning.

The first light of the new dawn was filtering through the cracks around the caravan door.

'The first thing we can do is get some sleep,' Rebecca answered, feeling suddenly unutterably weary. The spell that she had unconsciously woven about them unravelled, and she saw that her two friends could hardly keep their eyes open.

'Lie down and take your clothes off,' Emer whispered hopefully.

'I am lying down,' Galen pointed out. His eyes were closed now. 'Later,' he promised.

'I'll see where Spike's got to,' Rebecca said hurriedly. She heaved herself to her feet, and left the caravan, closing the door behind her. She sat on the steps as the sun rose, and was soon joined by the beek, who seemed calm now, and replete.

After a little while, Rebecca realized that there were no sounds coming from inside the wagon. Her eyelids drooping intolerably, she opened the door a fraction. Galen and Emer lay side by side on her bed, fast asleep in each other's arms. Galen was still fully clothed.

CHAPTER SIXTY-FOUR

Rebecca woke just before noon, and wondered for a moment why they had not been disturbed. She had no memory of any dreams, and felt almost cheated. Galen and Emer soon roused themselves, stretching cramped limbs and smiling at each other and at her. Kedar and Annis arrived shortly afterwards, their arrival doubly welcome as they brought food for a large, belated breakfast. Rebecca made the introductions, to which a bleary-eyed Galen responded quietly. His thoughts were obviously on the food.

'I'm glad you didn't wake us earlier,' Emer commented, yawning.

Kedar and Annis exchanged glances.

'It never occurred to us,' the artist said.

'We knew . . . ' Annis began, then fell silent.

'You three m-make a formidable team,' Kedar commented drily.

Galen looked up and swallowed a hastily chewed mouthful.

'You don't do too badly yourselves, from what I've been told,' he remarked.

'B-but our talents have only a local effect,' Kedar replied. 'Compared to the p-problems that confront you, our achievements are trivial.'

'Healing my face may have seemed trivial to you . . . ' Emer began – then stopped as she saw the solemn expressions of her companions.

'You don't know the half of it,' Rebecca told the newcomers. 'Galen has told us what is happening in Ahrenia – and it's even more frightening and confusing than we had thought.'

'We heard,' Annis responded simply.

A few moments passed in astonished silence before

527

Rebecca could find her voice.

'*All* of it?' she asked softly.

Kedar nodded.

'While we were asleep,' he said. 'Dreams are handy things sometimes!'

'We compared notes this morning and realized what had happened,' Annie went on. 'You have been very brave,' she told Galen.

'And lucky,' he replied, still struggling to come to terms with this new development.

They were all quiet for a while, each alone with their thoughts. Rebecca realized that much of what she did as a dream-weaver was instinctive, seemingly without control, and seemed to work of its own accord. This idea did not make her feel any more comfortable. *Your talent is unquestionable, but you have much to learn.* Leading Galen here had been deliberate – she hoped – but why had Kedar been drawn to her? *True magic reveals itself.* She was not sure about that – all it seemed to do was confuse her even more.

'All right,' Emer stated emphatically. 'We've got all these . . . "clues" . . . and you four have demonstrated certain talents . . . '

'You're in this too,' Rebecca put in quickly. 'Like it or not.'

'I can't see what *I*'ve done,' her friend replied, 'but I will gladly contribute my inestimable intelligence to the discussion. Between us we should be able to work *something* out. All we need is a bit of organization!' she declared.

Spike chose this instant to announce his presence, and the unexpected miaow seemed to emphasize his agreement with Emer's statement. The group looked at the beek, then turned back to Rebecca. She knew they were all assuming that she should take the lead, and knew that she *should*, but she had no idea where to begin.

'We know that Ahrenia is under a military threat from Jarlath and his mercenaries,' Emer prompted, 'and we know the surface reason for that. But it seems to me that there is something more behind it.'

'Something magical,' Annis put in.

'None of this makes any sense unless that's true,' Rebecca

528

agreed quietly.

'I'm sure the monks are involved,' Galen said. 'Davin told me as much, and it's obvious they're not . . . normal. You only have to look at them to see that! And the blue-stone Hakon gave me was magical,' he went on, warming to his theme. 'It was some kind of tracking device. They used it to follow me and Beth.' He paused briefly as something else occurred to him. 'Cluny said that the tide of magic was rising. "It has lain dormant for ages," ' he quoted, ' "but something is happening now, and it's growing stronger every day." '

'*Something*,' Rebecca whispered to herself.

'Why us, though?' Kedar asked. 'I m-mean, Annis and I have talent enough for a few fairground tricks, but that's hardly applicable to the p-problems facing our country. And it's obvious that Rebecca is a dream-weaver – but how does that help?'

'It's because we're together!' Rebecca exclaimed, sure of herself for the first time in ages. 'This *can't* just be accidental. You two are wizards. You shouldn't belittle that. And Sancia told me that dream-weaving can be used as a link to enhance the powers of true wizards.' She paused, and her face fell. 'Only I don't know how,' she added miserably.

'Perhaps we can help you find out,' Emer said, unwilling to let her friend lose heart now that they seemed to be on a positive track.

'The three of us are linked somehow,' Galen added hopefully.

'We proved that in the chess game,' Emer went on.

'And in the dreams afterwards,' he concluded.

'What did Sancia say was the final stage of dream-weaving?' Emer asked.

'Shaping dreams and using them in the waking world,' Rebecca quoted.

'Well, that's just what you did in the chess game,' her friend said triumphantly. 'Now you just have to do the same thing, only this time on a bigger scale! With these two to help you, who knows what you could achieve?'

'But . . . '

'All right,' Emer continued, brushing aside Rebecca's interruption. 'We're agreed that there's a magical threat, and that we have to do something to oppose it – even if we don't know *what* yet. So exactly what is it we have to fight? What's happening, and why is it so awful?'

'You *know*!' Rebecca accused, her face pale. Facing her innermost fears was not something she could do lightly.

'Of course I do,' Emer said, sounding mildly exasperated. 'I just want to make things clear for everyone. Step by step.'

'You'd better humour her,' Galen remarked, grinning. 'I know what she's like when she's in this mood.'

Emer pushed him playfully. Her eyes were smiling, but her expression remained stern.

'Well?' she demanded.

Rebecca made a forlorn attempt to marshal her chaotic thoughts.

'Something terrible that happened in the past,' she began hesitantly, 'is happening again. The story in *Beneath the Salt* about my namesake . . . ' She swallowed hard. 'The one I never got the chance to finish.'

'Tell us,' Kedar prompted.

Rebecca did as she was told, quoting the fateful words that were burned into her brain.

' "One of the most common, which exists in several versions, is that the city was banished by angry gods – many ages ago – to languish beneath the sea. Its people lived the cold-blooded lives of underwater creatures until a great battle restored it to the open air. Central to the battle was the conflict between opposite sides of the magical spectrum within the Web. The opposing forces were, to put it simply, good and evil, and they remained deadlocked until the intercession of a character known variously as the Child of the Web, the Seeress of Night and the Tears of the World. All the chronicles agree that she lived by the edge of the sea, and most versions state that she was the only child of a cruel, widower baron. Several give her name as Rebecka, though the spelling of this varies, and it was her death . . . " '

When she finished, even the air in the wagon seemed still.

'I don't know what came after that,' Rebecca said quietly.

'Let's assume it *does* refer to you,' Emer said, businesslike once more.

'What else . . . ?' Rebecca began.

'The references certainly make it sound likely,' Emer went on doggedly, 'but the book said "several versions". Not *all* of them have to be about you, and even so, there's no reason to suppose that the end is always the same.' The inference of her words sank in slowly. Perhaps Rebecka did not die in every version.

'But the Heretics believed . . . Alomar believed that certain events are repeated throughout history,' Rebecca persisted. 'Milden told me so. Why put that in his book if he thought it was only a myth?'

'Perhaps because it was just a good story,' her friend replied. 'You can't trust people who write books.'

'Cluny mentioned some old stories,' Galen remembered, 'which told of a conflict that would recur throughout history. And so far it has. Remember the snow-cluster marble that showed the chess game? It was exact in every detail, and yet that stone was eight hundred years old!'

'You see!' Rebecca cried, despair touching her voice.

'Then what are we doing?' Annis asked. She had been following the conversation closely, and chose her moment to enter it carefully. 'If we're not supposed to be able to stop the cycle, why have we been called together?'

'Exactly!' Emer exclaimed gratefully. 'We *can* change it!'

'How?' Kedar asked mildly.

'That's what we're trying to find out!' she retorted.

'Cluny had some marble carvings,' Galen volunteered, 'and I saw more in that room below the salt.'

'Go on.'

'There was a man on a horse,' he began, ticking them off on his fingers, 'but that could refer to anyone. A castle in flames . . . '

'Edgefield?'

'Not recognizably. And a group of musicians, I think,' he went on. 'Then there was a battle scene, but that was so worn that I couldn't make out any details. A huge ship . . . '

'That could m-mean the m-mercenaries from the south,' Kedar pointed out.

'It's all pretty vague, though,' Annis commented. 'Those scenes could fit almost anything.'

'The last two were very strange,' Galen remembered. 'One showed some men walking up castle walls . . . '

'That was us!' Rebecca exclaimed. 'We were walking *down* the walls, but backwards, hanging on to the ropes.'

There was an ominous pause as they each considered this confirmation of their involvement in the cycle of history.

'And the last one was really odd,' Galen said eventually. 'Very crudely carved, as though it had been done in a great hurry. There were three men, linked by lines from their heads.'

'Like us,' Emer said, smiling. 'At least when we're asleep.'

'Doesn't help much, though, does it?' Galen said, sounding disappointed. No one contradicted him.

'Let's get back to the book,' Annis suggested. 'If our assumptions are correct, and the salt-flats take the place of the sea, then Derith is going to be restored to the open air.'

'But that's impossible!' Kedar exclaimed. 'It would have b-been crushed into nothing centuries ago.'

'The tower room wasn't,' Galen countered.

'But how *could* it rise?' Annis asked.

'I've seen the salt move,' Galen told them. 'It's as though it's alive.'

'But it's still impossible to see how a whole city could suddenly emerge after having b-been b-buried for eight hundred years!' Kedar responded.

'True,' Galen admitted.

'I dreamt about the people in Derith waking up,' Rebecca said quietly. 'It's happening.' Her eyes flashed. 'Your tale, Annis, the one that nearly choked me – the ending is wrong. The evil king was preparing to come back. Don't you see – Tyrrell wasn't defeated at all! And now his time is near.'

'I heard the monks saying something like that,' Galen said, watching Rebecca's pale, anxious face.

'You think they're in league with him?' Annis asked.

'It wouldn't surprise me. They look as if they've been pickled in salt for a good few years.'

'But Tyrrell died centuries ago,' Kedar objected. 'How *can* they be working together?'

532

'I don't know how, but I still believe it,' Rebecca declared. She told them of Kavan's magic painting of the monk, discovered by her when a child. Kedar listened in awe as she described how the monk's expression had changed, how the strange chess pieces were often moved, and finally, how the seemingly benign figure had become a vision of horror.

When she finished, the young artist whistled in disbelief.

'It's a gateway to the Web,' he explained. 'B-but to have kept it open for so long! The p-power needed to do that would be *incredible*. I knew Kavan was good, b-but . . .' Words failed him.

'A gateway?' Emer asked. 'Was that the same thing that happened with your painting of Rebecca?'

'In a sense,' Kedar replied. 'But my creation was only a fleeting thing – and even then it almost destroyed me. Kavan's has lasted for hundreds of years.' He paused, lost in admiration. 'B-both p-paintings showed that something – or someone – is looking for Rebecca.'

'Perhaps Kavan's was meant as a warning,' Annis said. 'He was one of us, after all.'

'You mean he knew that Rebecca would find it – after all that time?' Galen asked.

'He knew there'd be a Rebecca,' she replied.

'You see what you need to see,' the dream-weaver said. 'Sancia told me it was no accident that I was the one to find the painting.'

'Well, I think he could have been more helpful!' Emer sounded almost indignant. 'Hints about chess games and monks are all very well, but if he'd told us what's going to happen on the salt, it would have been more useful.'

'The demon I saw when I was a child,' Rebecca wondered. 'Could that have been another warning?'

'P-perhaps what's under the salt recognized you,' Kedar suggested. Rebecca shivered at the thought.

'We know about the myths that surround the salt,' Emer rationalized. 'Derith and such like, and all the stories the Archaeologists tell. But the salt is only one of the common themes in all this.'

'And the other is?' Galen asked obligingly.

'Rebecca's dreams, of course. Most of the information we

have comes from them – even if it has been substantiated elsewhere. Perhaps their sequence can tell us something.'

She looked expectantly at her friend.

'But I've been dreaming all my life,' Rebecca said weakly. 'Right from the nightmares when I was a little girl. How can I remember them all?'

'Are you being deliberately obtuse?' Emer demanded. 'You *know* which are important!'

'Tell us,' Annis urged.

Rebecca collected her thoughts for a few moments, then began.

'The first was probably the one where I was trapped inside a picture frame.' She described how her musings in the Gallery of Edgefield Castle had led to her being trapped in Cadell's painting, with the subjects of the other portraits staring in at her. Then she described the dream that had been a precursor of the chess game – a bleached world filled with ruthless opponents – but also containing the first intimation of the link between herself, Emer and Galen.

'The next one was much later,' she told her intent audience. 'A long time after the game. Salt was pouring into my room, and then the first set of letters appeared. I couldn't remember what they were until Galen told me yesterday.'

'That was the set I saw at Cluny's house, after the game,' Galen put in.

'There was a woman in the dream, and she saved me from drowning in the salt,' Rebecca went on. 'She said, "For you, my child, the light will never fade." '

'So you have friends in the Web as well as enemies,' Kedar said, interpreting the images.

'I hope so.' She smiled wanly. 'Then, just before I went to Garadun with my father, I dreamt of a white city and a black pyramid. It was Derith, full of ghosts, all looking up at the sky.' She trembled at the memory of the spectres' dreadful longing. 'I saw two marble tablets there.'

'Those were the two I'd seen described in the book the day before,' Emer said. 'The Okran Stones.'

Rebecca nodded, white-faced and breathing with difficulty. Reliving these dreams was an unpleasant experience – and their implications made it even worse.

'The next was in Garadun,' she said shakily. 'I call it the Healing Dream. It didn't tell me anything, but it made me feel a lot better.'

'That was the one with Sancia?' Annis said.

'Yes. Just after she died. But she spoke to me in my mother's voice.'

'You'll be able to call on them again,' Annis said softly. 'Their help will be there when you need it.'

Comforted by this thought, Rebecca returned to her list.

'After I saw Montfort, there was the whirlpool dream,' she said. 'With another stone.'

'This one,' Galen said, holding up his find.

'I was trying to convince Montfort that he faced magical enemies,' Rebecca went on, realizing now how prophetic the dream had been. 'But he wouldn't listen.'

'We'll have to make sure he listens now!' Emer announced.

'But how?' Galen wanted to know. 'How can you convince him if he doesn't want to believe.'

'It's hopeless,' Rebecca said. 'He won't accept anything as outlandish as this. Not until it's too late.'

'We have to try, though,' Emer insisted, and was about to say more when Kedar overrode her.

'Any m-more dreams?' he asked.

'Only the ones I've had since I've been with the fair,' Rebecca answered. 'The last set of letters – the ones Galen saw in Riano – and Montfort's non-existent son. That ended with a bell tolling – and it makes my heart sink just to remember it.'

'The bell Drain thought he saw in the salt?' Galen suggested.

Rebecca shrugged.

'Possibly,' she said. 'Who knows? Then there was the dream that brought Kedar to us, and the one that brought us all to this place,' she concluded.

'So here we are,' Emer said dramatically. 'And it's obvious what we need to do in order to convince Montfort.'

'What?' Rebecca asked innocently. She was the only one there who had not realized in advance what Emer's reply would be.

Emer held up the sheet of paper on which the five sets of letters had been transcribed.

'Solve these,' she stated. 'Simple!'

CHAPTER SIXTY-FIVE

'Simple?' Rebecca looked at her friend as though she had gone quite mad. 'Of course! So simple that no one's been able to do it in *centuries*.'

'No one's ever had them all together before,' Emer retorted.

'How do you know we've got them all? There may be more – *hundreds* more!'

Emer pulled a face and waved her friend's objection aside. Kedar was the next to speak.

'Do you realize,' he asked thoughtfully, 'that you only dreamt of the sets of letters after either Emer or Galen had seen them?'

'You three *do* make a formidable team,' Annis commented softly.

'You see!' Emer exclaimed. 'Why would they appear in your dreams if we're not supposed to solve them?'

Rebecca felt all their eyes upon her as she pondered the truth of Kedar's observation. *Even when we were apart, we were together in some ways,* she thought, feeling the bond between them grow even stronger.

'All we can do is try,' she said quietly.

'Then let's get to work,' Emer responded triumphantly.

It was impossible for them all to look at the single sheet of paper at once, so Kedar was commissioned to make a copy. While he worked, the others considered what they knew about the letters and their origins.

'I remember the legends about the Okran Stones,' Rebecca said. 'One said that the fate of the land would depend on the nature of the person who reads them first.'

'Then you'd better get there before I do!' Emer replied, grinning. 'You may be pedantic and stubborn at times – when you're not being downright weird – but you've got a much sweeter nature than me.'

'You shouldn't joke about something like this,' the dream-weaver whispered solemnly.

'Oh, come on, Becky,' her friend urged. 'Don't be so glum.'

'Anything that people don't understand is bound to attract all sorts of myths,' Annis put in.

'And there were lots more, weren't there?' Galen added.

'Yes,' Rebecca admitted. 'Depending on which one you believe, translating the stones will allow you to command demons, find fabulous treasure, or bring a terrible curse down upon you.'

'We'll settle for the first two, I think,' Kedar said drily, without looking up from his work.

'And there's one that says their translation will portend a great natural disaster,' Rebecca went on. 'Like an earthquake . . . '

'Or a salt-quake?' Emer suggested.

This time it was Galen who found her flippant tone inappropriate.

'You wouldn't find that idea so funny if you'd *seen* the salt move,' he told her. 'Or seen it swallow a man whole.'

'If we're right, and Derith *does* rise,' Emer retorted, indignant and unabashed, 'we'll have a lot more to worry about than a few men getting pickled!'

Galen did not reply, and Kedar glanced up.

'P-perhaps there are other explanations for the stones,' he said. 'They don't *have* to contain a dire m-message.'

'There are plenty of suggestions,' Rebecca answered. 'Poetry, love-letters and such like, all absolutely harmless – but I can't believe it. Someone went to an awful lot of trouble with them. Their message *has* to be important.'

Kedar nodded, finished writing, and handed the original to Emer, who sat on the couch flanked by Rebecca and Galen. The artist retained his copy, and shared it with Annis, who sat beside him on the bed. They all stared at the enigmatic puzzles, hoping for inspiration.

```
T H E D R    W T H E S    A G I C F
D L N E       O D O A       M S N A
F L O A U    T L W L O    F E I T V
I O M C      O E T D       I N E E
W E H T T    F O B E W    L R O R R

    E W I Z A    A R T S S
    E N N R      P E O I
    O R N D E    S O I F X
    O H S E      F W T A
    B H T I R    E H T E C
```

Annis eventually broke their silent scrutiny.

'Anagrams?' she suggested.

'What?' Kedar asked, frowning

'Mix the letters around,' Galen explained, remembering his conversation with Cluny and Anselma. 'For instance, the top row of the last set could make STARS.'

'And the last lines of the fourth one could be SHOE and BIRTH,' Annis went on.

'The top row of the first would make DERITH,' Emer said, 'but there's no I.'

'It can't b-be that simple,' Kedar decided after a few moments. 'B-besides, some of the lines don't m-make *any* p-possible words.'

'What about columns then, or diagonals?' Rebecca suggested.

Further study produced little that was even vaguely sensible, and this approach was quickly abandoned.

'How about a substitution code?' Annis asked. 'Where one letter actually means another, according to a set pattern. A becomes B, B becomes C and so on. What do you think?'

'How could we possibly solve that?' Galen responded. 'Unless we know what the pattern is.'

'Perhaps it's determined by something we should already know,' Emer suggested. 'And all we have to do is work out what it is.'

'But that could be *anything*!' Rebecca objected.

'Then maybe we can find a clue in the letters themselves,' Annis put in. 'E is the most common letter in our language, so let's see which one occurs most here, and take that for E. Then we can try and work out what the others are, and build up the pattern.'

Time passed in silence as the group counted and made notes. Eventually, they all saw what was happening.

'Have you got the same as us?' Galen asked.

'Yes,' Annis said ruefully.

The most common letter, by a good margin, was E.

'Oh, well. It was worth a try,' Kedar muttered resignedly.

'No! Don't you see?' Rebecca said suddenly. 'It's important. Look. There are plenty of vowels, no J, K, Q or Y, and only one each of X and Z. That's much as you'd expect in a normal piece of writing, isn't it?' She sounded enthusiastic for the first time. 'That means we're *supposed* to read the letters as they are. Surely! And it makes having to move them around much more likely.'

'Perhaps you have to combine letters from more than one line or column – or even from more than one stone,' Galen suggested.

'But there would be millions of combinations!' Rebecca exclaimed, aghast.

'And we're not even sure we've got all the stones,' Kedar added.

'What about reading them as they are but not in straight lines?' Emer suggested. 'If you read round the top left corner of the third set, for example, you get MAGIC.'

'I saw that before,' Galen replied. 'But it doesn't fit with anything else.'

'The same combination in the fifth one gives PARTS,' Kedar said thoughtfully. 'But the others are just nonsense.'

'It's the same with WIZARD, if you read across and then down in the top right part of the fourth,' Galen added. 'Doing the same in any of the others only produces rubbish.'

'We're being stupid!' Rebecca exclaimed abruptly. 'These ideas must all have been tried over and over again since the Okran Stones were first found – and by far more clever minds than ours.' No one saw fit to dispute this statement, and her fervour was such that even Emer refrained from making any comment. 'What's so special about us? Why should *we* be the ones to translate them?' Rebecca went on, staring at each of her companions in turn. 'Why did the dreams find the letters and draw us together?'

'Dream-weaving for the three of us,' Emer answered promptly, 'and wizardry for these two.'

'And Sancia,' Rebecca completed for her. 'This is her home. What did her message say?' She fetched the old woman's note, and re-read it. But there was no immediate enlightenment, and she handed it to the others, thinking furiously.

'What does she mean by you being her "kin of the ages"?' Annis asked.

'I don't know,' Rebecca answered. 'At first I thought it meant that I was the one to take her place with the fair. Now I'm not so sure.'

' "Your friends are welcome too",' Kedar quoted.

'This time,' Emer said, remembering her earlier visit.

'She knew this was coming,' Rebecca said calmly. 'Why else would she have left the cards laid out like that?'

'Show us again,' Galen said.

She obeyed, laying the cards out on the box table between them.

'Perhaps she's telling us to look at the letters that correspond to the groups of cards,' Annis suggested.

Experiments to test this theory produced only meaningless jumbles. Rebecca lost some of her earlier enthusiasm, and lapsed into silence.

'Perhaps Sancia was showing us a pattern, not a message as such,' Kedar said.

'It is an odd shape,' Emer put in. 'Like a crown on its side.'

Kedar had been looking at the cards with an artist's eye, considering them from several different angles.

'The whole thing would have a neat symmetry if the two shorter lines m-moved half a space to the right,' he murmured, reaching out and sliding the cards on the cloth. 'See what I mean?'

Rebecca suddenly sat bolt upright, a surge of excitement coursing through her.

'You two are not only wizards,' she said hurriedly. 'You're Heretics too! Your song!'

'What about . . . ?' Annis began, puzzled.

' "Two parts shift and magic flows"!' Rebecca quoted.

540

' "The elders speak and p-power glows", ' Kedar completed for her.

'*This* is how Sancia had laid the cards out,' she went on, pointing. 'I moved them, thinking that they must have been displaced by the bumping of the wagon.'

She took the paper and quickly wrote out the sets of letters in the new alignment. After a moment's hesitation, Kedar did the same. Almost immediately, words began to appear. In the first set one diagonal line read ENACT, and HOLD and WILL formed part of others being read upwards. After that, the discoveries came thick and fast, amid exclamations, laughter, and great excitement. The second stone revealed BELOW, SALT, HOLD again, and FOLD. The third gave FATE, INTER and LIES, and the fourth, THREE and BORN. Only the last stone revealed little of interest.

They were all delighted by their progress. The problem had not been solved, but they were undoubtedly getting closer to a result. Their enthusiasm for the task renewed, each vied with the others to make the next discovery.

'All these diagonals, what do they remind you of?' Emer demanded, looking at the two wizards. She received no response, so answered her own question. 'Your emblem!' she exclaimed. 'The one on Annis's ring and your satchel . . . '

'And Sancia's pendant,' Rebecca whispered.

'Two Xs b-between two horizontal lines, enclosed in a circle,' Kedar said. 'Why haven't we seen it before?'

'These are Heretical stones,' Emer concluded. '*Your* stones.'

'The Okran Stones were found above Derith, and so was this one,' Galen said, tapping his marble tablet. 'Is that where the Heretics' society originated?'

'I don't know,' Annis replied, and Kedar shook his head.

'Come on,' Rebecca urged. 'We're nearly there. It must make sense soon.'

Further study only brought increasing frustration as they all kept seeing fragments of the answer only to miss the final key. Much to her own surprise, it was Emer who made the breaththrough. She had returned to the last stone, intrigued by its comparative obscurity.

'It's not two Xs,' she blurted out. 'It's two overlapping

triangles. See there. SIFT – that's what started me thinking. What if the song was a misquotation of one of these, as well as an instruction? This is the stone with PARTS as well, as well remember. Look! Begin at the middle of the bottom row. Read up the diagonal to the left, across the top, and then back down to where you started.'

'TWO PARTS SIFT . . . ' Galen read, astonishment clear in his voice.

'Then repeat that from the middle of the top,' Emer went on eagerly, pointing the way.

'TO FACE THE FOE . . . ' he read aloud.

'Gods!' Kedar breathed, looking at the fourth set of letters. 'Listen to this. THREE WIZARDS . . . IN DERITH B-BORN.'

Their excitement was now almost unbearable.

'HOLD THE DREAM . . . ' Rebecca read from the first set, then gasped. 'That was in Sancia's message! ENACT THE WILL.'

'This one is even better,' Galen almost shouted, pointing to the second set. 'BELOW THE SALT . . . HOLD WEB OF OLD.'

Annis completed the translations in a quieter voice.

'ONE MAGIC FATE . . . IN TERROR LIES.' She shuddered.

'Wait a moment,' Emer interrupted. 'That doesn't use the letters in the middle row.'

'F.I.V.,' Annis quoted.

'T.W.O.,' Galen spelt out. 'Two.'

'That's it!' Rebecca cried. 'All of them. The letters that match the fire-demon cards are the first three letters of a number. Four, Two, Five, One and Six.'

'So you're supposed to read them in order,' Emer concluded gleefully.

'But there's one missing, even now,' Rebecca went on. 'Where's Three?'

'Read what we've got,' her friend commanded, and Annis obliged.

' "Three wizards in Derith born; below the salt, hold Web of old." Then there's the missing line . . . ' she said, her eyes scanning the page. ' "Hold the dream, enact the will;

one magic fate in terror lies; two parts sift to face the foe." '

The group sat in silence for a few heartbeats, overawed by their achievement. The ancient riddle had been solved!

'Yes,' Emer said slowly. 'That's it.' She paused, then voiced the question that was surfacing in each of their minds. 'But what does it all mean?'

CHAPTER SIXTY-SIX

In the days following Farrand's surrender, Montfort had worked out his strategy. Naturally enough, he chose Edgefield Castle as his headquarters, but several squadrons of men were sent east and west and billeted in neighbouring villages. A series of look-out posts were established along the northern rim of the salt-flats, and beacons set up so that signals could be passed quickly along the length of the line. The majority of the king's troops were deployed in camps on open ground, ready to be called to any point of danger at a moment's notice. Then Montfort and his officers spent time bargaining for and organizing supplies for these camps. Apart from that, there was little that they could do, except wait for news.

Nothing came from the south – though they had not expected anything so soon – but the king did receive one encouraging message. This came from Redfern, and stated that Arledge was already on his way south across the salt with a group of Archaeologists. The innkeeper added, somewhat mysteriously, that Galen had ridden north again on a mission of his own. Ellard wondered why Galen was not heading straight back to Edgefield, but assumed that he had his own reasons for not returning. He was sure Arledge would bring back the intelligence they so desperately needed, but this obviously would not happen for a few days yet.

There was also a scarcity of news from the north, but what came through was uniformly unpleasant. Montfort's northern detachments had come under heavy pressure from the forces led by the rebellious upland barons – 'the old guard' as they were known. His army was being forced back towards Garadun, and had sustained many casualties. Although the

544

reports were sketchy and sometimes confused, the overall picture was clear. Montfort fumed silent about his inability to help his comrades, and fretted over the prospect of his capital being invaded. Nevertheless, he knew he must stay where he was, and be ready to face the even more dangerous threat from the south. His constant waking nightmare was the possibility that his northern allies would be defeated utterly, thus allowing the old guard to march south and attack his unguarded rear. Scouts were constantly on the look-out, ready to give warning of any approach, but if such an attack were to coincide with Jarlath's arrival across the salt, then Montfort's battle would be lost almost before it began.

The troubled monarch found it difficult to sleep, or even to relax. Logic told him that he had done everything possible to protect his country and his heritage, yet there were still many unanswered questions that nagged him. Even the peaceful surrender of Edgefield Castle – after Cranne's suicidal foray – had given him little satisfaction.

Farrand had yielded, but remained defiantly silent, painfully aware of his sullied honour, and determined not to betray his allies. Montfort had been filled with rage at the baron's intransigence, and had thought of ordering his execution, but he soon calmed down, and had him locked in a secure, thick-walled pantry – the nearest thing the castle possessed to a dungeon. His fate would be decided later. His soldiers had been disarmed and herded up. Most were being kept under guard, while several others had volunteered to join Montfort, swearing a new oath of allegiance. These new recruits had been accepted – though not without some suspicion – and had been dispersed among different units of the king's army. There they would either prove their loyalty or die.

Baldemar had all but wept with relief at his rescue. He had been almost craven when he met Montfort, loudly protesting his innocence and loyalty. The baron reminded the king of a piece of straw, blowing this way and that with every stray gust of wind. Like many bullies, he was weak at heart and was clearly now a broken man.

There was no sign of Baldemar's daughter. Montfort

thought of her often, afraid for her safety, but hopeful. He had interviewed many castle staff who claimed that they had seen her escape – some even believed that she had flown away over the roof tops – but none of their stories tallied. In his more optimistic moments, the king decided that Tarrant must have rescued her after all, but at other times darker possibilities occurred to him. All he knew for certain was that she was not there. This fact caused him a great deal of regret.

The other person Montfort would have liked to talk to was also unavailable, but for a very different reason. Baldemar's chamberlain had apparently known more about the running of Edge than the baron himself, but Radd was unconscious, in a deep and possibly fatal coma. He was receiving the attention of one of the army surgeons, as well as being tended by Nursey, but he had been viciously tortured by Cranne, and though his body still lived, his mind had retreated from the pain and horror. Montfort doubted that it would ever return.

* * *

In another town, many leagues to the north of Edge, Tarrant and Pike were making the final arrangements for their departure.

'Everything set?' Tarrant asked.

'Yes,' his lieutenant replied, looking and sounding unusually nervous. 'As ready as it will ever be.'

'Don't worry! He assured us that it was all quite safe,' the younger man told him.

'After what we've seen here, I'm not so sure,' Pike commented dourly.

'We've taken greater risks in our time,' Tarrant pointed out.

'Aye, but we've always known what the risks *were*,' the veteran muttered. 'This is all new to me. And I don't like it!'

'Come on, old friend,' Tarrant responded. 'Let's be on our way. At least we'll be able to shake things up a bit.'

The two men grinned at each other, and both pairs of eyes glinted with the fire of adventure.

'That,' Pike said drily, 'is the understatement of the *year*.'

'What harm can it do?' Tarrant asked. 'The old guard are pushing south. We must do something to stop them.'

'There's plenty we could do, without this!' Pike declared.

'We'll have some fun, never fear,' his captain reassured him. 'I've an idea or two I'd like your opinion on . . .'

As they mounted their horses, Tarrant went on to outline his plans, and as they moved further south, Pike recovered his usual composure. He even managed to stop glancing behind them quite so often.

'That's more like it,' he said with some satisfaction when Tarrant had finished.

'Then spread the word,' the younger man replied, grinning. 'We've no time to waste.'

* * *

In Rebecca's caravan, the discussion about the newly deciphered messages had gone on long into the evening. The dream-weaver had managed to work out the message Sancia had left in the cards. The kings formed one triangle, and the queens another. The lovers, one man and one woman, were in both, whereas the fire-demons were outside the pattern, not human and thus not part of the immediate message.

The group had speculated about the symbolic meaning of the two triangles. It seemed likely that the 'three wizards in Derith born' were indeed the original Heretics, and that they therefore formed one of the triangles. There were other possibilities, however. Rebecca, Emer and Galen were of course linked in a three-sided team, as they had proved in the chess game. Rebecca recalled the vision she had had during the game, of an infinite chess-board, its black and white squares stretching in endless diagonals, but joining herself and her friends in a triangle.

'It's all in threes,' Kedar said, looking at Annis. 'M-makes us feel quite inadequate. Where's our third p-part?'

He had meant his question half in jest, but Rebecca took it seriously.

'Perhaps you're the present-day equivalent of the old wizards,' she said. 'So we do need another person.'

'You can't compare us to them!' Kedar exclaimed. 'We don't have p-power like that.'

'How do you know?' Rebecca asked. 'Perhaps when you're all together . . .'

'This is crazy!' the artist said, shaking his head.

'In any case,' Annis put in, 'we have no idea who the third wizard is.'

'I do,' Rebecca replied.

'How?' Kedar asked. 'Who is it?'

'He's a musician,' she answered. 'His name is Newell. I met him at home just before the castle was invaded.' She told the story of Newell's incredible music, and of their subsequent, ill-fated meeting.

'It makes some sort of sense,' Annis said thoughtfully. 'A painter, a storyteller and a musician. But how are we supposed to find him?'

'Even if your theory is correct,' Kedar insisted, 'what can we do once we *are* together? We're artists! We don't fight wars.'

'I found you two, didn't I?' Rebecca replied, ignoring this outburst. 'So I can find him too.'

The others – Emer especially – were glad to see Rebecca's resolve, but to have unravelled the riddle of the stones and still have no definite instructions about what they were supposed to do left them all feeling bemused, almost cheated.

'Well, we'll just have to work on it,' Rebecca concluded.

'And look for the missing stone,' Galen added.

'One thing's clear, though,' she went on. 'We have to get to Montfort.'

'I'll tell the wagon-master,' Annis volunteered. 'It shouldn't take more than three or four days to reach Edgefield.'

The storyteller left with Kedar, and the other three sat quietly for a few moments. They were all desperately tired – but there was a spark in Emer's eye, none the less.

'I'm going for a walk,' Rebecca said quickly. 'To clear my head. Can Spike come with me?'

'Of course,' Galen replied. 'He's probably starving by now.'

Emer said nothing, but her smile was grateful and the message in her eyes was 'don't hurry back'.

Rebecca closed the door behind her, a strange, empty feeling in her chest. She wandered aimlessly amid the bustle of the fair, but took in little of its sights, sounds and smells. Spike darted here and there, finding new adventures at every turn, but even his enthusiasm could not lift her depression.

Spike yowled plaintively at her feet, and she bent down to pick him up, cradling the tiny creature in her arms.

'Are you lonely too, little one?' she whispered.

CHAPTER SIXTY-SEVEN

The fair had been moving slowly south for two days now, but there had been no further suggestions about the meaning of the stones' message. Nor had Rebecca's dreams revealed anything out of the ordinary. She still could not control them to any extent, and merely going to sleep hoping to find Newell or receive some other revelation was not enough. Her impatience with their slow progress was only making matters worse. She felt nervous at the prospect of returning to a home that might have been ravaged by war, and wished that she knew more about what had happened in Edgefield. She was worried about those she had left behind, and about what they might have suffered. Above all, she was worried about Radd, hoping now, in the light of everything she had discovered, that he would not refuse to let her read the full story of the earlier Rebecka. She must find out what had happened.

Rebecca was sorely tempted to borrow horses and ride on ahead with her friends, but knew that such an action would be both dangerous and wrong. Until this matter was settled, Sancia's wagon was her home. She took comfort in the continued presence of Kedar and Annis, who were both bewildered and a little scared, and especially in that of Galen and Emer – though she was careful to give them their privacy whenever possible. The belief that the three of them belonged together was one of the few pieces of firm ground in her rapidly shifting world.

She dreamt that night of a string of beacons, flaring like jewels in the darkness. Beside them stood a group of soldiers, looking out into the black waste beyond, the flames reflected on their armour. Behind them, unseen, marched a silent army, pillaging and burning, leaving only a devastated wasteland in its wake. Closer and closer it came, squeezing the narrow band of life thinner and thinner, until it almost disappeared between the dark salt and the black desert. Rebecca tried to cry out, to warn the waiting soldiers, but she was kept mute, her desperate voice swallowed by the vast silence of the dream.

Just before the thin line of light was about to be overrun, her vision changed abruptly. A group of musicians were playing, and the dream-weaver in her leapt for joy. *Newell!* she called. *Boomer, we need you!* But once again, she could not make herself heard. This time the music hid her words; the fractured chords and melody of a soldier's marching song swelled forth, but these musicians were out of step, producing an increasingly tuneless cacophony, each playing to a different rhythm. From somewhere a voice said, *Where's our third part?* But no one answered.

And then she saw him, his back to her.

Boomer!

He turned towards her, but where his face should have been was only a blank horror. Instead of eyes, nose and mouth, there was just smooth skin, a flat, featureless mask. Only his ears remained, but still he could not hear her.

He turned away again as the music was drowned by the languorous tolling of a huge bell.

* * *

The following morning, Rebecca felt dread like a weight inside her, but was at a loss to interpret her dream in any but the most obvious way. No one could offer her any help, not even Emer and Galen, who had both felt echoes of her nocturnal distress in her own sleep. But when an advance patrol returned to the fair and reported that a great army was camped in the next valley, all her fears were immediately confirmed. Montfort would indeed be facing foes from both sides of his precarious position.

Local farmers reported that the army was marching south, and it was obvious from the standards they bore that they were from the northern uplands. One of the banners depicted a wolf's head with three stars above it – and this fact only served to deepen Rebecca's dread. The fair slowed its pace, not wishing to become embroiled with a hostile army, and once again Rebecca wondered if she should ride on ahead to warn Montfort. She was dissuaded by Galen, who pointed out that such a venture would be horribly dangerous, with little chance of success, and that if she were to be captured, then their efforts would be doomed to failure.

'Montfort will have his scouts out,' he added. 'They'll bring him the news faster than you ever could.'

At the crest of the ridge, Rebecca looked down upon the army moving away from them, and knew that Galen was right. The fair followed at a distance, with the dream-weaver's tense group waiting for their chance.

* * *

Montfort knew what the tired messenger was going to say even before the man's words were spoken. He braced himself, trying to ensure that his face remained calm – but inside he was close to panic. His nightmare was getting closer by the hour.

'Sire, the northern rebels are little more than a day's march away,' the soldier reported. 'Our units have been scattered, and there's little hope of aid from any of the remnants.'

'How many men have the old guard brought with them?' the king asked, keeping his voice steady.

'I have no definite figures, sire, but they're here in full force. The equivalent of three detachments at least, with a full complement of archers and cavalry.'

'Then how many are marching on Garadun?' Montfort demanded, frowning.

'None, my lord. They're all coming to Edge.'

'That's something, at least,' the king muttered to himself, thinking with some relief of his undefended capital. Aloud, he asked, 'Where are they now? No. Wait. Let me gather my captains first.'

A council of war was hurriedly convened, and it was agreed that they would send all the men they could spare – about half their total force – to tackle the old guard. It was obvious that they needed a quick and decisive victory so that they could return and guard the edge of the salt. As the mobilization was organized, the consensus of opinion was that the strength of the northern army could be matched easily enough, but that Montfort's troops could not afford too many casualties if they were to face Jarlath and his mercenaries in the near future. Should that attack take place while half their own force was away, then all would be lost. Speed was therefore essential.

By noon they were on the march, with Montfort in command. He left Ellard in charge of Edge. By early evening, the two opposing armies were camped less than a league apart, each now fully aware of the other. The lights of their respective fires could be seen across the wide valley. Guards were set and patrols sent out to inspect the territory as best they could; Montfort knew, however, that any real action must wait until daybreak.

Morning brought an uneasy stand-off, with neither side willing to relinquish the high ground. Montfort and his captains studied the terrain. Between the two armies was a wide valley, a strong-flowing river at its base, crossed only by two stone bridges. The river divided to the west, being fed by two lesser tributaries which had formed narrower valleys running south-west and west respectively, between which stood a prominent, rocky hill that jutted out like a prow dividing the waters. The twin rivers were fordable above the confluence, but any crossing lower down would be fraught with danger. The bridges were therefore absolutely crucial. Further to the east, the valley widened into a flat plain of farmland and villages, dissected by the powerful, meandering river.

If either army attempted to cross the bridges, they would come under fire from the opposing archers, ready in their advance positions, and, once across, would face a long, hard fight uphill. Yet the geography of the region made any outflanking manoeuvre all but impossible – even if Montfort had the time for such a tactic. The board and players were in place, but none of them could move. It was stalemate.

They can afford to wait, the king thought angrily. *We can't.*

553

He stared at the battleground until his eyes hurt, hoping in vain to hit upon a solution. Many options had already been discussed and discarded. Time passed slowly, until at last Montfort had to make the inevitable, hopeless decision. He called his captains together at noon.

'Gentlemen, we can wait no longer,' he began, his heart heavy. 'Delaying us here is a victory for the rebels. We must take the initiative – at whatever cost.'

The veteran soldiers, all older than their king, listened in hard-faced silence. Each man was loyal, and regarded Montfort highly, but in their eyes this was the first time he had been fully tested. While they respected his decision, knowing that it had been a difficult one to make, they also knew the odds they would be facing in the field that day.

'We will send three of the four infantry detachments down to the west,' the king began. 'They can cross the southern tributary in safety, then move up the western valley to the far side. I will leave the location of the second crossing up to the individual commanders, but it must coincide with the cavalry getting over the bridges. By attacking on two fronts at the same time, we will divide their resources. The fourth infantry will follow the cavalry, and act as movable reinforcements. This way, we can hope to get most of our forces across the river before we are fully engaged.' He paused, looking at the grim faces that surrounded him.

'That still gives the enemy the high ground,' someone said.

'It can't be helped,' Montfort replied. 'Once across, the cavalry can circle round to the east. That will give them an easier approach to the hill, and spreading our assault over a wide front might confuse the enemy's defence. And it has to be a full-scale assault,' he emphasized. 'No quarter, no prisoners. This must be quick and final. Understood?'

His men nodded. They each knew that the plan was a desperate one, born out of dire necessity, but they also saw the need for action. They went to make ready, leaving the young king alone to beseech the Web for good fortune. Whatever happened, he knew, he would live with the consequences of his decision for the rest of his life.

Forgive me, he pleaded silently as he watched the first of his men move off. He knew that many would not live to see the sunset, and wished fiercely that he could go with them. To lose himself in the clamour of violent action, and leave the thinking and planning to others seemed an attractive notion. *But it is not to be,* he told himself sternly. *You have your path in life. And you have no choice but to walk down it as boldly as you can.*

Such a large movement could not hope to go unnoticed, and the enemy's response was soon clear. Several units were moving westward, ready to guard the approach Montfort's infantry was hoping to take.

At a pre-arranged signal, his cavalry charged downhill, dividing into two streams that flowed towards the bridges. There was no disguising their action, and the rebels were soon readjusting their own positions.

Montfort watched the scene unfold, his stomach knotted with tension. At first, all appeared to go well. His army's tactics had led to some confusion among their complacent foe, and a good number of foot-soldiers had now forded both tributaries, while the first of the cavalry units had reached the bridges. But then the enemy seemed to come to life. Archers took a heavy toll of those on the western bridge, and the way across became congested and chaotic. Those on the eastern span fared much better, and most of their number managed to circle the enemy position as planned.

Meanwhile, Montfort's infantry engaged the rebels on the slope of the more northerly of the two narrow valleys. The fighting was savage and bloody, and the monarch's soldiers proved themselves courageous and capable, making slow progress uphill in spite of considerable losses. The pressure on them eased slightly when the cavalry attacked from the east. Although the charge was slowed by the slope of the hill, and the enemy archers again managed to exact a heavy toll, the horsemen pressed on until battle was truly joined. The remnants of the mounted troops, together with the last of the foot-soldiers, slogged across the river and up the hill to complete the three-pronged attack, hemming in the rebels.

Watching from his distant position, Montfort wanted many times to join the battle, or at least get closer to it, but he held back, knowing that he had the best view from where he was. Instead he kept in touch with a constant stream of scouts, sending out instructions and receiving reports from the field. However, this did little to assuage his feelings of impotence. The real battle was amid the flashing blades and flying arrows on the far side of the valley. *Keep going*, he urged his troops silently. *Keep going. You're nearly there!*

The old guard commanders were no fools, however. They had prepared their positions well, and often seemed to retreat only to find better strongholds. After the initial confusion had worn off, they began to take advantage of the unexpected turn of events. They had not dared to hope for an all-out attack, because this would have so obviously played into their hands. Always fighting from the higher ground, and thus more aware of the best use of the terrain, the rebels' war of attrition began to be increasingly effective.

Montfort's advance slowed; the cavalry wheeled, turned, and tried again, while the infantry fought and died for every pace of muddy ground. And all to no avail. The hopelessness of their cause eventually became obvious, and Montfort, in an agony of helplessness, sensed total disaster. He saw the first signs of forced retreat, and prepared to make the best of a bad situation. Signals were sent, ordering his troops to pull back to the river. There he hoped to turn and hold the jubilant rebels. If his men could only have time to regroup, then they would continue the battle on more equal terms. It seemed a forlorn hope, but it was worth a try.

The king found that he could no longer stand aloof; if he failed now, then his country was doomed. He called for his own horse, and led the way down to the battlefield.

On the far side of the valley, the retreat had become a disorganized flight. Montfort could almost taste the fear and panic as he drew closer. The hillside was a maddened surge of noise, blood, and churning mud.

Many of the rebels had followed the retreating loyalists, despite orders to the contrary, and the carnage had spread to the valley floor. The bridges were the centre of the battle, but many men tried to swim the dangerous river; before long, the water was running red.

The archers on both sides were now reduced to scavenging for fallen arrows, or embroiled in hand-to-hand fighting. This gave Montfort's men some small relief, but even so, by the time he reached the eastern bridge, it was clear that it was only a matter of time before his troops would be overwhelmed.

Sword in hand, Montfort succeeded in rallying his men temporarily, but this could only delay the inevitable. Those who were still alive were back on the southern bank of the river by now, but some of the foot-soldiers were running away. Seeing this, the rebel leaders succumbed to the euphoria of victory, ordering their entire troops down to finish the fight. The battle for the bridges was almost won as the triumphant force swept down to complete their work. A huge roar went up as the resistance at the western bridge gave way and rebel troops poured across, sending the remnants of the royal army fleeing in all directions.

Montfort was on foot now, actively engaged in the defence of the other bridge. His men were keeping up a desperate rearguard action, but they knew it was only a matter of time before they were overrun. The king's sword was mired with blood, his face beneath the steel guard a snarling mask of defiance.

Then an unexpected break in the fighting allowed him to look around for a moment. Somehow, everything seemed to be happening in slow motion; a wounded man crawled painfully next to the parapet of the bridge; below, a terrified horse thrashed in the pink, foaming water; on the opposite bank the rebels regrouped for one final onslaught. Montfort could see the hungry, joyful cruelty of their expressions. At the front of the pack, his sword held aloft ready to give the signal to charge, stood a figure that he recognized. It was Glanville, Farrand's elder son. Their eyes met, and Montfort saw his destiny in the other's gloating, malevolent stare. Glanville smiled, knowing that he had won, and prepared to lead his men onwards to crush the last of the loyal resistance.

CHAPTER SIXTY-EIGHT

What happened next was like a scene from a nightmare.

With an ear-splitting roar that shook the valley floor and drowned all battle noise, the western bridge exploded. Balls of orange flame were hurled into the air. Huge chunks of rock defied gravity, rolling lazily skyward, while shards and lesser stones buzzed like maddened insects. Men and horses were butchered by this lethal fusillade; those on the bridge itself were torn asunder, dismembered in an instant with no time even to scream.

Some men flung themselves to the ground, while others, mesmerized in disbelief, stood rooted to the spot, watching as an enormous swell of water surged downstream.

The thunder died away, leaving an eerie, shocked silence broken only by the shrill screams of wounded horses and the thud of stone returning to earth. A pall of dark smoke hung over the spot where the western bridge had once stood. Not a stone remained in place.

The wave rolled down towards the eastern bridge, spray filling the air and soaking many of the soldiers nearby. For a while, that was the only movement; the battlefield seemed frozen. Then, suddenly, men were pointing up to the western sky, their enmity temporarily forgotten in the face of a new terror. There, tailing smoke and flame, a fireball traced a lazy arc as it flew towards the massed ranks of the rebel army still on the northern side of the river.

There was instant panic as terrified soldiers fled in all directions. In the chaotic scramble for safety, many tripped over and trampled their comrades. Many more plunged into the water, either by choice or by force, and were swept away. When the fireball landed, the effect was even more devastating. A vast explosion threw men and earth into the air with indiscriminate ease. Once again, the thunder faded, leaving behind it a legacy of screams. A huge brown hole had been torn into the land – a gaping wound of earth, surrounded by horror.

The men standing by the eastern bridge had watched these incredible events with utter disbelief. Even the would-be deserters from Montfort's beleaguered force had turned back to stare, and the few rebels who had already crossed the western span were now isolated.

A second fireball flew into the sky, originating from the hill between the tributaries, then hurtling towards the rebel army. The survivors stared at it as if hypnotized, until eventually Montfort broke the awful spell.

'The gods of the Web are on our side!' he yelled. 'Will you oppose us now, Glanville?'

The roar of approval from his loyal supporters was echoed by shouts of alarm from their remaining foes. Still no one moved.

'Are you with me?' the king roared, brandishing his bloody sword.

The response was overwhelming, coming from men who had believed themselves lost but who now had new hope. As they surged forward, the rebels melted away before them. Even Glanville turned and ran, deserted by his colleagues. The battle was renewed, and within moments, Montfort's men were across the bridge, turning to press westward.

A third thunderbolt struck, but the rebels were more thinly scattered now, and there were fewer casualties. The royal advance hesitated, but no more blazing missiles flew across the sky, so they pushed on, reinforcements pouring over the bridge behind them.

By now, any rebels trapped on the southern bank had been slaughtered. The traitorous army was no longer an organized force, each man being concerned only with his own survival. For Montfort's rejuvenated soldiers, the hunting was easy.

And yet the wonders of that day were not over. Unseen until now, a group of men on rafts had been travelling down the turbulent waters of the northern river, and were now within fifty paces of the smoking, vanished bridge. Although there were only ten of these men, they turned the tide of battle – already running strongly in Montfort's favour – into an unstoppable flood. As they drew close to the rebel forces, they began to throw what looked like fist-size rocks at the disordered, stupefied enemy. When these rocks hit the ground, they exploded in a blinding flash of noise and flame, and although their power was small compared to that of the fireballs, their effect on an already demoralized foe was devastating. Many men were killed or horrendously burnt by the infernal missiles, but even more were trampled underfoot as their desperate comrades tried to run from this latest nightmare.

The ravaged remnants of the old guard's army fled in a full-scale retreat in the only direction still open to them – uphill – easy prey for the king's archers.

The newcomers had now stepped ashore, and were still hurling their deadly weapons. As Montfort paused, blood-stained and begrimed with mud and sweat, to stare at the unknown warriors, recognition dawned – and he made his way towards the leader of the group, a smile on his face for the first time that day.

Tarrant turned a smoke-blackened face towards his sovereign, and grinned.

'I should have known you'd be responsible for this!' Montfort said.

'Not me, sire,' the envoy replied. 'Two of your loyal subjects. You'll meet them later.'

'I shall look forward to it.'

'I'm sorry we couldn't get here any earlier,' Tarrant went on. 'Looks like we made it just in time.'

Montfort knew that for many loyal men Tarrant had come too late, but the amazing, unhoped-for reprieve still buoyed his spirits.

'I owe you a great debt,' he said, 'however it was done. After today, few of our enemies will relish facing an army with the gods of the Web on their side.' He glanced up to the western sky.

'A slight exaggeration, perhaps,' the envoy responded. 'But a useful idea.'

'Come, then,' Montfort concluded. 'Let's finish this business.'

With their swords in their hands, the two men strode towards the final slaughter.

* * *

By dusk, the vast majority of the rebels were dead, and the remainder scattered far and wide. Montfort's weary but joyful army returned to their abandoned camp, already recounting bloodthirsty tales of heroics and wonder. Each man knew that the next morning would see the start of their march back to Edgefield, but tonight was for celebration, albeit a sober one. Although their victory was complete, Montfort detailed guards throughout the night. He was taking no chances now.

The king and most of his captains retired to his tent to assess their losses. These were worse than he had feared. In spite of the final, resounding victory, their reduced numbers meant that the salt-rim defences would be severely weakened.

Tarrant entered the tent, together with Pike, and two people no one recognized.

'My lord, may I present Cluny and Anselma,' Tarrant announced grandly, ushering the newcomers forward. 'A couple with many and varied talents – one of which was the invention of the fire-weapons that came to your aid today.'

The alchemist and his wife bowed awkwardly, looking both proud and nervous. Mountfort quickly went to them, and took their hands in turn.

'You are indeed welcome,' he said. 'Tarrant has told me a little of your exploits, but I never dreamed . . . Without your help, our cause, our country, would have been lost today. Can you explain these miracles to us?'

'Not miracles, your majesty,' Cluny answered. 'Simply alchemical research and the higher arts.' Behind him, Tarrant smiled at the alchemist's pomposity.

'Experiment and application, sire,' Anselma explained. 'Fire is one of the simplest chemical reactions. All we had to do was harness it.'

'But what we witnessed today seemed far from simple!' the king replied. 'Please, tell us more.'

For the next hour, the strange, outlandishly dressed man and his more simply attired wife held forth on a subject that made their eyes flash with enthusiasm and ardour. Their audience listened, most understanding little of what they had heard but fascinated none the less. Montfort tried to follow their unstoppable flow of words, but found that his thoughts wandered occasionally. *There's madness in their eyes*, he mused, *as well as a great thirst for knowledge. I wonder if they could have foreseen the results of their experiments.*

Cluny and Anselma were explaining that certain elements would burn fiercely when combined, whereas others would expand, producing inflammable gases – air that burned, in fact. These effects were harmless enough in the open, but when they were confined the results were, quite literally, explosive. The couple went on to relate how they had been researching these phenomena for years, and that their efforts had been intensified in the last few months – especially since Tarrant had arranged for their secret departure from Edge. The results of their endeavours had been evident that afternoon.

'Of course, we shall need more time and resources if we are to make such weapons truly effective,' Anselma concluded.

'That was effective enough for me!' Montfort exclaimed.

'The large projectiles were propelled by a primitive catapult from the hill,' Cluny said. 'It has a limited range, and is clumsy and inaccurate. Hitting the bridge was the purest fluke.'

'Perhaps the gods really *are* on our side, then,' one of the captains commented softly.

'The hand-held weapons are more sophisticated,' Tarrant put in.

'Correct,' Anselma agreed. 'The reaction there is caused by impact.'

'So you must handle them carefully,' the envoy went on.

'A self-propelled projectile should be possible,' Anselma said. 'There is energy enough to spare. That would truly revolutionize . . .'

'I'm sorry, but we have no time for theory,' Montfort interrupted. 'War is upon us, and we need more of the weapons used today.'

'That may not be possible,' Cluny said, his face a picture of dismay. 'Our supplies are gone, and it will take days to gather more, to mix them and manufacture the containers.'

'Then let us hope we have those days,' the king replied. 'You will receive all the help you need. When our enemies from the south arrive, we will need every possible advantage.'

CHAPTER SIXTY-NINE

Arledge and his guides left Riano on the morning of the day of Montfort's battle. Although they had no knowledge of the remarkable events taking place on the far side of the salt, they were subdued by what they had learnt in the city.

Abstaining from their usual behaviour, the Archaeologists had gone about their business with quiet efficiency, and had proved adept at their new profession. The mercenary camps had been spied upon and their numbers estimated. The soldiers' restless inactivity had not gone unnoticed, nor had the endless variety of rumour circulating in the town. One of the most common concerned the monks. Little had been seen of them since their arrival, and this had only fuelled the fires of gossip. Many people believed that the brethren had magical powers which would protect the army from the dangers of the salt-flats, and therefore could not understand their delay in marching north. Others said that the monks were, even now, performing arcane rituals in order to establish the most propitious time for the crossing. Arledge believed the reasons for the delay to be more mundane. Somehow, Jarlath must have learnt of Montfort's march upon Edge, and was waiting to be sure of his position. By now, Arledge hoped, the northern rim of the salt would be in loyal hands, but even so, he was dismayed by the size and strength of the baron's army.

During their stay in the city, Arledge and his group had avoided the castle, not wishing to share Davin's fate, and had also stayed away from the other Archaeologists in Riano. They had no wish to be recruited to help guide the rebel forces across the salt! Indeed, Peyton and his men avoided all their normal haunts, and amused themselves by pretending to be carpenters or farmers visiting from the country.

When the time came, they left town quietly, keeping away from the commonly used roads, and heading for the salt by a roundabout route.

'To Edgefield?' Peyton asked once they were clear of any possible eavesdroppers.

'Yes,' Arledge replied. 'Montfort won't like our news, but it's important that it reaches him as soon as possible.'

'Do you think we might meet some of Jarlath's spies coming back the other way?' Holmes asked hopefully.

'If we do,' Peyton replied, smiling, 'we can take care of them, eh?'

'It'll be a pleasure,' Holmes replied.

Peyton led his party on to the salt.

* * *

'My men grow restless,' Olin said, in a dangerously quiet voice.

'I am expecting news within the next day or two,' Jarlath snapped, barely able to contain his anger. 'In the meantime, I insist that you control your men.'

The mercenaries had been in Riano for seven days now, and the baron was aware of the tensions building up between them and the local people. Their alien presence was also putting an increasing strain upon his ability to provide for the armies, and his stores were running low. Jarlath was having to pay the mercenaries during their enforced idleness, and while the money in itself was of little concern – he had treasure enough for a dozen wars – the waste still rankled.

'We came to fight a war,' Nur growled. 'To claim the bounty of our courage and skill, not to sit around in stinking camps.'

'You were the ones who refused to cross the salt,' Jarlath pointed out.

'And it was you who had forgotten to tell us of its dangers,' Olin shot back.

'So we sit in the mud being paid a pittance,' Nur spat. The younger of the mercenary leaders had been drinking, and his face was an angry red.

Jarlath looked from one to the other uneasily, feeling as though he had invited a pair of wolves to share his home.

'The rewards will be plentiful once Montfort has been defeated,' he said coolly, trying to pacify his volatile allies. 'You will not regret your journey.'

'Our journeys are *always* worthwhile,' Olin replied, the threat barely concealed. 'And this one will be no exception. I shall see to that.'

The mercenaries left then, leaving the baron to fume impotently.

When the day comes that I no longer have need of you, he promised them silently, *then you will not live to see nightfall!*

* * *

Elsewhere in Riano, another discussion was taking place.

'We can brook no further delay,' the abbot grated. 'Our powers will begin to wane within a few days, and we have spent too long in their preparation to waste them now.'

'We will march soon,' Hakon replied determinedly, 'no matter what message comes from the north.'

'How can you be so sure?' the ancient monk asked.

'Because all men – even barons and mercenary generals – can be persuaded if sufficient . . . pressure – is exerted,' the chamberlain replied.

The abbot's bony face registered shock.

'You would make such a sacrifice now?' he asked. 'Even *your* strength would be dangerously weakened by such an act.' Both of them knew that using their sorcery to directly influence the minds of other men would mean such a drain on a brother's power that it would take him months to recover.

'Raliel has the skill.'

'But it will mean his doom!'

'Undoubtedly,' Hakon answered calmly. 'But our cause is greater than the worth of any single brother. He will be prepared to do whatever is necessary.'

* * *

When the fair arrived at the remains of the battlefield, passing dreadful scenes of carnage, they stared in horror at the mass of dead bodies and the inexplicable craters in the valley floor. Wisps of smoke still rose, looking like ghosts in the pale morning sunlight.

A few local people were around, burying corpses and scavenging for valuables, but the fair did not linger. Everyone knew that their dream-weaver had to reach Edgefield as soon as possible – and no one felt inclined to argue with her.

Once across the river, the travelling was easy and they made good time. The wagons rolled into their usual site beside the town in the early evening, only two hours after the last of Montfort's returning army. Rebecca and Emer were in a state of great anxiety, and went straight to the castle, with Galen at their side. Spike had been left behind, much to his annoyance.

There were soldiers everywhere in the town and signs of the recent conflict could be seen at every turn. A few buildings had been burnt to the ground, and many more had suffered some damage. Arrows still protruded from some wooden doors and walls, and there were dark stains on the cobblestones. The quiet atmosphere was balanced somewhere between shock and mourning.

The sentries on the castle gates did not recognize the three friends, but it took the baron's daughter only a few words to gain admittance. Ellard was summoned, and he hurried across the courtyard to greet them, then led them to one of the smaller rooms in Baldemar's apartments. They were all nervous, especially Galen. It was the first time he had returned to his former home since the fateful chess game.

Ellard knocked, but got no response. He opened the door, glanced inside, then stood aside to let Rebecca pass. Her father was slumped in a chair, a bottle and glass on a table by his side. On the other side of the table, also sprawled in a comfortable chair, was Scuttle. He was cradling his own glass, and his expression showed a similar mixture of drunkenness and blank despondency. Both men were staring into space, and a stranger would have had difficulty in deciding who was the master and who the servant. It was a tableau that would have been unthinkable only a few days before.

Baldemar looked up slowly as his daughter entered, and his face came alive as he got to his feet. Scuttle also noticed Rebecca's arrival and started to rise, but then apparently thought better of it. He sat down again and poured himself another drink.

The baron stared at her, and his eyes had lost their haunted appearance now. When he spoke, it was in a voice so quiet that it was barely audible.

'Gods, Rebecca. I thought I had lost you too.'

Rebecca was shocked. She hardly knew this man. And her astonishment increased when he held out his arms in an oddly childlike gesture of welcome. Feeling as though she was in a dream, Rebecca went to him and was enfolded by his large but gentle arms. She returned his embrace gingerly, not sure how to deal with this unexpected show of affection.

'I'm glad you're here,' Baldemar said simply, a catch in his voice.

'So am I, Father.' She looked up at him, and saw that he had tears in his eyes. 'Are you all right?'

The baron did not answer. He had seen Emer and Galen hesitating in the doorway. There was no anger in his gaze, only a guilty sadness.

'Radd . . .' he began softly.

'Where is he?' Emer asked.

Wordlessly, Baldemar led them to the adjoining room. Nursey was sitting at the bedside, her face grave. She glanced up as they came in, and when she saw the girls, her expression wavered between delight and sadness. Emer rushed forward, to where Radd lay quite still beneath the blankets, his face bruised and scarred. Sightless eyes stared at the ceiling, and for a dreadful moment Emer thought he was dead, but then she saw the minute rise and fall of his chest. She looked at Nursey, fear in her eyes.

'He's been like this for seven days now,' the old woman told her, shaking her head.

Emer took her father's hand in her own, and felt another wave of fear at its chill.

'He will wake up though, won't he?' she pleaded.

'I don't know, little one,' Nursey replied gravely. 'It's in the hands of the Web.'

'But there must be *something* we can do!' Emer cried.

'I've tried all I know, sweetheart,' Nursey answered sadly.

Rebecca joined them at the bedside, and put an arm around Emer's shoulders. It was the only way she could think to comfort her. No words seemed adequate. For herself, she was desperately disappointed as well as distressed for her friend. Now there was no hope of finding the book.

'How did it happen?' Emer whispered.

'I don't rightly know,' Nursey replied, 'but I know that Cranne wanted him to talk, and he wouldn't.'

'I'll kill him!' Emer spat.

'No need, my dear,' the old woman told her. 'Cranne must be dead already. Rode off on to the salt like a madman!'

Emer relaxed slightly at this, and Rebecca felt a wave of relief. Her thoughts returned to their main reason for coming back to Edge.

'I must talk to Montfort,' she said quietly. 'Will you come?'

'No. I'll stay here,' her friend replied, still gazing at her father's face.

Rebecca nodded, then turned to Ellard.

'Is the king here?'

'Yes, my lady. I'll take you to him.'

Rebecca glanced at the others.

'I'll stay here,' Galen said, indicating Emer.

'Father?'

'This business is beyond me,' the baron replied. 'I've played the part of the fool for too long, and now there's nothing I can do. Must you involve yourself?'

'I have no choice.'

Baldemar bowed his head in acceptance, and Rebecca felt sorry for him for the first time in her life. She knew, however, that this was not the time to show her compassion. She had more important concerns now. *Perhaps it's better that I do this on my own,* she thought.

'I'll come back as soon as I can,' she told him, then followed Ellard into the corridor.

As they left, the captain turned back to Galen and smiled.

'I'll want a report from you later,' he said. 'You've done well.'

Galen's thoughts were elsewhere, and he did not respond.

Ellard showed Rebecca into what had been Baldemar's study, and Montfort and Tarrant stood as she entered, their faces registering surprise, then pleasure.

'Welcome, Rebecca,' the king said. 'We had not hoped to see you so soon.'

'Thank you, sire.' Rebecca curtseyed.

'Welcome home,' Tarrant greeted her. 'How did life in the fair suit you?'

'Better than I could have dreamt possible,' she replied, then laughed at her own words and was forced to explain to the puzzled men.

'So dream-weaving has been added to the list of your accomplishments,' Montfort commented.

Rebecca thought she detected a hint of scepticism, but chose to ignore it.

'My *only* accomplishment,' she replied.

'Hardly . . . ' Tarrant began.

'I have important matters to discuss,' Rebecca interrupted him, suddenly impatient.

'We all do,' the king said calmly. 'And while I do not doubt your talents, I don't see how they can help our present situation.'

'But they *can!*' she said eagerly, then went on, more nervously. 'You face a magical as well as a human threat.'

Montfort's face creased in a frown.

'I have no time for this, Rebecca.'

'Please! Just listen for a few moments,' she insisted. 'We've discovered so much . . . ' She glanced hopefully at Tarrant.

'I always thought Rebecca was special, sire,' the envoy said. 'What harm can it do to hear what she has to say?'

'Not you too?' Montfort groaned. 'I have had enough of omens and the like from the gossip-mongers.'

'Please, my lord,' Rebecca tried again. 'I wanted to tell you in Garadun – in the garden, remember? – but I know so much more now. And you do indeed need help. We *all* do.'

The memory of their early morning talk clearly struck a chord.

'Very well.' He waved her to a seat. 'What have you to say?'

Rebecca plunged into the story of her dreams, the myths of Derith, the Okran Stones, Annis and Kedar, and all that she had discovered over the past few days. In her haste, some of the facts were garbled, and she watched as Montfort's patience waned, though he spoke little. To her disappointment, Tarrant remained silent throughout, offering no encouragement or support. When she told them of her dreams of the king's son, Montfort interrupted her.

'For the Web's sake, don't tell any of my advisers about that!' he remarked. 'They'll force me to marry before we fight!' He laughed, but Rebecca was not amused. She realized that she had made little impression, and that he had humoured her only out of politeness. She felt humiliated.

'I'm serious,' she protested angrily.

'Listen, Rebecca,' Montfort began, his face solemn now. 'I'll admit that you've uncovered some remarkable co-incidences, and some even more colourful tales, but none of it will matter once Jarlath and his mercenaries march over the salt. *That's* the reality we face.'

'No!' she cried. 'You have to see . . . '

'No, *you* must see, young lady,' he interrupted firmly. 'What is it, when all is said and done, that you have? Some legends, a few artefacts from a lost city and some "wizards", who by their own admission are not very powerful. Your own talents are remarkable, and I'll admit that the human mind may be capable of things that I do not understand – but even your most dramatic discovery is quite useless. The stones' message is hardly less obscure when translated than when it was a complete puzzle! We face an army of flesh and blood, swords and arrows, not demons or mythical cities. I do not fear Derith or Tyrrell. They have been dead and buried for centuries. It is Jarlath who frightens me – and would frighten you too if you had any sense.'

Rebecca sat stunned and speechless, tears of anger and frustration brimming in her eyes. Then a new resolve grew within her. *I have not come this far to fail now,* she vowed. *I will win this argument yet!*

'Forgive me for wasting your time, your majesty,' she said formally. 'I am sorry to have troubled you.'

She stood up and curtseyed, then walked to the door with all the dignity she could muster. After she had made her exit, both men looked at the door for a few moments.

'Gods, but she's pretty,' Montfort breathed.

'Yes,' Tarrant said. 'She is.'

CHAPTER SEVENTY

Jarlath derived great pleasure from his urgent summons to Olin and Nur, carefully calculating the timing of his message so that it would interrupt their evening meal. The news the baron had received was good; not perfect, but good.

The foreign generals arrived, their expressions wary, while Jarlath smiled inwardly. It had been two days since their last acrimonious exchange. When Hakon entered the chamber, looking flustered, the baron's pleasure increased. *For once the monks have not intercepted my messages.* His complacency wavered slightly when Raliel followed his master into the room. *Why has Hakon brought his assistant?* The chamberlain's aide looked nervous, and his face glistened unnaturally. *What's the matter with him?* Jarlath wondered, before turning back to the southerners.

'Good news, I trust, Baron?' Olin asked, his voice deceptively mild.

'Indeed it is,' Jarlath replied, beaming. 'My scouts returned this afternoon. As we suspected, Montfort holds Edge.' He paused, enjoying his audience's consternation – and noticing that Raliel flinched at his words.

'You call this good news?' Nur asked sarcastically.

'In itself, no,' the baron replied. 'It was merely inevitable. However, reports from our northern allies confirm that they have managed to do more than create a diversion. They have defeated Montfort's outlying detachments and are now marching towards Edge. His forces are already stretched. If we attack from both sides, he will be overwhelmed, crushed like an insect beneath our heels.'

'We march, then?' Nur demanded, fire blazing in his cold eyes.

'At daybreak tomorrow,' Jarlath confirmed. He noticed that Raliel had relaxed visibly, his expression drawn into as near a smile as his emaciated features could manage. *Why so relieved?* the baron wondered, then dismissed the monk from his mind. 'If you can be ready by then,' he added, needling his arrogant allies still further.

Nur bridled, an angry retort on his lips, but his partner restrained him with a small gesture.

'We will be ready,' Olin stated evenly.

The mercenary leaders left without further ado and Hakon turned to his assistant.

'You may go now,' he rasped. 'Inform the brethren that the time for action has come.'

Raliel hurried away to do his master's bidding.

'So it begins,' Hakon said. The chamberlain seemed inordinately pleased, but Jarlath was too busy gloating at his own prospects to notice the gleam in the monk's eyes.

'Yes,' he replied. 'You will soon be chamberlain to the king!'

* * *

Arledge and his spies arrived in Edgefield the day after Rebecca, and their detailed reports of the enemy's strength only confirmed Montfort's worst fears. His forces would be badly overmatched, and he would have to make use of every possible advantage to have any hope of victory. The salt-defences were his only tactical benefit, but he knew that a concentrated attack by the rebel forces could breach that thin line. The king was left to hope that Cluny, now working feverishly back at his old home, would once more provide timely and miraculous aid.

In the meantime, all Montfort could do was prepare his positions as best he could, and somehow try to outguess or outmanoeuvre his enemy. To this end, he assigned Arledge and his guides to look-out duty on the salt. The Archaelogists went willingly, enjoying their new adventurous role. Before they left the castle, they made a point of finding their former colleague.

'Hello, young lubber!' Holmes greeted Galen. 'Having a

nice rest while we do all the work?'

The young man grinned.

'I've not been idle,' he protested.

'Gods. Look at that smile!' Milner exclaimed. 'He's obviously found both his women.'

'He looks so tired, poor lad,' Holmes added.

'Join us if you can,' Peyton said, a twinkle in his eye. 'We're short-handed, and these northerners . . . ' He indicated Arledge, ' . . . are all right, but they've no feeling for the salt.' He was teasing. The soldier and the Archaeologists had become firm friends.

'You think they can stand the pace, Arledge?' Galen asked.

'They're an undisciplined lot,' the soldier replied, 'but I'll knock 'em into shape eventually.'

After they had parted company, amid much laughter, Galen went on to Radd's house.

Rebecca and Emer were already there. The girls had spent a miserable night. Emer had shared Nursey's vigil at her father's bedside, but there had been no change in his condition. Rebecca had spent time with her own father, trying to get to know this strange man. She was pleased by some of the changes in him, but annoyed by his self-imposed weakness. It was as though the events which had robbed him of his arrogance and cruelty had also drained his determination and spirit. He refused to discuss it, and Rebecca found him difficult to deal with, especially as she was still fuming over Montfort's rejection. When she had eventually given up and gone to bed in Radd's room, sleep was a long time coming. Her dreams were full of blood and pain, birth and death, with several scenes repeated or superimposed confusingly. Amidst all this had been brief images of paintings coming to life, and, more reassuringly, scenes from the fair. Even from a distance, she was keeping a watch upon the women there.

In the morning, she had persuaded Emer to help her look for *Beneath the Salt*. For the next few hours, they had ransacked Radd's library, study and bedroom, and had searched any likely hiding places in the other rooms. Their hunt proved unsuccessful, however, so they returned to the library to see if there was anything of use in the other books.

It was a mammoth task; there were so many that they hardly knew where to begin, and even those in the previously locked cupboard proved unenlightening. They continued half-heartedly, while Rebecca complained of Montfort's stubbornness. She had expected support from her friend, but Emer was preoccupied.

'If *you* can't persuade him, Becky, then we wouldn't stand a chance,' she said resignedly, then brightened as Galen came in. He hugged her, and smiled at Rebecca.

'How are you getting on?' he asked.

'Nothing,' Rebecca answered, her impatience mollified somewhat by the sight of her two friends together. At least something in the world was as it should be.

Galen told them of his meeting with the Archaeologists, and of the grave news they had brought with them.

'Montfort will never listen to me now,' Rebecca said dismally. 'We have to give him *proof*, something definite.'

'There's one other bit of news,' Galen added. 'Cluny's back in town.'

'Perhaps *he* can help,' Emer suggested. 'After all, he's supposed to be an expert on stuff like this.'

'I doubt it,' Galen responded. 'He's got his hands full at the moment.' He explained about the weapons the alchemist had created, and the effect they had had on the battle.

'That explains the craters,' Emer remarked, finding it hard to imagine a weapon that powerful.

'Even so, it must be worth a try,' Rebecca persisted. 'I'm sure he'd help us if he could.'

Their speculation was interrupted by a timid knock at the library door, and they all looked up expectantly just as Milden's head peered round.

'They said I might find you here,' the archivist said.

'Milden!' Rebecca was delighted to see him. 'Come in.' She introduced Emer and Galen, and the newcomer bowed uncertainly.

'Pack that in,' Emer told him good-naturedly. 'We're riff-raff!'

'What are you doing here?' Rebecca asked.

For a moment, Milden eagerly scanned the bookshelves, but then he turned back to her.

'I've something to show you that you might find of interest.' He reached into his robe and pulled out a leather pouch. Inside was a letter. 'I've been doing a lot of thinking since your visit, and I reached the conclusion that what you were looking for must have been important. Recent events confirmed this – and so I came looking for you.'

'What is it?' Rebecca asked impatiently.

'Remember the Okran Stones?' Milden asked.

'Yes,' she replied eagerly.

'I was going through some ancient correspondence, cataloguing anything that looked interesting, and I found this. It mentions another stone in passing, as a curiosity. It's different from the ones I know about.'

'You've found the missing stone?' Rebecca exclaimed. She took the proffered letter and carefully opened the fragile parchment, trying not to raise her hopes too high. *It might be one we already know about.*

But a new set of letters stared back at her – though her first glance told her that this was not the set she had expected.

```
E  B  A  L  A
E  S  N  N
S  R  E  C  V
A  H  E  I
E  F  T  N  E
```

'Well?' Emer demanded.

'It's a seventh!' she replied.

'Gods. How many more are there?' her friend exclaimed.

'What does it say?' Galen asked.

Milden gave him a sharp look.

'You've translated them?' he asked incredulously.

'Yes,' Emer replied proudly. 'We've six of them now, but the third is still missing.'

' "Three balance ancient fears",' Rebecca quoted.

'Show me!' Milden demanded, so Rebecca explained the stones' secret, and told him the whole sequence.

'Remarkable!' he breathed.

'So if this is the last one, then the message ends like this,' Emer said thoughtfully. ' "One magic fate in terror lies; two parts sift to face the foe; three balance ancient fears." '

'It keeps coming back to *threes*,' Galen put in. 'Three wizards in Derith born, three of us, three men on the stone carving.'

'Even the triangles in the design,' Emer added.

'We need Newell!' Rebecca burst out, filled with a sudden conviction. 'Annis, Kedar and Newell. It was three wizards then who started all this. There must be three now to finish it.'

'When we found Annis,' Emer said, as eager as her friend now, 'she was scared stiff on her own. "One magic fate in terror lies"!'

'Then, when Kedar joined her, we all had that feeling of searching. Sifting,' Rebecca went on. 'That's when we made our discoveries, and realized what we were facing.'

'But to balance it all, we need the third,' Emer concluded triumphantly.

'It *has* to be him,' Rebecca said. 'We must find him!'

They all turned to look at Tarrant.

'Newell,' Rebecca explained. 'He's a musician – and the third part of the wizards' power!'

'Better not let Montfort hear you talking like that,' he said drily.

'Will you help?' she asked, ignoring his comment.

'If I can.'

'Then you believe me?'

'I believe that your ideas are worth listening to,' the royal envoy replied. 'But you must admit that some of your conclusions do seem a bit far-fetched.'

'They won't seem far-fetched when Derith rises and we're not prepared,' she retorted.

'How can you prepare for something like that?' Tarrant asked mildly.

'That's what we're trying to find out!' Rebecca pointed out forcefully.

'All right. All right,' he said, holding his hands up defensively. 'Tell me why Newell is so important.'

Rebecca explained her theory, with occasional help from Emer and Galen.

'And you agree with all this?' Tarrant asked Milden when she had finished. The two men obviously knew each other.

'I'd like to,' the archivist replied hesitantly. 'There's a lot

I don't know yet, and more that I don't understand, but until now my life has all been concerned with books. When it suddenly becomes real, it's rather frightening.' He paused, then added, 'But it *is* real.'

Tarrant nodded, his expression thoughtful.

'Right. Where do we look for Newell then?' he asked.

'He was here with a group of musicians when Father and I got back from Garadun,' Rebecca answered, delighted that he had agreed to help. 'That was about twelve days ago. But then Farrand attacked us, and I don't know if anyone's seen him since.'

'Let's hope he wasn't killed,' Emer said.

Rebecca's heart sank. *Perhaps that's why my dreams haven't been able to reach him.*

'We'll find him,' Tarrant reassured her. 'Pike is very good at that sort of thing,' he added confidently.

'Thank you,' Rebecca said. 'Can you arrange for rooms for Annis and Kedar?'

The envoy nodded, smiling to himself.

'What are you smiling at?' she asked.

'I was thinking that you are a very different young lady from the one I first met,' he answered. 'I rather like being ordered about by such a beautiful woman.'

'Then get started!' she commanded, laughing. *Have I really changed so much?*

Tarrant saluted, bowed formally and edged out of the room backwards.

'Stop it, you idiot,' Rebecca told him as she followed him out.

'Where are we going?' Emer asked her.

'To see a mad alchemist,' Rebecca replied.

'Is he in on this too?' Tarrant asked.

'Yes,' Galen replied. 'He was the one who showed me the first stone.'

'Well, don't take up too much of his time,' the envoy advised. 'He's very busy at the moment, and what he's doing is extremely important.'

'We know,' Rebecca replied, undeterred. 'But so is this.'

'And be careful,' Tarrant added. 'I've seen the results of some of his inventions. I wouldn't like you to be caught up in one of his less *controlled* experiments.'

CHAPTER SEVENTY-ONE

Galen and his companions knew that they had reached the right place when a roar sounded from the basement room, quickly followed by billows of smoke.

He had led them through the streets of the town, and some of Edgefield's inhabitants had recognized various members of the party. Most stared curiously, especially at Rebecca, but she was too deep in thought to notice. Others called out their support, referring back to the chess game as well as to more recent events. Galen waved to some, replied in kind to others, and generally enjoyed his public return to the town. By contrast, Milden was silent, looking around with interest but not meeting any of the onlookers' stares. He was not used to being the centre of attention.

By the time they had reached the end of the alchemist's street, they had acquired an entourage of small children, who giggled, pointed and made comments as they capered along. However, when Galen's eventual destination became clear, the children melted away. There were soldiers at the end of the street, suspicious of anyone who approached too closely. Galen was relieved to see that he knew one of the guards, and explained to him that Tarrant had given them permission to visit Cluny. It was near enough to the truth; at least the king's envoy had not objected.

While the soldiers were obviously one reason for the emptiness of the street, it now became clear that ordinary common sense would have kept most people away. When they had recovered from the shock of the explosion, and the smoke had begun to clear, Galen led his friends down the steps to the cluttered basement. The eccentric room was even more of a shambles than usual. Anselma was nowhere to be seen, but Cluny was frantically beating out flames coming from the bed. In the centre of the room stood a strange, metallic contraption, from which more smoke was leaking gently. There were chunks missing from the stone-work of two of the walls.

'This is the man who will win the war for Montfort?' Emer whispered incredulously.

'Hello!' Galen called, but the alchemist did not hear him, too concerned with his efforts with the smouldering blankets. However, Anselma came in from the store-room, a jar of powder in each hand, apparently quite calm in spite of the mayhem around her. She saw Galen at once.

'Clue!' she called. 'We have visitors.'

Her husband completed his fire-fighting with one last thwack and turned to face his guests. His clothes and hair were slightly singed, but his grimy face lit up with pleasure when he saw Galen.

'My friend! Welcome!' he boomed, then noticed Rebecca, and bowed. 'My lady, I am honoured.'

The baron's daughter stepped forward.

'This is not the occasion for formalities,' she said. 'I need your help and advice.'

'Anything!' he responded eagerly, and made an ineffectual attempt to clear some room for his visitors to sit down, while Galen made the necessary introductions. Anselma made no attempt to help her husband, knowing the task to be hopeless, but contented herself with placing the jars carefully on a table and nodding a welcome to each of her guests. Eventually they all sat in a circle on the floor.

'So,' Anselma said. 'The three chess players. We've wanted to meet you for a long time.'

'A lot has happened since then,' Rebecca stated.

'Tell us,' Cluny said eagerly, adding, 'Please, my lady,' as an afterthought.

'How is your work on the weapons progressing?' she asked.

'We've done everything possible until new supplies arrive,' Anselma answered. 'Now, tell us everything.'

So the three friends related their tale of discovery once more, while the alchemist, his friend and Milden – for whom most of the story was new – listened avidly. Galen produced the tablet he had found, and compared it to Cluny's; the stone was the same size, and the craftsmanship identical. The listeners became increasingly impressed by Rebecca's dream-weaving talent, the way in which the riddle of the stones had been solved, and how all the other elements seemed to fit into a frighteningly plausible pattern. They agreed that they needed to find Newell, the missing stone and *Beneath the Salt*, but argued that there were several possible interpretations of the facts.

'We've always known of the cyclical theory of history,' Anselma said, 'but we've never come across anything as specific as the other Rebecka.'

'It's all very confusing,' Cluny added. 'The tide of magic has definitely been on the rise for some time now, and you and your friends are obviously one manifestation of it. But there must be more to it than that.'

Their discussion was interrupted then by a delivery of boxes. The soldiers who carried them in cast anxious glances at the chaos in the room, and left as quickly as they could after Anselma had supervised the unloading of a bewildering array of unknown substances.

'Don't put those two so close together!' she shouted at one point, making the soldier concerned jump nervously.

'Duty calls,' Cluny remarked gleefully, rubbing his hands in anticipation. 'We promised Montfort, you know. Work, work, work!'

'Come back in the morning,' Anselma told Rebecca. 'We'll have finished this lot by then, and we might have thought of something useful.'

'Where's the brazier?' her husband asked, already intent on his experiments.

'Where it landed,' his wife replied matter-of-factly.

'Come on!' Galen urged. 'Let's get out of here.' In spite of their lack of progress, his companions did not feel inclined to argue. Galen left the stone and the half-fossilized book behind, knowing that the alchemist was fascinated by them.

When they returned to the castle, they went straight to visit Radd. There was no change in his condition, but Nursey told them that Annis and Kedar had arrived, so they went in search of the two wizards. They were found in the servants' quarters, where Annis was sitting with a small child on her knee and others about her feet, telling a story about a tiny dragon 'no bigger than my fist'. Kedar sat cross-legged on the floor, sketching the scene.

They waited until the tale was finished, then prised Annis away and brought the wizards up to date. As evening wore on, the conversation turned to more practical matters.

'Have rooms been assigned to you yet?' Rebecca asked.

Milden replied that he was already installed in a room in the main building, and took his leave, explaining that he had some reading to do, but the other two shook their heads.

'We can all stay at my house,' Emer suggested. 'My father isn't going to object, is he?' She forced a wan smile, and added, 'There's more than enough space for you all, especially as Galen will be sharing my room.'

'And Kedar mine,' Annis said shyly.

'That's settled then,' Emer concluded, grinning at the story-teller. 'You can have my father's room again if you like, Becky.'

Rebecca nodded unthinkingly, trying not to let her feelings show. She was happy for the love and comfort her friends had found in each other, but she felt left out, awkward – and jealous. *Wonderful!* she thought, hiding behind her smile. *Now I get to play chaperone to two loving couples!*

* * *

The dream began in much the same way as that of the previous night, but this time it was much clearer. Rebecca saw the births of three babies, two boys and a girl. The events were simultaneous yet separate, each birth overseen by three old men who nodded approvingly. They were present at each nativity, yet unseen, unheard and unrecognized. The ancients faded, changed, becoming sticklike creatures, like the drawings of a child. Then they turned around, their heads linked by a triangle of light, before disappearing altogether. And yet Rebecca sensed that their presence remained within the dream, aloof guardians to the three stories that were unfolding. Although each strand of the dream was separate and recognizable as such, yet each life was woven into the pattern of the other two. Each was unaware and unfulfilled, complete only in their unknown comradeship.

The three stories were played out simultaneously, their realities superimposed, but Rebecca was not confused. *Seeing the past in dreams.*

Kedar had had an unhappy childhood. He had been born into a poor household, the third son of a farm labourer. He had discovered his artistic talent very early, and was forever making patterns, shapes and pictures with any material that came to hand – much to the annoyance of his parents. For much of his young life, he regarded his obsessive gift as a curse. He tried to join in with the children around him, but was constantly rejected. They did not understand him, and he had no real interest in their rough-and-tumble games. Even his brothers bullied him, mocking him whenever he tried to explain his pictures. Eventually the young artist developed a terrible stutter, and then withdrew into virtual silence. His father was unsympathetic and grew increasingly aggrieved by his son's failure to complete the tasks assigned to him, to pull his weight in the toil of their ever-expanding family. He took to shutting the boy away in a store-cupboard as punishment when beatings proved ineffective. Kedar cried in the darkness, prey to nightmares and a fear of blindness.

He finally escaped when he was eight years old. For a pitifully small fee, his parents apprenticed him to a journeyman painter who had recognized the boy's immense talent. He then proceeded to exploit it to the full, and Kedar's life became an endless round of drudgery. He was able to use his talent, but not in the way he would have wished, and his master often took the credit for his work. The boy's existence was made tolerable by the few secret moments he had to paint for himself.

Three years later, an elderly painter named Edel made Kedar's master an offer he could not refuse, and acquired the young man's contract. He immediately released him from it, giving him freedom for the first time in his young life. Kedar was stunned, grateful and frightened all at the same time, but the kindly old man treated him like a grandson and taught him much, including the true value of dedication. He also introduced him to the secrets of the Heretics. Edel was rewarded with a fierce loyalty and love that lasted until his death – and beyond. Kedar grieved for him still, remembering him as more of a father than his real sire.

The young man was now alone in the world, and he began a life of travel, living from his ever-growing skill, and gaining in confidence as the months went by. When he discovered his wizardry – by mistake – he was not frightened, but incredibly excited. He treasured the infrequent moments of magic, and became even more dedicated to his craft. His stutter was less pronounced, and he grew into an attractive young man who made many friends but formed no lasting attachments.

And he painted. Sketches, portraits, commissions, landscapes, and scenes drawn purely from his imagination. And to each he added his own mark, the emblem of the Heretics.

Rebecca's dream drew close to the present. Baldemar's portrait appeared briefly, and later the fair, and Kedar's meeting with Annis. Two strands had come together at last.

Although Annis's own story began in different circumstances, it was nevertheless similar in many ways. She had been born to well-to-do parents, her father being cousin to a minor nobleman. Learning to talk at an incredibly young age had ensured her popularity for a while, as an exhibit to be paraded before her parents' guests for their amusement and praise. However, her fertile tongue soon began to get her into trouble. She invented stories and told them incessantly to anyone within earshot, or to herself if she lacked an audience. While other children of her age played, she talked. The persistent, noisy child soon found that she was ostracized, and realized that the adults no longer found her entertaining.

After a time, her parents rejected her completely in favour of their more convenient children. Annis was sometimes cared for, sometimes neglected, by a succession of nannies, and was finally sent away, with most of the household believing her to be insane. 'She's living in her own world,' the servants whispered as they watched her go. The asylum to which she was sent proved fascinating at first, filled with people who were apparently interested in her stories, but before long Annis realized that this was a place of horror, and managed to escape.

She almost starved to death, living on her wits but very confused. A shepherd's hut provided refuge for one hard winter, but then she found the fair, and realized that she had a home at last. She found security in the constant movement and in the collection of eccentric travellers, and she learned to use her talent wisely, to know the value of silence and of friendship. Strangers always made her nervous, though, and she avoided telling stories in their company, preferring the ever-appreciative amd well-known audience of her companions.

Rebecca's dream drew close to the present, and she saw her own appearance, sensed the terror as she forced Annis to re-evaluate her life. Then Kedar arrived, bringing both a lessening of the fear and an ill-defined longing. Now they were together in reality as well as in the dream.

Newell's story lacked the overt cruelty of the other two, but was somehow the saddest of them all. He had been the only child of a successful merchant, and his early years had been happy enough. Later, music came to rule his life, and he showed absolutely no interest in trade. At the age of fourteen, after a blazing row with his father, he had walked out of their home, leaving his mother heartbroken. He was never to return.

Newell joined up with various groups of musicians, but did not stay long with any. He was brilliant, but restless and increasingly bitter. His own music consumed him, transported him to new worlds where he could forget his imperfect eyesight and soar on the wings of his imagination. The confines of the traditional music he was forced to play grated on his nerves, and gained him a reputation for being difficult.

The young man's only other obsession was history. He had become aware of the Heretics, and idolized the old masters – painters and storytellers as well as musicians – learning all he could about them.

His talent was always recognized – but not his magic. He made few friends, and earned the rather sarcastic nickname of Boomer. He was often filled with despair, but his talent drew him on, always searching, always yearning – and never content.

Rebecca's dream drew close to the present. She experienced once more the wizardry of his playing in the Great Hall, relived their meeting and unfortunate separation. She saw him put Radd to sleep, then go to the kennels to look for Old Growler. When he came out again, the yard was unusually busy, and he soon found himself in the midst of fighting. His only thought was to rescue his precious, unique viol, and so he escaped from the yard and plunged into the servants' quarters. His fellow musicians had already left, and he snatched up his instrument and fled, only to be confronted by a large soldier, bearing the emblem of a white wolf on his chest. Newell was unarmed, but the soldier still attacked him. The musician tried to avoid the sword's blow, and instinctively defended himself with the only thing possible. The sword shattered the viol, but left the young man unscathed as he fell to the floor.

The soldier moved on, and Newell ran for his life, tears of fury and resentment in his eyes. His only thought was to travel north, to the only man who could replace his lost treasure.

The dream drew a veil over the end of his story.

* * *

Rebecca awoke, touched with the contentment of Kedar and Annis, but sharing the unrelenting anger of Newell.

'He's heading for Garadun!' she said aloud. 'He's *days* away!'

She rose quickly and went in search of Tarrant, blurting out her dream-tossed discovery.

'Pike's already on his trail,' the envoy told her calmly. 'One of the musicians thought he'd go to the capital to get a new instrument. '

Rebecca nodded vigorously.

'You have to bring him back,' she said, now more certain than ever that the three wizards belonged together.

'We're doing all we can,' Tarrant assured her.

But we haven't got much time, she thought anxiously.

Cluny and Anselma had worked through most of the night, and then had slept for a while on the now cleared bed. A few hours later, they rose with the sun and organized the collection of their valuable produce by the soldiers.

'Don't drop them!' Cluny advised jovially as the specially prepared boxes were carried out. It did not seem much to spread amongst an entire army, but if used well the weapons would at least provide an element of surprise.

Cluny caught sight of the artefacts Galen had left the previous evening, and picked up the stone-hard book.

'I wonder . . . ' he murmured, turning it over in his hands.

'There's no time for that now,' Anselma reminded him. 'This mixture is volatile!'

The alchemist went back to work willingly enough, but an hour later, with yet another experiment completed, they decided to have a break and Cluny went back to the book.

'If we tried some of that green stuff that ate a hole in the floor . . . ' he began.

'Be careful, Clue,' Anselma warned, but half-heartedly; she was obviously as intrigued as her husband.

The corrosive mixture was found and a few drops carefully administered. It fizzled quietly in the book's cracks, a few popping sounds preceding curls of acrid fumes. The alchemist placed the book in the sealed chamber he called his 'oven', and left it while they found themselves some food. Then he donned heavy gloves and took the book out. His efforts to prise open the pages proved unsuccessful, and he muttered crossly to himself. Anselma watched carefully, thought she saw one of the cracks widen minutely, and went off to the tool rack. She returned with a large mallet and a steel chisel.

'Try this,' she advised. 'As if you were splitting slate.'

'You're a genius, my love,' her husband replied.

'When all else fails,' she answered, 'hit it hard with something heavy.'

They exchanged smiles, then Cluny lined the chisel up just behind the book's front cover.

'Here goes.'

588

He struck sharply, and with a loud crack the front binding sheared away completely, exposing the title page of fossilized parchment.

'Well I never!' Cluny breathed.

They stared at the page, on which seven circles were clearly inscribed, each with a familiar jumble of letters inside.

CHAPTER SEVENTY-TWO

'Could I see Kavan's p-painting of the m-monk?' Kedar asked.

'Of course!' Rebecca had forgotten all about her childhood discovery. *With his special knowledge, perhaps Kedar will see more than I ever could*, she thought as they set off for the East Tower.

They had gone only a few paces, with Emer, Galen and Annis tagging along behind, when she remembered that the picture was not in her secret lair, but in a wardrobe in her bedchamber. She had put it there before the fateful meeting with Cranne. Her rooms were now in use by Montfort's staff. She had been offered them back, but no longer wanted them for herself. Her memories of the place were tainted now.

Rebecca explained their change of direction, adding that she hoped the painting would still be where she had hidden it. The apartment was empty, and she felt uncomfortable; the rooms were familiar, yet she did not feel at home. *Has so much changed in only a few days?* she wondered, noting the new items of furniture, the maps and other military equipment spread around the chamber.

She retrieved the painting from the wardrobe.

'Oh!' At first she thought her eyes were playing tricks on her, but then she realized what had happened. She showed the picture to the others, who crowded round but allowed Kedar pride of place.

'He's gone!' Emer exclaimed.

'It looks as though he's just stepped outside for a moment,' Galen commented wryly.

Kaven's handiwork now depicted a bare wooden table; the

monk and the chess-board had vanished. The stone walls in the background were a little clearer than Rebecca remembered, their dim recesses filled with bookshelves. But in the centre of the wall, never seen before, was a door. It stood ajar, bright light shining round the rim of the wood.

Each onlooker saw the same images, yet each reacted differently.

Is the game over? Rebecca wondered. *Have I won or lost?* She still did not know the rules. And the light beyond the door fascinated her. It was white, pure but unnatural. *For you, my child . . .*

Emer shivered, finding the scene inexplicably eerie. 'Why has he gone?' she asked quietly, but no one had an answer for her.

The room looked oddly familiar to Galen, and he found himself thinking, *Where are the stairs?*

'Perhaps it's telling a story,' Annis suggested. 'The games, the changing emotions on the monk's face, and the monster. Now he's gone. I wonder where he is?'

'And is he coming back?' Rebecca asked.

Kedar was silent, prey to an almost overwhelming rush of emotions. He sensed much more than he saw – presences both ancient and unborn. Kavan was there in the room with him, as was Edel, and an endless line of others. The young painter revelled in Kavan's mastery of his art. Even now, with its commonplace subject matter and simple construction, the painting lived. Kedar would not have been in the least bit surprised to see the door open as he watched, for light to flood into the room as the monk returned. *What is he doing?* he wondered, but the painting gave no answer. *It's so old, but the paint hasn't cracked or faded at all.* He was mesmerized, feeling almost as though he could step into that room from so long ago.

'What was Kavan trying to tell us?' Rebecca asked. 'There must be a message in this somewhere.'

Kedar wrenched himself back to his own world.

'I don't know,' he said quietly. He felt unaccountably moved by the picture, but also frightened. This was true wizardry. He could never hope to aspire to such power.

'Perhaps it'll change again,' Rebecca said. 'I'll keep an eye

591

on it.' She tucked it under her arm, intending to return with
it to Radd's house.

* * *

In a nearby room, unaware of the speculation concerning
the ancient picture, Montfort and Tarrant were discussing
their defensive strategy.

'We need more of those weapons,' the king insisted,
frowning.

'We're doing all we can,' his envoy replied. 'Cluny won't
let anyone except himself and Anselma handle that stuff.
He says it's too dangerous, and I'm inclined to agree with
him.'

'He's a strange man to let his wife take those risks but
not allow soldiers near,' Montfort remarked.

'To tell you the truth,' Tarrant responded, 'I think
Anselma's less of a danger than *he* is. In any case, we'll just
have to make the best use of what we get.'

'So moving them is dangerous too?'

'Yes, but we can handle that. I'm training special units,
and we're working on special panniers for the horses. If we
spread the weapons out along the whole line, we'll have too
few to make any real impact. We need a good supply at the
point where we'll be facing the main thrust of Jarlath's army.'

'What about the catapults?' the king asked.

'Not mobile enough,' Tarrant answered. 'We'll place what
we have on the highest vantage points, but once the enemy
realizes they're there, they'll be able to avoid them easily
enough.'

'But it might slow them down a bit first,' Montfort said.

Tarrant nodded, grinning.

'Yes, though we'll be better off concentrating on the hand-
held stuff. They can be used anywhere.'

'Agreed,' Montfort said. 'Is that all for now?'

His companion rose from his seat, then hesitated.

'Have you thought any more about what Rebecca said?'
he asked.

The king regarded him with a slightly reproving smile

'If I didn't know better, I'd believe that young lady ha

592

turned your head,' he accused in a mild tone.

'She *is* special,' Tarrant replied.

'I don't deny that,' Montfort said. 'But I'm not about to start chasing phantoms. We have enough problems in the *real* world.' He held up his hand to forestall any further comment. 'No more.'

Tarrant nodded, accepting the decision.

* * *

It was early afternoon before Cluny and Anselma found Rebecca. She was alone in Radd's library, reading forlornly.

'We have a small success to relate,' the alchemist declared.

The baron's daughter was ready to clutch at any straws by now, and she looked up eagerly. Cluny laid the book down before her and she gasped, her eyes going straight to the third set of letters.

```
F  T  H  E  A
O  G  E  G
T  N  H  E  R
I  I  S  D
N  E  K  A  W
```

'It doesn't add much, I'm afraid,' Cluny remarked as Rebecca mentally worked out its meaning.

Oh yes it does! she thought, her heart sinking. *So it is all up to me.*

'Are you all right?' Anselma asked, noting that Rebecca had turned pale. 'Does it tell you anything?'

' "Kin of the ages, heed wakening; hold the dream, enact the will",' Rebecca quoted. 'In Sancia's message, she said, "I learnt too late that you were my kin of the ages." And later she told me to "hold the dream". So those lines are meant for me.' She had always feared that her role in the coming conflict would be important. Now it was clear that her fears had been justified.

'It sounds like an instruction,' Anselma commented.

'It is,' Rebecca replied. *But I still have no idea what I'm supposed to do!*

* * *

'Give us a tune, Boomer!' the drunk yelled.

Newell did not even look up from his corner of The Blind Husband tavern. His new viol lay on the bench beside him, but he was slumped on his seat, staring into the murky depths of his drink – one of several he had earnt by his music.

'Aye, lad,' the innkeeper added, knowing a good thing when he heard one. 'Play as good as you did earlier, and there'll be free board for you tonight.'

Still the musician did not react. He was sunk in depression, convinced that his new instrument was inferior to the one he had lost. It had needed new strings, and had proved fiendishly difficult to tune. Still, he could not afford to look a gift-horse in the mouth. The instrument maker in Garadun had given him the viol for free after Newell had played it for a few moments. The craftsman had explained that no one else had proved capable of managing more than a few screechy notes, and that the instrument was therefore of no use to him. He said that the viol was very old, and that some of the wood might have begun to warp. All Newell knew was that it took an enormous amount of patience and total concentration to make it sound at all melodious. When he was in the right mood, however, he admitted to himself that the instrument had a lovely tone.

'One o' the old songs'd be best,' the drunk suggested.

Newell raised his head slowly and fixed the man with a half-blind stare.

'What would *you* know of old songs?' he rasped bitterly. 'You wouldn't recognize *really* old music if you heard it. It's been suppressed. The Heretics have always been persecuted – even now!' In his ale-induced confusion, Newell had revealed the name of the secret society, but he did not notice. 'It's disappeared. I can't bring it back. I try – the gods know I try – but all I hear is whispers. Whispers! Even in my dreams now!' He was shouting, standing up and leaning forward, his hands flat on the table. 'Prying. Whispering.'

'I only wanted a song,' the drunk complained, looking offended as Newell's harangue faltered.

'Come along, lad. There's no need for a scene,' the innkeeper put in hurriedly. 'Give us a tune.'

Other drinkers took up the request, and made a chant of it. 'Give us a tune, give us a tune!'

I'll give you a tune! Newell snatched up his viol and bow, and launched into a high-pitched, flowing melody that was deceptively sweet at first. Murmurs of satisfaction were gradually silenced, then turned to angry muttering as the music became increasingly harsh and violent. Newell played on, piling discord upon discord, layering the pain and the madness, and filling the air with a blind fury as he tried to drown out the accursed whispers. The world ceased to exist as the magic swept him away in a torrent of bitter ice and screaming fire.

The tormented sound ended abruptly when someone grabbed his arm. Disorientated and alarmed, Newell stared at his assailant with the unfocused eyes of a lunatic.

'Out!' the innkeeper yelled.

Newell staggered as he was shoved towards the door, but managed to save his instrument from harm.

'You've no right abusing our hospitality like that,' the landlord told him angrily. 'Get out, and don't come back!'

Shouts of agreement sounded from his patrons.

Newell stumbled into the night, feeling the first chill of winter on his bare arms. He looked up at the star-kissed sky, the cold full moon.

The whispers in his head began again.

CHAPTER SEVENTY-THREE

Having to stay in one place on the salt during the hours of daylight was alien to the Archaeologists' nature, so Arledge and Peyton had agreed a patrol route that would keep them on the move – and give them the best chance of spotting the approaching enemy. They had headed due south for three leagues, then turned roughly north-east and walked parallel to the salt's rim towards Blackator, the upper reaches of which were just visible on the horizon. Their plan was to patrol back and forth along this line, which would surely cross the route of the army from Riano. They had supplies enough for several days, although they did not expect to use them all.

They camped the first night, as intended, at a site directly between Edgefield and Riano. A watch was set throughout the hours of darkness, but nothing untoward was seen. On the second day they continued as planned, keeping a careful watch to the south. By mid-morning they were nearing Blackator, its huge black presence dominating the eastern skyline. The day was cool but cloudless, and they were all looking forward to a rest before turning round and retracing their footsteps.

'How close would they have to be before we could see them?' Flank asked.

'Why?' Holmes responded, eyeing his companion's bulky frame. 'Don't you think you could outrun them?'

'An army that size would raise a cloud of salt-dust, and besides, we'd see the smoke from their campfires first thing in the morning,' Peyton answered more seriously. 'Don' worry – we'll see them long before they see us.'

Flank smiled, and seemed reassured.

'Perhaps they're not coming,' he suggested hopefully.

'And perhaps the sun won't rise tomorrow,' Milner countered. 'They haven't come all this way for nothing.'

'They've been waiting a long time in Riano,' Flank said defensively. 'Maybe they've changed their minds and gone home again.'

'I pity Jarlath if they have,' Holmes put in. 'Men like that don't like to leave empty-handed.'

'It's a nice idea,' Peyton began, 'but—'

He came to an abrupt halt, and signalled for silence.

'Feel it?' he whispered.

It was more of a vibration than a sound, a rhythmic tremor that they all sensed through the soles of their boots.

'They're coming,' Arledge breathed, scanning the horizon. 'Why can't we see them?'

'Because they're still too far away,' Peyton replied. 'We wouldn't have heard them if they weren't so well drilled.'

'Marching in step on the salt?' Milner said, aghast. 'They must be mad!'

'Aye,' Peyton agreed. 'Completely insane.'

'Can you tell where they are?' Arledge asked.

'Not yet,' the senior Archaeologist replied. 'But it won't be long. Let's walk on.'

The others obeyed without question. The black mountain towered above them a quarter of a league away, its convoluted surface the colour of night. Then the salt began to rumble, a deep, distant sound at first that rapidly grew louder. The booming seemed to set up its own echoes, feeding upon itself until the whole world trembled. The men exchanged glances while the beeks danced on nervous feet.

'Gods . . . it *can't* happen that quick!' Peyton's voice was cracked with horror, his eyes round with sudden fear. His companions had never seen him react this way before. He shook his head as if unable to believe what his special senses were telling him. Then a string of violent oaths burst from his lips and he looked around with panic in his eyes.

'Run!' he yelled.

'Which way?' Holmes shot back.

'Blackator,' Peyton replied. 'It's our only chance.'

'We can't climb *that*!' Milner exclaimed.

'You will if you want to live,' his leader replied.

He set off without further ado, throwing his pack aside and sprinting towards the black mountain. The others pelted after him, their beeks leaping alongside in the mad race.

Below the salt, the rumbling increased to an incredible volume, and another sound could be heard now, faint but unmistakable – the sound of an army on the move.

The Archaeologists ran into the shadow of the rock. Peyton did not slacken his pace, and Arledge and Milner matched him stride for stride. However, Flank was now panting hoarsely and lagging behind, and Holmes dropped back to urge him on, only to be stopped in his tracks as the salt shuddered violently beneath their feet. They turned to see the unbelievable sight of a vast column of salt hurling itself into the air with volcano-like fury. It was two leagues from where they stood, but was still awe-inspiring.

'Come on!' Peyton yelled urgently. 'It's going to hit in a moment!' He and his two companions had already reached the base of the mountain and were scanning the rock in a frantic search for a route upwards. They began to climb, scrambling precariously, urged on by Peyton's warnings. Flank continued to stare at the salt, mesmerized, until Holmes grabbed him and they both began to run.

They reached the base of the rock and followed their comrades. Ascending with desperate haste, they began to think that they must be safe. The roaring of the salt had lessened to mere thunder now.

'Can't . . . go . . . on . . . ' Flank gasped.

Holmes paused, a few paces higher, and looked back out over the flats. What he saw filled him with fearful dread, but also with a sense of childlike wonder. A tidal wave of salt, five times taller than any man, was bearing down upon them with unbelievable speed. It rolled and raged, tumbling and reforming, plumes of salt dust flying into the air above the enormous bulk of the main surge. In some ways this was more remarkable than the original eruption; it was more immediate, more beautiful, more deadly.

'Higher!' Peyton screamed from above.

'Come on!' Holmes yelled.

'Can't . . . ' Flank breathed. 'Legs . . . gone . . . '

Holmes reached out, pulled the younger man up to the next ledge, then climbed on again. He was about to turn round, to repeat the process . . .

. . . when the world went white. The wave struck Blackator with the force of a dozen avalanches, exploding as it hit. Clouds of salt were hurled hundreds of paces into the sky as the mountain shook under the assault. Holmes clung to the rock for dear life, his body battered and his ears deafened, and somehow managed to hold on. But when the white fury abated and he was able to open his eyes again, there was no sign of Flank. He had been swept away.

Peyton's voice drifted down from above.

'Holmes, Flank, you still there?'

'I am!' Holmes yelled, his voice shaky. 'But Flank's gone.' He climbed up to his colleagues, his limbs feeling leaden, and joined them as they stared out at the scene below.

The flats seethed, churning and boiling in the wake of the giant wave. It made the movement that had killed Kibble seem like a tiny flexing of the salt's muscle. Slow waves rolled over the surface, colliding and coalescing; islands rose and fell in the moving sea of quicksalt, and in the distance, the sky sparkled as the sunlight caught the falling crystal particles.

'The army?' Holmes asked.

'It must have begun right in their midst,' Peyton answered quietly. 'No one will have survived that.'

Looking more closely now, Holmes could see tiny flecks in the white sea, debris tossed in the dry waves. But there was absolutely no sign of anything living.

'The whole army?' he whispered.

'Looks like it,' Arledge answered. He supposed that he ought to be pleased – after all, the threat to his country had been destroyed in one fell swoop – but he was too stunned to feel anything. 'They were just swept away.'

'Swept clean,' Peyton added, awe and satisfaction mingling in his voice.

'Will it stop?' Milner asked, watching the seething mass below. They had no supplies – and there was no way home through that!

'It always has before,' Peyton answered. But even he

had never seen anything on this scale.

* * *

For two days, the march had gone without a hitch. After overcoming their initial nervousness, Jarlath and his troops had been in high spirits. The army moved in good order, unit by unit, with the mercenaries forming the front rank and the central core of the rear. The baron's own men guarded the rear flanks, and provided the scouting parties who kept a watch on all sides. The monks had stationed themselves in a huge circle spread around the main bulk of the army. This, Hakon had explained, was so that they could use their special powers to calm the salt should it become necessary. Jarlath had seen a demonstration of their talent, and felt secure within the protective ring. Even the mercenaries, who regarded the monks with superstitious dread, began to take them for granted after a while, and many of the soldiers marvelled at the way that their guardians – even the most ancient of them – were able to keep up the march with ease. For their part, the brethren were in jubilant mood, and though they spoke little, their eyes glittered as the crystals crunched beneath their feet.

It was during the mid-morning of their third day out from Riano that the abbot heard the first rumblings from beneath the salt. He immediately gave a signal which was passed around the circle of monks. Moments later, they halted, raised their arms to the sky and cried out in exultation. The soldiers stopped, suddenly afraid, as the strange guttural sounds vibrated in the air.

The salt heaved. Men stared in terror, screaming as a circular wave of salt rose up, ringing the army. Then it moved inwards, growing ever stronger. Whole units floundered, sinking into the quicksalt, while others struggled desperately for a few extra moments. The wave surged on, squeezing ever tighter, its power building inexorably until it became concentrated at one point, and all the forces merged into a huge explosion. A vast plume of salt flung itself towards the sky, feeding on its own fury, before rushing down and outwards once more. Its unearthly roar shattered eardrums and crushed lungs. Jarlath died with only an instant to realize that he had been betrayed, and unable to hear the sound of his own screaming.

But the monks' creation was not finished yet. It spread out again, even more devastating than before. Like the ripples of a monstrous stone hurled into a still lake, it turned the flats into a boiling sea of death. Survivors of the first onslaught stood no chance; they were sucked down into a cauldron of unfathomable depths as the glistening tower of salt dust rose into the sky. Olin and Nur, the strongest of the men, were among the last to succumb. They died, raging against their fate, but as helpless as all the rest.

The wave reached the ring of monks. They too succumbed, overwhelmed by the deluge, vanishing from the world of the sun . . .

. . . and appearing in the world below the white sea.

Each of the brethren joyously submitted to their fate. They filled their lungs with salt, breathing its crystal purity, and knew unconfined wonder. Their time had come.

Within the salt, the monks marched on, going about their dreadful business.

CHAPTER SEVENTY-FOUR

When Rebecca awoke from her uneasy but dreamless sleep, the first thing she did was glance at Kavan's picture. What she saw made her pause, blink, then stare. *What has happened?* she wondered, frowning.

The canvas was now entirely white, just a blank space within the frame – as though it was waiting for the artist to begin again.

Swept clean, she thought, utterly bewildered. Then a small voice inside her head added, *Or filled with salt.*

*   *   *

Arledge and his colleagues reached Edgefield Castle in the early evening. The scouts on the salt rim had seen and reported the disturbance on the flats, but it was not until the return of the Achaeologists that the real events of the previous day became common knowledge. They were ushered up to Montfort's room to tell their story, and were soon rejoicing with the king, their initial reticence swept away by Montfort's easy manner. They talked to their sovereign as though he were an old friend, their own natural gregariousness happily reasserting itself. For his own part, Montfort had warmed to his visitors immediately, especially as their tale was so welcome.

'You have brought news better than any I could have hoped for,' he said, fetching glasses and filling them with dark red wine.

'We nearly didn't bring any news at all,' Arledge commented, and told the king of the terrifying wave of salt and their desperate flight to Blackator.

'That was when your companion died?' Montfort asked.

'Yes,' Holmes replied, reliving the dreadful moment. 'The salt just swept him away.'

'Then we will drink a toast to his memory, to your own survival, and to the news that you have brought me,' Montfort said.

Five glasses were raised, and each man drank.

'As far as we could tell, the salt kept moving all that afternoon and most of the night,' Peyton continued. He shook his head, staring at the contents of his glass as though still unable to believe what he had seen.

'We were very nervous when we came down this morning,' Milner put in, 'especially as only one of our beeks had survived. But we had no choice. With no food or water we wouldn't have lasted long up there!'

'Besides, we needed to stretch our legs,' Holmes added, grinning. 'That wasn't the most comfortable night I've ever spent.'

'The salt was still very . . . *tense*,' Peyton said. 'But solid enough to get us here.'

'And you're absolutely sure that Jarlath's army was destroyed?' Montfort asked.

'I saw most of them go down with my own eyes,' the Archaeologists' leader replied. 'In any case, the movement was so big and spread so wide that nothing for leagues around could have survived.'

There was a sad note to his voice as he added, 'It shook me up, I can tell you.'

'Then it's over.' The king was filled with an almost unbearable relief. His mind turned briefly to the less dramatic but equally onerous tasks that now lay ahead, but first . . . 'We must celebrate our good fortune properly,' he decreed.

'Judging by some of the scenes we saw on the way here,' Holmes remarked, 'we already are!'

'Good,' Montfort replied. 'Then let us join in!'

The news spread like wildfire, and caused rejoicing among soldiers and civilians alike. A feast was being prepared for the Great Hall, and there were already impromptu celebrations in the town and the army camps.

The only person who felt no pleasure at the enemy's demise was Rebecca. Her immediate reaction when she heard the news was one of foreboding. *This is only the beginning.*

Even her staunchest allies, Emer and Galen, were swept up in the general atmosphere of euphoria, but they could say nothing to convince Rebecca.

'You just *want* to believe it,' she accused them. 'But it's not over yet!'

'At the very least, *one* threat to Montfort has been removed,' Emer countered. 'Can't we be pleased about that?'

'I must go and see him,' Rebecca decided, and left her friends without another word.

She found the king alone in his apartment, studying reports. He looked up as she came in, and smiled.

'The gods have favoured us, Rebecca,' he said. 'Isn't the news wonderful?'

She stood in silence, unable to return his smile.

'Why so solemn?' he asked, rising and coming towards her.

'It's not over,' she said quietly.

'What?'

'This is the beginning of our troubles, not the end.'

'You're not trying to tell me . . . ?' he began.

'Yes, I am!' she exclaimed vehemently. 'Don't you see? The real enemy wasn't *Jarlath*. His army may have been destroyed, but what happens next?'

'I celebrate my good fortune, return to Garadun and try to reunite my country,' he replied, smiling again.

'Don't go!' A sudden fear enveloped her.

'I have work to do, Rebecca,' he said calmly.

'But it's not over,' she repeated. 'The *real* battle hasn't even begun.'

'Please. Enough of this nonsense!' For the first time, there was a touch of anger in his voice. 'Don't you trust the word of Galen's friends?'

'Of course I do. What they saw was real enough . . . '

'Well then!'

'But even they cannot see into the future.'

'And you can?' he asked, half-amused, half-annoyed.

'Yes,' she answered defiantly, then added in a less certain tone, 'A little.'

'Then you will see that I must leave here tomorrow,' he said. 'Much as I would like . . . '

'How can you be so stupid?' she interrupted angrily.

'Even my courtesy has its limits, young lady,' he said coldly.

'I'm sorry.' But she did not sound it. 'It's just that I *know* the real war has yet to be fought – and that for some reason my role in it will be crucial.' She was pleading now, and looked very young and vulnerable. Montfort was moved by the uncertainty in her voice, but could not come to terms with what she was saying.

'How can that be, Rebecca?' he asked gently.

'I don't know,' she replied miserably. 'I don't *want* to be important. I find it so hard . . . '

'You find it hard?' Montfort exclaimed, his patience snapping at last. 'Do you have any idea what it's like for me? Hedged in by rules and tradition, being fed advice from all quarters – and most of it useless. Fighting inertia and vested interests on all sides, constantly striving to balance one against another. At least Jarlath was honest enough to try to fight me out in the open. Gods! I wish I could be more like my father. He did not find it hard to tolerate injustice.'

'I'm glad you're not like that,' Rebecca said softly, as he paused for breath.

Their eyes met, and when the king spoke again, his voice was filled with sorrow.

'Then why do you try to distract me with things that are not real?'

'My dreams *are* real,' she responded. 'The legends are real. The message of the stones is real . . . You may not be able to touch them, or see them, but none the less they exist.'

Montfort shook his head, at a loss, and Rebecca took her chance.

'Why should the salt suddenly be so active?' she asked. 'It's never been like this before. What if I'm right? What if you *do* need magic? Will you continue to turn away until it's too late?'

'The world is ruled by men, not by sorcerers,' he said.

'Well, perhaps you should have a few women to help you then!' she shot back.

'Where have I heard that before?' the unmarried king replied, laughing.

'Don't mock me!'

'I would not dare,' he exclaimed, still smiling.

'Then I'll do it without you,' Rebecca declared, furious now. 'The wizards will help me, even if you won't. Ask Tarrant, ask Cluny. They believe me.' The look of surprise on his face helped her continue. 'Something awful is going to happen, something that will make all the battles up to now seem like nothing more than drunken brawls. And if you won't fight, I will! You'll . . . '

Her prediction was never completed. Montfort suddenly stepped forward, took her face in firm but gentle hands and kissed her on the lips. At first Rebecca was too astonished to react, but then her body responded almost against her will, and she experienced a surge of pleasure at the warmth and contact. She was about to put her arms about his neck when he jumped away from her like a startled rabbit.

Shaken, Rebecca realized that there was a soldier standing in the open doorway. She looked back at Montfort, and saw that he was blushing slightly. The soldier waited awkwardly, not knowing where to look, while Rebecca stood unmoving, shocked into silence.

'What is it, Redmond?' the king asked.

'I thought you should know, sire,' the soldier answered. 'The scouts have reported more tremors on the salt. Big movements. It's been shaking the land for leagues around.'

'Really?' Montfort glanced at Rebecca, but she was not even listening.

'Yes, my lord,' Redmond said. 'That'll finish off any remnants of Jarlath's army,' he went on, with evident satisfaction.

'That's good,' Montfort said weakly.

'I'll . . . er . . . return to my duties then, sire,' the soldier said

Before he had a chance to move, Rebecca fled past him into the corridor. She was totally confused, and could not stay where she was a moment longer. Monfort reacted too late, stepping forward with a hand outstretched – but she was gone.

Redmond bowed and left, speculation in his eyes. After a few moments' reflection, Montfort returned to his reports. He turned the page, then realized that he had no idea what he had just read. *Damn the girl*, he thought woefully.

As he forced his attention back to the pages in front of him, a sudden tremor shook the room.

CHAPTER SEVENTY-FIVE

Something was stirring deep beneath the salt, as if the powers of the earth itself were awakening. The cold night sky, set with stars and a full moon, was the only witness to the events of that evening.

Dusk saw the first of the renewed tremors, and they continued thereafter with ever-increasing force. It began as a sort of bulging of the salt. A vast area of the flats rose several paces, then the crust cracked and shattered, and salt flowed outwards like streams of white lava from an underground volcano. The process was accompanied by a ceaseless grinding noise and vibrations that were felt for many leagues. Rivers of salt poured forth from the point at the centre of the disturbance. Hours passed as the remorseless flow continued, spreading wider and wider over the flats. The shaking intensified, until the very air itself seemed to tremble.

Then a small triangle of black appeared, pushing back the salt. Fraction by fraction, a huge pyramid rose into the air.

Before long, the remnants of a great city began to appear around its vast black heart. The last of the crystals ran away like water, in rivulets and sudden cascades, as pale, elegant buildings emerged into the open air. Their walls were cracked, and their roofs had collapsed, but the stone itself was still fresh and clean. Not one of the many tall structures had remained intact, but there was a spectral beauty in them still. The city was an ancient ruin, in which only the black pyramid had survived unscathed, its smooth surfaces like sections of a starless night. It dominated the scene.

In the centre of the city, next to the pyramid, the remains

of a fantastic crystal bridge lay in shattered ruins across what had once been a river bed. Moonlit rainbows danced in cracked shapes in the fragments – and soon the ghostly light flickered over an even more astonishing scene.

The salt's movement had stopped at last, leaving the city as the only thing standing above the plain – because, as it had risen, so Blackator had sunk, as though it was a counterbalance of a monstrous set of scales. Slowly but inexorably, the mountain went down, and the salt closed over its summit like water over the head of a drowning giant.

Derith was in the land of the sun and the moon again. But it had lain dead for eight hundred years, and its rebirth was not yet complete.

Feeding off some invisible source of demonic energy, the city began to rebuild itself, restoring its former glory. Impossible lights flared and died, and power whispered in the deserted streets. Time seemed to reverse itself. Cracks closed, walls righted themselves, great stones floated in the air and joined together once more, and roofs were miraculously reconstructed. The crystal bridge reformed amid a blaze of incongruous beauty, and the towers rose again, the tallest of them reaching up into the sky, their windows like dark eyes that looked out over their domain. And yet those eyes were still blind. For a few moments the city was as quiet as a graveyard. For all its renewal, it was still dead – but would not remain so for long.

The monks came first, bursting forth from the salt and gazing around with wonder at their reborn home. Physically they were unchanged, but now they wore the unmistakable mantle of power, fire burning bright in their cold eyes.

The soldiers came next, mercenaries and Jarlath's men alike, their weapons and armour gleaming as if newly polished, their muscles and sinew as strong and supple as ever. But they were changed. The men were mute and expressionless. They did not communicate, and mingled together with no distinction between officers and men, no privileges of rank. Jarlath, Olin and Nur were no different from the rawest recruit. They were all equal now – and all totally mindless.

They moved with the dream-like imprecision of puppets,

their eyes clouded windows that concealed the vacuum within their skulls. They had become the creatures of legend, dead men walking the face of the earth, marching to the irresistible commands of the jubilant brethren who had created these misbegotten abominations. They had become dreekers.

Last to emerge were the city's original inhabitants. They came slowly, awkwardly, as though still weighed down by their centuries beneath the salt. They were little more than skeletons, frail tatters of flesh stretched upon bone, preserved by the very element which had killed them. Men, women and children wandered aimlessly amid the growing throng, given unnatural life in a new world long after their unnatural deaths had fed the fires of evil sorcery.

With such, Derith repopulated itself.

The monks began to organize their charges, gathering them into the open spaces around the pyramid. The dreekers waited obediently.

Deep within the torgrist tomb, another creature stirred. He woke from his long, long sleep, and rose, a slow smile spreading over his cruel face as he drew the sources of power to him. He sensed his minions gathering around him, and gloated over his continued dominance. Rejuvenated by his long rest, his link with the Web was now so strong that it was invincible. Within his sphere of influence, the three ancient wizards lay trapped, in thrall to the man they had so desperately sought to oppose. He laughed for the first time in eight centuries, and the catacombs echoed and shook at the sound. His time had come.

The waiting multitude saw him emerge from the concealed entrance near the top of the pyramid to stand before them like a god. Thousands of pairs of eyes, fire-bright and blank alike, looked up and saw a figure whose appearance was that of a large man. He was tall and broad-shouldered, his black hair and beard shining in the moonlight. Yet about him was an aura of power and command that dwarfed the puny strength of the monks and made him seem like a giant in comparison.

Hawk-like eyes looked down on his subjects as he raised

his arms in a dramatic gesture. Lightning flared silently in the sky above, illuminating the city and the sea of eager faces, and rippling on the bridge of rainbows, sending livid flashes of colour slicing through the night.

'*My bargain has been fulfilled!*' Tyrrell roared in triumph.

As the waiting army responded to his mighty voice, a golden bell boomed forth its signal from the highest tower.

CHAPTER SEVENTY-SIX

The violent tremors – and the ensuing panic – had delayed Edgefield's planned celebrations, and had caused Montfort to postpone his departure. He still could not accept any of Rebecca's dire predictions, but was none the less more worried by the continued movement than he would have cared to admit.

The castle itself had been directly affected, when part of the West Tower – already weakened by the recent fire – fell into the courtyard below, crushing four people and destroying part of the servants' quarters. The damage to the town had been less severe, and while many citizens had been affected, for most, glass and crockery were the worst casualties. A few fires had started, but had been kept under control. Cluny and Anselma had had a terrifying time, trying to preserve and protect the many volatile materials and explosives under their roof. But both they and their scarred basement had survived.

Yet the worst damage was to the minds of the people. The ground beneath their feet – their ultimate security – was suddenly no longer safe. In a world where the earth itself shook, nothing was certain, and this lack of fundamental stability left everyone disorientated and afraid.

It came as a great relief when the shaking finally stopped around midnight. In the eerie silence that followed, many people thought they could hear the distant tolling of a bell.

* * *

The earthquake frightened Rebecca as much as anyone. But unlike most of the other inhabitants of Edge, she had an underlying knowledge of what might be its cause,

Is it happening already? she wondered. *It's too soon! I'm not ready.* She hoped desperately that she was wrong, that the world really was as straightforward as Montfort would have her believe, but she could not convince herself. In her mind's eye, Derith was rising – and she knew that there was nothing she could do to prevent it.

She tried to find Tarrant, to see if he had any news of Pike and Newell, but the envoy was nowhere to be found. Her subsequent searches, first for Emer and Galen, then for Kedar and Annis, were equally fruitless. In the chaos, all her friends, all the people she *needed*, eluded her.

Rebecca would have liked to climb one of the castle towers and get a better view of the moonlit flats, but that would have been too dangerous, so instead she retreated to her room in the chamberlain's home, her head still reeling from the day's events – and from Montfort's kiss.

Was he just trying to shut me up? she wondered. *Would any girl have been treated in the same way? Or is he really attracted to me?* The idea seemed ridiculous, but the kiss was certainly not the product of her imagination. *And how do I feel about him?* The answer to that was too complicated for her to even think about. She was filled with a mixture of emotions too complex to define. There were some she could identify; respect, admiration, anger at his stubbornness, even pity. He had always behaved in a gentle and courteous manner to her, and she knew that he had a sensitive streak that balanced his sometimes ruthless pragmatism and mental strength. Physically, she found him very attractive. But what did all this add up to?

Why did he jump away from me like that? As if I had poisoned him! Her confusion increased. *What would have happened if Redmond hadn't come in just then?* Each question led to more, and provided no answers. *And why did I run away?*

Feeling helpless, abandoned and extremely sorry for herself, Rebecca's thoughts went around in circles.

Eventually the vibrations stopped, and there was some small comfort in that. Then she heard the tolling of a distant bell – and her fears returned in full measure. She could not help recalling Derith's legendary bell, which apparently could only be rung in times of great peril. Then, according to the book in Milden's library, it could be heard in every part of the kingdom. Tolling the doom of the hour.

Much later, Rebecca fell into an exhausted sleep. But her sleep gave her no rest; her dream that night was a ceaseless internal battle. She knew that she should be weaving, trying to find Newell, to see into the future or reveal means of fighting against the fate that was threatening to overwhelm her. But all her efforts failed. The images of the dream returned again and again, delighting in the face that was drawing close to hers, in the touch of his hands upon her skin and the boyish wonder in his eyes. Whether it stemmed from her own imaginary fantasies or from some unlikely vision of the future, the dream showed her desires that her waking mind would never have admitted, and woke in her sensations that she never knew existed.

When she returned to the real world, she was flushed and happy. The pang of loss she experienced on finding herself alone was sharp and potent, a mixture of guilt and wonder.

Don't mock me, she pleaded.

I wouldn't dare, Rebecca heard him reply.

* * *

The king also spent a restless night. His men had dealt capably with the inevitable emergencies arising after the tremor, but that did not stop him from worrying. Montfort knew that he should be preparing for the next stage in his self-imposed, lifelong task. He must attend to affairs of state, healing rifts between opposing factions and putting his plans into operation. But he could not concentrate, and his traitorous thoughts kept straying to Rebecca. He saw her face before him in all its moods; happy, angry, defiant, uncertain, mischievous, determined and sad – and always beautiful.

He cursed himself silently for his stupid actions. *What must she think of me?* And then, in a vain attempt at self-justification: *Why must she taunt me with those silly theories?*

Montfort knew that Redmond could be trusted to be

discreet, but had anyone else seen his actions? He winced at the memory. *Why is she so important to me?* he asked himself.

One possible answer occurred, but he pushed it aside. Love had no place in his life at this time.

*   *   *

Galen came to Rebecca's bedchamber soon after she woke.

'Radd's come to,' he announced. 'And he's asking for you.'

She hurried to the chamberlain's bedside, where Emer sat holding her father's hand in her own.

'He's asleep again, but it's not the same as before.' Emer's eyes shone, and she looked tired but happy. 'His breathing's much stronger now.'

Rebecca wanted to wake Radd instantly, but controlled the impulse.

'The change started with the tremors,' her friend went on. 'It's as if the vibrations woke him up. Then this morning he actually opened his eyes and spoke.'

'What did he say?'

'It was a bit confused,' Emer answered contentedly. 'I think he said that my mother loved me. Then he talked about some light or other. He sounded almost as weird as you! But he did say one clear thing – about wanting to see you. He *is* going to be all right now, isn't he?' she finished, the suspicion of tears in her eyes.

Rebecca looked at Radd's pale, emaciated face and had her doubts, but she could not douse Emer's hopes.

'Yes,' she answered. 'I'm sure he will. Has Nursey said anything?'

'As soon as he opened his eyes, she rushed off to get him some food,' her friend replied with a grin. 'She's probably preparing a banquet!'

Radd's eyelids fluttered.

'Wait for me!' he cried in despair. 'Wait for me!'

'It's all right, Father,' Emer responded, squeezing his hand. 'I'm here.'

The chamberlain stared at his daughter, pain and loss reflected in his eyes. Then the confusion cleared, and he returned the pressure of Emer's hand-clasp. He turned to Rebecca.

'I'm glad you came,' he said in a quiet, weak voice. He looked so ill and battered, and sounded so tired that Rebecca's doubts redoubled in that moment, but she forced herself to smile. Emer made way for her, and she moved closer.

'I'm glad you're getting better,' she said, as lightly as the lump in her throat would allow.

They were silent for a few moments, neither knowing where to begin. They each wanted their reconciliation to be complete, but both knew that there were things that had to be said first.

'I'm sorry I betrayed your trust,' Rebecca ventured. 'I did not mean to hurt you.'

'I have been very foolish,' Radd admitted sorrowfully. 'It is I who should apologize. I was wrong in trying to hide things from you, but I was scared. You were like a second daughter to me. The idea that you could be involved in such . . . ' His voice faltered. 'I'm sorry.'

'So much has happened since . . . ' she began.

'I know,' he interrupted, staring at the canopy above his bed.

'But how can you know?' she asked, totally confused now.

'I have been dreaming,' he replied, the ghost of a smile touching his thin face. 'Though perhaps it was more than dreaming. I talked to my wife. She looked different, but her voice was the same. She was still my love, even after all these years.' There were tears in his eyes now. Behind Rebecca, Emer swallowed hard.

'Then you know how important that book is?' Rebecca asked, feeling heartless in her persistence, but driven by need.

'That dreadful book!' Radd whispered, grimacing. 'How I hated it.'

'Where is it?' she persisted.

Radd hesitated, reluctant still. Slowly and painfully, he raised his head from the pillow and looked directly at her.

'Do you forgive me?' He was crying openly now, his voice weaker than ever.

'With all my heart,' Rebecca replied, close to tears herself.

'Promise me one thing.'

'Anything.'

'Remember that no destiny is certain,' he said slowly. 'The future can always be changed.'

'I'll remember,' she promised. *Where is it?* she pleaded silently.

Radd's head fell back again, and he closed his eyes, obviously close to exhaustion.

'Is Emer still here?' he asked.

'I'm here, Father.'

'Don't leave me yet. Rebecca must go, I know, but . . . '

'I'll stay,' his daughter promised.

'Since your mother died, I've loved you more than anyone on this earth,' he whispered. 'I may not always have shown it . . . '

'I know, Father,' Emer replied, keeping her voice steady with some difficulty. 'Tell Rebecca where the book is,' she added gently.

'I've one more thing to say,' he breathed. 'I may not get another chance.' He paused, gathering his failing strength. 'I've often wished that you two were more alike, but now I know that you complement each other. I was wrong to want to change you. No man could be prouder of his two girls than I am of you, nor love them more.'

This last admission left both girls speechless. Tears ran down their cheeks. *Don't let him die,* Rebecca pleaded fearfully. *Please don't let him die.* For a few moments even the book was forgotten, but as the silence dragged on, she began to wonder whether he would have the strength to say any more. It came as a shock when he spoke again, his voice low but clear.

'The book is hidden where I thought no one would find it . . . It's in a room full of rubbish at the top of the East Tower . . . under a pile of old rags . . .'

My secret room! Rebecca was too filled with nervous anticipation to appreciate the irony of his choice of hiding place.

'Be careful,' Radd advised anxiously. 'The stairs are dangerous, and the floor is rotten in places.'

'I'll take care,' she promised. 'Thank you. I'll come back soon.' She leant over and kissed his cheek softly.

'May the Web protect you,' he added quietly as she left the room.

Emer took her father's hand once more, but Radd was fast asleep within moments.

*   *   *

At first, no one could believe the evidence of their own eyes. The salt had been still now for only a few hours, yet a vast army was marching from the heart of the flats towards the northern rim. Riders from several look-out posts headed for the castle at the same time, each carrying the same message. Montfort could not doubt them all; the impossible was happening, no matter how hard he found it to accept.

'From deep on the salt, you say?' he asked again.

'Yes, sire,' the first messenger confirmed.

'How many men?'

'Thousands, my lord,' a second rider replied. 'Though there was so much dust about it was hard to tell exactly.'

'And how long before they reach the rim?' Montfort asked, his heart sinking.

'Could be less than an hour,' was the answer.

The king was dumbfounded. *It can't be happening. It can't.*

'There's something else, my lord,' another messenger said hesitantly. 'There's strange lights in the sky above them, as if there's lightning but no thunder.' The others nodded in agreement.

'Aye. Some of the men reckon it's sorcery. They say those soldiers are dreekers,' one of them added.

'Rubbish!' Montfort exclaimed. 'They are men, and we'll meet them as men. Begin the preparations for the defence. I'll ride with you.'

Even while Montfort was shouting orders to his staff, he wanted to refuse to believe that his world was no longer that rational place he'd always thought it. But try as he might, the idea would not go away.

Has Rebecca been right all along?

CHAPTER SEVENTY-SEVEN

Rebecca walked the familiar route, her mood one of both hope and dread. Although she craved knowledge, she was aware that it might bring terrors with it.

The armoury in the lower part of the South Tower was in complete disorder, but she picked her way through the dangerous clutter without a second thought. The great southern wall had stood firm, however, and she soon reached the iron-studded door in the East Tower.

Once inside, Rebecca looked around with a feeling of trepidation. At some point during the earthquake, a large stone had obviously fallen from the top of the tower, crashing through the wooden floors and damaging some of the stairs. She began to climb, testing each step carefully, her heart thumping. The boards creaked ominously but held and she finally emerged into her hideaway.

The room was lighter than she remembered it. Pale sunlight streamed in through the narrow windows and the hole in the roof, which was much larger than on her last visit. Her eyes swept the familiar contents of the room – the rocking horse, the jars and handbells, the basket of candles, the broken furniture and pottery. The sight of some mildewed books made her heart beat even faster, but then she recognized them as her earlier, unreadable finds. The pile of clothes was on the far side of the chamber.

Rebecca edged her way across the room, skirting around the places where she knew the floor to be rotten. Outside, the wind moaned in the battlements like a frightened animal. She hesitated, understandably reluctant, then burrowed into the pile. She found the book immediately, and pulled it out. *Beneath the Salt* was slightly damp, but undamaged. The moment could be put off no longer. Rebecca sat down on the dusty, mildewed heap, feverishly turning the pages until she found the engraving of the black pyramid. Then she turned to the next page and skipped over the words until she reached the sentence that had haunted her for so long. Steeling herself, she read on.

Several give her name as Rebecka, though the spelling varies, and it was her death that apparently signalled the end of all hope for those who had sought to oppose the re-emergence of the city. Without her, it is assumed, their forces were unable to halt the enemy's advance, and, although the reason is never made clear, it is implied that she wielded considerable magical powers.

It was worse than Rebecca had imagined. If these dreadful events were happening again, it was *all* up to her.

But I'm not a wizard! she protested silently, then remembered her conversation with Sancia. '*Is dream-weaving magical?*' '*Not in itself. It can be used as a link to enhance the powers of true wizards.*' Rebecca's heart sank even further. Even with 'considerable magical powers', her namesake had lost. *And I don't have a full complement of wizards to help me!* She was angry now as well as frightened. *I'm not dead yet!* she told herself firmly. *The future can always be changed.* She forced herself to read on.

Depending upon which source one chooses to accept, the allegiance or nature of Rebecka is also uncertain. Some versions portray her as a tragic heroine who gave her life in the cause of justice, while others cast her in the role of a sorceress in thrall to an evil, tyrannical king, who is himself overthrown by the forces of righteousness.

Doubt flickered momentarily in her mind. Was Montfort really what he seemed? Then came her instinctive denial, and the realization that choosing between sides represented by the king and Cranne posed few problems. Rebecca was committed.

Your author offers no opinion on this matter, beyond stating that, in legend, as with history, one's attitude to truth is often defined by one's viewpoint.

She was growing impatient with Alomar's slightly pompous style, and was tempted to skip over some lines – but she did not dare.

One of the most complete and believable versions of this myth, and one which I myself have had the privilege of reading in the original manuscript . . .

Rebecca had a sudden vision of an old scholar sitting hunched over a yellow parchment in a cluttered, ill-lit room. *The story was ancient even when Alomar was alive!* she realized. *So it must predate the salt.*
The vision faded, leaving her with a feeling of affection for the Heretic of long ago whose life had been devoted to the search for truth. She returned to his text.

. . . is based upon the theory, now accepted by all scholars worthy of the name, that the Web is a vast circle, and that history therefore constantly repeats itself. Thus the Rebecka myth can be seen as a microcosm of all life in our world, an eternal struggle re-enacted for ever, in cycles which must be measured in hundreds, if not thousands, of years.
    The following is a faithful account of this version, though not in the archaic language of our ancient chronicler, whose name, alas, has been lost in the mists of time. I trust my reader will forgive the minor adjustments I have made in the translation in order to render the account intelligible to modern readers.

Oh, get on with it! Rebecca smiled in spite of herself, lost in the spell Alomar was weaving.

An evil king once ruled this land . . .

It's the story Annis told! She read on quickly, and found

that this tale soon diverged from her friend's version. It told of the king's obsession with immortality and his research into the subject much as Annis had done. But then it described the bargain with the evil side of the Web, by which he had hoped to achieve his ambition, in much greater detail.

The demons demanded a high price for their gift. Firstly, the king must die without an heir. All his children, legitimate or not, had to die. The king, by now insane with his lust for eternal life, agreed – slaughtering his royal heir with his own bloody hands and sending assassins to kill his other offspring.

The second demand was that the country's capital city be destroyed and its inhabitants put to death. The demons told the king that a vast deluge would annihilate the city, plunging it deep below the surface of a vast ocean. But beyond even that, the pitiless fiends demanded more deaths with which to feed their gargantuan appetites. Civil war was to follow, brought about by the uncertain succession and the seeds of jealousy already sown by the king among the rival, noble families.

And yet this carnage was still not enough to satisfy the demons. Their need for power-giving slaughter was to be projected far into the future, as a prerequisite for the completion of the bargain. These deaths were to take the form of a gift to the new sea, by the drowning of a great multitude – a further stipulation being that these souls, on which the demons would gorge themselves, were to be wrested from the soulless. This condition confused and worried the king, but then he solved the riddle and agreed readily.

The final part of the agreement concerned the king himself. He was to 'die' at a certain time, by drinking a certain poison, and was to be interred in a special tomb designed both to preserve his physical form and to accept power from the Web, thus building its potency until the time was ready.

Tyrrell's pyramid. In Rebecca's mind, the last piece of the puzzle fell into place. The parallels with her own time were frighteningly obvious. Substitute salt for sea and it was the same tale. Chilled in both body and heart, she forced herself to continue.

In return for his compliance, the demons pledged themselves to reveal a certain portion of their secrets, allowing a few of the king's trusted fellow conspirators to escape the deluge and to unnaturally prolong their lives. They would not yet be immortal – though that ultimate reward was promised – but they would be able to prepare, through the long generations, for the time when all would be ready and the bargain fulfilled. Finally, the king would return, reborn as a god, all powerful, to rule his country for ever.

Before this might come to pass, however, many centuries would run their course, thus allowing the power to accumulate and the configurations of the Web to be at their most favourable. In addition, other events must occur simultaneously, elements similar to those at the very beginning of the process. The land must once again be ruled by an heirless king, civil war must have been declared, and the soulless men must have set sail upon the demon sea.

The mercenaries! In Ahrenia, foreigners – especially those from the south, whose cold eyes and pale skin made them appear almost inhuman – were often thought of as soulless. And paid soldiers, men with no compassion or pity, were the least human of all their race. *And they are already upon the sea*, Rebecca thought. *The sea of salt. And if the Archaeologists are right, then they have already 'drowned'. All the conditions have been fulfilled*. Just as complete terror threatened to overwhelm Rebecca, she glimpsed a tiny spark of hope in the next paragraph.

The king had agreed to the demons' terms, and had sealed the pact in blood, but his plotting was spied upon by three wizards, who, though powerless to stop the bargain being undertaken, set out to prevent its fulfilment.

Three wizards in Derith born.

623

The king died, and was buried. Then came the deluge, the most terrible catastrophe that the world had ever witnessed. Yet the civil war eventually came to an end, a new king was crowned, and a new capital city proclaimed. The years passed, and the fearful events were gradually forgotten. Peace came to the land, and its people flourished. But in a remote corner of the realm, the old king's evil allies slowly increased their arcane knowledge, prolonging their lives by demon-fed power, always looking ahead to the ultimate prize. These men became sorcerers, feared throughout the land; as such they attracted acolytes, and passed their secrets from one generation to the next, until their power was at last sufficient for their task.

But the sorcerers knew that they had not been the only ones to escape from the doomed city. The wizards had themselves been trapped, and had died with the rest, but they had foreseen the disaster and so had been able to warn certain of their apprentices. These students had escaped before the deluge of salt, taking with them the knowledge, their most precious weapon, of how to fight against the king's bargain. And so a mortal enmity grew up between the two groups, each working to destroy the other.

However, as the sorcerers' power grew, so that of the apprentices declined. In such an ill-matched fight, much of the wizards' lore was lost. Yet even this had been foreseen by the three old masters, and they left clues in their art for those who would know how to read them. Thus, when the time came, wizardry might be reborn to face the evil foe.

Here, at last, was a slim strand of hope for Rebecca. *Jarlath's monks are the sorcerers*, she realized, fighting to keep everything clear in her own mind. *And the Heretics are the wizards' apprentices – Kedar, Annis and Newell.* So much of what she had discovered seemed obvious now. It was no wonder that the Heretics' history had been so clouded and vague. After centuries of attrition, it was incredible that the organization had survived at all. Not only had almost all its records been destroyed, but most of those still in existence had been transformed by the monks, making them seem like the ramblings of lunatics.

And yet the brethren and their allies had not entirely succeeded. The clues still remained – even if they had seemed absurdly obscure at first! The Okran Stones were the most obvious message, but Kavan's painting of the monk, the prophetic snow-cluster marble carvings, Galen's fossilized book, even Annis's story, had been the work of the ancient wizards. Rebecca was sure of this – and equally sure that all that effort could not have been in vain. *No destiny is certain.*

But in the end, even this was not enough.

When she read this, Rebecca's last hopes shattered, and she wanted to scream with frustration, to cast the book away and deny its existence, its uncanny accuracy. But she knew she must read the story to its bitter end. And it was bitter indeed.

The last battle was fought on unequal terms. Although the Seeress of Night, a prescient maid who lived by the seashore, made a belated attempt to harness the talents of the three wizards – whose spirits had re-emerged together from the Web for the first time in centuries – her efforts were doomed to failure. The conflict was over almost before it began. The reborn king was truly invincible, as was his soulless army. Magic and arms proved equally useless against them, and most of their opponents fled in terror, without even attempting to fight. Only the Seeress of Night resisted, but she was slain by the evil conqueror himself. All else fell in ruins.

The demon-king ruled from his newly-risen city, and exacted a cruel revenge for the age he had spent beneath the sea. His minions became purveyors of terror, as cold-blooded as their miserable underwater lives had been, and the sorcerers, themselves immortal now, indulged their depraved appetites with years of pain and suffering for the subjugated people of the land.

Eventually, as with all immortals, the king and his

sorcerers grew bored with such indulgences, and set off to torment other realms, leaving the land to rebuild itself slowly, and try and regain some measure of peace and happiness. Until, many years later, another king, all unknowing, began to wonder about immortality . . . and the whole cycle began again.

Rebecca stared at the page, though she no longer saw the words that were written there. Everything fitted. Everything! *What am I to do?* She shivered, the damp cold of the tower having settled in her bones. Knowing the certainty of defeat, was there any point in trying? The wind howled, and she remembered Newell's music, and wondered fleetingly where he was. *What can I do?*

Her own name drew her attention back to the final paragraph, and Alomar spoke to her across the centuries.

'I am too remote here in my northern home to speculate on whether this version of the Rebecka myth has parallels with our own time. My old bones are too weary now, and I do not travel far. Derith was buried by salt two hundred years ago, and Tyrrell did indeed die without a direct heir, but already the details of his passing are hard to find. Yet there *are* clues, many of them illustrated in this book. One day their meaning will be found, and on that day, all those of us of like mind will be with the new Rebecka in spirit, even as she fails. The dark age which will follow is not to be contemplated.

CHAPTER SEVENTY-EIGHT

Montfort stood on top of one of the earthworks that were the land's last line of defence against the salt. As he stared out over the flats, he tried not to let the disbelief and horror show on his face, but knew he was not succeeding. All about him, his men stood in silence, a palpable sense of dismay in the air.

The enemy army, only a few hundred paces away now, was huge, and advancing relentlessly straight into the teeth of the defences of the rim. Their massed ranks had raised a cloud of dust, and behind them, dwarfing such a petty haze, a salt-storm glittered in the pale sunlight. And above that, silent lightning flashed, staining the clear sky a lurid yellow. Even the sun itself seemed tainted.

'It's impossible to tell exactly how many there are, sire,' one of Montfort's captains told him. 'But they've brought their entire force here. There have been no sightings anywhere else on the rim.'

'It's as though they've deliberately chosen to attack our strongest point,' another officer added.

'So much the better,' Montfort replied, hoping his voice still carried some conviction. 'Have the outlying units been recalled?'

'Yes, sire. They're on their way.'

'Some have already arrived, my lord.'

Tarrant came up beside the king.

'I've sent for the other catapults, too,' he reported. 'I'm not sure they'll get here in time, but there's no harm in trying.'

They were standing a few paces from one of the wooden contraptions, an awkward-looking beast which appeared coiled and ready to spring. Tarrant stared southwards.

627

'They'll soon be in range,' he added.

'Then let's give them a taste of our fire-power,' Montfort decreed. 'To your positions! Remember, we hold our ground. This time the terrain is to our advantage.'

Combative instincts came to the fore, and officers hurried to take charge of their troops, messengers rode off to convey the orders elsewhere, and Tarrant's men made the final preparations to the four catapults. Tarrant knew their range from tests he had conducted earlier, and now he waited patiently for the enemy to reach the target zone. Then he raised a flaming torch as a signal to the other crews before lowering it to light the oily covering of the missile. Four wooden beams sprang up, releasing their fiery comets into the sky. Each trailed dark smoke in a lazy arc over the salt; each was watched by thousands of pairs of eager eyes. They landed in the midst of the front ranks of the enemy, with devastating effect. Four huge explosions flared within moments of each other, throwing bodies and great gobbets of salt into the air. A ragged cheer went up from the defenders, and Tarrant surveyed his handiwork with some satisfaction. But then the jubilant shouts died away. Apart from four gaps, which had obviously taken the full force of the explosions, the enemy's army had not been affected, and marched on as though nothing had happened. The panic and confusion that Montfort's men had expected were nowhere in evidence.

'Reload!' Tarrant cried urgently.

'Such discipline is not human,' one officer breathed. 'Even for mercenaries.' He was not alone in voicing this thought; whispers ran through the defenders' ranks as they waited behind their makeshift fortifications.

Again the fireballs flew, and still the enemy came on, their remorseless march uninterrupted. The level of fear in the royal army rose another notch.

Riders were hurriedly distributing Cluny's hand-held weapons to those who had been trained in their use, but first the archers had their turn. A wave of arrows formed a dark cloud in the air, but though the salvo was dead accurate for the most part, it did not appear to have much effect on the enemy ranks. Officers prepared their men f the inevitable close combat, and the hand-held explosives were brought into action, filling the air with noise and smoke. And through it all, the enemy pressed on.

In such scenes of bedlam, the full horror of what the defenders were facing became clear only as the enemy drew near. Many of the soldiers had suffered horrendous wounds; arms had been torn away, gaping holes ripped in torsos; arrows protruded obscenely from chests and limbs – and some men were even missing parts of their heads. For normal men, such injuries would have meant certain death, but the mercenaries marched on relentlessly. Worse still was the fact that among the soldiers were a number of skeletal creatures, lurching forward like visions from a graveyard nightmare. And behind them, a glittering whirlwind of salt towered in the sky, promising further horrors.

Montfort and his officers did their best to rally their men, but few had the stomach for such a fight. An enemy force that could walk unconcerned through such detonations, who could take arrows through their hearts and suffer mortal wounds yet still advance, spoke of such evil sorcery that even the king's most loyal followers knew they had met their match. Most fled; a few stayed to face the horror and clash swords with these fearful not-men, but it was soon obvious that their cause was hopeless. Everyone who knew the salt knew what these creatures were. Dreekers walked the earth once more, a nightmare come to life. Their very name was a watchword for terror, and it spread like wildfire on the lips of Montfort's army.

The king himself stood with his sword in his hand, feeling stunned and sickened. The appearance of the dreekers had dealt such a blow to his mind that he was teetering on the brink of insanity. His whole philosophy, the very core of his being had been shattered by the events of one hour – and now his body refused to obey him, paralysed as it was by helpless dread. He could not force himself to enter the battle.

Tarrant and a few others had thrown themselves into the cauldron of terror. The envoy hacked and hewed, inflicting terrible damage on the somehow ponderous soldiers of the enemy. One vicious blow severed an opponent's neck completely, sending his head spinning to the ground, yet

629

the body did not fall. It stumbled forward, flailing blindly with its own weapon while Tarrant stared in disgust and horrified disbelief.

'Take their legs!' he yelled desperately. 'They can't keep coming without *them*!'

He followed his own advice, disabling another soldier who had already taken one arrow through his stomach and another through his eye. The man fell to the ground, where he continued to squirm uselessly. None of the enemy soldiers had uttered a sound either in pain or fury, and their uncanny silence made them even more menacing. Even more revolting was the fact that they did not bleed. Open wounds resembled red jelly, embedded with bones and internal organs, but no blood spurted forth.

The dreekers' advance slowed a little as Montfort's rearguard defended the slopes at the rim, but the tide of battle was unstoppable. Deserted by most of their allies, Tarrant and his companions were forced to flee. The envoy had seen many good men cut down by the empty-eyed mercenaries, and it could only get worse.

Some of the most loyal soldiers retreated to the castle with their devastated king, while the enemy hordes poured over the salt-barriers and marched towards Edgefield.

In the town, all was panic. Civilians were leaving as fast as they could, taking only what they could carry. Looting was commonplace, and people were fighting over horses. The soldiers who knew the truth, and from whom the news had spread, were even more desperate to get away. Edgefield's streets and alleys were soon clogged with terrified people, and only the strongest and most ruthless made any progress as they struggled towards the roads leading north.

Barely three hundred men returned to the castle to await the siege – each certain in his heart that he would not live to see another day.

*   *   *

Only the Seeress of Night resisted . . . but what can I do Rebecca was still in the tower, paralysed by helpless drea *What if I don't resist at all?* She was desperate to find som way – any way – to move events away from the book's predictions. But she knew, even as she posed the question, that she could not just give in. She would play her role because she must. Although the prospect of her own death loomed in her thoughts, it merely left her numb; the fate of Ahrenia, however, left her utterly appalled. *The dark age which will follow . . .*

At least Rebecka tried! she told herself. *Can I do less?* She repeated Radd's words, trying to convince herself. *The future can always be changed. No destiny is certain.* Rebecca wondered whether the chamberlain believed his own statements. Why had he hidden the book for so long? Another voice penetrated her misery. *Accept the Web and all things are possible.*

She got slowly to her feet, and the fateful book dropped from her cold fingers. It was of no use to her now. Rebecca shivered, glancing around the room as if reacquainting herself with real world. *Kin of the ages, heed wakening. Hold the dream, enact the will,* she thought. *I'll try, Sancia. I'll do my best.*

She crossed the hazardous floor carefully and made her way down the steps. Her only plan was to find Kedar and Annis – and preferably Emer and Galen as well. Perhaps together they might find a way to weave their magic into something tangible.

As Rebecca stepped outside, she was buffeted by the wind. She turned the corner of the great wall and looked along the battlements of the south section. Two soldiers were wrestling just a few paces away. She hesitated, glanced down into the castle courtyard and saw chaos, with men running in all directions.

A cry brought Rebecca's attention back to the struggle ahead of her. One of the assailants had succeeded in throwing the other over the outer edge. The defeated man fell screaming to his death, while the victor stooped to pick up his discarded sword. Then he turned to face her.

Rebecca felt as though she had been turned to stone. She could not even scream. Cranne had returned from the dead.

CHAPTER SEVENTY-NINE

Cranne hesitated, his expression betraying no emotion. It was almost as though he was waiting for someone to tell him what to do. Eventually, he began to move towards her, his sword held out in front of him, and his face an impassive mask – which was somehow even more frightening than the anger or cruel gloating Rebecca had expected. There was a deep gash in his cheek and another on one arm, but no blood had come from either wound. His clothes were stained with a fine white powder.

Rebecca stood petrified, wildly running through her options. There was nowhere for her to run – she knew of no other way down from the tower. She could jump to her death, and end her torment, or rush at Cranne – and be killed by him. *What am I to do?*

Then a waking dream seized her as it had done during the chess game, its reality superimposed upon the world's. Everything seemed to move in slow motion. *Time is not constant in dreams.*

A small boy, his body ghostly and transparent, appeared between her and Cranne. He was brandishing a wooden toy sword at the approaching man, but Cranne did not seem to notice him. The boy turned round to face Rebecca, his face full of worry, his eyes round with fear.

'Don't let him hurt you!' the child cried. 'He mustn't!' He turned back to face Cranne, but the dreeker ignored him, his empty eyes still fixed on his prey. At every step, the child retreated, his image fading as he drew closer to Rebecca.

From somewhere in her memory, Rebecca heard Gale tell her about a theory of Peyton's. *Perhaps there are ghosts of the future as well as ghosts of the dead. The spirits of people who might have been born, but who never were – because their parents never met or died too soon.*

The boy was her own son! Rebecca knew this for the truth as soon as the thought occurred to her. *And he's trying to protect me!* Her heart almost broke at the sight of his forlorn efforts, the tiny toy sword matched against unforgiving steel. *If I die, he will never live.* An intense, impossible maternal instinct awoke within her – and she prepared to defend a ghost.

Rebecca stepped forward, and as she did so, Cranne halted, alert but still expressionless. His blood-stained sword was still held ready. The child also held his ground.

Help me! It was a cry in the wilderness, and Rebecca expected no answer. But one came.

A light appeared, formless at first but none the less instantly welcome; it surrounded the boy like a glowing shield as a familiar, longed-for voice spoke in Rebecca's mind.

You should have called on us before, child.

'Granma! Granma!' the boy cried, looking up at the light and smiling, no longer afraid.

For you, my child, the light will never fade, Rebecca thought. *Hello, Mother.*

The gentle glow became more distinct and Sancia's shape took form, standing beside the boy.

Hello, Rebecca.

Look after him, she pleaded.

Of course, her mother's voice replied. *But you must protect yourself.*

Cranne had paused, aware of something between them but obviously unable to see what it was. Rebecca realized suddenly that her son was vastly important – not just to her, but to the whole world. She *had* to stay alive. She had to give her son life!

The child and his spectral guardian disappeared, and the dream was over. Rebecca was back in the real world, with Cranne approaching ever closer.

A commotion erupted behind him as men emerged from the great South Tower. A frantic sword fight was spilling on to the battlements, and the air was suddenly filled with the clash of steel and angry shouts. Cranne glanced back over his shoulder, and Rebecca wondered whether to take advantage of his momentary distraction and run. Perhaps she could somehow trap him in the tower. But her plans came to nought as another voice froze her to the spot.

'Let me through, let me through!' Radd pushed past the flying blades, miraculously unscathed. He was pale and limping, and obviously in a lot of pain, but he seemed possessed by some unearthly form of energy. 'I heard her!' he cried, as he hobbled towards the unmoving Cranne. 'Where is she?'

Farrand's son watched the chamberlain's erratic progress for a few moments, then rushed towards Rebecca. As she turned to flee, she slipped on an uneven flagstone and fell, grazing her hands and one elbow on the rough stone of the battlements. Cranne loomed over her as she tried to scramble to her feet. His sword was raised, flashing in the sunlight, and in its deadly gleaming she saw her son fade from existence.

'No!' she screamed for him.

Cranne hesitated fractionally, and in that moment Radd crashed into him, shouting incoherently. The chamberlain was unarmed, but his insane attack meant that Cranne missed his target, and his blade struck sparks as it hit only unyielding stone. Rebecca slid away as Cranne turned upon his assailant, throwing him aside easily with his free arm. Radd landed heavily, but even that did not still his tongue.

'Where is she?' he pleaded, his eyes wild. 'Where's my Clara?' Rebecca had never known him speak the name of his long-dead wife aloud before. 'I heard her.'

So Sancia speaks for her too, she thought, filled with a great sorrow.

Cranne had recovered now, and turned on Radd as the older man got painfully to his feet.

'When you truly love someone, Rebecca,' the chamberlain gasped, 'the light never goes out. She's come for me at last.'

Cranne lunged. Radd made no effort to avoid the thrust, and the blade sank deep into his chest. Blood gushed forth as Rebecca looked on, stricken with grief and horror. But

Radd seemed to welcome the death blow, and reached forward to grab both the sword's cross-piece and Cranne's arm. He pulled them towards him, driving the blade even deeper, until it grated on the stone behind his back.

Taken by surprise, Cranne staggered, and Radd used the moment to lurch sideways, dragging sword and swordsman with him.

'It's up to you now, Rebecca,' her one-time tutor breathed. 'Fight for all of us.' He was smiling as he toppled backwards through one of the square openings in the battlements. Cranne was still gripped in a deathly vice, and both men disappeared, falling to the stony ground far below.

Rebecca rushed to look down, brushing the tears from her eyes. Radd lay still, at peace; Cranne's body was broken beyond repair. It still writhed, but he was no threat now.

Rebecca's resolve was complete. *It's up to you now. Fight for all of us.* She knew that she would fight to the end.

* * *

Pike and his companions reached the castle just in time. They had to fight their way through the town, battling against the press of people fleeing in the opposite direction. They managed to escort their unwilling passenger to the gates, and were admitted just before they were closed in preparation for the last-ditch defence.

'Well, young man,' the veteran remarked. 'I hope you're worth all this.'

Newell's habitual surliness had been replaced by fear and bewilderment. 'What am I supposed to do?' he asked, looking around at the chaotic scenes within the castle. The young musician grasped his viol like a talisman.

'There's others that will tell you that,' Pike answered. *I hope*, he added to himself. 'We'll find them.'

Soldiers were rushing to their positions, manning the many weak spots in the castle's defences. There was no thought of defending the great South Wall, but Pike had seen a grappling hook fly over the battlements there, and knew he must act.

'No time now,' he growled. 'Come on!' he yelled to his men,

and they followed him, leaving Newell alone and utterly confused.

A man and a woman emerged from the building to the right of the gate, and the three stared at each other. Although they had never met before, there was recognition in their gaze.

'Hello, Boomer,' Annis said.

'We've b-been waiting for you,' Kedar added, tapping his fingers on the blank canvas under his arm.

* * *

Pike found that Tarrant had got there ahead of him, their uncanny instincts drawing both to the South Wall and the unexpected danger. But on this occasion they were too late. Enemy forces were already inside the South Tower, and the fighting was fierce in the confined spaces. The two men had little time to grimace at each other in recognition before they were in the thick of the action.

'Who's that?' Pike yelled, pointing upwards with his sword.

'Radd,' Tarrant answered. 'What's he doing there?'

The chamberlain was high above them, making for the battlements. They were never to see him again. Tarrant and his men cut their way through the enemy, dismembering the deathless soldiers and leaving behind a trail of hideous twitching flesh. When they emerged on to the wall, they saw Rebecca at the far end. They stormed towards her, clearing the battlements and cutting down the enemy ropes. When Tarrant reached the girl, he held her while she sobbed, crying from a mixture of grief and shock – and relief at her own narrow escape from death. The envoy's own emotions were also in turmoil. He could not remember ever having been so affected by a woman's distress, and wished that his arms were not protected by mail; he longed for his embrace to be warmer, less impersonal.

At the same time, Emer and Galen emerged from the other end of the battlements, having evidently found a way up the entire height of the East Tower. Tarrant stepped back from the emotional reunion. Rebecca looked into her friend's face, unable to hide her pain.

'Your father . . . ' she began, then hesitated when she saw the fear in Emer's eyes. 'He saved my life.'

'He's dead, isn't he,' Radd's daughter said, her voice sad but resigned.

'Yes. He died with . . . with the man who was trying to kill me.'

'We couldn't stop him,' Emer said, fighting back her tears. 'He was shouting about wanting to join my mother.'

'They're both part of the Web now,' Rebecca tried to reassure her friend.

Emer nodded and swallowed hard.

'It's what he wanted,' she said determinedly. 'And we have other work to do.'

She nodded towards the south, and they all looked out over the flats. Only a few hundred paces away, a salt whirlwind towered into the sky. It was even closer than the edge of the salt. As they watched, it collapsed in on itself, clearing the air as though a glittering curtain had suddenly been drawn back. What was revealed was even more terrifying; a huge blaze of bright flames, a tower of demonic fire.

And within the tower, woven into the flame, were hundreds of skeletal figures, their thin bodies twisted in demented agony. Rebecca recognized the silent throng of her dream, and knew that the ancient citizens of Derith had been raised to the land of the sun once more. Yet this was not the escape they had longed for. Here, as below, they were the helpless, tormented pieces in a game played by greater powers.

On top of the tower stood a man – or what had once been a man. A voice like thunder rolled from his lips.

'I am Tyrrell. I hold your doom in the palm of my hand!'

The god-king laughed, and the sound shook Edgefield Castle to its foundations.

CHAPTER EIGHTY

Almost all the fighting ceased when both the monks and Montfort's soldiers became aware that the real battle – the outcome of which would decide all their fates – was between Tyrrell and those he faced on the castle's southern wall. The monks smiled, anticipating their victory, while the soldiers looked frightened and confused.

Rebecca stood rooted to the spot, feeling totally insignificant before her opponent's casual display of power. The dream world imposed itself upon her senses once more, giving her a tiny measure of security. She was aware of movement within that nether-space, of patterns merging and shifting. Triangles of light appeared in the infinite darkness. Clearest of all was the link between herself, Emer and Galen, both standing near her now, a firm base of love and strength. Beyond that, a little more distant, the three wizards stood together, awaiting her direction. Rebecca's heart leapt. *Newell's here!* She sensed the potential within the trio, but knew that they needed her instruction in order to harness it. Each of them held an emblem of their art; Kedar the salt-white canvas, Annis the now coverless fossilized book, and Newell his ancient stringed instrument. Each emblem was a gateway to the Web, waiting for them to express their wizard's magic. With a jolt, Rebecca realized that each item was a gift bequeathed by the first three Heretics. Old magic and new; it was her task now to bring them together.

Much further away, she saw yet another triangle. Kavan and his two colleagues of old lay dormant inside the Web. But they were held fast, enmeshed by the demonic power of Tyrrell's centuries of careful preparation. *They're trapped!* Rebecca realized that they needed their own dream-weaver, one within the Web, whose talent could unweave the evil king's malignant snare and free the wizards for the fight. As soon as she realized this, she knew that their dream-weaver was her son. *But if I die, he will not be strong enough.* She saw again the vision of the child fading as Cranne drew near, intent on her death. *A pale ghost.* Her death would deal a crucial, double blow, affecting the battle in both worlds. *Why not Sancia?* she wondered desperately. *She's in the Web.* The answer came back immediately. *The Web chooses its own partners. I have different work to do.* Rebecca wanted to ask more, but the presence faded.

There were countless other patterns within the Web, within her waking dream, but most were vague, shifting randomly. Rebecca knew that while some of these patterns were set, immovable, other strands were still free.

Weave well, my child.

This all passed through her mind in the instant after Tyrrell's laugh, but now he spoke again and everything became focused on the immediate conflict. Rebecca was hardly aware of the others on the battlements with her. More men had arrived since Tarrant and his colleagues had cleared the wall, but they were anonymous, mere spectators. Everyone stared, mesmerized by Tyrrell's image. Blood from the cut on Rebecca's elbow trickled unheeded down her arm.

'Well, Seeress, how do you choose to die?' The god-king's voice boomed out, rolling over the castle and echoing in the town beyond. He was obviously amused, enjoying the last few moves of a game which could only have one result.

'I choose to live!' Rebecca shouted back. Her voice was tiny by comparison, but resolute.

Tyrrell laughed again.

'That choice is not yours to make,' he roared. 'You see my power.' He flicked one gauntleted hand and a gout of flame shot forth, enveloping the top of the South Tower. The air was filled with cracking sounds as stones splintered in the intense heat and wood turned to ashes in moments. 'You and your puny friends cannot match me,' Tyrrell mocked. 'But perhaps you should try!' The evil face smiled, and Rebecca sensed a vague familiarity – but one she could not place . . .

'I am not the only one who opposes you!' she cried. 'The wizards . . . '

'Are in my power,' he completed for her, gloating. 'You know that now. They cannot help you, and you can never reach them. And as for your new *allies* . . . ' He laughed derisively. 'I have seen them. What are their pathetic talents compared to mine? They are fit only for the fairgrounds from whence they came.'

Rebecca had a sudden vision of the fair where she had met Sancia, and of the play she had witnessed there; the actors' words, the visual effects of scenery, lighting and costumes, and the music which had heightened the drama and emotion. Three arts combined as one. *True magic reveals itself.*

Now she knew how to weave the talents of her allies, and she cried out in silent appeal.

Help me!

Emer and Galen were with her immediately, and she took comfort from that, but it was the wizards she needed most. She could not see them, but that did not matter now.

Help me!

I have the canvas but not my brushes, Kedar answered.

You do not need them.

What should I paint?

A shield around us.

I can open the pages now! Annis sounded surprised. *Where should I read?*

The book is a gateway – nothing more.

The pages are all blank!

You do not need them – tell a story of your own.

I can play, Newell said. *But what?*

The old music – but your own.

I don't understand.

Just play. The music will teach you.

And so the combined talents of the three wizards fused into a whole. Music rose from the castle courtyard, a wailing, hypnotic sound that stilled every noise except the storyteller's voice. Her words were universal, and spoke directly to everyone who heard. Wedged between these two was a vision of creation that made the story true, the music

640

real. The colours of a wizard's imagination painted the very fabric of the world.

And the words told how true magic awoke for the first time in centuries, how it was woven into a shield of light. Newell's music forged a direct link through the substance of the Web, and Kedar's artistry gave it form.

Most of the mesmerized onlookers saw the arcane painting as a glowing sign, written on the air around Rebecca, and consisting of two overlapping triangles inscribed within a circle. But others, according to their own vision, saw it differently. Some saw a massive black shield of steel, others a crystal cloud of rainbow hues – but all were moved by the sight.

Together, the magic of the three wizards was not three times greater, but a *hundredfold*. Yet still it was not enough.

Tyrrell clapped his hands in thunderous, sarcastic applause.

'Very pretty,' he mocked. 'So my old adversaries' plans did not entirely fail. But what do you seek to achieve by this pitiful display?' His tone was amused and condescending.

Rebecca had sensed the growing power of the three wizards and, with the aid of Emer and Galen, had used her dream-weaver's talent to give it purpose. She had been as shaken by its strength, as amazed by the shield's appearance, as any of the onlookers, but she also knew that it was still desperately weak compared to Tyrrell's inferno of centuries-old malice. The three ancients were still trapped and helpless, their wizardry usurped and perverted to the god-king's purpose. Without their help, Rebecca knew, defeat was only a matter of time.

'How long can you keep up this charade?' Tyrrell roared, echoing her thoughts. 'Shall I tell the brethren to set my minions upon you again? Your shield holds you fast – and will not defend you against dreekers. Nor will it protect your friends. Don't you wish to avoid such useless slaughter?'

Help me!

In the real world, someone put their mail-clad arms about her from behind, embracing her with great gentleness. Within the Web, her son reappeared, stronger than ever.

Rebecca looked at him with renewed hope, but his little face was distressed.

I can't reach them, Mummy! the boy cried miserably. *It's too hard.* He was close to tears, distressed by his failure.

'Do not think to free the ancients, child!' Tyrrell boomed.

He knows everything we do, Rebecca thought helplessly.

'Give up the struggle, Rebecca. Accept your fate. You know it has already been foretold. My power within the Web is too strong.' Tyrrell's face creased into an evil smirk once more. 'You've had enough of this, eh?' One hawk-like eye closed in a grotesque wink.

Suddenly, Rebecca knew why the god-king seemed familiar. A dream-image from months ago flashed into her mind – and she was trapped within a picture frame inside the Gallery while characters from other portraits stared at her. One of them had winked at her like that.

There was movement again now below the walls. The dreekers had woken up. Shouts and screams mingled with the clash of steel as the fighting resumed. Tyrrell had lost patience with the game.

Above the tumult, Rebecca shouted as loud as she could.

'Your bargain is not fulfilled! *Cadell was your son!*'

Silence descended once more as the brethren sensed the danger in her words. Tyrrell seemed momentarily taken aback. Odd flashes of colour, crimson and purple, rippled through the tower of flame.

'I am your descendant!' Rebecca cried, flinging the words at him like poisoned arrows. 'The conditions were not fulfilled, and the bargain is void!'

'You lie!' Tyrrell roared.

For answer, Rebecca dipped her fingers in the blood that still ran from her elbow, and held up her red-stained hand.

'Your blood runs in my veins, Tyrrell!' she yelled. 'This is my proof!'

Behind the tower of flame, the air began to stir, shimmering like a giant heat haze.

'Absurd!' Tyrrell cried, but the absolute certainty had gone from his voice. 'I killed my heir with my own hands – and all my bastards were slain by the brethren.'

'All except one!' Rebecca replied, her voice quieter now

but even more resonant.

The Web confirmed her accusation as she spoke, and she glimpsed the faces of a long line of ancestors – from herself and Baldemar, through the generations to Cadell . . . and to Tyrrell. She was not the only one to see it. There was fear in the god-king's eyes for the first time. Fire lashed out in all directions, and men ducked instinctively, hiding behind blistering stone. Rebecca and those near her were protected by the magic shield.

The cage around the three ancients was unravelling now. Gateways within the Web were opening. Old and new wizards greeted each other in joy and mutual recognition as Rebecca and her son wove their strands of power together.

I've found them, Mummy! His young voice was full of triumph.

Well done, little one, she replied gently.

'No!' Tyrrell screamed. The ear-shattering sound was echoed by the brethren, their tasks forgotten in the face of new terrors. The shimmering in the air behind the god-king grew more violent.

Three wizards in Derith born,
Below the salt, hold Web of old.

All the triangles were working together now. Every Heretic who had ever lived added his voice to the recitation. Now that the ancients were free, the true magic was a thousand times more powerful. Newell was no longer playing alone, and his music became the sound of the whole world; of the plains, the seas, the mountains and the sky; the sound of the stars, sun and moon. Of every living thing. Of heath and farmland, desert and snow. And of the salt-flats.

Kedar's vision had joined with Kavan's; together they painted on a canvas the size of the world – the world as it *should* be.

Annis opened her book at a new, empty page, and with her ancient counterpart began to tell a story. A story that was different from any the world had ever heard.

CHAPTER EIGHTY-ONE

Kin of the ages, heed wakening.
Hold the dream, enact the will.

Annis's story was Rebecca's story. It was Rebecca who was the catalyst for all the others, weaving all the strands together. It was Rebecca who felt a surge of incredible joy, not for her own survival but for that of her world, her son, her ancient counterparts – all the Rebeccas who had tried and failed. Past and future met in her.

One magic fate in terror lies.

The fires beneath Tyrrell were growing more erratic now, the flames of variable colour and strength. He was screaming still, calling for blood, for deaths to feed his corrupt being, but his charges were lost to him now. The magic of the two sets of wizards and their allies had become an incandescent force, reasserting the justice of the Web. The human soldiers watched in awe as the hooded monks aged horrifically before their eyes. In a few short moments, the skin of the brethren, their emaciated flesh, even their bones, rotted and shrivelled, crumbling to dust and rags. Their death agonies, though brief, were hideous. Now that the tainted bargain which had supported them for so long had collapsed, they paid for their unnatural longevity in a gruesome manner. By contrast, the soulless dreekers simply fell to the ground and lay still. They had become men again – dead men, at peace at last. Tyrrell's army was no more.

Two parts sift to face the foe.

The shimmering in the air took shape, and two massive demons, creatures of fire and ice, loomed over Tyrrell. He seemed very small now, trapped within the dying flames.

'No!' he cried. 'I kept my part of the bargain. It's a trick!

The demons approached, their burning eyes implacable. Great talons stretched out towards their prey.

'You must have *known*!' Tyrrell screamed, desperate now. 'Why didn't you tell me?'

Still they did not reply. They were utterly indifferent to his hysterical ravings, their silence implying that the reasons for his failure were no concern of theirs. A debt was due – and they were here to collect it.

Before the astonished, jubilant, but still fearful eyes of those who watched from the castle, the demons tore the very fabric of Tyrrell's being apart. His body was ripped to shreds; so too was his evil-engorged soul, until nothing remained and his anguished screams were silenced. Tyrrell would not even survive in the Web. This was total annihilation.

Their work done, the demons glanced at Rebecca, recognizing the child on the salt from years before. She was not alone in her terror, wondering what would happen next, but the demons merely looked at her. After a few moments, they began to fade, and then the shimmering tower sank into the earth.

And with it went the last remnants of Derith's long-dead inhabitants. Their bones returned to their hidden resting places and their spirits were released from their vile subjugation. They went silently, feeling neither joy nor sorrow, but only relief. Their long torment was over at last.

Three balance ancient fears.

Far to the south, in the middle of the salt-flats, the reborn Derith trembled. Walls cracked, towers toppled, and the great bell was silenced – this time for ever. The crystal bridge shattered, and the black pyramid exploded in the grip of unimaginable forces. Huge pieces of torgrist were flung far and wide as the salt reclaimed its own.

The earth shook for leagues around as the city sank beneath the waves of a dry, crystalline sea. Everything sank down into the darkness, regaining its original resting place. The flats were silent once more, serene and unbroken save for the dark heights of Blackator.

When the earth finally stopped trembling, the wizards' shield faded. Its work was done. Tyrrell and all his evil was gone. Gone for ever.

In the courtyard, Kedar, Annis and Newell stood silent and still, their eyes shining with achievement. They fell into each other's arms, triumphant, yet utterly weary.

On the battlements, Rebecca sagged, too drained to fully appreciate all that had happened. Slowly, she turned in the circle of the strong arms that still held her, and saw who had supported her in the last moments of the conflict. Montfort's eyes looked back at her, wonder and more reflected in them.

'Now do you believe in magic?' she asked softly.

'I believe in you,' he whispered.

They were both aware of the hundreds of people watching them, those close by on the wall as well as the soldiers and castle staff below. It was a private moment of satisfaction for Rebecca, none the less.

'I was right though, wasn't I?' she persisted, smiling. 'Admit it.'

Montfort did not answer. Instead, he pulled her to him and kissed her. This time there was no drawing back, even when the cheers rang out from their delighted audience, cheers which grew even louder as the kiss went on. Rebecca responded willingly to his fierce passion, fully aware of what this act meant for the king. When they finally drew apart, her eyes were filled with tears of joy.

She knew now who was to be the father of her son.

EPILOGUE

Tarrant was drunk. Even in a city bent on anticipatory celebration, he would normally have remained sober, reckoning that he always needed his wits about him. This evening was different, however, and his drinking companion knew why. Pike watched his captain with indulgent amusement mixed with genuine concern. The younger man was as dear to him as a son – though he would never have admitted it.

'She was always special,' Tarrant announced. 'Knew it from th' start.'

'No one would deny that,' Pike answered.

'Right fr'm chess game . . . ' the young man mumbled, then roused himself and spoke more clearly. 'A' first it was th' practical matter of inheritance. She's a woman.'

'So I'd noticed,' his companion responded drily.

'Can't be baron if you're a woman,' Tarrant stated, emphasizing each word with a pointing finger.

Pike nodded sagely at this profound observation.

'So it's importan' who she marries. Hah!' The sometime envoy paused to take another swig of his drink. 'Bu' more than that . . . ' he resumed. 'I knew she was a wizard. I *knew*!'

'A dream-weaver,' Pike corrected him mildly.

'Same thing,' Tarrant said dismissively. 'I felt it in my bones.'

'I know.'

'How?' the younger man asked suspiciously.

'You told me.'

Tarrant looked at him in bleary-eyed surprise.

'I did?'

'Words to that effect,' Pike replied.

After a few moments' consideration, Tarrant laughed, then leaned forward to whisper in conspiratorial tones.

'Perhaps I get messages from the Web! P'raps I'm a wizard too!'

They decided to toast this idea.

'To Tarrant,' Pike announced grandly. 'Warrior-mage!'

Their joint hilarity lasted only a few moments before Tarrant lapsed into gloom again.

'Not that it's done me much good recently,' he muttered.

'Better not let the men see you in this state,' Pike advised. 'Not good for morale.'

Tarrant ignored the jibe.

'Know what I said t' her, after the chess-game?' he asked. Pike shook his head.

' "I travel too much to have need of a wife",' he quoted incredulously.

'Well, that's true enough,' his deputy replied. 'You've said as much to me many times.'

'It's true, old friend,' the envoy agreed. 'But if I *did* want a wife . . . I'd want her.'

'That's treason!' Pike grinned. 'You're talking about the queen.'

'Not till tomorrow,' Tarrant pointed out. 'Think I still have a chance?' he asked facetiously.

'Not a hope,' the veteran replied emphatically, still smiling. 'Have you seen Montfort and Rebecca together lately?'

'Revolting, isn't it,' Tarrant remarked, grinning himself now. 'They're never apart.'

'They will be this evening. It's bad luck otherwise.'

'Those two make their own luck,' the envoy claimed sourly. 'It's not fair. What's he got that I haven't?'

'Apart from a kingdom, a palace or two, the loyalty of all men of intelligence, the love of his people, a fair nature, gentle charm and amazing good looks, you mean?' Pike asked, his eyebrows raised.

'Yes!' Tarrant demanded. '*Apart* from those!'

The two men stared at each other for a moment, then roared with laughter.

* * *

Montfort and Rebecca were not the only couple whose wedding followed the dramatic events of a month ago. Galen and Emer had married only a few days later, while everyone was still in Edgefield. The king himself had witnessed their vows, and Rebecca had been the ring bearer for her friends. Emer's wedding ring had a special significance. It had been made from the coin that had been Galen's rookie find on the salt. Cluny had tested it out of idle curiosity, and when he found that it was made of gold, the alchemist had cleaned the metal with a special solution of his own devising, and Anselma had forged it into a delicate band for the bride's third finger. Both couples were now in Garadun as royal guests, but they had chosen to make their homes in Edgefield. The group had become close friends, and Anselma had confided in Emer that her husband would have been lost in the capital.

'He likes being thought of as eccentric,' she added fondly. 'Here he'd just be one of many, but in Edgefield he's a big fish in a small pond.'

After Galen and Emer had celebrated their marriage, Montfort had made two important announcements. The first was that Baldemar had expressed a wish to be relieved of the duties of the barony. Knowing of his daughter's plans, he wanted to move to Garadun to be near her. In earlier days, Rebecca would have suspected her father's motives, but she believed him now when he said he merely wanted to live quietly, without any responsibility. Baldemar was a shadow of his former self; even the knowledge that his daughter was to be queen had not restored his former arrogance or ambition. He was just glad that she was alive and happy.

The king's second announcement concerned the appointment of Galen as Chancellor of Edge, where he would rule as Montfort's representative in place of Baldemar. The People's Champion was a popular choice, both because of the well-known role he played in recent events, and especially because he had refused to join the ranks of the nobility, preferring a commoner's title. It was Montfort's first step in the long and arduous process of reforming his land.

Galen and Emer had moved into Radd's quarters, and

would return there after the royal wedding. The old baronial rooms were to be put to other uses. Spike travelled everywhere with the newly married couple, and while he was still fiercely protective of his master, he had learnt to tolerate Galen's wife. The beek became known as the Champion's Champion, and revelled in the attention paid to him.

* * *

Not all the events of the last month had been as pleasant. Farrand and the surviving rebellious nobles had been tried for treason, found guilty and executed. The process highlighted a side of Montfort's character that Rebecca found hard to come to terms with, but she recognized that he must punish those who fought hard against him if he was to establish a firm rule. The victorious king then took advantage of the ravages of the civil war to promote men who believed in his plans for Ahrenia, replacing those killed during and after the fighting.

One of the effects of Rebecca's triumph over Tyrrell had been unexpected. Within a few days of Derith's final disappearance, Peyton decided that the salt was no longer his home.

'It's not the same any more,' he told his colleagues. 'Any lubber'll be able to stroll across so long as he can walk in a straight line.' The future was to prove him correct, and the serenity of the flats was no longer deceptive. While other bands of Archaeologists kept up a meagre living by escorting any still nervous travellers, Peyton, Holmes and Milner made their own plans – involving their second love. Between them, they bought The Raven from Redfern, who had decided to retire from the distasteful business of selling alcohol. The Archaeologists renamed the tavern The Drunken Dragon, but it soon came to be known as the Archaeologists' Place. It became famous for its eccentric landlords, and for the tales they told at the slightest provocation. In the years to come, most listeners only believed a fraction of what they had heard – but that mattered little. It was an entertaining place – and the beek was still the best in the area.

Equally unexpected was the creation of the first official 'royal' fair. When Rebecca's plans were settled, she went to the travellers – to whom she owed so much – to explain and to apologize. She felt terrible about abandoning her charges. However, the fair people agreed to travel north to Garadun and make their home there, on ground granted to them by royal charter. They were willing to give up their mobile lifestyle, at least until a new dream-weaver arrived. Although it was a compromise that did not suit everybody, it was the best they could do.

* * *

However, in many ways, life in Ahrenia reverted to normal – as much as was possible in such a time of change. Montfort in particular, was glad of this. He knew now that his view of life had been too narrow, and he genuinely wanted to widen it as much as he could, trying to meet Rebecca half-way. His betrothed was still a dream-weaver, but even though she had tried to explain the meaning of this to him many times, and with considerable patience, there were still aspects of her talent and of course magic that eluded his grasp.

It was not that he wished to deny the importance of what had happened, but he hoped that the influence of such incomprehensible forces would diminish to levels that he could understand. For her part, Rebecca was happy that this should be so. Life would not be tolerable at such an intense level. She was also willing to compromise, knowing that her talents would still be there if needed.

On the evening before their wedding, Montfort found himself alone for once, and began to resent the old tradition that was keeping him from Rebecca. He missed her after only a few hours, and began to brood about a conversation they had had soon after the confrontation with Tyrrell. He ran through part of it again in his mind.

'So all of this has happened before?'

'Many times.'

'But now the cycle is broken?'

651

'Yes.'

'Because you won?'

'Not entirely,' Rebecca answered. 'Because of the way *we* won.'

'It was nothing to do with me!' he protested.

'Yes it was,' she said seriously. 'Without you, we could still have lost.'

'But . . .'

'When you came and put your arms around me, what were you thinking?' she asked.

'That I loved you,' he replied promptly.

'Is that all?' she asked, smiling.

'Isn't that enough?' he replied. 'I wanted to help you, to protect you – even though there was nothing I could do.'

'In other words,' she concluded, 'you committed yourself to me. And by doing so, you made him real.'

'Who?'

'Our son.'

'Our son?' he exclaimed disbelievingly. 'He hasn't even been conceived yet!'

'That doesn't matter to the Web,' she replied calmly. 'It knew that he *ought* to be born, and that was enough. The three of us became a new triangle, and he was the one who acted as dream-weaver in the Web, freeing the ancient wizards so that they could help us.'

'The original Heretics?' he asked, feeling dreadfully confused.

'Yes. They're sleeping peacefully now. No one will ever trap them again.' Rebecca was totally matter-of-fact, yet to Montfort the conversation seemed not quite real.

'You frighten me when you talk like this,' he said softly.

'There's no need to be scared,' she answered gently. 'All the elements of the cycle have gone. Tyrrell's destroyed. The ancients are standing guard over all of us. And I survived – to bear a child who will carry on a bloodline which cannot exist in the cycle. If another Rebecka comes along centuries from now, her life will be very different from mine.'

As he sat alone the night before his wedding, Montfort still found it all difficult to understand. The most puzzling thing of all was how a child who had not even bee conceived yet could have influenced events in such a way. His mind baulked at the idea. And he realized that he would just have to accept Rebecca's beliefs and get on with his life. And the next step in that life was their wedding.

Perhaps now the barons will stop pressuring me about an heir, he thought, then laughed quietly, wondering what their reaction would be if he told them that his son already existed – somewhere! *Better not try,* he advised himself.

* * *

Rebecca also spent the latter part of that evening alone. Her attendants had left, satisfied that all was in readiness for the morrow. Since her time of need, her dream-contacts with the Web had become less frequent. She did not feel the loss, and was more than content with her new life – except for one thing. She longed to see her son again.

Her dream that night began with a brilliant white light that filled her room. A voice beyond the brightness told her that the Web was granting her a gift, and that she would see her son once more before he was born. She accepted the gift gratefully, hearing many different tones behind the tender voice; Sancia, her mother, Radd and more.

Then all was silent. The light faded and became the gentle white of misty countryside; Rebecca could see hills and pale grass, and in the distance, cliffs and a calm sea. She recognized it as Montfort's southern estate; though she had never been there, he had described it to her, and had promised to take her there one day.

Rebecca stood quite still, savouring the cool, moist air and the absolute quiet. A small hand slipped into her own and, filled with contentment, she looked down at her son. There had been so many things she wanted to ask him, but none of them seemed important now. Except one.

'Will you be a dream-weaver too?'

'Like you, Mummy?' he asked solemnly.

'Yes.'

'Father says I'll be a king when I grow up,' he said carefully.

'You can be both,' she told him.

The boy considered this prospect for a while, then gazed up at his mother with a delighted expression.

'I should *like* that!' he said.

*   *   *

When Montfort and Rebecca exchanged their vows the next day, they restored the old bloodline to the throne of Ahrenia. Tyrrell's and all future claims to worldly immortality passed into history.

Garadun was decked out for celebration, with bright flags and banners everywhere; many thousands had braved the early winter cold to watch the processions pass by, and the city was full of music, laughter and merriment. Nowhere was this more true than in the Great Hall of the palace, where the royal couple and their guests witnessed the final performance of the three wizards. The combined magic of Kedar, Annis and Newell transported everyone present, and the visions, sounds and experiences became more real than life itself. It could have lasted only moments; it might have lasted hours; no one knew – or cared. But when it came to an end, the three were nowhere to be found. Rebecca was sad, but not surprised. She had been a privileged witness of the flowering of true magic. Now Kedar and Annis would test the future together, while Newell would follow his destiny alone.

The wizards left behind a magical legacy of wonder, joy and bemusement, not least in Nursey, Rebecca's ancient retainer, who was heard to remark, 'Now where have they gone? I haven't enjoyed a dance so much in years!'

She had not moved from her chair except in her imagination.

'Oh well,' she sighed. 'That's city folk for you, I suppose.' She puzzled over the disappearance of her dashing young partner, then fixed her gaze upon her neighbour, an elderly adjutant. 'Young man,' she asked politely, 'would you please fetch me another glass of wine? I'm about to expire of dehydrangea!'

*   *   *

From that day on, Montfort and Rebecca were rarely far from each other's side, although circumstances occasionally forced a temporary separation. On one such occasion, Montfort returned to their apartments and found the rooms filled with winter flowers. Rebecca smiled at him as he came in, and poured wine into two glasses.

'What are we celebrating?' he asked.

'An anniversary.'

'But we've only been married nine days!' he said, smiling.

'It's the anniversary of something that hasn't happened yet!' she explained. She had not needed the help of the Web, only her own dream-weaver's instincts, to know that her son would make his appearance in the real world exactly a year from today.

'Something that's going to happen?' he asked, looking at her oddly. 'What?'

His wife smiled at him.

'You wouldn't believe me if I told you,' she said.

THE END

A SELECTED LIST OF FANTASY TITLES
FROM CORGI BOOKS

THE PRICES SHOWN BELOW WERE CORRECT AT THE TIME OF GOING TO PRESS.
HOWEVER TRANSWORLD PUBLISHERS RESERVE THE RIGHT TO SHOW NEW RETAIL
PRICES ON COVERS WHICH MAY DIFFER FROM THOSE PREVIOUSLY ADVERTISED IN
THE TEXT OR ELSEWHERE.

*All Corgi/Bantam Books are available at your bookshop or newsagent, or can be ordered
from the following address:*

Corgi/Bantam Books,
Cash Sales Department
P.O. Box 11, Falmouth, Cornwall TR10 9EN

Please send a cheque or postal order (no currency) and allow 80p for postage and packing
for the first book plus 20p for each additional book ordered up to a maximum charge of
£2.00 in UK.

B.F.P.O. customers please allow 80p for the first book and 20p for each additional book.

Overseas customers, including Eire, please allow £1.50 for postage and packing for the first
book, £1.00 for the second book, and 30p for each subsequent title ordered.

NAME (Block Letters) ....

ADDRESS ....

....